Praise fo.
KRISTINE KATHRYN RUSCH'S DIVING UNIVERSE

"The Diving Universe, conceived by Hugo-Award winning author Kristine [Kathryn] Rusch is a refreshingly new and fleshed out realm of sci-fi action and adventure."

—*Astroguyz*

"Kristine Kathryn Rusch is best known for her Retrieval Artist series, so maybe you've missed her Diving Universe series. If so, it's high time to remedy that oversight."

—*Analog*

"This is classic sci-fi, a well-told tale of dangerous exploration. The first-person narration makes the reader an eye witness to the vast, silent realms of deep space, where even the smallest error will bring disaster. Compellingly human and technically absorbing, the suspense builds to fevered intensity, culminating in an explosive yet plausible conclusion."

—*RT Book Reviews* (Top Pick) on *Diving into the Wreck*

"Rusch delivers a page-turning space adventure while contemplating the ethics of scientists and governments working together on future tech."

—*Publishers Weekly* on *Diving into the Wreck*

"Rusch's handling of the mystery and adventure is stellar, and the whole tale proves quite entertaining."

—*Booklist Online* on *Diving into the Wreck*

"The technicalities in Boss' story are beautifully played.... She's real, flawed, and interesting.... Read the book. It is very good."

—*SFFWorld* on *Diving into the Wreck*

"Kristine Kathryn Rusch's *Diving into the Wreck* is exactly what the sf genre needs to get more readers…and to keep the readers the genre already has."

—*Elitist Book Reviews* on *Diving into the Wreck*

"Rusch keeps the science accessible, the cultures intriguing, and the characters engaging. For anyone needing to add to their science fiction library, keep an eye out for this."

—*Speculative Fiction Examiner* on *City of Ruins*

"Rusch's latest addition to her Diving series features a strong, capable female heroine and a vividly imagined far-future universe. Blending fast-paced action with an exploration of the nature of friendship and the ethics of scientific discoveries, this tale should appeal to Rusch's readers and fans of space opera."

—*Library Journal* on *Boneyards*

"Rusch follows *Diving into the Wreck* and *City of Ruins* with another fast-paced novel of the far future… [Rusch's] sensibilities will endear this book to readers looking for a light, quick space adventure with strong female protagonists."

—*Publishers Weekly* on *Boneyards*

"Filled with well-defined characters who confront a variety of ethical and moral dilemmas, Rusch's third Diving novel is classic space opera, with richly detailed worldbuilding and lots of drama."

—*RT Book Reviews* on *Boneyards*

"…a fabulous outer space thriller that rotates perspective between the divers, the Alliance and to a lesser degree the Empire. Action-packed and filled with twists yet allowing the reader to understand the motives of the key players, *Skirmishes* is another intelligent exciting voyage into the Rusch Diving universe."

—*The Midwest Book Review* on *Skirmishes*

"A combination of first-person and third-person narrative and flashback segments makes this a complex and compelling story. It's like having three tales in one, with an added peek into the bad guys' activities, all of them intriguing, classic science fiction. It leaves the reader eager to explore this universe again and see what will happen next with these characters."

—*RT Book Reviews* on *Skirmishes*

"A skillful blend of science fiction and murder mystery which keeps ratcheting up the stakes."

—*Worlds Without End* on *The Falls*

"[The Runabout] is so good, it will make you want to read the other stories."

—*SFRevu* on *The Runabout*

"Amazing character construction, building a plot that riveted me almost from the moment it began. I will now absolutely have to read the preceding titles and I cannot wait to see what will come as a result of *The Runabout.*"

—*Tangent Online* on *The Runabout*

"By mixing cerebral and investigative elements, emotional character segments, and the adrenaline of action, Rusch tells a complete yet varied tale that will please science fiction readers looking for something different from the usual fare."

—*Publishers Weekly* on *Searching for the Fleet*

"One of the most amazing science fiction series in recent years now has an exciting new installment."

—*Astroguyz* on *Searching for the Fleet*

The Diving Universe

(Reading Order)

Diving into the Wreck: A Diving Novel

The Application of Hope: A Diving Universe Novella

Becalmed: A Diving Universe Novella

City of Ruins: A Diving Novel

Boneyards: A Diving Novel

Skirmishes: A Diving Novel

The Falls: A Diving Universe Novel

The Runabout: A Diving Novel

Searching for the Fleet: A Diving Novel

The Renegat: A Diving Universe Novel

The Spires of Denon: A Diving Universe Novella

THE *RENEGAT*

A DIVING UNIVERSE NOVEL

KRISTINE KATHRYN RUSCH

wmg PUBLISHING

The *Renegat*

Published 2019 by WMG Publishing
Parts of this novel appeared in different form as the novellas *The Rescue of the* Renegat *(Asimov's,* January/February 2018) and *Joyride, (Asimov's,* November/December 2018)

Cover design by Allyson Longueira/WMG Publishing

ISBN-13: 978-1-56146-090-8
ISBN-10: 1-56146-090-7

ACKNOWLEDGEMENTS

My heartfelt thanks go to Dean Wesley Smith on this for supporting me throughout this book while moving, while doing some superhuman feats, and managing to juggle everything. He also kept me focused when I had no focus at all. I couldn't have done this one without you, Smitty. I love you.

THE *RENEGAT*

A DIVING UNIVERSE NOVEL

THE SCRAPHEAP

INTERNAL CLOCK MALFUNCTION
PERPETUAL NOW

THE SCRAPHEAP

The force field breach caught the Scrapheap's attention. It tried to enter the breach properly into its log, but could not cite a date. The Scrapheap did not have the capacity to manufacture a date, so its systems awoke.

It needed assistance. Human assistance.

The Scrapheap did not know how long it had functioned without human assistance. Its internal clock had doubled over on itself three times and had malfunctioned on the fourth reset. That malfunction did not trigger an alarm, because it was no threat to the Scrapheap itself.

The Scrapheap monitored and evaluated threats. Its protocols demanded that it record major breaches and threats from outside. Internal threats were dealt with routinely.

Energy spikes were minimized. Certain ships were contained within their own private force fields.

The Scrapheap had done such things since its beginning.

It did not think of its beginning as anything but the start of its internal clock. It was not self-aware, although certain systems had more awareness than other systems.

The Scrapheap knew its own history. It had started as five decommissioned ships, stored side by side in a region of space its creators believed to be little used and off the main travel routes for the sector. Those decommissioned ships were to be transferred to the nearest sector base, but the base had no need for the ships.

So the first force field was created. It protected all five ships. Those ships remained in the force field, and then other ships were added. Some were brought in under their own power. Others were towed in by a larger ship. Still others arrived using their *anacapa* drives.

On one occasion, those arrivals had caused a chain reaction. The energy wave from the arriving *anacapa* drive had triggered a malfunction in a dying *anacapa* drive, causing one ship to explode and resulting in damage to two more.

Humans had arrived three months later with a new core for the Scrapheap, and a control center to protect that new core. The Scrapheap's mission grew that day, to preserve and protect the ships and the ship parts inside its force field.

The Scrapheap followed its mission diligently, recording its activity, logging it, using the dates from its internal clock.

Over centuries, the Scrapheap grew from five ships to one million, three hundred and sixty-three thousand, seven hundred and one. Not all of the ships were intact. Many of the items the Scrapheap called ships were not ships at all, but parts of ships.

In the early centuries, the humans returned regularly, flashing their identifications and removing ships that still had value. The humans moved intact ships inside a secondary force field near the core, and did not touch those ships, although those ships routinely maintained themselves. If one of those ships malfunctioned, it would flag itself for removal from the secondary force field. If possible, the ship would then remove itself from the secondary force field.

If the ship could not move itself, the Scrapheap would do so, using a powerful tractor beam that only existed inside the secondary force field.

The Scrapheap maintained all of the external shields that belonged to the ships gathered in the main force field. In that way, those ships would not spark another disaster. The Scrapheap added and removed miniature force fields, rotated some ships away from others, kept those with dying *anacapa* drives isolated from ships that could possibly negatively interact with the dying drives.

The humans went in and out of the Scrapheap, removing ships and parts of ships as needed. Some ships' *anacapa* drives were activated remotely, and those ships left the Scrapheap on their own power. Sometimes humans entered the Scrapheap through various portals built into the large exterior force field, and removed ships.

One thousand years into the Scrapheap's existence, the humans ceased removing ships. The only changes inside the Scrapheap were the ones the Scrapheap initiated itself.

Until the breach.

A ship tried to enter the Scrapheap. That ship did not know the code to activate the portal in the force field, so the Scrapheap activated its defenses.

The ship left.

This was not unusual. It happened routinely throughout the Scrapheap's existence, so the Scrapheap did not create a log for the incident, although the incident remained in the short-term buffers.

Then the ship returned. It used a code that had not been used since the first four hundred years of the Scrapheap's existence.

The force field opened.

The ship entered the Scrapheap, flew around many of the ships inside the Scrapheap, and left.

The ship repeated this behavior for two hours on each of the next five days.

On the sixth day, the ship returned. It followed a path it had used before, and stopped near a DV-Class ship. Humans then emerged from the returning ship, and traveled to the DV-Class ship. The humans entered the DV-Class ship, and one-point-two hours later, the *anacapa* drive inside that ship activated.

The DV-Class ship left the Scrapheap.

The new ship remained inside the Scrapheap. The Scrapheap tried to contact that new ship. It did not respond. The new ship eventually left via engine power through the opening in the force field.

The Scrapheap then tried to identify the type of ship that the new ship had been. That type of ship did not exist in the Scrapheap's records. Nor did the ship seem to be a ship that could have been updated from any other ship in the Scrapheap's records.

The Scrapheap had scenarios programmed into its systems for such an occurrence. The scenarios postulated that the ship had stolen the entry codes and was now stealing vessels.

The Scrapheap would attack the ship when it returned.

But it did not return.

Instead, the DV-Class vessel returned. Humans, identified as the same or similar to the ones who had arrived earlier, traveled from the returning DV-Class vessel to another DV-Class vessel. Then the second DV-Class vessel's *anacapa* drive activated, and removed the second DV-Class vessel from the Scrapheap. Then the first DV-Class vessel left again.

At that moment, the Scrapheap attempted to log the interaction as a serious breach. It could not do so. It no longer had the ability to time-stamp a log.

The Scrapheap had a failsafe to send information to its creators should the log function break down. But that failsafe had limitations.

The Scrapheap had to send the information from its short-term buffers to the humans before the information was recycled out of the buffers.

Upon discovering that it needed to send the information from the short-term buffers, the Scrapheap acted immediately. It sent the information along the channels it had been using for its decennial updates.

The Scrapheap also requested a repair of its systems as well as an augmentation that would prevent the unwarranted theft of vessels.

It could not attack vessels that had been stored inside the Scrapheap.

But it could flag the breaches as suspicious, maintain the records of those breaches, until the human creators arrived and determined what to do with the information.

Because the buffered information needed to be protected differently than the decennial update and because the buffered information could not be permanently stored, the Scrapheap requested a receipt be sent when the information reached its final destination.

The Scrapheap had not made such a request in all of its existence. The request set different protocols into place, protocols the Scrapheap had never used before.

The information system was old. The buffered information first traveled to sector bases closed, abandoned, and forgotten. The information then routed back to the Scrapheap, which repackaged the information and sent the information again.

The Scrapheap repackaged six times before the information managed to get through that hurdle in the system.

The Scrapheap then deleted the previous sector bases from its communications channel. It sent information directly to the working sector base.

More ships disappeared weekly, so the Scrapheap sent buffered information weekly.

The Scrapheap did not get a response.

Its systems were programmed to continue to send information until it received instructions.

It received none.

So it continued to send, even as the buffer cleaned itself out, and the log mechanism jammed. The Scrapheap did close the force field and reactivate the defensive measures, but sanctioned DV-Class vessels continued to enter the Scrapheap, disgorge humans to another DV-Class vessel, and then remove that DV-Class vessel.

The emptiness inside the Scrapheap grew.

The Scrapheap was not alarmed by this change. The Scrapheap was not sentient.

But it responded like any powerless being under attack.

It asked for help.

It defended itself as best it could, while it waited for a response.

PART ONE
THE JOYRIDE
130 YEARS AGO

THE *BRAZZA TWO*

They assembled in the Third Level Mess Hall, the one designed for first-years. The furniture was tiny, built for small bodies, and the walls had painted murals of cats and dogs, the comfort animals kept in the arboretum wing, and not allowed on this level. Still, Nadim Crowe knew, a lot of tears got shed beneath those murals, hiccoughy tears, the kind that little kids couldn't hold back even if they wanted to.

He thought the murals cruel, but then, he thought sending little kids to boarding school while their parents gallivanted across the universe equally cruel. Last year, he'd volunteered down here until the sobs got to him. Then he requested a transfer, which had sent him to the medical wing, and that turned out to be infinitely worse.

Why he'd decided on the Third Level Mess as a meeting site for the two teams was beyond him. It went into that category of his existence that he filed under *It Seemed Like A Good Idea At The Time.*

Of course, he hadn't thought that through until tonight, while he was waiting for the others to arrive. Before that, he'd only thought about the competition. He had had a lot of prep to do, and that meant doing some of the prep here, in the Third Level Mess.

A week ago, he'd tampered with the Third Level Mess's security system, shutting down the audio and video tracking just to see if anyone noticed the system had been tampered with. He kept the environmental controls on and boosted the emergency warnings, just in case something bad happened here while the security system was off. The Mess was all about little kids, after all.

He had chosen the middle of Ship Night, when (in theory) no little kids were using the Mess. He'd kept the system down for three hours just to see if anyone noticed.

No one did notice, which disturbed him and relieved him in equal measures. He didn't like that it was so easy to tamper with the security systems on the *Brazza Two*, but at the same time, it made this little dare easier.

And, he knew, that the systems in other parts of the ship, systems that monitored kids his age, were better designed. The adults didn't think that little-little kids would meddle with security systems, but the adults knew that teens did. Crowe supposed if any of the little-littles had successfully screwed with a security system, they would have moved to the gifted track immediately.

He had no idea how the gifted track worked for the littlest of kids. He hadn't been on this ship when he was really little. He had arrived on the ship at age nine. Unlike most kids, he'd actually requested his berth. He'd already been old enough to know that anywhere in the universe was better than a landlocked life with his parents, so why not go to the best possible school which had the added bonus of being in space as well.

The fading bruises, two broken ribs, and evidence of other badly healed broken bones had convinced the Fleet's school administrators that Crowe had been right about his parents. His tests—off the charts when it came to mathematics, science, and technical aptitude—convinced the administrators to send him to the most prestigious school ship in the Fleet.

He never would have cried underneath these murals if he had arrived here when he was young enough to eat in the Third Level Mess. He would have celebrated.

He wasn't celebrating now. He was jittery.

He'd been the first to arrive in the Third Level Mess, and it was mostly dark. Five dim overhead lights failed to properly illuminate the space. Four of the lights were in the Mess's four corners, leaving pools of darkness over the tables and the back area.

The fifth light—the brightest light—was off to his right. It shone over the long rectangular counter designed for the adult staff to serve the little kids their food. When he volunteered here, he wondered why there was a serving station. After all, in the other messes, the students were monitored by computer and actually informed when they took a food item that didn't fit into their regulation diet.

He asked his question, and was told that computer diet controls caused most of the little-littles to melt down. Instead, it was better to have adult assistance, so when a child did break down, he did so with someone nearby who could soothe him.

Crowe had seen a lot of soothing here, more than he had experienced at home. He'd also seen a lot of unhappy children. Because of that, he knew, most people on the *Brazza Two* avoided the Third Level Mess.

No one monitored this section of the ship after dinner either. He had double- and triple-checked that himself when he had come here in preparation for the competition. He had gotten the idea, and before he had even told Tessa about it, he had gone to the three main competition sites—the Mess and two different ship bays—to see if the competition was even possible.

It was—just barely. It would take some luck and a whole bunch of skill. That was what he loved about it, and that was why he was so very excited.

In the last fifteen minutes, his team had started to arrive. Ten of his friends, sliding in one at a time, some of them fist-bumping him as they passed, others just hovering near the bench beneath the mural, which provided the only truly comfortable seating. The bench was at adult height, probably because whoever built it had had some kind of brain fart, and had forgotten that this room was for little-littles.

As the team arrived, Crowe stood with his hands behind his back, deliberately mimicking Captain Mbue's favorite posture. She impressed him. She had been the captain since he started here. She was no-nonsense. When she gave her annual do-your-best speech to the various classes, she meant it. Some of the other teachers and staff on the ship treated the students with barely concealed condescension, but Captain Mbue seemed to believe each word she said.

When Crowe became captain—a real captain, a captain of a DV-Class vessel—he would treat his entire crew with respect, from the oldest to the youngest. He would do his best to be exactly like Captain Mbue.

And tonight, he was going to captain a ship. If he pulled this off, no one on the *Brazza Two* would be the wiser. Or if they found out, they would think him brazen but brilliant. He hoped for the first, but he would take the second.

The question was whether or not he would still run the mission if Tessa failed to show up.

Tessa Linley, the most gorgeous girl he had ever seen. She was luminescent, with dark brown eyes that perfectly matched her smooth unblemished skin. She wore her long hair in dozens of tiny braids that fell down her back most of the time, but when she was working hard on something delicate, she would wrap those braids around the top of her head like a crown.

He had no idea if she knew that half of the competitions and challenges he had thrown at her had been because he wanted to see her marvelous brain at work and because he wanted to spend more time with her. He had yet to impress her, although he had won two of the past three challenges he had made to her.

None had been as elaborate as this one. They had come up with it together. They had found some redundant systems in the *Brazza Two*'s security protocols. Thinking they had happened on something the more experienced engineers had missed, Tessa and Crowe had asked one of their instructors if they could begin the process of removing the redundant systems.

The instructor had laughed, which surprised both of them. And then he had complimented them on their observations.

But, he had said, *those systems exist for a reason. This is a school ship with the best and brightest in the Fleet on board. We've learned over the years that no matter how hard we try to keep you students intellectually stimulated, you'll still venture out on your own. And one of the things you'll do is tamper with the systems. The redundancies make sure that the tampering and the damage from it are at a minimum.*

Crowe and Tessa said nothing to each other for days after that, but slowly they realized that they both had come to the same conclusion: they both decided to investigate the redundancies, to see what the "best and brightest" had tried before Crowe and Tessa had even thought of boarding the *Brazza Two*.

That, combined with the fact that the *Brazza Two* had followed a part of the Fleet to a nearby Scrapheap for some major learning opportunity for the officer candidates, had captured Crowe's imagination. Not only did he want to best the students who had come before him in the accelerated youth program, he also wanted to visit that Scrapheap, and he knew he wouldn't be allowed to.

Only the officer candidates—those in their twenties or older, with decades of schooling and experience beneath them—were allowed to go. And they would be supervised every moment of the visit, which sounded like torture to Crowe.

He loved working on his own. And that, combined with the other strictures, had given him an idea.

Tessa then refined it.

And like almost everything they came up with, they decided to turn it into a competition.

Unlike their other competitions, though, this one required the help of others. Together, Tessa and Crowe recruited half of their class.

Tessa sidled up beside him. He knew she was there before he saw her. The scent of her jasmine soap always preceded her. She leaned against him, her soft skin warm against his, and he felt a jolt of lust.

He took one step away. He didn't want to be distracted by his body right now.

"Wasn't sure you were going to come," he said softly.

"And miss this? Are you kidding?" She stepped forward just a bit, probably so that she could see his face in the dim light.

He could see hers, bright and eager and shining with excitement.

"You do a head count?" she asked.

"Not yet," he said. "I was waiting for you."

She punched his arm lightly. "We don't have a lot of time. You should've been ahead of this."

"You're the one who's late," he said.

"I'm not late," she said. "You were early."

"Still want to do this?" he asked, deflecting. Or maybe just deflecting the thoughts from his brain.

Maybe that was why he didn't win every contest he had with Tessa. Part of his brain was always busy controlling his body so that she wouldn't know just how much she affected him. Another part of his brain monitored his every word so that he wouldn't say something stupid. That part of his brain usually failed, especially as he got deeper into the contest and focused on the task at hand instead of his mouth.

Fortunately, Tessa didn't insult easily.

She didn't forget, though, either, and she often brought those comments back up, usually in a teasing way, but still. He found his missteps horribly embarrassing.

"If I didn't want to do this," she said, "I wouldn't be here. What I'm not sure about is whether or not we can finish before everyone gets up. I don't want to come back to a welcoming committee."

He bit his lower lip. They had discussed this problem earlier, and then she had said it didn't bother her.

"It's a possibility," he said. "A good one. That's why I'm asking you if you want to back out."

She let out a half laugh, and her eyes sparkled. She was so beautiful when she was smiling that it took his breath away.

"Are you kidding?" she asked. "It's been ages since we've done anything remotely exciting. I've been looking forward to this for weeks."

"So have I," he said, feeling a spike of energy running through him. "So let's get to it."

She nodded, then started a head count, whispering the numbers under her breath. He counted with her, mentally making note of which team the people present were on.

His team had gathered together near the mural wall. Hers was scattered around the room, huddling together in twos and threes. That one simple fact buoyed him. It meant his team was more cohesive than hers.

"Looks like everyone's here," she said.

Not only were both teams in place, but each member was the correct member. Once, he'd initiated a competition with Tessa, and half the people he'd handpicked to participate had sent someone else in their place. It had been a last-minute competition, though, and he really hadn't prepped anyone.

This time, he'd been running virtual drills with his team. He'd designed a three-part program that simulated what he thought would happen. The first part got the team to the docking bay. The second part was stolen from the flight simulator that first-year pilot training instructors used, and the third part was sheer guesswork.

Tessa had warned him not to do anything like that—*you'll get caught and then what will you say?* she asked; *I'll say that I was using my imagination just like they encourage*, he replied. But he hadn't gotten caught. And not only had he maintained the interest of his team in the adventure, he had also made sure they were as prepared as they could be.

"Okay." Tessa clapped her hands together to get everyone's attention. It was ten-thirty p.m. ship time. They weren't even supposed to start until eleven.

But Crowe had no problem with starting early. The earlier they left, the sooner they would return. If they managed to get back before four a.m., they were less likely to be caught.

Tessa had probably impressed that on her team; he certainly had on his.

"This is your last chance if you want to back out," Tessa was saying—to everyone, which kinda annoyed him. He didn't want anyone to back out and he didn't want to remind them that backing out was an option.

Everyone was watching her. He could see faces half-illuminated in the dim light, all of them focused on her with great intensity, which also irritated him. She was his friend, not theirs—although that wasn't true. Tessa somehow managed to be everyone's friend, even though she was closest to him—or so he hoped.

"There's a chance we could get caught," she said. "A good chance, really. But as I told you, or rather, as I told my team, there's safety in numbers. They might punish all of us, but not as severely as they'd punish one of us. So you'd be helping out in more ways than one if you stay. Besides, this'll be fun!"

Her voice rose with that last bit, and it actually sounded like fun instead of something scary and dangerous.

A bunch of people closest to Crowe smiled. He couldn't see the other faces clearly enough to know if they were smiling too.

He needed to take this over, though, before she scared them all to death.

He said, "Those of you who've been in competitions before with me and Tessa know the drill. We're going to have the computer start a thirty-second countdown. As soon as it hits zero, it'll say *Go!* and you go. You know where you're supposed to be, so you run there."

Or, he thought, his team knew where they were supposed to be. He had no idea if hers knew.

"You should have instructions from me or Tessa, so you should know what to do." He didn't look at her in case she failed at this for the first time ever. She used to be the most organized one of the two of them. She wasn't anymore—he had learned that lesson soundly and had started to beat her at her own game.

"If you don't know exactly," Tessa said, lending credence to the idea that she hadn't prepared as much as he had, "follow the other members of your team. My team is wearing a slash of lime green along one cheek tonight, so if you see someone with a slash across their face and you're part of my team, follow that person. Someone will put you to work."

He hadn't thought about color-coding his team, but that was only necessary for this part of the competition anyway. He had hardly given the front part of this any thought at all, because that wasn't the part that interested him.

The competition really didn't start until the teams got on board their respective ships.

"Remember," Tessa said, "the point of this is to have fun, and maybe learn something along the way."

Crowe disagreed: he thought the point was to learn something and maybe have fun along the way, but he stayed quiet. Tessa was better at rousing the troops than he was.

"So, ready?" Tessa asked. "The countdown starts...*now!*"

Apparently that was her computer command, because the androgynous voice started counting backwards from thirty.

Crowe moved slightly away from the door. He had instructed his team to let Tessa's go first. A few competitions ago, some of the team members had gotten trampled in the opening stampede, and that had cost him precious time (not to mention a long and convoluted explanation in the medical wing).

Besides, he hadn't just tampered with the security systems here; he'd also tampered with the door commands on the docking bay entrance his team was going to use.

The tampering wasn't as extreme as the tampering here—ship security would definitely have noticed any major changes to the systems in the docking bay.

All he had done was prep the redundant systems to operate more efficiently if given certain commands. He had figured, if he had gotten caught, that he would tell his teachers or security that he had been trying to improve the system. He'd been given permission to investigate the redundant systems after all.

The computer countdown hit *three... two... one... Go!* and Tessa's team took off so fast that they nearly trampled each other.

"See ya, sucker!" Tessa said to him as she raced by. He just smiled. She should have seen that as a warning that he had done some prep, but she hadn't.

Or maybe she just didn't care.

She was on her way to the secondary docking bay. It was closer to the Third Level Mess than the docking bay he had chosen. She probably thought the proximity would give her team an advantage.

But there was a lot that could eat up that advantage, including getting in, working the ship, and getting the bay doors to open. His team had worked through all of the scenarios he could think of, and he still worried that those hadn't been enough.

The sound of her team's shoes, slapping against the floor, receded. There was no laughing and giggling and catcalls, like there had been on some previous competitions, so she had done some work with her team.

"Okay," he said when he could no longer hear Tessa's team. "Let's go."

His team gathered around him, and they walked to the docking bay. No running at all. They even took the Third Level elevator to the First Level. Nothing wrong with students touring the public area of the ship. He'd learned that long ago. And if they weren't acting like they were doing something wrong, then no one would think they were.

Two of his team members—Omar and Erika—already had their personal computer screens up on clear holographic mode. They were the ones assigned with tricking the redundant systems so that the team could get into the docking bay undetected—at least for a few minutes. Long enough that they would be able to get to the ship he had chosen.

Two other team members—Igasho and Sera—were going to scrub the identities of the entire team, effectively removing them from the security system the moment the group entered the docking bay. He'd learned that trick by studying what students had done before.

The system was set up to catch that little maneuver, but he'd tested it (like he had tested everything), not with his own profile, but with the profiles of some of the kids one year ahead of him. He'd set up the scrubbing to look like it was accidental—a glitch in the system. And he'd deliberately chosen candidates who had no real technical expertise. These were the kids who liked the arts, who focused on languages or ship culture or Fleet history, such as it was.

There was no way those kids had the ability to scrub their own profiles, and they didn't have the wherewithal to hire someone (or bribe someone) to do it for them. If ship security didn't look too deeply at the scrubbing, no one would figure out what had happened.

So far, no one had looked to see if the scrubbing was anything more than a system error.

And Crowe had learned how long it took the system to recognize it had been spoofed and to solve the problem.

The fastest the scrubbing had been repaired had been seven minutes. The fastest it had been reported to a human had been ten minutes—and that had been on the same student. It had been an outlier, but Crowe used that figure as his figure.

He'd tested the team in their simulation. They had to move fast to the ship, and get inside within six minutes. That way, when their profiles returned to the system, they wouldn't be in the middle of boarding a ship they had no right to be on.

They hadn't done it physically—they hadn't done any of this physically—but they knew what the stakes were, and at least according to some of his instructors, virtual drills created brain muscle memory as effectively as actual drills created actual muscle memory.

He was counting on that.

The elevator door opened on First Level, and the team headed en masse to the docking bay entrance. Once inside, they'd run to the ship. Out here, they laughed and joked like kids on a walk, except for Omar and Erika, who were in the middle of the circle, mostly protected from the security imagery—so that the system wouldn't flag their behavior (or anyone's behavior) as suspicious.

The corridor was wide enough to accommodate four across, the ceilings high, and the floor made of a material he always meant to look up, designed to help anyone who had not yet adjusted to the peculiarities of the *Brazza Two* to maintain balance and stability. This flooring vanished on the main levels, but was part of the entire area around the docking bay, something Crowe had noticed, but didn't yet understand.

They arrived at the fifth entrance into this docking bay. This particular entrance had the most minimal security because it was the farthest from any access point. It also led into the part of the docking bay reserved for the lesser-used ships. No outside ships ever docked here, and no small ship in active use docked here either.

Crowe had spent nearly a week looking up each small ship in this area, its specs, its foibles, and its capacity. He knew he had an inexperienced team, so he wanted something easy to pilot. He also knew that the ship had to be large enough to handle ten, and with portholes big enough that the team could see the Scrapheap with their own eyes.

He also wanted a ship that could handle the distance to the Scrapheap rapidly, with minimum fuss, and could handle the one maneuver he was most afraid of on its own.

Bringing the ship back to the *Brazza Two* and docking in the same spot required piloting skills beyond anyone in this group. While all of the small ships attached to the *Brazza Two* had an autopilot function, not all of the autopilots worked well.

Most of that was by design. The *Brazza Two* didn't just train gifted students in their early years of study and scholars who would eventually train aboard a specialty ship; it also trained pilots, engineers, and the entire officer core. They all needed small ship experience, and not all of that experience could come from simulations.

Many of the small ships in this docking bay were training vessels with certain features disabled or removed. Crowe needed all of the features of a Fleet vessel to work well, just in case his little crew did get into trouble. He needed to be able to activate a part of the ship or give it over to the computer or contact someone on the *Brazza Two*, ask for help, and then be able to implement that help.

He hoped nothing would go that seriously wrong on this little adventure, but he also knew that hope wasn't something a commander could count on.

Captain Mbue had said that on more than one occasion. Speaking to his class, she had added, *Hope should give us the wings to pursue the experience that will then enable us to make the best decisions for that particular moment. Optimism and hope built the Fleet. Experience pilots it. Adventure keeps it moving, ever forward.*

She had never mentioned creativity in any of her speeches, but Crowe liked to think that creativity was part of the Fleet as well. Maybe one of the most valuable parts.

Certainly, his creativity had helped him catch the attention of every single one of his teachers. They always gave him assignments far beyond anything someone his age should do. And they praised his nonstandard way of approaching each problem they gave him, telling him they had never met anyone who thought like he did.

He hoped they would have the same reaction to this adventure. If they caught him.

The fifth entrance into the docking bay was also the smallest—a single door. The eleven crowded around it, and waited while Adil took point. He was slender and small, having not yet hit his full growth, which Crowe believed might make him even more valuable down the road.

Right now, Adil had to unlock the entrance. Crowe was suddenly breathing shallowly. He wanted to unlock the entrance. He had done every single thing in the simulation, so he knew what the crew would be up against, and some things he did better than others.

Like opening doors undetected.

Only his time had been fifteen seconds *slower* than Adil's time. And nothing Crowe could do in the simulation made his time faster than Adil's.

That was how Crowe had made the assignments anyway. The crew members who did the jobs the swiftest while being the most accurate were the ones who got the job.

That didn't stop him from shifting from foot to foot. Each passing second felt like an hour.

He hadn't thought about this, about the way it looked when eleven kids crowded around a door. If he had given that part thought, he would have had the scrubbing of their digital signatures begin sooner.

Adil finished in record time (even though it didn't feel that way) and the door slid to one side, just like it was supposed to. The crew walked in, with Igasho and Sera remaining just outside the door, as they finished the scrubbing.

Or, at least, Crowe hoped they finished the scrubbing. Because this was one part of the plan that they had no way to check.

Igasho entered first. His black eyes met Crowe's, and Igasho nodded. Igasho believed it was done.

Then Sera stepped inside and shouted, "*Go!*" just like she was supposed to do.

The crew ran for the first time, everyone heading for the scout ship that Crowe had designated as theirs.

His stomach tightened, and he was still having trouble breathing. He'd checked and double-checked the manifest all day, just to make sure that the scout ship was still in place.

The ship had the uninspired name of *Br2 Scout3*. Apparently school ships lost scouts in training so often that the scouts' names were simple.

This scout had been in service for almost a hundred years, and was on its last legs. It hadn't been used much at all, which was one reason why Crowe had targeted it. He knew no one was paying much attention to it.

He'd run a diagnostic a few weeks ago, piggybacking on engineering's standard small ship diagnostic. So technically, *he* hadn't run the diagnostic at all. He had just added *Br2 Scout3* to the list, and the engineering department had run its usual check. The ship came out clean.

Crowe scurried around some of the other smaller ships—a runabout, an orbiter, a few tiny ships that were little more than pods—following his team.

He was the one in charge of the scout ship, and he had to get there when everyone else did, but he had a stitch in his side from his uneven breathing.

He was a lot more nervous than he expected to be. This entire mission was a lot more real than he had ever imagined, and he was beginning to think they were in too deep.

If he hadn't made this into a contest with Tessa, he might have backed out right here.

But he had, and his pride was going to keep him moving forward.

The team arrived at the ship with two minutes to spare. They were all gathered around the back end of the scout. This ship had a cargo door, like many of the military vessels.

Usually small ships were coded to the pilots and bridge crew of the larger vessel they rode in, but not training ships. Training ships had entry codes for each class that was supposed to train inside.

Crowe had investigated which unit was using what type of training ship at the moment. None of them were actually training on scout ships in classes right now, but the classes on the scout ships would start up in a few weeks.

Fortunately for him, the instructors for that unit were already preparing—or maybe they had never changed the entry codes. He had dug into that part of the shipboard computer, using an instructor identification he had borrowed long ago. It wasn't the only instructor identification he had borrowed in his time here—he rotated through them when he needed to.

He'd actually burned three of them on this trip. If the team got caught, he wouldn't be able to use those identifications again.

His mouth was dry and his heart was pounding. He stepped up to the back control panel, hidden to the left of the door. Usually this part of a scout ship was opened in the ship's tiny bridge, but there were redundant systems in all of the Fleet's vessels.

Every type of ship had extra ways to enter. Ships that went off on their own without any backup, like scout ships, had several redundant entry points, so that no one could get locked out in a strange environment.

He opened the control panel with shaking fingers, wishing he had more control over his body right now. He didn't want his team to know how nervous he was, although they could probably guess.

Maybe they would chalk it up to adrenaline. Or maybe they were just as nervous, and even more excited.

No one said anything. He could hear some ragged breathing, but that was about it.

The panel revealed a triple-coded entry, just like he expected. That calmed him. He had to type in a pattern with his fingertips. The ship would then identify him as a student in the *Brazza Two*. In the past, the ships had to confirm that someone was in the program that was going to use the ship, but so many records weren't kept up that the instructor core abandoned that system and just put regular student records in place.

The instructors figured there were other ways to prevent students who didn't belong from getting on the ships.

And those ways were the ones that Crowe had discovered, overridden, or planned for.

He had planned for this one. The ship asked him for the class code. He'd found that about a week ago. He swept his forefinger across the flat-screen pad four times, then placed his entire hand on the screen.

Nothing happened.

Was he going to fail at this, lose this competition, because he had underestimated the access code to the ship he needed? What would Tessa say about that? She rarely teased him about his failures, but this would be too rich to ignore. She would—

Metal against metal squealed, followed by a rumble and a series of small clicks. Five of his team members stepped backwards. They had been too close to the back end of the scout ship—the end that was slowly opening like a cargo ship door.

Just like it was supposed to do.

He let out a half laugh, catching it before it became an exclamation of joy. Still, he couldn't keep the smile off his face as he nodded to his team.

He gave a one-finger symbol—index finger up—and then pointed at the dark interior. He stepped into the darkness first, even though a captain never went first. But he wasn't a real captain (yet) so screw it.

He wanted to run, but he knew better than that. Instead, his boots caught on the ramp, making banging sounds as he walked up it.

Lights came on around him the deeper he went into the ship.

His team—his *crew*—flanked him. Once they were all inside, he nodded at Maida, who would be his second in command on this journey. She grinned at him, her round face and green eyes filled with joy. He had picked Maida for this one because her scores on all of the tests they had done in the simulation were the closest to his.

She was the only other person who had managed each test along the way. Everyone else had failed at least one.

She walked over to the interior control panel for the door and the environmental system, and pressed it, shutting the cargo door and making sure the environment was suited for the team. Proper oxygen mix, proper temperature, full gravity.

Still, they would grab environmental suits as they passed through the armory on their way to the tiny bridge. In a couple of the simulations, things had gone so badly awry that the fake crew needed environmental suits.

Even though those simulations were outliers, they happened. And Crowe was cautious enough to prepare for the worst and hope that it would never come to pass.

He glanced at the crew. They were smiling at him, the nerves gone—so far as he could tell. Maybe the crew was all excited about this part of the mission.

In his estimation, this was the most dangerous part to them and their future careers with the Fleet. If they got caught at this moment, without having achieved their objectives, they'd join all the ignominious previous students who had tried to get a ship out of the docking bay.

Those students often lied about the reason they were leaving. Most of them were fleeing the school.

Crowe wasn't, and he figured he would have the simulations to back him up, but he still hated this part.

He led his crew out of the cargo area and into that narrow armory. The armory was empty; it wouldn't be stocked with weaponry unless the scout ship was going off on its own for real. But environmental suits had to remain with all ships at all times.

Still, he felt a thread of relief when he opened the uniform storage and found dozens of suits in various sizes hanging from pegs, just like they were supposed to be.

Apparently he hadn't entirely believed that the suits would be here.

Everyone grabbed a suit, then spent a few uncomfortable minutes sliding it on over their clothes. Crowe's suit was newer than the suit he had in his dorm room, and it took him a moment to figure out that the suit operated by touch-command. He left the hood down, and the gravity in his boots off.

He didn't wait for anyone else as he headed to the tiny bridge.

The *Br2 Scout3* was a midrange scout ship—or so its specs said—designed for regional exploration. The *Br2 Scout3*'s standard crew could expect to be on board for weeks, maybe months, as the exploration went on.

That meant there were two levels on the ship—operations and residential. He wasn't interested in residential; the crew wouldn't be on board that long. But operations had to have a fully functional engineering section, weaponry and defensive capabilities, and a bridge big enough to handle a minimal crew which, Fleet regulations stated, was five people at one time.

The bridge was on the opposite side of the ship from the cargo bay. So he jogged in that direction, a little surprised at the time it took. The simulation estimate for that seemed to be wildly off.

Of course, the simulation didn't take into account the equipment left in corridors from the *Br2 Scout3*'s last mission, or the way that the sharp angles of the *Br2 Scout3*'s design slowed down anyone scurrying across the ship.

The *Br2 Scout3* was just barely small enough for a crew of ten to run it, although crew compliment said that this ship needed a minimum of thirty, should the ship be gone for longer than a day or two.

Crowe finally reached the bridge, and was relieved to find the doors open. He had planned for four minutes of struggle with the control panel so that his crew could get into the bridge. He wouldn't need those four minutes, which was a good thing, since he had already wasted them and a few more getting to the bridge.

He wondered how Tessa was doing. He hadn't heard any sirens or notification of a lockdown, and he would have, since the *Br2 Scout3* was still on board the *Brazza Two*.

So she hadn't been caught.

The others of his crew joined him, environmental hoods down, looking a little flustered and sweaty from their own jogs across the ship. Maida reached his side.

"Ready?" she asked in a tone that told him she thought he was having second thoughts. If one word could sound like a shove in the back, that *ready* was it.

"Yep," he said, and stepped inside the bridge.

He had expected something small, but not something this claustrophobic. The ceiling was low, the lights old and a bit grey, the way that lights from a century ago were made. The bridge was designed like half of a bowl, with everything leading to the lower level down front. That level included a wide variety of screens, which could be toggled together to form a holographic representation of space itself.

He had thought that sounded exciting when he first found out about the design of this type of scout ship. He thought the bridge would seem vast. But now it seemed a little cheap, and the downward dip just looked like a hazard rather than a design feature.

Maybe that was because of the equipment. The equipment had been updated, but it looked grafted on, like a bandage over a particularly ugly wound.

The consoles were too large, for one thing, all of them a little too square for the design. The captain's chair, standard in larger ships, had been removed here. In fact, in order to make room for the extra equipment, every single chair in the bridge was gone.

He felt a little dizzy and then realized he'd been holding his breath. Not that it mattered. He hadn't tested with modern up-to-date equipment. His simulation had been based on the older ship, the design that *Br2 Scout3* had been built to, not the one it had been upgraded to.

"Wow," Adil said from beside him. "This thing has an *anacapa* drive."

He was looking at the *anacapa* container, near the navigation controls.

Crowe cursed under his breath. He didn't want to be anywhere near an *anacapa* drive. He thought he had picked a ship without one.

He'd studied the drives enough to know they were unpredictable, and the last thing he wanted was one of his people messing with one, and getting them all in trouble.

"We're not touching it," Crowe said. "In fact, we're not even opening the container. The first thing I'm going to do when I get to the controls is lock us out of the *anacapa*."

"No need," Maida said. "None of us want to touch it, right, gang?"

The entire crew chorused their unwillingness to touch the *anacapa* drive. He felt some of the tension leave.

This was why he had picked the ten people that he had. They believed in the same things he did. And they had that risk-taking attitude that he liked. Only they weren't reckless in their risk-taking. They took *calculated* risks.

"All right," he said. "I'm holding you guys to that, mostly because we're behind schedule as it is. Stations, everyone."

They all had assigned places and tasks. Navigation, shields (should they be necessary), and, most importantly, at least to him, recording the mission, not just on the ship's system, but on separate systems.

The crew was heading out to see a Scrapheap for the first—and maybe only—time in their lives. They needed a record of the visit.

"Here we go," he said.

And they all descended on the bridge, ready for the challenge of a lifetime.

THE *BR2 SCOUT3*

Fortunately, the captain's station remained in the middle of the bridge, even though the equipment had been changed out. Not that it would have mattered if the captain's station was in the back or near the phalanx of screens at the bottom of the bowl.

Crowe had run the simulations so many times that he could picture the station in his sleep. He was glad it was in the same place. That, at least, felt like he had expected it to.

He called up the holographic command screen. The structure of its menu looked like he expected as well, which was a relief. He glanced around the bridge. His crew was in place, all ten in their positions.

Maida was at the very bottom of the bowl. She had all of the screens on, plus a holographic replica of the area around the ship which was, right now, the interior of the *Brazza Two*'s docking bay.

Crowe's palms were sweating: he wiped them on the exterior of his environmental suit, not that it did any good. That material repelled liquid. It repelled everything.

He faced the biggest hurdle of all—leaving the *Brazza Two* without being detected.

Three days ago, he had found the automated exit controls for the docking ring. No one had to monitor exiting ships on most DV-Class vessels. But the *Brazza Two* monitored exits because of all the students on board.

But the default command/control inside the computer of a DV-Class vessel was an automated unmonitored exit, not the kind of exit the *Brazza Two* used. All he had to do was reset the *Brazza Two*'s command/control default, and he could leave easily.

Or so he had hoped when he reset that default. He had had no way to double-check what he had done.

He entered the command for decoupling from the *Brazza Two*. That system—like so many on board the *Br2 Scout3*—was automated.

In theory, the *Br2 Scout3* would contact the *Brazza Two*, and together, the automated systems on both ships would execute the departure of the *Br2 Scout3* from the *Brazza Two*.

A list of procedures appeared on his holographic screen, which he hadn't expected. Some things had been reprogrammed in other ways to accommodate the school ship, apparently.

One by one, each item on the procedure list checked itself off. As they got close to the final two—which would culminate in exiting the ship—he said to Igasho, "Activate the travel program."

Igasho nodded, and touched images on his holographic screen.

Crowe had decided a week ago to plot the coordinates of their trip alongside the Scrapheap. That way, he wouldn't be tempted to change the travel plans as they flew out—something he suspected he would do once he saw the Scrapheap.

He had plotted a trip that would take them along the edges of the Scrapheap, just far enough from its own protective barrier that the automated defense systems in the Scrapheap wouldn't notice his ship at all.

Technically, the Scrapheap was programmed not to worry about Fleet vessels, but Crowe had spent the last few months studying Scrapheaps—what little he could find. What he discovered was that most of them had been programmed when they were built and weren't updated by any ships that came within range.

There was also a lot about Scrapheaps that wasn't in the easily accessible file, which meant that there was a lot about Scrapheaps that were on a need-to-know basis, something that made them even more dangerous, at least in his opinion.

"Here we go," Maida said.

The door to the docking bay opened. It showed up on screen after screen and in the holographic recreation near her. The *Br2 Scout3* lurched forward, the way larger ships did when they had to leave some place at the lowest level of power.

Crowe's heart rate increased, but not with fear. With excitement. He was commanding his first ship. Yeah, this was an unofficial mission and yeah, he wasn't really captain, but it felt real enough.

It felt like his future was waiting for him right outside the *Brazza Two*.

The crew seemed to hold its collective breath. They watched as the *Br2 Scout3* eased out of the docking bay.

"When do I open the portholes?" Sera asked.

She was in charge of what Crowe had been calling the in-ship visuals. They had come to see the Scrapheap, and they were going to *see* the Scrapheap, not just on screens—which they could do from the *Brazza Two*—but up close and in person. Or as up close and in person as it was possible without going inside the Scrapheap itself.

"Now, I guess," Crowe said, and instantly regretted the *I guess*. Captains didn't speak in *I guesses*. Captains actually knew what they wanted, even when they didn't. They sounded certain.

He wasn't sounding certain at all.

Sera tapped her screen and then the bridge's ceiling opened, revealing the largest porthole Crowe had ever seen. He had been mentally braced for that, but being braced and actually seeing it were two different things.

Some of the documentation he'd seen on this type of scout ship had called the porthole over the bridge a design flaw, while others called it one of the most magnificent parts of the ship.

It was, he decided, both. Easy to attack and destroy (even with the protective layer provided by the ceiling) but it also provided one of the best views he'd ever seen on a starship.

The porthole curved downward and added extra width to the front of the bridge bowl. The porthole also curved along the sides of the bridge's walls as well. The only place the porthole didn't appear was behind him, where the door was. Bad design though it was, it was also a bit uplifting, and he found he didn't mind it one bit.

The *Br2 Scout3* eased out of the docking bay and into the space around *The Brazza Two*. The *Brazza Two* seemed impossibly huge next to the scout ship, dominating one entire side of the scout ship and towering over it as well, looming like a darkness over the porthole.

Crowe had picked this evening for the competition because in the morning, the officer contingent would begin its investigation of the Scrapheap, which meant that the *Brazza Two* was as close to the Scrapheap as it was going to get. He had figured that the officer training might involve day-long or week-long investigations of the Scrapheap, with other small ships hanging around the edges of the Scrapheap.

So he had calculated that this night was probably his best—his *only*—opportunity to see the Scrapheap up close.

The competition would keep him honest and get him back to the *Brazza Two* long before anyone got up for breakfast.

He was glad he planned that way, because the images on the screens before him took his breath away—and that was *before* he saw the Scrapheap with his own eyes.

He knew how big the Scrapheap was. He'd read the statistics. It was the size of a large moon. It wasn't perfectly spherical because it was an amalgamation of retired Fleet vessels, sent to the Scrapheap while the Fleet figured out what to do with them.

This Scrapheap had been in existence for more than four hundred years, if not longer. It was protected by a force field and had some kind of internal monitoring mechanism in the very center.

From what he could find in the records, the Scrapheap had a way of communicating with the Fleet should something go horribly awry. He had no idea what that meant, but it made him wary of going into the Scrapheap.

The other thing that made him wary about going inside—besides the force field and the notification—was the way that ships became part of the Scrapheap. They were either brought by other ships or they were sent to the internal coordinates of the Scrapheap using an *anacapa* drive.

Sometimes, he guessed, ships just appeared inside of it, and if they hit another ship, well then, oh, well. He didn't want to get hit, even if it were extremely unlikely that getting hit would happen.

"Wow," Erika said. She was looking up, so he did too.

Above him, the edge of the Scrapheap twinkled. That was all the confirmation he needed of a working force field. Then, beyond it, he could see the outline of an old DV-Class ship, and parts of some other ships, seemingly motionless, and much too close to each other.

His mouth gaped open despite his best efforts to remain calm in the face of something magnificent.

The *Br2 Scout3* moved slowly, but it seemed much too close to the Scrapheap. He glanced down at his controls.

Nope. The *Br2 Scout3* was following the edge of the Scrapheap exactly as he had programmed it.

The Scrapheap was just so large that it seemed like the *Br2 Scout3* was closer than it actually was.

He looked at the screens, saw his own ship as a pinprick against the edge of the large Scrapheap nearby. The *Brazza Two* was farther from the *Br2 Scout3* than the Scrapheap was, but he had designed this maneuver that way deliberately, although now he was wondering what, exactly, he had been thinking when he had done so.

The Scrapheap scared him. Contrary to what he had expected, he had no desire to break through that force field, to visit the inside of the Scrapheap, to see what he was missing. He was close enough, maybe even too close.

The Scrapheap hovered near his little scout ship like some malevolent creature, about to absorb him.

He wiped his sweaty palms on his pants, then realized that captains didn't do that. Captains didn't do a lot of things. They didn't recklessly put their friends in danger on a mission that they weren't trained for.

He had thought the simulations and the research would be enough.

He was wrong.

Crowe swallowed against his dry throat. No wonder the Fleet did not allow students near the Scrapheap. It was too dangerous.

They needed to turn back.

His team didn't seem anxious, though. For some reason, the scariness wasn't bothering them. Most worked their positions, as if they were regular bridge officers. Two weren't working at all. They were still looking up, gaping at the Scrapheap.

"Any sign of Tessa?" he asked. "Seriously?" Omar asked before anyone could answer Crowe. "We're touching distance from the Scrapheap, and you ask about *Tessa*?"

"Yeah." Crowe licked his bottom lip. It was chapped. He'd been tugging on it without even realizing it.

He wanted to declare the competition done. And if Tessa hadn't even gotten off the *Brazza Two*, then he could backtrack without fear of humiliation.

That thought had barely crossed his mind when another followed. Screw humiliation. He needed to get back to the ship.

"The other docking bay just opened," Maida said. She touched something on her holographic controls and another screen rose.

A ship that Crowe didn't recognize emerged from the docking bay. The design marked the ship as an Explorer-Class, one that was retired when the Scouts got bigger.

"Oh, crap," he said, maybe out loud.

Tessa was doing what he had initially thought of doing. There were a handful of Explorer-Class ships on the *Brazza Two*, for reasons he could not divine since no one had touched them in years. He wasn't even sure their systems had been maintained.

He knew it would be a lot of work to see if they had been maintained, which was why he had changed his mind about using one. He figured it would be hard enough for a group of teenage geniuses to pilot a ship larger than an orbiter when they hadn't done it before, but he figured it would be even harder for them to handle a crisis if something went wrong.

They just didn't have enough experience.

And he was smart enough to know that, at least.

He had felt a lot more confident about the scout ship. Although with all of the full simulations he had run, he had discovered a few crises that his inexperienced crew couldn't solve, and that the automatic controls couldn't handle either.

He called those simulations the *Kiss Your Ass Goodbye* scenarios, and fortunately, in all of the simulations he had run, the crew had only hit one of those once.

Once was worth the risk out of thousands of simulations.

He had thought, anyway.

He had no idea what kind of risk Tessa was taking, but it was a greater risk than he wanted to contemplate.

"Can you figure out how to hail them?" he asked Omar.

"Tessa's ship?" Omar said. "It might take some time. I have no idea what that ship is or what it's called or if they'll even answer us."

Crowe swallowed again, and it actually hurt. His throat was so dry that swallowing scraped. His heart was pounding.

This entire lark had gone awry, and not because of him.

"Figure out how." Crowe moved his own command screen closer. He would try to figure this out too. He hadn't investigated the communications on board the *Br2 Scout3* because he figured he wouldn't need it.

All he had imagined was someone—the *Brazza Two*—trying to contact him. Not him trying to contact someone else.

Through his clear holographic command screen, he could see the Explorer vessel. It was shaped like a stubby tube, and it rotated rapidly, something he had only seen a few Fleet ships do. He had no idea what the rotation meant. Rotation could be used for a variety of things, and he had no idea why it had been built into the design of the Explorer-Class ships.

And then the ship vanished.

"Don't get rid of the visuals," he barked at Maida.

"I didn't," she said.

He got cold. "What do you mean you didn't?"

"I mean," Maida said sounding as panicked as he felt, "Tessa's ship disappeared."

He swore. Explorers had *anacapa* drives. Tessa wouldn't be crazy enough to use one, would she? That took special training. Not even high level officers could use *anacapa* drives without clearance—

"Look!" Adil said, pointing at the Scrapheap.

There it was, the Explorer-Class vessel, butted up against the force field.

Crowe's breath caught. "Tell me that's not inside the Scrapheap," he said, but no one did.

He used his own controls, but their readings were inconclusive. Or maybe he just couldn't understand them.

"Hail her," he said to the crew in general. "Someone. Hail her *now*."

Three different people started pressing their fingers against their holographic consoles, searching for a way to contact Tessa.

Maida found it first—or rather, didn't find it.

"I think she's inside the Scrapheap," Maida said, answering his first question, "because I'm being told that the ship is outside of communications range, and that's just not true."

Crowe put a hand on the top of his skull, wrapping his fingers in his hair. Why would Tessa do this? Why?

But he knew the answer. She did it so that she could beat him. And she had. How did he let her know that she had?

"I think I got through," Adil said. "See if you can talk to her."

"Tessa," Crowe said. "You win, okay? Now get out of there."

"Do I have that on record?" Tessa's voice came through the console loud and clear, as if she was beside him.

"You do. You win. We all attest to it. Now get out."

"You should see this, Crowe," she said. "You have no idea how many ships are here. It's so neat."

"Great," he said. "Maybe next time. Take great video. And, um, do you think you can get out without using the *anacapa* drive?"

"Why?" she asked. "That's how we got in."

"I know," he said, and then stopped himself. He didn't want to say the drives were dangerous, because he didn't want to scare her. But they were, and no one in their group knew how to use one.

"Stop worrying," she said. "We're going to take a few touristy vids and then we are out of here. I promise. You get on your little trajectory up and down the outside. I'll meet you back in the Third Level Mess. And you better pay up, buddy."

She signed off. He wanted to clutch the air around him, grab onto her and her words and shake her.

"Pay up?" Erika asked, with a smile on her face. "What did you promise?"

He was about to answer her when something at the edge of the Scrapheap caught his eye.

"What's that brightness?" he asked Maida.

She saw it too, then augmented the screen and the holographic projection.

"I think it's an explosion," Omar said. He wasn't looking at the visuals. He was looking at the console in front of him. "And—shit—it's moving, like—I don't know—an infection."

It was moving, seemingly from ship to ship or piece to piece. It was far enough away from the Explorer-Class vessel that it hadn't hit them yet, but it would.

"Adil," Crowe said, "can you hail her again?"

"I'm trying." Adil sounded terrified.

Crowe swore again. He jabbed at his holographic console, trying to see if there was something stronger than a grappler on this ship.

The *Brazza Two* had a limited mechanism, a way of pulling nearby ships into the *Brazza Two* if need be. Most ships didn't have it—it was dangerous tech—but school ships did because they did so much training.

And maybe this Scout ship had something too, but he couldn't find anything like that, and he had no idea how to get through the force field, even if he did.

At that moment, the force field shimmered right in front of the Explorer-Class ship. The Explorer zoomed out of the Scrapheap, white and golden explosions lighting up the area behind it.

For a moment, the ship seemed to be free of the Scrapheap, and maybe everything would have worked out if the force field had closed behind the Explorer-Class vessel, but it didn't, and the light, looking almost like it was burning (not possible—there was no oxygen in space, not possible at all), traveled along lines straight for the Explorer-Class vessel.

"Put up your shields, put up your shields, put up your shields," Crowe said to Tessa, even though she couldn't hear him. And then he realized what he was saying. He found the controls for the *Br2 Scout3*'s shields, and activated them on full.

The fire lines—or whatever the hell that was—reached the Explorer-Class vessel, and outlined it for a half second. Crowe imagined he could see every deck and every person inside the vessel, the way that he had seen a human skeleton once, illuminated through someone's skin underneath some kind of irradiated light.

The Explorer-Class vessel seemed frozen—and then it exploded, bits of the ship flying everywhere.

"We need to get out of here," Sera said, reaching for her console. "That stuff is going to get us."

"I vote we try the *anacapa* drive," Maida said, sounding even more panicked than she had before. "I think we should—"

"No," Crowe said.

The explosions were continuing inside the Scrapheap, moving away from the force field deeper into the Scrapheap itself. The remaining parts of the force field were bowing from some kind of pressure, and Crowe thought he could see ships, stretching on into infinity.

"The *Brazza Two* is moving," Sera said.

He looked down at his controls. Sure enough, the *Brazza Two* was moving away from the Scrapheap at a rapid clip.

"Match their speed," he said to Igasho, who had been the one who tested best on the navigational controls. "Get us out of here."

And he hoped Igasho could.

THE *BR2 SCOUT3*

The *Br2 Scout3* wasn't moving. But the *Brazza Two* was, leaving them—and the Scrapheap—behind at a rapid clip. The Scrapheap looked like it was on fire. The fire kept moving, into and out of the Scrapheap, consuming everything in its path.

They were in its path. The *Br2 Scout3*. With his friends. Whom he had brought on board.

Just like he had gotten Tessa involved.

"Really, Crowe," Maida said, "the *anacapa*."

She wanted him to use the drive, just like Tessa had. Tessa, who had laughed and said *Stop worrying* in that chiding tone of hers.

"This is already a disaster," he snapped at Maida. "Let's not make it worse."

Although it was getting worse by the second. Through that opening in the force field, parts of ships were spiraling outward, some of them glowing just like the Explorer-Class vessel had glowed just before it exploded.

And sure enough, one of the ships that had spun out the farthest just exploded, followed by another, and another.

Crowe took over the navigation of the *Br2 Scout3*. Screw Igasho. Screw the testing. What mattered was the way everyone behaved in the field.

Crowe had just figured out it was easier to do things on his own than it was to give commands.

"I got this now," he said to Igasho.

Then Crowe changed the trajectory of his ship. He wasn't chasing the *Brazza Two* any longer. He plotted a course as far from the Scrapheap as he could possible go.

He needed the *Br2 Scout3* to go faster, as fast as it could go. He revved up the speed, ignoring the ship's warnings that flashed all over his screen.

This speed is not recommended, it said right near the *execute* button.

"Screw you," he said to the screen, and punched *execute* with all of his strength.

The ship yanked forward so hard that he could feel it inside the bridge despite the attitude controls. Something squealed, probably the engines.

"Our shields are getting pelted," someone said. "I don't know if they'll hold."

Crowe glanced at the holographic three-dimensional image that Maida had created. Debris was flying out of the Scrapheap in all directions and at all kinds of speeds. The explosions were still traveling inward at what seemed like an even more rapid clip.

And the *Brazza Two* was getting slammed as well. Its shields looked fragile. The entire ship seemed to be in the middle of the debris instead of getting away from it.

The *Br2 Scout3* on the other hand had moved away from the bulk of the debris, but a lot of it was still coming in their direction.

Crowe wasn't going to be able to outrun this. They were all going to die. Everyone, all of his friends, dead because he decided to do something stupid. Tessa...

He wouldn't let himself think about her. He had to get a grip on himself, think of this as a simulation.

He called up the *Br2 Scout3*'s weapons system. It wasn't online, but he knew how to get at least part of it to work.

"What're you doing?" Omar asked.

"Weapons," Crowe said.

"Got it," Adil said, as if that were a command.

"Can you bolster the shields?" Crowe asked Maida.

"I don't know, I—"

"Bolster them," he snapped. He hadn't expected her to be a panicker when he had given her the task of being his number one. She was great technically, but everything was a crisis for her, not that it wasn't a crisis, it was, but he didn't need her reacting like that.

"Yes, sir," she said, as if he were an actual captain. He wanted to look at her in surprise, but he didn't, because he didn't have time.

The weapons array appeared. *Targets?* It asked him.

Simulation, he reminded himself.

And then he programmed in all of the debris that was heading their way.

He didn't have the skill to run the weapons system himself, so he set it on automatic.

"Crowe," Erika said, "For God's sake, rule out the *Brazza Two*."

He hadn't even thought of that. Part of him wondered why she hadn't done it, and then he realized, he hadn't given anyone else permission to run the weapons system—within the system itself.

He protected the *Brazza Two,* and the actual Scrapheap, and then entered his entire team into the command structure for the weapons system.

After he did that, he realized with a start that the system had already targeted and destroyed the bigger pieces of debris. The smaller bits of debris were hitting the shield and—at the moment—bouncing off.

The *Br2 Scout3* was getting farther and farther from the Scrapheap, but he kept monitoring it. The *Brazza Two* was moving parallel to the Scrapheap, for reasons he did not understand. It was taking a lot of damage.

One large piece was spiraling toward the *Brazza Two,* and it looked like it was going to directly hit one entire side of the ship. If it hit, then the entire ship might be opened to space, and then everyone would die, because he had wanted to stage a competition—

"Simulation," he whispered. "Simulation."

Maida was staring at everything, not moving, and in that moment, he realized he wasn't the only one having trouble with all the events around them.

"You guys!" he yelled. "This is just a damn simulation!"

Yes, he was lying, but they didn't know that.

"It looks real," Maida said.

"All simulations look real," he said. "Now get to work."

And miraculously, she did. She started using her skills to boost the shields. He went back to the weapons system, because he couldn't control whatever it was that the *Brazza Two* was doing.

The debris was thinning, although he didn't know if that was because his weapons kept targeting it, or because the *Br2 Scout3* had moved beyond much of it, or because the explosions inside the Scrapheap were slowing down.

He couldn't do anything except continue to run. And as he had that thought, he paused for what seemed like forever, but really only had to be a half second.

Run. Because this was an unmitigated disaster.

Run. Because his life was over even if he went back to the *Brazza Two*.

Run—and never find out what caused this.

Run—and lose the only home he had ever known.

He wiped at his face—it was wet—and then made himself study the Scrapheap.

The explosions were continuing, but the force field was knitting itself back together.

It took him a moment to realize that something was being sent from the *Brazza Two* to the Scrapheap, some kind of beam or light or ray or something that seemed to be inspiring the Scrapheap force field rebuild.

And then he realized what that was.

The *Brazza Two* had taken the energy from its shields and was using that to encourage the force field on the Scrapheap to rebuild.

The *Brazza Two* was putting the entire ship in danger to stop whatever was cascading inside and around the Scrapheap.

The entire ship, from the officer cadets to the little-littles.

Who cried near the mural because they had been sent away from home.

The little-littles. If they died, it would be his fault.

It was all his fault.

THE *BR2 SCOUT3*

Crowe's breath hitched. He couldn't think about the little-littles or the risks he had forced everyone to take. He couldn't think about what could go wrong as the *Brazza Two* tried to rebuild the Scrapheap's force field.

He had to act.

He programmed a hard about into the *Br2 Scout3*. The *Brazza Two* needed reinforcements and they weren't going to come from any ship nearby.

He still had full shields.

"What are you doing?" Now Omar sounded panicked.

Crowe wasn't going to answer him. Crowe didn't dare answer him, because Crowe didn't want to get talked out of this.

"Maintain the speed," he said to Igasho, "no matter what."

The debris continued to zoom past, but the weapons seemed to catch most of it. Amazingly, the *Br2 Scout3* had very little damage—so far.

He programmed coordinates into the navigational system so that the *Br2 Scout3* would arrive on the far side of the *Brazza Two*, the opposite side from the Scrapheap.

"We can't go back to the *Brazza Two*," someone cried from the back. "Not now."

In his own head, Crowe deliberately did not identify the speaker. He didn't want to know who had given voice to his very thought from before. He would *not* get talked into running away.

Not now.

Not yet.

Maybe not ever.

"The engines are in really bad shape," Erika said. "They're not made to sustain this speed. The system wants me to use the *anacapa* drive."

"The system can screw itself," Crowe said, even though the system was the only thing keeping them alive right now.

He was keeping his eye on the *Brazza Two*. Maybe he was crazy, taking the *Br2 Scout3* to the *Brazza Two*—if the *Brazza Two* exploded, then everyone would die.

He had no idea what was causing the explosions nor did he know what was going on with the Scrapheap. Judging by the *Brazza Two*'s reaction, someone on board there knew exactly what was going on and they had done a calculation—the lives of everyone on board (including the little-littles) were less important than keeping whatever was coming out of the Scrapheap contained.

That whole idea just made him shiver.

He wiped at his face again—dammit—and let out a small ragged sigh as the *Br2 Scout3* reached the *Brazza Two.*

"Get closer," he said to Maida. He needed to try something, and he couldn't be bothered with micromaneuvering the *Br2 Scout3.*

"Closer to what?" she asked.

"Sera," he said, deciding to ignore Maida. "Get this ship as close as you can on *this* side of the *Brazza Two*. Keep us away from the Scrapheap."

"Got it." Sera sounded almost chirpy. He glanced at her. She wasn't quite smiling—more like a grimace—but she was concentrating *hard* on what she was doing.

Unlike Maida, who was still not focusing very well.

"Simulation, simulation, simulation," he whispered, thinking of the challenge before him as one that required accuracy in a short period of time.

He had no idea how to use all the permutations of these shields, but he was going to try. He had to assume they worked like standard shields on all of the Fleet's larger vessels.

If he was wrong, it probably wouldn't matter, since everyone was going to die anyway, but he had to give it a try.

"Need help?" Adil asked.

"No." Crowe sounded a bit curt, but he couldn't help it. He had to concentrate.

And—breakthrough—the shields were just like he expected. He took their power and moved it, just like the shield specs said he could. He poured that power at the *Brazza Two*, augmenting their shields.

For a moment, those shields grew stronger, repelling what he was doing. Then someone on board the *Brazza Two* must have realized what Crowe was about, because the *Brazza Two* started sucking shield power from the *Br2 Scout3.*

The *Br2 Scout3* command console warned him that the power output was too high, that it might have to pull from important systems.

He circumvented that. He guided the ship to pull from engines. Then he shut off the automated weapons response, and had the ship pull from that too.

If something came at them now, they were undefended completely. The *Br2 Scout3* would get damaged at best, blown up at worst.

But he didn't tell the others. He didn't dare. He didn't want them to question what he was doing. They might try to reverse it.

The *Brazza Two* glowed orange as the energy moved from the *Br2 Scout3*'s shields to *Brazza Two*'s shields to that ray-beam-light whatever that was funneling power to the Scrapheap.

Crowe clenched one fist, watching. He could only monitor now; he didn't dare do anything else.

"This ship is shuddering," Erika said. "Is a ship this size supposed to shudder?"

No one answered her. They were all working on something or looking at the scene playing out on the screens.

Crowe was watching the *Brazza Two*. It looked different somehow, maybe just because he had never seen it from this vantage.

The explosions continued, worming their way deeper into the Scrapheap. He could see spots of color, but they were harder and harder to read as the force field closed up.

Then something in the very middle of the Scrapheap lit up the entire area around it. That something looked huge. It was rectangular, with actual right angles and corners, which led him to believe it was human-made, not some layout caused by various ships.

The power coming off the *Brazza Two* intensified.

The force field was nearly closed.

And then that rectangle exploded.

Ships spun out of it, bright red and orange and yellow, surrounded with that light that he had seen before.

The force field was nearly closed, but something small whipped its way out of the remaining opening.

And then he realized that the something wasn't small. It was the size of a small ship, an orbiter or a runabout. And it was heading directly for the *Brazza Two*.

He couldn't do anything, and neither could the *Brazza Two*. Its entire power was being focused on that beam-ray-light that was closing the force field. It never wavered.

He wanted the beam-ray-light to shut off, weapons to appear, something to happen to that runabout-orbiter.

Instead, the small ship slammed into the side of the *Brazza Two*, sending it toward the *Br2 Scout3* at an amazing rate of speed.

"Stop linking us to them!" Maida shouted.

She was right. That would ease some of the pressure, give the *Br2 Scout3* some maneuverability, but she didn't realize that their futures were over anyway, and—

The *Brazza Two* grazed them, scraping over the top, damaging the stupid porthole that he had thought was so special.

He activated some emergency controls, or maybe they were already activating as the porthole cracked.

"Bring your hoods up," he said. "Activate your environmental suits."

Everyone did, just like they'd been trained to do in every single class they had ever taken. The hoods went up, the suits were sealed, the environment kicked in—cooler than the air on the bridge, and, at least in his case, staler.

This suit hadn't been worn in a long, long time.

The ceiling closed above them, but it wasn't going to matter. The ship was losing environment.

But only the bridge was populated. The rest of the ship was empty. And this ship was designed to preserve the environment everywhere.

He launched into the controls again, not giving instructions again, because explaining was just so damn hard.

He isolated the bridge and rather than siphoning its environment to other parts of the ship, he directed theirs here. He established a protective bubble around the bridge itself, so even if the ceiling didn't protect them from the cracked porthole (and seriously, who designed that? Because it was pretty stupid. Maybe that's why this Scout ship was being retired), then they would be able to survive until someone rescued them.

If someone rescued them.

He looked to see how the *Brazza Two* was doing, but all of the screens that Maida had set up were gone, as was the holographic model. His own control screen was flickering.

The *Br2 Scout3* was running out of power.

He suddenly felt lighter.

It took a moment to understand that sensation. He hadn't felt it in years—the transition between full Earth gravity and zero gravity, happening slowly. He'd gone to zero gravity workouts, but there was no transition. He'd just go from one environment to the next. This one was changing bit by bit.

He activated the gravity in his boots, and they clamped onto the floor as if they were magnetized.

"Anyone see what's going on with the Scrapheap?" he asked.

"Force field's closed," Omar said.

"The *Brazza Two* has shut off that thingy tying it to the force field," Sera said.

"Explosions are continuing inside the Scrapheap," Maida said, "but it doesn't look like anything else is getting out."

Crowe tried to make his screen work, but it didn't. There was a design flaw too. He needed to look at the command controls and they weren't accessible to him.

He tried to walk to one of the wall consoles, but the gravity in his boots was holding him back. His legs actually hurt as he moved.

He cursed.

"The *Brazza Two*," he said. "Is it holding together?"

"Seems to be," Sera said.

"But we're not," Adil said. "You getting these warnings?"

"No," Crowe said. "My console is down."

"We need to get out of here," Maida said, her voice rising with panic again.

He blinked, thought, wondered if the *Brazza Two* would even take a message from them.

He managed to get to the wall console, and slammed his fist against it with a bit more force than he expected. Fortunately, the slowly decreasing gravity mitigated the power of that blow. He didn't damage anything, and he would have if he had hit it that hard in full Earth gravity.

The console flared on. He saw a dozen different warning lights, and actually heard the voice of the ship filtering into his hood, stating each and every one of those warnings with a flat seriousness.

The *Br2 Scout3* was close to the *Brazza Two*, but he'd lost track of what part of the ship was right near them. He called up a two-D image on the flat screen before him, the best he could do.

As far as he could tell, they weren't far from the bay door they had exited from.

Could they be that lucky?

"Adil," he said, "send the signal to the bay doors to open for us."

"I'm not sure we can maneuver in there," Adil said.

"Just see if the damn doors open," Crowe said.

He was investigating whether or not the engines had any thrust at all, and if the helm would respond to commands he gave.

The power was flickering. The *Br2 Scout3* was dying or at least it thought it was dying, but it seemed like there might be just enough juice here to get them on board the *Brazza Two* again.

After that, he had no idea what would happen.

"Doors opening!" Adil sounded ecstatic. Had Crowe ever heard Adil sound ecstatic? Crowe had no idea.

"Okay," Crowe said. He rerouted the remaining power to engines and the helm, punching in the proper coordinates for docking—he didn't even want to try automation (not that he'd ever done anything as complicated as a docking maneuver) and then he hit *execute.*

The *Br2 Scout3* lurched again, which he hoped was a good sign. He focused on the two-D images on the screen before him, the small ship heading toward the larger one.

The *Brazza Two*'s shields were down. The ship seemed to be rotating away from the *Br2 Scout3*. He hoped that wasn't the case.

But the littler ship headed toward the open bay doors. He slowed the *Br2 Scout3* as much as possible, hoping that it was slow enough. He gave the ship one last thrust and then shut off the engines entirely, hoping the ship would ease through the doors on its own accord.

It didn't veer off course. It headed directly for the *Brazza Two*, directly for those doors, and then into the docking bay itself. The bay was dark and there was no power, and nothing was going to stop the *Br2 Scout3* from going through a wall if he wasn't careful.

He hit the inertial dampeners on the *Br2 Scout3*, demanded that they stop the ship as quickly as they possibly could.

For a minute he thought they weren't working either, but then they did. And the *Br2 Scout3* floated above the dock, just like it was meant to.

He didn't sigh with relief. He couldn't feel anything. He wasn't even sure he was breathing properly, but he had to be, because he had enough air to talk.

"Adil," Crowe said. "Shut the bay doors."

"Okay," Adil said.

And Crowe turned on the automatic pilot, instructing it to dock, and hoping that would work.

Then he leaned against the console, and tried very very hard to stay calm.

He had no idea why that was so important, but he knew it was.

THE *BRAZZA TWO*

It took them an hour to get off the *Br2 Scout3* and another hour to get out of the docking bay. They kept their environmental suits on, hoods up, just in case everything inside the bay was compromised.

Crowe's suit wouldn't tell him what the environment around them was, but the bay itself was much darker than it should have been. He kept expecting security around every corner. He thought they might show up with their weapons drawn, might take everyone into custody, but no one seemed to be monitoring the docking bay at all, which really bothered him.

He discovered part of the problem as they tried to leave the bay. The doors were sealed. He and Adil checked the bay doors to make sure they had closed properly—and they had—so they both figured the sealed exits were part of some security protocol.

They didn't discuss overriding it; they just did. None of them wanted to stay in the dark and creepy docking bay.

It didn't take long to override the security protocol, which should have bothered Crowe, but it didn't. He wanted to get back inside the *Brazza Two*. He wanted to find his room, and hide in it.

The exit doors slid open to reveal chaos. Bright red lights blinked everywhere. The floor was illuminated yellow so that they could find their way to a safe zone. The ship's automated voice, so different from the one on the *Br2 Scout3*, repeated that they were in an emergency and they needed to get to their designated shelter.

Designated shelter. He had forgotten about that. He'd always thought the drills stupid, and now, there was actual need for all of that practice.

He had no idea how to get to his shelter from here. And he wasn't going to go either.

He had a different destination in mind.

"Now what do we do?" Maida asked. She was shouting through the environmental suits' communications link, even though she didn't have to. Their voices came through clearly even with all the noise.

Crowe looked around. There was some damage here—the walls had scorch marks (at least, that was what he thought he saw), and it was pretty clear that the Earth gravity had vanished at one point. There was too much debris on the floor, not just ship parts and wall parts, but casual items—tools and gloves and a few plastic dishes (from where he did not know).

That probably meant the environmental system had been shut down as well, and who knew what other systems had been offline. If he had to guess—and it would just be a guess at the moment—he would say that the power from all available systems went to the shields or to that beam-ray-light thing that the *Brazza Two* had used to link with the forcefield on the Scrapheap.

"Get to your designated shelter," he said to his crew, his team, his friends. "Don't say where you were or what you were doing. Just go. They may not know that we were the ones on the *Br2 Scout3*. They'll know about me—"

"How?" Omar asked. "If they don't know about us, they won't know about you."

"I did a lot of work ahead on this," Crowe said. "My presence will be hard to hide."

Besides, he wasn't sure he wanted to hide it. He would think about that when he left the group.

"I just don't want you guys to get into trouble because you listened to me," he said.

"Well, we did," Erika said. "We chose to come along. We should take our punishment too. I mean, look at this."

She swept a hand toward the debris in the corridor before them. None of them had ever seen any part of the *Brazza Two* like this. It had always been pristine.

"We stole two ships," Crowe said flatly, "destroyed who knows how many in the Scrapheap, and damaged the *Brazza Two*."

And maybe killed Tessa and her team. Maybe. He refused to believe that yet. Because, after all, he had no proof they had been on that Explorer.

(*Except that she had talked to him. She had told him. She—*)

He shook his head, trying to get the niggling thoughts out of it.

"This is really serious," Crowe said, "and they'll probably pull anyone involved out of the program."

Maybe put them in the brig or take them to one of the sector bases for some kind of justice.

Or send them back to their parents.

His stomach twisted, and bile rose in his throat. He swallowed the bile down, trying to ignore it.

"So go," Crowe said. "You don't want to be involved in this."

"I'm not going to lie," Erika said.

"Then don't lie about yourself," Crowe said, "but don't implicate anyone else."

"You're going to lie?" she asked.

He shook his head.

"This is my fault," he said. "Every one of us knows this is all my fault."

THE *BRAZZA TWO*

His team left him after that. One by one, they walked down that corridor, until it curved to the right, and he couldn't see them anymore.

No one stayed with him. He hadn't asked them to, and would have encouraged them not to, if someone had tried.

No one did.

He didn't blame them. They probably felt as numb and lost as he did.

He unhooked his environmental suit's hood, and pushed it off his face. He figured he could bring it back up if there was no air, but there was, and he was glad—if he could actually feel something akin to gladness.

The air had an acrid odor that he couldn't entirely identify. Some of the stench was burnt plastic and rubber, but some of it smelled faintly like pepper, or ammonia or something that he didn't want to contemplate.

His eyes started watering immediately and his brain told him to put the hood back on. But he wasn't going to. He deserved the watery eyes, the headache already building in his sinuses. He needed to smell this, and taste it, and feel the greasiness of the air.

He had caused this by being reckless and arrogant. What had he thought? Geniuses, on a joyride. They wouldn't get caught, or if they did, they'd get their wrists slapped and maybe be rewarded for their ingenuity.

God, how wrong could one kid be?

He had shut off the gravity in his boots long ago, but his feet still felt heavy. The muscles were sore fighting that extra force. When he stepped over bits of debris, his knees ached.

The farther he went down the corridor, the blacker the walls were. It looked like some of the controls had exploded outward. There was a bit of foam on the floor, and the walls and ceiling had a slick wet coating look to them as well. That peppery tang was stronger here, along with the stench of burning.

His eyes stung, but the tears had stopped. His throat ached, although he was no longer sure the worst of the ache was being caused by the smell.

He walked along the corridor, saw the footprints from his friends illuminated in the yellow light. Sirens whooped out here, but they sounded anemic. They weren't coming from overhead; they were echoing from other parts of the ship.

If the sirens weren't blaring here, they were either burned out or had never come on. But that annoying voice, a little more robotic than the one on the *Br2 Scout3*—that was the difference, he had finally identified it, was still telling him (and anyone else who was in this corridor) to go to their designated shelter.

He hoped everyone had. He hoped the only losses were the two ships. He hoped that Tessa had been lying to him about what she saw.

Because she was good at winning these contests without following the rules. He always forgot to specify certain details.

He never said they had to be on the ships. He never said that. He never said they had to travel individually outside of the *Brazza Two*.

She could have sent that Explorer-Class vessel on its own mission, and recorded what it saw on her own equipment.

That was something Tessa would do.

That was something he *hoped* and *prayed* Tessa would do.

He walked to the ladder linking the docking bay to the other levels. He went inside the wide tube where the ladder was and slid inside. No soot here, no smell of pepper. But hand prints—glove prints—on the rungs. Boot prints too.

His people probably. His team, his crew, his friends. Going up and away from here. To their shelters.

He hoped all ten of them had the presence of mind to remove their environmental suits from the *Br2 Scout3* before going into the shelter. He had forgotten to say anything.

He climbed the ladder, his entire body feeling wobbly and stretchy from exhaustion. Mostly he had stood and worried when he was on the bridge of the *Br2 Scout3*, but it felt like he had been running and hitting things for three solid days.

Maybe the oxygen was thinner here than he thought.

Maybe the exhaustion came from something else.

He shook that thought away as he reached the third level.

It didn't smell bad here at all, but the ship's voice still reminded him to go to his shelter. The yellow lights covered the floor and the red warning lights flashed.

Nothing looked damaged, though. He wondered how that happened—all the damage below, and nothing here. Although the damage below seemed to have come from systems being overloaded and there were fewer essential systems here. Almost everything here had been designed for the little-littles.

He didn't see any of them. He hadn't seen anyone, not since his team had left him.

Everyone was probably still in shelters.

He staggered a bit on his way to the Third Level Mess. He wasn't sure what caused the stagger—those rubbery tired legs of his or the ship listing and the attitude controls not working or the floor buckling just a bit from whatever had happened below.

He would find out eventually, he supposed.

The doors to the Third Level Mess were open, just like he had left them. Or had he left them like that?

The very thought made his heart lift. Maybe he had been right in his assumptions; maybe Tessa had played him. Maybe she was waiting for him here—she certainly wouldn't have gone to her designated shelter, not after everything that happened.

He had declared her the winner, so he couldn't take that back.

He stepped through the doors, startled at the red lights blinking. This room was silent—something he'd learned when he worked here. No blanket announcements to panic the little-littles.

The dim lights in all the corners were still on. The light over the serving table was on as well.

But the floor was a minefield of utensils and dishes and toys. The toys made his heart clench. He looked around, terrified he'd see some injured or dead little kid crumpled against one of the chairs.

He switched on the knuckle lights on his glove, swept the entire Mess once, twice, and then a third time, all without moving from the door.

Nothing.

He was alone.

Unless Tessa was hiding, wanting to surprise him. She wouldn't do that, would she? That wasn't quite like her.

He stepped inside, his jangled nerves and his pounding heart ahead of his brain.

He was alone here.

She hadn't come.

If she had been on the *Brazza Two,* she would have come here. She had said, *I'll meet you back in the Third Level Mess. And you better pay up, buddy.*

She never let a challenge go unanswered. She never let him forget that he lost. She would be waiting for him, partly to see if he was okay, and partly to gloat that she had won, no matter what the cost.

Although the cost would have devastated her.

Instead, it had destroyed her.

He shook his head, trying to get that last thought out of it. No. She was fine. He was fine. They were all fine.

He went deeper into the Mess, smelled something sweet and sugary—spilled syrup?—and saw where the toys had come from. The box of extra toys for the distraught kids had toppled over. Or maybe it had risen in zero-G and then turned over. He didn't know, couldn't tell, didn't want to know.

He was just relieved as he walked that he didn't see anything else—anyone else.

Except Tessa.

"Please be here," he whispered. "Please."

But he knew he was talking to an empty room. He didn't just know it on a gut level. He knew it throughout his body.

That victorious trill in her voice, followed by the weird bright light, and the lines of fiery light that trailed to her ship, and the explosion…

The explosion.

His knees buckled. He clutched at a nearby chair, missed because it was shorter than he expected (*Stupid. This is the Third Level Mess. For little-littles*), and nearly fell over. His hand caught the low table going down, and he stood there, bent in half, breathing hard, his entire body aching.

The explosion. Tessa. God. What had she been thinking? Why hadn't she simulated it out? Why had she tried something so risky?

Risky like stealing ships and going to the Scrapheap in the first place. As a lark. A trick to fool the teachers and to see something forbidden. To prove how smart he was.

He hiccoughed—half a laugh at himself, half something else he didn't want to identify. His chest hurt, his throat was full, his eyes were watering again, and damn. Tessa.

He had no idea how long he stood there, shaking, unwilling to stand up, but eventually he did. Eventually, he had to. His back was giving out.

No one came for him. No one probably even knew he was here.

But the red lights had stopped blinking while he was bent over, and the floor was no longer yellow.

Someone would come to clean up this place.

If there was any reason to.

He should have started the cleaning process, but he couldn't bring himself to do so.

Instead, he made it to the mural and sat on the bench beneath it, wondering if those painted kittens and puppies had magical soothing powers.

Probably not.

He wasn't sure he believed in magic anyway. He used to like to say—to Tessa—that he was a man of science.

Tessa.

He closed his eyes and waited, hoping she would come back to him, and knowing she never ever would.

THE *BRAZZA TWO*

It took nearly a week for someone in authority to talk to him, and that someone ended up being the captain.

Crowe had spent the entire week confined to quarters, but the quarters he was confined to weren't his. The dorm rooms on his level did not have kitchens and had a shared bathroom between four rooms, and someone—he had no idea who—decided he was too dangerous to be with anyone else.

He concurred. He was dangerous.

He got bits and pieces of news in his luxurious prison. The brig had been completely demolished when some of the debris hit it, which was why he was imprisoned in the two-room quarters. The quarters had a large porthole, but it had been sealed closed. He couldn't look out of it, even if he wanted to.

He no longer had computer privileges either, and everyone seemed to forget he had been a student, because no one gave him homework or study materials or anything to read. He could access only the first level of entertainment, which he kept playing on repeat. He just had it on as noise.

He couldn't access any other news, but someone different stopped by every day, and each time, he would ask what happened. He got different snippets from different people.

The death toll finally settled at fifty. They had initially thought it would go higher, but apparently, the injured were recovering.

The damage to one entire section of the ship was catastrophic. Entire levels were closed off, but that was where most of the people had died—and they had died in ways he didn't want to think about, because their section had been ripped open and exposed to space, and while the ship could repair itself and put down a barrier to hold in the ship's environment, the barrier would go down wherever it was most likely to hold, and in that case, apparently, the barrier had sacrificed an entire wing of the ship.

Fortunately every nonessential person had already evacuated that area.

And no children died.

Except, as a woman had told him tersely, just as she was leaving the room, the eleven teenagers on board that ship.

Seven days afterwards, exactly, the captain summoned him.

Only Crowe hadn't been aware of the summons initially. Two guards got him, told him to join them *now*, and then marched him through darkened corridors that looked abandoned.

Halfway through the march, he wondered if someone was planning to hurt him physically for all he had done.

But by the time that he got to the ship's administrative level, he knew that no one was going to hurt him or beat him up or discipline him in unsanctioned ways.

The guards had taken him through a deserted part of the ship so that no one would see him or talk to him or come at him.

They were, apparently, protecting him. And he wanted to tell them he was not worth their time.

But he didn't.

Because they led him into a suite of rooms he'd never been in before. The rooms were brightly lit and beautifully decorated—or had been until last week. Some of the decorations had been put back, like images stuck to the walls, only those images were frozen rather than rotating through a panorama of views. Most were frozen on some planetside image—a waterfall, some flowers, but one of them was of a little-little laughing beneath the mural, and he had to look away.

The guards led him into a narrow room with too much light, and a gigantic black desk that almost resembled half a wall. Behind it, the captain stood, her hands clasped behind her back—that posture he had mimicked before everything changed.

She turned around. Her face had new lines, and her eyes were sunken into their sockets from lack of sleep.

"Leave us," she said to the guards.

They did, the door closing behind them.

That was when Crowe realized the room had no chairs at all.

"I'm not going to ask you why you did it," she said. "We found all the materials you prepared, figured out what systems you breached, and talked to your friends. If I really cared why you did it, I suppose I'd be more thorough and ask you. But I don't care."

She sounded tired too. That energy he had so admired in her was gone.

"I just want to tell you that you pose a hell of a dilemma." She raised her chin just a little, and with that movement, he realized that he was taller than she was. "You see, Mr. Crowe, we wouldn't be standing here without you."

"I know," he said miserably. "I've been thinking about it—"

"You did not let me get to my point," she said. "You saved every life on the *Brazza Two*. That maneuver of yours, sharing the energy from the scout ship with our ship, no one taught you that, right?"

He shook his head. Of course no one had taught him that. Who could have taught him that? He wasn't supposed to be on ships, let alone train on them.

"You had gotten your ship clear of the debris field. You could have left. You could have taken the ship far from us, and all of you could have escaped. Instead, you came back and made yet another risky maneuver, enabling us to close that force field. You saved lives."

He was still shaking his head. "I didn't though. People died."

"They did," she said, her tone flat. "And that's our dilemma. You were reckless, and your recklessness destroyed ships and cost fifty people their lives. And then you were brilliant, and you saved over four hundred of us. By rights, we should banish you from Fleet ships forever. But if we do, we'll lose one of the most brilliant thinkers we've encountered in generations."

She smiled, but the smile didn't reach her very tired eyes.

"See?" she said. "Dilemma."

"No," he said, since the head-shaking was doing no good. "It's not a dilemma. Send me away. It's all my fault. Everything. I coerced everyone else. I made them. It all happened because of me—"

"Actually," she said, "we both know that's not true. Tessa Linley made one fatal choice. She used her *anacapa* drive. No one is allowed to use that drive without nearly a decade of training, and somehow she managed to override all of those systems."

"Tessa didn't do anything wrong," he said. "It was all me. It—"

"You discarded that very same idea," Captain Mbue said. "You even told the others on your bridge crew that your friend Tessa had made a serious mistake."

"She wouldn't have made it if I hadn't challenged her to race to the Scrapheap," he said.

Captain Mbue's gaze met his for a long moment. He stopped talking. He felt heat creep up his cheeks. She was shaming him into silence without telling him to shut up.

"The Explorer Tessa took hadn't been touched in years. As far as we can tell, its *anacapa* drive was starting to decay."

He opened his mouth to ask about that. The captain held up a finger, stopping him.

"They do that. It's something you learn if you take the decades-long course in *anacapa* usage. The drives malfunction and cause serious problems, which is why they get replaced more often than some believe necessary."

The captain paused. She was studying him, but he wasn't entirely sure why.

"The energy from that *anacapa* caused a reaction inside the Scrapheap," she said. "It's too technical to explain, and I'm not entirely sure I understand it, since *anacapa* drives are not my specialty, but that reaction caused the energy to change, which caused all of those explosions."

"Then why didn't her ship blow up first?" he blurted, then caught himself. He almost put his hands over his mouth, but he didn't. He made himself stand perfectly still.

"Because *anacapa* drives can create a wave, and that wave moved outward from the point where she entered the Scrapheap, and that wave then found something else that caused the reaction, which threaded back through all the other ships until it found hers." The captain looked like she was going to say something else, but she stopped.

She looked down, ran her fingers along that long desk, tapped it with the forefinger of her right hand, and then stopped, drawing a circle.

"You probably don't know this since you've been in isolation," she said, "but the reaction continues inside the Scrapheap. There are continual explosions. That's why we had to close that force field."

"There are no other ships around," he said. "Why didn't you just leave? No one else would have gotten hurt."

She raised her head, gave him a grim smile, and said, "If only I could tell you, Mr. Crowe. I cannot. I was following orders."

"Everyone on this ship could have died," he said.

"Yes," she said. Simply. Flatly. She had known that, and had still done it. She had risked every child on this ship, every adult, every single little-little. "And they would have died without you."

He studied her. He had no idea how she could be so cold about what had happened, about what she had nearly done.

She tilted her head just a little, as if she were taking a measure of him.

"I'm not willing to sacrifice you, Mr. Crowe," she said.

His stomach churned, just like it had when he first got back to the ship. This felt so wrong. He didn't want her to defend him.

"You're talented," she said. "You've got a gift, a gift the Fleet needs."

He shook his head again.

"And you've learned humility—I hope, anyway," she said. "Have you?"

His gaze skittered away from hers. He wasn't even sure what she meant.

She reached across that table and grabbed his arm. Her hand was cold.

"They're going to punish you," she said.

He nodded, not looking at her, despite the power of her grip.

"And then," she said, shaking his arm, "you're going to rehabilitate yourself. For me."

He swung his head toward her. He hadn't expected that.

She gave him a small smile. "I'm being demoted, Mr. Crowe. I should be. It's—"

"It's not your fault," he said. "It's mine. All of this—"

"Of course it's my fault," she said. "I'm the captain. I let you and your friends steal ships. You were planning this methodically for weeks, and no one under my command caught it. That's on me. These deaths are as much on me as they are on you, Mr. Crowe."

Her fingers were digging into his skin. He didn't pull away, though. He couldn't, not without breaking eye contact, and he couldn't do that either.

He finally realized that she wasn't being cold. She was being contained, more than anyone he had ever seen.

"You and me together," she said quietly, "we owe the universe fifty lives."

He started. Her words made him catch his breath.

"It was our carelessness that lost those lives," she said. "I'm not going to diminish those lives by dividing them up—twenty-five for me, twenty-five for you. We each owe the universe fifty lives, Mr. Crowe, and we are going to spend the rest of our days atoning for that."

He was having trouble breathing. He wasn't sure what, exactly, she meant.

"You can't atone if you go home to those parents of yours or get banished to some planet around an abandoned sector base. You can only atone by serving. That talent of yours has to be nurtured until one day, it saves at least fifty lives that wouldn't have been saved. Am I clear, Mr. Crowe?"

He nodded. She was clear.

"I will be doing the same," she said, "from whatever post they assign me. But the last thing I'll do as captain is direct your punishment. You will spend three years in rehabilitation on a Fleet vessel. It won't be pleasant. And then you'll have to start your education all over again. Your scores here will be wiped off your record. You will learn everything you can, and you will do the best you can, and if you make even the smallest mistake, I will come after you. Is that clear, Mr. Crowe?"

"Yes, sir," he said. "It's clear."

"Good."

She let go of him. Her fingers had left red marks on his skin, and an ache in his bones. She gave him a fierce look.

"I hope this is the last time I ever see you," she said. "Because if I do see you again, it means you've failed."

He nodded.

"You're dismissed, Mr. Crowe."

He nodded again, and pivoted, feeling heavier than he had felt before he entered the room. Then he had had no idea what his future was going to be, and in some ways, he still didn't.

But she had given him a direction, and it was one he agreed with.

Except...

Tessa. She had been so much more than he could ever have been. They competed, but only so that he could aspire to her greatness, her brilliance.

She had gotten an *anacapa* drive working. That should have been impossible. And others would say that it was reckless and stupid, but the feat itself, somehow working that drive, that was years beyond where she should have been.

He couldn't have done it.

And now he wouldn't.

Because Captain Mbue was right; he needed to atone. And to do that, he had to learn a whole new way of being. A humbler, smarter, less risky way of being.

He stepped back into that ruined anteroom, filled with the stuck images. The guards flanked him, as he walked back to his quarters.

He no longer had any idea who he would have been if he hadn't challenged Tessa to the competition.

He had no idea who he was now.

All he knew was who he had to be—a man who could carry fifty deaths on his shoulders, and somehow make sure nothing like that ever happened again.

He had no idea if he could do that.

But he knew he had to try.

PART TWO
CONTACT
100 YEARS AGO

THE *SPRÁVA*

Vice Admiral Bella Gão sank into the chair in the center of her research room. She had deliberately designed the room to have as little furniture as possible. Her chair, cabinets built into the wall to store whatever she might need, and a table to set things like the occasional cup of coffee or some snacks if she was going to be here a long time.

She had a lot of tech in this room, though, most of it responding only to her voice command. The junior officers who worked with her could access the information on their own systems, but they couldn't see what she had changed—not without her permission.

Only her superior officers knew the other log-ins to her systems, and so far, in the twenty years she had worked in this room, no one else had tried to access it.

There'd been no need.

She worried that there might be a need right now.

Her chair was bolted into the floor, a decision she had made almost a decade ago, when the *Správa* had encountered some difficulties in a foldspace maneuver that had caused the entire ship to lose attitude controls. Generally, the DV-Class vessels that formed Command Operations for the Fleet didn't have any difficulties at all. They traveled with the core of the Fleet, stayed away from any military issues, and were usually the last to enter a sector, generally by a well-traveled foldspace route.

Still, that one incident had reminded her she was on a ship, and occasionally, troubles arose. Back then, she had thought herself so practical, bolting her chair into place.

This morning, she regretted that decision. She wanted to move the chair to the back wall, so she could move around. She could go through the commands to release the chair or to fold it into the floor, but that would take time, and oddly enough, she didn't feel like she had time.

So she would have to make do.

Spherical holographic projections of various Scrapheaps surrounded her, most of them about a foot in diameter. Sometimes she thought of the Scrapheap projections as if they were a series of human heads floating around her, as ghastly and lost as a decapitated head could be, filled with information no longer useful, memories nearly gone, and antiquated ideas best left unspoken.

But every now and then, one of those severed heads became an actual ghost, something she had to deal with. She would have to focus down and concentrate, spend a few days thinking about things that she hadn't considered before, and then the crisis—if it could be called a crisis—was over.

This time, though. This time worried her.

The gigantic three-dimensional holoimage in front of her was not the size of a head. The ball was the size of a small tabletop that seated four and even at that size, it didn't give her the information she wanted.

She had walked around it three times, always bumping against her chair. She had increased the size of the image so she could see inside it better, but she knew the size wasn't the problem.

The problem was the composition of that sphere.

It wasn't a real-time image of a Scrapheap. It wasn't even a replica of an existing Scrapheap.

Instead, the sphere was an amalgam of different pieces of information, cobbled together from data files so old that half of them were corrupted, new data that had streamed in after going through a dozen (or more) different communications channels, and her best guess.

Ironically enough, the guess wasn't what worried her. The guess was, in some ways, the only thing she was certain about. She knew what she had based her guess on.

The rest of it was as ephemeral, as speculative as an actual ghost.

She ran her hands through her short-cropped black hair, then made herself stop. Her hair was thinning—age, mostly, although her doctor told her that stress contributed as well. They could boost the hair follicles using some nanogenetic something or other which would stop the hair loss, but she had to take two days off for the procedure, and she hadn't had two days off in a row in more than a year.

Of course, she probably couldn't ask for time right at the moment, because she was the only one who understood the new data that had come her way, although *understood* was a large overstatement.

She glanced at the dozens of smaller holograms of the Scrapheaps floating around her. Those holograms were multicolored and sparkly. The dark bluish-black of their sectors of space shone through all of the area around the ships contained inside the Scrapheaps. Outside of the Scrapheaps, pinpricks of light winked at her or slashes of white cut across the edges of the image, promising galaxies beyond what she could already see.

The force fields around those Scrapheaps all sparkled just a little, showing anyone who came too close that something weblike and powerful would prevent entry.

And then beyond the force fields, bits of ships stored in the Scrapheap. Those ships appeared mostly as shadows or negative images, black and silver and gray, against the gleaming backdrop.

Even when there was a problem at a Scrapheap, she found the hologram reassuring. It reminded her of the Scrapheap's size and history, its place in the universe, the way that it was more than a single problem or a single incident.

She usually loved looking at the Scrapheaps, feeling as if they were bits of reassurance, resources that the Fleet had and almost never used. Sometimes she thought of them as a cascade of bubbles, the kind the children made with their breath and a bubble wand full of nontoxic soap in the rec area of one of the school ships.

But this…

First of all, the gigantic sphere wasn't multicolored. It was gray and white and black, with just an occasional flash of sepia or yellow or brown. Those flashes weren't something coming across the image. They were corrupted data, information she would never be able to retrieve.

Second, it made no difference if she was looking at the images in two-dimensions or three. The missing information still slashed across the data stream like someone had wiped a finger across condensation on the surface of a glass.

Every time she focused on those slashes, her stomach twisted—and she thought again of her options.

Option one: she could ignore this, pretend she hadn't understood what she was looking at. That wasn't too far off the truth. She was afraid she was interpolating what she was looking at according to her own biases, although she had just spent the better part of an hour arguing with herself over that. She wasn't exactly sure what her biases would be, in this instance.

Option two: call in someone else to help her make a decision. But that would mean getting them up to speed, which might mean infecting them with her biases again, and it would prevent option one from ever being implemented.

Option three: follow protocol.

Protocol, though, was what was making her queasy. Protocol, in this instance, would risk several hundred lives.

And over what? Something that didn't matter anymore?

Or did it?

She started to reach for her hair again, and then stopped. Instead, she stood up, her shoulders penetrating some of the nearby holograms. She commanded them to float above her so that she wouldn't become part of the images, then she walked around the gigantic sphere, not to see more information, but to consider it all.

Four days ago, data had bounced off a relay that still existed in Sector Base V, even though that base had been closed for at least a thousand years. Because that relay worked, the data found its way to the Fleet.

At first, the data was considered insignificant, something that was a glitch in the system. Until another stream of data arrived at the same time the next day, and then again yesterday.

Someone glanced at the data stream, saw that it related to a Scrapheap, and forwarded that data to Gāo's department. No one in the department understood what they were seeing, so they had called her in.

She had seen ancient data streams before, as a cadet when she was training in Scrapheap maintenance, but she had never seen data streams like this.

This one had clearly gone through several communications nodes, and not all of them clean nodes. Plus, this data wasn't in any kind of form, the way that data from a Scrapheap should have been.

Scrapheaps had maintained their own logs for as long as there had been Scrapheaps. And the data she should have received from a Scrapheap should have been in the form of a log. Or of some kind of incident report.

This one was not a log and did not have an incident report. These data streams that had come through seemed the same, although closer examination showed that they weren't.

At the beginning of each data stream, there was a request, in the same words and with the same signature. It was a request for repair and maintenance, so that the Scrapheap could *create* logs.

Scrapheaps had redundant systems, so if something ceased working, some other part of the system would take over. The reports and logs were the only way the oldest Scrapheaps could communicate with the Fleet itself, so they were designed to continue, even as other parts of the Scrapheap fell apart.

It took her half the morning to synthesize the data, and to realize that what she was looking at was unsorted images and technobabble from a Scrapheap's buffer. The Scrapheap, unable to create logs, was sending everything it had so that the information wouldn't be lost.

Gāo didn't even know a Scrapheap could do that. She had no idea anything had been built into the Scrapheaps' systems that would allow a buffer transfer, although it made sense if every other method of reporting broke down.

Still, she did a cursory search of Scrapheap reporting history and never saw anything about buffers or backing up information with the Fleet itself.

She did not look at the control core specs. She had never built a Scrapheap herself, although she had authorized two of them. She did not know if a data stream spew from buffers was the last resort of a modern Scrapheap that couldn't report or if that was an old system that got removed over the millennia.

She suspected the system had gotten removed, because if all of the Scrapheaps did that when there was a log problem, the Fleet would drown in data.

In three days, she had already received more information than she wanted, enough to cause her to isolate an entire computer system so that she could synthesize everything.

At some point, she would have to bring in other techs. But she didn't trust them yet.

Not because of the buffer information or the data overload, but because of the Scrapheap's identification number.

She had never seen it before.

It wasn't in the records.

But it fell into the numbering system that the Fleet maintained—at the beginning of that numbering system.

Which sent a little shudder through her every single time she thought about it.

She had believed that the first Scrapheap had been built four thousand years ago. The records went back that far.

But this suggested that the records were off by at least two thousand years. Scrapheaps had existed for *six* thousand years, not four thousand years.

And if that was the case, then this wasn't the only Scrapheap somehow dropped from the records.

There were others as well, meaning that there were ships out there, lost ships collected in forgotten Scrapheaps, and a small wealth of problems that fact created.

Which made option one seem like the best option. No one knew these old Scrapheaps existed. So they were no longer the Fleet's problem.

Although they could be.

Because what she thought she was understanding from the bits of data she gleaned out of the corrupted wealth of data that had come her way was that ancient DV-Class vessels, vessels the Fleet once called Dignity Vessels, with functioning *anacapa* drives, were being stolen from that forgotten Scrapheap.

And if that was true, that meant whoever had stolen those vessels could repair them, maybe even reverse engineer them, or simply use them—and the *anacapa* drives—to whatever purpose they divined.

The robbers could even threaten the Fleet itself.

Although that seemed like a silly proposition. All of this occurred so far away that the Fleet had no clear records of the sector. Even with an *anacapa* drive, it would take months, maybe a year, for the thieves to catch up to the Fleet.

And why would anyone attack a Fleet as vast as this one, when there were sectors filled with planets and wealth and territories also long forgotten by the Fleet, in between the Fleet and these thieves?

But that wasn't the only problem. There were dozens of other potential problems, including raids continuing on every single Scrapheap between here and there, taking ships the Fleet had decommissioned, and using them again.

Worse, someone might find the Ready Vessels, and use those as well to make war, to bring destruction, to take over entire worlds or sectors. Ready Vessels were specially designed warships, hidden inside each Scrapheap. The ships were large and state-of-the-art—whatever art existed at the time of the Scrapheap's creation.

Most of the Ready Vessels were larger than a DV-Class ship, and had so much weaponry and specialized defensive capability that the Fleet needed to protect those ships. The Fleet didn't want Ready Vessels traveling with the main body of the Fleet, partly because Command was afraid that the warships would make the locals in any sector think the Fleet was arriving prepared for war.

The Fleet was prepared for war, if it had to fight, but it usually used DV-Class ships, which were powerful enough to handle most challenges the Fleet faced.

But sometimes the fighting escalated, and the Fleet needed something bigger and even more powerful.

That's where the bulk of the Ready Vessels came in.

The Fleet wasn't supposed to look backwards, but sometimes it had to. Sometimes, it had to make choices to protect itself.

What to do about this situation was not a decision she could make on her own. Because the data would keep coming, unless she blocked it. And then it would stream somewhere else, searching for a way to reach the Fleet, sending information the Fleet wanted to keep private to places or peoples unknown.

She had not trained for this issue. She wasn't even sure she knew what real options she had.

She had to enlist help.

And she had to do it fast.

THE *SPRÁVA*

In all of her decades in service to the Fleet, Gão had never gone into a meeting with her superior officers as woefully unprepared as she was for this meeting.

At her request, the officers had come to the *Správa*, specifically to the conference room she preferred, just off her research room. At first, officers had asked why she couldn't hold a joint conference holographically, in some private space, but that was an argument she had been prepared for.

She didn't want any of this information to leak any more than it already had. As secure as holographic meetings were throughout the ships composing Command Operations, she wasn't sure the holographic meetings were secure enough for this.

Besides, she didn't want to send the data stream information to her superior officers via any link between the ships. She wanted to show them the problems she was having and hoped that maybe she would get some suggestions for onsite filtering.

She had linked the three days of data-streamed information to this conference room along with the holographic projection she had made from all of it. She had lowered the long conference table and its chairs into the floor, so the officers would have to stand as they looked at the hologram she created.

She had left the sideboards up, though, and covered them with food, so the officers wouldn't feel too uncomfortable.

And, she felt, that was all she could do.

The officers had arrived early, and had come to the room, clustering near the food, as if she were throwing a party. Everyone glanced at the gigantic hologram in the exact center of the room, but no one examined it closely. It didn't look like anything they had seen before, so they all knew that she would have to explain it to them.

Technically, four of the five officers who had arrived weren't her actual superiors. They were all vice admirals too, just like she was, with somewhat different focuses.

But she asked them here because they had either worked with Scrapheaps in the past or they had more seniority than she did.

Two of the vice admirals brought security details, which Gão thought of as overkill. Apparently neither of the vice admirals traveled to any ship without security, even other command vessels.

Gão managed not to shake her head in disgust as she asked the security details to remain in the corridor outside the conference room.

The only real superior officer in the room was Admiral Shannon Hallock. She had arrived last, and unlike those two vice admirals, did not bring a security detail with her.

Hallock had arrived alone and had slipped into the room about five minutes before the scheduled start of the meeting.

Admiral Hallock made Gão nervous. Hallock had promoted Gão fifteen years ago, and had praised her work on that day, but hadn't done so since. Hallock wasn't someone who said much more than she needed to, and usually what she needed to say was some kind of criticism.

She didn't look unpleasant, though, like so many people who spent their lives criticizing others. She had a square face with a firm jawline, skin a shade darker than Gão's, and thick brown curls that made Gão self-conscious about her own thinning hair.

Hallock was the only one who stared at the hologram in the center of the room, hands behind her back, and grey eyes sharp and questioning. She was probably the only person invited who actually understood what she saw—or didn't see—since she had spent more than a decade doing Gão's job.

Gão's gaze met Hallock's. Even though this was Gão's meeting, Hallock had to start it, because she was the most senior officer in the room.

"This is an interesting hologram," Hallock said, almost as if Gão had cued her. "I assume it's why we're here."

"Yes, Admiral, it is." Gão moved closer to the hologram, but still maintained eye contact with Hallock.

The vice admirals all moved so that they could see Gão, as well. She launched into an explanation of what the hologram was, and how it got created.

As Gão spoke, she watched their faces, so she could slow down or explain more if it looked like they didn't understand. She had a hunch Hallock would be the only one who would ask if she didn't understand something.

The other vice admirals probably didn't want to look stupid in front of a superior officer. Gão had yet to meet another vice admiral who was secure enough to admit they didn't understand something about the Fleet.

Scrapheaps were particularly mysterious. Some ranking officers in the Fleet had never even seen one.

Gão had to assume that everyone in this room had, judging by the way they nodded as she talked about typical behavior of Scrapheaps.

Only Vice Admiral Nabil Calixte seemed a little confused. He stood nearest the sandwiches, leaning against the counter, arms crossed. He was tall and very thin. He always made her think of old-fashioned images she had seen of scholars, with intelligent eyes in faces that were on the border between gaunt and starved.

Maybe she thought of him as a scholar because he handled the school ships, maintaining their personnel, re-evaluating their missions, and determining if the number of students indicated the need for another ship.

He had a well-rounded background in all of the disciplines, but none of his knowledge was deep—deliberately so. He needed to understand a lot of things, and trusted his underlings to help him should an additional layer of complexity be involved.

As Gão gave them the background, Jiu Rwizi had paced around the gigantic hologram, peering into it as if she could find out more information just by looking at it.

Rwizi was the closest Gão had to a good friend among the vice admirals. They had trained together as young women, although Rwizi had been promoted much faster than Gão. Rwizi also had a specific and rare specialty. *Anacapa* drives. She was a wizard at working them, understood them better than almost anyone, and got her promotions by training some of the best *anacapa* engineers in the Fleet.

Like Calixte, Rwizi was tall and thin, but she didn't look like a scholar. She looked like someone specially engineered to handle narrow passageways throughout the Fleet vessels. She wasn't genetically engineered—no one was—but sometimes the right person seemed perfectly designed to handle their job.

That was Rwizi. One reason Gão wanted her here was because she could accurately assess the risks that Gão was proposing.

So far, no one had called up their own screens or asked for the raw data. Gão expected that would happen, but apparently they wanted to hear what she had to say first.

The only person who seemed at all nervous was Vice Admiral Zaida d'Anano. She was one of the two who had arrived with a security detail. She wore perfectly pressed slacks and a crisp white blouse, looking like she had just dressed for the day. Her auburn hair looked pressed as well, plastered against her skull with some kind of product that made it seem as fake as her clothing.

Her hair matched her makeup, making her skin even paler than it usually was. Her dark eyes, hidden under her long brown lashes, narrowed as Gão explained the vast amount of data she had received.

Gão couldn't read d'Anano. Gão had no idea if d'Anano always fidgeted and adjusted the cuffs of her sleeves or if the topic made her more nervous than usual.

Gão had nearly reached the end of the background information when her gaze met Vice Admiral Claude Nguyen's. Nguyen was the other person who had brought a security detail, which had surprised Gão. He had never seemed like the paranoid type before.

At the moment, Nguyen stood a half step behind Admiral Hallock. He was shorter than she was, but had land-based muscles, even though he had never lived on land. He did a lot of workouts in full gravity plus. Gāo had run into him on the exercise wing of *Krachtige 3* back when both he and Gāo had been commodores, assisting the rear admirals.

Nguyen might have been the only other in the room who had an inkling about what that hologram was. He had worked the Abandoned Ships Detail early in his career, and many of those ships got taken to nearby Scrapheaps.

When Gāo finished the initial part of the presentation and took a breath, Nguyen looked like he was about to say something.

Somehow d'Anano managed to speak first.

"So," she said, "we have a malfunctioning Scrapheap. I do not understand why that's an issue for all of us. Normally you deal with such things, don't you, Bella?"

Not Vice Admiral, not even Gāo. But the first name, as a diminishment. Gāo took a breath, then decided not to take anything personally. She didn't dare.

They had a big decision to make.

"Normally, I do," Gāo said. "I guess I didn't make myself clear, Vice Admiral. This Scrapheap is not in our records. It predates anything in our files."

"Would it have Ready Vessels then?" Rwizi asked.

"I don't know if this Scrapheap has Ready Vessels," Gāo said. "That's the problem. I thought the Scrapheap system was four thousand years old. This Scrapheap predates the system by two thousand years. We have nothing in our records that states when, exactly, the Ready Vessel system began, so I can't even guess."

Calixte brought a clenched fist to his gaunt face, and tapped his thumb against his chin.

"One of our school ships has a department that specializes in Fleet history," he said. "We might be able to find that information there."

"Even if the Ready Vessels existed in that ancient Scrapheap," Rwizi said, "wouldn't the vessels be so old as to be useless to us?"

"To us, yes." Admiral Hallock poured herself an ice tea from one of the pitchers on the sideboard. "But not to a group finding them. We improve our designs, but we don't abandon them. I believe it would be a safe bet to assume that the Ready Vessels have *anacapa* drives, and early stages of the weaponry that modern Ready Vessels have. The ships would probably have similar defense capabilities as well."

Her words hung for a moment, because no one wanted to interrupt her before she was finished.

Once he realized she was done, Nguyen said, "I think it would also be safe to assume that if there were Ready Vessels in that Scrapheap, and some organization figured out how we had hidden them, that organization would search for other Scrapheaps."

"Fortunately," d'Anano said, "that Scrapheap will not have the coordinates of any Scrapheap built after it."

"That's not quite how Scrapheaps work," Nguyen said. "The core of the Scrapheap itself might not have that information, but we store ships built long after a

Scrapheap was completed in the Scrapheap itself. If the ships weren't properly decommissioned, then the location of the other Scrapheaps would be discoverable."

"Even if, it seems, the thieves never do discover the Ready Vessels," Rwizi said.

No one spoke for a long moment. Normally, in a meeting like this, Gão would have been pleased that the officers understood the seriousness of her presentation.

This group clearly understood the seriousness of what they all faced. They also knew, without her repeating the information, that the Scrapheap might have been losing ships for years, not just weeks.

One hurdle crossed.

But she was just beginning. And the other fact she wanted them to understand was that she couldn't accurately trace how long it had taken the information to reach her, so she had no idea whether the crisis occurred a month ago or centuries ago.

"I'll be honest," she said, "this Scrapheap is so old and faraway that I thought of ignoring the contact altogether. But I immediately realized that we might have a larger issue on our hands."

"The other Scrapheaps," Nguyen said.

"And the Ready Vessels," Hallock said.

Everyone looked at her.

"We like to think they're undiscoverable, but they aren't," she said. "We've protected and hidden them well. The flaw with the Fleet, as I see it, is that we don't change technology that works well. We change technology that isn't working in quite the way we want it to."

Gão swallowed hard. This was why she had brought the others in.

Hallock made eye contact with each person in the room before she spoke again.

"We have never had a challenge or a problem with our storage of Ready Vessels," Hallock said. "That *would* be in our records. So we have continued the practice. We have also discussed moving the Ready Vessels from older Scrapheaps to newer Scrapheaps, but we have never done so."

She gave the entire group a thin smile.

"It is something that the admirals discuss at least twice a year, and until today, we had no reason to change that practice. I suspect we will do so going forward."

Then her gaze met Gão's. Gão's breath caught just a little. Nerves kicked in, as if this entire ancient Scrapheap problem had just gotten worse.

Maybe it had.

"The question is," Hallock said, "what do we do about the past? Isn't that right, Vice Admiral Gão?"

"Yes," Gão said. "We have the personnel to examine all of our Scrapheaps, but the resources that would take would change our mission. The Fleet moves forward, not back, and a large number of our ships would have to move back to each Scrapheap to investigate any potential problems we might find."

"You're right," Rwizi said, "sending personnel is not the optimal method for any investigation, especially one that sends sections of the Fleet backwards."

Gão gave Rwizi a small, grateful glance. Rwizi was functioning exactly as Gão had hoped, as a support who understood what was going on.

"What about pinging the Scrapheaps?" Calixte asked. "We could ask them specifically for information on the Ready Vessels."

Gão nodded. "I thought of that. We can do that with some of the Scrapheaps. Some of the oldest Scrapheaps are not designed to handle information requests of that nature. We could try to upgrade their systems from a distance, but that would take time. We don't dare send upgrades through foldspace."

No one entirely understood foldspace, although the Fleet traveled in and out of it all the time. The common explanation was that the *anacapa* drives actually created a fold in space, that shortened a trip between two points, the way that a folded blanket would seemingly shorten the width of that blanket.

For Gão, that explanation always created more questions than it resolved. She tried not to think about those questions now. She needed to listen to what the others said before she expressed any opinion at all.

"We can't send upgrades through foldspace because of information corruption?" Calixte asked. He clearly did not know.

"Because we can't trace anything through foldspace," Rwizi said. "The only way we would know if the upgrade reached its target would be a successful communication. And if the upgrade went awry, we would also have no idea."

"We can send single ships back to repair or upgrade those systems in person," Hallock said. "We have done that in the past."

Gão knew that. She had just been starting her career in Scrapheaps when a team had to go back to one of the older Scrapheaps to reboot its entire internal system.

"We might be overreacting," d'Anano said, using a tone that irritated Gão. d'Anano used the word *we* but she meant Gão. "This all may have happened to one Scrapheap a thousand years ago, and the entire event might have been local."

"Exactly," Gão said, taking back control of her meeting and surprising d'Anano at the same time. The best way to defang a potential problem in a meeting was to agree with her.

Sometimes those agreements were false, but in this case, Gão actually did agree with d'Anano.

"I have an idea," Gão said, "but I don't like it. And it's based entirely on Vice Admiral d'Anano's point."

d'Anano looked at Gão as if reassessing her.

"I think we send one ship back to that Scrapheap," Gão said. "The ship evaluates the entire situation, lets us know if it's something we need to worry about, and then we make our next decisions."

"Sounds sensible," Calixte said. "Aside from the distance, which is daunting, what do you dislike about this?"

Gão was about to answer when Rwizi spoke up.

"There's no guarantee that the ship would ever get to the Scrapheap." Rwizi's voice was soft. "There's no guarantee that the ship would be able to communicate with us in anything approximating real time, even if it did get to the Scrapheap. And that's just the trip *to* the Scrapheap. The trip back would be just as fraught, just as difficult, if not more so."

"We go through foldspace," Calixte said. "We accept the risks. How is this different?"

"I haven't calculated the exact trip yet," Gão said, "but my preliminary analysis suggests that the ship would not be able to travel through foldspace to that Scrapheap in one trip. That would almost guarantee the loss of the ship. The safest method of travel would be to go in and out of foldspace a number of times."

"How many?" Nguyen asked, his voice tight.

"I don't know yet," Gão said. "Maybe five. Maybe ten."

The vice admirals glanced at each other, as if weighing the reactions of their colleagues. Hallock herself continued to stare at the hologram. Gão glanced at it too. She hated the fact that the information on it was incomplete.

"It is my understanding," Calixte said, "that going into and out of foldspace is as dangerous as traveling a long distance into foldspace."

Gão admired the way that he managed to ask a question without asking a question. Given the job that he had, such a skill was essential. He had to sound like someone who knew what he was talking about, but he also had to be open to new ideas.

"Every time we enter foldspace or leave it, we take a risk," Rwizi said. "Statistically, that risk remains the same. You have the same chance of getting lost in foldspace or having an *anacapa* malfunction in foldspace each time. The statistical weight is not cumulative. The chance, depending on the age of the ship and the *anacapa* drive, might be as high as fifteen percent, although I doubt that, for reasons I won't go into here."

She didn't say what she doubted about that percentage—whether it was too high or too low. Gão had never discussed it with her either. The command staff rarely discussed the dangers of *anacapa* usage. *It is what it is*, one of her instructors had said long ago, and she agreed. As long as the *anacapa* drive was the only effective way to travel extreme distances, the Fleet would continue to take the risks involved with using it.

"Fifteen percent," Calixte murmured, as if he didn't know. Gão wondered how he couldn't know. That was a statistic she thought of every single time the *Správa* went into or out of foldspace.

"However," Rwizi said, "from what information we can gather, it appears that danger increases the farther a ship travels in foldspace. Which is why I recommend each ship have *anacapa* and foldspace experts on board to calculate the best trajectory for travel. Sometimes it's worthwhile to go in and out of foldspace, and risk the fifteen percent each time. And sometimes, it's better to travel the long distance, without the big risk."

"And in this instance?" Hallock asked, although her tone suggested she already knew the answer.

"I wouldn't do it," Rwizi said. "I wouldn't travel back there at all. Not on one long trip, not with however many journeys into or out of foldspace in a short period of time. It's simply too dangerous."

Gāo was nodding. She had come to the same conclusion, but she had felt that her conclusion had been personal, not professional. As Rwizi had said, she wouldn't do it. Even if ordered to.

She would probably resign.

"And that doesn't count the trip back," Rwizi added. "If a ship somehow makes it to the Scrapheap, that's a miracle, in my opinion. And then, the ship would face the same potential problems coming back. And for what? Information that we might not need?"

Hallock made a small sound in the back of her throat, as if taking note of Rwizi's dismissive tone. Hallock then walked around the hologram, a frown on her face.

"Did you want all of us to sign off on a decision to ignore the events at that Scrapheap?" d'Anano asked Gāo.

Gāo's cheeks started to heat, but she willed the flush away. It was a trick she had taught herself as she rose up the ranks. She made herself focus on the content of d'Anano's question, rather than Hallock.

"I felt this wasn't a decision I could make on my own," Gāo said. "If I followed protocol, I would have to send several ships back and gather information. If I only send one ship, then we run the risk of not getting the information at all."

"And if you ignored the contact from the Scrapheap, as you considered doing, and something happened to the main body of the Fleet, then you would lose your command." d'Anano stated that last flatly, as if it was the primary consideration in Gāo's calculations.

"If I worried about losing my command whenever I make a decision," Gāo said, "I wouldn't have the command in the first place."

Hallock raised her head, probably at Gāo's tone. Hallock then glanced at d'Anano. Hallock's expression was impossible to read.

"You were correct in contacting us, Vice Admiral Gāo," Hallock said, shutting down d'Anano's argument. "This is a decision that must not be made lightly. As I see it, we have several issues to deal with. We have the problems or the past problems at a Scrapheap we did not even know existed."

Gāo nodded. So did Rwizi. The other three just watched Hallock, as if they were uncertain what she would say next.

"We also have the problem of more lost Scrapheaps. We thought this Scrapheap habit of ours was newer than it was. It is not. We might have suffered similar issues at other Scrapheaps and not received any notification at all. Do you agree, Vice Admiral Gāo?" Hallock kept her tone level, not revealing how she felt about any of this.

"Yes, I do," Gāo said. "It worries me."

"It concerns me as well," Hallock said. "We have a problem with our communications systems over these long distances. We haven't paid a lot of attention to those systems, because we go forward, as you said. But we have left a lot of tech behind us. We decommission the sector bases and the starbases. We might need to consider destroying the Scrapheaps."

Gāo felt a little dizzy. Destroying Scrapheaps? No one had ever mentioned that before.

"Why don't we?" Calixte asked.

"The Ready Vessels," Nguyen said quietly, as if he were passing the information to Calixte on a test.

Calixte nodded. "So we may have been arming sectors without even realizing it."

"Not that it matters," d'Anano said.

Everyone looked at her.

She shrugged, seemingly unconcerned by their surprise.

"Oh, don't pretend," she said. "We go into sectors, explore them, use them at times, settle there for a while with our bases, and then we leave. We have no idea if we leave the communities there better off or worse off, and more importantly, *we don't care*. If these thieves break into an ancient Scrapheap, are they stealing anything important? We didn't even know that Scrapheap existed."

"We know now," Nguyen said.

"We do," d'Anano said. "But we haven't been threatened by our own Ready Vessels. We haven't even fought a major engagement with another fleet in a long time. We've gone afoul with settled communities on various planets, but something spacefaring, like us? We haven't seen the like. Why should we care?"

Gāo looked at Hallock, to see how she responded to that. But Hallock's face remained impassive.

"It's my understanding," Gāo said, using Calixte's verbal trick, "that any ships we send back to that Scrapheap would be on a suicide mission."

"I think so, yes," Rwizi said.

"And we might not be able to communicate with them once they arrive," Gāo said.

"I think that's a solvable problem." Hallock had clasped her hands behind her back.

"The communications issue?" Gāo asked, surprised.

"The Scrapheap reached us," Hallock said. "It took several tries, but it did. We can figure out the relays, see if or where the links are broken, and get the information we need. The question on the table is whether that information is worth lives."

No one spoke. The vice admirals deliberately did not look at each other.

Gāo shifted slightly. She had called this meeting, after all. She was the one who should have had the most to say about what the Fleet should do.

"We have enough information to make major policy shifts," Gāo said. "They would probably be prudent shifts. We don't need to send anyone back to the original Scrapheap."

"And yet, I am curious, aren't you?" Hallock said. "That might not be the first Scrapheap. There might be a lot of information that we do not have lurking inside that Scrapheap."

"Is it important information?" d'Anano asked. "We have lived without it so far."

Rwizi went to the sideboard, picked up a plate, and placed a sandwich on it. The movement surprised Gāo. Gāo would have thought the meeting nearly over, but Rwizi clearly did not.

She turned, waving the plate at the others, as if asking them if they wanted anything. So far, two of the vice admirals waved a dismissive hand at her. Hallock ignored her entirely.

"There's one thing no one has mentioned," Rwizi said, picking at the sandwich. "The trip through foldspace."

"I think we've been discussing that," Nguyen said.

"Yes," Rwizi said. "The trip *backwards.* But a single trip that long has never been tried, at least that we know of, and it would be nice to know if our assumptions about such trips are correct."

Gāo shifted again. Something about this made her very uncomfortable, but she couldn't put her finger on what.

Calixte asked, "Meaning?"

"Meaning wouldn't it be better to send ships back to that Scrapheap to test the distance? We know we have communications nodes along the way. We have coordinates, and we have backup ships, in case the ships get damaged on the journey." Rwizi picked up her sandwich and held it, but didn't move it toward her mouth. "We would know how the trip works, and what the issues are. And as a bonus, we could get information from the Scrapheap itself."

"If it's still there," Nguyen said.

Hallock looked at him in surprise. Rwizi took a bite from her sandwich. Gāo frowned.

"No one has mentioned that possibility either," Nguyen said. "But there could have been enough raids to take out the Scrapheap. Or maybe it exploded like that one did, thirty…forty…years ago now. Your ancient Scrapheap might be gone."

"Or it might be a treasure trove of information," Calixte said. It sounded like he was warming to the idea.

"Your traveling once through foldspace argument has merit, Vice Admiral Rwizi," Hallock said. "Let me bring it to the operating committee and see what they think. In the meantime, Vice Admiral Calixte, get a team to research old Scrapheaps. See if we have records in that school ship you mentioned, records we haven't looked at in centuries. We might discover other Scrapheaps existing as well."

"Yes, sir," Calixte said.

"Vice Admiral Rwizi," Hallock said. "I want you to plot two different trips to that Scrapheap. One trip is a direct shot through foldspace. The other in small bites. Calculate the odds of success to get there."

Rwizi grabbed a napkin and dabbed at her mouth. "What about the trip back?"

"For the time being, we shall assume they'll come back the way they went," Hallock said. Then she glanced at Gāo.

Gāo braced herself, but Hallock looked back at the hologram.

"Vice Admiral d'Anano," Hallock said. "I want you to prepare a list of people whom we can spare from the Fleet. They need to be spectacular at their jobs, but not necessarily career material."

"Troublemakers?" d'Anano asked.

Hallock tilted her head back and forth, as if considering the word. "Not quite. People who do not fit in. We'll need enough to staff a ship, and they are going to need to work together. But..."

Her voice trailed off.

d'Anano's lips twisted.

"But," d'Anano said, "if they all die on this mission, it won't make any difference to the Fleet at all."

"Yes," Hallock said quietly.

"That means you don't want them to have family either, right?" d'Anano said.

"They can have family," Hallock said. "But not close family. If we decide this mission is a go, there will be no spouses or children or grandparents on board. Only people essential to the mission itself."

"What kind of ship are we going to send?" d'Anano asked, sounding like she believed the mission would happen.

Gāo didn't. She took Hallock at her word. Hallock was still exploring the possibility.

"I don't think we have any DV-Class vessels to spare," Hallock said. "And that might be too much ship for what we're considering."

"The ship will need to defend itself," Nguyen said.

"It'll also need to be able to survive for months, if need be, without backup," Gāo added, simply because she could remain quiet no longer.

"And it'll need a good, new, *anacapa* drive, properly integrated into its systems," Rwizi said.

"That's a DV-Class vessel," Nguyen said. "We'd have to send a relatively new ship."

"Not necessarily." Calixte sounded thoughtful. "We could send an SC-Class ship."

"A security vessel?" Nguyen said. "They rarely work alone."

"But they're designed to do all the things you mentioned," Calixte said, "and just because they don't normally work alone doesn't mean they can't. It's just tradition that makes us send several security ships to a crisis."

"Tradition, common sense, and good tactics," Gāo said.

She took a breath, about to suggest that they retrofit a DV-Class vessel from one of the closer Scrapheaps, and then realized that was silly. If they were going to send a ship, they would have to do so soon. They wouldn't have time for a retrofit.

"SC-Class," Hallock said to d'Anano. "Find the right staff for a brand new SC-Class ship. Give me double the names. Split up duties. And let me know the pros and cons of each."

"That's a minimum of eight hundred names, Admiral," d'Anano said.

"Yes," Hallock said in that same flat tone she had used earlier. "It is."

No one spoke for a moment. The flatness of her words made them even more powerful. People who were expendable. A ship that might not come back. A mission that had several purposes, none of them entirely obvious.

"Admiral," Gão said, "just before I came here, I was notified that another data blast arrived from the Scrapheap. I suspect we'll get the raw data every day until or unless we block it. May I bring in others to help me sift through that data? I'd like to see if it's all repetitive or if each day brings new information."

"By all means," Hallock said, "bring in your best team. Make sure they know the data and the information we glean from it all is classified."

"Yes, sir," Gão said. "If the information is a continual resend, do I have your permission to block future transmissions?"'

"Not yet, Vice Admiral Gão. We need to decide what we're doing next. There's more information than just the data stream. We also need to see if the communications nodes for each data burst are the same."

Hallock looked at the group, then glanced a final time at the hologram. She reached out, almost as if she wanted to touch it, and then brought her hand back.

"I think we've decided enough for now," she said to Gão. "I'd like to reconvene in two days' time. That will give us time to contemplate what we've discussed here. It'll give your people a chance to examine the data more thoroughly. We might learn more about Scrapheaps and Ready Vessels. And we should have a least a tentative list of names, right, Vice Admiral d'Anano?"

"Yes, sir," d'Anano said, already sounding weary.

"All right then," Hallock said. "Let's move forward with this. You're all dismissed."

The four vice admirals left, Rwizi carrying her plate and the remains of her sandwich with her.

Gão had to return the room to its usual status, so she remained. To her surprise, so did Hallock.

Hallock set her ice tea on the sideboard. She hadn't touched the liquid at all. She leaned against the sideboard. Her posture wasn't as rigid, and her expression was softer, maybe even compassionate.

"You find all of this disconcerting," Hallock said. "Yet you've ordered personnel to take risks bigger than this throughout your career."

Gão took a deep breath. That was true, and she hadn't thought about her reaction in this context. She'd made much tougher decisions on her own, but this time felt different.

She wasn't sure why.

She glanced at the hologram. It was large and gray and incomplete. The shadows and the blurs inside of it were unusual as well, but not that unusual. She *had* sent ships into dangerous situations with a lot less information than this.

"I...think it's the going backwards," Gāo said slowly. "We're not sending a ship or a group of ships to find out something new. We're checking on something old, something we've abandoned."

Hallock was nodding as Gāo spoke.

"It doesn't feel like we're doing our jobs when we go back, does it?" Hallock said. "It feels as if we're making a mistake."

"Yeah." That was it. Gāo finally understood.

"Even though it's not your fault that the Fleet lost track of the older Scrapheaps," Hallock said.

"It's my responsibility, though," Gāo said. "I'm in charge of Scrapheaps."

"And your work has changed or, rather, will change, now that we know about this one. Many of the items we discussed today will fall into your purview."

Gāo nodded. Hallock was right. The communications piece would end up on Gāo's plate, as would finding the older Scrapheaps, and figuring out what kind of shape they were in.

"This mission, if we do it," Gāo said, "will only be the first of many."

"Or not." Hallock pushed away from the sideboard. She pointed at the hologram. "Can you make that go away?"

Gāo called up her system on its own holographic screen, tapped a single corner, and the Scrapheap hologram disappeared.

The conference room suddenly felt huge. Hallock went to the wall panel, and tapped the controls. The floor shuddered and Gāo had to move closer to the sideboard.

The table rose first, long and gleaming. It always got cleaned when it was placed in the floor. Then the chairs rose back to their spots.

And now the conference room looked like it always had, a place where decisions were made easily and comfortably, where risks were discussed as if they were theoretical instead of real.

Gāo felt some of the pressure leave with the hologram itself.

Hallock swept her hand toward the table, inviting Gāo to sit. Gāo did. Hallock sat beside her, not at the head of the table at all.

So this was going to seem informal. It was a nice trick, one Gāo had used with subordinates as well.

"Let me tell you something," Hallock said, not adding that the "something" was in confidence, but implying it. "I have wanted to change this policy for years."

"Which one?" Gāo asked.

"Scrapheaps themselves," Hallock said. "You're feeling uncomfortable because you're sending a ship backwards. I have always felt that way about Scrapheaps. They don't fit with the Fleet's mission. We move forward."

The table dug into Gāo's side, and the seat of the chair pressed against her right thigh. But Gāo didn't move. She wasn't sure if she should agree or if this was some kind of test.

It would help if she could read Hallock, but Gāo had never been able to do that, not with Admiral Hallock. Some of the other admirals, sure. They never seemed to hide what they were thinking. But Admiral Hallock kept her opinions close.

Maybe that was why Gāo thought this was a test. Because she had never been in this circumstance with Admiral Hallock before.

"We close our sector bases, and remove all relevant material from them. We have had ships arrive at decommissioned bases," Hallock said, "and those bases are almost always unusable. The community has moved on, and is sometimes unrecognizable. Knowledge of the Fleet is mostly gone. But Scrapheaps remain part of our system. We upgrade them—or should. We monitor them. We make them report across vast distances. And, apparently, they can find us, against long odds."

"You think that Scrapheap knows where we are?" Gāo asked.

"Scrapheaps don't 'know' anything," Hallock said.

Gāo felt that as a bit of a rebuke. She didn't want to defend herself though. She needed to focus on what Hallock was saying.

"But the communications system tracked us, and anyone with sense and a bit of engineering ability might be able to back trace any communication we send to a Scrapheap." Hallock raised her eyebrows just a little, emphasizing her point. Clearly, she had made this point to others. "So I believe that makes us findable. Whether someone would want to is another matter altogether."

Gāo frowned. She sat up in the chair, relieving the pressure on her side. Then she shifted slightly. She had to consider her words before speaking. She didn't want to insult Hallock, but Gāo also wanted to make sure she understood.

"You want to send a ship, not for any of the reasons we discussed earlier," Gāo said, "but to gather information to bring to the other admirals. You want this be the first salvo in shutting down the Scrapheaps."

If Gāo were a different woman, she would feel threatened by that. After all, her entire job was about Scrapheaps.

But she didn't. Hallock had a good argument, and had put her finger on something that had always bothered Gāo about her work.

She never felt like she was doing a job that benefitted the Fleet, no matter what her superior officers said. She always felt like she—and sometimes she alone—was looking in the wrong direction, facing backwards while all of her comrades faced forwards.

She had spent the last few decades of her career making decisions about things that the Fleet had long since abandoned. And she had done a lot of mental gyrations so that she wouldn't have to think about that.

Hallock shifted as well, placing her elbow on the back of her chair, and turning slightly so that she faced Gāo more directly.

"It wouldn't be the first salvo," Hallock said. "Since I left your job, I've been pushing the admirals to shut down the Scrapheaps. My arguments have not made a lot of difference. Tradition counts for a lot more within the command structure than I like. What the others have asked for, and what I have been unable to provide, is evidence that the Scrapheaps do not function as intended."

Gão frowned. "But they do protect the abandoned and forgotten ships."

"Do they?" Hallock asked. "You have evidence of theft on a grand scale. Theft that might have taken place a century ago or more."

"In a sector we no longer care about," Gão said.

"Perhaps," Hallock said. "I care less about the theft of damaged ships than I do about Ready Vessels. Even so, what you have in that little bit of data you provided us, is the beginning of an argument *with evidence* to shut down the Scrapheaps, just like we shut down sector bases."

"What would we do without Scrapheaps?" Gão asked.

Hallock smiled. It was her first real smile of the meeting, and it transformed her face into a web of smile lines, showing her age, but making her seem more approachable at the same time.

"Now you sound like my colleagues," Hallock said. "This is where we get into trouble—the entire Fleet. We follow tradition and continue doing things the way they've always been done, even when the system is not logical and does not function."

Gão's cheeks heated. She couldn't stop that flush at all.

"We develop a new group of ships." Hallock lowered her voice as she said that. "We send them back, and we have them destroy any Fleet vessel that they find."

Gão's breath caught. Destroy a ship? A perfectly functional ship? That went counter to everything she had ever learned.

"See?" Hallock said. "Destroying a ship is harder for us than taking a life."

"But the ships might be useful," Gão blurted.

"Have they ever been?" Hallock asked. "In your entire command, have you ever known us to *remove* a ship from the Scrapheap? Have you ever known us to take spare parts from a Scrapheap?"

She didn't give Gão a chance to answer, not that Gão needed to. The answer was, of course, no. They never had.

"We are keeping the ships because we have been trained—perhaps indoctrinated is a better word—to maintain them. To keep them alive at all costs. Sector bases and starbases are easy to abandon. We do not live on them. But we live on the ships. They are as much a part of us as our hands."

Admiral Hallock's eyes twinkled, as if she knew that Gão—and anyone else—would see this as a radical thought.

Gão did feel distinctly uncomfortable even thinking about destroying a Fleet ship. Fleet ships contained lives and memories and more. They were homes; they were the Fleet itself.

Hallock watched Gão as if expecting Gão's reaction. That small smile grew on Hallock's face.

"You don't like this concept, do you?" Hallock asked.

Like. Dislike. Gão had no idea.

"I don't know," Gão said after a moment. "I had never given it any thought before now."

Hallock's smile seemed to have frozen in place. Perhaps Gão wasn't as big an ally as Hallock had thought. Or perhaps Hallock had thought Gão agreed with her, even though no one Gão knew had ever spoken of these concepts before.

"Did you know," Hallock said slowly, "that some land-based cultures actually put their dead into the ground?"

Gão had studied such things when she was in school. "Yes," she said. "It has something to do with crop nutrients."

"No, it does not," Hallock said. "Those cultures alter the bodies so that they will not decay. They remain preserved as best as the science allows."

Gão was stunned. "Preserved for what?"

Hallock opened her hands, as if to say *I have no idea*. "For some, it is a religious ideal. Something about being restored to the flesh. For others, custom, perhaps? But I have given it a lot of thought. For those cultures, the bodies are the vessels. The ships, if you will. Because they travel individually, and live on their planet. They do not live communally as we do, and they do not see the ships or other vehicles as anything other than utilitarian."

Gão had encountered that before, usually in cities that sprang up around a sector base. The culture in those cities was dramatically different than one on a Fleet ship.

"The Scrapheaps are nothing more than a burial ground, in space, for our most important bodies," Hallock said.

Gão pressed her lips together, not sure what she should say about that concept. She wasn't sure if she agreed with it. She wasn't sure what she thought.

Had this information come from someone else, Gão might not have considered it at all. But this was Admiral Hallock, who was not known for outré ideas. Admiral Hallock was known as one of the most sensible members of the command team.

"If I can prove that these Scrapheaps actively harm the Fleet," Hallock said quietly, "then we might be able to shut them down."

"And do what with the Ready Vessels?" Gão asked.

Hallock's eyes twinkled again. Apparently, she had been asked this question before. Or maybe she was just waiting for Gão to come up with it.

"I believe our warships should travel with us," Hallock said. "We train a different military staff, one that will run those ships at all times, rather than bring in staff when we need them."

"But other cultures will see our warships," Gão said. "They'll think we're going to attack them."

"That presupposes other cultures understand our ships now," Hallock said. "How do they know that DV-Class ships are also used for diplomacy? Those ships have weapons and defensive capabilities. Any culture sufficiently advanced enough to scan a DV-Class vessel could easily think that vessel is a warship. Sometimes, Bella, our culture is very egocentric."

Gāo frowned. Hallock was giving her several things to consider, things she hadn't thought of before.

Hallock flattened her hand on the table, and then stood. "Well," she said, "that's enough philosophy for the moment."

Gāo stood as well.

"What I want you to know, Vice Admiral Gāo—" apparently, they were back to being formal again "—is that unless some other information is brought to my attention in the next few days, *convincing* information, at least to me, I will be approving this mission. We will be sending one SC-Class vessel to that Scrapheap. Ostensibly, we will be testing an extra-long foldspace journey, as Vice Admiral Rwizi suggested, but you and I will both know that we will be watching for other information."

Gāo swallowed hard. "Why are you telling me this? Why not tell the others?"

"They will not lose their command if things change," Hallock said.

"Neither will I," Gāo said.

Hallock rocked back ever so slightly. "We won't have Scrapheaps any longer."

Gāo smiled. "We will be spending years decommissioning the Scrapheaps. I can guarantee that. And if that occurs, someone has to be in charge. That someone may as well be me."

Hallock laughed and clapped Gāo on the back. "I hadn't even thought of that. You are correct. So it shouldn't matter to you if things change. You might even end up with a more challenging job."

Perhaps. Gāo made herself smile back, although she still felt distinctly uncomfortable.

Hallock had succeeded in making Gāo feel uneasy about something she had felt certain about just that morning.

"I know this isn't common procedure," Hallock said to Gāo, "but I would like you to oversee this mission yourself. I will want regular reports from you once the mission is underway."

Gāo nodded, even though she wasn't sure the mission would happen. There was still a lot to determine.

And Gāo knew that, if she really wanted to stop this trip from happening, all she had to do was request a hearing with the other admirals.

That would make an enemy out of Admiral Hallock, though.

Gāo had to consider her next moves carefully. It might be better to take the risk, send the ship back to the Scrapheap, and see what happened next, than it would be to make such a powerful enemy.

Besides, the Fleet would then learn the fate of at least one of its Scrapheaps.

Gāo wished Hallock had said nothing, had simply given the order to send the mission, and let the rest happen as it may. Gāo wished Hallock had not brought her into the politics of the Scrapheaps at all.

Now Gāo was going to have to determine how she felt about Scrapheaps, Fleet policy, and these traditions.

Unless the ship they sent back to that Scrapheap discovered something definitive.

Gāo wasn't sure what that something would be.

But she half-hoped that she would find out.

THE *SPRÁVA*

True to her word, Admiral Hallock approved the mission. And, true to her word, she put Gāo in charge of it. Gāo could have assigned the mission to underlings, but she didn't want to.

She was hoping she could derail the entire thing.

The morning the orders came down, she was having a breakfast her father used to make in their quarters when she was a girl. Comfort food. Bean sprout rice, cold cucumber soup, seasoned kelp, and, of course, kimchi. She wanted grilled short ribs, but cooking them was difficult in her own kitchen, and she didn't want them that much. She was stirring up eggs to make a vegetable omelet for protein, when the little bell sounded, indicating important orders.

Still, she didn't look immediately. Her quarters were smaller than the average senior officer's quarters because she didn't like large spaces. She had a kitchen that opened to a dining area, and a comfortable living area. Because she was an admiral, she couldn't have quarters on the outside edges of the ship. Hers were buried deep inside the *Správa,* so she made do with large screens that rotated through images of some of the most calming places she had seen in her travels. She also had a small greenhouse between her living area and the single bedroom she had insisted on, and sometimes she just shut off the screens and looked at the growing plants.

She had toyed with doing that this morning after her stretching routine, but had made breakfast instead.

Now, she regretted it. Because she had known that the orders would arrive soon. The other vice admirals had done their assigned tasks.

She hadn't liked what she had seen, particularly from Vice Admiral Rwizi. The courses she and her team had plotted were numerous, because, as she said, there was a bit of guesswork involved. The maps of the sectors were old or relatively nonexistent. So she had gone with the areas that had surviving nodes that the information had come through. And even then, she hadn't liked what she had found.

The short trips, with any ship using an *anacapa*, no longer had a 15% risk factor, like most *anacapa* trips. The risk factor increased with each trip, not because the *anacapa* might fail, but because the odds of going off course increased with each trip.

However, Rwizi gave the long journey—one single trip through foldspace—a 50% chance of succeeding. She noted that she was being optimistic.

She said, if she were doing the trip, and here in her report, she had said (again) that she would not, she would take the short trips. Not because they were safer. In the end, they might have even more risk, but because there was a chance that the crew could leave the ship and live in a sector once inhabited by the Fleet.

Getting lost in foldspace, on the other hand, usually meant the entire crew died.

Gão had brought this report to Hallock's attention, and Hallock had nodded. *It is what I expected*, she had said.

I think it disqualifying. I don't think we should take this mission, Gão had said.

If it were just for the thefts, I would agree, Hallock had responded. *But it is not.*

And those words replayed over and over again in Gão's mind since that short discussion. The reason she needed comfort food this morning wasn't because she was feeling sad or out of sorts, but because she finally—deeply—understood what Admiral Hallock wanted.

She wanted the crew of that ship to die. She wanted the mission to fail. She would use that as an example of how the Fleet couldn't maintain its Scrapheaps. How, even though the plan to keep Ready Vessels and old ships in one place seemed good in theory, it was not a practice that worked for the Fleet at all.

Gão had spent the last two nights trying to figure out if she wanted any part of this mission. Yes, saying no to it would destroy her career. But that mattered less to her as she got older, a fact that sometimes surprised her, since she no longer had family to fall back on. She had never had children, never had a long serious relationship, except with the Fleet itself.

And she was willing to give that up to prevent a mission that would result in certain death for the handful chosen.

But, as Hallock had said, Gão had given orders like that before. She had sent crews to their deaths before. The difference was that they had known they were on a suicide mission.

They had known what they were fighting for.

She hadn't been given strict orders yet, but she knew, just from the way Admiral Hallock was acting, that Gão wouldn't be able to tell anyone what the real mission was. Once the mission failed, Hallock would present herself as the voice of reason.

We tried, she would say. *We planned the best mission we could. Our people couldn't even arrive.* Or couldn't get back, or whatever happened.

Gão also had a hunch that Hallock would insist on the short trips, not just because of Rwizi's recommendation, but because that was the only way to track the ship.

And then the Fleet could declare the ship lost, the mission a failure, and Scrapheaps a dead concept.

The orders pinged insistently. She finished the omelet and pushed it, steaming, onto a plate. Then she set it next to the rest of her breakfast.

She hadn't touched any of it. The act of making the breakfast had been as soothing—maybe even more soothing—than the act of eating it.

Besides, the orders were here.

Gāo opened the orders on a holographic screen near her dining room table. She stood, just in case Hallock had the guts to give the orders in person.

But of course, Hallock hadn't done that. The orders had come, as orders usually did, on official forms.

Vice Admiral Bella Gāo would oversee a mission to what might be the original Scrapheap, to fix that Scrapheap and find out whatever had happened to it. The ship would follow the plan outlined by Vice Admiral Rwizi. The crew would use maps synthesized from information gathered from that Scrapheap and stored in the Fleet's files, information compiled by Vice Admiral Calixte and his team.

Vice Admiral Gāo would choose the final crew from the list of possible crew members sent to her by Vice Admiral d'Anano. They would gather on an SC-Class vessel, already chosen in consultation with Vice Admiral Nguyen. That vessel, *The Renegat*, was being retrofitted and augmented to handle a long mission such as this.

The *Renegat* would leave in one month's time.

Gāo admired the way that Hallock had named each of the vice admirals who had consulted on this mission. The orders made it seem like the entire group had decided to make this work, when, in fact, they had all expressed doubts.

But that was why Hallock was an admiral and the rest were vice admirals. She knew how to play the political game better than anyone Gāo had ever known.

Gāo looked at her omelet, which was no longer steaming. She poked at the kimchi, then stirred the cucumber soup. Her stomach growled. She was hungry, even if she didn't deserve the comfort food, not with what she was going to have to do.

Then she tapped a finger on the table. What bothered her wasn't the mission, exactly. She had helmed missions she privately thought unwarranted before. That was one of the banes of her existence, part of her career.

What bothered her was lying to the crew, as she brought them onboard.

But what if she were honest with them? What if she told them that the mission had little chance of success? And what if she told them that they were being put on this ship, this *Renegat*, because they wouldn't be missed.

They would then be able to say no to the assignment. That no might force them to leave the Fleet, but the Fleet didn't value them anyway.

She stopped tapping the table and clutched her hand into a fist. She was well aware that her reaction in the moment was more about her than it was about the crew of the *Renegat*. Those people were, at the moment anyway, simply names on a list to her.

But if she was going to run this mission—and Hallock had told her she was—then Gāo had to do things her way.

And her way included honesty and choice. If Gāo said no to helming the mission, Hallock would simply find someone else. But if Gāo did the best she could, and still couldn't end up with a full crew complement, then the mission might not happen.

And if the *Renegat* had a full crew, then she could console herself with the idea that they were all informed. They knew what they were getting into, as best as anyone could.

Gāo took a deep breath, and nodded to herself. She hadn't come to a great compromise, but she had come to an acceptable one.

She could lead this mission and still hang on to what little integrity she still had left.

THE *KALUWASAN*

The captain's ready room smelled of whiskey, rotting fruit, and unwashed blankets. Not even the air purifiers in the environmental system had been able to clear the stench, which gave Gāo an indication of just how filthy the ready room actually was. Gāo nearly walked out right at that moment, without even talking to the man who leaned against the wall, his arms crossed.

But Commander Isma Fiorenza put her manicured hand on Gāo's arm, a silent reminder of her promise. Fiorenza had asked Gāo to approach Captain Ivan Preemas with an open mind.

Fiorenza was Preemas's superior officer and, apparently, his champion. Gāo had no idea why anyone would champion a man so clearly undisciplined.

The causes of the ready room's odors were obvious—overflowing garbage, wadded blankets (and clothing) strewn across the floor, and a desk littered with tablets, tools, and dirty dishes.

Preemas watched Gāo's reaction to his ready room without moving, as if he expected her to walk out without talking to him.

He didn't look like a man who deserved a conversation. He was as messy as his ready room, although he had known she was coming to talk with him about a new position. Technically, moving to the *Renegat* would be a promotion. Anyone else would have dressed up for it.

Preemas hadn't. He hadn't shaved in days. His blondish-brown hair, which desperately needed a trim, touched the edges of his wrinkled blue uniform.

The uniform was the only familiar thing about him. It had the gold captain's stripes and the word *security* emblazoned across the right breast pocket.

He wore nonregulation brown boots that looked like they had seen better days, and contrary to regulation, he wore rings on each finger of his right hand.

Fiorenza was his exact opposite.

Every part of her was coiffed and pressed. She wasn't wearing a uniform because it wasn't required for field commanders, even when they were on a mission.

But security teams all had to wear uniforms because the teams never knew when they would be called into action.

The *Kaluwasan*, Preemas's ship, hadn't seen action for nearly a month. Gāo had examined the files. The ship had saved three other vessels that had been stranded at the edge of the sector and had prevented at least one of the ships from exploding. The *Kaluwasan*, with the help of one other SC-Class vessel, also fought off five smaller vessels of unknown origin, thought to be regional pirate vessels bent on stealing the Fleet technology from the ships.

The files made the fight, standoff, and rescue sound both heroic and dramatic, and perhaps they had been. But Gāo was seeing nothing heroic about Preemas.

She saw attitude and incompetence. Shipshape was an adjective for a reason. A clean, well-maintained ship showed discipline and respect for the ship herself. That this room—the captain's room—was so filthy would have disqualified Captain Preemas from almost any command Gāo was considering him for.

Gāo's usual method for calming her nerves—taking a deep breath—would not work here. She was breathing shallowly on purpose. She had considered breathing through her mouth, but she had no idea what kinds of germs she would inhale.

"I thought I ordered you to clean up before our visit," Fiorenza said to Preemas.

"I have," Preemas said as if he were a teenage boy caught inside his filthy bedroom. "The *Kaluwasan* is spotless."

"Except for this room," Fiorenza said. "I told you we were going to meet in this room."

He raised his eyebrows, his green eyes flat. It felt as if he was daring Gāo and Fiorenza to walk out.

Gāo didn't have time for games. She had a short-list of possible captains for the Scrapheap mission, and Preemas was at the top of it.

She had reviewed his record. It started out stellar. He had done exceedingly well in school in every single discipline a captain needed. He fast-tracked through all of his training. He had worked his way to second officer on a DV-Class vessel by the time he was thirty.

Then that vessel, the *Esizayo*, got lost in foldspace for an entire year, but on the ship itself, only 25 hours had passed. Preemas was one of the few who did not need counseling afterwards, since his entire life had been that ship. He hadn't missed a year out of the life of his children or hadn't missed an important event like the death of a parent.

Either he had been able to convince himself that the lost year meant nothing to him or, indeed, it *had* meant nothing to him.

He continued on the fast track to captaincy, going through the various trainings with just a blip on his record here and there. A little insubordination, at the right moments, usually for the right reasons. He had charisma and lots of friends, and no one held those moments against him.

He got promoted until he received his own DV-Class vessel, the *Raadiya*, which had an undistinguished run under his command, until the Drauxhill Incident. A first-contact mission that went so seriously awry that it caused the Fleet to reconsider its first-contact protocols, the Drauxhill Incident concerned Preemas only in that he was captain at the time. He had not participated in the first contact, having followed protocol to the letter.

He was not blamed for anything. Every investigation exonerated him and his crew. The problem was that the protocols themselves had not been flexible enough to handle the situation.

After the incident, though, Preemas had slowly crumbled. He had requested a psychological and medical evaluation, which found him emotionally unfit due to unaddressed psychological stress, caused by everything from the lost year to the Drauxhill Incident.

He had to go through a therapeutic regimen, and then start his climb all over again toward a captaincy. But with that emotional breakdown on his record, he knew—everyone knew—it would be harder for him to regain his captaincy of a DV-Class vessel.

He didn't take orders well from other captains, and finally ended up as captain of the *Kaluwasan*, a lower level SC-Class vessel known for making the occasional daring maneuver and saving more lives than it lost.

He would have had a good reputation, based solely on his work on the *Kaluwasan*, if he had never been a DV-Class captain and hadn't had the breakdown.

And didn't tend to argue with his superiors.

Fiorenza was the first commander who could handle him. She actually seemed to like him.

But Gāo didn't.

"I've seen enough," Gāo said.

"Going to give up on me so easily, Vice Admiral?" Preemas asked.

She lifted her chin ever so slightly. "You have clearly given up on yourself, Captain. I need someone strong, who can handle a mission that is probably the most dangerous the Fleet has designed in centuries. You are not that man."

She pivoted and walked out of the ready room, and onto the *Kaluwasan's* bowl-shaped bridge. The small security staff tried not to look at her, and she tried not to act relieved that she was breathing actual clean air. She had crossed the bridge, around the captain's chair, which, to her surprise, was neat and pristine, when Fiorenza caught up to her.

"Give him a chance, Vice Admiral," Fiorenza said, not even trying to speak softly.

"I did," Gāo said. "He knew we were coming, and—"

"Respectfully, sir," Fiorenza said, "he is exactly what you want on this mission."

Gāo looked at the bridge crew. They all had their heads bent, trying not to pay attention to the conversation around them, but unable to ignore it.

Gāo sighed heavily, climbed up the incline to the back of the bridge and the exits. She left the bridge, waited for Fiorenza, and did not speak again until the doors closed on the bridge itself.

"I want a leader," Gāo said.

"He is one," Fiorenza said. "And he's creative. You're going to want that too. He breaks protocol to test you, because protocol got his entire first-contact team and his backup team killed in Drauxhill. He believes protocol is a bind that restricts thought and forces captains to make bad decisions."

"You could have warned me," Gāo said. "I would not have come."

"I made you promise that you would take him seriously, Vice Admiral," Fiorenza said.

"I did," Gāo said. "I examined his resume. I thought about him as a candidate. I need someone who is able to handle a difficult mission, not act like a sullen teenager who didn't get his way."

"This sullen teenager has always had his crew behind him," Fiorenza said. "Since his misadventure in foldspace decades ago, he has gone into and out of foldspace more than any other captain in the Fleet."

"Daring it to harm him again, no doubt," Gāo said. Then she softened her tone. "You see that as a good argument, Commander. I see it as reckless."

"He's always saved lives when he's gone in," Fiorenza said. "I know who your other candidates are, Vice Admiral. He's the best of the bunch."

Gāo nodded. "I realize that, and it's not a recommendation. The bunch is a sorry lot." She patted Fiorenza on the arm.

"I appreciate your enthusiasm, but Captain Preemas is not what I'm looking for on this mission." And, Gāo thought, she would not be bullied into taking him.

She left Fiorenza in the corridor, and headed to the docking bay where the orbiter she had arrived in waited.

Once again, Gāo would talk to Admiral Hallock. Gāo had interviewed every single captain candidate now, and found them all wanting. She had spoken to existing captains, demoted captains, and young officers who were good, but about to be passed over for the plum DV-Class assignments.

She could see just from the interviews why those young officers weren't being given plum commands. The existing captains usually were doing well enough not to dislodge them from their posts, and demoted captains, like Preemas, had too much baggage.

Gāo would tell the admiral that there was no one suited for this trip, at least that she could find. And she would be able to back that finding up with evidence.

No matter how much Hallock argued that expendables get sent on this mission, there was a counter-argument. The mission had to have even a slight chance of success. Bringing on incompetent captains would guarantee a failure.

There would be an investigation if (when) the mission failed; the mission couldn't look like it had been sabotaged in the first place.

As she headed to the docking bay, Gāo was already lining up her arguments for Hallock. Then an ensign stepped out of one of the side corridors.

"Vice Admiral Gāo?" the ensign asked. She was young—maybe twenty-five—and had the bright eyes of a woman who loved her job.

"Yes," Gāo said as calmly as she could.

"Captain Preemas requests another moment of your time," the ensign said.

"Thank him and tell him that I've given him enough time today," Gāo said.

"Vice Admiral, I'm to keep you from going into the bay until he arrives," the ensign said.

"I countermand that order, Ensign," Gāo said. "I'm leaving."

The young woman sighed, but didn't move. At least she understood protocol.

Gāo slipped past her into the docking bay. She half-expected other members of the *Kaluwasan's* crew to try to stop her. They did not.

She had almost relaxed by the time she reached her orbiter. There, outside of it, stood Captain Preemas. Clearly, the *Kaluwasan* had a quicker and more efficient way for the captain to get to the docking bay than the route that Gāo had taken.

"Our business is completed, Captain," Gāo said. "I am afraid you're not what I'm looking for."

He gave her a half smile.

"I know you're caught in a bind, Vice Admiral," he said. "I know that you've been given a task that requires maybe a dozen ships to complete and you're only allowed to use one. You've also been given a list of names to fill out that single ship, and none of them are stellar—including mine."

She felt a bit cold. She had thought all of that information was classified.

"If what you know is true, Captain," she said, "someone has illegally given you access to classified information."

He tilted his head slightly, as if acknowledging what she said.

"I work on an SC-Class vessel," he said. "When we're effecting a rescue, we often don't have time to go through channels to get information. I have maintained my DV-Class security clearance, which you can discover by going through the records. I have dreams of captaining my own DV-Class vessel again."

Then he gave her a self-deprecating smile.

"Of course," he said, "the longer I'm away, the more I see my chances of achieving that dream slipping away."

Gāo opened her mouth to tell him that those chances would be completely gone after her report, but she stopped herself, and made herself listen to him. If he did indeed have DV-level security clearance, then he had access to some of the information she was acting on. It wouldn't take much to figure out that she was putting together an important mission.

He would probably assume she was sending him to a Scrapheap, because she was in charge of Scrapheaps. He wouldn't know which one, because that was classified well above a DV-level.

Still, his willingness to approach her again intrigued her. Even though she knew that he was still not following protocol.

"I'll be blunt with you, Captain," she said. "This mission that I'm recruiting for is not the stepping stone you want to a DV-level vessel. After reviewing your record, and watching your behavior here, I doubt you will ever have another command like that. So you do not need to advocate for this job. Be glad. It isn't really a job that anyone should want."

He started to say something, then stopped himself. He frowned, as if he hadn't expected her words at all.

"Sir," he said quietly, "if I were to promise you that I could complete this mission, whatever it is, would you consider me for a DV-Class vessel the next time a captaincy opens?"

"No," she said.

He looked startled.

"I doubt you could complete this mission," she said. "I doubt anyone can."

His energy shifted. He went from pushy to still so fast that she almost thought she was looking at another person.

"An impossible mission," he said slowly. "You're setting this ship up for failure."

"I am not," she said. "The mission is what it is."

His eyes narrowed, as he thought. He seemed to be putting pieces together, words she hadn't said.

That strange expression crossed his face again. His eyebrows went up slightly.

"A mission that the brass consider worthwhile. A mission in which they—you—are sending a second-tier ship, one that can be written off, with an unestablished crew." That head tilt again. Apparently, Preemas did it when he was thinking. "A crew no one would miss."

Gāo should have moved away, because she didn't need to discuss anything with him anymore, but watching him think was fascinating. She was beginning to understand his appeal.

He was brilliant.

He was also emotional, moody, and difficult.

"This is a suicide mission, isn't it?" he said slowly, as if it were all being revealed to him. "You've been told to send a single ship on a mission that has been deemed impossible but necessary."

She didn't move. Thank the stars, she had learned how to keep her expression neutral.

"Which means that it's a fact-finding mission or it's an experiment." He gave her that quirky half smile again. Yes, appealing, but somehow dangerous.

She still didn't like him, but she had to respect his reasoning process.

He nodded, as if confirming his own assumptions to himself. "That's why only one ship will go when you wanted more. That's why the list of names I saw were…let's say 'compromised'…at best."

Gāo did not answer him. She just watched him think.

Then his gaze met hers, his green eyes even brighter than they had been a moment ago.

"I've heard about you, Vice Admiral," he said. "I've heard that you're blunt and a straight talker. You don't make promises you can't keep. So if you were to send me on this mission, a mission you don't think I'll survive, you won't make me a false promise of a promotion that you believe I won't live to see."

She still didn't speak, even though he was spot-on with his assumption.

"But what if I exceed expectations?" he asked. "What then?"

She smiled in spite of herself. Charming and arrogant. She had seen that combination before and didn't trust it. It led to entire ships following a leader who was promoted too quickly, didn't have the experience to make good decisions, and refused to listen to others when it was needed.

Although she had seen none of that in his record through his service on the *Raadiya*. When he had been on the career track, he hadn't behaved that way at all. If anything, he adhered to protocol too rigidly.

But there was evidence that his arrogance had overtaken him as the captain of the *Kaluwasan*. Or perhaps, he was simply trying to prove something—to himself, and to the Fleet.

"If you've looked at my record," she said to him, "then you know that I care less about the results than I do about the way they were achieved. I don't make promises based on results. I never use prizes as incentives, particularly for dangerous missions. Doing so leads to cut corners, which leads to sloppy work."

"You would rather a mission fail because it was neat and tidy?" he asked.

"I would rather that difficult missions not exist at all," she said. "But they do, and they require a specific kind of crew, one that can do the mission as assigned and maintain the dignity of the Fleet."

His half smile twisted into a full smile. "The dignity of the Fleet," he said, and his tone was mocking. "You believe such a thing exists."

"I know it does," she said. She had seen it. She had reinforced it. She did her best to maintain it, each and every day.

He raised his eyebrows again, letting his expression disagree with her instead of his words.

"So if I come back from this suicide mission," he said, "but you think I compromised myself or my ship to do so, you wouldn't promote me."

"That's correct," she said.

"And you've already decided that I'm not the right material for this mission, is that correct as well?" he asked.

"You needed to impress me, Captain," she said. "And you did. Just not in the way that you wanted to."

"You want a regulation captain, someone by the book," he said.

She didn't nod. She let her silence speak.

"Your list doesn't include any," he said. "If you want someone like that, you'll have to promote from below, and I suspect this mission takes an experienced leader, not some green kid, am I right?"

He was right, and that was her dilemma. But she didn't tell him that either.

"So what if you take a chance with me, Vice Admiral? And what if I end up doing something great for the Fleet? What if I survive this mission, complete it successfully, *and* do something beyond your expectations? What then?"

She had no idea how to answer that. She didn't believe he could do that. She didn't believe anyone could.

Preemas's eyes glittered as he watched her. He seemed to think he was convincing her to take him on as captain of this mission.

He had no idea she had mentally gone down a different track.

"You seem quite self-involved, Captain," Gão said.

He leaned back just a little, clearly surprised by her words. He must have thought that he had convinced her.

"I'm sure you will find a way to achieve whatever goal you set for yourself," she said, "Or rather, you might, if you start giving protocol a second look. Now, if you'll excuse me."

She really wasn't asking permission to walk past him. She said *if you'll excuse me* as a verbal shove, as a way of getting him to move aside.

He leaned against her orbiter for an extra minute, reminding her once again of a sullen teenager—defiant even when he had lost—and then he smiled politely, nodded, and stepped into protocol.

She brushed past him, and placed her hand on the exterior door panel. The door rose, and two steps lowered so she could go inside.

"Vice Admiral," he said, "self-involved or not, I'm the guy you need on this mission."

She smiled at him. Had he really said that? Reinforcing her self-involved statement as if it had meant nothing to him?

Her smile seemed to annoy him.

He straightened further. He was taller than she had realized. He had slouched as he stood, which was not something an overconfident person did.

Perhaps the bluster had been for him, and not for her.

His gaze remained on hers.

"One last thing." He sounded almost desperate. "If you can't find a victim you approve of to take command of your suicide mission, just remember that you have a volunteer."

He touched his chest lightly, in case she missed the point.

"Duly noted, Captain," she said, and climbed into the orbiter.

The door closed behind her and she stood for just a moment as if the airlock had been engaged, even though it hadn't been.

Victims and volunteers.

She didn't like how sharp his words were, mostly because they were on point.

She would have to give this meeting a bit more thought.

After she spoke to the admiral. After she tried to scuttle this mission one last time.

THE *COJ*

Gão felt like the lowest ensign whenever she boarded Admiral Hallock's DV-Class ship, the *Coj*. Gão felt that way even though she requested the meeting.

She had taken an orbiter to the *Coj*, and landed in the cushy docking bay it had for Fleet dignitaries. Everything inside the *Coj* was either designed for the dignitaries or to intimidate someone who didn't belong.

Gão belonged, and she still felt intimidated.

The *Coj* wasn't decorated the way that working DV-Class vessels were. It didn't have obvious black nanobit walls or floors. It wasn't low maintenance at all.

Every inch of the *Coj* required the kind of upkeep that the Fleet usually frowned upon. The walls and railings appeared to be made of real wood, expensively grown on one of the hydroponics decks of the so-called jungle ships.

Gão suspected that the walls and railings weren't made of real wood, because that would be wasteful, and Hallock was generally about conservation of resources. The walls and railings were probably made of nanobits, programmed to appear shiny and rich and expensive—in both time and resources.

The floors of this part of the *Coj* were expensive. They were covered in carpet, specially woven just for this ship. They had the *Coj*'s name written over and over again into an almost geometric pattern, repeated in various browns to accent the wood.

If Gão looked down, the carpets made her dizzy. She preferred a standard black floor that matched the standard black ceiling, so that if the ship lost attitude control, she didn't need to think about up and down.

She tugged on the sleeves of her uniform. She wouldn't have even worn her uniform if the meeting had been held on her ship. But because she was coming to the *Coj* and making a very formal request, she felt she needed the armor her uniform provided.

Crisp blue pants, even crisper white shirt, a perfectly pressed dark blue dress jacket with the whitish silver stripes denoting her rank on the sleeves. She didn't wear her medals or any of her commendations. She wasn't in full dress, after all. Just everyday dress, the kind that usually occurred on a diplomatic mission.

And perhaps that's what this was. She just hadn't been willing to admit it to herself.

She was going to need to use a lot of diplomacy to win Admiral Hallock over to her side.

An aide met her outside the docking bay. The aide didn't introduce himself, probably figuring that Gão knew who he was. She recognized him. He had a narrow face and a slight frame, and he was a favorite of Hallock's. She generally used him to enforce protocol at various meetings.

He led Gão to a very different kind of ready room than she had seen from Ivan Preemas or even from most captains of DV-Class ships. Admiral Hallock's ready room was filled with personal items. The walls contained rotating two-D images of the places Hallock had been. A blanket made by the Ededfds out of a plant native to their small corner of Idetan glistened like running water on top of a chair made of bright blue weeds from some other place that Hallock had visited.

Everything in the room—everything, from the desk to the mug to the dangerous light fixture hanging from the ceiling—came from some corner of Admiral Hallock's life. She collected artifacts and kept them in all of her personal rooms around the ship.

It made her parts of this ship feel almost like parts of an alien vessel. Most Fleet ships had a sameness to them, but everything about Hallock's ship seemed specially created just for Hallock.

She wasn't in the room. Gão waited, hands clasped behind her back, wishing she wasn't nervous. She looked at the images, most of them of different natural environments—skies of varying shades, some with clouds threatening to storm, some with two or three suns; waterfalls and ice flows, lakes and oceans, fields of grain and flat deserted land that looked like it had never seen water.

The door eased open behind her, and Gão started like a guilty child. So much for being the face of calm.

She turned.

Admiral Hallock wasn't wearing her uniform, of course. She was wearing slacks embroidered with green and gold flowers, a matching gold shirt, and big green bangles on her wrists.

"I hadn't realized this would be a formal meeting, Bella," Hallock said. Then she waved the unbangled hand. "Sit. Sit."

She indicated the chair made of weeds, but Gão couldn't bring herself to sit in it. She eased herself into the only regulation chair in the room, finding comfort in its sturdy and familiar black shape.

Hallock smiled ever so slightly, as if she had expected nothing less of Gão. Then Hallock sat on the weed chair. It creaked under her weight.

"You have doubts about the mission," Hallock said without preamble.

"I was hoping I could get you to call it off," Gão said.

"Based on what?" Hallock asked.

Based on a thousand things, from the hopelessness of the mission to the pointlessness of it. The way that it was the opposite of a normal Fleet mission. The fact that no one who was helping her plan the mission thought it was a good idea.

"I can't find the kind of crew we need," Gão said. "The young officers are not ready for this kind of mission, and I can't, in good conscience, send someone at the beginning of a career into something that will probably destroy them."

Hallock raised her eyebrows. "You weren't young and ambitious once, Bella?"

"I was, Admiral, and if ordered, I would have served. But I wouldn't have volunteered." That word echoed the phrase that Preemas had spoken to her. Victims, instead of volunteers. That phrase had haunted her ever since.

"Vice Admiral d'Anano gave you a list," Hallock said. "I saw it. One thousand names. None of them are suitable?"

Gão let out a small breath. "None of the captains are. I interviewed all of them. They're disasters, each and every one of them."

"Are they?" Hallock asked.

"Yes," Gão said. "They were passed over for promotions or demoted for a reason. Most of them are burned out and incompetent."

"Most," Hallock said.

"Yes." Gão felt irritated. Why couldn't Hallock just trust her?

Because Hallock wanted this mission to go, no matter what.

"If you think this mission should happen, sir," Gão said. "Then let's send an already staffed battle-tested DV-Class ship. Let's send good people back there, who can handle whatever they find."

Hallock folded her hands on her lap. "I wanted to send six DV-Class vessels on this mission. I was denied. Then I asked for two. I was denied. So I asked for an established crew with a DV-Class vessel. Again, I was denied."

She said this all with a flat voice, but it couldn't quite hide the thread of anger running through it.

She said, "I barely got approval for one SC-Class vessel with a crew of misfits and failures, and then only because the Fleet never knows what to do with such people, particularly if they refuse to retire to some sector base somewhere."

Gão's breath caught. She almost felt as if time had frozen around her.

She had often been in discussions with others in the Fleet about that very issue—the people who didn't do as commanded, who didn't live up to expectations, and who didn't follow the rules for those who didn't fit. Usually, people who didn't fit left the Fleet itself, moving to starbases or sector bases, getting left behind if they were alive when a sector base closed.

It became clear to them that they didn't belong in the Fleet, and they respected that clarity, maybe even liked it.

And then there were others, ones who made big mistakes or who seemed to rebel for no reason or who screwed up on levels that Gāo simply couldn't understand, people who refused to learn or budge or change in any way.

"You don't approve." Hallock sounded almost amused. "They're the problem, not us, Vice Admiral Gāo."

Ah, so they had gotten formal again. No longer a discussion between chums.

"If they left the Fleet as we encourage them to do," Hallock said, "we wouldn't have to find a place for them. They would take care of themselves."

"I met a few people who still believed they had a future with the Fleet," Gāo said, thinking of Preemas.

"Oh, they do," Hallock said. "Just not the future they thought they had. Not everyone can get promoted. Not every career moves forward."

"I know career people who are happy to stay in the same job," Gāo said.

"And none of them are on that list," Hallock said.

She was right, too. None of the people Gāo had interviewed had been happy where they were.

Gāo said, "Admiral, I know you like the idea of this mission…"

Hallock laughed. "You may stop being polite with me, Bella. You don't like this mission, and I'm not going to cancel it. I'm not going to put anyone else in charge, either. You know Scrapheaps better than anyone else."

"But if you send a ship, they'll also be experimenting with foldspace travel," Gāo said. "Can't you put someone else on this, like Vice Admiral Rwizi?"

Hallock gave Gāo a chiding look. "Are you worried that the failure of this mission will go on your resume?"

"Of course not," Gāo said. She hadn't even thought of that. She was shocked at the very suggestion.

"Then get this mission underway," Hallock said.

Gāo had to try one last time. "Admiral, we could send them to that Scrapheap, and never hear from them again. I know you want definitive results, but I don't think you will get them."

"Maybe not from this mission," Hallock said.

"Then why are we sending them?" Gāo asked.

Hallock's lips moved ever so slightly. Gāo couldn't tell if that was supposed to become a smile or a frown.

"You know why, Bella," Hallock said.

"I know what happens if the mission actively fails," Gāo said. "But what happens if we send this ship and only get silence in return?"

"Then we'll try again," Hallock said.

A chill ran through Gāo. This mission wasn't worth one ship, let alone two.

Admiral Hallock smiled at Gāo. "I'm shocking you."

Gāo didn't know how to answer that. The truth didn't seem like an option, especially since the first thought to cross her mind was to wonder at Hallock's grasp on reality.

And then Gāo realized something worse: Hallock had a firm grasp of reality. She just didn't care about the lives she was sending to that Scrapheap. Maybe she had never really cared about the lives under her command.

"Pick the crew, Vice Admiral Gāo," Hallock said. "And keep in mind that it will be better to have volunteers instead of victims."

Gāo raised her head in surprise.

Hallock's smile grew. "You reported on every candidate you met, Bella. Did you think those reports would go unnoticed?"

The reports were really logs, mostly for herself, so that she could remember everyone she had talked to. She had spent a bit of extra time on Preemas, but only because he had been so unusual, and she hadn't been certain of her response to him.

"I think if I only pick volunteers," Gāo said slowly, "I won't get the best crew."

"But at least you'll have an enthusiastic one," Hallock said. And then her smile faded. "Because it's not pleasant to deal with someone who doesn't believe in the mission."

The sideways criticism bit hard. And reminded Gāo who she was dealing with. The woman who confided in her and pretended to be her friend was not Admiral Hallock's usual behavior. Usually, Hallock made stinging comments like that, never balancing the sting with praise.

"Get the ship underway, Bella," Hallock said. "You've wasted too much time on this already."

Gāo stood, her teeth clamped tight. If this mission did succeed, she would waste even more time. And that didn't even count what might happen if the ship disappeared into foldspace or met with some other disaster.

"May I make a request, Admiral?" Gāo asked.

Hallock sighed. "What?"

"Would you please note my hesitation in your file on this mission?"

"Because you believe in I told you so's?" Hallock asked snidely.

Gāo shook her head. "I just want a record of this, so that when someone investigates—"

"*If* someone investigates," Hallock said.

"—they'll know the idea was yours, and not mine."

"Seems to me that you're focused on your career at the expense of everything else, Bella," Hallock said.

Gāo felt a surge of anger, and bit it back.

"Actually, Admiral," she said, "if I was focused on my career, we would never have had this meeting. I would have followed your dictates to the letter the moment you made them."

Admiral Hallock studied her for a moment, then inclined her head forward.

"You're a mystery, Bella," she said after a moment. "And I don't have time to unravel you."

She waved a hand, dismissing Gāo. Gāo left, feeling shaken and exhausted. And even more frustrated than she had been before she had gone in.

She was going to have to pick an inferior captain to lead the wrong kind of ship on a dangerous mission that would not succeed. She could find no way around this.

Even if she resigned, the mission would go forward.

All she could do was try to find the best combination of crew members that she possibly could.

And then she would have to wish for the best.

PART THREE
THE RESCUE
NOW

THE *AIZSARGS*

The ship appeared out of foldspace, leaking atmosphere on both sides. Captain Kim Dauber caught the white edges of the ship before her bridge crew even noticed. She had been staring at the wall screen, trying to see the planet Vostrim as a whole, wondering if she needed to run a sector-wide diagnostic to make sure no part of the just-closed sector base was noticeable even to ships not in orbit.

Then this ship appeared, close and in trouble.

The wall screen had been set on two dimensions, and was scanning for anomalies in nearby space, which was why she even saw the white edges around the ship. Sometimes, through the right screen setup, that transition between foldspace and regular space made a ship of any color look like it had been outlined in white.

The white faded around the edges, but the gray of the leak did not.

"We've got a ship in trouble," she said, without turning around.

With those words, her bridge staff would refocus and take action.

"Got it," said Nazira Almadi, Dauber's first officer. Almadi was working on a secondary console, her long black hair wrapped in a bun on the top of her head, her gaze focused downward, probably on readings on the console.

Usually Dauber and Almadi weren't on the bridge of the *Aizsargs* at the same time, because Dauber trusted her first officer to handle the bridge as well as Dauber herself did.

But, fortunately for that damaged ship, Dauber had her best officers manning their posts today.

She was in charge of closing down this sector of space for the Fleet, making sure that the people who remained on Vostrim, where Sector Base Z had been located, wanted to leave the Fleet and continue their lives in Z-City after the base closed.

She also needed to make sure that every Fleet ship had left the area, that no random ships had been assigned elsewhere and were returning, incorrectly, to the closed sector base.

"The ship's one of ours," said Brett Ullman. He stood stiffly near his console, his features half-hidden by screens opaqued and floating around him. He usually worked navigation, but he was handling data flow right at the moment.

"You sound surprised," Dauber said without turning around. She wasn't as surprised. The ship had come out of foldspace, after all.

But the ship did look odd.

"Configuration's old," he said. "We have nothing in active use that looks like that ship."

Dauber nodded, taking in the information, but not willing to examine it until later.

"Whatever that ship is," she said, "it doesn't matter. It's leaking atmosphere, and it needs help."

"I'm reading one hundred ninety-nine life signs on that ship," Ullman said.

"Let's get them off the vessel," Dauber said. "We'll tow the ship, but I don't want it near us."

She had learned that lesson years ago. Ships with foldspace capability could be touchy when they were in distress. Particularly after they had emerged from foldspace. *Anacapa* drives were delicate things that could malfunction. And sometimes ships brought back all kinds of other problems from that great beyond.

"The great beyond" was how she thought of foldspace, even though the description was incorrect. Foldspace wasn't beyond anything. It was something else entirely.

The science around foldspace was constantly changing. Some believed it was a different region of the universe, a region that the Fleet had somehow tapped with its *anacapa* capabilities. That seemed as unlikely to her as a ship creating foldspace.

All she knew was that ships could use the *anacapa* to jump to foldspace, and then return to the same spot in regular space hours later. She had used that technique in battle a dozen times.

She didn't think about foldspace or how it worked; she just used it.

"I've been trying to contact them," said Josephine Ornitz. Ornitz was short and round. She was reaching upwards on a new console, one she hadn't even bothered to reconfigure for her height. She headed Dauber's communications department, and hadn't worked on the bridge in months.

But Dauber had needed Ornitz for the sector base closure, so she was currently on the bridge. Which was lucky. Because, if Ornitz couldn't contact the ship, then no one could.

"Anything from them at all?" Dauber asked. "Distress signal? Anything?"

"No," Ornitz said.

"It looks like a number of major systems are down, sir," said Massai Ribisi, the *Aizsargs*'s chief engineer. He wore a nonregulation hat over his bald head, and was still in black exercise clothes. She had taken him from his daily personal routine to help her find any evidence of the closed base. "I'm not sure they can contact us."

Dauber frowned at the ship, no longer outlined in white. Any indication of foldspace had disappeared altogether, leaving the familiar pattern of stars—some of them faded and some of them glowing brightly against the darkness of space.

"Get a rescue vehicle, and tell them to be prepared for anything," she said. "Send fighters to escort it."

"You expect that ship to attack us?" Ullman asked.

"I expect nothing," Dauber said. "I'm preparing for everything."

Then she turned, faced the best bridge crew she had ever worked with. They were each handling a different aspect of this emergency, heads bent, fingers moving. Two security team members, who weren't part of the bridge crew, stood near the door. They were a necessary but unusual addition because the *Aizsargs* had been dealing with the final closure of a sector base (and final closures sometimes made the locals crazy). The security team were the only ones looking directly at Dauber.

Then she realized they weren't look at her at all. They too were looking at the large two-D screen imagery, watching that ship leak atmosphere as it wobbled forward.

"Prepare Deck Seven for the survivors on that ship," she said to her Chief of Security, Vilma Lauritz. "I want that deck sealed off from the rest of the *Aizsargs*."

"Right away, Captain." Lauritz had been working one of the stations near the door. She didn't head below decks, the way that Dauber would have. Instead, Lauritz's hands started moving rapidly as she isolated the deck.

First order of business for Lauritz, Dauber knew, was to establish a route for the strange ship's passengers to go from the docking bay to that deck, without passing crucial systems.

That was why Dauber had picked Deck Seven. It was the closest personnel deck to the docking bay. Lower level personnel decks had individual cabins for single crew members, a large mess, and two recreational areas, but no essential services and, more importantly, no access to them.

Even better, Decks Seven and Eight had been cleared before this last pass around the sector base, in case the *Aizsargs* had to pick up stragglers. Dauber wasn't displacing any of her crew members.

"Let's move," Dauber said. "At the rate that ship's venting atmosphere, it only has a few hours left."

She was guessing, based on the ship's size and its layout. She was also assuming that the atmosphere was venting at an even rate throughout the ship.

For all she knew, the ship had lost a lot of crew already. It looked pretty large to only have 200 people on board.

"What kind of ship is that, anyway?" she asked Ullman.

"I've been trying to match it so that the rescue vessel knows how to access it," he said.

She smiled to herself. She knew he was doing that work, because he was just that good.

"I'm not finding anything current," he said. "It looks like a Security-Class vessel from about a hundred years ago."

She wasn't sure how that could be. SC vessels had a very specific design. "It looks nothing like a Security-Class vessel to me," she said.

"I know. It threw me too at first," Ullman said. "The SC designations went through a complete redesign about fifty years ago. In theory, they're more efficient now."

"In theory?" she asked.

He shrugged. "There are always complainers."

And he said nothing else.

She turned, looking at the ship. It appeared dark, except for the gray atmosphere leaving. Had some of the whiteness she saw earlier been the ship's lights?

"What are the major differences between this SC ship and the current ones?" she asked.

"Too many to list," Ullman said. "I'm sending specs to the *Aizsargs Rescue One*, because they're not going to know how to get around this thing."

Aizsargs Rescue One was their newest rescue vehicle. It had just been replaced before this mission. Dauber almost belayed the order to send *Rescue One*, almost told Ullman to send *Rescue Five* because it was the oldest rescue vessel, and she didn't want to risk the new one.

But, depending on what was happening here, that ship's survivors might need all the upgraded tech on *Rescue One*.

The thought of both rescue vessels made her realize something.

"Was it standard practice for an SC vessel to work alone a hundred years ago?" she asked Ullman.

He raised his head, looked at her, and blinked, clearly surprised. He hadn't thought of that either.

But both of them knew how SC vessels worked now.

SC-Class ships were security ships. They were sent to the scene of a crisis, usually in twos or threes, and they handled the emergency. If the SC-Class ships went out alone, it was usually on a forward mission or somewhere planetside to do some preliminary research.

SC-Class vessels rarely did solitary work for longer than a few days, maybe a week. And usually the planetside work was at a sector base or a planet that might house a sector base.

She never heard of an SC vessel operating alone this far from the Fleet.

"I have no idea," Ullman said. "My understanding of systems and practices is that they remain the same."

"Until they don't," Ornitz muttered.

Dauber tilted her head a little, conceding that point.

But Almadi got to the heart of the matter. She raised her head, squinted at the two-D representation as if it could tell her everything, then said, "Systems and practices now means that we'd see dozens more of these ships coming out of foldspace."

Everyone on the bridge looked at her. Dauber frowned.

"Or," Ullman said, "they're still in foldspace."

Fortunately, he didn't use the word *stuck,* which was something everyone who ever traveled through foldspace worried about, whether they admitted it aloud or not.

Almadi's fingers hovered over her work screen. She was probably waiting to calibrate what the *Aizsargs* should do, depending on Dauber.

"I'm hoping nothing else comes out of foldspace while we're working on this ship. After that, we'll talk to them—" Dauber hoped "—and find out if they were part of a group. Let's just get over there now."

Almadi nodded, then bent her head over the screen, fingers moving.

Dauber said, "Tell *Rescue One* to have its shields set and make sure someone monitors the area around the injured ship and *Rescue One*. I don't want a ship to emerge from foldspace right near our vessels and fighters. Got that?"

"Already on it," Almadi said.

"Good," Dauber said.

That ship, whatever it was, was lucky. It had caught the *Aizsargs* at the right moment, when she was staffed with her best personnel, doing their best work. Had the injured ship arrived two days from now, it would have been alone in this sector. The base would have been shut down, and even though a lot of people still on the surface of Vostrim knew how to help a disabled ship, they no longer had the tools or capacity to do so.

"The ship is still not answering us," Ornitz said.

"Willfully?" Dauber asked.

"I can't tell," Ornitz said. "But I would be remiss if I didn't inform you that they might be deliberately avoiding answering our hails."

"Why would they do that?" Ullman asked. He sounded a little preoccupied. Or maybe Dauber thought he was. Because he should have known the answer.

"That ship is by itself. It's old, and it's not working well," Dauber said. "There's a good chance it's been stolen."

One member of the security team guarding the door to the bridge looked at her sharply. No one else seemed surprised.

Ullman's skin flushed. "Sorry, Captain. Wasn't thinking. Although where would someone pick up a vessel like that? Wouldn't we know if one was lost?"

"We lose ships all the time," Almadi said. "We keep track, but who pays attention to each and every one?"

"Something else to gather data on, then," Ullman said. He didn't sound discouraged at all. He sounded intrigued by the challenge.

Dauber had a hunch they all were. After all, they had thought this entire mission would be routine, and so far it had been. No DV-Class ship—the largest and most important vessels in the Fleet—liked being at the tail end of Fleet space.

Sector bases moved as the Fleet moved out of a sector. The main part of the Fleet itself hadn't been in this sector in over five hundred years.

Dauber hadn't protested the assignment—she had been too professional for that—but she had chafed when she received it. No DV captain wanted to take her ship backwards, not even for a few months.

She didn't like being in a sector that was well known, that held no surprises, and was, in fact, so unimportant the Fleet was pulling away from it.

Although she had been wrong, hadn't she, about the no surprises. That crippled ship out there was something new and different.

"We have one other thing to find out," she said to her bridge crew. General order, not to someone specific. "We are going to need to know what got that ship out of foldspace. Did it travel here on its own volition? Come out of foldspace here because that was what it had been programmed to do? Or has it somehow attached to the signal of our *anacapa* or a dying signal out of Sector Base Z?"

"I'll make sure *Rescue One* has that question front and center," Almadi said.

Good. Dauber was glad that Almadi was communicating with *Rescue One* on that matter. Because the way the ship got here would have a direct impact on the way the *Aizsargs* helped it. And what they needed to do with the *anacapa* drive on that ship.

Dauber straightened her shoulders, then moved to her own station. She had no captain's chair on the bridge, unlike many of her compatriots. The bridge was no place to sit down, although of late, a chair wouldn't have hurt.

Things had moved too slowly here for the past few months. She was happy for the distraction.

She only hoped that the distraction remained simply that—a distraction.

Because she didn't want this incident to become something bigger.

THE *AIZSARGS RESCUE ONE*

Nothing had attacked *Rescue One* yet. Attacks were common during rescues. Raul Zarges always braced for attacks first.

Zarges had run the rescue ships for the *Aizsargs* for more than a decade. He used to love the work, but even before his last mission, he was seeing any loss of life as a failure.

And in rescue work, it was all about who got saved, not about who got lost.

Zarges wasn't piloting *Rescue One*. Instead, he stood in the cockpit of the *Rescue One*, supervising. In theory, anyway. His pilot, Pascal Turris, didn't need supervising. Turris could handle *Rescue One* in the middle of a war zone, in his sleep.

Rescue One was always safer with Turris at the helm than with Zarges. Still, Zarges felt the need to watch the approach to that ancient SC-Class vessel that Captain Dauber had sent him to. Zarges wanted to see what they were up against.

Zarges was wearing his environmental suit in case he decided to go on the mission. The suit's hood was down, and the environment was off. He wasn't sure he would leave the cockpit at all, although he really wasn't needed here.

In addition to Turris in the cockpit, *Rescue One* had a navigator who specialized in close quarters, a life raft technician, and a weapons' specialist.

Every contingency planned for.

The *Rescue One* was a strange hybrid of a ship. It had a large hold in its belly that could fit three hundred people, but they couldn't access any other part of the ship. The rest of the *Rescue One* had been designed to work with a maximum of fifty crew members, and none of them would stay on board for longer than a day or two.

There weren't really crew quarters here. *Rescue One* had pop-out hammocks for overnight missions, and a barely adequate kitchen for the crew. Most of the resources on the ship, besides weapons and rescue tools, were centered near that holding area, including an automated medical bay.

Usually the rescued needed immediate medical attention, food, and water, and *Rescue One* generally provided such things on the way back to the *Aizsargs*—if, indeed, the rescued were going to the *Aizsargs*. Sometimes *Rescue One* took the rescued back to whatever planet they had left or the starbase they had traveled out of or the larger ship they had traveled from.

This past few weeks, *Rescue One* had taken half a dozen ships back to Z-City. Most of those ships were filled with young people who hadn't known how to pilot, but wanted to stay with the Fleet, and their parents didn't.

Sufia Khusru, his second and the person who had run *Rescue One* while he was on medical leave, had encouraged most of those kids to apply to school ships, so they could travel with the Fleet and leave Vostrim permanently.

Zarges had a hunch this mission wouldn't be nearly as easy as those had been.

Not that Khusru would have called it easy. But compared to his last mission, the Z-City rescues had been a piece of cake.

Khusru was in Staging, along with the rest of Zarges's rescue team. He wasn't sure yet whether they would use a grappler, a spacebridge, or something else to get the people off that SC-Class vessel.

He wasn't even sure they wanted off the vessel.

Hence the worry about an attack.

Zarges squinted at the damaged vessel. He was surprised at the SC designation. He had rescued a lot of ships, including several with an SC designation, and he had never seen one with this design.

The *Aizsargs* had sent over some specs for the ship, but Zarges hated using design plans to mount a rescue. He liked going into ships of a design he'd seen when it was fully operational, not one that was falling apart and in distress.

His team was studying the specs as he was watching *Rescue One* ease closer to the SC-Class vessel. He was watching on the three-D screen his pilot was using, seeing the tube-shaped *Rescue One*, with its wide belly, ease up beside the much larger SC-Class vessel.

Zarges had already ordered up life rafts, not just to get the stranded crew off the ship, but maybe to send them to the *Aizsargs*. A fully staffed SC-Class vessel—at least the ones he was familiar with—could have as many as five hundred people on board.

So far, the preliminary data showed closer to two hundred. But he didn't entirely trust information coming from a damaged ship. He had to have a contingency plan for the normal crew complement, just in case some kind of damper had activated on sections of the ship.

If there were five hundred people on board that ship, he would have to improvise the rescue even more than rescues were usually improvised.

He had already warned Captain Dauber that he might have to send some of the rescued directly to the *Aizsargs*, without the usual stopover on *Rescue One* for cleanup and debrief. Captain Dauber assured him that she was prepared to receive whatever and whomever he sent.

His heart was pounding. He was a lot more nervous than he ever remembered being, but this was his first mission back. And it looked like one he would have to be clear-headed about.

As he watched the image of the *Rescue One* move ever closer to the SC-Class vessel, looming against its side like a baby floating toward its father in zero-G, Zarges briefly toyed with letting Khusru run the mission. But that would be an admission that he wasn't ready to return to work, and if he wasn't ready now, then he might never be.

He had to get past his failures somehow, or retire. And the idea of having no real work to do on any kind of vessel, even if he remained with the main body of the Fleet, terrified him at such a visceral level, he couldn't even speak of it.

This SC-Class vessel seemed to be blind. No ship of its size—no Fleet ship of that size—should allow a ship like *Rescue One* to get as close as it was, without hailing it or putting up shields.

So far, no attack, which—as far as he was concerned—harmed Dauber's theory that the SC-Class vessel had been stolen. Thieves would attack another ship nearby, right? Particularly if that ship's designation showed it as part of the Fleet.

At least, that was what he assumed, and he knew that assumptions could sometime get him into trouble. As damaged as this ship was, it might not have the capability to do anything except drift in space. There might be no way anyone on board could know of the presence of *Rescue One*.

Besides, *Rescue One* had been hailing the vessel since it got within range, and no one had responded. Neither *Rescue One* nor the *Aizsargs* had even received an automated distress signal.

Zarges studied the SC-Class vessel. He could finally see its designation was etched into the side of the ship, which the Fleet had only done a few times in its history. The SC-Class vessel was called the *Renegat*.

Its hull was pockmarked and scarred, either by heat weapons or some kind of fire. Patched holes reflected blackly in the lights from *Rescue One*, showing that the *Renegat*'s nanobit repair system still worked.

Up close, Zarges could tell this was a Fleet vessel, albeit of a kind he had never seen before. The smooth hull, the rounded edges, even the shape of the exterior doors, looked familiar.

But the layout wasn't, and his team was going to struggle with that.

"Hail them again," he said to Turris.

"I have been," Turris said. "In addition to a verbal hail, I've been pinging, letting them know a ship was close. I've also sent some automated signals on other bands, and I'm not getting anything."

Zarges took a deep breath. He squinted at the ship.

"But there are life signs?" he asked.

"Yeah," Turris said. "The *Aizsargs* was right. There are exactly one hundred ninety-nine life signs. A couple of them seemed to have moved, but not very far. I can't tell if they're conscious or not."

Zarges frowned. If there were two hundred unconscious people on that ship, his rescue team was in trouble. He didn't have a large enough team to evacuate two hundred unconscious people quickly.

But Dauber's theory danced around his head. They could be thieves, in which case, they were working at stealing whatever it was, and they didn't care about the *Renegat's* problems.

"Is there another working ship on board that one?" Zarges asked. "Maybe inside one of the bays?"

"There's no way to know that," Turris said. "Nothing is powered up, and nothing is hooked to the outside. Not even us."

That comment set Zarges back a little. Grappling to the *Renegat* would be risky at best. Which made it essential that Turris remain in the cockpit. He'd freed *Rescue One* from tight situations before.

But the grapple couldn't hold for long. *Rescue One* had to stay in touch with the *Renegat* only as long as it took to let his team board.

"I'm going to finish suiting up," he said. "Let the team in Staging know we're going onto that ship."

"I don't like what I see near that ship," Turris said. "I'd recommend against grappling."

"It'll be a short contact," Zarges said. "We'll use a spacebridge, then we'll roll it up once we're on board. You'll deploy life rafts when we ask for them."

If they could. If the two hundred people on board were able to get to some kind of exit.

Zarges needed to see what they were doing, and figure out how to get them off the ship.

"I'm not sure that damaged ship can handle a grapple at all," Turris said.

"That's just one of our gambles," Zarges said, and he heard something in his voice that he hadn't heard in a long time. It wasn't fair to call his tone upbeat.

He didn't like to think he was happy about people being in trouble.

But he appreciated the challenge that was facing him. It made him feel alive, just like it used to.

That thought made him calmer. Maybe he had been right: maybe he was ready for this mission, counselor be damned.

He tapped a closed fist on the back of Turris's chair.

"Let the team know we're going to the bridge of that ship," Zarges said. "I'll meet them in Staging. We leave in five."

"Got it," Turris said.

Zarges headed out of the cockpit. He grabbed his hood, pulled it over his head, and sealed it. Then he activated the suit's environmental controls.

As he hurried to Staging, he let the team know what he was thinking.

"We have to get to the bridge of that ship," he said.

"We?" Khusru asked through the comm. She sounded surprised.

Apparently she had thought that he wasn't going with the team. He didn't blame her. He hadn't gone on a mission in six months.

"We," he said, and set the hookup in motion.

THE *AIZSARGS*

The crew on the *Aizsargs*'s bridge was quiet. All they could do right now was watch the rescue unfold.

They needed to be ready to spring into action the moment *Rescue One* left the *Renegat*. And that wouldn't happen for some time.

Dauber paced around the floating screens. She had the main rescue set up as a hologram in front of the closed portal. Everything looked frozen to her, waiting, just like she was.

The half-dozen fighters she had deployed to protect *Rescue One* should the *Renegat* attack hovered just out of the *Renegat*'s sensor range. The fighters could reach *Rescue One* in a matter of minutes. Their weapons could arrive even faster, and, judging from the information Dauber currently had, would destroy the unshielded ship.

Almadi monitored a variety of readings in the space around the rescue. She was watching for another opening into foldspace, in case more ships arrived, maybe ships that had been stolen alongside the *Renegat* (if the *Renegat* had been stolen, which Dauber wasn't sure of).

She was also monitoring the space around the rescue. She was deeply worried that more ships would appear from foldspace. The *Aizsargs* was a little more vulnerable than she would like.

If the *Aizsargs* was vulnerable, *Rescue One* was extremely vulnerable, particularly if the *Renegat* had been traveling in a tight formation with other ships. Those other ships might arrive out of foldspace an hour or two later, but still close to the *Renegat*. Which meant that the new ships could easily hit *Rescue One*.

The entire crew of this ship, and of *Rescue One*, were aware of that problem, and so far, no one had mentioned it. If it happened, they would deal with it.

Until then, all they could do was monitor.

Ornitz had stopped trying to hail the *Renegat*. That responsibility now fell on *Rescue One*. They had been trying to contact the ship during their entire trip to the *Renegat*'s side. If they couldn't contact it from without, they would try once they got inside.

If they got inside.

Dauber hated this part of an unexpected rescue mission. Because she had no idea how the *Renegat* got here, where it had come from, and what it had been trying to do before it arrived.

She had no idea if the *Renegat*'s 200 souls would be happy to find out about the team from *Rescue One* or if they would immediately go to war.

And she liked knowing things.

Ribisi was monitoring the *Renegat's* systems. He kept reporting on their continued decay.

Dauber could see that. The atmosphere still leaked out of one side, trailing like a cloud of smoke in a nonexistent wind.

"Anything?" Dauber asked as her pacing brought her beside Ullman. He was searching records, looking to see where the *Renegat* had last served and why it had come to this sector.

"Not yet," he said without looking up. His fingers moved quickly. He could go through data faster than anyone else on her bridge, faster than anyone else on the ship, almost faster than parts of the computer itself.

She paced past him, examining every console as she passed.

Her entire bridge crew was keeping busy, doing things that would help if the 200 people got rescued, things that would probably be a waste of time if they did not.

The *Aizsargs*'s medical staff had activated their triage teams, and expanded sick bay. Protocols for dealing with non-Fleet personnel had been put into place on every deck. On some decks, only people with clearance could even touch the ship's computer system.

Rescue One had deployed two grapplers, and was extending a spacebridge. The bridge would attach to a door, provide a small environment just in case that door opened directly into a ship without airlocks, and then her team could go inside.

The spacebridge wasn't designed for Fleet-to-Fleet rescues. In theory, a Fleet ship could easily tow another Fleet ship or bring that ship into the docking bay (if the larger rescuing vehicle was a DV-Class vessel).

Dauber had decided to treat this SC-Class vessel—this *outmoded* SC-Class vessel—as a non-Fleet ship. She hadn't even had to tell Zarges that. He had understood when she had mentioned the ship might have been stolen.

But he clearly understood why she was doing this. The methods they were using were going to be tough on the ship. Grapplers sometimes damaged an already crippled ship, and they weren't the only problem *Rescue One* now faced.

Because sometimes even the most experienced crews reacted badly to a rescue. They were oxygen deprived or battle-scarred and they didn't always recognize a rescue as a rescue.

Dauber gripped her hands behind her back, trying to run scenarios through her mind, hoping none of them would come true.

Because, if this rescue turned into a disaster, she had fewer resources than usual at her disposal.

Most of the Fleet ships had left the sector, since almost everyone from Sector Base Z was gone. There were no large ships left at Sector Base Z, either.

Dauber could send for assistance, and it would arrive within the hour.

But she'd been in battles that had lasted less than fifteen minutes, and had more casualties than fights that had lasted for days. Everything was unpredictable, particularly when there was a surprise attack.

This had many of the hallmarks of a surprise attack. Not all of the hallmarks, but enough to make her nervous. Strangely, she was taking the most comfort from the age of that ship, even though the age had taken the rescue from routine to strange right from the start.

And she was going to be prepared for anything. Because, out here, anything could happen, and often did.

The spacebridge was now locked into place. The grapplers hadn't moved. The *Renegat* looked like a gigantic bug trapped by a smaller, more deadly bug. The gray cloud continued off its side.

And no ships appeared out of foldspace.

Yet.

THE *AIZSARGS RESCUE ONE*

Staging was the most organized part of *Rescue One.* It had to be: Teams often deployed from this part of the ship very quickly.

Today's team wasn't moving quickly now, even though there was an urgency to dealing with the *Renegat.* There were procedures to follow, plans to figure out.

And the spacebridge needed to be double-checked.

Zarges arrived last. The other six members of the team were waiting, suited up, with small tool and medical kits attached to their belts. Given the number of people in the *Renegat,* the best thing the rescue team could do was get everyone off the ship. The medical kits were for triage, for injuries that might prevent movement.

Zarges grabbed his supply belt and slipped it over his waist. Then he grabbed glove lights, and a few other supplies from the nearest supply closet.

Sufia Khusru joined him. She was small, thin, and strong, perfect for this kind of work. She wasn't wearing her hood yet. Her dark hair was shorn close to her head, making her black eyes seem even larger than they were. She leaned into him, and spoke away from the comm on the edge of her hood.

"Do you really think you should be going on this mission?" she asked quietly.

They didn't stand on any kind of ceremony on *Rescue One.* Remaining silent about orders could cause a cascade of deaths.

"Yeah." He glanced over his shoulder at Morris Ogden, who was checking the seal on his gloves. Ogden was the second most senior person on the teams, after Khusru. "Ogden's good, but he's never handled a situation like this. Only rescues of known Fleet ships."

"I've done this kind of rescue before," Khusru said.

"Yes, I know," Zarges said. "But there are people scattered all over that ship. Usually when things go wrong, people cluster."

"You're worried that they'll, what, attack us?" Khusru asked. "This isn't a setup. That ship is in trouble."

"Clearly," Zarges said. "But how much of that trouble did they cause? We might have to make some decisions that..."

He paused. He didn't quite know how to say what he needed to say. They were a rescue vehicle, and what he was about to suggest went against all of their training.

"I know," Khusru said. "We might have to leave some people behind, and not due to their injuries. I already gave the team weapons."

"That's the thing," Zarges said. "I think we split into two teams, one to see if we can slow down whatever is causing the atmosphere leak so we can buy more time, and the other to get people off the ship."

Khusru's gaze moved from him to the team, and then back. She nodded. "You're right. That would be a better use of our resources."

"I want you to do a standard rescue," he said. "I'll handle engineering."

"Take Palmer and Iqbar," Khusru said.

He had just been about to ask for them. They were both fast workers and unflappable, and both could jury-rig on the fly.

"I'll take Cayden and Niane," Khusru said, and Zarges had to suppress a smile. She didn't want Ogden, mostly because she didn't want someone else trying to take over command. Ogden had been known to do that if he didn't like how a rescue was progressing.

"We'll leave Ogden here to handle the spacebridge," Zarges said.

Khusru gave him a tight smile, as if she understood completely. She probably did. Then the smile faded.

"One last time," she said. "I'll be happy to partner with Ogden and split teams, if you're not up for this."

Zarges felt a thread of anger, which wasn't like him at all. Which probably meant he wasn't quite up for this. Her question was a legitimate one.

But this mission would go much better with him than without him. He had handled non-Fleet systems before, and part of him was afraid this old ship, with a design none of them knew, would have other parts from other cultures grafted onto Fleet equipment.

He wasn't the best engineer in the universe, but he could sometimes see how certain systems worked at odds with each other.

He made himself breathe. "I'm up for it," he said, and hoped he was telling the truth.

PART FOUR

THE JOURNEY BACKWARDS

100 YEARS AGO

THE *RENEGAT*

Acting Chief Engineer Nadim Crowe crossed the bridge of the *Renegat* on his way to Captain Preemas's ready room. Crowe had only been on the bridge itself a handful of times since the *Renegat* left on its mission, and each time left him more and more uncomfortable.

Captain Ivan "Call Me Pre" Preemas liked to keep the bridge dark and uncomfortable. He kept the wall screens off, but had them set at black and reflective, so everyone on the bridge could see each other's movements. The portholes were closed not just on the bridge, but on all of the public levels, which made Crowe want to fling them open so he could see the beauty of space.

And then there was the crew itself.

Collectively, they were the worst crew he had ever worked with. When he had received his assignment to move to the *Renegat*, he had done what he had always done. He had requested that some of his trusted allies join him on the ship, and for the first time ever, that request had been denied. Not by Preemas, but by Vice Admiral Gāo who was actually in charge of this mission.

When Crowe saw that, he looked over the crew manifest, and hurriedly picked the most capable officers for engineering. Sometimes that meant moving them from some other part of the ship, but no one seemed to notice or care.

Which bothered him as well.

Preemas should have blocked him or Gāo should have complained. Neither of them had. Crowe wasn't even sure they had noticed.

Then, on the second day of the journey, Preemas had given the entire crew some kind of pep talk about the mission. He made the mission sound exciting and heroic—they were going to investigate thefts of a Scrapheap so far back that the Fleet couldn't send a lot of ships. And oh, yeah, they were going to experiment with foldspace travel too.

And because of that, you folks—all of you—you wonderful crew members you—were specifically chosen as the absolute best people in the Fleet to execute this mission.

Crowe hadn't believed any of that, particularly the "absolute best people" part. Unless the "absolute best people" were absolutely the most expendable people with a handful of passable skills in the entire Fleet.

Some of those people stood on the bridge now. Titus M'Ghan sat as he piloted the *Renegat*, or rather, as he let it run on automatic pilot, because Preemas wasn't on the bridge at the moment. Crowe had worked with M'Ghan on a scouting mission years ago, and found M'Ghan to be lazy and the kind of crew member who cut whatever corners he could.

His bald head reflected the lights above almost as much as the screens reflected the entire bridge. He didn't even have any floating screens in front of him so he could monitor the autopilot, or maybe he was doing so from the navigation console where his hands rested.

It was everything Crowe could do to keep from shaking his head.

He didn't dare show his displeasure too much. He wasn't well liked on this—or any—crew. People watched him warily from the moment they met him.

He was taller than the average Fleet member, with broader shoulders and actual muscles. He spent the first nine years of his life landbound, and that had given him height and strong bones, and a sense that he did not belong. He wore his straight black hair too long for regulation, but refused to cut it unless ordered to do so.

Most captains ordered it, but Preemas had simply looked at him, sighed, and shaken his head, then moved on to something else.

So Crowe's quiet rebellion, and his private reaffirmation of his own sense of self, remained, even though he had to pull his hair into a ponytail, and, when he worked on delicate things, tuck it inside the back of his shirt.

At least he wore his uniform like the crew of an SC-Class ship was supposed to do. Half of the bridge crew had already discarded that regulation, including the first officer, Danika Newark.

Newark also had long black hair, which Crowe always thought was vanity, not rebellion, and she kept it loose most of the time. This afternoon, it fell like a waterfall down her back, accenting her black-and-white shirt, and matching pants. The outfit looked like loungewear, not something someone wore on duty.

But apparently Preemas didn't care about such things, or he would have stopped her from dressing like she had just gotten up.

Newark glanced at Crowe as he came down the center of the bridge, skirting some of the consoles that were stuck haphazardly on the floor behind Preemas's chair.

Her gaze was flat, her skin sallow. She never went into the exercise areas, which had sunlamps, and it showed. Even though her skin was naturally darker than Crowe's, he made a point of exercising every day, which added just a bit of color to his skin, color hers would probably never have.

He tipped an imaginary hat to her. She curled her lower lip and looked away. She didn't like him any more than he liked her.

They had served together on three different vessels. He thought her incompetent, and she thought him disloyal. But somehow their opinions of each other didn't seem to matter with their superiors, because both of them had been promoted in the years since.

The promotions had often been lateral, moving to a lesser ship while gaining a higher rank, but they were promotions nonetheless.

Besides, Newark wasn't the most dangerous incompetent on the bridge. That award went to Yusef Kabac, who thought himself a specialist at anything he touched.

Currently, he worked navigation, which startled Crowe. He had demoted Kabac years ago when Kabac had nearly destroyed an engineering department on a training ship by trying to rebuild a blown drive.

The drive was ruined and needed to be discarded, but Kabac had done something even worse to it, something Crowe hadn't had time to investigate, because he'd had to jettison the drive from the ship.

The nearby explosion had dented the ship's sides. Crowe had taken the blame for the entire thing because Kabac had been in his department, but Crowe wouldn't take any punishment unless Kabac had been demoted and forbidden to work in engineering ever again.

Apparently, Kabac was the kind of man who landed on his feet, though, because he was on the bridge on the *Renegat*, and he was handling navigation.

Given the poor math skills Kabac had shown in his engineering work, Crowe doubted Kabac could plot any kind of course anywhere. Crowe hoped Kabac was as lazy as M'Ghan, and let the computers do the work for him.

Crowe didn't know the rest of the bridge crew, and he wondered what the difference was between them, why some of them continued to wear their uniforms and the others didn't. Maybe it was personal preference, or maybe the crew had already split into factions.

After all, they'd been on this mission for a full week now, traveling across a known sector, following some travel plan that had been approved by the admirals. Crowe hadn't seen the plan, and he should have, since he was the one who would be maintaining the various drives and coaxing the *anacapa* to do things it probably wasn't designed to do.

A pale-skinned blonde woman whose blue uniform was a little too big glanced at him, her blue eyes wide. Either she had heard stories about him or she was one of the Skittish—the people who had been yelled at or demoted so many times that they were terrified of everything.

He nodded at her, but didn't smile. He rarely smiled once a ship was underway. People tended to see smiles as encouragement, and he didn't like encouraging anyone unless they deserved it. And, in his opinion, the competent people of the world did not deserve encouragement, because that would be patronizing.

Of course, that attitude had gotten him in trouble with superiors, who told him he wasn't sufficiently positive with his teams.

That was why he liked to bring his own team with him, people who knew how he worked and didn't need silly back-patting time-wasting encouragement when all they were doing was the job they had been assigned.

The bridge on the *Renegat* was larger than the bridge on most SC-Class vessels he had been on. It was circular, which was also unusual. And the unusual design made it feel like he was walking forever by the time he got to Preemas's ready room.

Most captains that Crowe had served under rarely used that room. They might go into it to reprimand someone on the bridge crew, rather than do so in front of the entire bridge, or to have a private emergency conversation that needed to occur so fast the captain wouldn't have time to go to their quarters.

But this captain seemed to have moved into his ready room as if it were the base of his operations instead of that chair in the middle of the bridge.

Crowe was about to use the signal beside the door to let Preemas know he had arrived, but as Crowe reached up, the door slid into its pocket with an audible *whoosh.*

Crowe made note of that whoosh. It was something that shouldn't occur. Interior doors should be silent, not obtrusively loud. He would send someone to the bridge level to make the repair as soon as he left.

He stepped inside the ready room, and the door closed behind him—another *whoosh.*

The ready room was cooler than the bridge, which surprised him. It had the dry-air smell of a place that was being cleaned once too often. Because of that smell, Crowe half-expected it to be devoid of furniture, but it was not.

It had an actual desk in the middle, an old-fashioned one that looked like it had been carved from actual wood. That desk clearly did not recede into the floor to make room for other furniture, so it had to be bolted down. Two large chairs sat in the corners of the door side of the room, tiny regulation tables beside them. Two more chairs sat in the other corners of the room, without tables.

A big chair with a circular back sat in front of the desk, and a chair the size of a small throne sat behind it.

And on that chair sat Ivan "Call Me Pre" Preemas. Crowe had to stop thinking of him by his full name with that little moniker in between it all, because at some point, the full name and moniker would slip out, sarcastic tone and all.

Crowe was never going to call his captain by a nickname, even if that was what Preemas desired. Rank structures existed for a reason, and that reason was a subtle way of keeping everyone on the ship in line during a mission.

If anything, Captain Ivan "Call Me Pre" Preemas should have insisted that everyone on the ship call him Captain Preemas at all times, and should have done so during that very first speech. Of course, he hadn't, and there were already indications that some of the basic Fleet structures were breaking down—the extra-long hair, the lack of uniforms—indications that Crowe had as well, because he hadn't cut his hair either.

Preemas's hair was regulation length. He didn't even have stubble this late in the afternoon. He wore a uniform, and it was as pristine as if he had put it on five minutes ago.

"Sit," Preemas said, and waved a hand at the chair in front of the desk.

"I prefer to stand, sir," Crowe said, keeping his tone neutral. He had no idea why he was here, and he wanted to be able to leave quickly if need be.

He didn't think he had done anything wrong, but he had learned the hard way that new captains on new ships sometimes used one person as an example to prove to the rest of the crew that they could be tough.

"I prefer that you sit," Preemas said. "I don't like standing, and I don't like being the only person in the room who is sitting. So you're the one who has to modify your behavior."

Crowe suppressed a sigh. The chair was bolted down, so he couldn't pull it back, much as he wanted to. Whoever had placed that chair near that desk hadn't put enough space between them for someone of Crowe's height.

The chair did swivel, though, and so he turned it toward himself, settled in it, trying not to look too awkward, and then spun toward Preemas.

And then, because Crowe couldn't help himself, he raised his eyebrows slightly as if to say, *Good enough for you?*

"Thank you." Preemas put his hands flat on the empty desk surface. No screen activated. There didn't even seem to be one, although Crowe knew that to be an illusion.

There was an ever-so-faint hum that indicated working equipment over and above the environmental system. The only place that sound could come from was the desk.

"Tell me why there is a seal in your file," Preemas said.

Crowe's heart skipped a beat. He had been asked this question more than a dozen times throughout his career, and he had declined to answer it every single time.

Still, he hated it. Because that damn seal, which had been in his file since he was a juvenile, had prevented him from ever achieving his childhood dream of captaining his own ship.

"The Fleet decided that file should be sealed for a reason," Crowe said this time, just like he had said every other time before that.

Preemas raised that perfectly shaved chin ever so slightly.

"If we're going to continue this conversation, Crowe," Preemas said, his tone clipped and annoyed, "assume that I have a brain."

"I do, sir," Crowe said, then realized that sentence was defensive. He hated being defensive this early in a conversation.

"You do not," Preemas said. "You told me the file was sealed for a reason. *Of course*, it was sealed for a reason. That's how seals work. I want to know what's behind the seal. Tell me what's in the file."

No one had ever asked that bluntly before. Crowe blinked, hoping the surprise did not show on his face.

"I'm not supposed to talk about it, sir," he said.

"I don't care," Preemas said. "I'm your captain and I order you to."

"I'm afraid sealed files don't work that way," Crowe said, and then realized he was probably insulting Preemas's intelligence again. "I mean to say, that you need a certain level of clearance just to look at the file, and captains do not have it, sir. I'm sorry."

"You did something big, huh," Preemas said. "Something the Fleet doesn't want known."

Crowe did not move. He couldn't confirm or deny that. He hadn't thought about the sealed file as "something big." He didn't think about it as anything, except a barrier for him, a part of his life he couldn't undo, no matter how much he wanted to. The incident had happened when he was fifteen, and the seal had been a part of his life ever since.

Everyone wanted to talk about it and no one respected him after he told them he could not.

"Tell me what's in the file," Preemas said.

"I'm sorry, sir," Crowe said. "I must respectfully decline."

Preemas let out a sharp laugh, which surprised Crowe. "Did they tell you that you couldn't reveal the details of the file? Or did they just tell you that you weren't supposed to discuss whatever it was that happened to you."

Happened to you. No one had phrased it like that before. Everyone else had said something like *whatever it was that you did.* Not *what had happened to you.* Both were true, but one was more sympathetic.

Crowe felt a wave of gratitude toward Preemas, then caught it. Crowe was being played. Preemas had done this before with others, and he knew how to gain their sympathy.

"I'm sorry, sir," Crowe said again, "I cannot discuss the file."

"And that is not an answer to my question," Preemas said. "What did they tell you would happen to you if you told someone what's in that file?"

Crowe's heart fluttered. He felt nervous about this for the first time in years. Because he couldn't remember the answer to that question, or maybe he didn't know. Maybe they hadn't told him.

Maybe they had told him he couldn't talk about the incident, told him that the file was sealed, told him that the incident was classified, and never told him what would happen to him if he talked.

They told him what would happen to him if he didn't agree to their terms. He wouldn't have had a career at all. He would have been dumped at the nearest sector base, and forbidden to work inside the Fleet. He would have lived in some city, like Z-City, and watched Fleet staff go back and forth doing fascinating things with engineering and tech, things he would be forbidden from doing.

But they didn't tell him what would happen to him later in his career if he actually told someone what was in that file.

"See, that's the thing," Preemas said. "They seal files after they've doled out whatever punishment they deem necessary, and they assume you're not going to talk. Or they threaten you to remain silent. But here's my thinking, Nadim. May I call you Nadim?"

"No," Crowe said.

Preemas's eyebrows went up, and he leaned back, looking shocked. "Well, that's a first. You don't like me?"

"It's not about like or dislike, Captain," Crowe said. "It's about protocol."

"Well, I don't like using two words when one will do. Or four words, in your case, Acting Chief Engineer Crowe. It's kinda like sitting down. I prefer to be comfortable, and I prefer nicknames."

"I do not," Crowe said.

They stared at each other for a moment. Preemas's mouth twisted slightly to the side. An almost smile—or it was an actual smile, since his eyes were twinkling.

"Okay," Preemas said. "Here's my thinking, Acting Chief Engineer Crowe. I have been given no instructions regarding your sealed file. I have not been told that I must throw you in the brig if you reveal its contents or that I must demote you if I hear you talking about it. At the moment, Acting Chief Engineer Crowe, I am the leader of our merry band. In fact, I am the law here. I determine the rewards and the punishments, in absence from direction of the Fleet."

Now Preemas was insulting Crowe's intelligence. But weirdly, Crowe was interested in this, because Preemas was making a point Crowe hadn't considered.

Preemas was saying, "You could probably challenge my authority, but where would it get you? It would piss me off, and the controversy would have to wait for a settlement for months and months, until we return to the Fleet itself."

If we return, Crowe thought, but did not say. He hoped his face didn't say it either. He hoped he was keeping his expression under control.

"During that time," Preemas said, "I could put you in the brig or isolate you from the rest of the crew or keep you working, being peeved at you and you at me, each of us thinking about the controversy between us that we decided the Fleet needed to settle. Or..."

Preemas fully smiled this time, apparently enjoying that dramatic pause. Crowe didn't enjoy it. He hated drama.

"...you could tell me what's in the sealed file."

"Since we are speaking frankly," Crowe said, "I see no reason, sir, to tell you what is in that file."

Although there were reasons. Crowe knew things about Scrapheaps that most of the Fleet did not.

Preemas leaned back in his chair, looking intrigued.

"No reason." It was almost as if he could see the lie. Then he nodded once, and sat up straight, his chair rocking. "I'll give you a reason, Acting Chief Engineer Crowe."

Crowe braced himself for the threat: *If you don't tell me, I will put you in the brig for the entire trip.* Or *if you don't tell me, I'll make someone else the chief engineer.*

He might have arguments against both of those things, depending on how Preemas presented them.

"This crew has been together now for a little over two weeks," Preemas said.

Crowe tried not to sigh. Here it was—the threat of demotion. He had expected it. It had happened before when superior officer discovered the file, but never this fast.

"I'm going to be making personnel changes," Preemas said. "So the more information I have, the better off I, and the entire ship, will be."

That last sentence didn't fit into the script. Crowe frowned.

"If you're going to demote me, sir," Crowe said, "just do it."

Without the drama, he mentally added.

"Demote you." Preemas sounded surprised. "That's not what I was thinking of, Acting Chief Engineer Crowe."

Crowe frowned before he could stop himself. He hadn't expected that at all. "Sir?"

"You've seen the rest of the crew," Preemas said. "From what I can tell, you know some of their records. You don't respect at least a few members of my bridge crew."

"I never said that, sir," Crowe said.

"You didn't have to," Preemas said.

Crowe's heart started to pound. He thought he hid his emotions well enough. Did everyone know what he thought? Had he lost one of his main survival skills?

"I don't know if you know this," Preemas said, "but I did not have a say in staffing this vessel."

Crowe had assumed it, but he hadn't know for certain. And, he had figured, Preemas had some staffing say. Captains usually did. They were usually allowed to bring their own favorites with them, if they really wanted to.

Crowe had just figured that the bridge crew included some of Preemas's most trusted officers. Since Preemas didn't have the best reputation in the Fleet, Crowe had just assumed that he would bring some bad actors along with him.

"I was not allowed to veto any crew, nor was I allowed to bring in any of my own people." Preemas flattened his palms against the desktop again. It must have been a nervous habit. He sounded calm.

Preemas apparently saw that he had Crowe's interest. Preemas's smile had long since faded.

"The crew placement came from on high," Preemas said. "The jobs everyone has are the jobs that the admirals think they should have."

His tone suggested he did not agree. Crowe certainly didn't. He wouldn't have brought in at least half of the crew. He would have left them behind. They weren't the kind of people who should go on a long mission.

They were probably not the kind of people who should go on any mission at all.

Knowing that made Crowe feel a bit better about Preemas. He wasn't the kind of man, then, who chose only the half-wits and derelicts for duty. He had been saddled with people whose reputations were as bad as his was.

"The crew has had time to settle in," Preemas said. "And the newness has worn off. They're now performing at the level they will perform at throughout the mission."

In other words, they had relaxed—or so Preemas thought. And, given what half the bridge crew was wearing that afternoon, he was probably right.

"I can see their work ethic and their abilities. Maybe not as clearly as I would be able to after six months or a year, but enough to get a sense of who they are." Preemas slid his hands off the desk and onto the arms of the chair.

Was this conversation making him nervous? Was that why he was fidgeting? Or was he the kind of man who fidgeted all the time?

Crowe didn't know his captain either, except by reputation, and that reputation hadn't been stellar. After the Drauxhill Incident, Preemas's reputation went down, but he still managed to get adequate assignments.

But mediocre captains, which was what the Fleet considered Preemas to be now, didn't get assignments like this.

Crowe frowned. He had just realized he was in a stranger situation than he had thought when he boarded the vessel.

"I think," Preemas said, "some staff assignments were based on previous experience and not on ability."

Crowe agreed with the observation for some of the crew. Some of them seemed to have no ability at all, like Kabac. But that could simply be Crowe's prejudices.

"So," Preemas said, "I'm going to shake things up."

Crowe froze. He wanted to be more than the acting chief of the engineering department. He wanted to be the actual chief with the responsibilities that entailed.

And he didn't want to be anything else—not even for reasons of a "shake-up."

"But," Preemas said, "before I shake things up, I did my due diligence. I've been reviewing files, looking for hints, clues, the kinds of things you normally find when you've worked with someone for a long time. Most of the files are pretty straightforward. Yours is not."

Crowe wanted to shift in his seat, fold his hands together, lean back, something. But he didn't. He continued to watch Preemas.

Preemas's eyes were twinkling. He knew he was making Crowe uncomfortable.

"You're doing good work," Preemas said, "and, quite frankly, that's an understatement."

Crowe almost shook his head in surprise and caught himself at the last moment. He couldn't remember the last time someone had praised his work without adding a caveat in the exact same sentence.

For someone who has such a bad reputation, one captain had said to him, *you do surprisingly good work.*

Crowe swallowed involuntarily, knowing he was revealing some emotion.

He couldn't stop himself. This meeting was definitely not going as planned.

"I would like to promote you," Preemas said, "but I refuse to do so without knowing what's in your file. If you're the kind of officer who has a history of suddenly losing his mind and going after crew members with a dull kitchen knife, I want to know that."

"I wouldn't be serving on any ship if that were the case," Crowe said.

Preemas gave him a lazy smile, a victorious smile, almost a *There. I got you* smile.

"You know what I mean, Acting Chief Engineer Crowe," Preemas said. "I mean that there are certain things in sealed files that make someone ineligible for promotion, some psych evaluation that someone decided to seal because you were young, or whatever. And that's truly what intrigues me. You were very young."

Crowe did not move. He had his face back under control.

"You have an amazing facility for tech and engineering. The things that I could read in your files were astonishing." Preemas folded those nervous hands on his desk. "If you didn't have this sealed file, along with a reputation for outspoken bluntness and an inability to get along with superior officers, you would be working at the cutting edge of Fleet technology, designing stuff that would make us all happier or safer or more deadly."

Crowe almost nodded. He knew that. He knew his opportunities had been limited because of who he was, who he had deliberately become.

"Outspokenness can be forgiven in the Fleet," Preemas said, "Particularly when it comes from the truly gifted, which is what you are. So there's something in that file. I need to know it before I take another move. What did you do at fifteen—what could you have done at fifteen—that would have caused this?"

Well, he asked. And he would keep pushing. And he had some good points about silence.

So Crowe took a deep breath and said, "I caused the death of fifty people."

And watched as all the color left Preemas's face.

THE *RENEGAT*

Preemas made Crowe explain, of course, and he did. Slowly. Shakily. In fits and starts. Feeling like he was revealing himself to the one person he didn't want to see him.

Crowe had not discussed this with anyone since he left the *Brazza Two* in disgrace. He didn't even really know how to tell the story.

But he managed.

And when he finished, Preemas didn't move. His hands remained splayed on his desktop, his body leaning slightly forward as if he were still trying to encourage Crowe to confess to something Crowe never wanted to discuss.

Crowe remained in the uncomfortable chair, twisted slightly, his legs tense. He was ready to spring up and leave the ready room the moment Preemas invited him to.

And Preemas would invite him to leave, judging by the expression on Preemas's face.

At first he had looked shocked. Then he got that expression under control and his face had gone completely flat.

Crowe had an idea that flat expression was how Preemas had made it through the day in his previous postings. No one knew how he felt. And, apparently, he had decided that Crowe shouldn't know either.

Preemas leaned back in his chair. "Has Gão read your file?"

"I don't know," Crowe said.

"Because she insisted you handle the examination of the Scrapheap, did I tell you that?"

Of course Preemas hadn't told Crowe that. Preemas probably hadn't told any of the other people on the ship about any special instructions that Gão gave.

Preemas was going to make those decisions himself, depending on what he learned on the way to the Scrapheap.

"Half the people on this ship have never seen a Scrapheap," Preemas said.

"Have you?" Crowe asked.

"Not up close." Preemas gave him a sly smile. "And what's your record since? Kill anyone else?"

The question, phrased so sarcastically, so casually, that Crowe wanted to launch himself out of the chair and plant his fist in Preemas's face.

Which was probably what the question had been designed to do.

Instead, Crowe remained very still.

"Not like you have," Crowe said.

Preemas tilted his head. "Meaning?"

"I was fifteen when I killed people," Crowe said, his tone sharp and cutting. He couldn't put his actual fist in Preemas's face, but he could put a metaphorical fist in Preemas. Easily, in fact. "When you did, you were already a captain."

"The Drauxhill Incident wasn't my fault," Preemas said. "I followed protocol to the letter."

"You were captain," Crowe snapped. "Of course it was your fault."

Preemas froze. His expression remained the same, but his eyes went from alive to flat, almost empty. Dangerous, even. A man who shouldn't be crossed.

"If the Fleet considered what happened my fault, they wouldn't have issued new guidelines on first contact missions," Preemas said.

He didn't sound flip anymore. Nor did he sound like the defensive man who responded initially to Crowe. Preemas sounded almost belligerent, as if he truly believed he was right.

"Of course they would have issued new guidelines," Crowe said. "They try to mitigate human error all the time."

Preemas's pale skin flushed. "You seem pretty sure of yourself."

"I've been there, Captain. I know how the Fleet behaves when something goes wrong. They punish the human who erred and they try to prevent it from every happening again." Crowe felt a bit breathless. He was off-kilter from talking about the file, and he was angry at Preemas for being so casual about all of this. "The captain of the *Brazza Two* was named Loreli Mbue. Ever hear of her?"

Preemas's lips thinned, but he didn't say anything.

"Of course you didn't, because she lost her command. She didn't get a second chance, like you did."

"She didn't try for one," Preemas said. "She went on to some medical mission."

So he had heard of her after all. Maybe he had looked her up after discovering information about Crowe. Or maybe Preemas had known all along.

Not that it mattered. What mattered was who she had been, and how she had changed Crowe, maybe forever.

"She went on 'some medical mission,'" Crowe said, giving his words a sarcastic slant, "because she and I, we owe the universe fifty lives."

"Meaning what?" Preemas asked. He sounded as angry as Crowe felt.

"Meaning we are trying to make sure that we save at least fifty lives. Her idea.

Because she took full responsibility for what happened, even though she had nothing to do with my theft of the ship."

Preemas's eyes narrowed. He heard the criticism buried in the subtext of Crowe's words, and that seemed to make Preemas even more agitated.

"She had something to do with it," Preemas said. "She should have prevented it. She was in charge of kids, for godsake. Kids take joyrides. There are ways to prevent that."

"There are," Crowe said. "And there were then, as well. I went around every single preventative protocol. She couldn't have known what I was going to do. I made sure of it. But the Fleet changed policy after that as well, and she still accepted responsibility for her errors."

He let the words hang. Preemas raised his chin, his cheeks bright red, his eyes glittering.

"I was exonerated," Preemas said. "She was not."

"She didn't ask for exoneration," Crowe said. "You did."

Preemas's jaw worked for a moment, his flush so deep that it had gone down his neck to his chest. He was clearly furious.

Then he let out a slow breath. His flush faded, and he grinned.

"So this is what you do," he said.

The mood shift was so fast that Crowe hadn't seen it coming.

"What?" Crowe asked.

"The bluntness," Preemas said. "The insubordination. The other thing that kept you from rising in the ranks. You talk to all your captains like this."

That hadn't been a question. It had been a statement, and an accurate one.

Crowe was shaking with fury. His mood hadn't shifted at all.

"I do," he said. "I am not going to allow myself to work in service of more deaths. If I can prevent them, I will. And I will stand toe-to-toe with anyone who tries to recklessly destroy the people on board his ship."

Preemas's gaze held his. "You think I'm going to do that?"

"I can't predict what you will do, Captain," Crowe said, putting a little too much emphasis on the word *captain*. "I can see what you did do. You didn't take responsibility for your failures in the Drauxhill Incident. Which leads me to believe that you're the kind of man who never takes responsibility. But I don't know that. I can't know it, until we run into some kind of trouble."

Preemas smiled, then brought his hands together in a slow clap.

"Bravo, Acting Chief Engineer Crowe," Preemas said. "You managed to make me angry in less than an hour. I didn't think I was quick to anger. Well done."

Crowe took a deep breath. He hadn't intended to anger Preemas. But Crowe was glad it happened. That would prevent any future interaction between them, unless something went really awry.

"That's exactly what I'm looking for," Preemas said.

Crowe frowned. He had no idea what Preemas was referring to.

"Sir?"

"I need a first officer who will keep me honest," Preemas said. "One who isn't afraid to challenge me. One who is willing to take over this ship and save lives if need be."

Newark certainly wasn't that person. Crowe made himself focus.

"So you want me to give you some possible names for the job?" Crowe asked. "You're going to replace Newark?"

"I'm going to replace Newark," Preemas said, "with you."

Crowe's breath caught. Whatever he had expected Preemas to say, it hadn't been that.

"I don't want to be first officer," Crowe said. "I prefer to remain in engineering."

"You'll do that too," Preemas said. "You'll be my chief engineer—no more *acting*—and you'll be my first officer."

"Those jobs are both full time," Crowe said. "I need to sleep. I will remain in engineering."

"You'll do both," Preemas said. "We'll make it work."

Crowe shook his head. "I'm sorry, sir. I must decline."

"I'm the law here, remember?" Preemas said. "You can't decline. You're my first officer and my chief engineer. And you'll be honest with me."

"Honest?" Crowe straightened in his chair. "Here's honest for you. I won't follow your every order, and I won't follow this one."

Preemas gave that sideways smile again. "So continue to be honest with me, Chief Engineer Crowe. If I die tomorrow, will you go to the Scrapheap with Danika Newark as captain?"

"I won't have a choice," Crowe said.

"You do have a choice, though," Preemas said. "You tell me, right now, who in the crew is captain material? Who can get this ship to that Scrapheap and back?"

Crowe's frown deepened. There was something behind the question that he didn't entirely understand.

"Vice Admiral Gāo thinks you can, sir," Crowe said.

"No, she doesn't," Preemas said. "That's why I wasn't able to put my own crew together. Everyone on board is a loner, Crowe, either by choice or circumstance. If we die, no one mourns. This is a suicide mission, and Gāo hired me to lead it."

Crowe's heart pounded. That finally made sense. No wonder he couldn't bring his staff. Half of them had families.

"I'm going to prove her wrong, Crowe," Preemas said. "The *Renegat* will return to the Fleet, whether something happens to me or not. And the only way I can guarantee that is to make you first officer. You're the only other person on this ship capable of the kind of command we need to execute this mission with a minimal loss of life."

Crowe blinked, processing all of that.

"So," he said after a moment. "You want me to be first officer, not to be your right hand on the duty roster, but—"

"To be my successor should I die," Preemas said. "I won't need you on the bridge. I'll need you in engineering most of the time. But I will need you on the bridge enough to know what's going on if I need to hand over command."

Or if things went horribly wrong.

"It's not two jobs, Chief Engineer Crowe," Preemas said. "It's the same job. Because this mission is all about getting the *Renegat* to that Scrapheap and back. And that will take some incredible feats of engineering, both with the *anacapa* drive and without."

He was right about that as well.

"So," Preemas said, "let me ask you instead of ordering you. Will you be the first officer of the *Renegat* and her chief engineer?"

Crowe should have asked for time to think about it. He should have done an analysis to see if he could easily do both jobs. He should have studied Preemas more to see if they were compatible.

But he didn't.

Instead, he said, "Yes, I'll take the job—jobs."

Preemas extended his hand.

"Welcome to hell, First Officer Crowe," he said.

Crowe shook it. "Been here a long time already, Captain Preemas. Nice to be acknowledged."

Preemas grinned. "We'll make this work," he said.

And, god help him, Crowe actually believed him.

PART FIVE
THE RESCUE
NOW

THE *RENEGAT*

Raina Serpell's environmental suit was damaged. The damn thing kept telling her about all the leaks it was plugging up, and then giving her a timeline as to how long the plugs would last.

Advise leaving hostile environment as soon as possible, it was saying every fifteen minutes.

She was floating on the bridge of the *Renegat* because, about four hours ago, the artificial gravity shut off, and the gravity in her damn boots wasn't working the way it was supposed to. Or maybe she hadn't figured out how to turn it on.

She kept one hand on the edge of the console, her feet occasionally banging against the gigantic captain's chair that she absolutely hated. She would have strapped herself into it, but she wasn't able to work on any other console, which irritated her beyond measure.

So did the black reflective screens on all of the walls. She had hated them when the ship had been functioning well, and she hated them even more now.

She hated the whole ship right now. It wasn't responding to voice commands, now that she was wearing the super-tight helmet that came with this environmental suit.

It had taken her nearly five minutes, but she finally figured out how to toggle that warning to infrequent, but she couldn't shut the damn thing off. She couldn't do much of anything technical. She was a damn linguist for god's sake. She'd learned enough to survive in the harshness of space. She knew how to use her environmental suit—when the damn suit worked—and she knew how to program a computer to learn a new language.

She did not know how to program *herself* to learn a new skill, not on the fly.

The only other person on the bridge, Yusef Kabac, had gotten his boots to work immediately. That wouldn't have surprised her months ago, because he had once been the *Renegat's* chief navigation officer. But the fact he had gotten the boots to work so fast surprised her now. Because he was having trouble with everything—including navigation.

She had trusted him from the moment they took over the *Renegat*, but eventually, she had started wondering if she should have trusted him at all. He wasn't a hard worker and he talked a lot. He hadn't seemed scared, though, until they went into foldspace this last time.

Now, he seemed more scared than she was.

Of course, he had reason: he couldn't get the helm to respond, not since the attack. He had managed the *anacapa* drive kinda sorta. Then he had taken a risk without her permission and had sent them on the longest trip through foldspace that any ship had ever taken. Double the length of the longest foldspace journey they had taken when they were heading toward that horrid Scrapheap.

She had never liked foldspace, and after everything the *Renegat* had been through, she had hoped to avoid foldspace as much as possible. They'd been returning along the trajectory they had been given when the ship left the Fleet, and then, after the attack near that weird planet Amnthra, Kabac got it into his head that they had to hurry along even faster.

The others had listened. They took orders from whoever spoke the loudest, and after Amnthra, Serpell had been in the med bay for three crucial days.

Of course, her wife, India, had died right then, and as Kabac had told the so-called bridge crew, no one could expect Serpell to make the correct decisions at a moment like that.

Why Serpell had gone along with his decision, she would never know. Probably because she had come back to the bridge after he had launched the ship into foldspace, and she didn't want to change anything.

She hadn't thought the *Renegat* would make it through foldspace, not with a hole in the hull. But, Kabac had said, the nanobits would patch the hole and the environment would hold.

Only the nanobits had stopped repairing everything on that long trip through foldspace, and something else had gone wrong, something she hadn't been prepared for. The *Renegat*'s environmental system was compromised, and she wasn't sure why.

Kabac had asked her to search for the problem, and she had tried. But she wasn't set up for this. She had no idea what she was doing.

When they took over the ship, she had planned on searching through the personnel records to see who else on board had enough training to help in the bridge. The personnel records were damn near useless, considering that there weren't complete records for the crew members who had joined on Sector Base Z.

But she had managed to compile a preliminary list when the *Renegat* went into foldspace for the first time on the trip back. That foldspace trip made her lose focus, because she had to worry about other things. And once she had realized she needed to look again, she couldn't, not with the attacks, the long foldspace trip, and the slow leak of the atmosphere.

She had just been about to do a shipwide hail for help when the artificial gravity gave out. Followed by the lights.

Emergency lighting was dim at best. She could have turned on the lights on the exterior of her suit, but Kabac had asked her not to when she put the suit on.

"I'm going to be doing some delicate work," he had said, "and I don't want any distractions."

She had put the suit on when they were still in foldspace. So had he. She had sent a shipwide order for everyone to don their environmental suits just in case, but she knew only a handful of people had listened to her. She hoped to hell they had put on their environmental suits before the environmental system shut off to "conserve energy."

She wasn't the captain. That was the problem. There was no captain, and that was her fault.

She hadn't wanted the command. Everyone had given it to her. They didn't want to be in charge, and she didn't either. But she had taken over more and more duties as the trip went on. People deferred to her, mostly. But not enough to make this an efficient ship.

She had learned how to operate some parts of the ship, but never the ones she needed in the moment. She learned on the fly, and whatever she learned wasn't useful in the next emergency.

Like this one.

But Kabac didn't know what the hell they were doing either. By rights, he should have been running the ship. He was the ranking officer here. If they went by ranking officers.

But she also knew that no one trusted him. He had been on the bridge crew when the *Renegat* left on the original mission, and he had gotten demoted on the way to the Scrapheap. Then he had bitched about the demotion and had disappeared during the worst of the trouble. But he said he wanted to go back to the Fleet.

He had probably thought he could waltz back into the Fleet, claim he was the one who brought the *Renegat* back and get a promotion he had not earned.

Although, if he got them out of this now, maybe he would have earned a promotion. Especially considering he had lied to her, and he was still managing to make do.

He had said he knew how all the ship's systems worked.

She had learned over the last few months that he only knew how they *should* work, which was more than she had known. He knew what each part of the ship did, and how the ship looked when it functioned properly.

And until they had come out of foldspace into regular space the second time, until they encountered those attacks from the only planet they tried to orbit, everything *had* functioned properly.

She shouldn't have listened to the remaining crew's panic about supplies. She should have simply reminded everyone that they had left much of the crew back at the Scrapheap, and the supplies that they had needed to feed fewer people.

She had made that argument, of course, but not very forcefully. It had been pretty obvious that no one had been comfortable with the supply levels, even though the *Renegat* had more than enough to get the crew home.

She had found herself on a ship filled with people who were scared to enter foldspace, but who wanted to return to the Fleet. There was no returning without foldspace.

Somehow, she had thought they would bond in their fright, rather than take action based on that fright. Again, her fault for refusing to declare herself captain, and then acting like the captain.

But she wasn't qualified. Just like everyone else on this stupid ship.

She hadn't found that out, though, until the *Renegat* was on its way back to the Fleet, when she hadbroken into Captain Preemas's logs to see his insights about the remaining crew.

Breaking in had been another thing she wished she hadn't done. Maybe if she had remained naïve about what they were facing, maybe if she hadn't given it any thought at all, she wouldn't have listened to the crew about supplies, the *Renegat* wouldn't have gone into orbit around that stupid planet, and the ship would be all right.

But they weren't. They were losing atmosphere, the environmental systems had shut down, the lights were going out, and no one on the ship had the technical skill to repair anything at that level.

She wanted to curl into a little ball and hide away, but if she curled up, she'd be banging all over the walls and the ceiling, and her damn suit would leak even worse.

She was going to die here, and she didn't even know where here was. The *Renegat* had used the comm system inside her helmet to announce that the ship, of its own accord, was leaving foldspace. Kabac was trying to stop the *Renegat* from doing so. He thought they hadn't traveled far enough, that the ship wasn't following his navigation points.

But he also admitted that the navigation system had been compromised during the attack along with all the other major systems, so, Serpell had asked him—screamed at him, really—*How do you know the ship wasn't following instructions?*

And he had screamed back that he hadn't known anything for sure, and she should have let him captain the ship, and she had said that he didn't have the temperament to be captain, and he had said look at where her temperament had gotten them, and then she thought about the nights she had spent in her cabin—in her solitary cabin, with India gone—and wondered if he wasn't right.

Serpell used to have such an even temperament, and now, she was all over the map—angry one moment, nearly in tears the next, panicked a moment later. No one had ever seen her like this—she had never *been* like this, and it was driving her crazy.

The whole situation was driving her crazy.

And it wouldn't matter soon. Because in just a few hours she'd be dead. Or maybe less than that if her suit was to be believed.

Advise leaving hostile environment as soon as possible, it said, as if on cue.

"Shut up," she whispered. "Shutupshutupshutupshutup."

And, for the moment, it did.

THE *AIZSARGS RESCUE ONE* (SPACEBRIDGE)

Raul Zarges stood at the closed doors leading into the spacebridge. He had informed the team of the changes in plans quickly, with Sufia Khusru at his side. Morris Ogden didn't seem upset at all at being left behind.

Ogden was the only one of the seven people in Staging with his environmental suit hood down. He stood behind a small plastic screen, double protection for the person who was at the controls of the spacebridge. That person sometimes had to make tough decisions about the spacebridge.

Sometimes that person would have to leave colleagues behind on a dying ship. Other rescue vehicles had had to sever the spacebridge to prevent some kind of disaster from coming through it—anything from a fireball to weapons fire to an actual attack.

Ogden had the right kind of calm, sensible nature. He was the person Zarges wanted in that position—not sentimental enough to sacrifice *Rescue One* because he didn't want to leave colleagues behind.

That gave Zarges confidence. He could focus on the task at hand. He and his team, Palmer and Iqbar, would go through the spacebridge first. They would head to engineering to see if they could stabilize the ship from there.

Khusru and her team, Cayden and Niane, would go to the bridge, and maybe talk with whoever they found up there, before they could see if the controls worked.

Zarges grabbed the strap near the tunnel door. Dorthea Iqbar grabbed the strap beside Zarges', not crowding him, but as close as possible so they could get into the spacebridge quickly. Palmer clutched the strap just behind Iqbar, also close and ready to go.

On the other side of the tunnel door, Khusru and her team grabbed their straps. Zarges couldn't see their faces, since everyone had their hoods up. If it weren't for their different body shapes inside those environmental suits, he wouldn't be able to tell anyone apart.

Zarges hoped the specs for the old SC-Class vessel they were about to enter had been accurate, because he had uploaded them into his suit. The teams needed to move quickly, and the best way to do that was following the shortest route, rather than exploring and guessing.

Engineering was the most important task because, if he could get the systems working again, everyone could remain on board the *Renegat*, and the *Aizsargs* could tow them back to the nearest sector base for more extensive repairs. Or they might be able to send over a team and do the work themselves as the ships traveled side by side out of this sector.

He didn't see it, though. Something about this ship, something he couldn't quite explain, looked too damaged for that plan to work.

"We're ready," he said to Ogden.

Ogden shut off the artificial gravity, and Zarges slowly floated. So did the other team members, remaining in place only because they held the straps.

Then the door slid open, revealing the familiar sight of the spacebridge. It really didn't deserve the name "bridge," or even the word "space." It was a tunnel. On easy rescues, a person could walk the length of the tunnel, and step through the door on either end.

But on tougher rescues, like this one, the spacebridge's atmosphere was on, but not its artificial gravity. No sense in walking into the other ship when that ship's gravity wasn't working.

The tunnel was made of black nanobits, just like *Rescue One* (and the *Aizsargs,* for that matter) but looked less substantial. The tunnel's walls were thinner and more pliable than a ship's. They also had ripples every few feet, because the nanobits hadn't had time to reset so that the tunnel's surface was smooth.

Even though a thin circle of light illuminated the path every three feet or so, the tunnel was dark. Zarges couldn't see the door on the opposite side, which wasn't that unusual. But he didn't like it.

There had clearly been a slight curve to the tunnel so that it could reach the door, and curves like that caused the occasional problem.

"All right," he said into the comm. "My team will go first."

He didn't have to give any more specific orders than that. The team—and Ogden—knew the drill. The other team would follow according to protocol, and the spacebridge would remain until the life rafts were deployed or until Zarges or Khusru gave an order otherwise.

Zarges's team entered single file. Iqbar, as the second-most experienced member of his team, led, followed by Zarges, with Palmer bringing up the rear. They would use that formation as they made their way through the ship.

As Zarges pushed himself into the tunnel, using an old skill that made sure his pace matched Iqbar's, his environmental suit felt a little too tight. Sweat pooled under his arms and along his back. He had already double- and triple-checked the system, so he knew the problem wasn't the suit.

The problem was him.

The last mission he had gone on had ended in catastrophe, with only five survivors out of a team of thirty. They had managed to save over 100 people, but as the *Aizsargs*'s counselor had pointed out, he never saw that as a victory. Too many lives had been lost for him to ever consider that mission a success.

And that old mission was the last thing he should have been thinking about in this narrow passageway.

The circle lights that he floated through did very little to illuminate the entire tunnel. They only cast light in the small area around the circle itself. As a result, the lights from the gloves of the team's suits brightened the tunnel before them.

Iqbar pointed her hands forward to illuminate the darkness ahead of them, Zarges kept his hands trained downward to illuminate the path, and Palmer had his hands pointed behind him.

When Palmer's lights changed direction, Khusru's team would start their way through the tunnel.

The journey only took about twenty seconds, but it felt like an entire lifetime had gone by.

Iqbar stopped only a few seconds before Zarges arrived. She tapped the edge of the door. It had an old Fleet marking, one that meant the controls for the door were ninety degrees to the left of that point.

She looked at Zarges. As she did, Palmer arrived.

Zarges nodded, silently giving her approval to try the controls before they opened the door either manually or with weapons.

Iqbar slid her gloved hand to the exact spot on the hull, then pressed her palm against it. The glove had a chip that ran all the known security override entry codes for every ship registered with the Fleet, starting with the most current and working backwards.

Palmer had just reached for his tool belt to pry the door, when the door eased open as if it had opened just a few hours before. That easy movement surprised Zarges. For some reason, he had thought opening the door would be a fight—especially since the ship had just emerged from foldspace.

Sometimes, in some of the Fleet ship models, the doors sealed tightly for hours after the activation of an *anacapa* drive. That was to protect the integrity of the ship's interior, in case the ship unexpectedly found itself in a truly hostile environment.

Blackness extended beyond the door's interior. Palmer stuck his fist inside, exploring with the knuckle lights on his glove.

The interior was black and small. An airlock built to an old design, one Zarges had never liked. In this design, only one or two people could use that airlock at the same time.

Palmer's light caught the edge of another control panel as Iqbar had rejoined them.

"I don't know how long that door will remain open on its own," she said. "Better go inside."

"If the power's out," Zarges said, "we need to be ready to open the interior door ourselves."

Exterior doors usually worked on a mechanical system if the power was out, but on some of the larger ships, that system had not been designed into the airlock door. That door wasn't supposed to open until the environment in the airlock matched the environment in the ship.

Zarges put his hand on his tool belt, and Iqbar did the same. Palmer used his free hand to propel himself into the airlock. He examined every part of the airlock again, then encouraged both of them to join him.

Zarges went in next, followed by Iqbar as per protocol. They squeezed tight enough to fit in the small space. As the door eased shut, he saw bobbing lights at the other end of the tunnel.

Khusru's team was on their way.

Then the exterior door closed, and he was shoved against the other two members of his team so tight that it was almost impossible to move.

If they had to open the interior door from inside this airlock, it would take a lot of negotiation and work.

He had to brace himself for that. He had to be ready.

But he wasn't. His heart hammered against his chest, and he willed his entire system to settle down. It wouldn't do to have an attack of nerves in the middle of a mission.

"How long do we wait for the door to disengage?" Palmer asked.

Then the interior door opened. All three of them shifted in surprise.

Iqbar worked around them, so that she could go first. Zarges followed. He half-expected to tumble to the floor as gravity engaged, but there didn't appear to be any.

"I guess the environment in the airlock matched the environment on the ship," he said, feeling no small sense of irony. The airlock wasn't designed for the vacuum of space; it had been designed to protect an atmosphere that had apparently already vented out of this place.

"This does not look promising," Iqbar said as she moved to the side of the interior door.

Zarges entered and moved to the other side. Palmer entered and as he activated the gravity on his boots, pulling him downward, the door behind him closed.

He looked over his shoulder—nervously, Zarges thought, although he could have been projecting.

"We've only got a few minutes before the other team joins us," Zarges said.

He really didn't want to waste time joining up. His team needed to go to Engineering to see if they could stop the atmosphere dump.

Khusru's team had the tougher task: they were to go to the bridge, and try to work controls from there. The scans had shown that there were two people on the bridge, which meant that Khusru's team might have to deal with personnel first, and rescue second.

That would give Zarges time to determine if the ship was salvageable. If not, then he would let Khusru's team know and she would try to access the bridge communications system to inform the survivors that help was here, and that they would all be rescued.

He did not want to evacuate the ship one person at a time. He wasn't sure they could. There was a clock here, although he wasn't sure exactly what it was.

Not yet, anyway.

Iqbar pointed one fist down the long hallway. The light didn't illuminate much. A shiny path on the side.

"No emergency interior lights back here," Palmer said. "They're losing power as well as atmosphere."

Zarges double-checked the specs that he had uploaded to his system. They weren't that far from Engineering. Since Engineering was so close, they could move faster without gravity.

"Follow me," he said, and propelled himself forward.

THE *RENEGAT*

The *Renegat* rocked. The ship shouldn't be rocking, should it? It didn't have power, and it was huge, and there was nothing in space that would cause anything to rock.

Serpell only knew it rocked because she was clinging to the control panel. Bits of the panel floated around her, which she was convinced wasn't normal, not even in an emergency situation.

Kabac had looked up when the rocking began, then put his head back down, focusing on his work.

She wanted to scream at him again—hadn't he noticed the rocking?—but screaming at him never seemed to work. *Talking* to him didn't work either, so she was better off just keeping quiet.

She wanted the displays back on. She wanted to touch something or ask a question, and get an answer.

Advise leaving hostile environment as soon as possible, her suit said.

"Fuck you," she said under her breath.

"Excuse me?" Kabac sounded shocked. He had heard that? Everything else was going wrong on this damn ship and her communication link to his suit was set on *exceedingly touchy*? Great. Good. What else had he heard in the past several hours?

The backup power was sending pale yellow light everywhere, clashing with the white light coming from the arms of Kabac's suit.

He was using that light to poke at the equipment, trying to fix it—she hoped. Or at least, not screw it up.

"Something's happening," she said.

"No kidding." His voice was dry and filled with contempt. Damn near everything he said to her was filled with contempt.

She had accepted the contempt back at the Scrapheap—hell, she might even have deserved that contempt—but now she knew the limits of Kabac's expertise. He wasn't that much better at anything than she was.

In fact, he was worse at things. She had saved the ship all by herself at least once.

No one on board would be alive without her. Not a single soul, and none of them seemed to want to acknowledge that.

She deserved some kind of respect—or at least a hearing. Particularly now, when everything was going wrong.

"I mean it," she said. "The ship's moving."

"E-yeah." That contempt again.

"It's drifting. It shouldn't be rocking." She sounded strident. She wished she didn't care about how she sounded. But she did care. "Something's going wrong."

He lifted his head and sighed audibly. "You realize you're interrupting my work."

"What work?" she asked. "It's not work. What are you even doing?"

"Trying to get the power back on," he said, and bowed his head again. He had told her more than once he knew nothing about the engineering systems on this ship, and now he was trying to get the power back on? Maybe he was the one who was causing the rocking.

And what was he even working on? None of the control panels worked anymore. Not even the control panel near the captain's chair worked, and it should have, right?

At least Kabac had tools out and was doing something. All she was doing was poking at the dark control panels, hoping something would spring to life.

Advise leaving hostile environment as soon as possible, her suit said.

That couldn't have been fifteen minutes. Was the warning's timing accelerating? Had the stupid suit overridden the commands she had given?

Programming only got overridden like that when something was about to go catastrophically wrong.

She pushed off the control panel and headed to one of the utility closets built into the wall of the conference area just behind the bridge. She had to push off a lot of equipment to get there—her traveling skills in zero-G had devolved to damn near nothing.

"You're not just leaving me up here, are you?" Kabac asked, a bite to the words. It took her a second to hear what was beneath the bite.

Terror. He was as scared as she was—maybe more scared, because she already figured out that she was going to die. Figuring that out was both calming and motivating.

She wasn't panicking about staying alive, per se, but she was focused on staying alive *longer*, maybe until they could get the ship's systems back up and running.

"My suit's dying," she said. *Dying* was an interesting word choice, when she could have used so many other words—*failing, been compromised, leaking.*

But she had said *dying.*

"I've got over twenty-four hours of oxygen," he said. "I can share."

She had no idea how. These stupid suits were supposed to be self-contained. And then there was the matter of the leaks in her suit. The pinprick leaks were everywhere.

"Won't help," she said, and didn't explain.

Her suit was leaking. The ship was leaking. She was screwed. *They* were screwed.

All she could hope for at the moment was that someone on some lower level figured out how to get into engineering and get the systems back online.

Because she had a hunch that getting anything back online was beyond Kabac's skills.

Just like it was beyond hers.

THE *AIZSARGS RESCUE ONE*

The cockpit of *Rescue One* had the normal mid-rescue silence. But this rescue wasn't normal, and that made Pascal Turris nervous.

He sat stiffly in the pilot's chair, monitoring everything. Usually he had a lot more information at this point in a rescue. He would know the layout of the ship in trouble. He would be able to call up the crew complement, figure out who his people needed to talk with, or who would be in charge if the captain was unavailable.

He would know where the best exits were. He would know where to deploy the life rafts if necessary.

He would know how close he needed to be for *Rescue One* to remain safe.

He knew none of these things. Oh, his crew had tried, and so had everyone else on the *Aizsargs*. They had sent several diagrams of the interior of SC-Class vessels of the same make and model as the *Renegat*, but they had no information on the *Renegat* herself.

No history of repairs, no history of missions, no idea what the ship had been doing for the last hundred-plus years or why it hadn't been upgraded to a new ship or if it had been stored in a Scrapheap or left on some sector base.

He wanted all of that information, and he wouldn't get it in time, even though he knew the *Aizsargs* was working on finding it for him and for the rescue team.

His crew had volunteered to search for more information, but he had stopped them. He needed them to monitor the *Renegat*. He didn't like the way the exterior looked. He couldn't get the kind of readings he wanted, because the *Renegat* wasn't communicating with *Rescue One*.

Even when he deployed the grappler, he didn't get the kind of information he usually did. He hadn't thought the deployment would work, but it had. The grappler had dug into the proper ports on the *Renegat*, and held.

His two rescue teams had no trouble going through the space bridge—or so Ogden reported from Staging.

And that was the last Turris had heard from anyone.

Zarges had wanted Turris to roll up the spacebridge the moment the rescue teams left it, and Ogden had already pinged Turris to ask if the bridge should be disconnected.

Of course it should, but Turris didn't want to, not quite yet. He wanted to give it just a few more minutes. Time, he figured, for the rescue team to start to go deep into the *Renegat*, and maybe realize that they couldn't remain.

Then they could turn around and exit through the spacebridge.

Even though they probably wouldn't do that, especially now that Zarges was in charge.

Turris had no idea what, exactly, was making him so uncomfortable here. He had successfully performed dozens of rescues in the past year. But he had always relied on his gut as well as his brain, and his gut told him that something was very wrong with the *Renegat*.

"The atmosphere's still venting," Corrado Ranaldi said. He was a short man, fastidious and precise, the perfect person to handle any crisis. Ranaldi was usually their navigator, but while *Rescue One* was tied to the *Renegat*, there was nothing to navigate. So he was offering little helpful sentences, as reminders of the duty that Turris wasn't quite performing.

"You'd think they would have shut that down first thing," said Anna Vail, who was going to coordinate all of the rescue details on this mission. She often led rescue missions, so she knew what she was talking about.

Turris couldn't look at her, though. She was bouncing on her toes, clearly restless. She wanted to be part of this mission, on the ship, not in the cockpit.

"Maybe they can't," said Mackay Adeon. He was thin and anxious, constantly moving, always completing something. He didn't normally come to the cockpit. He always handled the technical details of the life rafts. He worried about everything, and knew, if he screwed up any part of life raft duty, a whole bunch of people would die.

He overcompensated by working too hard. So, in the time it had taken to send the in-person rescue teams, Adeon had already set up the life rafts in their bay belowdecks. But he could deploy the rafts from here, if need be.

"They haven't been on board very long," Turris said, trying to keep the second-guessing at a minimum.

"Then they need to hustle, because this is a real mess." Ranaldi was bent over the navigation controls, but it was clear he was talking about the *Renegat*. He probably saw the same readings that Turris did. "We should get as far from this ship as possible."

"I know," Turris said. He hadn't wanted to grapple onto the *Renegat* in the first place, but now that *Rescue One* was attached, he was afraid to release the grappler. He was worried that removing the grappler would cause even more damage to the *Renegat*.

To his eye, it seemed like the exterior of the *Renegat*'s hull was compromised, and the nanobits hadn't repaired the ship the way they usually did.

He glanced at the ship's clock. The rescue teams had been on board for ten minutes now. If the team was going to dive back into the spacebridge, they would have notified him of that already.

So that meant they either believed they could get the *Renegat* running well enough to take her to the relative safety of the nearest starbase or they could get the two hundred people on board off the ship with enough time to spare.

But something niggled at the corner of his eye. He checked and double-checked what he was seeing—in data, in two dimensions, and in three. He couldn't quite figure out what was making him so very uneasy.

"Anyone else worried about removing the spacebridge?" he asked. Not the best way to ask the question, he knew, but he would rather get the honest answer than have people dance around it.

"I was worried about getting close to the ship at all," Adeon said.

"I don't like the idea of pulling it," Ranaldi said, "but we have no choice."

"They're not coming back through no matter what they find," Vail said. "They think you've already pulled it."

She was right; he hadn't told the rescue teams he was doing anything differently.

He felt a little odd about that. It wasn't that he failed to think clearly; it was just that he was so preoccupied with what he had been seeing on that ship.

"Adeon," Turris said, "do we have any of the records of that ship coming out of foldspace? Something in the way that it's operating really bothers me, and I can't put my finger on it."

"I'll see," Adeon said. "But if there were serious, easy to find problems with the *anacapa*, I would think that the *Aizsargs* would tell us."

First rule of rescue, Turris almost said, was do the work yourself. But he didn't say that. His team knew what the priorities were. Right now, the priorities on board *Rescue One* were getting ready to assist the teams in the *Renegat*.

"The team might not have had a chance to check the *anacapa* drive," Vail said. "They have a lot to do from the moment they get on that ship."

Turris knew that, mostly in theory. He had gone inside a crippled ship on a few rescues, but not many. He was always better served to act as a pilot for the rescue vehicle.

"I don't like the readings I'm seeing," Adeon said. "They're uneven, and I didn't even know that was possible with an *anacapa* drive."

"It's almost as if the drive didn't shut down when the ship came out of foldspace," Vail said.

That was it: that was what bothered Turris. The energy readings were abnormal, but energy readings were always abnormal on a ship in trouble. It was the *kind* of abnormal that bothered Turris the most. He hadn't seen anything like it.

His stomach twisted. Time to get *Rescue One* untethered from the *Renegat*.

Turris sent a message to Ogden, telling him to roll up the space bridge and seal *Rescue One*. As soon as Ogden let them know he was finished, *Rescue One* would move away from the *Renegat*.

"Ranaldi," Turris said, "figure out where we can move so that we'll be able to best deploy the life rafts, if we need to."

"We won't know where to send the rafts until the teams contact us," Vail said, as if Turris had never run a rescue before.

To be fair to her, there were two schools of thought on life rafts. One was to take a neutral position as far from the damaged ship as possible. The other was to hover as close to the damaged ship as possible so that the rafts would get to the ship quickly.

Both had their dangers. The first was that the life rafts might not arrive in time. The second was that any explosion on the damaged ship might damage *Rescue One* instead.

Turris would rather risk *Rescue One* than lose lives on board a ship in need of rescue. So he ignored Vail, and waited for Ranaldi to plug in the coordinates.

While he waited, Turris monitored the grappler. There were sensors on its claws, but their readings were strange as well. The nanobits that composed the *Renegat*'s hull seemed active, but they were also losing their bonding. He couldn't tell if they were actively repairing the ship, or not working productively at all.

"Okay," Ranaldi said. "I've locked in the coordinates."

Turris nodded, then hit the command to unhook the grappler. He didn't alter the way it was done; he didn't do it more slowly or more carefully. Sometimes slow was as bad as fast. Sometimes normal was the best way to succeed.

The grappler started to disengage, and then stopped. A red light flared across Turris's console.

"It's stuck," Ranaldi said, sounding surprised.

Turris nodded. He had half-expected that. Maybe more than half.

He opened a holographic screen, hit the virtual grappler controls and watched as an image of the bent black arm rose in front of him. He scrolled it to one side, so that he could see the actual claws.

Five of them, resembling a hand, which was not an accident of design. They gripped the side of the ship the way that someone might hold a ball that almost exceeded their hand's span. The only difference was that all five claws were the same length.

"Manual," he said to the controls. Behind him, he heard Vail gasp. He knew her objection; it was the Fleet's position that the automated grappler controls worked better than any single person could.

But he felt like the sensors weren't working properly—not through the fault of the grappler itself, but because of the communication it was receiving from the other ship.

The grappler holographic image created an extra slot for his arm and hand, measured to his specifics. He slipped his right hand inside that holographic image, placed his fingers over the claws, and settled in.

"Sir," Vail said.

"I've got this," he said curtly. "I'll need to concentrate to do it right."

She didn't say another word.

The entire cockpit was silent. He had to ignore them all, so he didn't even know if they were watching him. He hoped that Ranaldi was also monitoring the controls, stepping into his occasional role as copilot. But Turris didn't check that. Right now, *Rescue One* wasn't going anywhere, so unless something attacked it or hit it from the side, he could ignore the piloting controls for a few moments.

He had worked grapplers half a dozen times before, and he practiced with them monthly, just to—pun intended—keep his hand in. He needed to know what normal felt like. He did those double-checks on every system that allowed him to access it manually.

He was glad he had done all of that practice. It might make a difference.

He twisted his right hand ever so slightly, feeling for abnormal resistance inside the grappler. Twisting his hand like that should have been difficult, but possible. Instead, his hand felt stuck.

So he tested micromovements, not with the whole hand, but with his fingers.

He started with his thumb, partly because he had practiced with the thumb and the little finger the most. Those were the ones that didn't quite work the way the other claws worked—mostly because of the way the thumb and the little finger were structured.

The little finger had the right number of joints, but not the strength or the length that the other fingers had. The thumb was the most difficult, because it not only lacked the strength and length of the other fingers, it was also missing a joint.

He had learned, over the years, to use the tip of his thumb as if it were that missing joint.

He did that now, turning inward, toward the palm of his hand, using the tip of the thumb as a kind of pivot. The claw moved, just the way all the others moved when he tried that maneuver.

So he rotated the thumb-claw back into position, and tried the index finger. That finger-claw he moved straight down, toward the palm, and the claw moved easily.

But doing that simple maneuver caused a strange ache in his middle finger, and an echoing ache in his ring finger.

He moved the index finger-claw back into position, and tried the same downward motion with the middle finger-claw.

It didn't move at all.

He tried three times, and at no time did that claw budge.

Then he tried with the ring finger-claw. It moved ever so slightly.

The little finger claw moved perfectly.

So the middle-finger claw was stuck.

He removed his hand from the holographic image, and went back to the grappler controls. He deactivated the middle finger-claw, and gave the grappler permission to tear it off, if need be.

He did not mention what he had done to his team.

Then he activated the grappler again, and had it follow normal protocol to disengage.

For a moment, the grappler didn't move, but there were no flashing red warning lights, nothing that indicated something had gone awry. He watched the claws on the holographic rendering, saw the exact moment that the grappler decided to leave behind its claw, and knew, even before it happened, that the claws would turn.

They did, pulling themselves out of the hull of the *Renegat.*

The middle finger-claw ripped at the upper joint, causing a damage alert, but no other troubles.

"What the heck?" Adeon asked. He obviously saw the alert.

Turris said nothing. The grappler retracted, folding up as it was designed to do, as it headed into its compartment on the side of *Rescue One.*

"Ship disengaged," the computer said, even though Turris hadn't programmed it to speak through this procedure.

Ranaldi was nodding, though. Apparently, he was the one who had programmed that little surprise.

Turris reached the controls, ready to start *Rescue One* on its journey to the coordinates that Ranaldi had programmed in, only to find that *Rescue One* was already moving.

Turris pointed at the screen. Ranaldi knew he was referring to the fact the ship was already underway.

"You think we're in that much danger?" Turris asked Ranaldi.

Ranaldi's gaze met his.

"No," Ranaldi said softly. "I think we're in a lot more."

PART SIX

THE JOURNEY BACKWARDS

100 YEARS AGO

THE *RENEGAT*

Crowe sat beside Preemas in the captain's dining room off the main mess. The captain's dining room was designed for intimate gatherings of no more than six people. If the captain wanted to have a meal with a larger group, there was another formal mess on level six, where the officers' quarters were. Those quarters were designed for officers with families or such high-ranking officers that they got two-bedroom suites, with a small living and kitchen area.

The captain's living quarters were also there, as were the first officer's living quarters. Crowe did not ask if Newark would lose those rooms, which were plush and well-apportioned. Crowe didn't care if he got them; his own living quarters were large enough for his every need.

Unlike this dining area. It had no portholes, but did have drop-down screens that could show every section of the ship. There were controls on the wall beside the head of the table, so the captain could run the ship from this room, should something go seriously awry.

Preemas sat there now, with all of the screens shut down. Screens off seemed to be his default in every room he was in. Crowe's default was the exact opposite. He liked information, the more the better. Sitting in this barren dining area, with a simple rectangular table, a built-in bench, and chairs that could be added to one side of the table, made Crowe distinctly uncomfortable. Only his self-control prevented him from fidgeting.

He didn't want Preemas to think he was nervous about the changes when, in reality, Crowe thought most of them were a good idea. But, over the last few days, he had learned that Preemas jumped to his own conclusions about pretty much everything, often on very little information, so Crowe had already settled into the habit of monitoring his every movement so that Preemas wouldn't misinterpret it.

The ship's main chef—who was about to be demoted, even though he didn't know it yet—had set the table with a variety of snacks. Crowe had tried the roasted watermelon seeds, and wondered how something that simple could be ruined. They tasted burned, even though they didn't look burned.

The other snacks looked promising—beautifully sliced carrots, perfectly cut zucchini, orange wedges, and some glistening tahini with pita chips.

Preemas had sampled the pita chips, made a face, and shoved them away. Crowe was actually scared to try any of the "fresh" vegetables. He'd been to hydroponics. The gardeners there were as incompetent as the rest of the crew. The easy, quick-grow items were yellow and brown, unless they were supposed to be yellow and brown, and in that case, they were either green or black.

Even the coffee was awful. Crowe had a cup in front of him that he wasn't going to drink. He had brought a bottle of water with him, and he was glad he had. Clutching it gave him something to do with his hands.

A pile of plates sat near the food, and only one had been used—still stacked with Preemas's rejected pita chips. Still, it looked like a proper sit-down meeting, which Crowe and Preemas were only going to have with one crew member—Danika Newark.

The others would find out about their reassignments a few minutes later, in the large mess hall, where Preemas was going to make a speech. Initially, Crowe thought they should tell each person individually, but with 267 staff changes, telling each person individually would take too long.

Besides, Preemas was bound to screw up. He'd tell someone that she would be replacing someone else before informing that someone else that he was being demoted.

Everyone was concerned anyway. For the past three days, Crowe had shadowed Preemas, and no one knew why. Newark had even demanded to be told, and that was when Preemas told her she would learn everything this afternoon, just before the big meeting.

She had an inkling, because she'd been giving Crowe strange sideways looks for the past 24 hours, but she probably didn't know how big the change was going to be.

"Ready?" Preemas asked Crowe.

Crowe nodded. He had been ready for two days. He didn't like keeping his new position secret, and he didn't like messing with people's lives. That wasn't his usual purpose. Usually he tried to keep them alive, not change how they lived.

But he said nothing. After he took the first officer position, he had decided to keep as quiet as possible about most things. He would reserve his bluntness for a true crisis.

And frankly, these staff changes were not a crisis at all. They were sensible. Preemas had done a lot of research all on his own. He had gone through each crew member's records, finding what their initial interests were in school or the level of job at which they had performed the best. He figured out where many of them had gone sideways—usually because of ambition and the promise of promotion—and decided to move them back to the sweet spot for their career.

His hope, or so he said to Crowe over the past three days of work, was that the ship would become more efficient, not less.

Right on time, the door to the captain's dining room chirruped, and slid open. Danika Newark entered, wearing her uniform, her hair pulled back. Her eyes widened when she saw Crowe. She opened her mouth as if she was going to say something, and then seemed to change her mind.

"Please sit," Preemas said.

Newark slid into a nearby chair without any protest. Her gaze found Crowe's again, but he kept his expression impassive. He didn't want to give anything away.

"I am going to make changes on the *Renegat*," Preemas said. "I wanted you to be the first to know."

"Second," Newark said, looking at Crowe.

His heartbeat increased slightly, not because she made him nervous, but because he couldn't believe her audacity. He would never have challenged his captain like that so soon in a meeting.

Perhaps she knew exactly where this was going and thought she had nothing to lose.

Preemas stared at her for a moment. Crowe glanced at the side of Preemas's face. His jaw worked, as if he was grinding his teeth together.

"Vice Admiral Gāo gave me the crew compliment and their positions before we left," Preemas said, apparently deciding to ignore Newark's comment. "I was unable to bring in other crew members, some I've worked with for years. Crowe here had made the same request for engineering and had been denied."

Newark swiveled her head toward Crowe, her eyes filled with contempt. Crowe actually had to work to keep his expression neutral.

She turned back to Preemas.

"You've looked at the crew," Preemas said. "You know that some of them are ill-suited to the tasks they've been assigned."

"Some of them are ill-suited to the Fleet," she said.

Crowe folded his hands together on top of the table, so that he wouldn't fiddle with his bottle of water or the horrible food.

"That remains to be seen," Preemas said. "I think everyone on this crew has been ill-served by the Fleet."

That was part of his upcoming speech. Crowe had heard parts of it already, and he agreed with some of it. He wasn't sure he agreed that everyone on this vessel had been ill-served by the Fleet. In some cases, Crowe believed that the Fleet had been too lenient.

His case, for example.

"You're being awfully charitable to a shipload of idiots and incompetents," Newark said.

Crowe wanted to caution her. She was part of that shipload. But he didn't move.

"I'm going to experiment," Preemas said. "I'm going to reassign much of the crew into positions that they haven't served in, sometimes for years. But these reassignments seem better suited to the crew's experience than the positions they're now in."

Newark's cheeks grew dark, and she glanced yet again at Crowe. "Your idea, huh?"

He started to answer but Preemas held out a hand, a single index finger up.

"You and I are talking, Danika," Preemas said, using the disrespectful first name.

Crowe had been unable to break Preemas of that habit, except with Crowe himself. For the last few days, either Preemas hadn't referred to him by name at all or had referred to him as Two-Assignment Crowe, which seemed just too blatant for Crowe. But no one else seemed to have caught on.

Newark's lower lip curled just a little, and she begrudgingly turned in her chair so that she faced Preemas directly, almost blocking Crowe's view of her face.

"The changes you'll hear about today are my idea and mine only," Preemas said, even though that wasn't true. Crowe had recommended some of the staff changes and Preemas had taken him up on those recommendations. "You're here as a courtesy."

Newark glanced at Crowe one more time, as if she couldn't stop looking at him.

She clearly knew he was going to replace her. She might have known for a couple of days now. And she clearly resented it.

"The courtesy is this, Danika," Preemas said. "You are nominally my first officer—"

"Nominally?" she asked.

Her gaze was now directly on Crowe's and remained there. He met her stare with one of his own.

She looked away first.

Preemas waited until her eyes returned to his before continuing.

"You never really warmed up to the job," Preemas said. "I asked you to go through crew files the day you were assigned to this vessel. To date, you haven't opened a single file."

"We were putting a ship together from scratch," Newark said. "I didn't have time for that kind of work."

Crowe knew that, on some Fleet vessels, officers had latitude to do what they thought was best. He usually got that latitude for engineering, simply because most captains didn't have the experience to micromanage that department.

But first officers were generally different. Unless they had the full trust of their captain, they were often glued to the captain's side, learning the job one tiny detail at a time.

"'That kind of work' is essential to putting together a new ship," Preemas said.

"Well," Newark said, her tone vicious, "I see that you found someone who was willing to do your scut work."

She glared at Crowe. He met her gaze impassively, still not moving.

"It's not scut work, Danika," Preemas said. "In fact, I spent much of the early weeks going through every file, making notes, and making decisions."

"Because you want to have control of your ship, not Gão," Newark said.

"If you'll recall," Preemas said, his words clipped, "this mission is a very dangerous one. I haven't told you all of the details, because I wanted to work with you for a while before I trusted you fully. But you did know that the mission was going to be hard and long and risky. It's essential that we have the right crew in place before we get to the difficult part of the mission."

Her eyes glittered with anger. "You just don't want me as first officer," she said.

"That is correct," Preemas said. "I don't. You are not up to the job."

Her nostrils flared, and her lips pursed. "So what are you going to do? Leave me on a starbase somewhere?"

Preemas let out a grunt of surprise. "That's not a bad idea." He looked at Crowe as if Newark wasn't even there. "We need to schedule a stop at Sector Base Z."

"Technically, we are supposed to go into foldspace before that," Crowe said.

"Yeah, have you looked at those plans?" Preemas asked. The question was unnecessary. It was clear from Crowe's comment that he had. "I don't like them. We have to refigure some of it. That's our next task."

"*He's* your first officer now?" Newark asked. "Do you *know* what kind of person he is? Do you *know* what they say about him?"

Preemas looked at her as if he had forgotten she was there. Crowe expected Preemas to either defend him or to say that what she knew was irrelevant.

Instead, Preemas said, "What do they say about him?"

"That he's so careless he murdered kids," she said.

"Is that in his file?" Preemas asked.

She closed her mouth, suddenly aware of the mistake she had made.

"Because I investigated his file," Preemas said. "I even know what's in the sealed section. And I can tell you categorically that he did not kill kids."

"If the file's sealed, you can't see it," she said.

"I have a higher clearance than you'd think," Preemas said, even though that wasn't how he knew what Crowe had done.

Crowe felt ridiculously grateful for that, and grateful, too, that Preemas hadn't corrected her facts. He was also aware that gratitude was a dangerous emotion, and Preemas had made Crowe feel it twice now, concerning that sealed file.

"This is why you're not suited for the job," Preemas said. "You don't want to do the hard work of dealing with the crew. I need someone at my side who can handle the crew and any crisis that may come up."

"I can do that," Newark said.

"No." His voice softened. "Your file is pretty clear on that point, Danika. You don't know who to turn to when things get rough."

She put her hands on the table, looking like a woman who was about to push her chair back so she could stand.

"Are we done?"

"No," Preemas said, surprising Crowe. "We're not. As I said, Danika. I read your file."

She raised her chin.

Preemas shoved the tahini at her. "Try this."

"I'm not hungry." She sounded deeply offended.

"I know that," Preemas said. "That's not why I'm telling you to try this."

She gave him an angry look, almost like a child who was being scolded by an adult, and then she dragged the plate toward her. She grabbed one of the pita chips and dipped it into the tahini.

The tahini should have been a blond-brown, but it was darker than that, and it didn't have any consistency at all. It dripped like a sauce. She grabbed a plate, held it under the dripping chip as she brought it to her mouth.

Then she took a really tiny bite, and grimaced.

"Terrible, right?" Preemas asked. "I could use the computer program to give me a better tahini, but we have customs on Fleet ships. We actually have a chef to make specialty dishes."

Newark set the chip onto the plate and put the plate down.

"What's wrong with the tahini?" Preemas asked.

"It's awful, like you said." She sounded furious.

"No," he said. "What did the chef do wrong?"

"He burned the sesame seeds," she said. "They're supposed to be toasted. Then he added some kind of oil, probably olive oil that was processed, not made here, and lemon juice, as well as some salt. I prefer tahini made only from toasted seeds, nothing else added. You can add other things if you're using the tahini in hummus or halva."

Her very specific answer surprised Crowe. He had no idea tahini was made out of seeds or that there was more than one way to make it. He also didn't know it was in hummus or halva. He didn't know anything about food, either having it prepared for him in the mess or using the computer processor in his room.

"You just made my point, Danika," Preemas said softly. He didn't sound like an angry captain now. He sounded like someone who actually liked Newark. "You didn't initially go into officer training, did you?"

She looked down. "No."

"You spent years in culinary classes, and were going to be a chef, weren't you?"

She nodded once, still not looking up.

"Your mother objected, didn't she? And then she died…?"

"She captained the *Lume,*" Newark said, with both defiance and pride.

Crowe let out a breath. The captain of the *Lume* was famous for sacrificing her ship in the middle of a battle to save dozens of ships around her. She received some kind of posthumous medal.

"She wanted you to follow in her footsteps," Preemas said.

Newark nodded.

"And after she died, someone convinced you that was what you wanted too—"

"No one convinced me," Newark said. "I knew that was what she wanted. And I…"

She shook her head.

"Being a chef isn't as important," she said quietly, almost to herself.

In fact, Crowe suspected she had been saying that to herself for years.

"You want to have another bite of that tahini?" Preemas asked. "It's worse without the chips, which are pretty awful all by themselves."

"We don't have to have a chef," Newark said. "We can live on prepared meals."

"For months?" Preemas asked. "That won't help morale."

Newark raised her head. "What are you saying?"

Preemas leaned toward her. "I'm going to run this ship without demoting anyone. Which is going to make rank confusing. But I think rank has been misused by the Fleet anyway."

She frowned. She didn't understand this any more than Crowe had when he first heard it.

"I'm going to move you to the chef's position," Preemas said to Newark. "You're going to work with the kitchen staff that's in place, but if you need to move them around, please do. I'm replacing almost everyone in hydroponics—they can't grow anything anyway—so your ingredients will eventually be better than the ones we currently have. But you will run the entire mess system. You'll be in charge of every bite we eat."

Newark's eyes brightened for a brief moment, and then the joy in them faded.

"I never completed the training," she said.

"I've eaten your meals," Preemas said.

"No, you haven't," she said.

"Yes, I have," he said. "You've been cooking on this ship. I've made sure that I got some samples."

"You're behind Romano's request for food?" she asked.

Preemas nodded, with a small smile.

"And you think I'm good?"

Crowe would have answered in a deprecating way, saying anything would be better than their current chef. (Which was true.)

But Preemas nodded. "I think you're gifted. Your baba ghanoush is the best I've ever had."

She laughed. Crowe didn't quite understand why until she said, "So that's why you have tahini here. You're sneaky, Captain."

Preemas shrugged ever so slightly, as if it didn't matter to him at all.

But Newark was right. He was sneaky and manipulative and several steps ahead of all of them.

Crowe made a mental note of that as well.

"Will you accept the transfer?" Preemas asked.

She frowned, but this frown was unlike her earlier one. There was no anger behind it, no fear.

"What about our current chef?" she asked.

"He's being moved to entertainment," Preemas said. "He won't be in your way. You'll let me know if there's a problem."

"Yes," Newark said, apparently not realizing that "yes" was an agreement to the entire shift. Then she laughed again, a sound with real joy behind it. "You're going to let me run the kitchens the way I want to?"

"Please," Preemas said.

"All right then," Newark said. "I'll accept the transfer. Although I think it's a mistake to take Crowe here out of engineering. He's really good at it. He's in the right job."

"I know," Preemas said. "He'll be doing both jobs."

She glanced at Crowe. "You know that's two full-time positions."

He nodded, but didn't say anything else.

"Well," she said, her tone doubtful. "If you think you can do it…"

"Danika," Preemas said, clearly trying to shut down that aspect of the discussion. "I wanted to talk to you before I talk to the rest of the crew. I can't go through this one-on-one with everyone, so I'm going to have an overall meeting with the entire crew. Back me on this?"

"Of course," she said, as if she hadn't been furious with him when she came into the room.

"Thank you," he said. "I'll be out in the mess in a few minutes."

She glanced at both of them, then stood. Her expression faded, but she seemed lighter.

"Captain," she said.

"Pre," he said. "No titles, remember?"

She shook her head just a little. She didn't seem to be any more comfortable with that than Crowe was. She inclined her head toward Preemas, and said, "Thank you."

"It's going to be my pleasure," Preemas said, waving a hand at the food.

She grinned and walked out of the captain's dining room.

Preemas leaned back. "That went well, didn't it?"

Crowe wasn't sure how to answer. It had gone better than he initially expected, because he had known that Newark would be furious about her loss of rank.

He hadn't expected Preemas to make her the chef of the ship. That hadn't been on the revised crew manifest, and Crowe felt as if he had been blindsided.

He thought he had been consulted on all of this.

It took him a moment to make sure he had control of his voice.

"I didn't realize you were going to move her to the kitchens," Crowe said.

"I didn't think she'd go," Preemas said, smiling just a little. He swept his hand at the food. "Then, last night, I got this idea. The entire crew has been complaining about the quality of their meals. I think having her in charge will improve everything."

Crowe nodded just once, a tiny nod, not sure what else to do. He didn't want to yell at Preemas for failing to consult him, because that would set their relationship on the wrong foot, but Crowe felt like he had been used.

Or maybe it was just the way that blatant manipulation made him feel. He hated seeing what Preemas had done, not because it had worked, but because Preemas had essentially used Newark's dreams against her.

Or had he? She was clearly bad at her assigned job, and she had wanted to be a chef since she was a child. She cooked in her spare time, which couldn't be easy, even in the first officer's quarters.

So it was the correct decision. It was just an odd way of getting there.

Preemas was watching Crowe, apparently seeing Crowe think.

"You don't approve," Preemas said.

Crowe shook his head once. "I didn't say that."

Preemas leaned back in his chair and grinned. "Unorthodox methods, First Officer Crowe. Get used to them."

"I guess I'm going to have to," Crowe said, as much for himself as for Preemas.

"They wrote us off, Crowe," Preemas said. "Remember that every time you feel a need to follow regulations coming on. Examine if those regulations are there for us or if they're there to make some higher-ranking asshole happy."

"Even if you're the higher-ranking asshole?" Crowe asked.

Preemas laughed. Then the laugher left his eyes, almost as quickly as it arrived. That was the second time Crowe had seen that kind of mood shift from Preemas, and it bothered him a great deal.

"I'm the law here, Crowe," Preemas said. "Remember that, and you'll be fine."

The air inside the captain's dining room felt stuffy. Crowe grabbed his bottle of water.

"They're waiting for us, sir," Crowe said.

"Pre," Preemas corrected.

"Sir," Crowe said, with force.

They stared at each other for a moment. Then Preemas grinned again. "I do like you, First Officer Crowe. You're going to keep me honest."

"I hope so, sir," Crowe said. "I truly do."

THE *RENEGAT*

Raina Serpell remained in her chair at the back of the largest mess hall on the *Renegat.* Her wife, India Romano, was already standing, shifting from foot to foot as she watched the rest of the crew file out of the room.

The conversation was low and uncertain. Serpell couldn't ignore all of it. Some voices just carried.

"...don't get what he means, rank won't matter. Of course it matters..."

"...know that I hate maintenance. It's like he read my mind..."

"...disrespects me. I worked my whole life for that promotion, and I'm here to prove that I belong in that position..."

Serpell still had the revised manifest open on her personal screen. The manifest was covered in red, which was the color that Captain Preemas had chosen to show the changes. She thought the color choice was a mistake. Red was for alarm and anger and uncertainty, not for something he had trumpeted as good news.

He had stood not six feet from her, with Chief Engineer Crowe and former, now anyway, First Officer Newark at his side. Captain Preemas had given some speech about everyone being in the wrong position, or the wrong position for this trip, and how he liked experimenting, and how it was going to work so very well for the ship.

Serpell had no idea how it could work well. Two hundred and sixty-seven people were in brand new positions, some in positions they had never worked before on a starship. Maybe in training. Or maybe not. How could they run a security vessel with so many people in brand new jobs?

She hadn't been moved to a new job, and she was grateful for that. But, then, it was hard to move a linguist. Linguists had specific training to deal with all kinds of languages, and all kinds of language mutations. Linguists worked tightly with the Fleet's computer system to make sure that translations were accurate.

Captain Preemas would need her the farther back they went. Who knew what kind of cultures had taken over the sectors in the years after the Fleet left? She certainly didn't.

India was a linguist too, but hated the work. Truth be told, she was the reason they were here. She did sloppy work, feeling that "close enough" was all most translations needed. She didn't love the work like Serpell did.

Serpell's friends all tried to talk her out of coming on this trip, but she couldn't leave India. India needed her. Serpell kept India steady, made sure she did her absolute best whenever possible. Serpell kept them organized as well, and India appreciated it. She always said she had no idea how she had gotten along before she had met Serpell.

Serpell wasn't sure how India had done it either.

India was leaning against the wall now, watching everyone leave. She had one booted foot resting on the nearest chair, a habit that drove Serpell crazy. India had a lot of habits that drove Serpell crazy, but Serpell kept telling herself that it was all part of the package.

She had fallen for India because they were so very different. India was taller, prettier, more gregarious. She changed her hair's color almost daily, and sometimes matched her eyes to the hair. Today's color was copper. India coated the top strands of her normally dark hair with copper, added some copper highlights to her irises, and covered her skin with some kind of copper powder. Her shirt had copper accents, and so did her boots.

If only she took as much time on her work as she took on her appearance, she would be the best linguist in the Fleet.

Not that she cared any longer, because her name was one of the names marked in red. India was moving to security. She had let out a small eep when she found herself on that list, and her entire expression brightened.

Serpell had found her own name as well, and she had felt a large thread of relief. She hadn't wanted to move away from the linguistics team, which was pretty good. She had been looking forward to putting her skills to practical use, with India by her side.

And now, India wouldn't be there.

Serpell kept staring at the names, hoping there had been some kind of mistake.

Others were thinking the same thing.

"...haven't done any work on navigation systems since school..."

"...would rather be in the diplomatic corps..."

"...not fair that she would get a promotion over me..."

Serpell wanted to chime in on that last one. Captain Preemas had been really clear that none of these moves were promotions or demotions. Just adjustments, ways of making the ship more efficient.

Now, the captain was nowhere to be seen. Former First Officer Newark was talking to a cluster of people near the kitchen door. Chief Engineer Crowe was gone as well.

Most of the crew had left the mess hall. It looked different than it had when Serpell had arrived. Chairs were scattered now, and mugs littered some of the tables.

Serpell had never served on a ship like this, where the common niceties like cleaning up after yourself were not observed. She was half-inclined to get up and start clearing off tables, even though she knew someone else was supposed to handle it.

"You being moody?" India asked. She was rocking the chair back and forth with her foot, almost as if she was mocking Serpell.

"I'm just looking at all the changes," Serpell said, hating the "moody" accusation. It was a new one. When they first met, India had liked Serpell's reflective nature, just like Serpell had liked India's sense of adventure.

Serpell wasn't sure when "reflective" became "moody," but she knew it had occurred before they arrived on the ship.

"The captain said he did a ton of research before making these decisions, and I, for one, believe him." India took her foot off that chair and gripped its back with both hands. She leaned down so that her head hovered near Serpell's shoulder. "You're not going to find the research in that list."

"I know," Serpell said. Her stomach was a hard knot of tension. Everything felt wrong to her. She liked the order on board a ship, and this totally upended the order, in every way possible.

She closed her personal screen, and pocketed it. But she still didn't stand.

Three different groups were scattered throughout the mess hall, talking animatedly to each other. Each group had at least one person whose name had been highlighted in red. Two of those people looked happy, and one looked terrified.

"You're not trained for security," Serpell said without looking at India.

"You don't need training for security," India said. "I've read the position descriptions in the past. You need physical strength, an intelligence that can handle fluid situations, and preternatural calm."

India didn't have preternatural calm. She barely had calm. It took very little to arouse her, whether that was arousing her to anger or arousing her sexually. India's moods shifted with the situation in front of her.

If anyone in the relationship should be called "moody," it was India.

"You know I've never stopped training," India said.

She was obsessed with her physical condition. She was one of the strongest people Serpell had ever met. She liked the physical work. That had been one of her big complaints about linguistics—how much time it took in quiet, studious places.

After she and Serpell met, India used to joke that they were a two-fer. Two linguists who could go into any situation. One would keep translating no matter what the circumstance, and the other would keep them safe even if the circumstance turned dire.

Serpell had liked that. She had liked the way that India saw the universe as a hostile place that needed to be conquered. Serpell had always thought that learning someone else's language was a way to conquer anything, and it wasn't until weeks after they had spoken their vows that, Serpell realized that India didn't agree.

India thought getting rid of the language barrier was a good first step toward dominating a situation. And sometimes India didn't even want to get rid of the language barrier. She wanted to learn the other side's language, and not translate anything, as a form of power.

"Ah, come on, Rains," India said, pressing her head against Serpell's. "You know this is better. I wasn't cut out to spend my days translating other people's words."

One of the groups across the mess hall had devolved into an angry whispered fight. They kept gesticulating at each other, as if they could change whatever situation they were in just by flapping their arms.

"I was thinking," Serpell said quietly, still not looking at India directly, "that maybe we reevaluate our positions here."

"That's what the captain did." India sounded practically gleeful. "And he put me in a job I've wanted for years."

The conversation was going to go nowhere. Serpell could see that now. If she pushed it, she and India were going to fight.

But Serpell had to push it. Because if she didn't, she would miss an opportunity.

"I mean, re-evaluate being part of this crew." Serpell spoke as softly as she could, given the people across the mess. She didn't want them to hear what she was saying.

India raised her eyebrows, and sank into the chair across from Serpell. "What are you saying? This is a great opportunity for me."

"He said this is going to be a dangerous mission," Serpell said. "He implied we might not survive it. And you know, everyone I've talked to here has no family with the Fleet or they're estranged from their family. Even you and me."

India's entire face had fallen flat. "You know they said I couldn't come if you stayed behind."

Serpell's breath caught. "What?"

"They said I couldn't come—"

"I thought you told them we were a team. I thought you told them that we couldn't be separated. I thought that's why they let us on this ship." Serpell's voice went up. She felt off-balance.

Had India *lied?*

"They didn't want you to come here," India said. "You could've kept moving up in the Fleet. I told you that a long time ago. They said you were too good to come along, and I said we go everywhere together, and then, remember, they had that meeting with you, and you said—"

"I said we were a team," Serpell said numbly. "I said we did everything together. I said that our careers were intertwined."

Were those lies too? She had believed them at the time, but now, they weren't going to be a team.

She swallowed the hurt, and went back to her point.

"If you take this assignment, India, we're not a team anymore." Serpell sounded a bit shaky, even to her own ears. "And frankly, what the captain wants to do sounds even more dangerous to me. He said we're going into foldspace after we leave this sector. I think this is our last chance—maybe our only chance—to get off this ship, and go back to our lives. I think we should take it, India."

India stared at her as if she had never seen Serpell before.

"And do what, Rains?" India snapped. "What would I do? Be your linguistic assistant on some assignment? I certainly won't get the chance to do security anywhere else. Going back will remove every single career opportunity that I have. Do you really want to sink me?"

"No," Serpell said. "But I don't want...I mean, I want us to be the team I told everyone about. I don't want to lose you in linguistics. You're—"

"A drag on you," India said. "You know it. You've taken work from me because you said that you could do it faster. What you meant was you could do it better. Everyone can. I hate linguistics, and I have a new opportunity now, because we're on the *Renegat.* So rather than run away to the safe parts of the Fleet, let's stay here. Let's see what happens."

"We could die," Serpell said, her voice a near-whisper. "That was the subtext, India. They put the wrong people in the wrong positions on a ship that has no support, and they're sending us somewhere mysterious which is a long way from here, and the implication is that we could die."

"And if we go to some planet and I misinterpret the language, we could die there too. Or we could get injured or sick or something bad can happen, Rains. We've had this discussion. You don't take risks because you're afraid. You need me to help you make the right choices, remember?" India didn't speak with her usual passion on this. Whenever she made a version of this speech in the past, she'd put her hand on Serpell's arm or pull her close or kiss her.

This time, India seemed almost angry.

"This doesn't feel like the right choice," Serpell said.

"For you maybe," India said, and then she waited.

Serpell got the sense that India was testing her, was trying to see if Serpell would get off the ship on her own volition.

And if she did, and the ship never came back, how would she feel? Vindicated? Lost? As if it was her fault that India had not come back? And what if Serpell never knew if India lived or died or died horribly? Could Serpell live with not knowing? Could she handle it?

If Serpell left without India, their relationship, their *marriage*, was over. They both knew it. That's why India didn't push that last little bit. Because India wanted the relationship to last too.

"Staying means that much to you?" Serpell asked.

"It's the choice between a future with a career and hope and possibilities, and a future where I'm a drag on you and everyone around us," India said. "So yeah, it means that much to me."

Serpell let out a small breath. One of the other groups was disbanding, everyone going in different directions. Former First Officer Newark's group was still together, and Newark was laughing.

Newark seemed comfortable, even though she had been demoted. After all, how else could you describe the loss of the first officer position as anything but a demotion? She had no reason to stay on board the *Renegat*, and yet she was doing so.

She had to know how scary this trip was going to be. She had to know what dangers they were facing. And she seemed happy.

That had to mean something, right?

Serpell ran a hand along her upper thigh, a nervous gesture she hadn't made in months. She recognized it, and couldn't stop it. It was part of her.

Just like the nerves.

Just like India.

"Okay," Serpell said, even though she was shaking, even though her stomach ached, even though a little voice in the back of her head was telling her that she was making a mistake. "We'll stay."

India hugged her.

Serpell leaned her head on India's shoulder, felt the warmth of the person she loved the most in the entire universe, and hugged back.

They had each other. They always had each other, no matter what.

And this time, that had to be enough.

THE *RENEGAT*

The *Renegat* was a ship in turmoil.

Crowe had known that would happen after Preemas made his announcements, but hadn't realized exactly how that turmoil would manifest.

The entire ship lurched forward as if it hadn't already been traveling across the sector. Some people took to their new jobs with great joy. Newark was one. Crowe had thought Preemas had played her, and maybe he had, but she loved working in the kitchens. Crowe had always thought Newark was bad with people, but she wasn't when she was cooking.

For the first time since he boarded the *Renegat*, the meals were good, fresh, and timely.

Dozens of others were just like her—thriving already, and it had only been a few days.

But, it seemed, even more people hated being moved, or demoted (no matter what Preemas said about rank), or just hated the unpredictability of their new world.

All of those people found their way to Crowe. Most of them came to engineering, which was starting to irritate him.

Engineering had always been the safest place on the ship, at least as far as he was concerned. He loved the hum of equipment, the way that it talked back to him, on the panels, through the sounds, with familiar smells and sights all around.

He liked conversing with every nonhuman thing in engineering. He understood all of it. He even understood the equipment that wasn't in engineering, but fell into his purview, like the *anacapa* drive on the bridge, which gave off a sharp odor reminiscent of hot dust when he ran diagnostics.

He could fit everything in engineering into its place. He knew what the problem was by the manifestation of the problem, and he usually knew the solution. If he couldn't find the problem immediately, he enjoyed the search for the problem. And if the problem didn't have an obvious easy solution, he liked looking for the hard one.

People weren't like that. He tried to convince himself that they were, but it wasn't working. They weren't tidy. Even if the problem was the same (and it seemed to be, dammit, Captain Preemas), the solution never was.

Some people just wanted to vent at Crowe. Others wanted him to reassign them. Still others wanted a new captain, a new mission, a new something.

Crowe was going out of his mind.

He had spent the last day hiding in engineering. None of the crew shifts had occurred in engineering. When Preemas wanted to switch some of the people in engineering to other parts of the ship, Crowe had blocked him. Crowe demanded that he remain in charge of engineering or said he would quit.

This time, Preemas backed down without a fight.

He probably had known just how difficult the transition would be, and the last thing he needed was his first officer fighting him as well.

Engineering was a good place to hide, not just because of the staff, but because of the design. This section of the ship was huge, with equipment everywhere, most of it impossible for visitors to understand at a glance. This particular engineering section had been built with alcoves for various control panels, almost like mini-cockpits, so that anyone working in engineering could have privacy.

Other engineering sections on other ships he'd worked in were one large room, with a few designated workstations. This one was designed so that you couldn't see all of its parts as you stood in the door.

He liked that. He even knew the reason for the unusual design.

SC-Class vessels were security ships, and often transported dangerous and difficult people from one place to another. In the Fleet's long history, sometimes those people escaped or lied their way into engineering. In a few cases, they had tampered with the equipment in the few minutes they were alone, before they got caught.

So, the SC-Class vessels (and the prison transports), had a non-intuitive design, particularly for critical systems. It meant that no one could run into engineering, find what they were looking for, and sabotage it within minutes of arrival.

It meant that Crowe could find privacy to work.

Or so he thought.

He had been working deep in the room, working on a problem with the foldspace travel plan to get the *Renegat* to that Scrapheap when Yusef Kabac found him.

Of course Kabac had been able to find Crowe relatively easily, because he had worked in engineering all over the Fleet before his demotion.

Kabac had always been an untidy man. His clothing always looked like he had picked it off the floor rather than from his closet. His hair rose around his head as if he were hanging upside down in zero-G. But when he had served with Crowe, Kabac had been clean-shaven.

Now he sported a beard that looked as bristly as the rest of his hair. Only his dark eyes and large nose rose above the beard. He smelled like he hadn't showered in days, and his clothes looked like he had lived in them.

In the close quarters of the communications alcove, Kabac's stench was eye-watering.

"It was your idea, wasn't it?" Kabac said without any introduction at all. No hello, no sorry-to-bother-you. Just that aggressive, blaming question, preceded by the stink.

Crowe was actually trapped against the wall. He would have to slide sideways to get away from Kabac.

"If you're referring to the crew changes," Crowe said in his most level voice, "then no, they weren't my idea at all. I didn't find out about them until the day before the announcement."

"Then you could have stopped it," Kabac said.

"I tried." Crowe wasn't lying. He knew that the changes would strain the relationships on the *Renegat*, and he thought that was a bad idea.

But Preemas had argued that the relationships were already strained by incompetence and inefficiency, and he actually had a point.

"I am not captain," Crowe said. "And as Captain Preemas likes to remind me, his word is law on this vessel."

"You could have at least moved me back to engineering," Kabac said, eyes glittering.

Kabac's audacity made Crowe's breath catch. Crowe knew Kabac hadn't forgotten the demotion. Apparently, Kabac thought that demotion meant nothing. Or perhaps, he thought he had more skills than anyone currently in engineering.

The level of delusion in this man was unbelievably high.

So, this time, Crowe decided to lie. "Again, Yusef. I had no say in the crew changes, no matter how hard I argued."

Kabac clenched his left fist and started to swing it toward the wall. Crowe caught Kabac's fist with his right hand.

"Engineering, remember?" Crowe said lightly, as if he didn't want to take Kabac's hand and twist it off his stupid arm. Didn't Kabac realize he had been about to slam his fist into a critical system?

Kabac pulled his fist out of Crowe's grasp. "I think you told him about me," Kabac said. "I think you told him that you didn't like me."

Kabac had gone off some kind of mental deep end.

"I didn't," Crowe said, and that was true. Preemas had moved Kabac to systems maintenance, which generally meant that he would run diagnostics and make sure the robotic equipment—what little there was on the *Renegat*—remained in working order.

The assignment was a real downfall for someone who had as much engineering training as Kabac did. If Crowe had been given that assignment, he would have been angry too.

"I'll admit," Kabac said, as if he hadn't heard Crowe at all, "that navigation wasn't my strong suit. It was where they moved me after retraining. Math skills, computers, systems, you'd think I'd be able to do that even without a computer backup, but I wasn't as good as I wanted to be. I am admitting that."

Maybe the repetition was coming from the fact that he looked like he hadn't slept since the announcements.

"But I was good in engineering. I was the best guy you had, and you know it." Kabac leaned into Crowe and pointed a finger at him. "You only demoted me because the others were jealous."

Was that how Kabac dealt with the demotion? By lying to himself? That seemed like a terrible strategy, but then, Kabac was all about terrible strategies. That might even have been the name of his engineering career.

Crowe decided diplomacy was the best route for him, not confronting Kabac with the truth. The stench of the man was making Crowe's eyes water, and the faster he cleared Kabac from the alcove, the better.

"Unfortunately," Crowe said, "I had no say in any of the staffing changes, not even in engineering."

"You argued for me, though, right?" Kabac asked.

It took all of Crowe's strength to keep from letting his surprise show. "I argued a lot with the captain," Crowe said, leaving off the fact that he hadn't argued for Kabac at all. Crowe hadn't even mentioned the man's name. "It did no good."

"Then I'll argue with him," Kabac said. "You can't protect him forever."

Crowe almost said, *I'm not protecting him*, but decided that sounded too defensive.

"May I give you some advice on how to handle the captain?" Crowe said.

Kabac blinked at him, clearly derailed by that sentence. Apparently, Kabac had thought Crowe would try to convince him not to talk to the captain.

"Sure." Kabac sounded a little surprised. "Yeah. Of course. What?"

"Wear your uniform," Crowe said. "Look your best. Maybe shave. Look like you belong in the officer corps."

That last might have gone too far. Kabac's eyes narrowed, and then he nodded.

"I thought Captain Preemas was a radical. I thought he didn't like uniforms and order like that," Kabac said.

That was actually an accurate assessment, at least as far as Crowe was concerned. But he didn't say that.

Instead, Crowe said, "Captain Preemas is a radical when it comes to staffing and running a ship. But he appreciates the little gestures of respect as much as the rest of us."

And he probably wouldn't appreciate having his eyes water by being so close to another crew member. Crowe was breathing shallowly, and that wasn't helping at all.

"Good thought." Kabac slapped Crowe on the shoulder once, a gesture of camaraderie. "I knew you were on my side."

And then Kabac left the alcove—or rather, his body did. His stench remained.

Crowe waited a few minutes, then peered around the alcove's side. No sign of Kabac.

So Crowe set the environmental controls to scrub the air as quickly as they could.

What an idiot. And the *Renegat* was stuck with a number of people just like him. Sacrificeable, apparently. They should simply have been removed from ship duty altogether.

Crowe let out a breath, then headed for his own cabin. He would wash his face, maybe even change his clothes after that. And while he did so, he would think about other solutions.

Because his meeting with Kabac wasn't the worst meeting he had had since the change. It was the most delusional, however.

Crowe needed to investigate how well the *Renegat* would run without the full crew compliment. Maybe they could shed some of the dissatisfied before the *Renegat* entered foldspace for the first time.

He would take a quick look at that, and if it looked possible, he would talk to Preemas.

Because some of these people shouldn't be on a ship at all, and, Crowe suspected, the *Renegat* would be better off without them.

THE *RENEGAT*

Preemas agreed to see Crowe that evening, in the captain's quarters. Crowe had never seen captain's quarters on an SC-Class vessel. These quarters weren't as elaborate as the quarters on a DV-Class ship. Everything was smaller, including the living area. It wasn't really built for meetings the way that the living area in the captain's quarters on a DV-Class vessel was.

But there was a captain's command closet here, just like there was on a DV-Class vessel.

Preemas had let Crowe in and then had gone to the small kitchen, setting mugs of coffee on a tray. Crowe waited near the door, just behind the small kitchen, looking at everything.

The quarters were smaller, yes, but they also felt more claustrophobic.

The ceiling was several inches lower here than in most DV-Class captain's quarters, and the living area seemed composed of the kitchen, a dining table pushed against the wall with screens that mimicked portals, and doors, everywhere.

The doors to the two bedrooms were on opposite sides of the room, and a door to the only bathroom in the entire apartment was near the kitchen. Not to mention a fourth door, barely outlined in the wall—almost impossible to see if you didn't know where it was—which was pushed up against the kitchen.

That door had to be the one that went to the captain's command closet. Crowe knew that because it was in the SC-Class vessel's specs, although he hadn't been requested to maintain the command closet.

On a DV-Class vessel, the closet wasn't really a closet. It was another room with a command console. The captain could take over all of the bridge functions from his command area in his quarters.

It wasn't an ideal setup, but it worked in an emergency, which was what it was designed for.

Given the specs of the captain's quarters on this ship, that command closet had to be the size of a bathroom in an officer's quarters, barely big enough for one person to move and do what he needed to do.

The entire captain's suite was claustrophobic and badly designed. Not comfortable at all.

"You gonna stand there or join me?" Preemas asked as he moved the mugs from the tray to the small table. He set the tray on the third chair, then sat down with his back to the shut-down screens. At least they weren't reflective in here.

Crowe came deeper into the room. It smelled of coffee and peppermint—Preemas's drink. Crowe sat down. The chair wasn't even comfortable. It was hard, and curved oddly against his back.

The coffee didn't seem like it had come from a pot, so Preemas had been using the dispenser, which was a good thing, since Crowe was particular about his coffee. And it looked like Preemas might have gotten the coffee right. It was the correct light tan color, indicating the proper mixture of cream and vanilla.

"We have a lot of disgruntled people," Crowe said, deciding to start with the understatement.

"Oh, I'm aware of that," Preemas said. "I expected it."

"Many of them are really angry," Crowe said.

"Yup." Preemas didn't even seem surprised. "You appear to be calming them, though."

"Some," Crowe said. "Some won't calm no matter what."

As he said that, he realized how very tired he was. He didn't like dealing with people, particularly stressed and upset people. Especially when the problems they were having were not problems he had created, although the problems were ones he had to defend.

He shook his head a little. "The situation seems untenable to me. I have no real idea what we'll do. I wish we could replace the whole crew and start again."

Preemas picked up his mug and slurped the coffee. Crowe winced. Preemas grinned. Clearly the man liked baiting him.

"Technically, we can't," Preemas said. "But they can leave of their own accord."

Crowe had been reaching for his mug, but he stopped mid-movement. "They can?"

Preemas nodded. "I was never told that the crew had to stay against their will."

Crowe felt a quick surge of anger, followed by admiration, topped with annoyance. He was pretty sure there were other emotions involved as well, but he couldn't identify them.

Damn Preemas. He had planned this all along.

"That's why some people are still in the wrong jobs," Crowe said softly.

Preemas shrugged. "You told them that there aren't enough of the right jobs to go around. I thought that was a great cover story."

It wasn't a cover story if that was the only option. But apparently it hadn't been. Crowe remembered that Newark had mentioned leaving the ship in her meeting with them.

So what are you going to do? Leave me on a starbase somewhere? she had asked after being told she was losing her position.

And Preemas had let out a sound that Crowe had thought was a grunt of surprise. But maybe it had been something else. Maybe it had been the sound of a man whose plan had been discovered.

He had recovered quickly, then told Crowe that they needed to schedule a stop at Sector Base Z. Crowe had told him that it wasn't possible with the foldspace plan that the vice admirals had given them, and Preemas had told him to revamp the plan.

Setting up one final stop at Sector Base Z, ostensibly for supplies.

Preemas was the most manipulative person Crowe had ever met. And he had scheduled the entire crew reorganization for the ten days before the sector base stop. Ten days was long enough for each person to try their new position and decide if they liked it or hated it.

Ten days was long enough for the other people on the ship to force someone out, if they had the option of leaving.

"You did this on purpose," Crowe said.

"Of course I did," Preemas said. "We had this discussion. The ship's crew is more efficient now that it was when we came on board."

"That's not what I meant," Crowe said.

"Oh?" Preemas asked. He sounded innocent, but a glimpse of his eyes told a different story. They smiled. He was proud of himself.

"You're stopping at the base, not for supplies, but to let people leave. And they'll do it because they don't like how you're running the ship." Crowe shook his head. "What if you lose good people? Competent people?"

"Like you?" Preemas asked.

"You want me to leave?" Crowe asked. To his surprise, his stomach twisted at the thought. He had settled into the *Renegat.* He actually liked the dual role he was playing, even though it had forced him to deal with upset people for the past several days.

"Not at all," Preemas said. "But I'll take the risk of losing some good people to get rid of a whole bunch of…shall we say…baggage?"

"And replace them with what?" Crowe asked. "This ship can run with a couple hundred people, but not efficiently and well. I thought you wanted to complete the mission and show Vice Admiral Gão that you are captain material for a DV-Class ship."

"Or maybe I just like a challenge," Preemas said.

"That too," Crowe said. "But you want to crush this mission. You want to succeed even though they want you to fail."

Preemas's expression changed rapidly just like it had those other times. He had looked joyful a moment before, and now he was extremely serious.

"They don't want me to fail," Preemas said. "They believe I *will* fail. They think it's dangerous to travel backwards at all. And to travel that far backwards? They think it's impossible. They know intellectually that we're heading into populated sectors, but they believe that those sectors are filled with warmongers and other dangers we can't foresee. So they didn't give us the right tools to go back there. We're a sop to some admiral. I'm guessing Admiral Hallock. She wants to get rid of the Scrapheap program."

Crowe frowned. "What does that have to do with us?"

"If we fail at this mission, then the Fleet will believe that it can't defend its Scrapheaps, so there's no point in littering the entire universe with disabled ships that we're no longer paying attention to. The Fleet will have to come up with some other way of dealing with them." Preemas sipped his coffee this time.

"Like blowing them up," Crowe said.

Preemas nodded.

"Our failure benefits Admiral Hallock," he said. "Our success might actually change the Fleet. It might change the way that the entire Fleet operates. It might actually look at the way it discards good people, like you, First Officer Crowe."

Crowe tensed. "I haven't been discarded."

"No? They sent you on this mission, didn't they?"

The words hung between them. Crowe liked to think he'd been sent on this mission because he had seen what happened when something went wrong in a Scrapheap.

But he couldn't lie to himself the way Kabac did. Crowe had also been sent along because he had no family, and very few friends outside of the engineering departments. No one would mourn him if he died.

"We change out a good third of the crew, and we have a shot of completing this mission, First Officer Crowe." Preemas emphasized *First Officer Crowe* as he spoke, the emphasis adding just the right amount of sarcasm. "Especially when another third of the crew has been moved into the correct jobs for their skill sets."

"I still don't know what you plan to do with an understaffed ship," Crowe said. He wasn't sure he wanted to travel the distance the Fleet expected them to travel without the full crew on board the *Renegat.*

"I've been researching the potential crew members at Sector Base Z," Preemas said. "I'm going to make offers to quite a few people. My wish list is long. Would you like to see it?"

Was that why Crowe had been brought here? To see the personnel that Preemas wanted to bring on board?

"You can't approach them right away." Crowe didn't answer the question. "And I'll be honest. I think the Fleet got one thing right. I don't think anyone with close family ties should be on this mission."

"I don't either," Preemas said. "That's why my list only contains young people who want to leave Z-City. They're ambitious, and they want to see the universe. Trust me on that one. Land-based people working for the Fleet often want to see the stars."

Crowe knew that. He'd grown up planet-bound. He'd applied to the best schools hoping they would send him to a school ship. The openings in those ships were limited, especially for the planet-bound. He had been both lucky enough and talented enough to get a berth.

But he had known other kids who had also had skills who hadn't had the same kind of luck.

"You have to be honest with them about the nature of this mission," Crowe said.

"Why?" Preemas said. "The Fleet wasn't honest with us."

Crowe hated it when Preemas exaggerated. "The Fleet was honest with you."

Preemas grinned. "I figured it out for myself. Gão prides herself on her honesty. So when I challenged her, she admitted what kind of mission it was. Didn't change my mind any."

"It might change some of theirs," Crowe said.

"There are a million ways to let the possible recruits know that this mission is dangerous," Preemas said. "One way is to tell them they might not see their home and family again, because of foldspace travel. Another way is to tell them that they might not see the Fleet again for years and years. That'll make some people balk."

He sounded as if he were speaking from experience. Maybe he was. Crowe had no idea.

All Crowe knew was that as a young man—before the incident at the Scrapheap—he would have ignored every one of those warnings.

He might have ignored those warnings after the incident as well.

"You're taking quite a gamble," he said to Preemas.

"No more than the gamble that we're already taking," Preemas said. "I suspect I'm improving our odds of survival greatly, depending of course on who leaves and who stays."

Preemas had a point. Better to have a few hand-picked people on the ship to go with the good ones they managed to keep than it was to have the disgruntled and the truly awful make this mission even more difficult.

"There's no way to guarantee that the worst of the worst leave?" Crowe was thinking of Kabac.

"No," Preemas said. "I can't force them to leave. Gão would know. She told me that she will judge this mission not just on its success, but how we achieved the success. She believes that the way any mission operates is as important as achieving the goal of the mission."

Preemas shook his head as if the very thought of discounting a successful mission because of the way it was achieved was a stupid way to work.

Crowe felt his stomach tighten. He agreed with Vice Admiral Gão. How success was achieved mattered as much as the success itself.

And yet he was here, with Preemas, on the *Renegat*, talking about manipulating the system.

Preemas picked up his mug of coffee and cradled it against his chest. "If Gão thinks I deliberately countermanded her orders, she'll probably be pissy."

Crowe would be. Part of him already was. This entire situation made him uncomfortable.

"So," he said slowly, "it's better that you manipulate your way around her orders."

He wasn't really asking a question, but Preemas nodded as if Crowe had asked him one.

"Yes, it's better." Preemas spoke with great confidence.

Crowe's eyes narrowed. He was walking a fine line here, between listening to his captain and trying to be the best officer possible. He could step up now and stop all of this. He could contact Vice Admiral Gão and tell her that Preemas was circumventing her orders.

Crowe could also tell her that he changed the staff assignments.

But he didn't really want to. There was a large part of him that found this entire mission to be a great challenge. He hadn't felt this excited about the technical part of a mission since—well, since he had been a boy and had the bright idea to see a Scrapheap up close.

And that precedent did not bode well.

Still, he couldn't quite let Preemas's strange way of manipulating the crew go. "What if I tell Vice Admiral Gão all the ways you circumvented her orders?"

Preemas's expression changed. He suddenly seemed wary. "You won't stay on the ship."

Crowe was not surprised by Preemas's answer. Apparently Preemas didn't like being crossed.

"And what if I tell her when we get back?" Crowe asked.

Preemas raised his eyebrows, then broke into laughter. "After a successful mission, with the right crew? Go ahead, First Officer Crowe. Tell her. The order of events will make it your word against mine. And I will have the added benefit of completing an impossible mission to bolster my side. Yours might simply be sour grapes."

Preemas had a point. If Crowe was going to tell Vice Admiral Gão anything, he had to do so before the mission. If the *Renegat* did not complete the mission, then what Preemas did wouldn't matter, except maybe to the usual completists who always wanted to find out why a particular mission succeeded or failed.

If the *Renegat* did complete the mission, the success would mean a great deal for everyone. For the members of the crew whose careers had been on a downward slide, the success might make them promotable, might give them another chance to move forward in the Fleet. For the rest, who had been moved to different assignments, it might open up an entirely new career path.

And there was even more that could come out of a successful mission here. The Fleet itself might review how it handled people who didn't always fit into the neat organizational plans—people like Preemas himself. People like Crowe. People whose brains didn't work in a linear fashion, but managed to come up with something better by working problems from three dimensions instead of two.

Maybe all of that was what was exciting Crowe. Maybe he wanted to stay on this ship because, for the first time in a long time, he felt challenged. Not just because he was doing a new job as well as his old one, but also because he couldn't predict what would happen next.

"Nothing to say?" Preemas asked.

This was the moment. This was the only remaining chance Crowe had to stand up for the values the Fleet claimed were the most important ones for its mission.

But, if the Fleet really had wanted this mission to succeed, it would have sent a DV-Class vessel. Maybe more than one.

Preemas was right: this wasn't just a suicide mission. This was a mission designed to fail on every single level.

"First Officer Crowe?" Preemas said, leaning forward. "You look like you have something to add. I'm giving you permission to do so."

Crowe spun his mug, watching the coffee inside swirl. "You believe Admiral Hallock will use a failure for her own purposes. But wouldn't it be wiser—and less costly—to say that it's impossible to deal with a Scrapheap so far away, and then use the so-called emergency to change policy? Why, exactly, are they sending us on this mission?"

Preemas reached out and stopped Crowe from twirling the mug. Finally, Crowe had irritated Preemas, and hadn't even meant to.

"I wondered about that," Preemas said. "I gave it a lot of thought, in fact. And then I realized one thing."

He paused dramatically, like he often did. Which irritated Crowe to no end.

"You're assuming," Preemas said, "that the loss of us would be costly to the Fleet. But we're not valued. If anything, we're costly when we remain in the Fleet. Getting rid of us—all of us on this ship—one by one isn't easy. It requires evaluations and procedures and panels and agreements. At what point does each person on this ship cost more in management time than we generate doing our jobs?"

Crowe sat very still. He hadn't thought of that at all. And yet, here he was, talking with Preemas about managing difficult people on the *Renegat*. In fact, almost everything Crowe and Preemas had done since Crowe became first officer was make staffing decisions.

"For the cost of one ship," Preemas said, "five hundred problems leave the Fleet, maybe never to return. If we do return, we will bring success with us. In theory, we will cease to be problems. If we return and have solved the Scrapheap issue, we've become valuable. Do you see the calculation?"

Crowe wanted to say that such a calculation wasn't possible, that they were dealing with human beings, after all, and no one would think that way.

But he knew better. He had seem the same calculation in action when he had stolen that ship and cost eleven of his friends their lives—not to mention all those lives on the *Brazza Two*.

Even though he had been the mastermind, even though he had *directly* caused an incident that resulted in serious damage and major loss of life, the Fleet decided he was worth saving. Some of the other kids on his ship, kids who had just been following his orders and who had survived, hadn't been as lucky. They weren't allowed to move forward with their education. They were kicked off the school ships and sent elsewhere.

"You're being awfully quiet, First Officer Crowe," Preemas said. "Is my argument making sense or am I just filling the air with sound?"

Crowe slid his mug closer. The coffee was separating from the cream. It no longer looked appetizing.

"You're making sense," Crowe said. He set the mug aside. "But there's one flaw in your reasoning."

Preemas leaned back in his chair as if he wanted to move away from Crowe's argument—whatever it was going to be.

"What's that?" Preemas asked.

"When we pick up people on Sector Base Z," Crowe said, "we will be taking people who have value to the Fleet. We will suddenly change their calculations."

Preemas nodded. He apparently had already thought of that. "And then, First Officer Crowe, we leave Sector Base Z, and immediately take our first foldspace leg. If the Fleet wants to, they can send someone after us."

"You're gambling that they won't," Crowe said.

"I know that they won't," Preemas said. "Land-based people aren't worth much to the Fleet either. Think how many land-based families we leave behind every single year. Whenever a sector base closes, everyone gets to choose whether to stay or to move to the next sector base. They don't get to choose whether or not they want to serve on a ship."

Crowe sat very still. He hadn't thought of that, but it was true.

"The Fleet values its *ships*, First Officer Crowe," Preemas said. "That's why we have trouble destroying them. But we close bases all the time. There's a contempt for the land-based folks. You should know that. You were raised on land."

Crowe met Preemas's gaze. It was unreadable. Crowe couldn't tell if Preemas was baiting him, letting him know that he wasn't worth much to Preemas and to the Fleet, or if Preemas was just stating a fact.

"We're going to be fine," Preemas said. "If they want to send someone after us, great. If they want to verbally reprimand us when we come out of foldspace, fine. It won't matter because we won't be turning around, and they won't order us to."

Crowe had a hunch Preemas was right about that.

"You watch," Preemas said. "They won't say a word. Because our contact is Gão, and she knows the limitations. She's under orders to get us to that Scrapheap. She'll discipline us when we get back, if we get back. Otherwise, she's going to let me make all the mistakes I can possibly make. If anything, us taking on crew that she hasn't approved gives her a strong argument that I've gone rogue.

She'll make that argument if we fail. I'd say watch for that, but if we fail, then we won't be around to see the argument she makes, so it won't matter to us."

Crowe sat very still. Preemas seemed rational. But sometimes, when he made arguments like this, he made Crowe as uncomfortable as Kabac did. Were the two men equally delusional? And how could Crowe tell?

"You're hard to read, First Officer Crowe," Preemas said. "Do you approve? Disapprove?"

Crowe decided he wasn't going to let Preemas know, exactly. If Crowe remained hard to read, then he had an advantage. For what, he didn't know. But he might need that advantage going forward.

"Does it matter whether I approve or disapprove?" Crowe asked. "You're moving ahead with this plan."

"I want to know if I should continue to consult with you," Preemas said.

"We've already had that discussion," Crowe said. "I'm your first officer."

"For good or ill," Preemas said with a grin. "Like a marriage, apparently."

If that was how he wanted to see it, Crowe wouldn't disabuse him of that notion.

When Crowe didn't say anything, Preemas's grin widened. He looked like he had just won at some game. Crowe wasn't exactly sure what that game would be.

"All right then," Preemas said. "You need more coffee?"

Crowe clearly didn't. He hadn't touched the original cup.

"I'm fine," he said.

"You might want to rethink that," Preemas said. "You're going to be here a while."

Crowe frowned.

Preemas stood and walked to the counter in the kitchen. He pulled a tablet off of it.

Crowe hadn't seen Preemas use an actual physical tablet before. Preemas had always used a networked holoscreen, at least in Crowe's presence.

Preemas tapped the tablet on. The screen blinked open, but didn't create a holoimage. Instead it remained flat, and lit from behind.

Preemas approached Crowe, and then held out the tablet.

"I want you to look at my wish list from Sector Base Z," Preemas said. "Tell me if you agree or disagree with my choices."

"On the tablet," Crowe said.

Preemas nodded.

"You want me to change them or mark them in any way?" Crowe asked. "Because I'll need access."

"I have it set up so that you can tap yes or no," Preemas said.

"But not lay out my reasoning," Crowe said.

"I don't care about your reasoning," Preemas said. "If I can't figure out your objection on my own, I'll ask you."

"Because you want me to stay here while I do it, right?" Crowe asked.

"Yes," Preemas said. "This tablet doesn't leave my quarters."

The words hung between them for a moment. Preemas wanted deniability. He didn't want anyone to know he had already found replacements for crew members who weren't off the ship yet.

But why? Because he was afraid of being caught? Or was this the long game? Was Preemas doing this for the day he returned, the successful captain who completed an impossible mission?

"I suppose this list only exists on this tablet," Crowe said.

"You catch on quick, First Officer Crowe," Preemas said.

"And if I delete the list?" Crowe asked.

Preemas's hand tightened on the tablet. He looked annoyed.

"You ask a lot of questions about thwarting me," Preemas said.

"I like to know all the contingencies before I start," Crowe said. "Besides, I might accidentally delete the list."

"You, the most talented engineer I've ever seen." Preemas made a dismissive sound.

"Everyone screws up now and then," Crowe said.

"I'm sure they do," Preemas said. "But not you. Not anymore."

That was mostly true. If Crowe made a mistake, it was a small one or it was connected to a misunderstanding of the human beings around him. He rarely made technical errors.

He was probably too cautious these days.

Or he had been, before he became Preemas's first officer.

"Wish list," Crowe repeated.

"Yes," Preemas said.

Crowe took the tablet.

"You want coffee?" Preemas asked.

"I'll get it when I'm ready," Crowe said, already looking at the list of names in front of him. The number in the right hand corner told him he had three hundred names to go through.

Names and short resumes. If he touched a name, he got the summary. If he wanted more, he had to tap twice.

He looked up at Preemas, who was still watching him closely.

"If you want me to go over this carefully," Crowe said, "I'll be here for hours."

"I know," Preemas said.

"I have duties," Crowe said.

Preemas grinned, and then the grin faded as if it had never been. Those shifting expressions were eerie.

"This is more important than anything else we can do right now," Preemas said. "If we pick the right people, this mission will succeed."

Which meant if they picked the wrong people, the mission would fail.

Crowe's grip tightened on the tablet. He didn't want the mission to fail, any more than Preemas did.

It was beginning to gall Crowe that the Fleet wanted them all to screw up. He hated the idea that they had already been written off.

No wonder Preemas wanted this so badly. He wanted to prove that this ship of misfits and fools was actually worth something.

And he was right: if they picked the best possible crew, they had a good chance of success.

Whatever that meant.

PART SEVEN
THE RESCUE
NOW

THE *RENEGAT*

Zarges turned on the light on the top of his helmet, kept his knuckle lights on, but shut off the lights on his palm and the bottom of his boots.

The corridor in the old SC-Class vessel was dark. But as he passed doors, he realized that the team had entered the ship right-side up for the interior design.

Which was good. He always hated reorienting himself.

The corridor to Engineering looked wider in the darkness than it did on the specs. He turned right, just like he was supposed to, and pushed through the wider corridor.

He was probably moving too fast. But he couldn't slow down entirely. Some of that was his elevated heart rate, and some of it was the small clock he had installed under his right eye. He had to keep track of time, because he knew they didn't have a lot of it.

Lights bobbled behind him, letting him know that Iqbar and Palmer were close. Technically, Iqbar should have gone ahead of him, even here, but Zarges didn't care.

He wanted to slow down and examine the ship around him. There was a lot more damage inside than he expected. The walls had holes in various places, and because the lights were so dim, he couldn't tell if those holes had come from weapons' fire or from some kind of internal deterioration.

If he had to guess, he would go for deterioration. Bits and pieces of ship floated around him—the occasional tool, a glove, a cup. Silverware had gone by too, which shouldn't be on this level at all, if he was near Engineering. At least, not on any Fleet-run ship he had been part of.

Food did not belong on the Engineering level and neither did most personal items. There was too much open equipment here—or the possibility of half-open containers with dangerous items inside—for anything small to be nearby, because of moments just like this one. When the gravity shut down, small items got tangled in everything.

He batted a fork away from his arm (and tried not to think about those prongs puncturing his suit), and continued forward. Either the ship's gravity had been off longer than a few hours or the ship was not being run according to Fleet protocols.

Or both.

He had to assume that the gravity had been off for longer than a few hours and prepare for someone else running the ship, both at the same time. That niggling worry he had had at first, the one concerning the size of the crew, came back. Maybe there were two hundred immobile life signs because people were dying, and another hundred or two crew members were already dead.

By now, Khusru and her team should have arrived on the *Renegat* and started their trek to the bridge. She hadn't come onto the comm either to discuss bodies or anything out of the ordinary.

Although none of them would discuss small, disquieting things, like silverware on the Engineering level.

He finally reached Engineering proper. The doors were open, which was against protocol. But then he realized that the exterior control panel had been destroyed. The doors might have been stuck open.

He peered at the control panel. It had been reconfigured. From what he could tell, the damage to the panel might have been caused by someone *inside* of Engineering, not from someone outside of it.

He glanced over his shoulder at the wall on the far side of the corridor. He thought he saw black slashes along it, burn marks, but he wasn't close enough to tell.

He lifted his head, saw Iqbar looking at the same marks he was looking at. She shrugged. He did too.

They couldn't solve the mystery of the *Renegat* at the moment. At the moment, they had to figure out how to save lives.

He entered Engineering as if he knew exactly where he was going. The interior glowed blue. The emergency lighting worked in this section, which meant that the power system was triaging. Only important areas were getting any kind of emergency power at all.

He changed the specs to Engineering only, and superimposed a clear image over what he could see through his hood. The general control panel was deeper inside Engineering, in an alcove behind some of the equipment.

Not logical, but then, a lot of the Fleet's smaller ships did not have a logical build, especially in ships that didn't have the array of defensive equipment and weaponry that a DV-Class vessel had.

He propelled himself toward the alcove, careful to avoid equipment jutting out at him. He was having trouble identifying what it all was in the weird lighting.

There were no sharp edges on Fleet ships (at least the ships he was familiar with), partly for moments just like this. The rounded edges made sure nothing punctured an environmental suit. But banging something too hard could still damage a suit. He didn't want to become part of the emergency himself.

The bobbing lights had faded in the blueness, but he didn't look back to see if Iqbar and Palmer had kept up with him. He assumed they had. He wondered if they were as unsettled as he was.

He couldn't see well enough in the blue light to know if anything had been displaced or even stolen out of Engineering. He maneuvered his way around another corner, and slowed as he reached the alcove.

At that moment, Iqbar reached his side. Palmer was just behind her.

Zarges nodded at both of them, and continued forward.

The alcove was exactly where it was supposed to be, with enough room for all three members of his team. He took the center panel, and they took the side panels.

The center panel looked like it was not functioning at all. He put his glove on the surface, hoping that perhaps codes would work or perhaps his identification as a member of the Fleet.

The panel sputtered to life. For a moment it glowed red—caution lights everywhere—and then they faded out, leaving only a pale white glow around a few of the command functions.

The illustrations were older—clearly from another era. And try as he might, he couldn't get the virtual screen working. He would have to do any work on the control panel itself.

He ran his glove along the edge, hoping to funnel more energy into the panel.

"Is your panel working?" Iqbar asked through their team comm link.

"Barely," Zarges said.

"Mine isn't working at all," Palmer said. Without being asked, he dove beneath the panels and opened the controls from underneath. "It's getting power. There just isn't enough to operate this equipment."

Iqbar activated the gravity on her boots, so that she could crouch beside him. She handed him a short-term energy pack from her belt. Zarges waited in front of the main panel.

The team had done this drill a hundred times, but never on a ship this old, and never under this kind of time crunch.

Still, they worked like it was an everyday mission. Calmly. In control.

The panel powered to life in front of him, nearly blinding him with the layers of red, blaring everywhere.

"Got it," he said.

"There's a flaw in the system," Palmer said. "Something's draining the energy at double time. That means we only have two hours, tops."

"If we're still here two hours from now, we've failed." Zarges didn't like the red. "Dorthea, I need you over here."

Iqbar stood beside him, and gasped. He had never heard her gasp during a mission before. If he had been asked just a few moments ago, he would have said that of all of them, Iqbar was the most unflappable.

Her hand hovered over the panel, as if she was afraid to touch it.

"What do you need me to do?" she asked.

"Help me figure out which of these caution lights is the most critical." But just as he said it, he saw which of the lights was the most critical.

Something was wrong with the *anacapa* drive.

He touched that caution light, and, for once, the virtual screen appeared. It had even more caution lights and something he had never seen in a ship this large—an ice-blue flare.

Evacuate immediately.

"What the hell?" Iqbar asked.

"Someone's tampered with the *anacapa* drive," he said.

"I see that," she said. "But it's not—"

"Looks like they started it incorrectly, then taxed it. If I could figure out what they did, then maybe—"

"That's not reversible." Palmer spoke from behind him. He was leaning over Zarges's shoulder.

The reason Palmer had gone under the control panels was that he was the most adept at handling unfamiliar equipment. He could process information faster than anyone else Zarges had ever worked with.

"Can we forestall it?" Zarges asked. "Maybe buy ourselves more time?"

"Maybe," Palmer said. "I think we're better served getting everyone off this ship, and getting as far away from it as possible."

Zarges was afraid he would say that. "I'll let the other teams know they're on point. Dorthea, contact the *Aizsargs*. Tell them that they're going to have to move as far away from this ship as possible."

"Yes, sir." Iqbar toggled her comm system so that she contacted the *Aizsargs* directly.

Zarges contacted Khusru.

"Sufia," he said, "we have to evacuate. We have an *anacapa* problem. And our timeline just got a lot tighter. This ship isn't going to last much longer."

He didn't want to explain the *anacapa* in depth. It would be too complicated.

"Got it," she said. And he felt a small measure of relief.

She knew what to do. Once she was on the bridge, she would begin evacuation procedures from there. She would also make a shipwide announcement if she could.

After he contacted *Rescue One*, he would see if he could find the shipwide comms from down here.

If Khusru couldn't make the announcement from the bridge, Zarges would make one from Engineering.

It was always better to have an announcement come from the bridge, though. It gave the order more authority, and often guaranteed faster compliance.

They needed fast compliance. They were going to need every single minute they had.

And even then, he wasn't sure they would be able to save everyone.

Just his luck. Another impossible mission.

Because nothing was ever easy in this job.

THE *AIZSARGS RESCUE ONE*

One had just reached the coordinates that Ranaldi had deemed safe when a message came in from Zarges.

Turris opened the comm so the entire cockpit crew could hear Zarges. It saved time. That way, Turris didn't have to repeat the information.

"This ship is critical," Zarges said. "We went to engineering, found most systems already gone, and a seriously malfunctioning *anacapa* drive."

The cockpit crew froze, even though Turris knew none of them were surprised. Ranaldi's gaze met Turris's over the navigation controls. Vail stopped fidgeting, her hands folded.

The cockpit still had a quiet, but it wasn't a mid-rescue quiet. It was that moment of quiet just before everything changed.

"How long will it take to fix the *anacapa?*" Turris asked. He didn't want to send an *anacapa* expert over to the *Renegat.* He needed a stable ship before he did that, and the *Renegat* was anything but stable.

Adeon had already left his post and grabbed an environmental suit out of one of the storage. He wasn't the best expert on the *anacapa* drive, but he was accurate and he was precise. He would be a great assistant.

Turris held up a hand to stop him, though.

"We can't fix it," Zarges said.

"Nonsense," Vail said before Turris could answer. She really wanted to be on that team. "*Anacapa* drives just need to be babied. It looks like this one wasn't shut off—"

"It was tampered with, and then taxed. Someone didn't know what they were doing." Zarges didn't quite sound panicked, but he did sound impatient. "Palmer estimates that we have two hours before the drive explodes. Or whatever it's going to do. We don't know, exactly, because none of us have seen this before."

Vail placed a hand on her console, as if she was prepared to use it to rescue everyone by herself. "We could bring in—"

"No." Turris glared at Vail. She was always trying to fix things. "We have two hundred people to get off that ship. Two hours is barely enough time."

"Exactly," Zarges said. "I've already let Sufia know, and I'll be contacting the *Aizsargs* next. But if you're anywhere near your old position, I suggest moving now. Get as far away as you can and still send out the life rafts. The ship's map we're using seems pretty accurate, so we'll be using the bay doors. We'll let you know more when we know more."

And then he signed off.

Turris felt something in his stomach ease. He had known there was something wrong with the *Renegat*'s *anacapa*. He just hadn't known exactly what it was.

Now that the problem was diagnosed, he could work on solving it.

"Corrado," he said to Ranaldi. "Do we have to move again?"

Ranaldi held up one hand as he moved the other on his console. He had probably started investigating the various positions of the ship the moment Zarges had mentioned two hours.

There was a lot to figure out here. The life rafts only held so many people, and moved very slowly. *Rescue One* only had two life rafts, so the rafts would have to make more than one trip. Their speed factored into this mess, along with the number of bodies that needed rescue.

"Figure three trips per raft," Turris said. "That's probably too many, but just in case…"

"I'm figuring four," Ranaldi said.

"We'd have to be too close for that," Adeon said. "If we get people here only to lose them when the *Renegat* explodes—"

"Then we won't know," Ranaldi said.

Sometimes the fatalism of certain members of his crew irritated Turris more than he wanted to say. He would rather take a risk at pushing them too hard than risk losing people.

"Three," Turris said firmly. He was in charge of this mission, and he had the same concerns that Adeon had. "We'll cram them into the rafts if we have to. Vail, let Zarges know that's the plan."

"Yes, sir," she said, her tone not letting him know either way how she felt about his orders.

Not that he cared. He needed to make sure *Rescue One* was in the right position so that it could save as many people as possible and escape with all of their lives.

"Yeah," Ranaldi said as if someone had asked him a question. He was focused on his work. He probably hadn't even realized that he had spoken aloud about how the crew would feel if everyone they tried to rescue died. "We need to move *Rescue One* again. I've locked in the coordinates."

With the movement of three fingers, Turris executed the command. *Rescue One* moved a little closer to the *Renegat*. He didn't like that, but he knew they only had so much time.

A little under two hours to rescue two hundred people scattered all over a large ship. That was a tall order in five hours. But two. Everyone would have to move quickly, and they would have to be willing to get on board the life rafts rapidly.

When Zarges had initially said he was going, that comment worried Turris.

Now, he was relieved. Khusru and Zarges were the most experienced at this kind of rescue. Maybe Zarges had known how difficult this would be, after all.

Turris let out a small breath. And it might be even more difficult. Because Zarges didn't say whether or not the people on board were supposed to be on board. If they had stolen the ship, then the rescue teams might be in even more trouble.

Turris had piloted a few rescues where the people on board the ship weren't ready to leave, for whatever reason. They had fought the rescue teams, fought getting onto life rafts, tried to escape with the ship—sometimes, people like that had to be subdued.

He hoped his team hadn't encountered anything like that. He hoped they would be all right.

But he couldn't worry about it, except to plan what to do with the strangers who would arrive on the *Rescue One*. He had to keep them isolated while he transported them to the *Aizsargs*.

The rest would be the rescue team's problem.

Turris moved *Rescue One* into place, then looked at the real-time holographic image of the *Renegat*. Part of the grappler's claw was visible sticking out of the ship. It drifted, atmosphere still venting. There were no lights that he could see.

He felt his mood lift. Now that he knew what he had to achieve and how quickly he had to achieve it, he had a sense of purpose.

He knew how to do this.

His team knew how to do this.

They would do it well, and everyone would survive.

Or, as Ranaldi had said, they would never know the difference.

THE *AIZSARGS*

"Why is *Rescue One* moving again?" Dauber asked.

She stood in front of the hologram of the entire area, watching as the *Renegat* still vented atmosphere. The space bridge had been retracted, and *Rescue One* had removed the grappler, then had gone into the nearest safe position.

Dauber had instructed the fighters to back even farther away, since no other ship had come through foldspace. Her bridge crew was busily researching the *Renegat*, but so far had found nothing.

She hated this part of the mission; she had no word from the crew on board the *Renegat*, and now *Rescue One* was moving sideways from its best position.

She had been multitasking before she noticed the movement of *Rescue One*. She'd been monitoring her people inside by watching the small gold dots that represented her team as they worked their way through the old ship. So far, the schematics Ullman had found in the Fleet records matched what Dauber had been seeing.

She hadn't monitored communications in real time, though, because she'd learned long ago that doing so gave her the wrong focus. It made her remember that those gold dots represented human beings she knew and cared about, rather than people upon whom the success or failure of a mission rested.

She couldn't make good decisions, when she remembered that she cared.

Still, she needed to keep an eye on them. And as she did so, she also worked on moving her people around on the *Aizsargs*. She needed to make plans, quite quickly, because 200 people might have to board this ship within the next few hours.

They needed a place to clean up, food, and probably medical attention. She was also going to have to figure out exactly what to do with them. She had just helped close the nearest sector base, after all, so she couldn't just dump them on the base.

She had to make several levels of contingency plans, because she still didn't know if the people on that ship belonged on that ship, or if they were criminals, or what had happened to them.

Brett Ullman had found a crew manifest—he thought. He was having to dig through a lot of sketchy information. But Dauber had him send the manifest to Khusru and Zarges. Maybe if they called the people on that ship by name, they might gain some trust.

Since *Rescue One* was moving away from the *Renegat.* Which meant what, exactly? That no one was worthy of being saved?

"Anyone?" she said because no one had answered her previous question. "Do we know why *Rescue One* is moving?"

Josephine Ornitz had a hand on one ear, something she did when the information coming through her comm was either too loud or too soft. She was still reaching up to work on the console before her, which, considering she'd been doing that for hours, couldn't have been comfortable.

She had been the one who had been monitoring the chatter between *Rescue One* and the team on the *Renegat.*

Her gaze met Dauber's, mouth a thin line.

"*Rescue One* is running into some difficulties," Ornitz said.

"Clearly," Dauber said.

Her sarcasm was lost on Ornitz, who had grown pale.

"They're saying the *anacapa* drive on the *Renegat* is failing. They want us to get as far from the ship as possible. They'll come back to us, if and when they have completed the rescue."

The entire bridge was silent for a half second. If and when. Dauber didn't like the sound of that.

"Did this come from Zarges?" she asked Ornitz.

"From Zarges directly, yes," Ornitz said. "He had been talking to *Rescue One* ahead of us. His message to us was short, sir. He needs us to get out of here now."

Dauber nodded. She took a deep breath. *Anacapa* explosions were scary for surrounding ships. Sometimes they could get sucked into foldspace because of an *anacapa* explosion nearby.

Sometimes, they could explode as well. One exploding *anacapa* drive could set off something in another drive, and that drive could go critical in a matter of seconds.

Even when an *anacapa* went critical and *didn't* explode, the energy waves could still catapult another ship with a similar drive into foldspace, or destroy the other ship's drive.

Dauber knew better than to ask if Zarges could shut down the *anacapa* drive on the *Renegat.* He would have sent a different message if he had thought there was time to save that ship.

If and when.

If.

He wasn't sure he would get anyone off the *Renegat* before it exploded.

But she would act like he was going to.

"Let me see what I can do for that *anacapa* drive," Ribisi said. If anyone could repair an *anacapa* drive, it would be Massai Ribisi. He was the most gifted engineer she knew.

"From a distance," Dauber said. "We're moving the *Aizsargs* as far from the *Renegat* as we can and still provide support to *Rescue One*."

She reached over to Brett Ullman's holoscreen. He'd been researching the *Renegat*. She tapped the screen with her forefinger. The screen vanished.

He looked at her, surprised.

She needed him on navigation right now, not handling data flow.

"Plot the fastest course without using foldspace," she said. "We need to move. Now."

"Yes, sir," he said, and got to work.

THE *RENEGAT*

Serpell felt stupid being on the bridge. What could she do here, anyway? She couldn't do anything. She had been slapping her hand on the console for a long time now. Every once in a while, she'd pause and try to speak some shorthand voice commands she had learned during her time as the person nominally in charge. Those voice commands weren't working either.

Nothing was working. It was dark, it was creepy, the power was gone, the atmosphere was leaking, and her suit was dying. The best thing she could do was save herself. There were escape pods somewhere on this vessel. All she needed was to carry a new environmental suit with her, and she was good to go.

Let Kabac continue frantically slapping panels and cursing the dwindling power. He wasn't asking for her help. He wouldn't want it if she offered it.

He probably wouldn't even notice if she propelled herself out of this bridge, maybe wouldn't even notice if she took one of the escape pods.

So she got off the ship. Then what? A pod with a month, maybe, of life support, as she drifted—where? And what did she know about escape pods anyway? Her training in escape pods had been DV training, nearly a decade ago, before she gave up her career to follow the downward spiral that had been India's lot.

India.

Serpell's heart clenched, and she forced herself to think about something else.

"You know," Kabac said. "You could try to fix something."

Serpell could. And she could fail.

"I'm going for a new suit first," she said. "Do you know of any extras close?"

"I'd be able to find you something if the ship's computers were up and running," he said.

She could have too. They could do anything with computers. That was the beauty of it. That was why she thought the *Renegat* would be able to make the trip back. Hell, the ship did 90% of the work—most of the time.

When the ship was functioning.

Before it had gotten attacked.

A beam of light hit Kabac, outlining his shadow against the dead screen on the wall.

"You did something," Serpell said, feeling excited for the first time. "You got partial lights—"

"That's not me," he said. "I'm not working the lights at the moment."

She would have snapped at him, she *should* have snapped at him, because the lights were part of the environmental system, and if he could fix that, then the atmosphere would return and it would buy them time.

Another light hit him, and then a third. Suddenly light blinded her.

She had to turn sideways to get the light out of her eyes.

"What the hell?" Kabac snapped. He looked up and cursed.

Serpell looked over, saw three people in unfamiliar environmental suits near the entrance to the bridge, glowing in the darkness.

"Captain Preemas?" a woman's voice said. It sounded thin and crackly as if it were coming from very far away.

Serpell glanced at Kabac, but couldn't see his face through his helmet. He was staring at the three people like he couldn't believe they were there.

Serpell couldn't either. They were looking for *Captain Preemas*? He wasn't here. If the woman was part of the crew flying home, she would know that.

"Who are you?" Serpell asked, because Kabac hadn't done anything—not since he'd looked up and cursed. It was as if his brain had stopped working.

"I'm Sufia Khusru," the woman said. Serpell couldn't tell which of the three people was speaking. With the way the lights fell on the environmental suits, Serpell couldn't even tell if all three of the people facing her were women or if only one of them was.

"I'm from the *Aizsargs,*" the woman was saying. "We saw you, saw your distress, and are here to get you off this ship."

Serpell hadn't heard of the *Aizsargs,* but she wasn't sure that meant anything. She wasn't sure she could recite the names of all the ships in the Fleet.

Still, it should have sounded familiar, right?

She swallowed hard. "What's the *Aizsargs*?"

The newcomers glanced at each other, or rather, at the person in the middle. That had to be who was speaking.

"It's a Fleet vessel," the woman said, and she sounded a bit cautious, as if she wasn't sure Serpell would know what the Fleet was. "DV-Class. We have enough room for everyone on board, but we have limited time to get you to our ship."

Fleet vessel. DV-Class. The biggest the Fleet had to offer outside of a few warships—at least these days. Serpell's eyes filled with tears, and she willed them away.

Someone who knew what they were doing. How had that happened? How had they found a Fleet vessel?

"How do we know you're who you say you are?" Kabac said.

The woman held up the palm of her hand and an image flared, showing a woman's face, and something that looked like a file about her and the Fleet.

Serpell had seen such things buried in the personnel files, but never attached to an environmental suit.

"We're with the rescue unit," the woman—Khusru—said. "We need to hurry. And we need to let everyone on the ship know they need to evacuate. We want to use the bridge systems to do that."

"This is too fast," Kabac said. "We don't know who you are—"

"Shut up," Serpell snapped. She didn't care if these people were lying about being Fleet. It didn't matter at all. They had come from outside the *Renegat*, they clearly had a ship, and they were offering rescue. "Control panels aren't working here."

"Cayden can handle that," Khusru said, as if Serpell knew who this Cayden was. Serpell guessed it didn't matter. He—she?—would do what needed to be done anyway.

One of the newcomers detached from the others and entered the bridge. He—?—moved toward the communications panel. The third member headed toward Kabac, who held up his hands like he was trying to stop that person.

"Can we help?" Serpell asked, trying to forestall any crisis. She didn't care what Kabac wanted. Serpell wanted—she *needed*—to get off this ship.

"Get me the captain," Khusru said. "We need him to verify the evacuation."

Serpell's face grew warm. She was trembling. If they were Fleet like they said they were, then they would want to know what happened to him.

"Um." God, Serpell had no idea how to handle this. Not that she had had any idea how to handle any of it in any way all along. "He's not...he's not...a lot of...we're..."

She looked at Kabac who was watching the third new person. Kabac stood near the *anacapa* and that person was heading toward it.

Serpell tried again. "We're...just trying to get home."

"Home?" Khusru asked.

"Back to the Fleet," Serpell said.

"Well," Khusru's tone was all business. "You've done that. Now go to the cargo bay on, I believe, Deck Four. Right? You have a cargo bay on Deck Four?"

Serpell swallowed. Her mouth was dry. Her heart was hammering so hard that she could feel it throughout her system. Maybe that was because the suit was failing, not because she was scared.

"We have a cargo bay on four," she confirmed. "Um, and I don't know how you're getting us out of here, but you should know my suit's failing."

"Are there other suits on board that you could use?" Khusru asked.

"I don't know," Serpell said. "I was just going to look."

"I'd rather have you evacuate than search for a new suit," Khusru said. "Can you make it to Deck Four without assistance?"

Serpell dry-swallowed again, an involuntary movement. God, she was scared.

"Yeah," she said.

"Good. I need both of you off this bridge," Khusru said.

"We have no idea you are who you say you are." Kabac finally found his voice. "We're not leaving the bridge to you."

"Then die with the ship," snapped someone else—another woman. "Because that's what'll happen if you stay here. The problem is, if you don't let us use the comms, the rest of your crew will die too."

"Kabac," Serpell said. "Let's go."

"I'm not leaving the bridge," he said. "I'm the only bridge officer left. It would be wrong—"

"You were demoted," Serpell said, because she felt she had to. "You were asked to leave the bridge before we even made it to the Scrapheap. You are only up here because I needed the help."

The Cayden person wasn't paying attention to anything she was saying. He—?—was doing something to the comm center.

"Arguing won't help anyone," Khusru said. "Our people have determined that this ship will blow, and it'll be an *anacapa*-based explosion. None of us will survive that."

Khusru pushed herself further into the bridge, heading toward Kabac just like the other person had.

"You can choose to stay," Khusru said. "I have no authority over whether or not you evacuate. Only your captain had that, and I assume he's no longer with the ship. So, it's your choice. But stay the hell out of the way of my people."

Serpell didn't want to hear any more. She wasn't cut out for any of this. She wasn't heroic. That was why she had come home in the first place.

She swallowed a third time. Dammit, that was irritating.

"Deck Four, Cargo Bay One," she said. "Someone will be there?"

"My team knows what to do." Khusru's tone alone dismissed Serpell. And Serpell didn't care.

People were here.

They could save her.

She might live after all.

PART EIGHT
CREW ADJUSTMENTS
100 YEARS AGO

Z-CITY

Land made Raina Serpell nervous. It was so solid beneath her feet. She couldn't punch through it and get to another level. She couldn't activate the land or change it or adhere to it with gravity boots.

The city itself catered to the base. The city sprawled out from the base like wedges of a gigantic pie. Each wedge seemed to have a different focus, from stores that catered to the locals in one wedge to several education facilities in another. The wedge that Raina found herself in right now was mostly geared to the transient population that came through the base—ship's crews and short-term engineers and builders—people who really didn't care about Z-City, but just wanted a place to sleep while they were in Sector Base Z.

Her hotel was only a block or so away. It was a structure made of brick, made locally, with carpets on the floors and a gigantic, luxurious bed that made the bunk she shared with India back on the *Renegat* seem like a tabletop.

It was cold here as well. She had to rent a jacket at the hotel, which had an entire clothing rental store behind the main desk. The clothing rental was apparently something most ship crews needed because they weren't trained to think about the environment on any planet they went to.

Instead, they went in environmental suits, did their jobs, and left.

She had a wardrobe back on the ship that she had brought but she had left there. As a linguist, she often stayed planetside for a month or two, getting to know a language.

She had been in and out of planetside living for years. She hadn't liked it.

But she could get used to it, maybe.

India's words from their conversation after Captain Preemas made his announcement kept sliding through Raina's head.

They didn't want you. You could've kept moving up in the Fleet.

Maybe if she stayed here—maybe if *they* stayed here—she could get a promotion. She would end up using her brain, not endangering her body. Perhaps that had always been the appeal of India. India would take the physical risks while allowing Raina the time she needed to think.

India, who wasn't anywhere near Raina at the moment. India had gone bar-hopping with some of her new friends in security, figuring they wouldn't have the time or the chance to get drunk once the *Renegat* was underway again.

At least India was being responsible in that way.

Raina blinked. Her eyes had started tearing the moment she stepped outside the hotel. She liked to think that was because of the chill wind, but she wasn't certain. It might also have been because she had stepped out of the hotel with one purpose in mind: she wanted to see Z-City.

She shoved her hands in the pockets of the thick coat they had given her, sniffled a little, and stepped onto the street. Z-City had some flying vehicles, but none were allowed this close to the Sector Base. In fact, there was a ring around the base beyond which flying vehicles were allowed.

Down here, all that went by on the roads were wheeled and railed vehicles. Most people used underground transport from the parking areas around the ring.

The streets were mostly empty in this part of Z-City except for the visitors from elsewhere. The streets were empty right now because it was the middle of the workday, according to the man from the hotel who helped her find the right coat. She had thought it was the weather. Right now the weather was cold by her standards, but within two months, it would become cold by local standards. So cold, in fact, that most locals didn't go outside for weeks. They would travel underground, using transports and basement entrances.

The fresh air that everyone said they came to land for when they moved off-ship would be completely unavailable (and deadly, he said) during that time.

She had to think about that, because if she left the *Renegat* and stayed in Z-City, she might end up stuck here for the rest of her life, doing linguistic make-work, not being on the cutting edge of language discovery.

She reached the other side of the street and stopped in front of yet another hotel. The sides of this one actually looked like someone had taken rocks and glued them to a wall. She supposed that was some kind of design, but she didn't understand why it even existed.

She gazed down the street, saw more nonuniform buildings, all of which caught her eye and made her very uncomfortable.

She had grown up on a ship. Ships were regulation for a reason. You didn't have to think about what the walls around the next corner would look like. You *knew*. Just like you knew what your cabin would look like. You could personalize it a little, but the retractable furniture, the surfaces, the floor, it was all the same level to level, room to room.

This, where everything was different, made her tense. She sniffled again, knowing that some of the tension came from the decision she was sneaking around.

If she stayed, she lost India forever. And Raina might not gain anything. India had said that the Fleet would have promoted Raina had she stayed off the *Renegat*, but she hadn't stayed off the *Renegat*. She had accepted that assignment.

If she abandoned the ship here, would that reflect badly on her? Would that label her as difficult a crew member as India? Or maybe even worse?

Raina sniffled a third time. Her eyes were burning from the cold. She shoved her hands deeper in her pockets, and wished for the easy comfort of an environmental suit.

She looked in the other direction. The street actually ran diagonally down to sector base. The pavement continued into the sector base itself. She'd seen the map. The roads all ended up in some lower level turnaround, where the automated vehicles (wheeled or railed) drove in a circle, picked up more passengers, and left.

The wind played with her hair, making her shiver. When was the last time India had touched her like that? Raina had no idea.

She let out a large sigh, and actually saw the white condensation of her breath.

If she stayed here, she would be in a city she didn't like much. She might not have a job anymore, although she could probably teach, not that teaching interested her.

If she stayed here, she would be alone. Because she wouldn't be able to talk India into staying. That had become clear the day Captain Preemas made his announcement. India liked the idea of working security on the *Renegat*.

Raina had thought as the *Renegat* landed inside the sector base, that maybe, just maybe, she would scout a place to live, see what the advantages to staying in Z-City were.

But as they walked off the *Renegat* for their short two-day leave, India had said, "I wish we weren't stopping. I'm ready to move to the next phase of my life."

"You're not afraid of all the danger ahead?" Raina had asked.

India had laughed. "It would be a nice change of pace from our humdrum life, don't you think?"

Raina hadn't said anything. She had realized, over the past several days, that India loved her new assignment. India wanted to stay on the ship, and India didn't really seem to care what Raina wanted.

Apparently, as far as India was concerned, Raina had already made her decision.

And maybe Raina had. She had always put India first.

But Raina was also acutely aware that this was the last chance to abandon this mission, her last chance to stay behind.

If she stayed, she would lose contact with India. They would probably be able to talk, but communication across foldspace took time, and was more prone to monologues than serious discussions.

And if Raina left India—and it would be Raina leaving India if Raina stayed behind—India might take that as affront.

India already seemed to take it as an affront that Raina even considered staying.

Raina let out a shuddery breath, seeing that condensation again. Then she inhaled, feeling the chill air fill her lungs. Weather conditions would only get worse here.

And there was all that gravity, the solid land beneath her feet. The night sky, filled with stars she might never visit, the ships arriving and taking off, ships she might not be able to work on again.

If she stayed, she would gain nothing.

She would definitely lose India.

There were no good choices. So Raina might as well continue on the path that she had assigned herself.

If something went wrong on that path, she had India. They had promised to be together always.

That, at least, was something she could hold on to.

With that one thing, she could build a future.

No matter where she ended up.

THE *SPRÁVA*

Vice Admiral Gāo bent over the large table screen in front of her, her right elbow on the screen's smooth surface, propping her right fist against her cheek. She wasn't comfortable—the seat of the chair that she had pulled over to the table was now resting against the backs of her knees—but she didn't want to be comfortable.

She had too much information, much of it contradictory, and she had no idea how to synthesize any of it.

She was in the study she had built off her main research room on the *Správa*. The study looked deceptively tiny, with wall art modeled on ancient rice paper scrolls and beautiful calligraphed symbols from Earth languages she did not speak. Usually the art calmed her, but she was thinking of shutting it off this afternoon, and putting some of the data files on the walls themselves.

But, she knew, where the data was located wasn't the problem. The problem was she didn't know how to organize the data, and as long as she didn't know how to organize it, she didn't know how to command an assistant or the system itself to organize it.

Gāo had pulled all of the data from the Scrapheap that the *Renegat* was going to. She still got daily updates from that Scrapheap. She had commissioned a small study group to investigate how this information was actually reaching the Fleet. Rwizi's group had already used some of the information—the easily accessible stuff—to plot the *Renegat*'s foldspace course. But Gāo wanted something more in-depth.

The study group was back-tracing each communications node, figuring out which ones were still active, which ones got skipped, and where, exactly, the information got rerouted.

Some of that information was easy to get, particularly on the nearby nodes, but some of the older information was proving difficult. Mostly, it seemed, the data from the Scrapheap had gone through decommissioned sector bases. The equipment in those bases should have been removed centuries ago, but Gāo was worried that the nanobits rebuilt some of the removed equipment.

She had no confirmation of that, and she hadn't said anything about it to the other admirals either. She didn't want Hallock to send yet another suicide mission to some decommissioned sector base to see what was going on there.

Gāo's back twinged. She stood up and wiped off her face, feeling completely overwhelmed. She had data from the Scrapheap, data from Calixte on some other possible Scrapheaps that the Fleet had forgotten about, and some truly scary data about the kinds of Ready Vessels possibly left behind in these Scrapheaps.

The Ready Vessels were keeping her awake at night when she wasn't worrying about the crew of the *Renegat*. She kept revisiting that decision nightly, because she had felt pushed into it, and she had never completely agreed with Hallock. Now that the ship was underway, Gāo felt even more responsible, especially since Preemas's updates were too short for her tastes, and too upbeat for the man she had met.

But the Ready Vessels bothered her even more than a single suicide mission. The old Ready Vessels, the warships, were often decommissioned because the weapons systems or a propulsion system or some other bit of tech was deemed dangerous. Some of the weapons systems destroyed entire populations in ways that Gāo—and the current version of the Fleet, anyway—believed to be unethical.

Calixte had pulled the research away from the students and only had his officer trainees in engineering and history handle some of the research, primarily because it was so terrifying. As of right now, no one knew if those weapons systems were decommissioned and left in place or if they were decommissioned and destroyed.

Gāo hoped for destroyed, but she kept thinking back to that conversation she had had with Hallock, the one about ships being so valuable the Fleet couldn't easily destroy any part of them, which was why Scrapheaps existed.

The longer Gāo thought about that argument, the more sense it made. And that actively terrified her. Because if that argument had as much truth to it as she thought, then a lot of these weapons systems or dangerous fuels or exploding propulsion systems might still exist, buried deep in a mostly unguarded and forgotten Scrapheap so many sectors away that she couldn't count it.

The Fleet had never been attacked by its own abandoned ships, but what if some other culture had? What if the Fleet had inadvertently destroyed entire races of people? What if the Fleet, in its haste to leave an area, had also left a way for the worst people in that area to take control of it?

She placed her hands on the small of her back and stretched.

The what-ifs were driving her crazy. She had no control over them, so she shouldn't worry about them, but the more she tried to make sense of all the information coming at her, the more she worried about what the Fleet had inadvertently done.

The door to her main research room chimed. The chime also caused a small blue light to appear on the table screen before her, just in case she had been very deep in the research and hadn't heard the sound.

Her personal assistant, Lieutenant Cali Baker, had actually come to the door rather than contact Gão through the system. That couldn't be good.

Gão let Baker into the main research area, and opened the study door.

Baker was a thin officer who wore her uniform even though Gão didn't insist on it. The blue with red trim looked good on Baker, accenting her light brown skin and shockingly pale eyes. She was older than some of the personal assistants to ranking officers, but Gão liked that about her.

Baker had transferred to one of the school ships early in her career, so that she could be near her children, rather than on separate ships for all but vacations. Career officers rarely made that choice. If they wanted to trade career for family, they usually remained at sector bases, or took research work on some of the support ships.

Baker hadn't abandoned her career as much as put it on hold. And then, when her children were grown, she returned. Gão took her on as soon as she was available, appreciating Baker's unflappable nature, which was partly due to her age, and partly to the way she was.

Baker didn't look unflappable at the moment, which bothered Gão. Baker knew how Gão conducted her business, so Baker's expressions were often predictive of what Gão's would be after Gão heard whatever news Baker had to impart.

Gão wanted to ask in a light tone, *Who died?* but knew better. Baker's expression was close enough to one that might have been caused by someone's death.

"Vice Admiral," Baker said, and Gão silently cursed. Baker had decided on formality in her tone as well as her words. "We…um…got a message from the head of Sector Base Z."

Gão frowned. She had little to do with sector bases. Baker knew that, which made this moment even more unusual.

Sector Base Z had just reached the point where it would be slated for decommission. Decommissioning would take decades, and would happen in stages, but it was going to happen. A location had just been approved for Sector Base C-2.

"He had just found out that you are in charge of the mission for the *Renegat*," Baker said.

Gão's stomach clenched. She had known the *Renegat* was heading to the area, and that Preemas was going to make an extra, unplanned stop, to pick up supplies and have the *anacapa* checked. She hadn't really approved that, but she understood his caution. The foldspace trips he was facing were going to be arduous, and he had no idea what he might encounter in the old sectors.

Gão didn't even ask if there was a problem. She knew there was, or the head of the sector base wouldn't contact her.

"What are we facing?" Gão asked. Was she going to have to call this mission off before the *Renegat* even got into its long foldspace journey?

She half-expected it. The crew was difficult, and Preemas had his issues. His enthusiasm for this entire mission might have waned.

"The director wants to know if you approved the personnel changes. He found something in the files that said you were in charge of personnel, not Captain Preemas, and figured he should notify you."

Baker's expression was a study in calm exasperation. This time, Baker had gotten Gāo's reaction wrong. There was no calm exasperation here.

Gāo felt a deep fury.

What kind of game was Preemas playing?

"What's going on?" Gāo asked.

"From what I can tell, several crew have left the ship, and Preemas is replacing them on his own," Baker said.

Which was the logical thing for most captains to do. But Preemas didn't have clearance to do anything like this.

"Get him for me," Gāo said.

She was going to stop this once and for all.

SECTOR BASE Z

Breaux had never done anything like this before. She didn't consider herself impulsive or even daring, and yet she was standing in the information line to talk with a representative from the SC-Class vessel the *Renegat* about maybe joining the crew.

The line snaked its way around the employee dining room on the top level of the base. The dining room had slitted windows, so that the employees could watch the mountaintop open whenever a ship asked to land inside the base.

Ships with *anacapa* drives didn't ask. They just signaled the *anacapa* drives inside the base and appeared in the gigantic service areas on the lowest level of the base.

She'd been taken down there a few times, mostly as part of a base tour for employees. The sector base wanted everyone to know where they worked and who they worked with, if possible. Lots of areas were marked classified or specialized, and of course, she wanted to go in those as well, even though she had never been able to.

The lower levels with the big ships felt like another world. She couldn't ever take in an entire ship. They were so huge that she really couldn't comprehend them, not even when she got to see them on the monitors.

On the monitors, the ships looked like finite things, bird-shaped and black, built for speed, it seemed to her, rather than long-distance travel.

Then she walked up to one, and couldn't even reach its nose when she raised her arm above her head. The ship was so huge that it looked like the mountain itself.

That had been a DV-Class vessel. She had seen several of those, because she took the tour whenever it was offered. But she had never seen an SC-Class vessel.

She had tried to bone up on them all night. They were Security-Class vessels, and they were supposed to work in groups, securing sectors, handling problems.

It seemed to her that the crew of a Security-Class vessel had to be highly specialized, but the more research she did, the more she realized that even SC-Class vessels had large crews with very diverse jobs. The major differences between an SC-Class vessel and a DV-Class vessel were of size of course, but mission as well. SC-Class vessels went on shorter trips, and usually didn't include families.

From what she could tell about the *Renegat*, it wasn't fitting into any of the SC-Class patterns. It was going on a long trip, alone, and it was having problems.

The crew admitted that much in the broadcast they'd sent to everyone on Sector Base Z. They said some of the crew were leaving, but didn't explain why.

The rumors Justine had already heard were about dissention in the ranks, and a hatred of the way that the captain was running the ship. But she had also heard that some of the crew who were leaving were terrified of the distance the *Renegat* had to travel in foldspace.

That very thought made her stomach twist. She had once vowed that she would never ever ever travel through foldspace. It seemed weird and scary and dangerous.

But it wasn't as weird, scary, and dangerous as Prescott. She had thought him so wonderful when she met him. He had one of the best jobs in the sector base, working on some classified project on a level she could never access.

He got a lot more respect than she did, and a lot more perks in the base. He had access to base housing even though he didn't have a family—*yet*, he would say to her when he mentioned that, his blue eyes twinkling, as if he expected them to have a family.

And truth be told, she had originally hoped to have a family with him. He'd seemed perfect—those marvelous eyes, that unusual blondish hair, the smile that would make everyone else smile. He was smart and witty and charming, and so very angry underneath.

She shifted slightly, then looked around. She half-expected him to walk through the dining hall, to see her standing here, gambling her future—on what? On an opportunity she wasn't sure she wanted?

She swallowed hard, then wiped her hands on her best black slacks. She had already asked her supervisor to find her a position off the base, maybe on a starbase somewhere or even on a ship, and she had been told that as a general researcher, her skills weren't in high demand in areas that had limited personnel.

She couldn't quite understand that: it would seem to her that someone who could research anything quickly and in depth would be more valuable on a ship than, say, someone who specialized in only one thing.

She had even made that argument to her supervisor, who shrugged, saying she didn't make the rules. But her supervisor had also added that the general researchers on the starships were usually born in space, not on land.

Justine had heard that anti-land prejudice a few weeks later when she'd gone to one of the job-opening offices on the base. She had skipped over the one for established employees and gone to the one kids who had just gotten out of school went to. The people there had told her the same thing, but they said they'd try.

She had mentioned Prescott—not by name—but she had said that she wanted to get off the base to get away from him, that she was worried he was using the tools he had at his job to spy on her. They asked for his name to report him, and that had scared her away.

Very far away, in fact. She hadn't gone back.

But someone in the office had called her the day before to tell her about this opportunity.

There seemed to be two different levels of interviews. First, the applicant would go to the table where a man who looked vaguely familiar sat. He would ask two or three questions, and either send the person through a door or ask them to leave.

Most everyone left.

She supposed she would as well. Because who needed a general researcher, particularly on some scary foldspace trip?

Last night, as she thought and thought and thought about this opportunity, she wondered if she had enough courage to go if someone offered her the position.

She would have to leave everything she knew, and get to know a brand new environment, doing different things than she had ever done before, while convincing people that she actually knew how to do her job.

And, to be fair, she did know. She was one of the best (if not *the* best) general researcher on the base.

She just needed to leave. She wanted to keep her job, at least, because the work would be familiar, even if nothing else was. She loved the work, and she didn't want to leave it too.

It took less than an hour for her to reach the front of that long line, which surprised her. She would have thought she was going to be in line for half a day if not more.

When she reached the desk, she realized why the man sitting behind it looked familiar. He was Fyodor Labhras, her supervisor's supervisor back when she was just starting out, someone who didn't know a lot about research, but who knew a lot about running things.

"Justine Breaux," she said as she stepped up, just like she was supposed to do.

She held out her wrist so he could scan the chip inside for all of her information.

"I remember you," Labhras said. "You were one of the best young researchers in the department. You don't want to get on this ship. You should stay here."

She opened her mouth to answer him, but didn't exactly know how. If she disparaged Prescott, would that make her unhireable?

"I suppose you want adventure," Labhras said a little sarcastically. "That's what everyone else says when I try to discourage them."

She swallowed hard. "Is that your job then, to discourage us?"

He shook his head. "I'm supposed to filter you through, is all. For some reason, they didn't want to automate this, but I think they could. I think they want a human to ask questions."

Justine frowned.

"And maybe discourage," he said a little more softly. "Because you need to think about this before you go. More than two dozen career Fleet people are leaving this ship, and they won't tell me why. I think that's a gigantic red flag."

"You don't think it's the mission?" she asked.

"The longest trip ever through foldspace? Maybe," he said, but he didn't sound convinced. "I think most long-term spacers on an SC-Class vessel would consider that a challenge, don't you?"

She didn't know. She didn't know long-term spacers. She had no idea what people who lived their entire lives in space were like.

She dry-swallowed for the third—or was it the fourth?—time.

"You probably want to come back later," Labhras said, "maybe see if all the openings were taken."

She shook her head. The movement came before she even had a conscious thought about it.

"I want to try," she said. "It's an adventure."

"One a lot of experienced people don't think is worthwhile," Labhras said. "The questions I'm going to ask you are also a red flag."

Her frown deepened. Why would he think that?

"And these are more personal than anything you've ever been asked here at the base before," he added.

She took a deep breath, bracing herself.

"Are you in a relationship?" he asked.

"Like, married?" she asked.

"Like, any long-term relationship. The kind you value," he said.

She thought of Prescott, thought about the future she had once imagined, felt her heart ache.

"No," she said.

"Your personnel record says you have no children," Labhras said. "Do you have any foster children or close relationships with the children of friends, distant relatives, anyone?"

"No," she said, not understanding why that question was even there. "I don't even have distant relatives."

She didn't have relatives. Her parents had died in an accident at the base, and they had left family behind at another sector base. She was nearly grown when the accident happened, so she wasn't raised by anyone special.

"Close friends you couldn't survive without?" Labhras asked.

For some reason, these questions felt wrong. "What is this about?"

He gave her a flat look, and she could almost hear his thoughts. He thought she was slow. Maybe she was. Or maybe she just wanted to hear him say what was implied.

"They don't want to take anyone who will be missed," he said. "They think you're not coming back."

She felt the blood drain from her face. That was blunt. A lot more blunt than she had expected.

But the way he phrased that first sentence sent a chill through her. Not because of this mission, but because of Prescott. Had he known that he could do anything to her that he wanted because she wouldn't be missed? Had she surprised him when she left the relationship?

Did he know how very vulnerable she was?

The answer was probably yes.

"Okay," she said. "That's clear."

She took a deep breath. Labhras leaned back in his chair, as if he expected her to leave now.

"No one will miss me," she said. "I want the adventure. What do I have to do to qualify for it?"

His entire face fell. She had never before had someone she didn't really know look so disappointed in her.

"All you have to do is walk through that door," he said.

"Okay, then," she said, and skirted the table, her heart hammering.

She usually wasn't an adventurer. But she could be. Anyone could be, right, if they only tried.

She stopped for a half second in front of that door. It slid open, revealing a wide, well-lit corridor beyond.

One step, and she was in a completely different future.

One step, and she would be someone else.

She took a deep breath—and then she took the step.

And completely transformed her life.

THE *SPRÁVA*

Lieutenant Baker couldn't raise Preemas on her own. He wasn't responding to hails from Vice Admiral Gāo's office. So Gāo did the next best thing. She had the head of Sector Base Z round up Preemas.

While that process was happening, Gāo spoke directly with the head of Sector Base Z, a man named Rufus Gerlik. He had chosen an open full-size hololink to speak with her. She sat in the chair in the center of her research area. She had shut off the art on the walls, so that they looked blank.

Gerlik's holo stood in front of her, threading his hands together. He was a small, balding man who looked like the stress of his job was too much for him. Or maybe he was worried that she was going to file some kind of complaint.

On Sector Base Z, he stood in front of some kind of black nanobit wall, which looked like part of a corridor rather than someone's office. But there wasn't enough for her to see to make a real determination. And, truth be told, she really didn't care what part of the sector base he was in.

It looked to her like he stood in front of her, with a black wall behind him that held him in place, with the walls of her study farther back. It felt a bit disconcerting for him to just stand there, while she was sitting, but, she reminded herself, she had not opted for the full holographic screen. She was just showing him a view of her face.

Gerlik already informed her that he had sent for Preemas, and would step aside once Preemas arrived. She told Gerlik that when Preemas arrived, she and Preemas would need a private conversation.

Gerlik snickered, then nodded. The snicker bothered Gāo more than it probably should have. It suggested Gerlik didn't like Preemas or maybe Gerlik didn't like the situation Preemas had put them both in.

Gāo really didn't blame Gerlik for believing that Preemas needed his help. Having a captain arrive at a sector base was a normal occurrence; making certain that captain had the crew he needed was an occasional function of a sector base.

But this had gone even farther than that. It sounded like Gerlik helped Preemas set up a full recruitment fair.

"Before he arrives," Gão said to Gerlik, "tell me how many crew members have left the *Renegat*."

Gerlik shifted, tugging on his left wrist as if he were trying to detach the hand. The man had more nervous quirks than anyone she had ever seen.

"I don't know exactly," Gerlik said. "We're not required to keep track of ship personnel. But I can tell you that fifteen from the *Renegat* asked for reassignment here at the sector base."

Then he lowered his voice and leaned forward, as if he were actually in the room and needed to get close to impart a secret.

"I must say, though, Vice Admiral, none of those fifteen are qualified for a commensurate position on my base. They were sent through personnel, of course, but personnel contacted me, a bit surprised that these people had even served on an active Fleet vessel." His voice went lower still. "Do you have any idea how many reprimands these people had between them?"

"I have a hunch," Gão said. "Captain Preemas was supposed to be working with a difficult crew. It's a rehabilitation project. No one was supposed to leave the vessel. They were all supposed to be working together on this particular mission."

She didn't add that the *Renegat's* arrival at Sector Base Z had not been approved through her, either. It was one thing to have Preemas ignore her orders on the crew—most Fleet personnel would understand his desires to do that—but adding other things that showed disobedience would not do her reputation much good either.

"Well," Gerlik said, "according to what we've been hearing, your Captain Preemas has made some waves that the crew did not like. I'll be honest with you, Vice Admiral. I wouldn't want to command a difficult mission with people who did not want to serve under me."

Gão knew nothing about Gerlik. She had no idea if he had ever served on a Fleet vessel or any kind of mission. People who ran sector bases did have to manage an incredibly large staff, but sector bases had a luxury that starships did not—there was usually a large employment pool to pull from.

"I understand he's been recruiting," Gão said, and did not add that she knew he had the assistance of the base. "I do not want anyone to leave with Captain Preemas."

"Um," Gerlik tilted his head, then gave her a small smile. She half-expected him to tug at his remaining hair, like a little boy. "I don't have that kind of authority. While a lot of people at the base serve the Fleet directly, many do not, and others are retired or inactive. I don't have the authority to prevent everyone from traveling with Captain Preemas."

Gão kept her frustration off her face. *She* would have been able to find a way to prevent Preemas from taking anyone with him.

"Then get him off the base," she said. "Revoke his access, now."

"We're completing an assessment of the ship now," Gerlik said. "It can't leave until we're done."

"An assessment?" she asked, suspecting he was trying to confuse her. "If it's just an assessment, Director, then you can stop at any time. If you're effecting repairs or improvements, then I can understand. Those were not authorized either."

"Um," Gerlik said again, doing that same silly forehead tug. That made Gão mentally vow that she would never tug at her own hair again. It looked ridiculous. "I'm sorry, Vice Admiral, but my mission here requires me to complete improvements for any Fleet vessel that arrives, should the vessel make that request. No one has to go through channels to get an extra *anacapa* drive or to make certain that all of the attitude controls are up-to-date."

Gão crossed her arms. "Are those two things he asked for?"

"Um, no, sir," Gerlik said. "I don't know what he asked for, only that the ship is undergoing assessment right now, and some kind of upgrade on certain systems that Captain Preemas and his Chief Engineer believe will be heavily taxed on this mission."

Preemas's Chief Engineer, Nadim Crowe, was one of the few crew members that Gão had met personally. Crowe had a terrible reputation, mostly because he disagreed with almost every single captain he had ever served. But she had investigated his files and discovered that Crowe's disagreements were usually over something that was about to go wrong; the captains rarely listened to him, and got angry when it turned out that Crowe had been right.

Combine that mouthiness with a terrible incident he had been involved in as a young man, and he was almost unhireable on a normal Fleet vessel. She had spent a lot of time with Nadim Crowe's file, trying to figure out if she could find him a different position in the Fleet.

But he had already used up most of his opportunities, and she had finally put him on the *Renegat*. When she had done so, she had comforted herself with two thoughts. The first was that Nadim Crowe wouldn't put up with any of Captain Preemas's craziness, and the second was that Crowe could save the entire crew with a fork and some spit if the situation called for it.

"Nadim Crowe asked for the repairs?" Gão asked, mostly as clarification.

"Um…" Gerlik frowned, and she could tell now that he was looking at a different floating screen. Apparently, he hadn't remembered Crowe's name. "Yes. Yes, Chief Engineer and First Officer Nadim Crowe."

First Officer. Hmm. That was new. The first officer had been a woman with very shady credentials.

Maybe these changes weren't as bad as Gão had feared.

"All right." Gão couldn't do anything with Gerlik then. She couldn't tell him how to do his job, and he certainly couldn't do hers. "Just get the *Renegat* off the base as quickly as you can, and shut down this recruitment effort."

"Will do, sir," Gerlik said. "And I have just received word that Captain Preemas has arrived. I'll have them send him in…?"

"Please do," Gāo said. "But be advised that my communications with the captain must remain private. Is this particular node secure? Because I don't want anyone listening in on our discussion."

Particularly you, she wanted to add, but didn't. If she could trust Preemas to contact her, she would have had Gerlik send him back to the *Renegat* for this communique. But she didn't trust Preemas at all, not anymore.

"Um, yes," Gerlik said. "Completely private, and I'll switch you to a more secure node now."

The image blacked out for a half second, then returned. A man stood beside Gerlik, and Gerlik was gesturing, the sound off.

Then Gerlik turned, reached forward, and pointed at something near Gāo with great force. It took her a moment to realize he had pressed something on a screen.

"I have secured the area, Vice Admiral," Gerlik said. "No one will interrupt you or your captain."

She thanked Gerlik, and he headed out of the range of her vision. She was about to call him back to tell him to take that other man with him, when the other man turned.

It was an almost unrecognizable Captain Ivan Preemas.

His long hair was cut shorter than regulation. His facial hair was gone. He wore a casual uniform, a lighter blue than the formal uniform. But his gold captain's bars were on his shoulders, looking like he'd actually burnished them so that they reflected any available light around him.

His eyes, brighter green than she remembered, twinkled when they met hers across the distance.

The twinkle made her angry. He had expected this.

He bowed ever so slightly. "Vice Admiral."

"Captain," she snapped. "I understand you've been augmenting crew changes without my permission."

His mouth rose in a half smile. "Do you want the honest answer or the one that will work with your coven of Admirals?"

The phrase, a *coven of Admirals,* revealed the kind of attitude problem she expected when she dealt with Preemas. Until that moment, she had been a little off balance.

She almost said, *What do you think, Captain?* but if she went the snide route, she would be playing his game. She did not want to do that.

She didn't answer him at all. Instead, she gave him her most stern glare, one that usually sent her staff cowering.

He didn't cower, but the twinkle slowly left his eyes and that half smile faded.

"You do realize that the crew you gave me was a complete and utter horror show, right?" he asked.

She wasn't going to answer that either. She raised her chin slightly.

"Half of them can't do the job they're assigned to, although some of them are very good at the jobs they were trained for but had to abandon for behavioral reasons." He spoke almost angrily now.

She didn't care about all of the details of his assignment, nor did she care about the blame he was trying to apply to her.

"I'll be honest," he said, his tone even angrier, "it's been a struggle. And some of the people you saddled me with are dead weight."

That didn't surprise her. But she kept her expression impassive. She didn't want him to know she had expected that. Nor did she want to insult his intelligence by saying she had hoped he could inspire them.

She had picked the best she could find from the list d'Anano had given her. The fact that some did not work out was less surprising than the fact that some did.

"All I did," he said into Gāo's silence, "was give them an opportunity to leave before we headed on the longest and most dangerous part of the journey."

Truth be told, she might have done the same thing. Better to run a ship with a small crew than run a ship with a crew that was trying to compensate for crewmembers who were not able to do the job.

Preemas's eyes narrowed. There was no twinkle left in them at all. It was almost as if there had never been a twinkle. Ever.

"My mistake, apparently, was talking to my man Gerlik, wasn't it? Enlisting his help, right?"

She didn't answer that either. She would figure out later if she needed to deal with Gerlik in even more depth.

"I should've just recruited people on my own," Preemas said, his tone filled with not-quite-suppressed fury. "Then you would have never known."

Time to speak up.

"I thought you saw this trip as a way to rebuild your reputation, Captain," Gāo said, her voice flat. Her expression still hadn't changed.

"I did, and I do," he said. "But you're making that very difficult, you know."

She knew that, and she wasn't surprised that he did.

"If I wasn't concerned about my damn reputation, I would have handled this on my own." He crossed his arms. "But, I care, so I am following the rules as best I can. Because someone told me that the end result doesn't matter if the method I use to get there isn't something she approves of."

Again, the blaming. She hadn't liked Preemas from the beginning, and she liked him even less now. The man was even more passive-aggressive than she expected, and that wasn't a good trait in a captain.

"If you were following the rules," Gāo said, "you would have continued with your crew and not stopped on Sector Base Z."

"Impossible," he snapped. "Some of these people are dangerous dead weight. I didn't tell them to leave, but they were figuring it out on their own. I did tell them they wouldn't be penalized if they did. They would get to keep their rank. I hope that wasn't out of line."

She wasn't going down the sidetrack.

"If that is the case," she said, and she made sure he understood—both from her tone and her stern expression—that she didn't entirely believe him, "then you did the right thing in giving them the opportunity to disembark on Sector Base Z. What you are not sanctioned to do is replace them. You will have to run with a minimal crew."

"Too late," he said. "I already hired replacements."

"Let them go," she said.

"No."

Then he closed his eyes, as if he was disappointing himself. She watched him. She had given him an impossible task, without enough ships to do it and without the right kind of crew.

Even though she didn't like him, he was the best of the choices she had had, and she did need to give him a small chance to succeed.

It was that feeling, that need to give him a chance, that was keeping her in this discussion.

He took an audible breath, and opened his eyes. "I request permission, Vice Admiral, to keep my new hires. We need them. I lost some key personnel—although 'lost' isn't the right word, since the people in those positions could never have done the job. I want a good crew. We're on a dangerous mission. I think I have everyone arranged so that we can make it to the Scrapheap and back. All I need is about two dozen more folks, and I should be able to run the ship to the best of my ability."

She didn't know how much of that he meant and how much of it was Preemas's attempt at charming her, trying to get her to do what he wanted.

But he did have a good point.

"Send me all of the information you have on your new hires," she said. "I will go through them within the next few hours. If I disagree with anyone you want to bring on board, they will not join the *Renegat*. If they do despite my orders, I will revoke your mission. If you do not return when I revoke your mission, I will send ships after you, as if you are an enemy of the Fleet. Is that clear?"

He actually leaned back as if she had struck him.

"You would pursue us as if we were your enemy?" he asked, sounding like a vulnerable child.

"If I have to revoke the mission, absolutely," she said. "This trip to the Scrapheap is the last chance for your career, Captain. You have taxed my patience to its breaking point, and you aren't even in the dangerous part of your mission. So, if you violate any procedure I set up from here on out, I will make sure you regret it until the end of your days. Is that clear?"

The color had left his face. She didn't think someone with such pale skin could get even paler, but somehow he did.

"Yes, sir, it is," he said. "I'll send the information to you as soon as we end this conversation."

"And one last thing, Captain," she said. "These people that you bring on board, they can't have family or close ties. Your mission is more likely to fail than to succeed. I don't want you to take promising career Fleet material or people who are well loved by friends and family and destroying their lives."

He pursed his lips, before he said anything. Then he managed, "Even if they want to come anyway? Even if they understand that they might never return?"

"Even if," she said. "Are we clear?"

He sighed, a little dramatically. She half-expected him to put a hand over his forehead as if she had given him some kind of headache.

"I don't like it," he said. "You're tying my hands."

"You knew the terms of the mission when you took the assignment," she said.

Not that it was a comfort to either of them. But she wasn't going to tell him that either.

"You'll get your list," he said.

"Good," she said, and severed the connection.

She stood still for a moment, wondering if she had been played or if she had played him. Then she wondered if *playing* was even the right term, given how many lives were on the line.

And now, after watching him, she had two responses to his command. His decision to improve his crew encouraged her. She understood it. It showed that he wanted to succeed. Just like his clothing, his haircut, and his demeanor did. He was acting like a captain, just like she had hoped he would.

Except, that passive-aggressive blaming behavior didn't belong in any command structure. A captain had to be willing to take responsibility for everything on his ship, the good and the bad. If he had a bad crew on a long mission, he had to bend them to his will and make them the best possible crew they could be.

She ran a hand through her hair, tugging a little, then noting the movement, and smiled at herself. She had vowed not to do that after watching Gerlik. Preemas was slowly driving her crazy.

Or maybe this mission was.

SECTOR BASE Z

Preemas slammed his fist against the wall. It didn't vibrate the way that walls on the *Renegat* did, and he brought his hand back swiftly as if the action had hurt him.

To his credit, he didn't cup his hand, though. That would have deliberately called attention to what he had done, and clearly, he didn't want to do that.

Crowe knew better than to grin at Preemas's obvious distress. Sometimes Preemas's behavior was childish, and it was nice to see him actually pay a price for that childishness, however small.

Crowe had just brought Preemas a communique from Vice Admiral Gão. Preemas had been in the "small" office, as Rufus Gerlik called it. The scale of everything on Sector Base Z was so much bigger than anything on the *Renegat*. The *Renegat*, like most starships, was efficient, built to maximize the available space.

Sector Base Z sprawled. Based on eyeballing the measurements of Gerlik's office suite alone, Crowe figured the suite was one quarter the size of an entire deck on the *Renegat*. Much of the space was completely wasted, like this "small" office that was, as far as Crowe could tell, only used for secure communications inside the Fleet.

The built-in shelves even had a layer of dust. And now, there was a smudge on the wall where the side of Preemas's fist had connected.

Of course, Crowe was probably being childish just thinking that way. But he didn't really care. Working with Preemas was nothing, if not an adventure.

"She shut us down," Preemas said. "I *told* her why we were doing this, and she shut us down."

Crowe had looked at the communique. Gão had shut down their recruitment efforts and that had not surprised Crowe at all. But there were some surprises in her communique, at least for Crowe.

"I don't know if you had a chance to look at all of it," Crowe said, trying to be as diplomatic as he could. He did know that Preemas had not had a chance to look through everything. It didn't matter how brilliant the man was; no human could scan that much information that quickly. "But, you'll see that she's allowing us to keep most of the recruits."

"Most." Preemas spit the word. "She got rid of the good ones."

She had not cleared some of the more promising candidates. Crowe had noticed that. But he had had a chance to look at her reasoning.

She hadn't taken their word for the fact that they were unattached. She had actually investigated, and most of them had close family in Z-City. She had been following the protocol she had set from the beginning for this mission.

But Crowe knew better than to say anything like that. Considering the mood Preemas was in, Crowe didn't want to be in the position to defend Gão for any reason.

Let her be the villain, as far as Preemas was concerned. He wasn't going to have to deal with her much after they left Sector Base Z, so she would be a convenient scapegoat for a lot of things.

Crowe rocked back on his heels, noting how he was thinking. He was already trying to figure out ways to manage Preemas, ways that were counterintuitive to good command.

Crowe clutched the communications tablet tightly. Preemas was a difficult man, and there was no real evidence yet that he was a good commander. He was certainly a volatile one.

Over two dozen people were leaving the *Renegat*, and hoping their careers weren't over. Crowe could join them.

"You're staring at me, First Officer Crowe," Preemas said.

Crowe blinked. He hadn't realized he had been staring. He had been thinking too hard to process what he was seeing.

What he was seeing was a man who wore his uniform lightly, looking like the ideal of a captain, with his hair perfectly cut, his jaw smooth and square. Only the fury in his eyes revealed that he might not be as ideal as he looked.

And fury was sometimes an appropriate response for a captain, particularly when he had a lot of things to deal with.

"She didn't get rid of all the good ones." Crowe saw some names on the list that he had recruited, people who would be of great benefit on this trip, including Natalia Stephanos, who was an *anacapa* expert. Crowe had done some fast talking to get her on board.

"We should just tell the others that they can come with us anyway." Preemas created a fist with that same hand, and then opened the fist again, as if closing it had hurt.

He had probably hit that wall with a lot of force, expecting the wall to absorb the impact, and instead, his hand had.

There were a lot of tiny details about life on land that living in gravity on board a ship did not prepare you for.

"If we're going to do that," Crowe said, "then let's get rid of the last of the stragglers. For example, I saw that Kabac has chosen to remain on the ship. Let's just get rid of him and all of his incompetent friends, hire a new group, and leave before the vice admiral knows what we're about."

Preemas gave Crowe a surprised look. "I thought you were about following regulations, First Officer Crowe."

Crowe shrugged his right shoulder. "If you're going to break one order, you might as well break another, especially if the orders are related."

Preemas's eyes narrowed, as if he were seeing Crowe for the first time. Then Preemas smiled halfway, the kind of smile he had given before when he was amused and uncertain.

"Except," he said slowly, "the orders are not related. Vice Admiral Gão has given me several orders in the past few hours. She wants me to stop recruiting here at Sector Base Z, so I am doing that."

Crowe felt his breath catch. He knew where some of this was going.

"She has now looked over everyone I have recruited here on the base, and has disallowed several of my recruits." Preemas was speaking more to himself than to Crowe.

But Crowe was beginning to understand. Preemas hadn't given her every name. Some of the people weren't on the list because Preemas hadn't put them there in the first place.

"She has expressly told me," Preemas was saying, "that I may not get rid of anyone she brought on board. She made a face when I told her that some left on their own accord, but she did not tell me to rehire them."

Crowe frowned. Did that mean Preemas was going to force more people off the ship?

"Frankly, First Officer Crowe," Preemas said, his voice turning snide as it always did when he used Crowe's new rank, "I wish I had come up with that plan before we stopped at Sector Base Z. I would have preferred to lose a few people at Sector Base A-2, and then lose the rest at Sector Base Z. I hadn't planned well enough."

And here Crowe had thought Preemas had planned the second sector base stop all along.

"She also didn't tell me that I had to get rid of everyone we brought on board. She understood that we are going to have difficulties and a minimal crew would not help the situation."

Preemas clasped his hands behind his back and started pacing. Then he let his hands drop to his sides.

"So, she's not unsympathetic," Preemas said. "But she is going to scrutinize us greatly."

"What does it matter?" Crowe asked. "They're sending us on a hell of a mission. If we survive, that's a tribute to us."

Preemas smiled slowly. It was a full smile.

"I love this mission, Crowe," Preemas said. There was no *First Officer Crowe* this time. Just Crowe's name. "It's just perverse enough to appeal to me. I love the idea that my personal success—bringing the *Renegat* back in one piece with as much crew as possible, and with all of the things that we were sent to discover—will be seen as failure by the vice admiral and her cohorts. I love that. If we do this right, Crowe, we'll have incredible power over them. We will prove them wrong. We will show them that we can do anything, against all odds. And, even better, we can do it with one hand tied behind our back."

He lifted his fist. It was slightly swollen on one side, and bright red.

"A hand that they tied behind us, I might add," Preemas said. "I'll be happy to say that when we return. With the right emphasis, of course. I'll sound as positive as I can. But they'll know. Gāo will know. I will show them that I'm a much better captain than they ever were, and that this ship filled with misfits and fools can do better than the most elaborately built and beautifully staffed DV-Class ship."

He sounded completely confident, convinced he could do all of this. His optimism was breathtaking, compelling—and a little frightening.

That Preemas believed he could not only succeed at this mission, but also turn it into a personal triumph when he returned, was both inspiring and delusional.

And yet, Crowe was standing on the edge of that delusion. If he stayed with Preemas, he had other choices. He could watch from the sidelines, participating ever so slightly. Or he could join Preemas in his quest to complete the mission and have a triumphal return.

Crowe wasn't sure there was any other way to be. He was convinced he had an either-or here.

Preemas tilted his head at Crowe, then let the fist drop.

"Do you disagree, First Officer Crowe?"

Crowe swallowed. "Disagree with what, Captain Preemas?"

Apparently, Preemas heard the slight mimicry in Crowe's tone, that slight sarcasm on Preemas's title.

"With my plan for success, First Officer." Preemas made it sound like a challenge.

This time, Crowe shrugged the other shoulder. "We have no idea what we're going to face. I would prefer that we go into it with the best crew possible. If that means ignoring some of the vice admiral's strictures, then I would like to do so."

"Noted," Preemas said. "But I'm not going to ignore. I'm going to bend the regulations as far as I can, but I'm going to follow them."

Then he leaned back a little and looked at Crowe.

"I had thought," Preemas said, "that you would be the one to force me to follow regulations."

And if someone had asked Crowe weeks ago if he was going to be the one who enforced regulations as opposed to Preemas, Crowe would have agreed. He would have thought he was that man.

But this mission had made him cautious in a way he hadn't expected. He had thought he would be rules bound. Instead, he wanted the best possible people beside him. People he could predict, people who knew how to handle themselves on a Fleet vessel.

"I want this mission to succeed," Crowe said. "I am not certain if we can do so with some of the crew that remains."

"There aren't enough of those people now," Preemas said. "If need be, I'll confine them to quarters if they get in the way."

"We're short, because the vice admiral has cut some people from our list," Crowe said.

"Ah, perhaps," Preemas said. "You see, regulations, First Officer Crowe. They work for us and they work against us. In this instance, they work for us. Because I don't have to submit the names of people who are no longer registered with the Fleet. Nor can I submit the names of people who walk on board and get hired on the spot, as I'm sure a few people will do, especially those who refused to go through the on-base recruitment."

Crowe nodded. "So we have a full crew compliment?"

"If we count people like your friend Kabac, yes," Preemas said.

Crowe wanted to say that Kabac wasn't his friend, but he didn't. Because Preemas had only wanted to irritate him, anyway, and Crowe had decided to remain unflappable.

"Then, I guess we're ready to leave," Crowe said.

"We need a few more supplies," Preemas said. "I thought we'd be here one more day, so I delayed on a few things. You might want to use that time to convince some names on your list that life on a sector base is a lot better than life on an SC-Class vessel traveling backwards."

"I am not the persuasive type," Crowe said. "You can be, sir."

"Sir." Preemas grinned. "Yes, I suppose I can be persuasive. I persuaded you, didn't I, First Officer Crowe?"

The answer Preemas wanted was a resounding yes. And the fact that Crowe knew that made him want to deny Preemas his *yes*.

But Crowe couldn't help it. Sometimes Preemas was appealing. That was probably how he had gotten so many promotions as a younger man.

"I am not persuadable, Captain," Crowe said. "I am swayed by certain types of logic."

"Keep telling yourself that," Preemas said, and slapped him on the shoulder, then winced. "I, on the other hand, have some people to scare off. You can come with me if you like."

Crowe shook his head. He wanted to walk around the sector base, see if it made him change his mind. He doubted he would.

He was about to embark on the grandest adventure of his life.

He would be a fool if he walked away from it now.

PART NINE
THE RESCUE
NOW

THE *AIZSARGS RESCUE ONE*

Mackay Adeon had the Fleet checklist open in front of him, a floating red screen of lists and to-do items, and he had his own personal checklist open beside it.

No one else could see the checklists. Some of the crew on *Rescue One* actually believed Adeon did all of his work from memory.

If he had done that, he would be doing a severe disservice to anyone he was supposed to rescue.

He was in the life raft deployment area, a small alcove off the larger life raft bay. The alcove had a door that could close automatically if he wanted it to.

He didn't want it to. He was working quickly, double-checking the lists, and using his own identification to access all of the life raft controls.

Essentially, he had to guess at what the rescued passengers would need immediately, before they even arrived on *Rescue One*. A quick diagnosis of their condition was something that every rescued person needed, and he set that up automatically.

But other things took more thought. He needed to decide things like which languages would greet the passengers, and whether or not the holographic medical units should perform some traumatic injury repair while the life raft was traveling.

He also had to decide if only living, breathing human beings were allowed on the life raft or if creatures, plants, and things like food supplies could be brought as well. He tried to leave that open, because more than once a life raft had tried to prevent newborns from entering in their parents' arms.

He tried to base his decisions on what he knew about the ship that was failing—the *Renegat*, in this instance—and not on what had happened before. He doubted anyone had serious impact injuries, for instance, so he didn't set up emergency wound repair.

But power and life support were failing, so he had to have some available medical treatment for those who entered with breathing issues and frostbite and other complications.

He only trusted himself to do this, although he had trained assistants over the years. They were manually setting up the rafts right now, working as fast as possible.

If his assistants screwed up, they would hear from him.

If they screwed up badly, not only would they be demoted, they might even be court-martialed, for letting vulnerable people die.

The court-martials, some argued, weren't fair, noting that the life rafts were 100% automated, after all, and whatever happened on them couldn't be predicted.

But Adeon couldn't do his job with that attitude. He believed he could predict enough of the rescue to save as many lives as possible.

He counted any death on a life raft as a personal affront. He also counted anyone who was unable to board the life raft and later died as another personal affront.

He went through both checklists again, then stepped out of the alcove. The life rafts were lined up in their bay, ready to deploy. Their back ends were open, revealing the interior.

The rafts were little more than gigantic padded rooms, with life support and handholds. No one was supposed to be on a life raft for more than thirty minutes.

The Fleet had learned long ago that no one should pilot a life raft. Sometimes the people being rescued rebelled—in one incident that he knew of, actually killing the pilot and attempting to steal the life raft, not that it would have done them any good. The life raft wasn't built for long distances, just for the short trip between a disabled ship and *Rescue One*.

He double-checked the interior controls, made sure the interiors were as sterile as they could be, and everything was in its place.

They looked fine.

His stomach knotted. He hated sending the life rafts off on their own, even though they were only transports. He wanted everything about them to be perfect, so that the rescued felt like they had finally reached a place of safety.

He wanted the life raft to give the rescued comfort, rather than make them feel as if they were on a fragile little vessel that barely protected them from the dangers of the space around them.

He patted the side of the nearest raft. The nanobits were solid outside, rubbery and soft on the inside. His hand left a faint sweaty palm print on the exterior.

"Good luck," he whispered to the raft, like he did every single time he sent one of these off.

Then he closed the doors on all of the rafts, and gave the command to have his team leave the bay.

The team left, and he stepped into the little alcove, sealing it closed behind him. He activated the life rafts, sending them to the *Renegat*, at the coordinates Zarges had specified.

One bay to another. The life rafts would arrive, remove passengers, and return to yet a different bay, where Turris had placed his best medical and organizational personnel.

They would get the passengers off as fast as possible, then send the raft along the automated passageway between that bay and this one. The raft would leave again from this bay, even though Adeon wouldn't check it the second time (much as he wanted to), and the procedure would continue with the next raft, and the next, and the next, until everyone was off the ship.

Or until it became impossible to get them off the ship.

His mouth was dry. He faced the rafts, and watched through the clear alcove door as the first raft departed through the open bay exit.

He wanted to program it to move faster, but he couldn't. The life rafts' maximum speed was slow because of its construction.

It would take as long as it would take.

The rafts would rescue everyone they could.

And all he could do now was watch.

THE *AIZSARGS*

The *Aizsargs* had moved farther away from the *Renegat* than Dauber wanted to be. She had watched the *Renegat* get smaller and smaller on her various screens, and finally tapped away from them, preferring to concentrate on the details of the rescue.

Her bridge crew had become a bit sparse. She had sent Vilma Lauritz, her chief of security, to the lower decks to make certain the correct precautions were in place.

Lauritz was going to reinforce the security barriers to those lower levels in case the 200+ people that the *Aizsargs* rescued required incarceration rather than protection.

Dauber would give them protection, of course, as she ferried them to the nearest starbase, one that could take over in whatever ways she needed—whether that meant taking the 200+ into custody or whether that meant figuring out where they actually belonged.

Now that the *Aizsargs* had reached its new destination, Dauber had moved Brett Ullman back to researching the *Renegat.* He had brought up a dozen more screens, so he was completely encircled in them. Most of them were clear rather than opaque, so from Dauber's perspective, it looked like files were scrolling across his skin.

She wasn't even certain he knew where he was at the moment, because he was so intent on everything he was doing.

Nazira Almadi was moving around the bridge, checking the work of the remaining bridge crew—not because she didn't believe they would do a good job, but because she was as uncomfortable as Dauber.

Almadi stopped beside Massai Ribisi, looking down at his screens, a strand of her dark black hair escaping the bun she had piled on top of her head. Ribisi pointed out something on the screen before him, and Almadi shook her head.

"Captain," he said as if he had known she was watching him. "Did you know the *Renegat* has a communications *anacapa*?"

Dauber blinked in surprise. Communications *anacapa* drives used to be a normal feature of ships that traveled through foldspace, but that practice ended about fifty years ago. Usually the communications *anacapa* drives were in DV-Class vessels only.

The communications *anacapa* drives were small, tiny slivers of a normal *anacapa* drive, and that had caused a lot of problems over the years. Sometimes the communications *anacapa*'s energy blended with the main *anacapa* creating a whole new set of problems. And sometimes the communications *anacapa* created its own little opening into foldspace without being directed to.

"Is that what's causing the problems?" she asked.

"I don't think so," Ribisi said. "It doesn't seem to be tied into the main systems. Should I tell the team on the *Renegat* about it?"

"If you think it'll help and not distract them," she said.

"As if I know." He hadn't moved his head through that entire conversation. His fingers had continued to poke and prod at the screens as if he could punch through them into the *Renegat*.

He had reached the limits of her *anacapa* knowledge as well. The situation was so fluid she had no idea what would help the team on the *Renegat* and what wouldn't.

"More information is always better," she said to Ribisi.

"Yeah," he said. "I agree. I'll let them know."

She hoped the new information wouldn't slow them down.

"Captain, I found something." Ullman sounded like he was speaking to her through comms. He wasn't, but he wasn't looking at her either. Instead, he was frowning as he stared at those clear screens, his eyes reflecting the backlight.

Dauber wound her way through holoscreens and consoles, past her very intent bridge crew. She stopped at the edge of Ullman's protective screen barriers, and almost asked for permission to enter.

He beckoned her to his side. It surprised her to realize he was braced against the stool he sometimes used to rest his legs. Even when he was sitting, he was nearly as tall as she was.

"Files," he said, pointing at one of the clear screens.

She leaned so that she could see what he was seeing. The files were displayed against the backdrop of the bridge, the blinking of the equipment and the movement of the other members of the crew distracting her.

That was why Dauber usually kept her screens opaque.

"Where?" she asked.

"Here," Ullman said, expanding the screen he was working on and opaqued it without waiting for her to request it. Now, she could see the information scrolling by.

Not that it mattered: Ullman processed data faster than she did.

"Summarize for me," she said, knowing she wouldn't be able to see half of what he had already absorbed.

"The *Renegat* is, like we thought, an SC-Class vessel. It has an undistinguished service record." He pointed a finger at another one of his clear screens. On it was a three-dimensional image of the ship, spinning in its little informational cocoon.

She couldn't help herself. She looked through his screen at the screen where Almadi was working. The structure of the ship was exactly the same—at least from here.

"So," she said, "what's the story?"

Because there had to be one. An SC-Class vessel didn't just disappear. Fighters sometimes did. Runabouts got stolen. Smaller ships always had troubles. But an SC-Class ship usually had a crew of 400-500, and an important mission.

"About a hundred years ago," Ullman said, "the *Renegat* went on some kind of secret mission, and never returned."

"What kind of secret mission?" she asked.

He shrugged. "I have no idea. It's still blocked off. I need higher clearance than I have to find out what the *Renegat* was working on."

That made her frown. Missions over 100 years old shouldn't have that level of classification.

"Let me try," she said, and called up her own screen. She opaqued it, put in all of her identification, and looked up the *Renegat*.

She found a bit more about the ship—it had apparently reported in for the first half of its assignment. But once it arrived on-site, information slowed, and then vanished.

"Huh," she said, studying the information in front of her, wondering if she could let Ullman look at the file. A peek would be a small breach of protocol, but her superiors might overlook that in this situation.

He would certainly be able to make sense of the information quicker than she could.

"What did you find?" he asked.

"I'm not sure," she said, and she wasn't. The file was filled with information, some of which seemed odd to her. She couldn't tell if the oddities came from the age of the information and the protocols in use at that time, or if the oddities came from something else.

She frowned, still thinking about letting Ullman handle this. While she worked on that problem with one corner of her mind, she could discuss some of the things she saw.

"From what I can tell," she said, "the *Renegat* vanished on a mission 100 years ago."

They already had that information, but not in quite the same way.

Everyone on the bridge was listening now.

"The mission was strange from the start." Dauber folded her hands behind her back and peered at the files. Some of what she saw, she didn't want to say aloud, not yet. "It was classified from the very beginning."

"Classified?" Almadi asked. She walked over. She could look over Dauber's shoulder because she was cleared for everything that Dauber was, but Almadi didn't look after all.

She waited, like everyone else.

But they all knew how strange the classification was. Most missions had layers in their files—protected information that only the officers could access, for example. But the Fleet rarely classified any mission. There was no need. The DV-Class vessels were moving forward, exploring, and there was little to hide.

The sector bases had classified areas, but that was to protect research and researchers, not to keep information away from the rest of the Fleet.

But Dauber had only seen an entire classified mission a few times in her career, and even then, those tended to be about diplomacy, not about anything else.

This trip didn't seem to be about diplomacy. It seemed to concern Scrapheaps.

"I'm seeing references to a foldspace journey," she said slowly, making sure she wasn't revealing too much. "And it seemed to be going back, through sectors long since abandoned."

That very idea made her shiver.

"And it seems..." she said, frowning at the screen, "that the *Renegat* went alone."

"They sent a single ship on a long foldspace run?" asked Almadi. "A *Security*-Class ship?"

Almadi's tone reinforced Dauber's surprise. But the fact that Almadi *was* surprised was even more important, because she had served on SC-Class vessels, and had briefly captained one during her officer training.

Dauber didn't address Almadi's surprise, because right now, Dauber had no answers for her. She had more questions.

"According to this," she said, "the *Renegat* left Starbase Rho with a new crew."

"Starbase Rho," Ullman said softly. "Wow."

Yes, wow. Starbase Rho had closed decades ago. Dauber had never even seen it.

"The crew compliment," Dauber said, "was 487. But at a stop at Sector Base Z, they added quite a few new crew members."

"'Quite a few?'" Almadi repeated. "What does that mean?"

Dauber shook her head, then glanced at Ullman. She needed him to go through this. To hell with the classified label. It was 100 years out of date. The *Renegat* was dying. She needed as much information as she could get, as fast as she could get it.

"I can't tell," she said. "They might have had crew abandon ship on Sector Base Z, but it's not clear to me."

"And why the uncertainty on the crew complement?" Ribisi said. "Either there were 507 crew members or 517."

"Or something in between," Ullman said.

The vague number was unusual. Everything about this mission was unusual.

"There's a chance that is the same crew," Ribisi said. "The *anacapa* drive is malfunctioning."

Everyone knew that one of dangers of foldspace travel was time displacement.

Dauber nodded. "We'll need a list of original crew members, just in case," she said. "Not just the officers, like we sent to Khusru."

"If it is the same crew," Almadi said, "then what happened? There should be three hundred more people than there are."

Dauber bit her lower lip. The ship had come through foldspace damaged, with atmosphere leaking and a malfunctioning *anacapa* drive. But there was no evidence that the ship had been breached by someone else.

Had something gone through the ship? An unidentified virus maybe?

"We're going to need environmental clearance as well," Dauber said. She looked at Almadi. "Make sure *Rescue One* knows this ship arrived three hundred people short. Make sure all of the medical information is accurate, and make sure that anyone who gets off those life rafts goes through full decontamination for every damn thing we can think of."

She was not going to bring a virus on board this ship.

But she didn't think that a virus was the problem. She was seeing other intimations of a greater issue, something she didn't entirely understand.

She handed her tablet to Ullman. He took it with surprise. She had left her clearance open.

She trusted him not to use that clearance to look at files he shouldn't look at. She knew him well enough to know that such a thing would never cross his mind.

"Figure out what happened to this ship," she said. "Then report to me."

"Yes, sir." He climbed onto the stool he had been leaning on and set to work.

She eased out of the cocoon made by his screens and walked to the main part of the bridge. She looked at Ribisi's screens as she passed, saw glowing and vibrating *anacapa* images.

"It's bad, isn't it?" she said to him.

"Yeah," he said.

"What do you think caused it?" she asked.

He shook his head. "I've never seen that kind of damage before," he said. "But I do know this: SC-Class vessels were never built to spend a lot of time in foldspace. Not even the older vessels, at least that I know of. They're meant to dive in and out, usually with a lot of support from other SC-Class vessels. And yet, you think this one went alone somewhere?"

"That's what it looks like," Dauber said.

"That makes no sense," he said.

"Yeah," she said. "I know."

And that bothered her more than she wanted to say.

PART TEN
INTO FOLDSPACE
100 YEARS AGO

THE *RENEGAT*

The captain's ready room was crowded. Crowe would have preferred to have this meeting in one of the actual conference rooms, but Captain Preemas was preparing to send the *Renegat* into foldspace, and he wanted to be as close to the bridge as possible.

The ready room's amazing amount of furniture made the meeting uncomfortable. Two of the chairs didn't move, and neither did the elaborate desk. At least Preemas had cleared off the desk.

Six people crowded around it, looking at the surface as if the screen there held answers.

Six people were, in Crowe's opinion, four people too many.

Although they all belonged in this meeting. He was the one who had brought three of them in—Natalia Stephanos, Tindo Ibori, and Milton Atwater. Preemas had also brought along one of the newbies, a woman named Justine Breaux.

She seemed the most out of place. She suffered from a series of embarrassed flushes, turning her light brown skin a dusty rose. She didn't really like the attention placed on her, and she had apologized for her lack of education on all things shipwide more than once since the meeting started.

Crowe wanted to tell her to shut up, at least about her inexperience with starships, but he didn't. It wasn't his place.

He stood next to Stephanos, who kept shifting from foot to foot. She was a slender dark-haired woman who was quiet until she couldn't take whatever it was that irritated her anymore. He had managed to snag her from Sector Base Z, where she had gone to teach for a few years. She had hated it, thankfully, so she was willing to come onto the *Renegat,* even with its problems. She had no family or close relationships, but her prickly nature precluded most of them.

He was glad to have her, considering the length of the foldspace travel that faced them. She knew more about *anacapa* drives than anyone else he had ever worked with.

Atwater knew a lot about them too, but his knowledge was all theory and history. He was the palest person Crowe had ever seen. Atwater had bright red hair and even brighter green eyes. He knew how the drives were supposed to work, the history of the drives in various ships, how the drives interacted with foldspace, and what kind of limits the drives could be pushed to.

Atwater wasn't an engineer. He was a foldspace researcher, the only real foldspace researcher on the ship, and he was in his element. Like Breaux, he was new to space travel and where she was frightened of it, Atwater was giddy.

Both responses were headshaking as far as Crowe and Preemas were concerned, but they knew that was one of the risks they were taking when they brought inexperienced travelers onto the ship.

The final person in the room, Tindo Ibori, was almost as tall as Crowe. Ibori had worked in maintenance until Preemas changed everyone's jobs. Preemas moved Ibori to navigation, which had turned out to be a brilliant move. Like the best navigators in the Fleet, Ibori could actually see space in all of its dimensions in his mind's eye. He needed equipment, but only to augment his imagination.

He was there to help the entire team replot their route if need be. And the need would happen, since Preemas had assigned Breaux to research where they were going, based on the old information from past Fleet missions and sector bases. Atwater was to figure out the best way to protect the *anacapa* drive, and Stephanos was supposed to be the one who would execute the plan—with Crowe's help, of course.

They had two major assignments: the first was to make sure they got through foldspace without taxing the *anacapa* drive, and the second was to make sure they ended up where they were supposed to end up.

Right now, the screen on the desk displayed two different maps side by side, in two dimensions. Crowe preferred holographic three-dimensional maps. He would have overlaid one on top of the other, but when he suggested that, he had been overruled.

Apparently the older map only existed in two dimensions, so the computer would have to guess and fill in the three-dimensional map. No one else wanted a computerized guess in the middle of their decision-making.

Crowe was of the opinion that the computer's guesses were better than theirs, but he had been overruled.

They were looking at the sector that had once housed Sector Base Q. The old maps from the days when Sector Base Q was in operation were detailed, but the current map was not. It wasn't much more than a guess, since no Fleet ship had been back that way in centuries.

Breaux had already complained that Preemas hadn't told her what her job would be, so she didn't have complete access to Fleet archives. She said, more than once, that she could have copied the pertinent archive material before she left.

Crowe had put in a request with Sector Base Z for that information, but no one had sent it to the *Renegat*. He suspected that Rufus Gerlik wasn't willing to do any more business with the *Renegat*.

If Preemas wanted to blindly follow the map that the Fleet had given him, the *Renegat* would already be heading toward the abandoned Sector Base Q. But Preemas didn't trust the Fleet any more than Sector Base Z trusted him.

The Fleet's maps took the *Renegat* into and out of foldspace ten times. Crowe had developed a different map that made each foldspace trip the same length, which meant that the *Renegat* would go into and out of foldspace a dozen times.

But neither set of maps—the Fleets and Crowe's—were based on anything concrete. Preemas got to the heart of that matter fast when he asked the one question no one could answer:

When we emerge from foldspace, how will we know we're in the correct place?

The question, asked more than a week ago, set everyone back. Because a star map wouldn't answer that question, particularly the farther back the *Renegat* went. Space changed, just like everything else. Stars cooled and winked out. Asteroids hit moons, sometimes destroying most or all of them. Inhabited planets sometimes exploded, especially when the humans on that planet went to war with each other.

Humans also built things, like moon-sized bases, and in one historical case, something planet-sized.

So eyeballing the area wouldn't work. Nor would the oldest maps.

The implication of Preemas's question wasn't just whether or not they arrived in the right place on the old maps. But the idea was that they could jump, then jump again, then jump a third time, all without checking against any map, and suddenly, they would be three foldspace trips away from wherever they were supposed to be.

They would never figure out where they had gone awry, particularly if they went into that part of foldspace that no one quite understood. The part where ships vanished or lost time or became becalmed.

Ships did escape from those places, but usually those ships had only taken one foldspace trip, not several.

Preemas wanted to make sure the crew of the *Renegat* knew where it was at all times.

Crowe wanted the same thing, although part of him wondered if that was even possible.

"Here's what bothers me," Breaux said, her voice shaking with nerves. Her fingers shook too. She wasn't used to brainstorming with people who outranked her, and it showed. "We're making other assumptions besides the one saying the maps are accurate. We're assuming that these sectors are at peace. Sectors aren't static, and we know there's lots of human habitation throughout. Humans make war, and sometimes, they make war across an entire sector. Suddenly our big ship arrives in the middle of all that?"

Everyone looked at her, and Stephanos didn't even try to hide her astonishment. No one who served on the *Renegat* and had served on other ships thought of the *Renegat* as "big."

"What?" Breaux asked. "What did I say?"

Crowe took pity on her and spoke before someone could correct her. She felt humiliated enough. He didn't want to lose her insights, because mostly, they were fresh. Humiliating her further would make her clam up.

"That's a good point," he said, a little more loudly than he needed to. "We don't know what we're heading into. We could land right in the middle of someone else's conflict."

"That's why we stocked up," Preemas said. "We'll be in and out of these sectors before they even know we arrived."

"We hope," Ibori said. "If we arrive near those sector bases like the Fleet map wants us to do, we guarantee that we arrive near human habitation. If we assume that those habitats monitor the space near them, then they will know where we are."

"And there's another problem." Atwater spoke up for the first time. "There's a long history of sector bases being improperly shut down. What if our *anacapa* drive hooks into an ancient sector base's arrival drive? We might end up not in the space around the sector base's home planet, but inside the closed base itself."

Crowe sucked in a breath. He had no idea such a thing was possible or that there was a "long history" of it. But he had brought Atwater onto the ship for precisely this kind of knowledge.

Preemas cursed softly. "So, we can't leave yet. We have to redo the maps."

"Maybe." Breaux sounded even more tentative than she had before. "But I've been talking to Milton, and I wonder if we should avoid the active nodes."

"The what?" Stephanos asked. Crowe was glad that she had, because he had the same question.

"The data that we received from the Scrapheap went through about thirty-five active nodes to get to us," Breaux said. "I've been studying its route. That data was rerouted about twenty times. I think that means it hit an inactive node, waited some requisite amount of time, and then was resent to a different node. I think maybe we go to the sectors with the *inactive* nodes, not the active ones."

"Because...?" Stephanos asked, clearly not following.

Breaux swallowed hard. "Because my guess is that the sectors with the active nodes have improperly shut down sector bases or starbases. Starbases aren't a worry because we can't get trapped inside, but sector bases...Milton says..." Then she waved a hand at Atwater, letting him take over her part of the conversation.

Which he did.

"In the historics I studied long before I joined the *Renegat*," Atwater said, "I found at least five cases of ships that were called back to old sector bases by the bases themselves. Three of those ships were just fine, although it took the crew some work to get out of the base once they were inside. Usually they needed to repair their own *anacapa* drive, and leave, but in one instance, they had to actually physically climb out of the base."

Crowe frowned. Preemas looked impatient. He didn't want to hear any of this. Crowe wasn't sure he wanted to hear it either, but it felt as if he needed to.

"But," Atwater said, "there are two instances where a ship ended up inside a destroyed base. One of the ships sent a distress signal as it got pulled, and it got found, shattered, inside."

"How is that possible?" Stephanos asked. "Our ships are built strong. The nanobits alone—"

"Wouldn't be enough to compensate for landing inside solid rock," Crowe said softly. He didn't even want to imagine how the last few minutes on that ship went.

"The other ship was greatly damaged, but the crew managed to survive," Atwater said. "I was actually thinking of studying this phenomenon more on Sector Base Z after they told me I couldn't study in space."

Preemas's mouth thinned. "You're citing five instances out of hundreds of thousands of trips inside and out of foldspace."

His tone said it was all irrelevant. Crowe wished he could agree.

"Beg pardon, sir," Atwater said, "but thousands of ships have vanished into foldspace over the centuries. We have no idea where or how those ships ended up. We only *know* of five instances. There could be many more."

"Or no more," Preemas snapped. "Let's stay focused on the possible. This ship has enough facing it without making up a sector base problem."

Crowe hated this part of Preemas. The man made a lot of decisions based on what he wanted to believe, not on any kind of fact.

"This sector base problem is not made up," Crowe said. "I think Justine's caution is a good one. Active nodes might be dangerous for us."

Preemas shot him an irritated look.

"All right, then," Preemas said, sounding even angrier than he looked. "I suppose we'll need to replot everything."

Crowe understood Preemas's irritation. Preemas wanted to leave this area as fast as he could, before Gāo realized he had gone around some of her orders again.

"Actually," Breaux said, and then swallowed convulsively. Clearly that was a nervous habit for her. "Um, we won't have to replot."

"Justine," Atwater started.

She held up a hand, stopping him, looking more confident than she had a moment ago.

"I...I...knew that I was going to suggest this," she said, "so I did some reworking. We'll still have to look up a few maps, but not as many as you think. We'll have to skip two of our planned stops."

"Two out of a dozen," Crowe said.

She nodded. "I'm guessing, you have to understand that, okay? But when I compared that information I saw in the data stream from the Scrapheap to the coordinates for old sector bases, it looks like there were only two active sector base nodes in this mix. The rest came from nodes nowhere near a sector base, and if it's not a problem to maybe end up in or near a starbase, then I think we'll be fine."

"We can avoid a starbase," Preemas said, his voice dripping with contempt.

"Then," she said, no longer meeting anyone's gaze, "in that case, only two. And they're farther down the route. Older bases. I mean, much older. Way back. So we'll have time to research them."

Preemas let out a breath. "All right. When can we comfortably leave?"

Comfortably? It was all Crowe could do not to give Preemas an incredulous sideways look. They were heading on a major trip into the great unknown, a trip that the Fleet figured they would die on, and Preemas had used the word *comfortably*?

No one else seemed to notice.

"Realistically," Atwater said, his head bent down as he looked at the flat maps, "let's give it one more day. I love Justine's idea, but I haven't had a chance to check her route yet."

"I'd like to check the coordinates as well," Ibori said.

The team was acutely aware that Breaux was not a navigator. Crowe gave her the sideways look he had avoided giving Preemas.

She stood, hands clasped in front of her, twisting awkwardly together. She was nodding as she bit her lower lip.

"I like that," she said, surprising him. Most people didn't like their work challenged. "I would prefer it, in fact. This is all new to me. In the past, everything I've done has been theory, and this…isn't."

"One more day." Preemas turned so that he could see Crowe. Their gazes met over Breaux's head, and Crowe saw both anger and reluctance in Preemas's look.

"I agree," Crowe said. "We need the double check."

Preemas's lower lip curled, something he sometimes did just before launching into a foul tirade.

Crowe raised his eyebrows, warning Preemas away from saying anything—or so Crowe hoped.

Everyone turned toward Preemas. His expression remained the same—tight, angry, controlled.

Then it relaxed and he grinned. If no one looked at his eyes, they would think he was fine with the decision.

"Tomorrow it is," Preemas said. "But that's it. We leave tomorrow no matter what. No amount of planning will prepare us for this trip. At some point, we're just going to have to leave. No matter how frightened we are."

"I'm not suggesting this because I'm frightened," Breaux said, clearly thinking that she was causing the problem.

Crowe held up a hand, stopping her. "The decision to double-check is a good one," he said, "even though we don't know what we're facing."

"We'll never know what we're facing until we get there," Preemas snapped. "We need to get this trip underway."

Everyone leaned back, the force of Preemas's anger clear. Crowe wanted to challenge him, but didn't dare. He wanted to say, *You want this trip to succeed? Then we take some precautions.*

But he didn't.

Because on some level, Preemas was right. On some level, they had to go with what they had. No one had done this before. No amount of planning would change that.

Crowe turned back to the team. He gave Stephanos a pointed glance.

"Let me know if you find anything major," he said.

She had worked with him before; she understood what he meant. He meant, *Let me know if you find something terrifying.* Otherwise they would be on their way.

"I will," she said, in a tone that Crowe recognized. It was a tone that she reserved only for him, only in times of greatest emergency.

Then Stephanos was the one who turned to Preemas.

"Do we have leave to get started, Captain?" she asked.

He waved a hand dismissively. "Of course, go," he said, keeping his gaze on Crowe.

The other four left, heads down, moving quietly out of the room, almost as if they expected Preemas to shout at Crowe.

It was possible.

"They're wasting time," Preemas said.

Crowe shook his head. "They're making sure we don't die before we arrive at the Scrapheap."

"I suppose," Preemas said. Then he narrowed his eyes. "Well? Go help them."

"Yes, sir," Crowe said, and left the ready room.

He wasn't going to help the team at all. He had other things to work on. Because Breaux had brought up a point that made him realize there was an aspect to this trip that he hadn't even considered.

He needed to make certain the *Renegat*'s communications *anacapa* drive was active. He usually paid no attention to a communications *anacapa*, leaving them off. They weren't needed most of the time, especially on ships that operated inside a sector, like most SC-Class vessels.

The *anacapa* was well protected in its little panel, but it was always better to have the drive inactive. He would have to set it now, because there would be no communicating with the Fleet without it.

He also needed to set up a slow backup data stream, one that would send any recorded messages to the Fleet by the very subchannels that Breaux had mentioned.

Crowe could probably do that work while they were double-checking Breaux's research.

And unlike Breaux, Crowe wasn't going to mention this to Preemas at all.

Crowe wasn't quite sure why. But he was beginning to think that telling this captain everything that was happening on his ship wasn't always the best idea.

Crowe sighed softly as he made his way across the bridge. He wasn't sure if he was behaving this way because he rarely trusted his superior officers or if his response was because he was trusting Preemas less and less as each day went on.

And Crowe wasn't sure he wanted to figure that out.

THE *RENEGAT*

Breaux stood on the bridge of the *Renegat*, hands clasped in front of her. The crew was scattered around various stations, some of which had floating screens and others had consoles. No one was sitting down. The overall screens on the ship—the ones that had given a view of the outside of the ship on every other trip she had ever taken on a starship—were off. Black, shiny, reflecting the tense tight faces of everyone here.

The people she knew were crowded toward the front. Natalia Stephanos was standing beside a console that was close to a small black box on the floor. Atwater had told Breaux that was the container for the *anacapa* drive. Stephanos wasn't even looking at the drive.

Neither was Ibori. He was at the console that he called the navigator's station, moving his hands rapidly. He seemed unconcerned by what they were about to do.

Maybe that was how all Fleet crew were trained to look. The ones who seemed tense might have been the screw-ups she'd heard so much about.

Because she didn't think her team was a group of screw-ups, and neither did Captain Preemas.

He stood near his captain's chair, looking at even more tablets and screens. He barely seemed to acknowledge her, and that was all right with her.

She felt like she was on the bridge as a courtesy.

That was what Atwater had said about both of them. He was also here, standing toward the back just like her, watching everything with eager eyes.

The only person who seemed to acknowledge their presence at all was First Officer Crowe. He had nodded at her, then smiled just a little, before going to work on a console near Stephanos.

Breaux felt useless, even though up until this point, she had worked very hard. The fact that her eyes were scratchy didn't help. She had had hardly any sleep at all.

She had been up all night with the team, checking the numbers, discussing routes, being asked over and over and over again if she actually thought that the recalculations were worthwhile.

How was she supposed to know? She didn't have the same skills as a navigator. She had just done basic calculations, then passed everything to the rest of the team. Some of the calculations she had cribbed from the information she had received from the Scrapheap communications file.

Most of the Fleet's archives were lost or, she suspected, the Fleet never really kept them. The Fleet never really cared about its history as history. Only about certain events as they pertained to decision-making—the fight that had led the Fleet to veer away from its first choice for Sector Base A-2, for example, would be something that had gotten placed in the records.

She found countless examples of battles that led to a change in Fleet technology or classified discussions of discoveries and weaponry. But she hadn't yet found any established maps or routes that the Fleet thought necessary to maintain. After the Fleet left a sector for good, it no longer cared about maintaining the maps.

It all frustrated her.

She twisted her hands together tightly, feeling even more nervous than she had before. Part of her nerves were caused by the fact that her research wasn't esoteric any longer. She wasn't doing it to get a promotion or to be seen as the most knowledgeable expert in her field.

What she had discovered—or hadn't discovered—was now a matter of life and death.

This entire ship's trajectory depended on information she had found, surmises she had made, and she was brand new. She didn't know anything.

Except how to understand the maps. Everyone seemed to value that, even Captain Preemas.

He was the most mercurial man she had ever worked for, and that made her even more nervous. But he didn't seem to see her except when he needed her, so she didn't take his moods personally.

Atwater did, but Atwater was a career man. He was hoping to turn this mission into something that would enable him to travel with the Fleet on other missions in the future. He was bright-eyed, and he seemed to believe nothing could go wrong. Especially after First Officer Crowe tried to reassure Breaux.

Don't worry, he had said when she had fretted about the *anacapa* drive itself. *We have a backup drive with us on the ship.*

Until that moment, she hadn't realized ships could carry backup drives.

Her mouth was dry, and she swallowed against it, heart pounding. Nothing was happening on this bridge, and yet she felt like she had run for miles.

She was terrified and exhilarated at the same time.

"Are we ready?" Captain Preemas asked First Officer Crowe. There was some edge to Captain Preemas's voice, almost an accusation. He had seemed so impatient the day before, even though he hadn't directed it at her.

She had had the sense that if he felt he could reasonably do so, he would have simply sent the *Renegat* through foldspace, calculations be damned.

"As ready as we're going to be," First Officer Crowe replied, his voice calm but filled with warning. Almost as if he were trying to tell Captain Preemas that nothing was going to go as anticipated and he had to stop expecting that.

Or maybe she was just projecting. Maybe she was the one who needed to hear the warning.

What she could hear was her heartbeat pounding in her own ears. She had been holding her breath.

She released it.

She glanced over at Atwater. He gave her a goofy sideways grin, filled with excitement. This was the fulfillment of one of his dreams. He had always wanted to be here, on the bridge of some starship.

She had never expected to be, and now she had stumbled onto this ship, this circumstance, about to take an adventure that made even the most seasoned officers nervous.

"All right then," Captain Preemas said. "Let's do it."

His fingers moved on the screen floating in front of him. First Officer Crowe moved his hand slightly as well, and Stephanos crouched just a bit, so that she could get closer to the *anacapa* drive.

No one else on the bridge moved. Breaux had expected something else at this moment—everyone to look up, everyone to acknowledge that this moment was the moment when they would officially become unreachable, a true explorer ship on a crucial mission back to a place the Fleet never thought it would return to.

But everyone seemed calm, as if this were an everyday event, as if nothing had changed.

Maybe heading into foldspace was an everyday event for all of them. It wasn't for her or for Atwater. She glanced at him again, but now he was watching Stephanos, that goofy grin still creasing his face.

Breaux should have crossed the bridge and stood beside him. At least then, they could share their own giddy excitement.

But she didn't want to move. The journey into foldspace was going to begin any moment, and she wanted to pay attention to it.

She stared at the darkened screens, only because she didn't know where else to look. That, and she could see most of the faces, looking serious as everyone continued their work.

Her hands gripped each other tightly. Her heartrate had accelerated so much that it felt as if her heart couldn't go any faster. She had to force herself to breathe.

Once they crossed into foldspace, she would feel better. She had to. Then they would be underway.

Or maybe, she would feel like this for the rest of the trip: scared, on edge, uncertain.

Then, the *Renegat* bumped and skidded, sliding forward as if it were a ground vehicle crossing ice on one of the mountaintops near Sector Base Z. But bumping and skidding was impossible: the *Renegat* wasn't on any kind of surface. Space didn't have turbulence like air did. Space was a vacuum.

In all of her time on ships (which wasn't that much, if she was being honest), she had never felt anything like this—a continual rocking, bumping, shifting.

She wanted to grab a console, but she didn't dare. She would have to walk to one, anyway, and even if she did find one, then she might grip it wrong, making something happen when she didn't mean to.

The skidding feeling continued. No one had warned her about it, and no one else seemed concerned.

Which meant this bump and change was *normal* when a ship entered foldspace.

Normal.

She exhaled. She had been holding her breath again.

Stephanos's face had relaxed. So, apparently, she wasn't worried about the *anacapa* drive. At least not anymore.

First Officer Crowe hadn't moved, though. His expression hadn't changed either. He was still looking at his console.

Captain Preemas gripped the top of his holoscreen and pulled it into a small ball, before it vanished.

The bumping stopped, and the screens came alive. Planets, stars, something white and filmy on the righthand screen, a bit of winking red to the left, none of it familiar. The closest planet wasn't blue and white and green the way that Vostrim was. It was orange and brown and purple, with a dot of bright red on one side.

Breaux's breath caught. She was somewhere else. Somewhere very far from where she had started.

And that felt…awe-inspiring and weird at the same time.

Then she made herself breath. In. Out. Trying to remain calm just like everyone else. Only they weren't trying. They *were* calm.

As she settled, she realized her chest hurt from the breaths she had been holding, a headache had started, and she was slightly nauseated—maybe from that weird bumpiness—but she was *here*. Somewhere else.

They were somewhere else.

She was here with the entire ship. They were in this adventure together.

She hadn't really felt that before.

"Breaux!" Captain Preemas barked.

She lifted her head, felt slightly dizzy, made herself breathe. Everyone was working except her and Atwater. And now, Captain Preemas was calling her.

"Yes, sir?" she asked.

"Come here," he said. "You need to check something."

She did? Her? She blinked. Atwater was watching, but no one else was.

She wended her way past the consoles, past the bridge crew hard at work, trying not to look at those magnificent stars, strange planets, and colorful moons on the screen. Somewhere else. How very exciting.

She reached Captain Preemas's side quickly. "Yes, sir?"

He had opened a two-dimensional screen with a map on it. A second screen was open beside it.

"Did we end up where we meant to?" he asked.

How would she know? He was the one with the team and the equipment and the navigators. He understood these things.

She didn't.

And then she realized what he was asking. He wanted to know if the two-dimensional map he had before him was anything like the one she had used for this sector. She had changed some of the perimeters in her work, as she searched for nodes and arrival spots and the old sector bases.

The first map he had called up was the one she had designed. The second one looked nothing like it.

He was worried, and she didn't blame him.

She swallowed, willed the headache away (and that didn't work, but at least she could pretend that it didn't exist anymore), and looked at the two maps. The new one looked familiar, as if it were the first one before she had tweaked it.

But she didn't want to say definitively.

What if they were in the wrong place? Would they jump again? Go back? Try to find the other coordinates from here?

No one had told her what the procedure was, and she didn't know. She had no idea what she would do if the maps were significantly different.

Then she realized that she wouldn't do anything. She had given her life over to this man, these people, and they would decide for her. The only decision she had made was the one to join this ship.

"Do you mind if I alter this image?" she asked, pointing at the second map.

"Tell me what to do and I'll change it," he said.

He didn't want her touching that screen. Maybe there was special access needed or something. Not that it was her concern.

She told him all the steps she had taken to change the first image, imagining it as if she were actually changing the image herself.

His fingers deftly moved across the image, much more accurately than she had managed the first time she tried it.

It only took a few seconds, and then the map refocused. She didn't have to say anything, because it was obvious that the two maps were the same, but she said, "Yes, according to this, we're in the exact right spot."

She was so relieved, her knees started to buckle. She caught herself just in time.

"Excellent," Captain Preemas said. "Do you concur, *First Officer* Crowe?"

Breaux had no idea why Preemas had put such emphasis on the words *first officer*, but he had. And First Officer Crowe didn't seem to mind.

"Yes," First Officer Crowe said in a flat tone. "According to our sensors, we are in the right place."

Someone applauded, just once, before they stopped mid-clap. Breaux knew without looking that the someone who had done that had been Atwater.

She turned her head ever so slightly. His face was red. She gave him a small smile, and he shrugged sheepishly.

"All right then," Captain Preemas said. "We'll cross the sector, just like our Fleet masters suggested, and then we'll take the next foldspace leg of our journey."

Breaux already knew, from the discussions the day before, that they weren't following the Fleet's suggestions just because the Fleet wanted them to travel slowly across sectors, but because both First Officer Crowe and Natalia Stephanos believed that the *anacapa* drive would work better on this long journey if it had time to rest.

There's no proof of that, though, right? Captain Preemas had asked, as if he wanted to cram a foldspace journey back-to-back with another foldspace journey until they got to the Scrapheap.

We're already taking a lot of risks, First Officer Crowe had said in that calm voice he had just used a few moments ago. *We don't need to take any more.*

And Captain Preemas had listened to him then. Apparently, they were following that protocol now as well, and Captain Preemas was just letting everyone know.

Captain Preemas surveyed the bridge crew, then looked pointedly at Breaux. She was standing too close, and she knew it. She just had no idea how to extricate herself from her position beside the captain.

Her gaze met his. His was filled with amusement at her obvious predicament.

"Anything else, Breaux?" he asked her, as if it had been her idea to bring her close to the captain's chair.

She swallowed, hating her nervousness. Since she had him here, she might as well ask about one other thing.

"Yes, sir," she said. "If someone could make sure that I get all the telemetry from this sector, I will use it to calibrate my work."

The amusement left his gaze. Had he really been happier when she was uncomfortable?

"You heard her, everyone. Make sure she gets the proper information." Then he nodded at her, and she understood. She was done here.

"Thank you," she said softly and made her way to the exit. As she passed Atwater, he fell in beside her.

"I'm giddy," he said softly, as if that wasn't obvious, as if he had been hiding his emotions all along.

Breaux was many things, but giddy was not one of them. Relieved, focused, and beneath it all, slightly terrified. She felt like they were traveling to the past, even though they weren't. They were simply reversing the track that the Fleet had followed for centuries.

And she had that thought as if it were a minor thing.

It wasn't.

THE *SPRÁVA*

Gāo's eyes ached. She'd been doing a lot of close work for hours, going over data and reports, trying to figure out if it was possible to change the way that the Fleet handled Scrapheaps without getting rid of the idea of Scrapheaps themselves.

She had gone to the officers' mess on board the *Správa*, mostly to see other faces and partly to look through the curved portholes at space beyond. She needed to see something pretty and uncomplicated, and even though she knew the universe itself was infinitely complicated, the winking stars and fading blue of the area around the ship calmed her like nothing else could.

The officers' mess wasn't as large as the regular crew mess, so it felt homey. Lots of brown and black wood taken from forests near the last two sector bases added an unusual design. The real greenery, vines whose type she couldn't identify, looped around the booths, above the windows, and along the walls, added to the comforting feeling.

It was as if the designers had brought just enough of planet living into the mess, but not so much that it would intimidate the crew members who had spent their entire lives in space.

Gāo had a favorite table, in the corner between the curved windows and a vine-covered wall. She sat with her back to the vines, and she had learned early on to not push her chair too far back or it would split the vines open and cover her with a gooey mint-scented sap.

Still, when she sat like this, she saw what was going on in the mess, as well as the entire length of the curved windows, and the activity outside of the ship. Sometimes, when the *Správa* flew in formation with the rest of the command ships, dozens of small ships with their lights and their sleek black bodies filled the view. Other times, like this time, the vastness of space itself, with the pale white and deep gold of distant stars, provided a light that made her heart sing.

After a day of hard work, she needed a bit of inspiration, as well as sustenance. No one would approach her in the officers' mess unless they were part of her team or unless she beckoned them. And when she sat here, she rarely beckoned anyone.

She sipped the blackest coffee made on the ship, ate a meal of spicy lentil soup with a side of cucumber salad—all ingredients grown in the *Správa*'s gigantic hydroponics bay. The bay was something she had ordered long ago, when she had transferred to the *Správa* and it had become her permanent home. She had asked that hydroponics become a major focus of the work on the ship, so that the food would not only be fresh, but varied.

"Forgive me, Vice Admiral." Lieutenant Cali Baker's careworn face appeared in miniature in the corner of Gāo's right eye. "I know you don't like to be disturbed when you're eating, but this can't wait. We have contact from the *Renegat*."

Gāo leaned back and dabbed her mouth with a napkin, doing her best not to sigh. "Another message?"

Preemas had sent two direct messages since that fateful discussion about his behavior on Sector Base Z. The first thanked Gāo for her quick review of the new crew members he had unceremoniously hired for the *Renegat*.

The second informed her that the *Renegat* was heading into foldspace for its long journey back to the Scrapheap.

The messages had been in line with what she had expected from him. The fact that he had contacted her directly right now was ever so slightly alarming.

"Problem, Lieutenant?"

"I don't know, sir. He didn't tell me." Baker's pale eyes seemed almost translucent in this small form. "But he is waiting."

"Transfer him to the communications room here," Gāo said.

She stood and put her napkin on the table beside her food, hoping she would be able to come back to it while it was still warm.

In all three of the major mess halls, there were small communications rooms off the main dining area, just in case someone needed to have a one-on-one conversation without traveling to a different part of the ship, and without the entire mess listening in.

The communications room off this mess hall was only a few yards from where she was sitting. She entered her command code to access the room, and slipped inside, hoping she was moving fast enough to catch Preemas.

Sometimes communications across any foldspace divide were uncertain.

But a wavy hologram of him stood in the center of the tiny room. He looked very professional. His hair was even shorter than it had been before, he was closely shaved, and he wore a casual uniform that looked pressed. The image occasionally fuzzed, revealing the controls on the wall of the communications room, but mostly, it looked like a glowing version of Captain Preemas stood inside the room with Gāo.

She activated her hologram, and then realized she hadn't even checked her face for an errant bit of soup, nor had she combed her hair. She had been tugging at it, and it was probably a mess.

Ironic that she would be the one who was a mess, not Preemas.

"Captain," she said as soon as she got the signal that the communications link was active.

There was a tiny delay, and then he said, "Vice Admiral," mimicking her tone. That was the Preemas she knew.

"I received your previous messages," she said.

"Sorry I didn't contact you one-on-one like you asked," he said. "I wanted to get the foldspace part of the journey underway before my crew changed its mind."

The question he probably wanted her to ask next was *Have they changed their minds?* But she didn't.

"So," she said, "your report...?"

He clasped his hands behind his back, like she usually did. He stood even straighter, as if he was actually reporting to her in person. "We have completed our first foldspace journey, and I am pleased to say that it was uneventful."

She let out a shallow breath. Not quite a sigh of relief, because she didn't want him to know that she was relieved. But relief all the same.

"I brought on two new crew members from Sector Base Z," he said, "and they specialize in research. I have one digging through the information that we have stored on board this ship about the places the Fleet has traveled and settled over the millennia. She is finding maps and imagery of where we've been. It's been highly useful so far."

He was digging at Gāo, letting her know that her instructions to him were ill-considered, and his own leadership was so much better than hers.

She had had other captains treat her this way as well. It was a passive-aggressive form of dominance, and one she found best to ignore.

Right now, she could do nothing about Preemas's attitude toward her, but she didn't need to. He was doing the job, and apparently, doing it well.

"Her old maps and data confirmed that we came out of foldspace at the exact coordinates that we had planned. Our *anacapa* is working well, and the ship seems to have no issues, not with personnel, not with supplies, and not with the trip itself." He sounded almost triumphant.

Gāo was startled at her own mixed response. She was pleased that the first leg of the foldspace journey had gone well, and she was happy that the *Renegat* was doing well.

But Preemas himself irritated her, and she wanted to shut him down with a sharp phrase accompanied by a haughty look.

"Our researchers are also studying that communication you got from the Scrapheap," he said.

Communications, plural, she almost said, but she wasn't willing to derail him yet.

"And because we're not sure quite how information got to you and how long it took," he continued, "I decided that I'd better contact you in person after each foldspace leg, just so that you get the message."

As if that were his idea. This one she wasn't going to let slip.

"I prefer live communications," she said. "I had told you that when I gave you this assignment."

He didn't move for a long moment. Then his eyes narrowed. She processed that little moment, and realized there was a lag. Not much of one, but enough to be noticeable.

Her stomach clenched. She had had a lot of communications across foldspace, and occasionally, there was a time lag or a data lag. It was usually nothing to worry about, but this was the first leg of a twelve-part journey. She hoped it was a problem between the sector the *Renegat* was in and the sector the *Správa* was in, and not something to do with foldspace itself.

"To clarify," she said, "we have received almost daily data packets from the Scrapheap, and we have an entire unit here studying the information that the Scrapheap is sending to us. So far, there is nothing new, because it believes we have not received its messages. But we can help you with the data flow or the way that the packets have traveled to us."

He raised his chin slightly, his eyes focused on her as if he were in the room. She realized, as he did that, that he had done so while she was speaking, not after.

Again, there was a slight pause before he responded.

"We would like that information," he said, "as well as any historical information on the sectors we're traveling through. Not the items in the normal Fleet database, which we have, but in your database. The more information we have, the better off we will be."

That was true, and something she hadn't considered. And, to his credit, he had brought on two researchers who could comb through the information.

"How long do you plan to be in this sector?" she asked. "I can have it sent before you leave."

"We're traveling to our next coordinates to make the foldspace journey. Those are the coordinates the Fleet mapped out. It will take us more than a day from here, so you have time."

Some interesting phrasing there. *The coordinates the Fleet mapped out* implied that they were going to use other coordinates at a different time.

Ah, well, that was a normal feature of longer journeys. At some point, a ship's captain had to make decisions to alter a route because of unforeseen obstacles along the way.

"I'll make sure you receive what we have," she said, making a mental note. She wasn't sure the Fleet archives contained much more than he already had.

"I don't know if you noticed this on your end," she said, "but on mine, there's a slight time lag. Maybe thirty seconds at the most, but enough that it's visible."

He lifted his head, and then nodded. She wished she knew exactly what he had nodded at, but she couldn't really tell with the time differential.

"I've noticed," he said, clearing that up. "I'm not sure if it's my equipment or if it has something to do with the distance we've traveled."

She hadn't given the equipment any thought. She was working out of the communications array in the mess. She normally didn't do that.

Transferring from her office here shouldn't have caused any problems, but shouldn't have didn't always mean anything. Sometimes just because something shouldn't have happened didn't stop whatever it was from happening.

"Generally," she said, "it's not the distance. I've communicated easily with a ship that went through foldspace."

But not backwards through foldspace. Tech in new sectors the Fleet was traveling to was always different, but in the old sectors, it might have pieces of the abandoned Fleet tech, and that could cause interference.

She would check on that theory with some of the engineers.

"I'll have my chief engineer go over the communications equipment to make sure we don't have any problems here," Preemas said. "Because if this is some kind of foldspace lag, it'll only get worse."

"We can't make that kind of assumption," she said. "We don't know how communications will work after you've traveled four or five sectors away from here. But we shouldn't have problems on two or three sectors. We've done that before. And you've only traveled one."

Or so she hoped. Because, she realized, she had no easy way to check where he was or how far he had gone.

"You don't think the effect is cumulative?" he asked, and then caught himself. Had he tried to interrupt her and failed because of the time lag? She couldn't tell.

She was going to answer the question he asked, as if he had waited until she had finished speaking before asking it.

"Each foldspace trip is different," she said. "The distance is more of a concern than foldspace itself. Technically, foldspace shouldn't cause any communications problems. The problems will come because at a certain point, our connection will be bounced through so many nodes and data streams that any discussion we have will, of necessity, slow down."

She waited for more than a minute, watching him. He didn't shift or even react to what she was saying. After about thirty seconds, she wondered if he had even heard her.

Then he frowned.

"I wonder if the different nodes in the different sectors can cause problems," he said quietly, and it seemed like he was speaking more to himself than to her.

"I don't know," she said. "I will have my people research that idea here as well."

Preemas's lips thinned. He held that expression, a frown creasing the space between his eyes, and then his face relaxed. He nodded.

"Thank you, Vice Admiral," he said, apparently deciding their communication was done. "I will contact you again when we've completed the second foldspace leg."

She had no reason to hold him in this conversation, although she felt oddly reluctant to let him go.

"Send me a formal report an hour or so ahead of when you will contact me," she said. "That will give me time to prepare questions, if I have any, and it will also serve as a double check if these communications break down."

"I will," he said.

She signed off, but remained standing, facing where he had been for a minute longer.

She had to separate herself emotionally from this mission. She was holding it too tightly and she was taking it too personally.

What was bothering her was not Preemas or the *Renegat* or even the type of mission itself. What was bothering her was the very thing that Preemas refused to let bother him.

It was a suicide mission. She knew it, and she had assigned the crew based on that designation.

Preemas had known it too, but he decided to work harder, to prove that he and his crew were not going to be the ones who died on this mission.

She needed to help him do so.

The first step was to send him all of the possible records that her people could find concerning the sectors he was returning to. And maybe even some information from the school ships, beyond what Calixte had given her at the beginning.

Gão straightened, her stomach finally settled, the tension in her shoulders gone for the first time in weeks.

She was going to make this right.

PART ELEVEN
THE RESCUE
NOW

THE *RENEGAT*

Serpell pushed her way out of the bridge, heading toward Deck Four and the cargo bay. Her heart was pounding, and her emotions were all over the place.

She was happy there were people on the bridge, people who said they could do something, but she was still here, on the *Renegat*, and she knew she wasn't safe until she was off the ship.

But at least there was an *off the ship* now. There hadn't been a realistic one, at least for her, as recently as thirty minutes ago. The question was, could she get off the ship fast enough?

It was dark in the corridors, although there was some emergency lighting still glowing along the floor. The ship was still in severe distress. And the distress was worse than she even imagined.

An *anacapa*-based explosion. No one would survive that, the Khusru woman had said.

Anacapa-based.

Kabac had been working on the *anacapa*. Had he made things worse?

Serpell took a shaky breath, and realized just how thin the air was in her environmental suit. She needed to get to that cargo bay fast, and gliding forward in the dark wasn't going to cut it.

"Suit," she said. "I need lights."

Advise leaving hostile environment as soon as possible, her suit responded.

"I'm trying, please," she said to the suit, as if it were a person, as if it would respond to begging. "Just a few lights, so I can find a new suit."

But the suit lights did not come on. Rather than fight with the suit, she kept moving. The emergency lighting extended through this section. The emergency lighting would have to do for right now.

She didn't know what she would do when she got below. She suspected the only reason emergency lighting worked on this level was because it was the bridge level. The emergency lighting would probably be off everywhere else.

She swallowed and mentally ordered herself to calm down. No one ever escaped something bad because of panic. The shadows, the dark, the thin emergency lighting (the stupid suit), she would deal with all of it, if she took it one step at a time.

She needed to get to Deck Four. Once she was on Deck Four, she needed to get to the cargo bay.

Once she got to the cargo bay, she would either escape or get a new suit or both.

One step.

Deck Four. That was next.

Then lights flared around her, casting her shadow, large and imposing, on the closed black door of the elevator to bridge level. Her heart continued to pound much too hard. It was nerves *and* the suit. It had to be.

When she got to the cargo bay—if she got to the cargo bay—she would definitely grab a different suit.

The lights got brighter. She propelled herself forward, not sure what or who was following her.

"Raina," Kabac said in her ear. "Hold up. I'm coming with you."

She wasn't sure if she should be relieved he was joining her or worried that he was no longer on the bridge. Those three people probably kicked him off the bridge. They probably suspected him of screwing up the *anacapa* drive as well.

And what if they were right?

She shook her head a little. She couldn't think about that right now.

Nor could she stop or even slow down.

"Can't hold up," she said. "My suit…."

And she let her voice trail off so that he would think that the problem with her suit was causing her to hurry along. Maybe it was. Maybe they could save her in that cargo bay.

Or maybe she would die there, while three strangers took over the *Renegat*.

"They're trying to steal the ship," Kabac said as he caught up to her.

"You don't know that," Serpell said. "And why do you care? The ship is falling apart."

She should care too because it was trained into her. She should always care about the ship. The ship was more important than the crew. The ship would outlast the crew. That was what she had learned over all the years.

Protect the ship.

"They pulled me away from the *anacapa,*" he said. "They lied. They say it's going to explode."

"I thought you don't know anything about *anacapa* drives." Her throat constricted, making it hard to get the words out. The three had said that on the bridge. What if they were right?

"I know enough to know that alarms would have deafened us by now if the *anacapa* was malfunctioning," Kabac said.

He moved ahead of her, and grabbed her arm, using his momentum to pull her forward. She was getting lightheaded. Was the suit finally completely compromised?

"Even with the power gone?" she asked.

He didn't answer, and she had worked with him enough recently to realize that when he didn't know the answer, he often remained silent rather than firmly stating something that could later be proven wrong.

"Let's just get to the cargo bay," she said. "We'll find out soon enough if they're telling us the truth."

She wasn't sure how they would find that out, exactly, because cargo bays could be locked off from the rest of the *Renegat*. That much she knew.

But she had to trust, just a little.

"We're going to die, you know," Kabac said softly.

"I know," she said, just as softly. "Believe me, I know."

THE *RENEGAT*

Zarges huddled over the central console in the alcove in Engineering, his visor reflecting the blinking red from the board. Palmer, beside him, was still trying to solve a bit of the *anacapa* problem from here, even though they all knew it was futile.

Palmer was adding another small energy pack to the console itself, because Zarges had ordered her to.

He had had his team contact both the *Aizsargs* and *Rescue One*, and he hoped to hell they moved the ships, because he couldn't guarantee that his timeline was accurate.

He had thought they would have two hours to abandon this ship and move everyone away.

But it was all a guess, compounded by the fact that this was an *anacapa* drive malfunction. He needed to get the communications array behind them functioning, because inside it, apparently, was a communications *anacapa* drive, a feature the Fleet had abandoned more than fifty years ago.

He hadn't even been able to get into the array, not with the power as low as it was. He needed to check that communications *anacapa* drive. They were getting no readings from it, but that meant nothing. He had no idea if the communications *anacapa* had extra containers around it to prevent its energy from reaching into the ship.

He could feel each moment slipping away. Fifteen minutes had passed already, and so far, there had been no announcement from the bridge.

He had to get the crew and passengers of the *Renegat* moving to the cargo bays, so that the life rafts could ferry them off the ship.

The communications array sputtered weakly to life, thanks to the energy pack Palmer had just placed on it. Now, all Zarges had to do was figure out how to make an announcement that everyone on the ship would pay attention to. Then he would see about that communications *anacapa.*

He took a deep breath and was about to toggle an actual button that supposedly started the process for a shipwide alert, when the array lit up even more.

Then a captain's code came through the array, verbally stamped from the bridge. Zarges's helmet picked up the code and the announcement itself.

This is the bridge: Evacuate the Renegat *immediately. Head to both cargo bays. Follow instructions once you arrive.*

The announcement was so loud that it hurt his ears. He hoped the announcement had gone through on all possible channels. He glanced at Palmer, who gave him a thumbs up, and Iqbar, who pulled herself level with him using the console to hold herself in place.

They both had heard the announcement as well.

Zarges let out a small sigh of relief. He wouldn't have to contact the *Renegat*'s crew from down here, where he wasn't even certain such a contact was possible.

Then he made himself focus. The announcement was only step one. The *Renegat's* crew had to follow the announcement. Zarges wasn't sure they would.

The announcement hadn't come from the captain of the *Renegat.* Instead, the announcement had started with *This is the bridge.* That sort of phrasing wasn't standard procedure.

Zarges had to figure that the crew of the *Renegat* wouldn't know exactly what standard evacuation procedure was. They'd hear about standard procedure in their training, and then again when they first boarded a ship, but for most folks that kind of training was years in their past.

He hoped this crew would hear the urgency and act on it immediately.

He needed to as well.

He twisted inside the communications alcove. He placed a hand on the side of the array, and hoped that the identification in his glove would force it to open.

It did, sliding sideways to reveal a small interior shelf. He turned on his glove's knuckle lights. They illuminated the small space perfectly. He could see the bed for the communications *anacapa*, but he didn't see a drive.

He peered sideways.

No drive at all.

The shelf was empty.

"I don't think we have a communications *anacapa*," he said to Palmer.

"The *Aizsargs* says we do," she said.

"Well," Zarges said. "We don't have time to search for it. Our priority is clearing this ship."

If there was a communications *anacapa* and this ship was going to blow, the explosion would increase exponentially. Although he wasn't sure that mattered. One *anacapa*, a large one, would cause an explosion that was catastrophic enough.

He pushed himself away from the communications area.

"All right," he said. "We can't do anything else here. Let's help with the evacuations."

THE *RENEGAT*

This is the bridge: Evacuate the Renegat *immediately. Head to both cargo bays. Follow instructions once you arrive.*

The announcement was strange. It sounded official, but it wasn't official. An official announcement would have had more identifiers—who was talking, who was issuing the orders—or it would have had none at all.

Still, Justine Breaux felt a tiny thread of relief.

She was wearing her environmental suit, her boots clamped to the floor of the third deck recreation room. She wasn't alone. Five other people were here, although she didn't know most of them except by their determined faces.

All six of them exercised at the same time every day, using one of the treadmills built into the floor. Only, since that attack the *Renegat* had suffered a few sectors back, the treadmills hadn't worked. Still, there was exercise equipment here that could be pulled out of lockers—big heavy balls that could be swung back and forth, when there was gravity, of course.

She made herself take a deep breath. The air in her environmental suit tasted like metal filings, but she didn't mind.

She wasn't quite used to the adventures she had been on, but at least she didn't freak out about them anymore. The first few scared the crap out of her and made her remember Labhras's words to her:

They don't want to take anyone who will be missed. They think you're not coming back.

Missed or not, she was coming back. A different person, just like she had expected. And if she saw Prescott, she was strong enough now to not just tell him off, but to hurt him physically if he even tried to touch her.

Funny that thoughts of Prescott would occupy her right now, when she had faced far worse than him. When she *was* facing far worse right at this moment.

When she decided to remain with the *Renegat*, she had assumed the ship would run like it always had, even without half the crew. The ship hadn't done as well as she expected, but ship life had been somewhat normal.

She researched the way back. She made sure they went to the right sectors. Meals were on time. Her tiny cabin didn't change, although she could have taken a larger suite.

Breaux had clung to the normal. She hadn't had much else.

That was what the treadmill was for. The exercise cleared her mind, and she had done way too much of it in the days after the *Renegat* left the Scrapheap.

The trip back seemed too easy, sometimes.

Then the attack, and the loss of the treadmills. Even then, she had tried. She came down here daily, just to stretch her legs, walking the entire way to get her exercise.

And sometimes there were others here. The same five, whom she grunted at whenever she saw them, or grinned at them a little dismissively, because she really wanted to get to her workout and then return to her quiet research, and then—

The loss of power, the loss of gravity, the ship in trouble. No one made an announcement then. She had gone to the lockers when the gravity went because she knew (guessed, really) that the next loss would be the rest of the environment, and she had handed out the environmental suits.

A couple people said thank you, one woman couldn't figure out how to put on her suit (fortunately someone else had helped her), and they were all suited up and ready to go to the bridge to find out what was going on when the environmental controls just shut off.

And that was when Justine's ideas failed. Because she and her five friends would be useless on the bridge. She couldn't do anything in engineering either, or any other part of the ship where technical stuff was going on. All she could do was research something before or after the event. Valuable, yes, except at moments like this.

So, she had learned throughout this trip, the best advice was to shelter in place. Which was what she had done (and the others had stuck with her) after she got the suit on.

Then she had calmly waited for more instructions, convinced there would be more instructions—or that someone would fix the problem.

She had waited and waited, and she was almost ready to give up, find an escape pod even if that wasn't normal procedure, when the additional instructions came.

She knew exactly where one of the cargo bays was, because she had entered the ship on that level all those months ago. But finding that bay in the cold and the dark was a whole other matter.

This is the bridge: Evacuate the Renegat *immediately. Head to both cargo bays. Follow instructions once you arrive.*

The repeated announcement jolted her. Whoever was making the announcements—Raina? One of the old bridge crew?—was completely serious about it.

Breaux flicked on her suit lights, nearly blinding herself. She had to shut off the lights around her shoulders, but she left the helmet lights on.

The other five people did the same thing.

They were doing what she was doing, which irritated her more than she could say.

Not only was she responsible for herself, she was going to end up being responsible for them too.

The announcement gave no timeline. Just said *immediately*. Which she was taking to mean *yesterday*.

She started forward, realized walking in gravity boots when she was in a hurry was just plain stupid, and hoped she still had the zero-G skills she had acquired at school as a child.

If not, she could always turn the gravity back on and try to run. That would be hard enough.

She had to clear the negative thoughts from her mind.

She could do this.

She walked to the door, the gravity boots making her feel like she was walking underwater, and then grabbed the edges of the door frame.

With a single voice command, she shut off the gravity in her boots.

Her hands remained gripped on the frame, but her feet lifted. She felt like she was floating on air, even though she knew she wasn't.

"Okay," she said, more to herself than her little flock of followers. "Here goes nothing."

And then she pushed off into the darkened corridor.

THE *RENEGAT*

Sufia Khusru floated above the only working console on the bridge of the *Renegat.* She had been on board a lot of ships in distress, but she had never seen anything like this.

The power to the bridge was thin, something she hadn't thought possible. The environmental systems were gone, and the emergency lighting itself was so faint as to be almost nonexistent.

Her team had moved into position to see if they could do anything to buy some extra time for the rescue. Ford Cayden was crouched beside the *anacapa* drive, its weird reddish purple color accenting his narrow features, making his frown of concentration seem even deeper than it was.

Jala Niane had levered herself beneath one of the other consoles, trying to boost the energy readings here. She had already put one of the small energy packs on top of the console.

It hadn't done much good.

Khusru had achieved her objective: she had sent an announcement to everyone on the ship, telling them to get to the cargo bays. She should probably move her team as well, but it felt wrong to simply abandon the work.

If they could buy a few extra minutes, then they should. Because a few extra minutes might mean a few more lives.

"Anything you can do, Ford?" she asked Cayden. He knew what she meant. She was referring to the *anacapa* drive.

"No," he said. "Not even if I had all the time in the universe."

He let go of the side of the *anacapa* drive, and floated upward. That weird light had left his face, but it did show the dirt on his environmental suit. The dirt glittered red.

Dirt. There shouldn't have been any dirt at all. This ship had been in trouble for a very long time.

Systems must have shut down bit by bit. Some of the problems that the *Renegat* was experiencing might have been caused by that slow decline.

It was the kind of thing that engineers generally fixed as a matter of course. The kind of maintenance even the lowest crew member understood needed to be done. The kind of thing that a handful of people on a ship should be able to tell the computer control system, and hand over to that system.

Khusru turned on the spotlight in the palm of her suit's right hand, and shone it around the nooks and crannies of the bridge. Dirt floated everywhere, which she hadn't noticed when they had arrived.

Dirt not only floated, it coated the walls and the floor, and hung from the ceiling.

That sense she'd had from the moment she arrived on this ship, the sense that something was horribly wrong, returned a thousandfold.

No matter what had happened to this ship, no matter what had happened to the officers, the ship should have remained spotless. It was one of those things everyone in the Fleet knew as a matter of course.

That odd bit of conversation suddenly rose in her memory. That reluctant man who said he was the only bridge officer left. The woman, who had seemed both desperate and reasonable, correcting him.

You were demoted, she had said. *You are only up here because I needed the help.*

Something bad had happened, and it had happened to the crew, before things had fallen completely apart.

But Khusru couldn't solve that now. No matter who these people were, she had to save them.

That was her job.

Niane used the legs of the console to push herself out from underneath it. She floated upwards, like a small child playing in zero-G for the first time.

"Cayden's right," she said. "We're useless here. I can't even access the information on who remains, who is gone, how many people are supposed to be on board."

"Let's move, then," Khusru said, sweeping her hands toward the door in a go-quickly gesture. "We'll have to rely on the *Aizsargs* or *Rescue One* to let us know if we get everyone off the ship."

If they could get everyone off the ship, before it completely fell apart.

Cayden and Niane left the bridge ahead of Khusru, moving at a rapid clip. She paused in the door and peered backwards. The bridge looked like it belonged to any damaged ship. Some of the damaged ships she'd been on had floating nanobits and other signs of decay.

But this was *dirt* and an *anacapa* drive that had been tampered with and people who had been demoted.

"What happened here?" she whispered, comms off.

Something awful.

Something she wasn't sure she would ever understand.

THE *RENEGAT*

If the schematics the *Aizsargs* had provided him with were correct, Zarges had a long way to go to get to Cargo Bay One, and not a lot of time to do so. He was pushing off the sides of the corridor, following the map his hood had placed across his vision, hoping each detail was correct.

Palmer had remained for one last moment in Engineering, and Zarges hoped to hell Palmer would get out while there was still time. Iqbar had headed to Cargo Bay Two.

Zarges had just received notification from Khusru that there wasn't much she could do any longer. Her team was leaving the bridge.

They had set the announcement on repeat, and he had heard it a number of times already, enough that he had tuned out the specifics. Khusru told him she could alter it if need be—or, at least, she hoped she could.

And then she had gone silent.

He was moving through the dark corridors alone, which unnerved him. He kept expecting to find more passengers, maybe someone to assist along the way. But so far, he had his team hadn't found anyone on board.

It was almost as if the information they had received through their scans was wrong. The ship felt empty and abandoned, even though every bit of information they had received from the *Aizsargs* said it wasn't.

Khusru had encountered two people on the bridge, but so far, those were the only two people any member of his team had seen.

He hoped his team wasn't risking their lives for nothing.

And risking the loss of a life raft or two. Those things were automated, but they were valuable and not always the easiest to reprogram. He'd only lost one on any of the missions he'd been on, but that life raft had been full.

His heart rate had increased. His suit sent a little beep of warning. He was forgetting to breathe regularly.

There was a very good chance that this mission would go awry as well. *Go awry*. Such innocuous words for so much loss of life.

He needed this mission to go well, and it already looked like that was impossible.

Although at this stage in his previous mission, everything had been on track. It had just been that one final instant, that moment when the ship and the life raft had disconnected improperly, and the raft sprang out of control, and he had been jettisoned into space, his tether still attached, his mouth open as everything—

Once again, he shook it off.

This was what his team had been worried about when they sent him here. This was what *he* had been worried about. This lack of focus.

He blinked, made himself concentrate on the map, and followed it closely, moving faster and faster through the empty corridors, wishing he could ask one of the ship's computers where all two hundred survivors were.

He had this terrible fear that they were unconscious, that the people on the bridge were space pirates of some kind who had harmed everyone else, and that the ship was compromised. Announcements wouldn't work if the entire crew was unconscious and unable to move.

The corridor dead-ended in a plethora of sealed doors and interior elevators. The elevators wouldn't work if the power was off, so there had to be ladders or stairs somewhere.

He didn't see them on the map he had, but logically, they would be right here, right nearby.

He pushed himself to the walls, grabbed door handles, tugged, and finally found one that jostled as he pulled. But it didn't open. So he investigated the side, saw that it pushed open instead, leading him to believe it was a stairwell or maintenance tube.

He pushed, and the door eased back as if it were on springs. It revealed both stairs and a ladder, the ladder for moments like this, apparently.

He used both—the ladder to pull himself up with his hands, and the stairs to guide him.

He was sweating now, not from overexertion or an incorrect temperature in his suit, but from nerves. Two levels up and he would reach Cargo Bay One.

He had no idea what he would do if the bay was empty.

Then he made himself shake off that thought.

He would help the life raft dock, then he would wait until the last possible moment before boarding the raft himself and getting off the *Renegat* with his team. If no one showed up, then there was nothing he could do.

No matter how much he wanted to.

No matter how much he tried.

PART TWELVE
FOLDSPACE AGAIN
100 YEARS AGO

THE *RENEGAT*

Breaux hadn't become used to the way the *Renegat* traveled through foldspace, but at least this time, she knew what to expect. She stood on the bridge for the second trip into foldspace, just like she had stood on the bridge for the first trip, only this time, she stood next to Atwater.

This time, she expected the bridge crew's extreme focus. The same crew was on duty, and in the same positions as the last time. Natalia Stephanos monitored the *anacapa* like it was a dog she expected to bite her at any moment. First Officer Crowe looked even more haggard than he had before as he monitored everything at his station.

Breaux had the sense that he wasn't getting much sleep.

She wasn't either. Whenever she was in her exceedingly small cabin, she felt like she was missing something or doing something wrong. She needed to be out and about, even though out and about was often the research wing of the *Renegat*.

She had been working hard there, preparing for this second trip through foldspace. She had even more information on the next sector of space than she had for the last one, which she found somewhat ironic, given that the previous sector was closer in distance and time.

But that new data stream from the Fleet had added a lot to her research. She didn't know what kind of cultures the *Renegat* might run into in this next sector (if any), but she did know what the coordinates should look like, how the nearest sector base got shut down, and what had happened to the starbase not far from where the *Renegat* was supposed to appear.

She had no idea if Captain Preemas and the bridge crew would find that information valuable, but she had to think they might. She was starting to think in contingencies—research contingencies, she had said to Atwater, during one of their late night discussion sessions.

He was working as hard as she was, trying to figure out if any sector they were going to had areas with improperly shut down *anacapa* drives. He was also trying to figure out if there were changes in *anacapa* technology over the millennia. He had said more than once that he worried about changes, not just in the *anacapa* technology, but in *anacapa* handling.

The Fleet makes positive changes after terrible events, he had said to Breaux one night, when he had had a little too much to drink. *I'm worried that they changed their* anacapa *handling after something horrible happened, something horrible that they then did not make a record of.*

Such a thing was possible, especially considering the gaps in the historical record (if you could call it an historical record) that she was finding.

She didn't want to think about what could go wrong, though. It was the job of other people on board to have those thoughts. Her job was to confirm that the area around the ship resembled the area around the coordinates the ship had been heading to.

If she found that nothing matched up, and they couldn't account for the change based on the passage of years, then the problem became someone else's. She would have to step aside and let the experts figure all of that out.

Which she was happy to do.

That didn't make her any calmer as the *Renegat* prepared to head into foldspace for the second time on her journey.

She shifted from foot to foot, trying to tamp the anticipation down. This time, she brought her own tablet, with the proper map of the section loaded onto it.

This trip was a tad dicier than the last. Not only were they traveling over more distance through foldspace, but they were arriving near an abandoned starbase. She trusted that the base was completely dead, but she didn't know, exactly.

Atwater hadn't said anything about the starbase. He had questioned her phrase "traveled over more distance through foldspace." He had launched into a long, and mostly pointless, discussion of the way that foldspace worked (or rather, the way he thought it worked, since no one really knew), reminding her that the name described how it worked—a fold in space.

So they weren't traveling *across* foldspace. They were folding a bigger part of space, like folding a blanket instead of folding a scarf. Or something like that.

She truly didn't care about the technical details, which she knew irritated Atwater. He lived for the technical bits.

She just wanted things to work, and to work properly, when she needed them to work.

She was trying to learn bits about the ship, but she didn't care as much as she should. She tried to pay attention to aspects of the ship that didn't concern her, if someone felt it was important to tell her about whatever it was.

Mostly, though, she did her job and did it as well (she hoped) as everyone else was doing theirs.

Captain Preemas had three holoscreens open in front of him. She couldn't see the information on them, and neither could anyone else.

But she could see the two-D tablet on his chair, and she knew it would have the old maps, just like the tablet she was clutching.

The captain gave the command to send the ship into foldspace, and Breaux clenched her fists, digging her fingernails into her palms instead of grabbing Atwater's hand for support the way she wanted to.

She didn't even glance at his face, because she didn't want to see that goofy grin again. She was working very hard at keeping hers from devolving into complete silliness.

The *Renegat* bumped and slid, just like it had the last time. But this time, instead of feeling as if she was experiencing an out-of-control slide on ice, the experience felt as if she were rattling down a gravel road in a wheeled cart with no airborne capability.

Her teeth chattered, her body bounced, and she almost felt as if she were bouncing toward the aisle.

Breaux kept an eye on Stephanos and First Officer Crowe, again, figuring if something went seriously wrong, they would be the first to see it.

Their expressions said nothing. They just stared downward as if nothing were happening at all.

The outlines of Captain Preemas's holoscreens surrounded him like small sketches. He wasn't looking at those screens, though.

Like Breaux, he was watching Stephanos.

Then the chattering stopped, the bumping eased, and the ship eased into its familiar movement.

The thought that the ship's movement was familiar made Breaux smile. She couldn't help herself: now she looked at Atwater.

He looked at her too, and his entire body moved forward a tiny bit as if he thought of hugging her and then changed his mind.

Instead, he nodded, and she knew that later this evening, they would be discussing this in the bar off the main mess, clutching drinks in their hands and speaking softly about how miraculous this all was.

She nodded back, then started across the bridge to the captain's chair, even though he hadn't called her yet.

The screens around them sprang to life, revealing a starscape she hadn't expected. Darker, bluer, fewer stars than she had seen on her information.

There was no starbase at all, at least that she could tell visually.

"The *anacapa* drive is fine," Stephanos said in a low voice, even though no one had asked her about it.

Breaux glanced in her direction, and saw that she had been speaking to First Officer Crowe. He was nodding, his mouth a thin line.

No one was looking at the big screens with their panoramic view of this new sector (this *old* sector, actually) except her.

Then she glanced over her shoulder, and saw Atwater. He was looking too, eyes sparkling.

"What do you have for me?" Captain Preemas asked.

Breaux jumped, her heart pounding. Maybe he had been talking to someone else.

But as she brought her head back around, she realized he hadn't been. He had been talking to her.

She forced as much of the smile off her face as she could manage. Then she clutched the tablet to her chest and hurried to his side.

"I brought my data this time, sir," she said to Captain Preemas, "so that we wouldn't have to reconfigure yours."

He nodded, then pushed another tablet aside. Maybe he had already done the calculations.

She had asked Tindo Ibori to provide her with all of the navigational information on the *Renegat* from the moment the ship went into foldspace this second time to the moment it emerged. Her tablet was ready to do the flat side-by-side comparisons. She had even altered the information a bit so that she could add a holoprojection, even though the computer would be adding information on the older material.

She thought it might be worth the risk, just so that the entire bridge crew could see where they had arrived.

If Captain Preemas approved, of course.

"There should be a decommissioned starbase not too far from here," she said as she set her tablet down. "Or there was a thousand years ago or so."

Then she let out a small chuckle, mostly at her own expense.

"I mean, I have no idea how long they last or anything, but you'd think someone would have repurposed it or something." She was babbling now, and no one else had commented.

Maybe no one else could. She was talking to the captain after all, and he had nothing to say.

"Anyway," she said, "let's look at this."

She slid the tablets next to each other, and then the captain set a third near her. The third already had interpolated the new information. She didn't have to do any of it.

That was really different from life on the sector base. Even when she asked someone to do something, they would only do it once. They'd never think for themselves.

But of course, the captain would. How else had he become captain, after all?

She peered at the images. The starbase, which had been her focus as she worked with these coordinates, wasn't anywhere nearby. That made her stomach twist.

But she really didn't know how long a starbase could exist in space. Nothing decayed here, right? So, in theory, it could just remain. Or maybe its moorings—whatever passed for moorings in space, whatever held it in place—maybe that part of the starbase eventually declined or someone had taken it for parts or…

Or they were in the wrong place.

Her stomach ached, and she felt lightheaded. She was holding her breath again.

She needed other markers. Not human markers. Natural markers.

She looked at the planets, and they appeared to be the ones she had been dealing with from the old maps. But a planet with six moons only had five, and there was a small asteroid cluster that had spread out nearby.

"It's not...it's not...perfectly aligned," she said. Then her finger touched that planet. "We're...we're...missing a moon."

She hated that she was stammering, but she couldn't help herself.

Missing a moon and a starbase, and one of the distant stars seemed smaller than it had been before. And something whitish surrounded it—a nebula? Something else?

She looked up at the screens surrounding the bridge. The whitish surround seemed clearer on those screens. The star was in the right position, as far as she could tell just by eyeballing it, but the star was a different size.

Or maybe the two-dimensional images that she had showed the star incorrectly. Maybe they magnified it or changed it or the information she was using was so old that it didn't translate well.

"Systems change over time." First Officer Crowe had joined them. "We cannot know if this system has changed as well."

"We've hit the correct coordinates," said Ibori. He was looking at the console just like he was supposed to, but his voice sounded a bit odd. As if he were surprised that they had hit the right place.

It made Breaux uneasy—or even more uneasy than she should have been.

"That's my reading as well," Captain Preemas said.

"And mine," First Officer Crowe said.

"The *anacapa* drive functioned properly," Stephanos said.

"So, as far as we can tell, we're in the right place," Captain Preemas said. "What we're seeing—what you're seeing—is the natural changes in a sector. We're usually not privy to them."

Breaux swallowed. While she had researched the information the Fleet had left tantalizingly in its wake about these sectors, she hadn't ever really researched what happened over time in a universe. How stars decayed. Or what could have happened to the starbase.

Everyone here seemed to know it, but she didn't, and she felt so naïve.

"That loss of a moon wasn't a natural occurrence," Yulia Colvin said. She was at another console, and Breaux had no idea what Colvin's duties were or what her past rank had been. Breaux had just started wondering about those things, because she had no idea how to address anyone.

Colvin tucked a strand of blonde hair behind her ear.

"That debris field in the planet's orbit is most of that moon," she said, "mixed with all kinds of garbage. I don't know if the moon was inhabited or not, but it was obliterated."

Captain Preemas raised his head and stared at the larger screens, a frown on his face. Breaux's heart was pounding hard.

"Any nanobits in that debris field?" he asked Colvin.

"Not that I can find," she said. "I'm seeing no evidence that there was a starbase anywhere near here. Not that it means anything."

"Why?" Breaux asked the question, then immediately regretted it.

"We might build our starbases in their permanent location," Colvin said, giving Breaux a compassionate look. Breaux wasn't sure why she was getting compassion from Colvin. Because Breaux didn't know these things? Or because her questions were incredibly stupid and Colvin took pity on her? "But that doesn't mean someone can't disassemble them and move them elsewhere."

"Was there something in the record that led you to believe the starbase still existed?" First Officer Crowe asked.

"The information said it was decommissioned," she said. "And from what I can tell about procedure, starbases that were decommissioned were left in place."

"Even a thousand years ago?" Ibori asked.

"I don't know that for certain," Breaux said, and everyone started to turn away. But before their attention completely left her, she added, "But I found information from fifteen hundred years ago, and that said that the Fleet left starbases empty and in place, because the pieces were too big to reuse and the nanobits too compromised to trust in any other structure."

"Sounds familiar," Stephanos said softly. She was speaking to First Officer Crowe, but no one else had spoken at that moment, so her voice carried.

"Missing starbase, missing moon, evidence of mass destruction surrounding a planet that should have had six moons, but now only has five. Who knows what kind of damage the loss of that moon is doing to the planet itself. Or has done, depending on how long ago all of this happened." Captain Preemas handed Breaux her tablet.

She took the tablet and clutched it to her chest.

And then, to her surprise, he smiled at her.

"I think you're right, Justine Breaux," he said. "I think we have arrived at the correct spot, and we have seen the changes a thousand years have wrought to this place. I also believe there are signs that this sector of space is not—or was not—a very peaceful place. So we're going to get out of here as fast as we can."

"You want to enter foldspace from here?" First Officer Crowe asked.

"I don't want the *anacapa* drive to work for at least two days," Stephanos said, but she looked at First Officer Crowe as she did so, as if he were in charge.

"I agree," Captain Preemas said, putting a slight emphasis on the word *I*. He had obviously seen Stephanos's deference to First Officer Crowe, and apparently had not been pleased by it. "We need to let the *anacapa* drive have some time between activations. We'll head across this sector, but quickly. Plot a course that takes us far from any planet or moon or anything else that might be inhabited. And let's have the sensors on full, searching for other ships. I don't want to be surprised."

Breaux swallowed hard, her heart rate on the rise again. She didn't want to be surprised either, but she already was.

She was having trouble with the idea that the maps she had used were a thousand years in the past, and the damage she saw might be contemporary. Part of her was still inclined to believe that nothing had happened in this sector after the Fleet left.

She glanced at Atwater. He raised his eyebrows and gave her a slight smile. Ever so slight. He was still feeling giddy.

She needed to remember what she was doing here, and that there would be surprises, maybe even more of them as the ship went in and out of foldspace.

Around her, the bridge crew got to work.

"Um, Captain?" she said, still clutching the tablet.

He looked up at her, his eyes darkened. He was irritated now, and she wasn't quite sure why. Perhaps because she had interrupted him.

"You do want us to leave from the same point and arrive at the coordinates we already decided on, right?"

"Yes," he said curtly. She could hear in his tone that she should have divined that on her own. "I'll inform you whenever there are changes. There won't be this time. So I will need one of your magic maps."

She nodded. "The information gets spottier the farther back we go."

"I'm aware of that," he said, and then went back to his work. He didn't dismiss her. He didn't even properly end the conversation. He just looked away as if she was nothing.

And compared to everyone else on this bridge, she was.

She held the tablet tightly and headed for the exit.

Atwater fell in beside her.

"Let me help you with the maps," he said.

"I thought you were compiling data on the foldspace journeys and *anacapa* histories," she said.

"I think that's part of the data," he said. "Don't you?"

She shook her head a little. This research was her contribution. She didn't need him in the middle of it.

"I'll let you know when I need something," she said, and hoped that didn't sound as dismissive as Captain Preemas had sounded to her.

Then she scurried past Atwater, not looking at his face. She didn't want to know if she had disappointed him or not.

So far, he was her only friend, and she wanted to keep the friendship.

But not at the expense of her work.

PART THIRTEEN
THE RESCUE
NOW

THE *RENEGAT*

The way out of the third deck recreation room should have been second nature to Breaux. She exercised here *every single day*. But in the dark and the cold, without the lights or the landmarks, she had only a vague sense of where she was.

Her habits were ingrained into her feet, not into this floating thing she was doing (which was making her vaguely nauseous). She would grab onto walls and push herself forward. More than once, she doubled back, having missed the corridor she had meant to take.

The five people in the exercise room were following her, as if she knew what she was doing.

She didn't, but they probably thought that because she used to go up to the bridge every time the *Renegat* slid into foldspace. Captain Preemas had trusted her, which made her untrustworthy to the new crew on this return trip.

She had screamed at them to get their attention, reminding them that she was one of the few people who actually knew how they had gotten to the Scrapheap. She was one of the only people who knew what the area should look like as they headed back to Sector Base Z, coordinate by coordinate, crossing foldspace trip by trip by trip.

If the *Renegat* hadn't stopped for those supplies, if they hadn't gotten embroiled in that attack, then maybe they wouldn't have lost power now.

She bit her lower lip, using the pain to help herself focus.

She needed to get to the nearest cargo bay, and she had only actually been inside them a few times, once helping with supplies.

She'd gone past a lot, though, on her walks.

Walks. Not floats. Not in the dark. And she really hadn't paid attention because, as she said to Atwater in one of their nightly debriefs way back before everything changed, the corridors all looked the same.

Except on bridge and engineering levels, he had said, correcting her. And someone else had added that in some of the crew cabin corridors, nothing looked the same either.

This is the bridge: Evacuate the Renegat *immediately. Head to both cargo bays. We are on the clock. You must hurry.*

The voice sounded rote. Breaux didn't recognize it, either, which had bothered her at first, and bothered her now, but she had no idea what to do about it.

"Anyone else know who's talking to us?" she asked through the comm link.

But just like every other time she had tried to talk to the five people trailing her like puppies, no one responded.

She was beginning to think her comm didn't work.

Or, more likely, she had no idea how to turn it on. But shouldn't it be automatic? When you put on your suit, the comm link should activate, right? Like the information about her body and the suit itself that ran along the base of the hood that she had somehow managed to attach tightly around her neck.

So far, the suit's oxygen levels were good, and despite the cold in the corridors, which was actually frosting things up, she was warm—not hot from exercising, but comfortably warm enough to get through all of this.

Her heart rate was elevated, but that was normal. She expected that, since deep down (or maybe not deep down), she was absolutely terrified.

She had made two turns out of the recreation room, the same two turns she made every single day, and had been about to make the third when she realized she had been leading everyone to the research room, not to the cargo bays.

She had had to stop, and think. How did she get to the bays from here?

And then she guessed.

She didn't like guessing, especially now that the faceless voice from the bridge had said they were on the clock.

Of course, they were on the clock, but she hadn't really thought of it that way.

Wouldn't they wait for everyone on the crew to get to the cargo bay?

She bit her lower lip so hard she tasted blood.

No, they wouldn't, and she knew it. Not this group. This group wasn't just in it for themselves, but they also had no real sense of camaraderie. They screamed at each other at moments of crisis, and they didn't listen, and they kept trying to do things that didn't work, and when they had been attacked on the way back, no one could figure out how to use the weapons array at first, not that it mattered because at least two people on the ship thought it was bad to fight back.

She had gotten the foldspace coordinates ready, and that was the trip that had scared the piss out of her, because they entered foldspace in a completely different area than they should have.

They didn't go to the spot where they had emerged the first time. They just left as these little ships were shooting at them, and making the shields flare, and Kabac kept saying shield flares weren't normal, and the ship's computer said that they were taking on damage, and no one knew how to fix that, and then they went into foldspace, and she fretted the entire time, while others tried to repair things.

Then the *Renegat* emerged in the right place. She had compulsively checked and rechecked and checked the maps over and over and over again.

They had come out in the right place.

She had no idea if they had done so this time, because Raina had banned her from the bridge.

They were having *anacapa* problems and Kabac said that Breaux made him nervous, as if she was supervising his work, which she wasn't.

She had just been trying to get them home.

Just like she was trying to get these five crew members—why, why, why hadn't she introduced herself to them in the past few months?—to the correct cargo bay.

She had to be going in the right direction, because if she wasn't, someone would have spoken up, right? They would have moved ahead of her, and gotten them on the right path.

They had to.

They were all in this together, whether they liked it or not.

They had to reach the cargo bay, and they had to do it fast.

She rounded another corner and hoped to god she was going in the right direction.

Because she was on the clock—and she didn't even know how much time she had left.

PART FOURTEEN

TIME LAG

100 YEARS AGO

THE *RENEGAT*

Crowe huddled behind the communications array in Engineering. The communications system came in several pieces. One was near the main engineering control panel, in its own alcove in the heart of engineering. That part of the communications system attached to the bridge. If Crowe needed to, he could route all of the communications into Engineering and cut off the bridge entirely.

The only section he couldn't completely control was the engineering equipment inside the captain's command closet in the captain's quarters. That command closet was built in such a way that isolated it from almost all of the major systems in the ship, so that the captain could retain control of the ship if he needed to if something went seriously awry, such as some outside group taking over the ship.

The fact that Crowe couldn't control the command closet was beginning to worry him. But he would set that aside for the moment.

He needed to check something that most of the crew did not know about. There were parts to the communications array that someone needed special clearance to access. It had become customary for the crew to be kept in the dark about that part of the array, which wasn't something he approved of. But he followed those rules.

And that meant he had to clear Engineering while he worked on the array. He told everyone who worked there to take a break whether they needed to or not.

Engineering without the crew felt different than Engineering when the crew was working. The sounds were muted, the low-level hum of equipment almost soothing.

Crowe loved the coolness that each alcove had. The alcoves with the most equipment had their own environmental systems to maintain air purity (or a slightly higher oxygen density, in the case of the system near the engines) and the proper temperature for the equipment itself.

The communications array remained cool as a matter of course. If he felt any heat near this array, he would know that something was wrong.

So far, though, he wasn't finding anything wrong.

He had removed the panels, and stood, hands on his hips, staring at the array's interior. Everything looked good. Blue lights glowed, golden lights blinked, pale white chips—each barely larger than a speck of dust—dotted the surface of the main board, covering the black nanobits like spilled sugar.

He had half-expected to find blinking red lights or pulled connectors or black nanobit coating on everything.

Or rather, he had half-hoped to find something like that. Because the fact that everything was fine meant something else was going wrong.

Preemas had contacted him as the *Renegat* sped across the last sector, the one with the exploded moon. As the ship traveled swiftly as far as possible from any possible habitation, the crew found more evidence of destruction. An asteroid field where none had been before, a hollowed-out continent on a once-inhabited planet, satellites around another planet, which was mostly enshrouded in blackish-greenish goo.

Preemas had contacted Vice Admiral Gão directly to make his reports, and there had been a lag in the contact between them of nearly two minutes. Apparently, Preemas had contacted her after their first foldspace journey, and there had also been a lag. Preemas called the first lag barely noticeable. At most, fifteen seconds, he thought.

A lag, no matter how long, was a problem. Crowe wished Preemas had reported it then, so Crowe could see the progression on all of this—if there had been any progression. But Preemas hadn't reported it, figuring the lag was a product of the distance or the foldspace travel or something else.

At the end of their meeting this time, however, Gão had ordered Preemas to figure out what was causing the lag on his end, if, indeed, something was.

After the first lag, Gão had done some kind of search on her ship to see if there was a local cause. She hadn't found anything. But she told Preemas she expected a bit of difficulty.

But something about this lag really bothered Crowe.

That was why he was down in Engineering alone, investigating the communications panel without talking to any of the others. If he had to, he would bring in Stephanos, and see what she had to say.

He rubbed his eyes with the thumb and forefinger of his right hand. So far, the array looked fine. Vice Admiral Gão's very competent people hadn't found anything either.

Crowe leaned into the open panel, and looked at all of the pieces one by one. He found nothing strange. Then he ran every diagnostic he could think of, one for each system. He ran the simple diagnostics, the diagnostics he usually cycled through monthly, and the most extensive diagnostics he could think of.

He found nothing.

Then he leaned back on his heels, closed his eyes, and thought about the array, the way he had seen it from the beginning of his journey here. Some of his subordinates had thought the eye-closing and the silence he required when he did this was weird and showy. But it wasn't. It allowed him to listen to the little voice within, the one that sometimes told him when something had gone wrong, something he had seen, but which hadn't registered deep down.

He listened to the quiet within himself, heard his own heartbeat, and felt the movement of the air around the array. He took a mental step back and listened, trying to see if he could hear anything in Engineering besides the standard low-pitched hum.

He couldn't. Nor did his little interior voice have anything to say about the array.

It all looked normal to him.

He opened his eyes. They focused, not on the array itself, but on a panel to the left of the white-flecked chips. That panel had a series of complex locks. Inside that panel was an *anacapa* container that was the size of his hand. The container was much larger than it needed to be, but unlike the container on the bridge, this container had walls so thick around it that nothing could get through without special equipment.

The tiny *anacapa* drive inside was encased in yet another container, that one set to a frequency that allowed the drive to interact with the communications array when the correct signal hit it, but prevented the drive from interacting with the *anacapa* drive that took the ship into foldspace.

In theory, of course. Everything the Fleet did with *anacapa* drives had to be chalked up to theory.

The size of the drive made diagnosing it difficult. Crowe would have to do so by sight. If the tiny drive was malfunctioning, he had one other under lock and key. Technically, he wasn't supposed to have a backup at all. The Fleet only issued these drives on request.

But once he discovered that he would be going on this long journey, he had requested an additional communications *anacapa* from an old friend in the Fleet, someone who owed him a favor, someone who not only couldn't say no, but wouldn't tell Vice Admiral Gão or Preemas.

Crowe sighed. He wanted to check on one more thing. He wanted to see if there was residual *anacapa* energy in the sector the *Renegat* had just left.

Preemas had been the one to suggest this. He had pointed out—rightly—that there was evidence of a major cataclysm or a major war in that sector. There might have been *anacapa* energy near the area where Preemas had tried to contact Gão.

Crowe never believed the old chestnut that only the Fleet used *anacapa* drives. The Fleet hadn't encountered any other culture that used the drives—not in modern memory. But the Fleet hadn't developed the drives itself, so *someone* had developed the technology.

And the Fleet could be sloppy about rounding up old drives. Since the Fleet had reverse-engineered the tech, some other culture could have done the same thing.

He moved to a different part of Engineering, around two more alcoves and into one of the scanning alcoves. He set up a search throughout the records of that sector they had traveled through, looking at energy readings that were out of whack and other red flags.

He hadn't searched for any of that while the *Renegat* was in the sector because Preemas wanted to get out as quickly as he could. Crowe was more determined to get the ship out, and monitor the equipment, than trying to figure out what exactly was going on in the sector itself.

The fact that the Fleet's starbase was gone, with no record of it having been there, really bothered him. The starbases were established, difficult to disassemble, especially for non-Fleet personnel, and hard to destroy.

If some group had taken parts of the starbase, the nanobits that made up the starbase should have compensated, regrowing the sections over time or, if the nanobits were running low (which they eventually would), blocking off a section and showing a new, shiny part of the older base.

The Fleet had been gone for a very long time, but that shouldn't have made a difference. The starbases were built to last. Besides, there was no wear and tear in space. Sector bases changed, damn near annually, particularly when they weren't being kept up any longer.

But starbases were the closest thing to a permanent structure that the Fleet built.

And there was a lot of *anacapa* equipment in a starbase. Not just the *anacapas* that were stored in an active starbase to help damaged ships, but the *anacapa* drive that enabled the base's ability to pull damaged ships out of foldspace or across long distances also was one of the largest the Fleet built.

Those drives should have been removed from any decommissioned starbase, but they weren't always removed or removed properly. Sometimes they were stored tightly in their own container, and left behind.

Starbases also had the tiny communications *anacapas*, and those remained, because starbases were supposed to be long-distance communications hubs, even after the bases were decommissioned.

Since almost no one knew about those tiny *anacapas*, there was no threat of theft. The drives were almost impossible to find, and when someone did find one, they couldn't use it to power a ship. The drive was too small.

So the Fleet left those.

Which meant that if the Fleet's starbase had been blown up or obliterated, it should have left some kind of *anacapa* energy signal in its wake. A small one, but one that might have had an impact on the *Renegat*.

Crowe searched for that too, and found nothing. Not even the *anacapa* signature near the spot where the *Renegat* had come out of foldspace.

He shut down the search and felt dread build up inside him for the first time since the *Renegat* left Starbase Rho. If he couldn't find what was causing the time differential, and Vice Admiral Gāo's people couldn't find it either, then that raised the possibility that the trips through foldspace were having some kind of temporal impact on the *Renegat*.

Not the kind that had lost Preemas his year. Or the kind that made ships disappear forever (seemingly forever, anyway). But something else entirely.

Crowe ran a hand over his face and sighed so hard that he felt his breath against his wrist.

He would have to bring in Stephanos.

Because the last thing Crowe needed—the last the Preemas needed—hell, the last thing the *Renegat* needed—was panic over the trips into foldspace. Everyone was on edge enough.

This might make tip them all over.

And he had no idea what that would do.

THE *RENEGAT*

They found nothing.

Crowe sat with Stephanos in his cabin. He had made her dinner—a stir-fry with the last of the flash-dried vegetables he had picked up in Z-City—and they were sipping chicory coffee, a luxury he had discovered on one of the ships he had served on almost a decade ago.

The coffee added to his nerves, which were jangling, despite the calm he had tried to restore by going through the simple act of cooking. He had learned long ago that cooking focused his energies in ways other forms of hands-on work did not.

But the time lag problem bedeviled him, and worried him more than he could say. He had given Stephanos the same assignment Preemas had given Crowe—figure out what (if anything) was causing the lag.

Stephanos wasn't as intuitive an engineer as Crowe was. She was more deliberative, more traditional. She worked through problems in the kind of order that would make professors of engineering proud.

But she turned that method into a way of doing things that could end up being as creative, if not more creative, than Crowe's. Crowe trusted her, more than he trusted anyone else on this crew. If there was a physical problem that caused the time lag in Preemas's conversations, Stephanos would find it.

She hadn't found anything.

Crowe had called her into engineering without explaining any bit of the problem. He had simply said that he believed the communications' *anacapa* was malfunctioning. Together they opened the panel, pulled out the container, and examined the tiny *anacapa*.

That drive was smaller than he remembered, more the size of the fingernail on his pinkie than on his thumb. But the little *anacapa* was golden and warm, just like it was supposed to be.

Stephanos even ran a standard *anacapa* diagnostic on it, and the drive had passed with some of the best readings she had ever seen.

They reassembled the container, sealed the panel, and that was when Crowe gave her the assignment to find the time lag.

She was the one who had suggested sending out a small ship, and seeing if the entire array had failed somehow.

He had done so, sending a runabout with her on board. They used standard communications techniques and found nothing. Then she shut off the runabout's array entirely, using only emergency channels that didn't access most of the Fleet's equipment, and that worked beautifully as well.

Finally, when she returned, he had her work on her own to see what she could find.

He had scheduled dinner so that she could debrief him. She had contacted him half an hour before to say she had nothing to report.

He still had her over to dinner, so that he could talk to her.

He also wanted her present when Milton Atwater arrived.

Crowe had given Atwater a different assignment. Atwater was to scan the Fleet records and see if there was any history of time lags becoming an actual problem in Fleet communications. Crowe wanted to know if growing time lags translated into something like actual lost time or if they were just a mere nuisance.

"You know we might not ever be able to find anything," Stephanos said. She had her long fingers wrapped around a black mug that Crowe had picked up in Z-City. He had picked up a lot of tchotchkes on that trip, maybe because he felt he needed something to remember the sector by, bringing with him just a little bit of home.

"I know," he said.

That thought bothered him a lot. He was worried that the lag might translate into some kind of superstition—the *Renegat* was losing time because it was traveling into the Fleet's past.

"It's probably some kind of weird little ghost in some machine part we wouldn't think of looking at," she said.

Crowe shook his head. He sank into the chair opposite her, which put him just a little too close. The cabin was small, but cozy. He liked it here, but he wasn't used to having other people inside his personal space.

"You don't think that's what it is?" she asked.

He was still shaking his head. He wasn't sure how to break the next piece of news to her.

"While you were working, I got some more information," he said. "It—"

The door announced Atwater's presence in the corridor. Crowe had set the door to tell him when Atwater was getting close, just in case Crowe and Stephanos had to conclude one of their more sensitive conversations.

But because Stephanos hadn't found anything, they hadn't had to wrap anything up.

Crowe got up and unlocked the door, instructing it to open when Atwater arrived.

"More information?" Stephanos asked, as they waited for Atwater.

Crowe held up a single finger. "I'll loop him in."

"He doesn't have clearance for this," she said.

"He doesn't even have a rank," Crowe said. "I'm not sure what counts and what doesn't anymore. And I'm not going to worry about it today."

The door swung open, revealing Atwater in his pasty-faced glory. His cheeks were red, probably from uncertainty. With one hand, he knocked on the door. With the other, he held a covered plate that smelled like freshly baked chocolate brownies, a specialty of Danika Newark, which was saying something, since she turned out to be quite a chef.

"Come all the way in," Crowe said.

Atwater slipped in as the door closed. He extended the plate. Crowe took it from him, removed the cover, and set the plate on the table. Then Crowe grabbed three smaller plates and set them on the table as well, along with forks and napkins. He went into the small kitchen, held up the coffee pot as a question.

"Sure," Atwater said.

He walked into the cabin, and looked around, seemingly startled at the space.

Crowe couldn't remember where Atwater was bunked, but he probably had one of the smallest crew quarters available. They all had private rooms on the *Renegat*, but those rooms at the lowest crew level were barely as wide as the bed.

"This is nice," Atwater said as he sat down. His voice had just a hint of envy.

He smiled at Stephanos, who didn't smile back. She didn't like the new crew members and hated the fact that they had been land-based. She felt that the rest of the crew now spent too much time trying to train land babies who had no idea how to behave on board a ship.

Stephanos leaned back, not even looking at the perfectly cut brownies.

Crowe had no idea how she could avoid them. He couldn't.

He took one.

"What I was about to tell you," Crowe said to Stephanos, "was that the captain spoke to Vice Admiral Gāo earlier today. It was difficult. The lag was eight minutes, instead of the five he had reported in the previous sector."

Stephanos shook her head. "I'm not seeing anything in our systems that would cause a lag, and even if something did, it would be a consistent lag."

Crowe nodded. He thought the same thing. He turned slightly in his chair and faced Atwater.

"Which brings us to you," Crowe said. "Is this something other ships reported? Is it a feature of foldspace?"

Atwater took a sip of the coffee, and winced. He looked at the cup. "What is this?"

"Chicory," Crowe said. "A delicacy."

Atwater tried to smile, but still managed to look somewhat tormented. He set the cup down.

"Foldspace," he said, as if orienting himself. "This is our third trip through it in less than three weeks. That in and of itself is unusual—"

"We know," Stephanos said drily.

"So," Atwater said, as if she hadn't spoken at all, "there isn't a lot of data. There are the dramatic time shifts in foldspace—the ones where ships lose months or years inside foldspace, but outside of foldspace it seems like they've been gone an hour or two."

"Or vice versa," Crowe said.

"Yes," Atwater said. "We have lots of information about all of those events, although most of the information is useless. What the Fleet collected was coordinates of journeys across foldspace and, for the most part, urged ships not to make the journeys in the same way."

Crowe bit one of the brownies. It was soft and moist, chocolate with a hint of caramel. Better than he expected.

"Were any of the coordinates near us when we experienced the lag?" Stephanos asked, as if she had personally been talking to Vice Admiral Gāo when the lags occurred.

"Not that I could find," Atwater said, "but the historical record is thin, and it gets thinner the farther back we go. The Fleet jettisoned a lot of this information, even from school ships and research facilities, because we never expected to return to these sectors of space."

Stephanos sighed softly, then eyed the brownies. She glanced at Crowe, who took another bite of his. He almost groaned with pleasure.

"So I drilled down to see what I could find about time lags in general." Atwater swirled his mug. He hadn't taken another sip from it, nor had he taken a brownie. "I didn't like what I found."

Stephanos froze. Only her eyes moved. She looked like she had gone on full alert.

Crowe continued to eat the brownie. He wasn't going to get upset by the opinions of a new crew member. Atwater didn't have the experience to put some of the information he was finding into context.

"What did you find?" Crowe asked, wiping the chocolate off his fingers with his napkin.

"That some ships went through foldspace and experienced communications lags. Those lags accumulated with each trip the ship took into foldspace, no matter when those trips took place." Atwater finally took a brownie of his own.

Stephanos sat up straight. "And?"

"From what I could tell," Atwater said, "and realize it was a small sample source, about twenty-six percent of the ships that had the time lag got lost in foldspace and were never recovered."

"Twenty-six percent?" Crowe asked. "That's very specific."

"Yes." Atwater picked up his fork and held it over the brownie, before setting the fork back down again. "And there's more."

"Okay," Stephanos said, her irritation clear. She hated anyone who presented information slowly. She wanted them to get to the point so she could move on and do whatever needed to be done with that information.

"Another ten percent," Atwater said, "not part of the twenty-six, but a completely different subset, were among the ships that lost years in foldspace. They'd travel into foldspace and wouldn't come out again at the expected time."

Crowe frowned. Something about that nagged at him, as if there was an important piece of information buried in Atwater's numbers. But Crowe couldn't grasp it. Not yet, anyway.

"So, to be clear," Stephanos said, "thirty-six percent of the ships that had this lag problem had disasters with foldspace."

"Maybe more," Atwater said, moving the fork away from his plate. "Because what I didn't have time to look for was the ships that only lost a day or two in foldspace or ended up emerging from the wrong coordinates. I saw a few ships with those issues as well, but they weren't in my complete analysis. No time."

Crowe's frown deepened. He let Atwater's words seep into him. There was definitely something else here, something lost in Atwater's near-panic about the facts.

"A number of the ships were older," Atwater said, "and got retired shortly after the troubles began, so that had an impact on our samples as well. I have no idea if they might have had problems had they stayed in active duty."

"Or if they wouldn't have had any problems at all," Stephanos said.

Atwater inclined his head toward her. "That too," he said in a way that led Crowe to believe that idea that they wouldn't have had problems had never crossed Atwater's mind.

Which meant that Atwater's information was inherently biased toward the lag causing problems.

"Was there any information on the ships' *anacapa* drives?" Crowe asked.

Stephanos gave him a sharp look. Apparently that question had occurred to her as well.

"The drives?" Atwater sounded surprised.

"Were they old? New? Damaged? From the same type of ship? Were they the same kinds of drives? Were they installed in the same sector base? Repaired in anyway?" Crowe asked.

He had hoped Atwater would have been looking all of that up. Atwater's specialty was *anacapa* drives and foldspace, after all. So when Crowe sent him after this information, he had expected Atwater to have looked at the drives as a matter of course.

Crowe set his brownie down, awaiting the answer. As he did, Stephanos caught his eye.

She held her hand just above the tabletop, her thumb and forefinger extended, a space of about an inch between them.

Crowe understood the movement. She wasn't thinking of the *anacapa* drives that powered the ships. She was wondering if the little bits of *anacapa* that powered the long-distance communications on the ships had come from the same large *anacapa* drive. Usually one gigantic drive was chosen, then sliced carefully, each little bit tested before it was placed into a ship.

Atwater wouldn't know that. He wouldn't have the clearance.

Atwater was sliding his fork back and forth. It made a slightly scratchy sound on the surface of the table. He didn't seem to notice.

"You know how Fleet records are," he said slowly. Crowe braced himself for an excuse. "I could only access clear records from the past five hundred years or so."

That was more than Crowe had expected.

"The ships were different versions of DV-Class and SC-Class vessels. There were a couple of smaller ships, because the Fleet kept toying with putting *anacapa* drives in cargo vessels and some orbiters for a while, but I disregarded that information." Atwater kept sliding his fork around.

Crowe wanted to grab his hand and make the noise stop. Then Stephanos did grab it, and took the fork away from Atwater.

She waved it at him. "Either use it for what it's intended for," she said, "or leave it alone."

"Sorry," he said. "I get nervous."

Stephanos rolled her eyes at him, which was better than what she would have normally said.

Crowe gave her a small smile. She did not smile in return.

"The ships were not the same, then," Crowe said. "Not built at the same time, not put together in the same place."

"I didn't check repair records," Atwater said, "but given the span of time that I looked at, I don't think they even got repaired in the same sectors, let alone at the same base."

Crowe nodded. If only it had been that simple.

"Which means we have to trace the *anacapa* drives," Stephanos said to Crowe.

"Or not," he said.

He stood up, suddenly empathizing with Atwater's nerves. Crowe grabbed his mug and walked to the tiny kitchen, ostensibly to pour himself more coffee. But he didn't need more coffee. He needed to think.

"Could you tell if these ships tried to trace the lag in their communications?" he asked, back to Atwater.

"No," Atwater said. "Ship repair records are impossible to find."

"This wouldn't even be in the repair records," Stephanos said. "They'd be in ship records."

"I didn't go that deep," Atwater said. "I could try."

"Don't," Stephanos said.

But Crowe turned, already shaking his head. Atwater had his back to Crowe, but Stephanos was looking at him.

Crowe left his mug on the counter, and walked back to the table.

"No," he said. "Try. See if you can find anything, particularly on the *anacapa* drive. More information is always better than not enough."

"Yes, sir," Atwater said.

"Now," Crowe said, "grab some of those brownies for yourself for later, and head back to research. I need to talk to Natalia."

"Yes, sir," Atwater said, then waved his hand over the plate of brownies. He had no idea how to take any.

So Crowe pulled four off the plate and put them on his plate. He put two on Stephanos's plate, even though she hadn't touched the first one.

Then he slid the original plate at Atwater, along with the cover.

Crowe almost said, *Run along*, but that wouldn't be fair. Atwater had given them a new direction.

Atwater covered the brownies, picked up the plate, nearly dropped it, then gave Crowe an apologetic smile. Crowe nodded, heading for the door. Atwater followed.

Crowe opened the door. Atwater walked through it, and Crowe thanked him, then closed the door, not even giving Atwater time to answer.

Crowe took a deep breath, and returned to the table.

"The communications *anacapas*," Stephanos said as he sat down.

"Yeah, possibly," he said.

"Two different problems then? The communications *anacapas* are malfunctioning and creating the lag?""Or they're interacting with the ship's *anacapa* as we go through foldspace," Crowe said.

She made a face. Then she picked up her first brownie with her fingers—no fork—and ate the thing in two rapid bites.

"The only way to test that," she said around the food, "is when we're in foldspace itself."

"Yeah, I know," Crowe said. "And even then, it might not give us the answers we want."

Stephanos wiped her mouth with the back of her hand. Then she wiped the back of her hand on her pants.

"What do you mean?" she asked.

"What if the interaction of the drives is causing the problem?" Crowe asked. "Do we get the captain to return?"

"And which problem are we talking about?" she asked. "The lag or getting lost in foldspace?"

They stared at each other for a moment.

Then Crowe let out a small breath. "I got a replacement *anacapa* for the communications array. Should we swap it out now?"

Stephanos opened her mouth, clearly surprised that he had gotten another *anacapa* drive for the communications array. She knew how hard they were to come by.

But she didn't address it.

"I don't think so," she said. "We don't know if that's the problem yet. We don't know if there's a problem with the ship at all."

He nodded, not liking that last statement. He could fix a problem with a ship. He couldn't fix a problem inherent in the travel system itself.

"I didn't ask Atwater to check something," Crowe mumbled, more to himself than to Stephanos.

"What?" she asked.

He pushed his full plate of brownies away, his stomach suddenly aching. "Has anyone ever looked to see if there's *always* a communications lag after travel in foldspace?"

"We would have noticed," she said. "The Fleet would have noticed."

"Even if it was less than a second?" he asked.

She brought a fist to her face, and tapped her thumb against her lips. Then she stopped, pressing her fingers against her mouth as if she didn't want to speak at all.

Finally, she dropped her hands. "Less than a second, and after the trips were over, things would return to normal?"

"Maybe," he said. "Probably."

Then he frowned.

"But," he said, thinking out loud, "not a lot of ships communicate with the Fleet after going through foldspace. The ships go wherever they're going and then return to the Fleet. DV-Class vessels are mostly autonomous. They don't report in. What we're doing is odd. We're reporting regularly."

She brought her hand back up to her face, continuing that tapping all over again. Her eyes moved ever so slightly as she got lost in thought.

Then she brought that fist down and lightly pounded on the table.

"I could check our records," she said. "Maybe the *Renegat* has a history of time lost communicating across foldspace."

"That would only tell us about this ship," Crowe said. "The ship we're having a problem with. Maybe."

"Still," she said, "we would know if the problem predates us."

He nodded. He almost wished Gão hadn't had them check the lag. It all made Crowe nervous. It got him thinking about all the ships that got lost in foldspace and never returned.

No wonder Gão wanted the communication problem solved. If the ship had a small percentage chance of returning, then the communications between the *Renegat* and the Fleet became all the more important.

Preemas had to get the information Gão wanted back to her, whether the ship returned or not. A lag meant the information might not arrive until days, months, years after it would have been useful.

"Yeah," Crowe said after a moment. "It probably would be good to know if this lag predates us. If it's cumulative. If the problem is building somewhere."

"I'm hoping it's just a communications issue," Stephanos said.

He nodded. "We're heading back into foldspace in a day or so. Let's see if we can set up some kind of test to monitor that communications *anacapa*."

"I'd like to do it," Stephanos said. "But then I won't be the one watching our regular *anacapa* drive."

He nodded. He still didn't have the staff he wanted. "Give me some recommendations as to who you would trust monitoring the main drive," he said.

"That's simple," she said. "I trust you."

THE *RENEGAT*

In the end, Crowe sent Stephanos to the bridge to monitor the ship's *anacapa* as the *Renegat* made its fourth journey into foldspace. If something went awry with the main *anacapa*, she was the best person to fix it.

He could handle the communications *anacapa* just fine on his own.

He was in engineering, alone. Stephanos had come down here an hour before the ship was scheduled to head into foldspace, and helped him set up all of the monitors.

The communications array was open, with the *anacapa* panel open as well. He had activated the tiny built-in cameras on the containers. He and Stephanos had gone back and forth about doing that. The fact that the camera was active would create an unplanned variable in their test, but it couldn't be helped.

If he had pulled the little drive out of its nest inside the panel, then he was materially changing the observation, and perhaps causing more problems.

There was no way he could wriggle himself any closer to the little drive, and he couldn't send in an extra camera. So they had tested the container camera about thirty hours ago.

Those container cameras were usually used to help put a drive into place, to make sure it hadn't been bumped or jostled in the normal business of traveling. The cameras were so rarely used that Crowe hadn't even been certain that camera would work.

But it had.

He had also activated every tool that the Fleet had set up to monitor those little drives—also something that would tamper with his experiment. But that couldn't be helped.

Either he monitored it or he didn't.

With all of this equipment going, he could have stepped to another part of engineering or even gone to the bridge. He didn't need to be physically in front of the array—if everything went well, that was.

Part of him didn't expect it to go well. Part of him expected to see a tiny flare of blue light or a little piece of foldspace open here in engineering itself.

And because he had had that thought, he couldn't in good conscience let Stephanos work down here. He would never forgive himself if he lost her. He had lost too many people already in foreseeable engineering accidents. He didn't want to lose another.

He didn't tell her that, of course. He kept such things very private. So she fought him every step of the way, reminding him that she was the expert on *anacapa* drives, not him. Reminding him that she might be able to see a problem just by eyeballing it, while he would have to rely on diagnostics.

He let her vent. He was almost as good as she was, maybe better because he knew his own flaws, and he still didn't change his mind.

Finally, when it became clear that she wasn't going to relent, he told her, quietly and simply, that he would rather have her monitor the large *anacapa* drive, the one that could take the entire ship with it if something went wrong.

He had a hunch, he had said, that all the tiny *anacapa* in the communications array could do was harm the communications array.

She had given him a disbelieving sideways look—she clearly disagreed about the kind of harm the tiny *anacapa* could do. But she didn't argue any longer.

"Just make a note on the record," she said. "A big note. One that says I vociferously disagree."

Crowe did feel odd, though, not being on the bridge for a foldspace trip, but he couldn't figure out any other way. He didn't trust any of the other crew members to work with Preemas on the journey—not if something went wrong.

And Crowe figured that, if something was going to go wrong, it would start soon.

He picked up the flat tablet connected to the container with actual wires. That was a double check. He opened three holographic screens so that he could monitor everything in real time. But if something went wrong with the energy readings, holographic projections were often the first things to disappear.

He wanted something tactile. Normally, he would just use the tablet as is, but he added wires for information (and it had taken him nearly an hour to set that up) because he wanted redundancy upon redundancy upon redundancy.

The holographic screens showed the same thing. The tiny *anacapa* drive looked like a fleck of gold lying on a white satin surface. It wasn't gold and the surface wasn't made of satin, but it looked rich and convincing.

It also looked the way it should look, ready for anything to tap its energy so that it could use its tiny bits of power to send messages out of this sector of space rapidly.

Engineering was too quiet. As he stood there, waiting, he found himself second-guessing his original decision to send everyone out of engineering. If something went wrong, he would need the crew.

And why was he keeping knowledge of that little drive secret? Sure, that was what the Fleet wanted, but the Fleet had sent this entire crew on a mission that the Fleet believed they would not return from.

If someone complained that he had given away Fleet secrets, he had a justifiable defense: *We weren't supposed to return, so I figured they could know.*

Unfortunately, he couldn't convince himself. Not because he thought the ship might return, but because he didn't want anyone tampering with this part of the equipment, no matter how well intentioned the tamper was.

The *Renegat* was only a minute or two away from the coordinates designated for their next run into foldspace. So Crowe braced himself, and forced himself to concentrate on that tiny *anacapa* drive.

Then the *Renegat* bumped and shuddered in a way that Crowe had never felt before, not all the times he had entered foldspace. He didn't like it.

He wanted to take over the bridge controls and see exactly what was going on, but he didn't.

He forced himself to concentrate on the tiny *anacapa* drive—and he was glad he did. It flared white. Just once, but that was one time too many. The flare was brief, less than five seconds, but that didn't reassure Crowe.

The drive should have remained inert. It shouldn't have done anything unless someone was sending a communication—and who would do that in the middle of a foldspace journey?

Still, he made a note, with a time stamp, so that he could return to this moment after the *Renegat* was out of foldspace. He didn't want to lose focus. He needed to keep his gaze on that tiny drive.

It looked so innocent now. Golden again, as if that single flare hadn't happened.

The *Renegat* kept bumping and shuddering. Then the bumps and shudders escalated. The tiny *anacapa* drive flared again, and winked out, just before the *Renegat*'s abnormal bumping abated.

The *Renegat* suddenly felt motionless, which was how it always felt when the ship emerged from foldspace.

He suspected getting stuck in foldspace would feel the same way.

He didn't dare look to confirm. Not while he was monitoring that tiny drive.

Then the external message system chirruped.

"We're clear." Stephanos spoke in that hollow way people used when they were subvocalizing as they sent a message. "And it looks like we're where we should be."

The external system chirruped again. She hadn't given him a chance to respond, not that he would have known what to say.

He needed to make sense of this data anyway. As soon as Preemas was done with her, Stephanos would come to Engineering. By then, maybe Crowe would have some idea as to what had just happened with the tiny communications drive.

He had hoped that he would see nothing.

But that hadn't happened. Instead of eliminating part of the problem, he had discovered something he didn't even know existed. Now, he had even more questions than he had before this experiment started.

And he wasn't quite sure how he was going to answer them—or if he should even try.

THE *RENEGAT*

Crowe wasn't getting much sleep. He had spent most of the last two days sequestered with Stephanos and Atwater, as they examined the data from the communications array and from the ship itself.

They had split up the duties: Atwater was looking at missions that predated this crew, trying to see if any problems were reported with communications after a trip into foldspace.

Stephanos was comparing readings from the main *anacapa* drive with readings she had from other ships she worked on.

Crowe was working Engineering, going through energy readings, looking for the slightest shift in *anacapa* energy. Every time the entire ship used the *anacapa* drive, the ship got flooded with *anacapa* energy, so Crowe was looking for something slightly different—a reading that would show what the little communications *anacapa* was doing.

And now, Crowe had a summons from Preemas. Crowe didn't have a lot to tell Preemas—not yet, anyway. Just some hunches, backed up by incomplete data.

When Crowe had received the summons, he had actually told Preemas that Preemas should wait a day or two, so that Crowe could compile all of the information he needed.

But Preemas wanted him now.

If that was the case, Preemas was going to hear something he wouldn't like.

Preemas was in his ready room. He had told Crowe not to knock, to just enter.

As Crowe crossed the bridge, a few of the crew glanced sideways at him. It felt strange to be on the bridge. Except for a few journeys late at night to check information from one of the navigation stations—information that the console itself stored—he hadn't been here since before the *Renegat* went into foldspace the fourth time.

The screens were off, as usual, so he could see a reflection of himself moving across the bridge. Tindo Ibori had a small hologram of the entire sector floating above his console. The information that created that hologram had come from scans the *Renegat* was doing now.

Crowe glanced at the floating cube of information—the slice out of the vast array of everything that filled this part of space—and didn't recognize any of it, not that he would. He wanted to stop and study it, even though the *Renegat* wouldn't be here long.

Ibori gave Crowe a weak smile. Crowe nodded, then put his head down. He needed to concentrate on the meeting. He was going to try to convince Preemas of something that Preemas would instinctively say no to.

Crowe had to get past Preemas's prejudices. If only Preemas had waited a day or two, then Crowe would have had—*might* have had—more data to use to convince Preemas. But Preemas hadn't waited, and Crowe had a hunch he knew why.

The door to the ready room slid open before Crowe had a chance to activate it. He stepped inside, nearly walking into Preemas.

Preemas wasn't behind that massive desk. He was pacing, somehow finding space to walk among all the chairs, his hands clasped behind his back.

"Took you long enough," he snapped, then waved his hand.

The door slid shut, nearly catching Crowe's back in the process. Crowe felt the breeze that the door created, sending a little chill through him.

Crowe didn't respond to Preemas's irritated comment. Crowe knew saying that—saying anything defensively—would be a bad way to start this discussion.

"Sit," Preemas said, waving a hand at one of the chairs.

"I prefer to stand," Crowe said, like he said every single time he had a meeting with Preemas.

Preemas shook his head and sighed. "Then don't move. I need to be able to walk, and I don't want to run into you again."

"Perhaps we should walk the corridors," Crowe said. "No one would be able to hear the entire—"

"*No.*" Preemas stopped walking, then turned and leaned on the desk. "This won't take long. I need to know if you've resolved the problem with the communications lag."

"No, sir," Crowe said. "We're still working on it."

"That's unacceptable," Preemas said. "We need it resolved."

"I know, sir," Crowe said. "But I think we have a larger problem than simply communications."

"You *think?*" Preemas seemed off, angry, as if something else had gone wrong.

Crowe wished he could gage the man's moods better. "I take it you spoke to Vice Admiral Gão."

Crowe worked hard to make sure that sentence wasn't accusatory. He had asked that Preemas wait until Crowe had finished his tests before speaking to Gão.

"Of course I did," Preemas said. "We have to get across this sector faster than we traveled through the last one. If you had been on the bridge when we arrived, you would have realized that the part of the sector we arrived in was being patrolled by warships of some kind or another."

Stephanos had mentioned that, but she said that the ships didn't seem to be aware of the *Renegat*, and that the *Renegat* had moved out of that part of the sector pretty quickly. She hadn't seen those ships as a major threat, but apparently Preemas had.

"We don't have a lot of time here, and Gão wants me to speak to her from each sector we travel to." Preemas ran a hand over his short cropped hair. "So, I couldn't wait for you any longer."

Crowe nodded, but didn't apologize.

"The lag makes a discussion damn near impossible," Preemas said. "Eleven minutes this time. The lags aren't even following a pattern. They're not doubling up on the time. They seem random."

"I don't think they are, sir," Crowe said.

"That damn word again. *Think. Think*," Preemas snapped. "I don't care what you *think*. What do you *know*?"

This was not how Crowe wanted to have this discussion, at all. But he didn't see a way out of it.

"I *know* that we have a serious problem with our communications *anacapa* drive," Crowe said, deliberately leaning on the word "know." "Whenever we go through foldspace with the *Renegat*, the communications *anacapa* opens an entrance into foldspace all on its own."

Preemas rocked back, as if the news touched him physically. "What does that mean?"

"That's what we're trying to determine," Crowe said.

"Well, fix it," Preemas snapped.

"I'm worried that if I try to fix it without the right information," Crowe said, "I could make things worse."

Preemas cursed, then pushed himself off the desk, as if he were launching himself into a standing position. He started to pace again, hands clasped behind him, ostentatiously walking between Crowe and the desk.

"So," Preemas said after a moment, "this just affects the communications array."

"No," Crowe said. "That's not what I'm telling you. The data suggests that ships which have a time lag in their communications eventually get out of phase with the entire Fleet. That could be where time differentials come from."

"Could be?" Preemas asked. "*Could be?*"

"We just don't know at this moment," Crowe said, hating how Preemas was trying to provoke him. "I have Atwater searching for more data, but the data he has already found is disturbing. Over a third of ships with this problem end up getting lost in foldspace or coming out of foldspace with a different perception of time than the Fleet itself."

Preemas shook his head. "Not possible," he said. "I'm pretty sure the *Esizayo* didn't have one of those communications *anacapas*."

That was the ship Preemas had served on, the one in which he had lost a year of his life.

"Forgive me, sir," Crowe said, "but you weren't a high-ranking officer on that ship, were you?"

Preemas shot Crowe an angry glare.

"And it was a DV-Class vessel, right?" Crowe asked.

"Make your damn point, First Officer Crowe," Preemas said.

"My point, sir," Crowe said gently, "is that I can guarantee you that the *Esizayo* had a communications *anacapa*. The Fleet has had them as long as we can trace back."

"You're saying I'm wrong about a ship *I* served on?" Preemas asked.

"I'm saying, sir, that you didn't have the clearance to know what was in the communications array. Only a handful of us know about it on this ship. I'm not even sure Newark was briefed before she became first officer." Crowe swallowed hard, realizing there was another gap. "I suspect that Tindo Ibori doesn't know either, and he probably should, given that the extra foldspace bubble might have an impact on navigation."

"*Might have*," Preemas said. "I need firm information."

"We don't have firm information, sir. We're dealing with *anacapa* drives." Crowe lifted his chin slightly. "If you want firm information, take that up with the Fleet. They're the ones who saddled us with these drives."

Preemas's eyes narrowed. He clearly felt the rebuke. Which, apparently, was making him angrier.

"So," he said, "you're telling me that a third of all ships with those tiny little *anacapa* drives disappear into foldspace? Give me a break, First Officer Crowe. If that were the case, then we'd lose most of the Fleet every year."

"No, sir," Crowe said, wishing Preemas was calmer. "I said a third of the ships that experience time lag in communications after going through foldspace end up experiencing time lag with the entire Fleet. Or disappearing into foldspace altogether."

"Great," Preemas said, almost to himself. He stopped walking. His back was to Crowe.

"What I do not know," Crowe said, "is if the communications *anacapa* is tied to this problem or if it is a separate problem or if it is completely normal."

Preemas shook his head, then leaned it backwards and then exhaled, clearly showing his irritation.

Crowe did not want to take that irritation personally, but somehow Preemas's emotions stirred up his. Crowe had never experienced that before. He was beginning to think that something about Preemas drew people to him, and then made them feel the way Preemas wanted them to feel.

This was probably some kind of charisma, which wasn't all that common in the leadership of the Fleet. In fact, the Fleet often discouraged charismatic leaders, because they could go rogue and disturb the way the Fleet functioned, particularly if the leader decided to take action against the Fleet.

Preemas hadn't moved. It almost seemed like he was studying something infinitely more interesting on the ceiling of the ready room.

He clearly wanted some kind of reaction from Crowe. And Crowe wasn't going to give him the reaction Preemas expected.

"I take it your conversation with Vice Admiral Gão did not go well," Crowe said as flatly as he could.

Preemas whirled. His face was mottled, his eyes flashing with not-quite-suppressed fury.

"'Did not go well' is an understatement," he said. "She does not like this problem. I'm pretty sure she's going to ask us to abort the mission the next time I talk to her. I don't want to do that, First Officer Crowe. That means we have failed."

Preemas had opened the conversational door to the very thing that Crowe had wanted to talk with him about.

"I think we are now faced with an opportunity," Crowe said.

Preemas's eyes narrowed. He seemed automatically suspicious of whatever Crowe was going to say.

"There's a distinct possibility," Crowe said slowly, "that the problem with the communications *anacapa* is not isolated to the *Renegat*."

Preemas's lips thinned. "Possibility," he repeated. He always seemed to hear Crowe's hedges, and give them too much weight.

"I don't think anyone," Crowe said in that same deliberate tone, "has ever observed a communications *anacapa* while the regular *anacapa* is going through foldspace. I could find no reference to it. Neither Natalia nor I were ever trained to look for it, nor was anything mentioned in our schooling or in our internships as young engineers."

"That doesn't mean anything," Preemas said.

Crowe could feel just how quickly Preemas wanted to dismiss all of this.

"It does, actually," Crowe said. "We don't know a lot about *anacapa* drives."

"You and Stephanos?" Preemas asked.

"The Fleet," Crowe said.

"That's what you were alluding to earlier? That the Fleet 'saddled us' with drives we don't understand?" Preemas made a dismissive sound. "No wonder they put you on this ship *Chief Engineer* Crowe. You're prone to exaggerating to prove your point."

His captain had just called him a liar. Crowe's face heated. He was many things, but he didn't lie.

And Preemas knew that.

Which meant that Preemas had jabbed at him deliberately, and was probably quite proud of the hit he had just made.

"I am not," Crowe said, making sure his face did not register his fury. He kept speaking slowly. "Everyone who trains on *anacapa* drives learns this. As you know, the Fleet did not invent the drives. There is much we don't know about them."

"What do you mean, we didn't invent the drives?" Preemas asked.

Crowe let out a slow breath. He tilted his head slightly. "You didn't get this part of the training?"

"I didn't have to work with *anacapa* drives," Preemas said. "We got one class in basic drive mechanics as part of the officer track. I assume that's what you got in your officer track courses as well."

"I never took officer track courses," Crowe said drily. "My education is purely engineering."

Preemas made a face. He was clearly getting impatient. He didn't understand that Crowe was laying the groundwork to make an important point.

"Why wouldn't officers learn the history of the *anacapa* drive?" Preemas asked.

Crowe shrugged one shoulder. "Perhaps because the word 'history' does not go well with anything the Fleet does."

"But you got that history," Preemas said.

"Years into the *anacapa* training. After I had been cleared to work on the drives. The entire system is designed to weed out most candidates. Working with *anacapa* drives is part knowledge, part finesse, and part educated imagination. But they don't tell you that up front, perhaps because so many people wash out of the program."

Crowe had thought everyone knew how difficult *anacapa* training was, but as he considered it, he realized there was no reason anyone outside of the engineering school would have any idea about the way that *anacapa* training worked.

Those who had failed wouldn't broadcast the fact that they had failed, and those that rose through the ranks were cautioned the farther up they went not to talk at all about the drives or anything they had learned.

"I got some training in the history," Crowe said. "Mostly, it was connected to the drive itself. We build the drives based on specs that the Fleet has had for millennia. We do not change anything about the drives. We build them the way we've always built them, never changing any aspect of the drive itself in any way."

"Including the communications *anacapa*?" That question had a different tone to it, and in that moment, Crowe knew he finally had Preemas's full attention.

"Yes," Crowe said. "I don't think we ever would have come up with that on our own."

Preemas frowned. "If we didn't come up with the drives, who did?"

"That I don't know," Crowe said. "I do know that everyone who is an expert on the drive knows that there's more about the drives that we don't understand than things about the drives that we do understand."

"That's just ridiculous." Preemas walked to his desk, pulled back the chair, and sat down heavily. "Why would we use something we don't understand?"

"Because it's the only thing we've discovered that allows us to travel vast distances," Crowe said.

"But we didn't discover it," Preemas said.

"No," Crowe said. "We use it, though. Every day. In a wide variety of contexts."

Preemas shook his head. Crowe recognized the twist of Preemas's mouth. The sentence Preemas was holding back probably had something to do with how stupid the Fleet actually was.

"Everyone who works on the drive," Crowe said carefully, "knows that there's a lot we don't understand about the drives. That's why you see a lot of concern and caution from the informed engineers when they approach an *anacapa* drive. I don't know if you've noticed how the engineers who specialize in *anacapa* drives are a lot more conservative about their use than those who have never had full *anacapa* training, but the reason is we've learned to respect and fear those drives."

Preemas crossed his arms over his chest and leaned back in the chair. He looked furious, as if it was Crowe's fault that the *anacapa* drives were one part mystery.

"I assume you have a reason for telling me this now, as opposed to weeks ago, when we planned this fiasco? Twelve trips *one way* through foldspace, using a drive we don't understand?"

Crowe slowly breathed in, and willed himself not to answer in kind.

"We all knew the risks when we planned this trip, sir," Crowe said.

"Not all the risks," Preemas snapped. "I didn't expect the time lag in communications."

Really? Crowe wanted to ask. *We're covering a distance the Fleet has never done in one large lump, and you expected to have instant communication across all of those sectors?*

He had to actively fight himself to prevent himself from saying that.

"The time lag led us to an important discovery, sir," Crowe said.

"That tiny foldspace opening in communications is an important discovery?" Preemas asked. "For us, maybe, First Officer Crowe, but only if we solve it."

"Beg pardon, sir," Crowe said, reverting to formal language to get Preemas's attention, "but that is incorrect. I believe no one in the Fleet knows about that little foldspace opening in communications."

"You *believe*," Preemas said.

"Yes, sir, I do," Crowe said. "We would have learned about it in training. We would have been told the purpose of that opening or how to avoid it or how to use it properly."

Preemas leaned forward, uncrossed his arms, placed his right elbow on the desk and braced his head against his open hand, running his fingers across his forehead as if he had a terrible headache.

"So what do you think we should do?" he asked, without looking up at Crowe.

Crowe wasn't sure how to present this, not in the middle of this discussion. He had initially imagined himself saying, *We can return as heroes*, but that wasn't going to work, not now, maybe not ever.

Preemas might be the kind of man who could manipulate others with grandiose talk, but it was tough to manipulate Preemas. And Crowe wasn't good at grandiose talk anyway, not like this.

"I think we have made a major discovery," Crowe said. "I think it's one that was worth our travel time, worth the difficulties we've experienced, and worth all the effort we put into planning this trip."

Preemas raised his head. His gaze met Crowe's.

"You want us to turn around," Preemas said flatly.

"I do, sir," Crowe said. This time he couldn't keep the excitement from his voice. "I think if we turn around and go back, bring this information to the Fleet, and let the *anacapa* specialists study it, along with the foldspace problems with the larger drives, we will be hailed as heroes."

That word finally left his mouth, and as it did, he wished it hadn't. It sounded wrong. Stupid.

Preemas smiled with only half of his mouth.

"Or idiots," he said, "if those specialists already knew about that little fold-space opening over the communications array and had deemed it insignificant."

Crowe felt the heat from his cheeks move into his chest. "I don't think so, sir. I think that they don't know about this. I think—"

"You don't know, Chief Engineer Crowe. You've been out of the major loop for years. You have no idea what the Fleet knows and what it doesn't." Preemas put his hands flat on the desktop, and levered himself up. "If we go back, and *I'm* right, that's the end of all of our careers. We'd become laughingstocks within the Fleet."

"And if I'm right," Crowe said, deciding to let the anger out, "then we have discovered something that will save countless lives."

"Maybe you didn't get the message, *Mister* Crowe," Preemas said, his voice filled with sarcasm. "We're not supposed to save countless lives. We're supposed to waste five hundred lives on a trip for some admiral's whim."

Crowe stiffened. He didn't like that "Mister," and he also didn't like the "admiral's whim."

Crews were subject to their commanders' orders. That was how it worked. That was how it was supposed to work, and a captain, like Preemas, should have made his peace with that fact a long, long, long time ago.

"Well, then." Crowe spoke softly, like he always did when he was extremely angry. "You should take my advice. We can surprise everyone by saving lives—including the five hundred who would die going to that Scrapheap."

"By disobeying our orders," Preemas said.

"That hasn't been a problem for you in the past," Crowe said.

Preemas's eyes narrowed.

"I frankly don't understand why you're worried about our reputations, Captain," Crowe said. "We had none going into this. It is a last-ditch effort to repair our relationship with the Fleet. If I'm right, then we will do just that."

"*You* will do that, Mister Crowe," Preemas said. "As you told me, captains know nothing about the history of the *anacapa* drive or the vagaries of the way they interact. You and Stephanos and that new recruit, Atwater, you'll all be heroes. The rest of us will have been along for the ride."

So that was what was bothering Preemas. That no matter how he twisted this, he wouldn't get credit for the discovery.

"It would be your decision to return," Crowe said. "Your decision to abort the mission and make a huge change inside the Fleet. You were the one who gave the orders that led us to this discovery. You would be the one who would get all the credit, Captain, not us."

"Nice angle," Preemas said, leaning back in his chair and putting his hands behind his head. "But it doesn't work, Mister Crowe. Because anyone with a brain would figure out who briefed me, who discovered the issue, and who—by the time we get home—might actually have a solution."

Crowe took a deep, steadying breath. Unfortunately, the breath didn't steady him at all.

"So," Crowe said, trying not to let all the anger he felt into his voice, and failing miserably, "you don't want to return with something that might possibly change the way the Fleet does things, preventing people from disappearing into foldspace for good, you don't want to do anything about that, because you won't get credit? Is that what I'm hearing, *Pre?*"

Using the nickname Preemas had wanted him to use was a bit passive-aggressive, but Crowe hadn't been this mad in a long, long time.

Preemas's posture didn't change, although his body stiffened just enough to be noticeable.

"I can't verify your work, Mister Crowe," Preemas said. "I have no idea if you're lying to me because you're scared and you've decided that the *Renegat* would be better off returning to the Fleet. You know I won't order that on my own, so maybe you're taking the matter into your own hands. Maybe you've decided that you know what this ship needs much more than I do. Maybe you feel that you can manipulate me into aborting this mission and therefore saving lives, no matter what the cost to the rest of us."

"That's the second time you've called me a liar," Crowe said. "I. Don't. Lie."

Preemas moved his right arm away from his head, waving his hand in a dismissive motion. "All humans lie," he said. "Especially when they have something to gain."

"What," Crowe asked, "do you think I have to gain?"

"Your life for one," Preemas said. "We've been talking about this as a suicide mission. You don't believe I can get us through this, so you're afraid that the changes we've made—the changes *I've* made—will kill us all. So you want to turn tail and run back to the Fleet, no matter what the cost to your reputation."

A reputation is worth spit if you're dead, Crowe nearly said, but stopped himself. He didn't care about his reputation. He never had. He would have just said that as an argument for arguing's sake.

Crowe took two steps forward until he was as close to Preemas's desk as he could get. Crowe then leaned down, and placed his hands on the surface.

His eyes were completely level with Preemas's.

"This ship started in trouble," Crowe said. "We were sent with the worst possible crew into an impossible situation to investigate something no one cared about except on some intellectual level."

"We agree on that, at least," Preemas said.

"We got into more trouble when it became clear that many on the crew really weren't up to the job at even a minimal level." Crowe leaned toward Preemas, lowering his voice even more. "At that point, I agreed with you. I thought we needed to take some drastic action. I thought your methods were flawed, but then, I thought the Fleet's methods were flawed too."

"So, two wrongs make a right," Preemas said, snidely.

Crowe ignored that. "I figured we could live with the communications time lag, especially one at thirty seconds or so. Even two minutes was fine. I figured we could adjust for that."

Preemas nodded. "We're not disagreeing yet, Mr. Crowe."

"But lag grew, and you demanded we investigate, and when we did, we discovered major threats to the ship. If we get lost in foldspace, no one will try to rescue us. There won't be a sector base nearby that will attempt to ping the ship. We'll be lost."

"That was an expected risk from the very start, Mr. Crowe," Preemas said. "And you know it."

"We may have found the cause of the problems with foldspace travel, not just for us, but for all Fleet ships," Crowe said, "and you're ignoring that."

"I am ignoring nothing," Preemas said. "As far as I'm concerned, nothing has changed except your opinion, Mr. Crowe. And your opinion counts for nothing."

The blood left Crowe's face. He could feel it, draining down, as his fury grew.

"Then you don't need me to fix that communications *anacapa*, do you?" Crowe snapped.

"No, I don't," Preemas said. "I'm going to let the vice admiral know that our communications across this vast distance no longer work. I'll send her reports, verbal ones, but the one-on-one communications will stop."

Crowe waited for Preemas to continue, to order him to stop investigating the communications *anacapa* and its interaction (if there was any) with the regular *anacapa* drive.

That half smile of Preemas's seemed cold. "Is there anything else, Mr. Crowe?"

Crowe stood upright and clasped his hands behind his back. "Who do you want me to send in here, sir?"

"No one." Preemas frowned. "Why would I?"

"You'll need a replacement for me," Crowe said. "Both as first officer and as chief engineer."

"Are you resigning?" Preemas asked.

"No, sir," Crowe said. "But you have made it clear that you think I'm unqualified—"

"I did not say that, Crowe," Preemas said, leaving off an honorific altogether. "I said we did not agree."

And your opinion is based on nothing, while mine is based on decades of expertise. Crowe wondered if he should say that. He wasn't sure what he had to lose.

"And," Preemas said, "since I'm the captain, I win."

As if it were a contest. As if winning and losing was more important than doing the right thing.

"At least let me speak to Vice Admiral Gão, sir," Crowe said.

"There's no need," Preemas said. "I'll let her know that the communications problem stems from the distance."

Which might not have been true at all.

"Sir," Crowe said as firmly as he could, "I would like to request from her all the records the Fleet has concerning the communications *anacapa* drive. As you said, this could be nothing, and I would like to know that before we waste future resources on it—"

"As you said, if there was a regular problem with the communications *anacapa*, the Fleet would have notified everyone working with communications and *anacapa* drives. There's never been a notification. There is no regular problem." Preemas spoke with heavy emphasis on *no regular problem.*

"Then, sir," Crowe said, "we have a problem, and it could be dire."

"Or it might not be. Swap out the little drive," Preemas said, "and see if that one interacts like the first one."

Crowe blinked at him. He hadn't told Preemas about the other drive. And that surprise must have shown on Crowe's face, because Preemas smiled.

"You think I don't know when one of my crew makes a bargain to get a piece of equipment. Now I understand why there was a discrepancy between the request you put in for a backup *anacapa* and the size of the delivery." Preemas's smile grew. "And here I thought you were asking an old friend in some kind of code for something specific, something other than an *anacapa* drive. I was half right. You were asking for something specific, a part of the ship I hadn't even known existed."

Crowe's mouth was dry.

"I don't miss much, Mister Crowe." There it was again, that verbal demotion. Crowe didn't like it. "It would do you well to remember that."

Crowe nodded. He would remember that.

"I would like to stay on as Chief Engineer, sir," Crowe said.

"Of course." Then Preemas's frown returned. "You didn't say anything about remaining as first officer."

Because Crowe didn't beg. And he wasn't sure he was as enamored of the job as he should have been.

"I am waiting for you to ask me to tender my resignation, sir," Crowe said.

"And who the hell would I replace you with?" Preemas asked. "You think anyone else on this ship is competent enough to command it? You're the best I've got, and you barely are."

The insult was deliberate. Apparently, this was going to be their relationship from now on, because Crowe had dared to think they should turn around.

"There are others who would do just fine," Crowe said.

"I disagree," Preemas said. "You're the first officer, whether you like it or not, Mister Crowe. And you will do as I tell you."

Crowe's interlaced fingers tightened painfully behind his back. "As you wish, sir," he said.

And it wasn't until Crowe left that he realized *As you wish, sir*, was not an agreement. *As you wish, sir*, was a dodge.

Crowe couldn't follow Preemas's orders. Preemas's orders were wrong.

And there was only one way to overrule them.

Crowe had to talk with Vice Admiral Gāo. She could order Preemas's return. And he would have to listen.

Because if he didn't, he wouldn't have that triumphant return he had been looking forward to. No matter how well Preemas performed on this mission, disobeying an order to return would guarantee that he got no credit, no matter what he did.

THE *RENEGAT*

Crowe stood inside engineering near the communications array. He had told the Engineering crew that he was working on part of the array they couldn't handle, but that wasn't true.

He was going to contact Vice Admiral Gão.

His stomach twisted as he did the planning for this. He had disobeyed a number of captains in his career. He had refused to execute orders that he believed would harm or kill crew or innocents. He had created a lot of reports that outlined the reasons for his protests. He had testified in front of a large group of officers, after incidents had occurred. He had justified his positions to vice admirals and admirals more than once.

But he had never gone over someone's head before, not in the middle of a mission.

This time, though, he felt justified. This time, he believed that he could make a difference for the entire Fleet, not just for this crew.

Although, he knew there was also a lot of self-interest here.

He didn't want to get stuck in foldspace, and he felt the *Renegat* was careening down that course.

Engineering was quiet, except for its usual equipment hum. The air smelled faintly of coffee: he had caught one of the new recruits from Sector Base Z drinking from a sealed mug near her station. He had sent her away with a reprimand, telling one of the other crew members to make sure that the recruit knew why her actions were so damn dumb.

He didn't have time for tiny dumb today. He needed to deal with Big Deal Dumb.

Initially, Crowe had planned to contact Gão by himself, then realized that wouldn't work.

If Preemas was on the bridge when Crowe initiated contact, the ship herself might notify Preemas that there was a long-distance message going through.

Stephanos was on the bridge to monitor Preemas and the communications system. If he had any questions, she would tell Preemas that Crowe was testing the system.

A captain who understood how all of the equipment worked down here would not have believed that for an instant, but Preemas let the engineers handle engineering. He was much more interested in the other systems on the ship, as well as the interactions between the people in his newly redesigned crew.

Even though he knew he probably wouldn't get caught, Crowe was nervous. He had packets of information to send to Vice Admiral Gão, although none of it was conclusive. And he wasn't really sure if it would all reach her. He knew that the communications array was acting up; he didn't know how it would work with large packets of data—larger than what he was creating by talking to her.

He also knew that eleven-minute lag would be an issue, especially for him. He wouldn't be able to see her reactions in real time.

If he was going to abandon this path, now was the moment.

He stood very still and thought about what he was going to do. Again.

Then realized he could bat this around in his mind forever, or he could actually take some action.

He took a deep breath, straightened his back, and then contacted the vice admiral directly, using the *Renegat's* command code.

Then he added a visual, as he said, "First Officer Crowe to speak privately with Vice Admiral Gão on a matter of life and death."

Of course, there was no immediate response. He had set up a timer on the communications array, so that he could time the delays between contacts in real time, which was what he would tell Preemas he was doing if he got caught.

It only took a few minutes for a response, which surprised Crowe. He had planned on the eleven-minute lag that Preemas had talked about, or maybe even something more.

A holoimage opened, showing a thin woman in a lieutenant's uniform. Her features were severe, her expression serious. Behind her, he could see brown walls with rotating images cycling through. Most were of the Fleet itself.

"We were not expecting contact," the lieutenant said. "I will get Vice Admiral Gão. Be patient. This may take some time."

She didn't mention the lag. Maybe she assumed he knew about it or maybe she didn't think it was relevant.

She did not wait for him to respond, which was a good thing. Instead, she walked away from the area, leaving him staring at the rotating pictures on the far wall.

Only they had ceased to rotate. They remained stationary, showing the DV-Class ships of the Fleet, with their names etched beneath the images. He had served on at least two of those ships. He didn't miss them, although he missed the size.

Then he blinked, wondering why the image had paused. Had she done that? Or was it part of the lag? Did the imagery freeze on the walls or did it just freeze when it hit a certain amount of data to be sent through the nodes?

He wasn't certain, but he made a note of it on a small tablet he had beside the communications array. From the start, he had planned to make a list of the technical things he had noticed in this communication.

Then he started sending the data packets. He wanted them to arrive as he was talking to Vice Admiral Gāo, so that she couldn't order him *not* to send them.

The image in front of him shifted and split. It became two images—the room itself, empty, and another room in which a small woman stood. That room was decorated in blues and golds, and looked official, although Crowe couldn't quite say why he thought it was official.

Maybe it was because the small woman was wearing a uniform, her shoulders squared by the piping that trailed down the front of the navy jacket. Side tables stood behind her. They gleamed—or, at least, Crowe thought they gleamed. He wasn't certain if the gleam was a trick of the light, or some anomaly in the holographic image.

It took him a moment to realize the woman was Vice Admiral Gāo. In person she looked so much larger. She had a forceful personality, one she usually kept carefully restrained, and only unleashed when she seemed to believe that emotion was necessary.

She had reprimanded him years ago and then had given him a second chance (or was it a third chance? Or fourth? He had stopped counting his supposed comebacks years ago). She looked older. Her hair was still black, but it was slightly tousled, as if Crowe had disturbed her while she was doing something important, and she hadn't had time to check her face in a mirror.

There were lines under her dark eyes, and around the edges of her mouth. But those eyes—they were still formidable. Even at this distance.

Crowe glanced at the clock he had set up. Six minutes had passed.

Her image shimmered and grew, as if it was trying to become a holographic image, but couldn't quite achieve it. He pressed the side of the communications array, bringing down the resolution just a tad, and the woman's image became clear.

It was definitely Gāo. Her expression was wary.

"Where's the captain?" she asked, letting Crowe know from the very start that she found this communication unorthodox.

"He does not know that I have contacted you," Crowe said.

Gāo did not move. Her image was definitely in some kind of stasis. The resolution grew and faded. Edges of the image leached away and then returned.

Crowe wasn't quite sure what he was waiting for. He had initially thought he would spew the information at Gāo. But as he stood here, watching the holographic image try to recreate itself, he wondered if that was the best approach. The image wasn't really static, and he was afraid some of what he had to say would get lost in the long-range communications.

After six minutes, Gāo said, "This is irregular, First Officer Crowe. Technically, all communications up the chain need to go through the captain. Is he incapable of communicating with me?"

"No, sir," Crowe said. "I'm going to tell you something in one big long lump of words, since conversations are hard through this interface. When I'm done, please ask for clarification if you need it. I'm afraid my words might cut out and you'll miss something important."

Still he waited for her response, which probably wasn't the most practical thing to do. He hoped that, on the bridge, Stephanos was keeping Preemas occupied.

Or better yet, Crowe hoped that Preemas hadn't noticed at all.

Then, less than five minutes later, Gão seemed to nod. Crowe had no idea if that was a trick of the data stream or if she actually had, but he took it as a go-ahead.

"I don't know if you know," he said, "I started as the Chief Engineer of this vessel, and continue to act in that capacity. Captain Preemas alerted me to the time lag in your communications, and asked me to investigate..."

Crowe told her everything, from the time lag research that Atwater had done to the conclusions he had made. Then he told her about the opening of the separate foldspace bubble inside the communications *anacapa*, and said he had no idea if that was normal.

He would have paused at that point if they were having a regular conversation and asked for questions, but he didn't feel like he could. Especially since, in the middle of his speech, Gão's head moved just a little more, and she said, "Proceed," as if he hadn't spoken at all.

They were talking over each other, in lag-time anyway, but he had a hunch she didn't mind any more than he did.

He told her about his fears, that the two *anacapa* drives interacted badly on some ships. He said he did not have enough information to know if the problems stemmed from the communications *anacapa* or if something else was going on. He also said he didn't know if the communications *anacapa* was part of a slice from a larger *anacapa* that routinely malfunctioned.

"I have sent you all of the information we have," he said. "I told Captain Preemas I believe this is a life-saving discovery and we needed to return to the Fleet to work on this technology. I think we're courting disaster if we continue to the Scrapheap. If Atwater's research is correct, we will either get lost in foldspace or lose years as we travel through it."

He swallowed, wishing he could see her reaction. He also wished that he had thought enough ahead to have a bottle of water nearby. He wasn't used to talking this much all at once, and he was growing parched.

"Captain Preemas does not think this discovery is important. He would like to continue to the Scrapheap, no matter what the consequences are." Crowe hoped he didn't sound too dramatic. He was going for matter-of-fact. "At this rate, I am not sure if we're going to make it to the Scrapheap. If I had to lay a bet on it, I would say that we are not going to make it there. This trip will have been for nothing."

He stopped, then thought the better of it. He needed to add one more thing before he found out if Vice Admiral Gão was angry at him for going around Preemas.

"Vice Admiral," Crowe said, "I think we should return. I have argued repeatedly with the captain about this, and he has done everything except demote me. I would hope that you would take my opinion under advisement and cancel this mission. I truly believe there is no hope of completing it and no hope of the crew surviving it."

There. He wasn't going to add any more. Not yet. He would see what she had to say.

He glanced at the clock. The lag down here wasn't as long as the lag that Preemas had experienced in his quarters. Either Preemas hadn't timed the lag well or equipment interfered.

Then the door to engineering rattled as someone tried to come it. Crowe had sealed it with his command code. No one was coming it without getting Stephanos or the captain to open it.

Still, the sound caught him off guard.

Then, out of the corner of his eye, he saw Gāo move. He had no idea how long she had actually been reacting to his words.

He wished he could compare her reaction in real time. Maybe he would try to sync up his audio later with her movements, just as a guess.

"I see," she said, sounding quite solemn.

That was how people became admirals. They didn't let anyone see their full reactions to the things they were learning.

He had tried that with Preemas, and doubted it had worked at all.

"I will review what you have sent, speak to our *anacapa* experts here, and see what their reaction is." Gāo had shifted slightly. It looked like she had taken a step to the side.

When it became clear she had not added anything, nor had she promised to get Captain Preemas to return, Crowe suppressed a sigh. Part of him had hoped she would do more than *take matters under advisement*, to use the usual parlance.

"Vice Admiral," Crowe said, "I have one other request. Can you have your people send me all the information they have on the communications *anacapa* drives. I'd like to know where our drive came from, if that's possible, and what ships share that small slice."

He wasn't sure if she could do that, especially since he had the secondary communications *anacapa* drive as well. They might end up giving him information on the wrong drive.

But that was a risk he was willing to take.

"I would also like to know if someone has already studied this or is studying it. One thing the captain did say was that he expected the Fleet already knew about this problem and we would be laughingstocks if we returned because of this. For the sake of my knowledge, and the future of this voyage, I would like to know if that assumption is true." Crowe had caught himself midsentence, since he almost said, *for the sake of my ego.*

He wasn't sure if he had meant that or not.

As he was speaking, he noted that Vice Admiral Gāo had shifted again. He wanted to finish before she spoke, although he wasn't sure he could.

"And one last thing, Vice Admiral," he said quickly, just like he would in a normal conversation if he was trying to prevent someone from speaking immediately. "We are heading back into foldspace in a day or two. A decision before we travel even farther from the Fleet would be advisable."

His breath caught. He wished he could take back that last word. He had learned long ago that superior officers didn't like words like *advisable.* It made them feel like any decision that came from a discussion like this wasn't theirs.

The edges of her holographic image faded in and out. She remained stable, however, but motionless.

No one moved in the area around her. The room where her assistant had been, on the split side of the image, slightly behind Gāo, remained empty. Crowe wondered if the assistant was still in the area near Gāo, listening to this conversation.

"Thank you for your concerns, First Officer Crowe," Gāo said. "If we have the information you requested, I will send it directly to you, through the same channel you used to send information to me."

She turned toward her right, as if letting someone know that it was now their responsibility to handle whatever was supposed to be sent to Crowe.

"Now," she said, "I have one question for you. How long has your lag been in this conversation?"

"Six minutes exactly, sir," he said.

Then he double-checked the clock as he waited for her to respond. The other times made him uncomfortable, but this one seemed interminable. He had no idea why.

"Have you any idea why the time shortened again?" she asked.

"I am contacting you from engineering," he said. "Directly through our communications array. That's the only difference on this end."

Six more interminable minutes. Not one second more.

During that time, no one rattled the door to engineering, and no one else contacted him down here. The air felt colder than it had earlier, and he wasn't sure why that was, but he decided not to let it bother him.

"Ours remains the same as the last contact," she said. "Almost eleven minutes. I have no idea how that factors into our equations. I'll leave that to the experts, with whom I will share your theories. I understand the time constraints you sent to me. I hope you understand mine. Information isn't always readily available. We will do what we can here. Gāo out."

And then her image disappeared entirely. The empty room grew to replace it, and then it vanished as well.

Crowe felt his shoulders relax. He had been too tense about this meeting, and it had gone as well as it possible could have.

He needed to save all of the information from the discussion, and he needed to do so in a way that only he could access it. If he chose to share that information with Stephanos or Atwater, he would. But he would choose.

So he still had some work here.

As he stepped into the array, he stopped for just a moment, wondering if he should check to see who rattled the door to engineering. Then he decided that was a problem for another time.

He had too much to do to chase problems that didn't exist.

He turned to the array, and went back to work.

THE *SPRÁVA*

Gão paced her study. Information floated around her, some in holographic form, some as scrolling data. All of it masked the artwork on her walls.

Usually the artwork gave her perspective, but today it just annoyed her—particularly since she knew it was there, but buried in the data she had been studying.

She didn't like what she saw. She had contacted a wide variety of experts after speaking with Nadim Crowe, and those experts hadn't heard of double foldspace openings when a regular *anacapa* drive was activated. They didn't dismiss the information, but they told her, as Crowe had, that they hadn't looked before, so they had no idea if it was normal.

They also believed it might be important.

She had forwarded all of the information Crowe had sent to as many experts as she could, including the various engineering and research vessels that were part of the school contingent. *Anacapa* drives and engineering were not her specialties, so she had no idea who to send the information to at the sector bases or on the various starbases.

And even if she had known, she wouldn't get any kind of confirmation from them soon enough to aid her with her decision.

That had to be her decision. And buried in the middle of it was that stupid order from Admiral Hallock, trying to find out more information about Scrapheaps.

Gão knew if she took all of this to Hallock, Hallock would agree with Preemas, that the trip should continue.

Gão could even hear Hallock's opinion, expressed in her crisp no-nonsense style. *If the captain in the middle of the mission believes it to be worthwhile continuing, then we shouldn't second-guess him.*

But Hallock hadn't met Preemas, and Gão had. She had also met Nadim Crowe, and as dicey as that man's history was, it was filled with solid analysis about any situation he found himself in.

He didn't say it. He would never have said it—but he was frightened. He saw each trip into foldspace as more risky than the last.

And he had contacted Gāo with over twenty foldspace trips still ahead of him.

Hallock wouldn't have counted the return trips. Hallock didn't care if the *Renegat* returned. Somehow, Hallock had made peace with her conscience on this.

Gāo hadn't.

She waved her hand, commanding most of the data around her to disappear. She had seen enough. She needed to contact Preemas, and she had to do so in such a way as to avoid getting Crowe into any more trouble.

Fortunately, she already had a way to do that, without bringing Crowe's name into the discussion at all.

"Baker," she said on her comm, to her assistant. "I am heading into engineering. Tell them that I will be using their communications array to contact the *Renegat*. I will need the area cleared before I get there."

"Consider it done," Baker said.

Baker didn't even have to ask why Gāo wanted to go to Engineering. Baker was helping Gāo organize all of the material she had received from Crowe, figuring out who could make the best use of it.

The one fact that had stuck in Gāo's brain, the one *she* could use, without sending it to someone else, was that Crowe had contacted her from Engineering on the *Renegat*. Crowe's time lag was shorter than hers.

She wasn't sure if that was because of his location when he contacted her, but that was something she couldn't ignore.

Gāo hesitated over her desk for one moment. She thought about bringing information with her, as a kind of show-and-tell for Preemas. But that wouldn't work with the time lags.

She didn't have to convince him of anything. She just had to tell him what to do.

She let herself out of the study, and walked to engineering. She had to go down five decks, to a part of the *Správa* she hadn't been to in maybe a year or more. She went into engineering when she was summoned, which was rarely, since the captain of this vessel handled most everything about it.

As the elevator opened on the proper deck, some of the engineers were waiting, looking slightly annoyed. They stood at attention when they saw her. She waved a hand dismissively.

"No need for formality," she said as she stepped into the corridor. "I'm only going to be using your area for a half an hour or so, and then you can return. They have a lovely apple crisp in the main mess today; have some and take a breather. By the time you're done, I'll be gone."

She didn't wait for a response, but headed toward engineering. The wide corridor was well lit and clean, the blue lights along the top making the light seem fresher than it was in other parts of the ship.

She knew that the engineering staff often played with ambience on this level, to see if anything they did raised spirits. The subtle things worked as well (and sometimes better) than the overt ones.

She would remember to remark on this to the captain; Gāo's spirits had lifted just by walking under those lights.

The engineering doors stood open, contrary to the usual orders on any DV-Class vessel. Chief Engineer Sinead Molsheim waited for Gāo just inside the door.

Molsheim was as petite as Gāo, but could lift three times her weight rapidly and without any problems whatsoever. Molsheim had been raised on ships, but she concentrated on strength, figuring she would need it inside of engineering as she reconfigured things.

That kind of thinking ahead had always served her well. She had been one of the most creative chief engineers in the Fleet, and had surprised everyone when she took the assignment to run engineering on the *Správa*. It meant fewer chances of adventure, fewer opportunities to work on the fly, fewer ways to broaden her horizons as an engineer.

She had disagreed with that, reminding everyone that the command ships were as important, if not more important, than a standard DV-vessel.

She was using her time on the *Správa* to improve systems, something Gāo appreciated.

"Vice Admiral," Molsheim said as Gāo entered. "I know you ordered us all to leave, but I would like to stay. In light of the information you sent me from the *Renegat*, I think it would be a good idea for me to monitor the communications array in real time, as you're speaking to the *Renegat*."

She said all of this rapidly, as if she was afraid that Gāo would interrupt her.

Gāo was both surprised and pleased by the request. She had not thought to have anyone monitor what was going on with the *Správa's* systems—not while she was talking to the *Renegat*. She had always thought they could examine the data after she had finished.

But this made sense, in light of Crowe's suspicions. And Gāo wouldn't be having a conversation that needed to remain private from another officer. Baker was going to be here, after all. One more person would make no difference.

"All right," Gāo said. "But just you."

Molsheim raised her eyebrows in surprise, but said nothing else.

"What do you need to do to set up?" Gāo said.

Molsheim moved aside. "I already set up, just in case you agreed. If you hadn't, I would have had to change two things before I left."

"Do you have a place for me, so that you will not be visible to Captain Preemas?" Gāo asked.

"Yes, sir," Molsheim said, "I do. Come with me."

She led Gāo around towers of glowing lights. Panels were half-closed or dark, indicating work paused, but not finished, just because she had decided to contact Preemas from down here.

Engineering was always the cleanest part of the ship, something Gão appreciated. Nothing was out of place. No clothing hung from the back of chairs.

Not that there were many chairs at all. Mostly, the Engineering staff moved around the gigantic room, altering and changing things or monitoring the ship's functions. Hardly anyone sat down for any reason. If there were chairs, they were lined up in front of their console, the seats neatly tucked underneath it.

Gão remembered her stint in Engineering decades ago, as part of her officer training. She had learned quickly that the meticulous work done here was not her strong suit.

But she always appreciated the Fleet's hands-on methods of training. Captains knew every department of their ship. She was beginning to think Admirals knew none.

Because half of the equipment here was modernized and light, no obvious nanobits, nothing that looked familiar to her at all.

She had gotten too wrapped up in the details of her work to remember that she was a part of this ship, someone who might have to command it if something went terribly wrong.

Molsheim led Gão around one final towering alcove until she was in what could only be described as a circular cubby made up of several alcoves curved inward.

Lieutenant Baker was already there, a holoscreen up and prepared for Gão. Baker was taller than either Gão or Molsheim, but sensitive to that. The screen was at Gão's level, not Baker's.

"Thank you, Lieutenant," Gão said as she stepped in front of the screen. "Are we ready for this?"

"Not quite." Molsheim answered. She stepped out of the alcove, and her voice receded as she said, "I will let you know when I'm in position."

"Have you already pinged the *Renegat*?" Gão asked Baker. Since they were communicating across such a distance, and the lags were increasing, it was better to let the *Renegat* know there was an incoming communication.

"Yes, sir," Baker said. "I used a standard notification. Chief Engineer Molsheim helped me send another one, augmented, as a kind of experiment. So the *Renegat* should know that you'll be contacting Captain Preemas."

"You haven't gotten any response, I take it," Gão said.

"I didn't ask for one," Baker said. "I didn't want to give the captain a chance to say no to this contact."

Gão smiled at her. Baker understood the problems and apparently had acted on them.

"I'm ready." Molsheim's voice sounded very far away. The various alcoves and equipment dampened sound inside Engineering which had made it one of the more comforting places Gão had worked in her training, even though she was unsuited for a crew position here.

"All right then," Gão said. "Let's do this."

Baker pressed the center spot on a screen inside a nearby alcove. The screen in front of Gão shimmered and then an image on it resolved itself into Preemas.

He was sitting at a desk, apparently waiting for her contact.

If he was in his ready room, it looked nothing like the room she had initially found him in. It was tidier than her study. Surfaces around him shone in the overhead lights.

It took a moment for him to look up. His expression seemed neutral but those bright green eyes of his narrowed just a little, as if he didn't want to talk with her at all.

She couldn't dissect the expression, although the lags gave her time, but if she had to guess, she would have guessed that he was annoyed about the contact, maybe even angry over it.

That micro-expression sent a little warning bell through her, although what that bell meant, she wasn't exactly certain.

"We don't have time for formalities," she said to him. "These lags are increasing, and we don't know why. Before I say anything more, I need to know you can hear me talk to you, right now."

Then she waited.

His gaze moved over her and then focused on the walls behind her. They weren't really walls, of course. Behind her were the alcoves, with their cool white and blue lights and darkened screens.

Preemas wasn't a dumb man. He would realize she was talking to him from Engineering.

She hoped he wouldn't realize that the switch of venue had come about because of Crowe.

Five long minutes went by. Then another two. Finally, Preemas's head bobbed, just a little bit, as if he were acknowledging her.

"I can hear you, Vice Admiral," he said. "I am now aware that this is not a social call."

His voice was filled with sarcasm. They both knew she wouldn't be making a social call of any kind. He knew something was up. He just didn't know what it was.

He said nothing more. She clasped her hands behind her back, holding herself rigid.

"Good," she said. "As we have discussed, you and I, your mission as designed concerns me. You complained about your crew, with good reason, and I looked the other way as you tried to improve it. I have also been doing a lot of research here on the way the data continues to arrive from the Scrapheap you're supposed to investigate."

She held up a hand, as if they were having a normal conversation and she was forestalling his answer.

"And before you ask, there is nothing new in that data," she said. "It is the same message and data stream that the Scrapheap has been sending for months now. Apparently, our responses, with inquiries, are not getting through. We have sent dozens, including many responses in older versions of Standard, and also using some codes that we could find in the archives. We are still not getting any kind of response."

She had a mental list of things she was going to tell him. That was just the first thing. She was going to ease her way into commanding him to abort the mission.

"Even with long-range sensors, we cannot verify that the Scrapheap still exists," she said. "Some of our scientists here are now postulating that this was a data dump, sent when the Scrapheap was in some kind of extremis, as its entire systems were being overrun or destroyed."

Preemas opened his mouth, then closed it. She assumed that was because she had held up that hand, forestalling him, several minutes earlier, but there really was no way to know.

"And then," she said, "we have the problem of the time lags in these communications. You have gone through foldspace four times by my calculations. That's one-third of the distance you need to travel just to get to a Scrapheap that might not be there."

Preemas's eyes had narrowed even more. Even though she was looking at his expressions from minutes earlier, it was clear he was getting angry and not hiding it well.

He knew what was coming. If they were having a regular conversation, he would probably have told her to hurry it up.

"The time lags disturb me, Captain Preemas," she said. "They're getting worse, not better, and we don't know what's causing them. There is a possibility that they're being caused by actual time displacement. You might have lost minutes as you traveled through foldspace. My concern is that the *Renegat* will lose days next, then months, and then years. That will do us no good, Captain. We will have sent you back, you will have lost time, and we won't be able to communicate any longer. This entire mission is predicated on the fact that you have to find out what's going on at that Scrapheap and let us know what, if anything, that something is. It doesn't appear you can do that."

He looked away, then back at the image of her inside his ready room. Then his image froze. She wasn't sure if he did that or if there was some kind of time limit on how long she could talk before the time lag caught up with her.

"So, Captain Preemas," she said with as much authority as she could muster, "rather than continue on this mission, I am ordering you to bring the *Renegat* back to the Fleet. We will deal with the Scrapheap in some other way."

And she would deal with Admiral Hallock, even if it meant some kind of reprimand for Gão herself.

"I need you to acknowledge that order," Gão said. "I will be sending the official order at the end of this communique."

So he couldn't say that, with the troubles communicating, he didn't hear her order him to return.

Now, she waited for him to respond.

He moved again. His head tilted back, his eyes narrowed, and his lips thinned. Then he stood up, and the image froze for another moment.

She couldn't keep track of all the freezing, when it occurred and for how long. It was easier to time the moments between responses than it was to communicate this way.

"Beg pardon, sir," he said, his tone insolent.

Her heart sank. She had hoped she wouldn't see this side of him.

"But I'm the officer on the ground. I'm not seeing the problems that you are. My crew now works well together. I have gotten rid of most of the dead weight. They remain at Sector Base Z for someone else to waste time with."

The Preemas she had dealt with recently wouldn't have been so blunt. But he was clearly angry. He didn't like the order to return.

"I moved others to different positions more suited to their skills. The ship now runs the way a ship should run." He raised his chin. "I think we are more than suited to this mission. I would ask you to rescind that order, sir. We deserve a chance to finish this mission."

He stopped speaking, then crossed his arms, as if his movements somehow could let her know that he was done and not being interrupted by the time lag.

"I appreciate your candor, Captain Preemas," she lied. She didn't think he was being candid at all. "I am glad you alleviated some of my concerns about your crew. However, you did not address the time lag. You will have to travel through foldspace four more times just to return to us. That's all the risk I'm willing to take. We are seeing an actual problem here, not a theoretical one, and therefore, I am aborting this mission."

He hadn't moved at all. She didn't know if that was the lag. She studied him as if she could get a sense of him just from his posture.

Finally he shifted from foot to foot, then took a deep breath. She knew he was reacting to what she had said.

"I don't understand your concern now, Vice Admiral," he said, his voice dripping with contempt. "You were willing to send us to our deaths to garner some information for Admiral Hallock. And now you're telling me you're concerned about our lives? Forgive me if I don't believe you."

Gāo stood rigidly, glad her hands were clasped behind her back so that he couldn't see her fingers twisted against each other.

"You're telling me," he said, "that you don't believe you'll get the information from us, so we should return. It's the information you value, not our lives. Don't make this about us. Here's the truth, Vice Admiral. You didn't think the mission would fail before we got to the Scrapheap. As long as it looked like we'd get there and you could find out what the hell happened a century ago or whenever that breach occurred, you were fine with losing an entire ship full of misfits. But now that it's become clear that you might lose the ship without garnering a bit of information, you want us to return. Failure is failure only when the mission doesn't get accomplished, not when the crew dies. Am I right, Vice Admiral?"

She was twisting her fingers so tightly that it actually hurt to move them. But she knew her expression remained impassive, which was good. Because she wanted to yell at him. And she also wanted to deny everything he said.

Deep down, she wasn't sure she could deny it.

So, she lifted her chin slightly and peered at him through hooded eyes.

"You have your orders, Captain Preemas. Abort this mission," she said.

His jaw moved. Then he didn't move at all. For a moment, she thought he had severed the connection.

But he hadn't. Five minutes after she spoke, he straightened.

"All right, Vice Admiral," he said. "Consider your mission aborted."

And then his image winked out.

That left her even more unsettled. Had he just shut her down or was that some kind of glitch?

The time lags had never been so definite. They had never shut down the communications. And he had just agreed with her, but in a way that filled her with doubts.

Consider your mission aborted.

He didn't say that the *Renegat* would return. Nor did he assure her that he was following orders.

He had said: *Consider your mission aborted.*

And that unnerved her. Because he left her with the sinking feeling that he was going to continue with the ship, heading to that Scrapheap, maybe as a way to prove himself.

She unwound her fingers from each other and let her arms drop to her sides. She shook out her shoulders, knowing that she was holding a lot of tension in them.

He had bested her, over a long-distance communication. If she contacted him right now, she would cede whatever power she had left. If she waited, she could reiterate her order. If he had moved farther away from the Fleet, she could instate Nadim Crowe as captain.

She would see if Molsheim could help her figure out how to broadcast that message to the entire *Renegat.*

The problem was that Gão wouldn't be able to enforce her command—not from this distance—and Preemas knew it.

She formed a fist with her right hand, thumb inside, feeling the pain against her skin. Damn him.

Crowe had told her the *Renegat* was heading into foldspace within a day or two of his contact with her. That meant that if the *Renegat* was continuing to the Scrapheap (and she was willing to bet money that it was), they would go through foldspace in 24 hours or less.

She would contact Preemas in 48 hours. If he refused to abort, she would see if she could force Crowe to take over the ship.

That was the only hope she had of getting that crew back alive. That was the only hope *Crowe* had of returning to the Fleet. She had to impress that upon him somehow.

She squared her shoulders and relaxed that fist. She had a plan now.

She would execute it as best she could.

PART FIFTEEN
THE MYSTERY OF THE *RENEGAT*
NOW

THE *AIZSARGS*

Dauber felt an odd jangling throughout her entire system. She leaned over the console before her, hating the uncertainty she faced.

She had never been in a situation like this one. She had rescued many ships, but none as strange and mysterious as the *Renegat*. Through the screens on the bridge, she could see the events unfolding in real time. *Rescue One* as far from the *Renegat* as it could get, the *Renegat* continuing to vent atmosphere and God knew what else, and the life rafts heading toward the *Renegat's* cargo bays.

That was all enough to make her nerves jangle, but she had done big rescues before. Successful or unsuccessful, those rescues had all had a pattern. This one was squarely in the middle of that pattern.

Her people were working the situation, doing the very best they could with whatever faced them. She trusted them, she trusted their training, and she trusted the equipment.

She did not trust the *Renegat* itself.

The unstable *anacapa* drive was bad enough. The low number of crew members was worse. The fact that the ship had once been part of the Fleet and had gotten lost bothered her more than she could say.

But this latest bit of information, which she had just managed to pull using her security clearance, disturbed her in a way she couldn't quite put her finger on.

"Brett," she said to Ullman, "have you found anything on time lags?"

"With the *Renegat*?" he asked. He was sifting through all the data she had found as fast as he possibly could, which was much faster than anyone else on the ship. "No. I've been seeing something about problems with the communications *anacapa* drive. It opened another window into foldspace as the main *anacapa* worked."

She let out a breath. That wasn't good. She couldn't remember exactly why the Fleet had jettisoned communications *anacapa* drives, but she had a hunch this might have been why.

"And don't ask me if I think that's what happened," he said. "I'm seeing lots of drama here and nothing definitive. This is the strangest mission I've ever seen, and the strangest ship I've ever dealt with."

She nodded. She felt the same way, and perhaps that was why she was feeling jangly. Shortly, she would bring the people from that ship onto hers, and she had yet to figure out who these people were or why they had arrived in this sector.

"Well," she said, "I was digging into the mission and I found notes on a time lag between the communications with the Fleet and the *Renegat*."

"It happens," Almadi said. She was helping with the rescue, but she was also keeping track of the flow of information. Almadi had always been fascinated by *anacapa* drives, even more than most of the people Dauber had served with.

"Yeah, and it's dangerous," Ullman said.

Dauber decided not to acknowledge the obvious. "The time lag grew each time the *Renegat* went through foldspace. After the lag reached eleven minutes, she was ordered to return to the Fleet. The captain received that communication, and was apparently irritated at it, but said he would abort the mission. And that was the last the Fleet heard from the *Renegat.*"

"Until now," Ullman said, raising his head out of his research and looking at that disabled ship.

"You think they got caught in foldspace?" Almadi asked Dauber.

"I don't know what I think," Dauber said. "There's a lot of subtext here. The vice admiral who sent them on this mission handled the captain herself. And she recorded a lot of thoughts about the mission. It would take me hours to go through all of this, maybe days."

Her words hung in the bridge. They all knew they didn't have days.

"A malfunctioning *anacapa* would cause time lags," Ribisi said. Apparently this conversation had gotten his attention as well. He had been focusing on fixing the *Renegat*'s *anacapa* drive.

"So would many other things," Ullman said.

"It might also have caused the ship to go wildly off course." Dauber frowned at the dying ship, looking at it through the screen. She wanted to contact Zarges, wanted to have him pull all the records from the *Renegat*, so she had that part of the ship's story. But he had already left Engineering and was now focused on getting those 200+ souls off the ship.

Dauber studiously avoided looking at the time. She didn't dare. She knew the rescue was going well, but she couldn't help feeling that they were already behind.

"Massai," she said to Ribisi, "can you pull the records off the *Renegat*?"

"I don't know," he said. "I'd have to stop trying to contain that *anacapa* drive."

"I can try," Almadi said. "I won't interfere with what you're doing, Massai."

"Let's hope," he said, sounding doubtful. "Is it necessary, Captain?"

She almost said no. She knew that the information wasn't necessary for the next few hours, but it would become necessary when she was trying to figure out what to do with the strangers who boarded the *Aizsargs.*

"Yes," she said.

"Consider it done," Almadi said.

Dauber nodded. Deciding to pull that information did not settle her nerves. In fact, it made them jangle even more.

Something was truly wrong here, and not just because the *Renegat* was dying. Something else.

Something she didn't understand.

PART SIXTEEN
COMMUNICATION PROBLEMS
100 YEARS AGO

THE *RENEGAT*

Crowe stood in the alcove in Engineering that was the farthest away from the main doors. It took a lot of winding turns and an in-depth knowledge of Engineering's setup to find this part, which was why he had commandeered this area.

He was using it for foldspace and *anacapa* research, and he didn't like what he was finding.

The *Renegat* had gone through foldspace a fifth time two days ago. Crowe had remained in Engineering, monitoring the communications array like he had the last time, and once more, a tiny foldspace opening appeared over the small *anacapa* drive.

He had been surprised and angered, mostly at himself. He wasn't acting like the scientist he was; he was acting like a scared crew member on a doomed ship.

If he had thought this through, he would have had a small probe prepared, one he could send into that foldspace opening to get readings out of it. If he had really thought it all through, he could have altered one of the tiny probes to see if it could venture into that foldspace opening and out again, before the opening closed.

He had done none of those things.

He had consulted with his best engineers, though, which wasn't as impressive as it sounded. He had Stephanos, and she was working as hard as he was.

Atwater was going through the data that Vice Admiral Gão had sent, but slowly, thinking that a bigger team was working all of this. Crowe wasn't so certain.

He hadn't heard from Vice Admiral Gão, and, as far as he knew, neither had Preemas. Gão wasn't the kind of person who let things slide. She knew how important it had been for her to make a decision *before* the *Renegat* went into foldspace this last time.

Something had held her up, perhaps her own superior officers. She would have responded otherwise.

Or maybe she had thought Crowe was stepping out of line.

Crowe looked at the data flowing around him like water. On three sides, he had set the data streams on scroll, just so that he knew the computer systems were working as hard as he was. The black-and-white images that the data became were on a clear background, so that he could see the blue-and-gold equipment behind it.

Everything was working; he was working. And so was his team. But he was also now one more foldspace trip away from the Fleet, and he didn't like it.

Especially since all of the indications were that the tiny foldspace opening over the communications *anacapa* drive led somewhere other than the foldspace opening that the *Renegat* had traveled through.

He closed his eyes, still seeing the data stream as a ghost along his eyelids.

He needed a break.

And then he had a thought he didn't like: What if Preemas had spoken to Gão already? What if she had gone on, doing business as usual, and no one had bothered to tell Crowe?

He opened his eyes, feeling annoyed at himself more than anyone else. He hadn't communicated much with Preemas, figuring they were both working on their various jobs. Crowe hadn't really thought that maybe Preemas's silence had a lot to do with an irritation with Crowe, or a desire to keep things from Crowe.

Preemas had never really told Crowe everything, so that wasn't all that much different than before. But then Crowe had stayed close to Preemas, so Crowe had remained on top of everything.

Lately, Crowe had been concentrating more on the *anacapa* drive, the communications array, and the time lags.

Although he hadn't been completely neglecting his first officer job. He had been working with the crew. Several crew members still felt out of sorts in their new positions. Others weren't up to the job, even though they had been moved. And there was just a lot of disgruntlement, particularly at Preemas's desire to get rid of rank (or the strictures of rank) wherever possible.

Everyone on this ship—competent or not—had been raised in the Fleet, and all of them were used to the rank system. Being without it or being told to ignore it for most things made almost everyone uncomfortable on a level that Crowe couldn't have predicted.

All of this meant that, while he was waiting to hear about Gão, he hadn't sought out the information. He hadn't tried to figure out if she had contacted the captain or not.

Preemas wouldn't have kept that from Crowe, would he?

Crowe shook his head as he had that thought. If Preemas didn't think the meeting was important, he wouldn't have told Crowe. The conversations with Gão were both routine and required, two things that Preemas chafed against. Crowe did know that Preemas worked hard at keeping Gão in the dark about most things. He didn't like having a commanding officer, particularly on this mission.

Crowe sighed heavily, then reached his hand through the data stream to the controls beyond. The data ran across his skin like a mobile tattoo.

He opened the logs for the communications array, then delved into the captain's log. The captain's log was mostly sealed—only a few others could examine who the captain spoke to, and no one, except the first officer, could see what those communications were about, provided that the communications had been recorded.

Crowe moved the screens running the data stream aside, and then stepped a little closer to the open logs. There, days ago, was a contact that had come from the *Správa.* It had arrived before the *Renegat* had taken its most recent trip through foldspace—about 24 hours after Crowe had contacted Gāo.

He felt chilled. He had heard nothing about this. Had it been a routine contact?

What, exactly, would routine be?

He scanned the log to see if there was a recording of the contact, but apparently Preemas didn't activate that part of the system. Crowe, feeling paranoid, checked to see if Preemas had activated the record function on any of his previous conversations with Gāo.

If Preemas had done it previously, but hadn't done it since, then it would be safe to assume that Preemas felt he had something to hide—from Crowe, since no one else could access any of this.

It only took a minute to find the previous contacts. This ship had been on its own for some time, and except for a flurry of communications around the time the *Renegat* docked at Sector Base Z, there weren't a lot of outside communications with anyone, not even the captain.

Crowe stared at the list: Preemas didn't save the recordings of any of his contacts with Gāo. Not a one.

So nothing had deviated there.

Crowe let out a breath he hadn't realized he had been holding. At least Preemas had been consistent. He hadn't changed his behavior at all, which meant, at least as far as Crowe was concerned, he had nothing to hide.

Crowe touched another sector of the control panel, and instructed it to find the captain.

Preemas was in his quarters.

Crowe shut down all of the data streams before he even gave them a second thought. He was shaking. He hadn't wanted to take this fifth trip through foldspace, and if it could have been prevented, he...well, he wasn't sure what he was going to do.

He stepped away from the alcove and rubbed his face with his hand, a nervous habit that he really needed to get rid of.

Then he straightened, and headed out of engineering, contacting Preemas as he went.

Captain, he sent. *I'm coming to your quarters. I need a few minutes of your time.*

That would give Preemas a few minutes to prepare himself for Crowe's visit, and not really long enough to forestall Crowe's arrival.

Door's unlocked, Preemas sent back.

Crowe checked the time as he walked. He hadn't realized it was late evening. He had worked through lunch and dinner, skipping both. He wondered how many meals he had missed while working on all of this. That was an old habit from his school days, his post-*Brazza Two* school days, when he had to prove himself.

He hadn't realized just how many of those old habits were ingrained.

He took the elevator up one deck, and walked to Preemas's cabin. The door was open, as Preemas had said. The scents of coffee and peppermint had filtered into the corridor, and Crowe braced himself. If the scents were so strong out here that the environmental system couldn't automatically whisk them away, then they had to be very strong inside the captain's suite itself.

Crowe walked in, knocking on the door as he did so.

"Captain?" he said.

"First Officer Crowe," Preemas said, his tone welcoming. Apparently, Crowe was in his good graces again. "What is so important that it couldn't wait until tomorrow?"

Crowe stepped past the bathroom door, past the small kitchen, and into the badly laid out living area. The coffee and peppermint smell wasn't as strong as Crowe had expected. Maybe it had all wafted into the corridor.

The living area was even more claustrophobic than it had been the previous times Crowe had been here, and it took him a moment to figure out why.

Just like he did on the bridge, Preemas had the wall screens off. Only here, the portholes were designed to show programmed imagery to mimic an actual outside view. Crowe had specially programmed the portholes in his generic officer's cabin to show the actual outside view, but most officers didn't bother.

It seemed Preemas couldn't be bothered to look at anything at all.

"The timing was my mistake, Captain," Crowe said. "I was so busy with my work that I had lost track of the hour. Once I finally realized what time it was, I had already contacted you."

Preemas's mouth twisted in something that resembled a smile. He hadn't been giving Crowe—or anyone, it seemed—a real smile lately. Crowe wondered what that meant.

"You seem to be quite lost in your work these days, First Officer Crowe," Preemas said. "I'm glad you're finding it interesting."

Interesting wasn't the word Crowe would use. All-consuming might have been better, but even that paled with what he was doing.

"You've been spending a great deal of time in engineering," Preemas said.

Crowe wasn't sure if that was a rebuke or not. He had to take a deep breath to keep himself from responding defensively.

"I have also been working on my first officer duties," Crowe said. "There's quite a bit of crew management that I seem to do as a matter of course these days."

As he said that, he wondered if that was one reason he was avoiding the mess halls. He seemed to be dealing with a lot of emotional issues whenever he went for a meal. Maybe he should consider eating in his cabin, as it was clear Preemas had been doing. There were dishes piled alongside the cleaner, as if Preemas couldn't be bothered to set them inside.

Just the sight of that little pile in the kitchen made Crowe realize that the environmental scrubbers were working overtime in here.

"Noted," Preemas said, with something like amusement. "Would you like to sit down?"

"No," Crowe said. "I've disturbed you enough. I just have one question."

"All right." Preemas leaned against the table, and crossed his arms. That was an interesting movement. He wasn't ready to hear any questions from Crowe, apparently.

"When you spoke to Vice Admiral Gão a few days ago, you didn't mention the time differential. I assume it was still bothering you." That was the only way Crowe could figure out how to bring up the subject—indirectly, and without rancor.

Preemas's odd smile had faded. "I don't recall telling you I had spoken to the vice admiral."

"You didn't," Crowe said. "But you usually talk with her around a foldspace trip, so I checked the logs to see if the discussion had taken place. I didn't want to bother you any more than necessary."

"Thank you," Preemas said in a tone that said he wasn't thankful at all. He seemed a bit resentful.

"Knowing what's going on with the differential will help us," Crowe said.

"I figured you had it under control," Preemas said. "The differential on this last discussion was less than it had been before. We were back to eight or so minutes. That looks like we're on the right path to me."

"I'd love to see any record you have of that," Crowe said. "Because we didn't implement any changes. If there were changes, they were from the vice admiral's side. I seem to recall that she told you the Fleet would also be working on this issue…?"

"She did." Preemas's gaze was flat, matching the expression in his eyes. "Apparently, they seem to be resolving it. Which means the problem isn't ours after all."

Crowe silently cursed himself. He had set himself up for that. But then, he hadn't realized that the differential was shorter. Had Gão spoken to Preemas from a location other than the admiral's suite? If she had done what Crowe had done, speaking near the communications array, that might have cut some of the lag.

"Wouldn't that have been embarrassing?" Preemas said. "Returning because there was a problem that wasn't a problem at all."

"Let's not celebrate prematurely, captain," Crowe said. "A few minutes shaved off the differential might mean only that the lag is unpredictable, not that it was being resolved."

Preemas grunted, letting his disagreement show, but without stating anything.

"I would like to see those records, if you have them," Crowe said again.

"I don't understand why," Preemas said. "It's resolving itself."

"No, sir," Crowe said. "I respectfully disagree. As we traveled through foldspace, I monitored the communications *anacapa*. Another tiny foldspace window opened inside that container again. I'm quite concerned about this."

And irritated that Preemas wanted to dismiss it.

"Did the vice admiral say anything about the differential?" Crowe asked.

"All she said was how much it continued to annoy her," Preemas said. "We agreed that it might be an issue as we moved farther apart. I will be sending individual reports without trying to talk once the differential becomes too great."

That didn't sound at all like the discussion Gão had had with Crowe. But she might have investigated or she might have changed her mind. Or she might have been humoring Crowe.

After all, he wasn't the commander of this vessel. Preemas was. Gão might have been treating Crowe differently than she would have treated the captain.

But that didn't explain why she had contacted Preemas *before* the foldspace trip, just like Crowe had asked.

"Have you been in contact since our trip?" Crowe asked, even though he knew that Preemas hadn't been in contact.

"No," Preemas said. "I do need to send the information I promised. Thank you for the reminder, First Officer Crowe."

Crowe nodded, as if that part of the conversation mattered.

"And she said nothing about the differential," Crowe repeated. "Nothing about the way her people were working on it? Nothing about their conclusions?"

"They didn't have conclusions yet," Preemas said. "Once she said that, everything else was just noise."

In other words, Preemas had ignored the scientific information. Crowe felt his frustration grow.

"Did you tell them about the problems with the communications *anacapa*?" Crowe asked.

"I might have said something," Preemas said. "After all, we want to point them in that direction. She said they would be deep in the research and when they had something, they would contact us."

Crowe wanted to say to Preemas: *You're risking lives here!* But they had already had that argument, and Crowe had lost. He had brought the information to Gão, and apparently, she hadn't cared enough to abort this mission.

He wasn't sure why she should. As far as the Fleet was concerned, everyone on this vessel was already dead.

But he would have thought that she might have cared that they wouldn't be able to get any of the information she wanted. He wasn't sure they would make it to that Scrapheap.

"You look uncertain," Preemas said.

"We just need that information about the *anacapa* drives," Crowe said. "I think we're on to something here."

"The Fleet doesn't seem to think so," Preemas said. "They would have acted if they did."

Crowe felt an odd chill. There was no reason for Preemas to say something like that, unless he suspected that Crowe had been in touch with Gão. Or was Crowe just being more paranoid than usual?

He didn't know. He had no way to gauge it.

And now, he had no idea whether he should contact Gão or not.

"Let me know when you're going to talk with the vice admiral again," Crowe said. "I will monitor the communications array, and see if there's anything going wrong with the communications *anacapa*."

"All right," Preemas said. "I will do that."

"Thank you," Crowe said. He suddenly felt very uncomfortable in Preemas's suite. "I appreciate it."

Preemas smiled at him—a real smile now—and said, "You need some sleep, First Officer Crowe."

Crowe nodded. "I think you're right. If nothing else, I'll leave you to it."

He headed to the still-open door. Preemas followed. They said their good-nights, and suddenly Crowe found himself in the corridor.

Feeling off balance. Feeling like he had entered a world he didn't entirely understand.

Which defined this entire journey for him. He was entering a world he didn't understand—a universe he didn't understand.

He had learned long ago that he couldn't control everything. He had discovered a way to approach his work and his life with that knowledge firmly at the forefront of his mind. It made a difference in how he interacted with others.

He needed to reclaim that knowledge. And he needed to act on it.

Because, nothing on this ship was in his control. Not even engineering. And he had to be okay with that.

Whether he liked it or not.

THE *SPRÁVA*

The doors to Engineering slid open. Vice Admiral Gāo had not announced that she would be coming to the *Správa's* Engineering wing, so her presence caught everyone off-guard. The engineers near the door, young officers whose names she did not know, looked at her in shock. Another, older engineer leaned around one of the glowing towers, apparently to see who had entered without permission, and then leaned back when he saw who it was.

The Engineering wing smelled faintly of warm equipment and human sweat. Here, more than any other department except hydroponics, the crew could get so involved in their work that they would often forget the niceties like food, sleep, and showers.

Gāo had noted the faint funk in Engineering before, and always had to remind herself that things would be a lot worse without the extra-strong environmental system, running at full power.

Chief Engineer Molsheim hurried toward Gāo from one of the aisles created by the hulking towers. Molsheim had deep circles under her eyes, and she looked like half of her staff did—tired and drained.

Gāo had not given them any orders, so whatever they were working on had probably come from the captain of the *Správa* or some other project Gāo was not aware of.

"I'm sorry, Vice Admiral," Molsheim said. "I somehow did not get notified that you were coming."

Her tone suggested that heads would roll for that little slip-up—not that failing to notify her of the vice admiral's pending arrival would have been a "little" slip-up.

"Your staff is doing just fine," Gāo said with a smile. "I didn't tell anyone I was coming here."

Molsheim smiled in return, but the smile didn't reach her eyes. She was definitely preoccupied with something.

"We can go to my quarters if you like," Molsheim said. "I don't have an office here."

"No need," Gāo said. "I came here because I would like to know if the messages I sent to the *Renegat* yesterday and today actually reached them. No one has responded to my hails, which hasn't happened before, and I'm concerned."

Molsheim let out a breath. Something in her face suggested that Gāo's request was a difficult one, but Gāo wasn't sure why. Molsheim didn't tell her either.

Instead, Molsheim led her through the towers of equipment, blinking and faintly humming. The warm smell that Gāo had noted when she had entered Engineering grew stronger as the distance between the towers narrowed.

Gāo had no idea how Engineering was laid out. Even though she had been here less than a week before, she couldn't have found the way to the communications array on her own, no matter how hard she tried.

She had terminated the *Renegat's* mission days ago. She expected to hear from Preemas as the ship entered foldspace, heading back to the Fleet. She hadn't heard a word.

If Preemas wouldn't talk with her, she expected Crowe to contact her, but she hadn't heard from him either.

She hadn't been entirely clear with Molsheim. When Gāo said she was contacting the *Renegat*, she was deliberately obfuscating. After Preemas had told her that he was aborting the mission, she had waited twenty-four hours to hear his plans. When he hadn't contacted her within a day, she contacted him directly, and had gotten no response.

She figured Preemas was being temperamental. But she also knew she couldn't assume, especially given the things Crowe had told her. So she tried to contact Crowe.

She hadn't gotten a response from him either.

And, if anyone should have responded, it would have been Crowe.

Something was wrong, and she wasn't sure what that something was. Preemas's words kept going round and round in her head:

Consider your mission aborted.

He said *your mission*. Not *the journey*. Not *the mission*. He had said *your* mission, as if someone else had given him another mission entirely.

Or he had given himself one.

Molsheim stopped in front of the communications array. The alcove seemed brighter than it had been, the lights rolling up the towers like water moving up a waterfall.

Gāo recognized this area, but she knew she hadn't arrived here this way before.

"All right," Molsheim said. "Let me check the logs."

She moved to Gāo's right, closer to one of the towers. Gāo took a step back. She and Molsheim were both small women, but this alcove wasn't that large. There wasn't a lot of room for the two of them to stand.

Molsheim opened a screen inside the array instead of using an outside screen. She worked on the screen itself, almost as if she didn't want Gão to see what she was doing.

"Your messages went out," Molsheim said, her back to Gão. "Standard hails, right?"

"Yes," Gão said.

"Sent through the communications array which, considering the distance involved, used the communications *anacapa.* I see no problems with the hails, and no problems with the *anacapa* or our systems here."

Molsheim opened another panel, then another, her fingers working rapidly. Gão felt useless. Perhaps she should have contacted Molsheim directly and let Molsheim report back to her, rather than watch the woman work.

Molsheim's broad shoulders went up and down as she inhaled, and then exhaled, as if she were bracing herself.

"We have no record of receipt," Molsheim said.

"Which means what, exactly?" Gão asked.

Molsheim closed all three panels, and then turned around.

"It means what I said, I'm afraid," she said. "It means we have no record of receipt. Our ships are set up to automatically acknowledge a hail, whether or not someone on board chooses to respond to that hail. I can find out if the ship received the hail and then ignored it, for example. I can also tell you if the hail was responded to."

Gão felt cold, despite the warmth near the equipment. "Neither of those occurred, I take it," she said.

"That's right." Molsheim frowned.

Gão sighed. "The captain was supposed to abort the mission and come back, which meant a lot of foldspace travel."

"Yes, I know." Molsheim sounded a little odd, and that frown grew.

"But…?" Gão asked.

"You're afraid the ship is lost in foldspace, correct?" Molsheim asked.

"Yes," Gão said, glad that Molsheim had put the words to that possibility, not her.

"Generally," Molsheim said, "when a ship is lost in foldspace, the hails bounce back. It's almost as if the ship doesn't exist—almost as if the ship *never* existed."

That was what Gão had been taught.

"There are exceptions, though," Molsheim said. "If you've been communicating over a long distance, and have done so recently, sometimes the hails…I wanted to say 'get through,' but that's not accurate. The hails don't bounce back. It's as if our system would know that their system exists already, and so doesn't send the same return message. It makes for confusion."

"Explain this to me," Gão said. She rarely had to deal with foldspace in this way. When she had captained her own vessel, she hadn't paid a lot of attention to foldspace communications. She had simply done it.

"Usually," Molsheim said, "the confusion comes in the Fleet's response. When we know that a ship has disappeared into foldspace, we respond quickly. We send foldspace search vessels and in those situations, they have very good luck finding the missing ship."

Gão had heard that before. But she also knew that many of those missing ships had lost significant amounts of time. They experienced time in months, perhaps, while the Fleet experienced it in hours.

"But," Molsheim said, "in the cases where the hails don't come back, we don't respond fast enough to find the lost ships. We think the ships aren't communicating for another reason."

Gão's chill increased. She was thinking that Preemas hadn't responded because he was being passive-aggressive—or because he was ignoring her order. But he might have been unable to respond. The *Renegat* might actually be lost in foldspace.

"Then," Molsheim said, "when we do respond..."

She shook her head. Gão frowned. This was clearly emotional for Molsheim.

"Um, sorry," Molsheim said. "One of my early assignments was on a foldspace search vessel."

"You saw a lot, then," Gão said.

Molsheim glanced back at the array, as if it could save her from this conversation. "Yes, I did."

She squared her shoulders and turned back toward Gão.

"The worst of it," Molsheim said, "wasn't the ships we couldn't find. We had hope that they went elsewhere inside foldspace or ended up in a different time, one when we couldn't search for them."

She shook her head, her gaze distant. Gão waited.

"The worst of it," Molsheim repeated, "was the ships that had clearly been stuck in foldspace for *decades,* at least from their perspective. Sometimes twenty, thirty, forty years. The ships would run out of food or other supplies. Some of those ships would only have a few people left on staff, waiting for us, or guarding the ship, or something. The others took the escape pods and went...somewhere. But I would have—"

Then she closed her eyes just a little, as if she regretted starting that sentence. She opened them, and sighed.

"—I still have nightmares about that," she said quietly. "Being stranded forever. Hoping, waiting, for a rescue that, from your perspective, never came. From the Fleet's perspective, we responded as quickly as we could. We'd get to them maybe a week later. But to them, it was a lifetime or more, and their lives would be over."

Gão nodded, not quite sure how to respond. Gão had heard about these cases, but she had never actually seen them. She understood it intellectually, and she had seen others who had worked on those rescues who were just as affected as Molsheim.

Gāo's mind had jumped along a whole different track. She wondered how Preemas, who had experienced the terror of being stuck in foldspace for a year, managed the mental side of his command.

Why would he be so willing to take the risk?

"I have a terrible question," Gāo said. "Is it possible to shut down the hailing system in such a way that it mimics the lost-in-foldspace response?"

"The one that confuses the Fleet and makes it think that the ship in question doesn't exist?" Molsheim asked.

"Yes," Gāo said.

Molsheim nodded. "There are several ways to shut down the hailing system so that the Fleet wouldn't know it. Most of them are very complicated."

Gāo was not surprised. "Chief engineers know this, then."

"Depends on their levels of experience," Molsheim said. "Someone serving on an SC-Class vessel would not know it, generally."

But this wasn't a standard crew. Molsheim knew that as well as Gāo did.

"And captains?" Gāo asked.

"I don't know what captains know," Molsheim said. "Especially someone like Captain Preemas. He served in a lot of capacities on a lot of vessels."

"But never in engineering," Gāo said. "So he would need help shutting down the hailing system?"

Molsheim was frowning. "You think he would do that?"

"I don't know," Gāo said, realizing that was almost as damning as answering yes.

Molsheim turned around, pressed an unmarked flat surface on a nearby tower, and then watched as the image of the *Renegat* rose between her and Gāo.

"Has the *Renegat* been retrofitted in any way?" Molsheim asked.

"Updated for this journey," Gāo said. "But not retrofitted. Parts were replaced so that this ship would be in the best shape possible for such a long trip."

Molsheim nodded. "Well, then," she said, "if he wanted to shut down the hailing system, and completely disappear from our records, he could do it."

"But he would need assistance, right?" Gāo asked.

"It takes a minimum of two people to shut the system down," Molsheim said. "Two different access codes, working at the same time."

Then she reached out, as if she was going to touch the *Renegat*. Her fingers floated across the curves of its arch. The *Renegat* wasn't as elegant as the usual SC-Class vessel, but it did have a kind of chubby prettiness.

Gāo doubted it was the prettiness of the vessel (in its pristine form) that caught Molsheim's eye. It was something else.

"Let me check something," Molsheim said, pulling her fingers back.

She called up the specs for that type of SC-Class ship, scrolled through diagrams that Gāo had never seen before, and sighed. Loudly.

"He could do it," Molsheim said.

"By himself?" Gāo asked for clarification.

"Not easily," Molsheim said. "But he could. He wouldn't even need that much special knowledge."

"Why not?" Gão asked.

"Because the *Renegat* has the same basic design specifications as the *Kaluwasan*. If he knew that ship really well, then he knows this one too."

The *Kaluwasan* was the ship that Preemas captained before the *Renegat*. Gão had no idea if Preemas knew that ship really well. Judging from the condition of that ready room, he didn't. But Gão was making a judgment based on her own ways of doing things, not the way someone else might.

"Forgive me, Vice Admiral," Molsheim said, "but the likely scenario is that the *Renegat* opened a window into foldspace, entered it, and is lost in there."

Gão frowned at that image of the *Renegat*. Molsheim was right: that was the likely scenario. And the entire Fleet had been trained to act on likely scenarios, not unlikely ones.

"All things being equal, I agree with you," Gão said.

"But you believe things are not equal," Molsheim said.

Gão wasn't going to admit that out loud.

"We're going to continue to hail them," Gão said. "Various times on different days, using different methods. We can't rescue them or even try to rescue them if they're lost in foldspace, so if that's what happened..."

Her voice trailed off. If that was what happened, then five hundred souls were essentially dead, gone without any way to confirm their loss.

"But...?" Molsheim asked.

Gão met her gaze. Molsheim had a tiny frown over the bridge of her nose, making her dark eyes look fierce.

"Captain Preemas told me he was determined to prove that he could run an impossible mission," Gão said. "He saw this mission as his way back into the Fleet. I just canceled that mission."

Molsheim was shaking her head before Gão even finished. "Even if he succeeds," she said, "the cancellation of the mission negates his victory. He's disobeying orders."

"I know," Gão said. "But he might believe that success will outweigh the disobedience."

Molsheim was still shaking her head. "Only someone who sees a future with no hope would even try that."

Gão thought about that initial ready room, about Preemas and the mess he was when she met him, about the spit-polished man she had seen on board the *Renegat*, a man who thought he had a future—or had a revived future.

Would he be willing to gamble that future with a charge of disobedience?

She almost smiled at the thought. Of course he would. He was already willing to gamble his life on this mission. He would take an even greater risk to save the mission, so that he wouldn't lose this chance.

"If we can't raise the ship in a day or so," Gāo said, "I want you to trace the contact I received from Chief Engineer Crowe on the *Renegat* and see if he did something different in contacting us than Preemas did. If so, we'll contact Crowe. Given his level of concern when he spoke to me a few days ago, I believe that he would not be going along with anything Preemas did counter to my orders."

"All right. I will do that," she said. Then Molsheim reached out a hand and lightly touched Gāo's arm. "But, the most likely scenario is—"

"Is that they're out of our reach, forever," Gāo said. "I know, Sinead. I know."

"Don't get too twisted up in what-might-have-beens," Molsheim said. "That's not good for anyone."

Gāo patted Molsheim's hand, then slipped her arm out of Molsheim's grasp.

"Noted," Gāo said.

It was good advice. Gāo just hoped that she would be able to take it.

THE *RENEGAT*

Nearly a month had gone by, and still no word from Vice Admiral Gão. Crowe had trouble believing the vice admiral, who had looked at him with such concern, would ignore what he had told her.

Particularly since she had sent much of the information he had requested almost immediately after he had spoken to her. Her message had promised more, but that hadn't arrived either.

Crowe wasn't sleeping much. He was juggling his two jobs, trying to pay attention to the crew and also to all of the engineering challenges on board the *Renegat.*

The ship had been upgraded, but it was beginning to show some wear. It had been two days since their last foldspace journey—their seventh. Crowe had spent the last two like he had spent the previous two, in engineering, monitoring the communications *anacapa.* The little foldspace window had opened each time, and on the sixth trip through foldspace, he had sent in a tiny probe—and instantly lost it.

He spent the last journey seeing if he could recover that probe, and of course, he couldn't. He and Stephanos had figured out that something in that open foldspace window had blocked the channel he was working on.

He had made modifications to the probes, so that the next one he sent in would be sending telemetry on multiple channels as it entered, rather than just one.

He had been so focused on sending probes through that foldspace window—probes that worked and sent information back to him—that he didn't consider why that one channel had been blocked.

That was odd. And it bothered him. There shouldn't have been any blocks at all.

Those were the kinds of thoughts that came to him in the handful of hours of sleep that he managed to get. He would wake up thinking about what he missed, or what he should have noticed.

Or, worse, how they were all going to die.

The other reason he didn't sleep much was that he kept seeing the Scrapheap explosion he had caused as a stupid young man. The way that explosion spiraled out from a handful of ships, heading backwards, igniting the space between the ships, where there should have been nothing, and there was something.

There had been something.

This on-edge feeling he had had ever since he had discovered that tiny fold-space opening—hell, ever since Preemas had told him about the time lag—that feeling was coming from Crowe's desire to save lives, not cost them.

And he was beginning to realize that by joining this crew, by accepting this potential suicide mission, he would be complicit in costing lives rather than actively saving them.

That fear, which made him sit bolt upright in the narrow bed of his officer's quarters, was like a thrum underneath his skin, part of him, every minute of every day.

And when he had the nightmare, when he saw that Scrapheap exploding again and again, just like he had seen it in life, the fear changed from a thrum to a drumbeat, consistent with his heartbeat.

Which was why he found himself in Engineering in the middle of the night, trying to track down whatever was causing the block on the probe.

The night crew in Engineering wasn't his best crew. Two of them—both young men—had half-assed training. They'd been pulled from their engineering internships after the engineer who trained them nearly destroyed the ancient DV-Class vessel he served on. That it had been a training vessel was an irony lost on no one. But the interns who trained with him were given a choice: return to school and repeat two years of study or move to less important technical jobs.

Both of these young men had moved, rather than return to school, something Crowe couldn't respect at all.

They had glanced at him as he entered Engineering, but hadn't spoken to him. They were clearly scared of him, which didn't surprise him; he didn't like them much, and that was probably obvious.

The other person on the night crew was Daria Willoughby. Crowe had chosen her for the crew himself after looking at her record. She had been an engineer longer than he had, and had served on small vessels. She had gotten tangled up in some kind of criminal activity with a lover on a vacation at a sector base. The details were sealed, but the Fleet hadn't stripped her of her rank or pulled her out of the Fleet altogether. Nor had she been charged with anything.

Which led Crowe to believe, with his own experiences with Fleet-designed justice, that she hadn't initiated anything. She might not have even done anything wrong. She had probably been in the wrong place at the wrong time, involved with the wrong person.

He had never asked. Nor had he told her what he had done.

She stepped out of her work area. He had assigned her the task of monitoring the equipment during the trips across the sector, making sure everything worked as it had in the previous sector.

"Sir?" she said.

She was a large woman, with a round face. The roundness hid her age, filling out the wrinkles, except for the ones near her mouth. Her hair didn't hide it, though. It was threaded with gray, something that she either allowed or was proud of. He wasn't sure which.

"Had a thought I need to check." he said.

He hadn't cleared her to work on the communications *anacapa*. He still hadn't told half of his team that the *anacapa* existed.

Old habits died hard.

"Let me know if I can help," she said.

He nodded, and headed to the communications array. Then he stopped, and peered around it.

She was looking at him, a small frown on her face. He had been coming to Engineering late at night for weeks now, and he had thought it didn't bother her. But maybe it did. Maybe she thought it was about her, and not about the work.

"Have you noticed a channel being blocked?" he asked.

"Sir?" She had resorted to that verbal trick, just like other long-time Fleet crew, because Preemas had said that the crew should ignore rank whenever possible.

"I sent out a probe a week or so ago, and didn't get any telemetry. I was using the usual channel to filter it back to me…" and then he paused, realizing the "usual" channel he had used was the usual channel for foldspace communications.

"Sir?" she asked.

He held up a finger, then headed toward the communications array, walking fast. He didn't like what he was thinking. He didn't like it at all.

She followed, probably worried that she had done something wrong. He didn't have the time or the emotional energy to calm her down.

He reached the array, then accessed one of the back panels. He fumbled through the small pockets, cursing the size of his fingers. Finally he accessed the side array, pulling up a screen and magnifying it thousands of times.

"May I help, sir?" she asked, her voice hesitant.

It was the right question. It was even the right time for that question. But he didn't answer. Because he was looking at a part of the array he never looked at.

The foldspace communications channel.

It wasn't just dormant. It was completely disconnected. There was no way that the Fleet could use any bit of equipment that communicated quickly across a long distance, and reach the *Renegat*. Any communications that came from the Fleet to the *Renegat* would have to go outside of the foldspace channel—and a communication like that could take months, years. Decades.

An oath escaped his lips.

"Sir?" Willoughby said again.

He started to whirl toward her, then caught himself. He wasn't angry at her, and she would think he was, if he wasn't careful.

He willed himself to be calm, then turned around slowly, monitoring his expression as best he could so that he didn't look fierce.

But he knew his eyes were filled with fury. He could do nothing about that.

To her credit, she didn't step away from him. She held her ground.

"I haven't checked the logs yet," he said, his voice so much calmer than he had even been trying for. Apparently, his body knew how to do this, no matter how angry he was. "But did anyone come down here and shut down foldspace communications?"

He wasn't really asking about *anyone* because only one person could make that order without him being present. Only one person had the power to direct people to do whatever he wanted.

She inclined her head just a little sideways, as if about to nod, and then rethinking it.

"Y-yes, sir," she said. "The captain. A while ago now. I thought you knew. He said you did. He said you trusted me to help him."

It took all of Crowe's self-control to hold back an epithet—or maybe a string of them. The bastard. What the hell had he been thinking?

"So, you helped him shut down that channel," Crowe said. "It took both of you, right?"

She nodded this time, looking terrified. Poor woman. Her entire career had been about following orders from people she shouldn't have listened to.

"I thought you knew," she said in a small voice.

"It doesn't matter whether I knew or not," Crowe said. "He is the captain and you were following his orders."

She bit her upper lip, winced, and then looked determined. Every thought was written across her face. Every single one. She hadn't wanted to tell Crowe something, then she had imagined telling him, and finally she had decided to tell him.

It was quick and not at all surprising.

"He—um—he may be the captain, sir," she said quietly. "But we all listen to you."

That last was surprising. Crowe hadn't expected to hear that "we all" listened to him.

"We all?" he asked. "Engineering?"

Which made sense. Of course everyone in engineering would trust him over the captain. That had happened on several ships Crowe had served on. Engineering was its own enclave, and the captain gave the orders, but the chief engineer made those orders happen—or belayed them, if the orders were difficult or impossible to carry out.

"No, sir," she said quietly. "Everyone who—I don't know how to say it. Everyone who knows what they're doing, sir."

He felt a little cold. They trusted him, and he had led them this deep into some unknown territory, on a ship that might not have been working properly.

He didn't really want to know this at all. If they all died because of this journey, it was apparently now on him, not on Preemas.

Five hundred souls. Not fifty. Five *hundred.* If they died, it would all be because they trusted him.

His knees wobbled. He knew better than to put out a hand to catch himself on the array. He might dislodge something. But for a moment, it felt like he would crumple if he didn't brace himself.

She reached toward him, then seemed to think the better of it. That small movement of hers steeled his spine.

He remained upright, cursing himself now for being such a damn fool.

"All right then," he said when he was sure he had control over his voice. "We need to re-engage that system, you and I. Are you up for it?"

She nodded. "Wasn't he supposed to do that, sir?"

"Do you really want me to answer that, Willoughby?" Crowe asked.

She bit her upper lip again, then shook her head. She knew the answer to that question. So did he.

"If the captain comes down here again and wants something," she said, "what do you want me to do?"

Crowe almost didn't respond. Because if he didn't respond, he was leaving it up to her discretion. But was that fair? He needed to decide if he was going to fight Preemas's crazy orders or if he was going to let the crew take all of the risks.

A decision that wasn't a decision at all.

"If he wants you to do something," Crowe said, "you contact me. Stall him, whatever it takes. But get me in here."

She smiled. She actually seemed relieved.

"Thank you, sir," she said. "I will, sir. That makes things so much easier, sir."

For her, maybe. But not for him. Or for the ship.

He didn't like the direction this was going in.

But he had waited too long.

And now he was going to have to figure out how it would all play out.

PART SEVENTEEN

THE RESCUE

NOW

THE *RENEGAT*

A dozen people were already in Cargo Bay One when Serpell and Kabac arrived. Everyone wore regulation environmental suits, and most had their knuckle lights on. Most were standing on the floor, which meant the gravity in their boots was working.

The lights illuminated the space where the dozen people were standing. The light was focused and small, rather than the bright lights that usually revealed every part of the cargo bay.

Beyond that cluster of people, the bay was dark and a lot more dangerous than it usually was. All of the cargo that didn't have artificial gravity built in or hadn't been tied down in one way or another floated. Serpell had to be careful as she moved past boxes and round metal containers. As she floated in closer to the group of people illuminating the center of the bay, she saw another group huddled near the extra-wide bay doors. A few of them had helmet lights trained on the bay doors.

The light formed competing circles that barely overlapped, leaving parts of the doors in darkness.

She had no idea if standing so close to the bay doors was a good idea. There was no airlock in this bay. If those doors opened, then everyone could be sucked into space.

If the doors opened, in theory, the door to the corridor would seal shut, and the rest of the ship would be protected. But she had no idea if that would work now that everything else had failed.

Both groups were eerily quiet. There was no chatter like there had been when the *Renegat* left the Scrapheap, or even in the aftermath of the most recent attack.

Maybe everyone knew this was their last chance at survival.

Or maybe they had already given up.

At least there was one blessing in these weird little gatherings of people. At least they couldn't see each other through the helmets. No one would recognize her if she didn't identify herself. If everyone inside the cargo bay knew Serpell had arrived, they would start peppering her with questions she couldn't answer.

Now she wished she had told Kabac not to mention her name.

He hadn't said anything so far, but he was the kind of man who would screw something up just because he touched it.

Which made her wonder about the *anacapa* comments the rescuers had made. Was the problem the drive? Had it been hit like Kabac had said? Shouldn't it have exploded if it had?

Or had he screwed it up by trying to fix it?

Her stomach hurt. She didn't know if that was because of the slowly leaking oxygen or because her entire body knew Kabac had screwed up, and she simply didn't want to admit it to herself.

This is the bridge: Evacuate the Renegat *immediately. Head to both cargo bays. Follow instructions once you arrive.*

Third announcement. This was serious.

And then she realized: she had arrived in the cargo bay. Where were the extra instructions?

She glanced at Kabac, an unsettled feeling making her cold.

Were there only three intruders, not three rescuers? Space pirates, come to kill everyone on the *Renegat* by leaving them in the bay, hoping for rescue?

Somehow that would be so much worse than actually killing everyone.

Serpell glanced at the closed bay doors. The rest of the rescuers just weren't here yet, that was all.

She was going to be fine.

They were going to be fine.

She had to believe it, because if she didn't, she would go completely mad.

PART EIGHTEEN
BETRAYAL
100 YEARS AGO

THE *RENEGAT*

They went into foldspace unexpectedly. At least, it was unexpected to Crowe. He had just awoken from that short nap he took after working with Willoughby to fix the foldspace communications system, and was heading to the mess to grab something to eat before heading back to Engineering, when the ship bumped and stuttered and lost attitude control long enough for Crowe to slide into a corridor wall with some force.

The contact sent a shudder of pain down his right side. He scraped the knuckles on his right hand, banged his elbow, and felt a jar along his shoulder strong enough to make him accidentally bite down, narrowly missing his tongue.

He grabbed the edge of a doorway just as the ship righted itself and smoothed. He stayed in place for a moment, letting the pain echo through him. New aches identified themselves, including a wrenched knee. He must have twisted it on the way down.

He stood slowly, shaking off the pain, and feeling a fury the likes of which he hadn't felt in years.

What the hell was Preemas doing?

Crowe tried to hail Preemas, but didn't get any response at all. That made the anger dissipate. Maybe this was an accidental trip into foldspace. Maybe the bridge crew was in worse shape than Crowe had been.

He changed direction, hurrying down the corridor to the ladders between decks. He knew better than to take the elevator, particularly since the attitude controls had blinked for a half second.

That wasn't ever supposed to happen. He had never felt it happen when the ship had gone through foldspace. At least, not to him.

He reached the ladders. No one else was on them, so he was the only one heading up to the bridge. His right hand ached as he gripped the rungs, and his right hip hurt as he climbed. The pain in his knee was getting better, though, so he had that, at least.

He climbed quickly. Each time he passed a deck, he heard voices, many of them loud or in distress. A few sounded frightened.

Apparently, Preemas hadn't warned anyone. Or there had been no way to warn people.

Crowe climbed faster, letting the worry propel him.

But part of him was well aware that if he thought this was a real emergency, he would have gone to Engineering first. He could have seen what was happening with the command controls while he was there; he could have done something to augment or fix any problem that had originated on the bridge—except a problem with the *anacapa* itself, since it and its container were on the bridge.

He reached bridge level and wasn't surprised to find the corridor nearby empty. He stopped for a moment, rubbed his sore elbow, and gathered himself.

He wasn't going to go into the bridge angry or panicked. He needed to be calm in case something was seriously wrong.

He needed to go in with no preconceptions at all.

It only took him a few steps to get to the bridge doors. They parted as he arrived—a very good sign. He stepped inside, and was surprised to see the screens on, showing yet another unfamiliar starscape. The entire bridge crew was in place, except for Crowe.

Even Atwater was here. He turned and smiled when he saw Crowe.

Stephanos was near the *anacapa* drive, standing near Ibori, who seemed to be doing Crowe's old job.

Preemas was in the middle of a circle of screens, and he was studying two more, comparing them back and forth. Breaux was standing near Atwater. She had a tablet in her hand and was studying it as well. She hadn't noticed that Crowe was on the bridge.

A few of the other crew members had. Yulia Colvin nodded at him. Crowe nodded back.

"Well," Preemas said, still looking down. "It appears that we're where we need to be. Right, Justine?"

Breaux nodded. "From everything I see, Captain. But the information I have is—"

"Exceptionally old, I know." Preemas said that as if he had heard it a million times and it didn't concern him at all. "Still. I might have expected a different outcome, given—"

"That you had gone in a day early?" Crowe asked. "From the wrong coordinates?"

Preemas looked up. He hadn't realized that Crowe was on the bridge. Neither had Breaux. She looked surprised.

Stephanos's cheeks colored and she, at least, had the grace to look a little guilty.

"Good morning, First Officer Crowe," Preemas said. "I figured—"

"You want to have this discussion here?" Crowe asked. Because that anger he had suppressed was rearing back up. It was obvious to everyone. And he realized he wouldn't be able to contain it.

The crew's eyes were wide. Stephanos had moved away from the *anacapa* ever so slightly, as if standing near it condemned her.

Preemas gave Crowe an evaluating look, and apparently did not like what he saw.

"Well, I have an empty ready room," Preemas said. "Natalia, you have the comm. I think we're in the clear. If not, I'm sure First Officer Crowe will tell me."

Preemas set the tablets down, and headed outside that circle of screens. Crowe walked across the bridge to the ready room. He didn't wait for Preemas to open the door inside. Crowe let himself in.

Preemas followed.

Crowe stopped in front of the desk. He had almost gone around it as if he were captain, not Preemas.

Preemas stepped through the door, and as the door slid shut, Crowe snapped, "Half the ship had no idea you were taking us into foldspace."

"Half the ship never knows we're going into foldspace," Preemas said. "You know that. It's *procedure*, First Officer Crowe."

Again with the sarcasm. Crowe clenched his right fist, felt an ache in his sore knuckles and then unclenched it.

Preemas didn't seem to notice the movement. He continued.

"So, it was a bumpy ride this time," Preemas said. "We didn't expect that."

"*I* didn't expect it," Crowe said, "and I'm your first officer."

Maybe Preemas had found out that Crowe had reported him to Gão. Maybe Crowe had read the entire situation all wrong from the start. Maybe that was why Preemas hadn't notified him that they were going into foldspace.

Preemas's eyes narrowed. He seemed to finally understand that Crowe was not hurt that he wasn't brought into the loop. Crowe was angry.

Preemas shrugged. The movement seemed calculated, not natural.

"You haven't been on the bridge for the last few trips into foldspace," he said. "You're not needed up here anymore. That became clear. So, I figured there was no reason to contact you."

"No reason?" Crowe's voice rose on the last syllable. He was perilously close to losing control. "During the last four foldspace journeys I was monitoring the communications *anacapa* drive, *as I've reported to you*. We have a problem there, one you denied me the chance to monitor this time. Obviously Natalia wasn't monitoring it, because she was on the bridge. Did you just decide that something that might endanger the ship was of no concern and you didn't need *anyone* to monitor it?"

"There hasn't been a problem for some time," Preemas said, as if Crowe was overreacting. "I figured you could get your sleep. You've been looking haggard, First Officer Crowe. People have noticed."

As if his lack of sleep was the problem, not Preemas himself.

"Hasn't been a problem?" This time, Crowe managed to keep control of his voice. "How would you know? You haven't contacted the Fleet for weeks."

"I've been sending messages," Preemas lied. "They've been responding. We haven't gone back and forth in real time, because there's no point. We knew it would become a problem the farther away from the Fleet we got. It became a problem, and we coped. Now we're moving on. You should too, First Officer Crowe."

The lie sounded so convincing. Or the lies, rather. The *lies* sounded so convincing, that Crowe would have believed Preemas if Crowe hadn't seen the evidence otherwise.

And now Crowe had a choice. Did he let Preemas know that Crowe had checked the logs? Or did he let Preemas think he was fooling Crowe?

"First Officer Crowe?" Preemas said. "Do we have a problem here?"

Clearly they did. But how Crowe should handle that problem was Crowe's current concern.

He decided avoidance, just for the moment anyway.

"Do you want me to step down?" Crowe asked, letting some of the anger back into his voice. "Because you have clearly deemed me unimportant to the command of this ship."

Preemas half-smiled. Crowe had seen that particular expression on Preemas's face a number of times these past few weeks. It was the expression Preemas used when he was trying to calm down an out-of-control crew member, one who had no real complaint.

That thought infuriated Crowe as well.

"I didn't realize you were so sensitive, First Officer Crowe." Preemas's tone didn't sound patronizing, even though his words were. "Perhaps your exhaustion or the unusual nature of this mission made you forget something."

Oh, there it was. The *understanding* that Preemas used many times with his crew. The fake understanding.

Preemas had paused here, so that Crowe could ask, *What did I forget?*

It was a little game, one that always ceded power from the crew member, even if the crew member was in the right.

Crowe kept himself completely still. He wasn't going to move, he wasn't going to take the bait, and he wasn't going to get visibly more angry than he had already been.

"You forgot," Preemas said into Crowe's silence, "that I am the captain."

Here was the space where Preemas expected Crowe to deny that. Any other crew member would have sounded defensive, upset, angry.

Crowe waited a half beat, so that Preemas would understand that Crowe had firmly considered his response.

"I didn't forget," Crowe said quietly. "It seems you forgot procedure. Again. I'm the first officer. I need to be informed about anything important. A course change, which this is, is important."

"We haven't changed course," Preemas said. "We're still heading to the Scrapheap."

"Oh, Captain," Crowe said, using that same sarcasm that Preemas usually used on rank. "You told the bridge crew while I was there that we entered foldspace from different coordinates than our planned route suggested. That's a major change in course."

"It made no difference," Preemas said. "We're where we're supposed to be."

"According to Justine's maps," Crowe said. "I heard that too. And that makes you lucky, not right."

"Me?" Preemas said.

Crowe nodded. "The decision was clearly yours, *Captain*, not ours. And if we had gotten stuck in foldspace, which was a possibility, then that would have been your mistake."

Preemas opened his mouth as if to argue with Crowe.

"And if we ended up in the wrong sector," Crowe said, not letting Preemas get a word in edgewise, "that would have been your mistake as well."

"We didn't," Preemas said.

"We were lucky," Crowe said. "Especially considering that momentary loss of attitude control."

He held out his right hand. The knuckles were turning black and blue. The scrapes were raw and red. It looked like he had beaten someone to a bloody pulp.

"I wonder how many other crew members got injured because of that little lapse," Crowe said.

"It's an engineering problem," Preemas said.

"And I am your Chief Engineer," Crowe snapped. "I should have been in Engineering, monitoring this trip. Instead, I was unaware of what you were going to do."

He crossed his arms and leaned on that desk as if it was his.

"Did you neglect to tell me because you thought I would fight you over the proposed change?" Crowe asked, his tone vicious. He wasn't trying to hold back the anger now.

"You wanted to run back to the Fleet," Preemas said.

"I did," Crowe said. "We have some problems on this vessel. They have to do with *anacapa* drives and travel into foldspace. You're ignoring those problems. I can't tell you if they're getting worse—"

"They aren't," Preemas said. "I told you that."

"Oh, but you don't know that, *Captain*," Crowe said. "You—."

He almost said that Preemas hadn't contacted Gão in a month, but Crowe refrained. He finally made a decision, doing it on the fly, of course.

He wasn't going to let Preemas know at all that Crowe was on to him, at least not in this way.

"I do know it," Preemas said into the silence. "We're fine."

"Then tell me what happened with the attitude control," Crowe said.

"That's a different system from the *anacapa* drive," Preemas said. "It probably got jostled, that's all."

"Keep telling yourself that," Crowe said.

"I don't appreciate the sarcasm, First Officer Crowe," Preemas said.

"And I don't appreciate the way you're playing with my very existence," Crowe said. "I'm assuming you're in denial here, not that you're being intentionally reckless."

Preemas's face flushed a deep red.

"Because, *Captain*, you know—you had the damn training—that every system gets affected when the *anacapa* activates. And whatever happens when the *anacapa* drive is active, then that's most likely *related to the drive*." Crowe crossed his arms. "Or did you conveniently forget that?"

"There's no proof that it—"

"There's no proof because no one in engineering was monitoring anything." Crowe finally raised his voice to a yell. "And the only way we can test it is to recreate the conditions, which I recommend we do not do."

"You would have us stay in this sector?" Preemas asked. "Forever?"

"I think this ship needs a top-to-bottom deep inspection," Crowe said. "I think we need to examine every single system. We've been taxing the ship too much, and you've been neglectful, *sir*. You're putting us all at risk."

"We're on a suicide mission," Preemas said, his anger matching Crowe's. "Of course, I'm putting us at risk."

Crowe took one step closer to Preemas, then Crowe deliberately leaned in, so that he was encroaching on Preemas's personal space.

"You want this mission to succeed," Crowe said very quietly. "If it's going to succeed, we need to *survive*. You and I have had this discussion before—"

"When you wanted to turn tail and run back to the Fleet," Preemas said. He didn't seem at all intimidated by Crowe's nearness.

"When I saw that this mission will fail given the information that we already have."

"They expect us to fail, if you consider failure not returning," Preemas said.

"I consider failure not being able to even get to that Scrapheap," Crowe said, leaning even closer.

This time Preemas did take a step back. The red in his cheeks had grown darker, almost purple, and his eyes flashed with fury.

"If we go back to the Fleet, *First Officer* Crowe," Preemas said, "we don't get to the Scrapheap. We fail."

"So you say," Crowe said. "But I always figured we could try again. We could fix whatever needed to be fixed, and then they would send us right back out again."

"Or laud us as heroes as you initially pitched to me, and keep us with the Fleet. Only the heroics would have nothing to do with anyone outside of Engineering. Your ego is getting too big for this ship, *First Officer* Crowe."

"I could say the same thing about you, *Captain* Preemas."

They stared at each other, their faces so close that Crowe could smell the coffee on Preemas's breath.

And then, to Crowe's surprise, Preemas took a step to the side. He couldn't back up or he would have hit the door.

"All right," Preemas said, his tone completely different. He was now going to try conciliation, when anger clearly hadn't worked. Crowe had seen this game in Preemas's bag of tricks as well. "We'll pretend this little incident didn't happen. I was wrong not to include you in this trip through foldspace. From now on, you will be notified in both of your capacities."

Notified, not consulted. Crowe heard the difference, and knew that Preemas had intended it.

He probably expected Crowe to thank him for recognizing that Crowe needed to be notified. Other crew members, when they challenged Preemas and thought they had won, thanked him.

Crowe wasn't going to. Preemas was still in the wrong, and they both knew it.

"You will, of course, check on what went wrong with the attitude controls," Preemas said.

"If it's possible to do so, now that we're out of foldspace," Crowe said. "I will find whatever the problem was, and I will see if it hasn't moved to other systems."

"However," Preemas said, "I don't think a general inspection is necessary at this time. The ship is doing just fine. These small glitches were expected—at least, I expected them. Didn't you, *Chief Engineer* Crowe?"

Crowe wasn't going to answer that. That was one of those on-the-record trick questions that would remove all liability from Preemas and put it on both of them. Or maybe even on Crowe himself.

"I think the ship is in distress, sir," Crowe said, "and I think we need to take that into account before we go any farther toward that Scrapheap."

"We're going to have to go into and out of foldspace several times no matter where we go, *Chief Engineer* Crowe. We're going to continue on the mission. We're over halfway there now. You can do your inspection at the site of the Scrapheap itself."

If they ever arrived. What Preemas had just said was a worthless plan, and they both knew it.

Crowe could keep fighting him here, in this room, or he could move forward, like members of the Fleet always did. And forward, this time, meant something else entirely.

It meant taking a chance that he hadn't planned on when he signed on to this mission.

"Do you understand me, *First Officer* Crowe?" Preemas asked.

Crowe moved his lips in a smile. He knew the smile did not reach his eyes, and he didn't care if Preemas knew it as well.

"I do, Captain," Crowe said, staying as level as he could. "I take this to mean you still want me as First Officer."

"If you remember who is in charge," Preemas said.

"Oh, believe me," Crowe said. "I'm not about to forget that."

"Good." Preemas eyed him, as if he was trying to see if Crowe meant something else. When it seemed like Preemas was satisfied, he said, "I promise. I will notify you of any small course correction or trip into foldspace. You will let me know if you're going to be on the bridge for those trips."

"Yes, sir," Crowe said. "I will."

"Good." Preemas looked over his shoulder, through the clear ready room door. Neither of them had opaqued it closed, so the entire bridge crew had seen the fight.

Not that it mattered to Crowe. Preemas probably hated the fact that the crew had seen Crowe's anger, but Crowe didn't. They had to understand that what Preemas was doing was not normal, and that Crowe did not sanction it.

"I take it you're returning to Engineering?" Preemas asked, swiveling his head back toward Crowe.

"Yes." Crowe wanted to see what had happened with the attitude control. He also had to do a few other things.

"Good," Preemas said, again. "We're staying in the sector for that minimum two days Natalia recommends. Just so you know."

He put a bite on the last four words, as if he resented even telling Crowe that. Then he let himself out of the ready room. Through the clear door, Crowe watched Preemas make his way back to his chair and that circle of screens. He beckoned Breaux as he did so.

Stephanos looked at Crowe from across the bridge. His gaze met hers, but he didn't smile or acknowledge her in any way.

He would deal with her later.

Right now, he had to investigate that attitude control. After he contacted Vice Admiral Gão. His message would be urgent. Because what had happened today hadn't just been reckless, it had been dangerous.

Crowe rubbed his sore right arm, and then stopped, and cursed silently as he realized something. Preemas *had* distracted him, after all.

The reason Preemas hadn't wanted the deep inspection had nothing to do with the fight over the Fleet or the location of the *Renegat*. Preemas still had no idea that Crowe knew about the disabled foldspace communications channel. As far as Preemas knew, Crowe had believed those lies Preemas had told about Gão.

Preemas didn't want the inspection, because Preemas believed that Crowe would discover that Preemas had been lying.

Lying cleanly and easily. As if it was something that he did as often as breathing. Which he probably did.

It made Crowe wonder what else Preemas had lied about. Probably everything, in one way or another.

Preemas might still be captain, but that didn't mean that Crowe had to trust him. Crowe would verify everything from now on.

And he would keep an eye on Preemas—until Crowe could convince Gão that she needed to issue an order to make the captain step aside.

THE *RENEGAT*

By the time Crowe reached Engineering, he had contained his fury behind a very calm exterior. He couldn't achieve anything when he was deeply angry.

However, he could use that anger as a fuel to drive every single action he made from now on.

He had a mental list of things he needed to do. He needed to contact Vice Admiral Gão. He needed to check the attitude control. And he needed to slowly disable the perks of Preemas's command.

Gão first.

As Crowe walked into Engineering, he instructed everyone inside to take a fifteen-minute break, effective immediately.

He stood near the door, and watched his crew filter out of the various towers and alcoves, a handful of them giving him sideways looks. The crew clearly didn't understand what he was doing. They were probably as unnerved as he had been by that sudden trip into foldspace.

They probably wanted to investigate whatever had happened to the ship. Some of them probably *were* investigating what had happened to the ship.

But, in the spirit of the captain, who believed ignoring problems was the same as solving them, the crew could wait until Crowe was ready to have them work the issues.

The last person left. Crowe checked to make sure his was the only life sign in Engineering. Then he closed the doors and sealed them.

He needed ten minutes, not fifteen. Ten. Just long enough that he could send a message to Vice Admiral Gão.

He whirled and headed to the communications alcove. He opened the panel that hid the communications *anacapa*, but didn't open the container, since no one was here to monitor it. So, he checked to make sure that the foldspace channel still looked active.

It did.

Then he closed the panels, and set up a communications window, coded to Vice Admiral Gāo. He started recording, making sure that he made several backups as he went.

"Vice Admiral," he said as the recording started. "The situation on the *Renegat* has become dire. I waited to hear from you after our last contact, and heard nothing. I consulted with Captain Preemas, who told me that you had convinced him to forge on to the Scrapheap. Later, I discovered that he had completely disabled our foldspace communications channel. If you have been trying to reach us, and cannot, that is why. In the meantime, he continued to tell me about the various conversations that you have had with him, conversations that I now know could not and did not happen…."

He outlined what he had found. Then he told her about the unplanned trip into foldspace, done without his knowledge. He lifted his arm as high as he could, showing her the purpling knuckles, the broken skin that he had yet to fix. He told her there were other injuries, and that Preemas was becoming more reckless rather than less.

Then Crowe said, "Vice Admiral Gāo, I humbly request that you relieve Captain Preemas of duty. I ask that you do so by patching into our entire communications system shipwide. I would prefer not to do that myself, so that I will be less compromised than I already am."

He shifted a little. His arm ached from trying to lift it over his head. He might have to go to the med bay after all.

"If you do not want me to run the ship, that is fine. You have a few other candidates who might be able to do a good job. I will assist whoever you choose."

Crowe was pleased that his voice remained calm. He was feeling a tad breathless, but it wasn't obvious in the way he spoke.

He had never asked to have a captain relieved of duty before.

"I am contacting you because I believe in the Fleet, in her rules and regulations, and in the proper way of doing things," he said. "Captain Preemas is guaranteeing that the mission you sent us on—discovering what happened to that Scrapheap—will not succeed. I don't think the *Renegat* will be able to handle the foldspace journey. I am not certain we can make the journey back to you, either, but we have a chance of that, if I can inspect the ship."

His heart rate had increased. On top of the anger, he was frightened. He had never done anything like this before.

"I suspect you tried to send me the rest of the information that I requested, and that it did not arrive because of the captain's perfidy. I am assuming that you also believe the communications *anacapa* might be causing some of our lag. I have no idea if the lag remains, because of what Captain Preemas did. We are also two trips through foldspace past our last contact, so our data gathering isn't as clear as I would like it. That's why I am sending you this message on all channels that I possibly can, in as many ways as I can. It's not worth even trying to talk at the moment."

She probably understood that. If he wasn't careful, he would start repeating himself. Some of this one-sided conversation felt like him trying to get something off his chest, rather than informing a superior officer.

"Vice Admiral," he said, "I hope you see fit to follow my advice. Please do let me know if I am overstepping."

Hell, he was overstepping by any measure. He knew it, and so would she.

But this wasn't a normal circumstance. He had to remember that.

"I hope you consider my proposal. I hope to hear from you soon. Thank you for your time."

He stood very still for a moment, then ended the recording. His knees wobbled, and he caught himself against the edge of the communications alcove.

He was tired, he was banged up, but that hadn't caused his body to nearly collapse.

He was trying not to break rules, trying not to revert to the kid who had cost fifty lives because he thought he knew better than everyone else.

But here, he did know better—at least, better than Preemas. And Crowe needed to remember that.

He was trying to save lives now. Trying to save a ship.

He hoped he wasn't too late.

PART NINETEEN

THE RESCUE

NOW

THE *RENEGAT*

Zarges had nearly reached Cargo Bay One. The emergency lighting here worked better than the lighting anywhere else on the ship. The walls of the corridor glistened in the lights from his suit.

New black nanobit coating. This part of the ship had been repaired and recently. Automatically repaired, judging by the way that the shiny part had a jagged connection to the older section.

His breath caught. Surely someone would have told him if Cargo Bay One had been compromised.

He forced himself forward. Iqbar was already at Cargo Bay Two. They only had about fifteen minutes left to manage a rapid evacuation.

People in environmental suits pushed past him, in a hurry to get inside the cargo bay. He glanced down the darkened corridor and saw more movement.

Well, none of the *Renegat's* crew seemed to think there would be a problem with Cargo Bay One. Which relieved him and worried him at the same time.

This ship had been through a lot, and he wasn't sure how much the crew had simply accepted the damage, and no longer thought about it.

But he couldn't worry about that. He had more than enough to think about right now.

He hoped that Palmer's time estimate was off, because, judging by the number of people in the corridor, nowhere near 200 people had reached the cargo bays yet.

"Sufia," he said to Khusru through the suit's comm link, "you need the change the announcement. Tell everyone they have less than five minutes to get here."

"Or what?" she asked. "We leave them behind?"

"If we have to put it that way, yes," he said.

Then he pushed himself inside Cargo Bay One. His suit lights illuminated floating cargo, some right in front of his face. He saw no obvious damage here, which relieved him even more.

Two groups of people looked like beacons in the darkness. One group stood a little too close to the cargo bay doors.

He had to get to them first.

"You've got forty to fifty people inside that bay," Palmer said. He was still in Engineering, still trying to see if he could buy them all more time. "You want me to contact one of the life rafts?"

Zarges felt a surge of irritation. Why was Palmer looking at the number of people in the bay, rather than working on stopping the upcoming explosion?

"I've got this," Zarges said. "You finish up."

"I have," Palmer said. "There's nothing I can do. I'm heading to your bay now. You're the one with the crowd."

Zarges didn't respond. Instead, he threaded his way through the floating cargo to the cargo bay doors. He illuminated his face ever so slightly so that the group of people could see him, and toggled his communications link so that it broadcasted on all frequencies.

"My name is Raul Zarges," he said. "I am with the Fleet."

Someone moved their hands together, and then everyone did. White gloves slapped against white gloves, but of course, he couldn't hear anything.

For a half second, he wondered if this was some strange custom that he had never heard of, and then he realized they were applauding him. Even though they knew he couldn't hear them.

He felt a small rush of relief. He had been wondering if the people on board this ship had stolen it or if they even knew what the Fleet was.

Maybe they didn't. Maybe they were just applauding the fact that he was an outsider.

Those details didn't matter, though. What mattered was getting these people off this ship.

"I need the group nearest the bay doors to move to the middle of the bay. I don't know if you're familiar with the Fleet's rescue technology, but in case you aren't, we're attaching ships we call 'life rafts' to the side of the ship. In a few minutes, you'll be able to step through the doors onto the life raft."

Everyone was facing him. He couldn't see through their helmets. All he could see were images of his face, illuminated in pale brown light, reflected back at him.

"The raft can only hold fifty people."

He paused there, and he shouldn't have, because they stirred, as if they were afraid a large number of people would be left behind.

"Our scans show that there are about two hundred people on this ship," he said. "Is that right?"

No one answered him. On the far end of the bay, he saw more lighted figures entering.

And then another announcement:

You have less than five minutes to get to the cargo bays. We are beginning evacuations, and we are on a clock. The ship is falling apart. You have to hurry.

The group in front of him stirred again. He was beginning to think they were Fleet, because if they weren't they would have already started pushing and shoving to get as close to the door as possible.

"I need to know," he said as the announcement ended. "Are there 200 people on this ship? Or are there more in some area that my scans can't reach? The brig, maybe, or some kind of container in one of the medical bays?"

Again, no one answered him. He was beginning to wonder if they could communicate through the comm links.

"I'm not starting the evacuation until someone answers me," he said, even though that wasn't true.

"We have 199 people on board," said a woman's voice. She sounded like an authority. The farthest group parted slightly, as she used the shoulders and helmets of her colleagues to propel herself forward. "No one is in the brig, and there's nothing in the medical bay that should block a Fleet scan."

"Good," Zarges said. "Thank you. Then we're starting the evacuation."

The woman was only a few feet from him. He reached up, grabbed her arm, and pulled her closer.

She struggled.

"My suit…" she said. "Please."

"This won't hurt your suit," he said. "Stand near me."

"My suit is failing," she said. "Please let go of it."

Instead of letting go, he pulled her with him toward the bay doors. If her suit was failing that meant others probably were as well.

"*Rescue One*," he said on a private channel, "prepare the life rafts. I will be opening the bay door and sending evacuees to you."

"Copy that," came the response.

"Do you know how to operate the bay doors manually?" he asked the woman he was holding.

"No," she said. "And please, let me go."

He did, since it was causing her so much distress. "Does anyone know how to manually operate the bay doors?"

Someone toward the back raised a hand, with palm light on, nearly blinding him. He turned away because he had to.

"You, then," he said, sounding as authoritarian as he could. "Help me open the doors. The rest of you step through them in a *calm* and *orderly* fashion. I will be informed when we reach the fifty-person limit. At that moment, I will close the bay doors while the first life raft leaves and a second takes its place."

He couldn't ask them if they understood. He wouldn't be able to see their responses and he didn't want the comm links filled with chatter.

The person who had raised his—her?—hand was already heading to the wall nearest the doors. Zarges followed, just as another announcement resounded through the comm links.

You have less than three minutes to get to the cargo bays. We are beginning evacuations, and we are on a clock. The ship is falling apart. You have to hurry.

The person who knew how to work the doors was hanging on to a handle near an open panel.

"Now?" he asked.

"Yes," Zarges said.

The panel looked familiar, but Zarges was glad he had asked for help. His new assistant hit two different buttons, then pulled a small lever. If this panel worked the way similar manual controls worked, the lever activated some pulleys and the doors would slide on the built-in rails as smoothly as if the computers had guided them.

For a half second, the doors remained closed, and Zarges's heart started hammering. He didn't know if he could wedge open doors that large, and he didn't want to fire on them, not with people this close, and not with the life raft attached to the outside of the ship.

Then the doors wobbled. They opened unevenly—the door closest to him moving faster than the door on the other side.

Light from the life raft poured into the bay. The life raft looked surprisingly small compared to the bay, but it didn't matter. Evacuees poured onto the life raft before he could even give the order.

He hadn't even set up his counting system.

On the private channel, he asked, "You're monitoring the numbers?"

"We have it," came the reply.

Which was good, because he didn't.

In less than a minute, the evacuees closest to the life raft had already entered it. A handful more stepped across the threshold when a voice said, "That's it. Make them stand back."

"That's it," he repeated on the comms. "That raft is at maximum capacity. We have another waiting. Step back and we'll set up."

Those who had started into the raft continued forward as if he hadn't spoken, but the next group of people did stop, thank heavens. He'd conducted rescues where he'd had to hold off the evacuees with weapons, just to keep things orderly.

He was glad that wasn't happening here.

He looked, saw that no one stood in the actual doors, and he said to his helper, "Close the doors."

The helper hit another button that Zarges hadn't seen, and then pushed up on the lever. The doors closed much more easily than they had opened.

More people lined up, some leaving their head and shoulder lights on. The junk floating around the bay seemed like it was aiming at the lights, when he knew it wasn't.

The evacuees shifted again. He recognized their movements. They were on the edge of panic. It wouldn't take much to tip them over.

The last thing he wanted was another announcement. That would frighten them worse, particularly since they had probably passed the time deadline that Khusru had set.

He switched to the private *Rescue One* channel. "Sufia, no more announcements. We need to finish the evacuation."

"Already ahead of you," she said. "We left the bridge a few minutes ago. There was no way to make that announcement automated. Do we know if everyone has arrived at the cargo bays?"

"I don't," he said. "*Rescue One*, do you have the figures?"

"There are 68 people in Cargo Bay One, and 23 remaining in Cargo Bay Two."

Great, he thought but didn't say, they would have to move people from this bay to the next one over.

"Can we make three stops here?" he asked.

"We can, but that doesn't solve one issue. Nine people have not yet arrived at either bay."

He felt cold. Either he could send some team members to find the remaining evacuees or he could abandon them. He'd never abandoned people in a rescue before, although with this kind of emergency, the Fleet policy was to abandon those who hadn't arrived before the time limit.

"Are they on their way?" Zarges asked.

"Looks like it."

"Then I'll wait for them," he said. "I'll get them off this ship."

Somehow. After he evacuated 91 more people.

Before the exploding ship killed them all.

PART TWENTY

DECISIONS

100 YEARS AGO

THE *RENEGAT*

Thirty-six hours later. Thirty-six hours after Crowe had sent the message to Vice Admiral Gão and still no word. No response at all.

He had started compulsively checking the communications array about 24 hours in, expecting some kind of contact. He even thought that perhaps a message she had sent got caught up in the equipment.

He checked every system, cleaned every possible channel, made certain that she could both contact him directly and contact the ship overall.

Nothing.

No word.

The silence unnerved him more than he thought it would, and he counseled patience to himself. He had more than enough to do, after all.

He had spoken to Stephanos about her work on the last foldspace trip. She had apologized profusely, said that Preemas had called her to the bridge and ordered her to help.

Preemas is the captain, you know, she had said, and she was right. He was still the captain, although it made Crowe sick to his stomach.

Preemas hadn't ordered Stephanos to keep Crowe in the dark, like Crowe had initially thought. Instead, Preemas had lied, saying he had contacted Crowe, and Crowe was in Engineering.

Which was why Stephanos had given Crowe such a strange look when he arrived on the bridge and was so utterly furious. Why everyone had given him a strange look.

They had all thought he had known about the foldspace journey when he actually hadn't.

So, to them, he looked a little off. But Stephanos immediately figured out what had happened. She had told a few others.

There was that, he supposed. Mostly, they thought he had overreacted to something, or that he was angry about the loss of attitude control.

He wasn't angry about the loss of attitude control; he was worried about it. The ship recorded the momentary loss—it had lasted less than a minute, even though it had felt like hours—in its logs, but he still hadn't pinpointed the cause.

He wanted to do that deep investigation of the systems, to make sure everything was working properly, but that was hard to do without Preemas's permission.

Crowe could do a lot of things without Preemas noticing, but to have the entire engineering crew dig through every system on the ship would be impossible to hide.

Still, Crowe spent most of his time in Engineering, partly because he was waiting for the contact, but partly because his anger wasn't as contained as he wanted it to be.

The crew knew they could find him here—and they did. He was dealing with what he was beginning to think of as the usual First Officer stuff—people relations, mostly, trying to keep this ship together by the sheer force of his personality.

In his past assignments, he had never noticed the First Officer doing anything like that, but maybe the situation on those ships wasn't as fraught, or maybe he had just paid attention to Engineering and ignored the rest.

Part of him suspected that on his previous assignments, the captain had handled the toughest part of crew relationships, if not directly, then through various intermediaries, not just one.

Preemas noticed how his crew got along—he wouldn't have been able to make such good reassignments if he hadn't noticed the people on his ship—but he didn't seem to care if emotions were high or someone was unhappy, so long as it didn't interfere with his damn mission.

Crowe tried not to think about the damn mission. Because getting to the Scrapheap was only the start of their work; investigating, sending information back to the Fleet (somehow) and then getting home—those were the other three parts.

He still wasn't sure they would be able to complete the first part.

While Crowe waited for Gão to respond, he started doing something else, something he told no one about, something he was doing so stealthily that if he got caught, he would probably be up for court-martial himself.

He was slowly dismantling the command centers in the captain's mess and in the captain's suite. As First Officer and as Chief Engineer, he had access to both locations.

And as Chief Engineer, he knew how to wipe any trace of his entry so that no one could figure out he had been there.

The equipment in the mess was easy to deal with. He didn't have to disassemble the equipment at all. He simply had to block access to the controls.

Blocking access from the mess was a major part of the design since any officer could enter that mess hall. The captain had to be able to shut off mess access to the controls at a moment's notice.

The captain's suite was another issue. Crowe had gone in once so far to see how old the equipment was and to see if it had been updated with the rest of the ship.

The command center had been inspected and made shipshape, but it hadn't been upgraded—which showed just how rarely those things were used.

Then Crowe had done most of the work inside Engineering, slowly dismantling the captain's ability to command the ship from his own quarters. The last thing he was going to dismantle—more as a *screw-you* than anything else—was the captain's ability to communicate from his quarters to the Fleet.

While Crowe dismantled the captain's command center, he built one in his own cabin. The one in his cabin wasn't as elaborate as the one in the captain's suite. Crowe just wanted the ability to communicate and to hold the ship until he could contact someone else on the crew or until he could consolidate command of the ship on his own.

He hoped he would never have to use either rebuilt command center, but he now discounted nothing. He had spent his entire career—ever since the screw-ups of his youth—following rules, staying within the lines, protesting if need be but doing so at risk to himself and his career, not by inserting himself into a process he didn't belong in.

And, if truth be told, he was doing the same thing right now, by contacting Gão.

But she was staying maddeningly silent.

He had just checked the communications array for the fifth time that morning when Preemas contacted him directly.

"Per your request," Preemas said, "I'd like to notify you of a course change. I'd just tell you, but you're going to yell at me, so come to my ready room right now."

Crowe went cold. There should be no course correction. There shouldn't be any changes, not yet. Crowe hadn't figured out what, exactly, caused the loss of attitude control, and he had told Preemas that it was essential they know as much about that particular event as they could know before they headed back into foldspace.

Of course, Preemas wouldn't listen to him.

Crowe was noticing that Preemas wasn't listening to anyone anymore.

Crowe gave the communications array one final look, silently begging for a message from Gão to arrive right away. He wanted the entire ship to hear about the change of command before they heard about yet another change of course.

Then he half-smiled at himself, hoping that someone (like Gão) would save him. The smile was also for his pessimism. He knew—*knew*—that the change of course meant something bad, not something that he wanted.

He knew Preemas would not announce that they were heading back to the Fleet. Preemas was going to do something else, something that Crowe suspected he would not agree with.

Then Crowe mentally chided himself for having the wrong attitude. Maybe Preemas had changed his mind.

And maybe Crowe would wake up from this nightmare to find that he had never boarded the *Renegat* at all.

He walked quickly to the bridge, greeted the afternoon crew, most of whom were people who had never worked on a bridge crew before Preemas found them, and then slipped through the open door of the ready room.

Preemas was leaning against the desk, exactly where Crowe had been the last time they met in the room. No, they weren't playing passive-aggressive games with each other. Not at all.

Crowe suppressed a sigh.

Behind him, the door audibly whooshed shut. The sound had to be programmed. Normally, it was silent. Then the door and wall to the bridge opaqued.

Either Preemas was getting rid of Crowe as First Officer, or Preemas was expecting a fight. Crowe wasn't sure which it was, although he suspected that, if Preemas was going to demote him, he would do it with the window between the ready room and the bridge clear, because he would want the entire crew to see Crowe's humiliation.

"Captain," Crowe said, deliberately sounding as neutral as he could. He found it slightly fascinating that he had trouble saying the title without some sarcasm attached.

"First Officer Crowe." Preemas managed the same tone, but the half smile on his face belied that professional sound. "As I said, I am letting you know of the course correction."

Crowe felt a chill run down his back. After he had seen the door opaque, he had hoped the course correction notification was just a pretext to get him up to the bridge. Apparently not.

"I have been thinking about all you told me about the difficulties with the various *anacapa* drives and with foldspace," Preemas said.

Crowe held himself still. Preemas didn't believe him now, did he? After all this time?

"We are finally going to follow the Fleet's original plan," Preemas said. "More or less."

Crowe frowned. Original plan? He wasn't even sure what that meant.

Then Preemas chuckled. "Less, I guess, since we're only going to cover less distance."

That chill ran through Crowe again. "Sir?"

"Considering all the problems you and Natalia and the others have flagged," Preemas said, "I decided it's prudent to just rip off the bandage, as they used to say."

Crowe bit the inside of his lower lip. He didn't want to jump to conclusions. Getting a major emotional reaction out of him was part of what Preemas wanted.

Preemas waited a half a minute. He wanted Crowe to quiz him. Preemas wanted this to be a dramatic reveal and Crowe wasn't playing along.

So, like a kid who couldn't contain a secret, Preemas said, "We're going directly from here to the Scrapheap. One long foldspace journey. Just not as long as the one the Fleet wanted us to take. But since the danger is going in and coming out, we're better off doing that once, wouldn't you agree?"

There was so much wrong with what Preemas had just said that Crowe didn't even know how to start. He finally understood why Preemas wanted a fight.

Preemas wanted to show Crowe, in every way possible, that Preemas was captain, and as long as Preemas was captain, he would be the most reckless captain Crowe had ever served with.

Preemas hadn't opaqued the door to hide a fight. He had done so to protect himself. If the crew saw how angry Crowe had been with Preemas on this day, then realized the order had come down that they were taking the long foldspace journey, everyone would be able to put two and two together and figure out the reason for the anger.

Now, though, they would think Crowe was in on the decision.

He could simply open the door. He could walk away. He could resign.

He wasn't sure if any of those things would be valuable.

No matter what, the *Renegat* would have to go through foldspace—or it would remain trapped here, wherever here was.

If the *Renegat* wanted to rejoin the Fleet, it would have to go through foldspace. To continue the mission, the *Renegat* would have to do the same thing.

"What?" Preemas said. The word wasn't really a question. It was a taunt. "You have nothing to say?"

"Would my comments make any difference?" Crowe asked, using that same neutral voice.

Preemas's face flushed. "I am the kind of captain who listens to my First Officer. That's why I made this decision."

Sure, Crowe wanted to say, *you're the kind of captain who listens to his first officer, and then disregards every single word spoken.*

Crowe said, "You might listen to your first officer, but you failed to consult with your Chief Engineer."

Preemas's half smile grew just a little bit. He thought the fight he had planned for had arrived.

"If I had known you were going to do this," Crowe said, calmly, "I would have briefed my engineering crew. We would prepare for the long journey. We would make sure systems are ready. We would like to do similar things any time we go into foldspace—"

He couldn't resist that dig.

"—but the opportunity isn't always there. This time, I would think it essential. No ship has ever taken a trip this long, that we know of anyway, and we do not know what kind of stress the journey will take on us."

Preemas's half smile froze. Preemas no longer looked as amused as he had just a moment ago.

"You agree with me." He didn't quite make that a question either, but it wasn't an insult. It was surprised, shocked even, as if Preemas couldn't believe what he was hearing.

"We have to travel through foldspace," Crowe said, warming up to this. "I prefer to be prepared whenever you order the journey, Captain."

"Huh." After saying that he was following Crowe's suggestion, Preemas couldn't then say that he expected Crowe to disagree with him. This cagey sound on Preemas's part told Crowe that Preemas was recording this conversation, and probably had planned to use it with the crew later, when Preemas emerged triumphant at the Scrapheap.

Because Preemas never believed he could be anything other than triumphant, of course.

What Preemas didn't know was that if he gave Crowe permission to do the inspections, Crowe could buy time until Gāo's message—whatever it was—reached them.

"So..." Preemas said, speaking slowly. "You see no problems with this foldspace trip then."

Definitely on some kind of record. Preemas was still trying to save his career. For some reason, he believed that despite everything he was doing, the Fleet would see him as some kind of hero.

"Oh, I see a million problems," Crowe said, thinking of the record as well, the one he might have to send to Gāo, "but we might be able to mitigate half of them."

Preemas's mouth tightened. His eyes narrowed. He seemed to know that Crowe was playing some kind of game, but what kind, Preemas clearly had no idea.

"These problems would exist whenever we went into foldspace," Preemas said defensively.

"They would," Crowe said. "These are the ones we know about. We might encounter more on the longer trip, but we won't know that until we're taking that trip."

We might get stuck in foldspace. We might emerge somewhere completely unplanned. We might lose the entire ship. Crowe didn't say any of those things, even though he wanted to.

"We need to take some extra time to prepare for the journey," Crowe said. "We want to get through foldspace with no problems at all."

"More time," Preemas said quietly, as if he was actually considering it. "Would more time make a difference on the quality of the trip?"

"Yes," Crowe said. If Preemas gave them long enough, they might not have to make the trip at all.

"Can you finish all of these inspections and fix the 'half-million' problems that you're somehow seeing?" Preemas asked.

"I would prefer more time than that," Crowe said, "especially considering how much time we're lopping off the journey by not going into and out of foldspace four other times, and crossing some sector in between to get in position."

"I recognize the time savings," Preemas said. "That's one of the reasons I want to do this. The crew is restless, First Officer Crowe."

Crowe couldn't tell if that comment was meant to be blaming or if Crowe had just heard it that way.

"Yes, they are," Crowe said. "Not all of them are fitting into their new jobs."

"At least they have that new work to keep them occupied," Preemas said. He was still frowning, still considering Crowe's proposal.

But Crowe waited patiently, wanting Preemas to feel that the decision to give Crowe more time was beneficial to the *ship* and Preemas's ambitions, not beneficial to Crowe, or Crowe setting up some kind of roadblock.

Preemas nodded, as if he had just settled an argument with himself.

"More time makes sense to me," he said. "But not too much. That's why a week is best. If you find something serious, we might have to reconsider. But for now, one week."

One week. Crowe hoped that was enough. He had no idea if it would be, but if he felt he needed more time, he would find some kind of problem that would convince Preemas to remain here.

That loophole helped.

Crowe hoped he wouldn't need it. He hoped he would hear from Gāo soon.

He hoped this nightmare journey would end, before the situation got worse.

PART TWENTY-ONE
THE RESCUE
NOW

THE *RENEGAT*

Everything looked the same in the dark. The walls, the floor, the ceiling. The doors weren't even labeled. Not with real printing. When the power was working, all Breaux had to do was touch a door, and the name of the department would flare at her.

She hadn't memorized the ship, not in that unconscious way that would have allowed her to get around it in the dark and the cold, leading five other people, none of whom had corrected her, and said, *You're going the wrong way.*

She was, though. She had to be. Because she should have been to Deck Four by now. Had she gone down too far? Not far enough? Taken the wrong ladder? Turned the wrong direction?

She had no idea, and her suit—the regulation, ill-fitting suit she had pulled out of the recreation room, had no map. What kind of suit had no built-in map?

"Does anyone know where we are?" she asked. "Does anyone have a map?"

One of the others brushed against the wall, and tapped it, as if expecting one of the built-in maps to appear. But of course, it didn't. The *power* was off. Hadn't these people realized that? There wasn't even enough atmosphere for them, because otherwise they wouldn't have to wear the damn suits.

Those tears that had been threatening came back and she blinked them away.

Had she missed the opportunity? Had the rescuers, whoever they were, already gotten everyone else off the *Renegat*?

Was she going to die here, with five people whose names she didn't even know, on a failing ship because she got turned around?

Because she never bothered, in all the time she'd been here, to learn how to find her way around without electronic help?

What was wrong with her, anyway?

She was panicking. That was what was wrong.

If she continued to panic, she *would* die. And these hangers-on, these people who couldn't think for themselves, they would die too.

And she would have them on her conscience.

She giggled. She wouldn't have a conscience. She would be dead. And dead people didn't have a conscience.

Or at least, she didn't think they did.

She stopped, patted her damn suit, then pushed on the fingertips of her gloves. Some suits she'd used, some of the really sophisticated new ones, brought up maps that way.

But of course this one didn't.

"Suit," she said, "can you put a map of the *Renegat* on my visor?"

She hoped she wasn't broadcasting to the others. But then what did it matter if she *was* broadcasting? She was trying to save all of them. And if she didn't say anything, she would literally—*literally*—die of embarrassment.

No map appeared.

And no one else stepped up or said anything. These people were starting to drive her crazy.

She could only try one more thing.

"Suit," she said, "show me how to get to Cargo Bay One from here."

Lights flared around her eyes. A red trail led to her right. She turned, then spun. She had limited zero-G skills, and that movement hadn't helped. In fact, it had probably contributed to her getting turned around.

She grabbed part of the wall, saw a hand on her leg, and realized she hadn't even felt it. She looked over, and someone—one of the others, another woman—was holding onto her, helping her out of the spin.

The red trail was now behind Breaux. She had no idea exactly how that had happened. And to make matters worse, she was dizzy.

But there was a red trail. And it led down a corridor. And even if the damn trail was wrong, it was a chance.

She couldn't let a chance go by. She just couldn't.

"Thank you," she said to the person who stabilized her. "Thank you."

And then she eased herself around, using the wall as a brace. When she faced the corridor exactly, she pushed off, careened a little to the side, had to push off that wall, and force herself forward.

Like swimming, her father had told her all those years ago. He had actually served on a Fleet ship. Maybe she had joined the *Renegat* because she had been emulating him. *Think of it like swimming but without the force of the water, pushing against you.*

She hadn't understood that until now. She could handle swimming. She would use the walls like water, using them to propel herself forward when she needed to.

And she needed to.

Because that *be here in five minutes* announcement had occurred at least ten minutes ago.

Please don't leave without us, she thought, forcing herself not to whisper the words out loud. *Please. Please don't leave without us. We'll be right there. We're trying. We just got lost. Please. Please don't leave us behind.*

The knot in her stomach told her that she didn't believe she would make it to the cargo bay in time. She would die here.

But at least she would die trying.

PART TWENTY-TWO

LONG-LOST COMMUNICATIONS

95 YEARS AGO

THE *SPRÁVA*

"Vice Admiral," said Lieutenant Octavia Vasiliev, "you need to see this."

Vasiliev stood in the doorway to Vice Admiral Gāo's study, but Gāo could only figure out where she was by the change in light and the sound of Vasiliev's voice. Gāo stood in the center of the room. More data than she wanted to contemplate surrounded her. It flowed in black and white strands from the ceiling to the floor, forming holographic columns. The information she wanted from each column automatically got highlighted and moved to yet another column. But that information was color-coded. So an entire ribbon of colors across the spectrum congregated in the far corner of her study, where her art was usually displayed.

She hadn't seen the art in days. She'd been buried in information about Scrapheaps, trying to figure out where most of them were located.

It had taken five years to collate all of the information that the Fleet had on Scrapheaps. Five years, and three separate research projects, not counting the brand-new field of study that Calixte had started on one of the school ships. That brand-new field focused on improving Scrapheaps, determining their future, and trying to figure out if anything was needed from the past.

Gāo swept her arms outward as if she were parting curtains, and the data columns bent and moved as if they actually were curtains. Vasiliev remained in the doorway, a tablet clutched to her chest. She was short and curved, unlike most female Fleet officers. Most of them lost their curves given all of the exercise required to rise in the ranks. Yet she was as trim as her body type would allow her to be. If she lost any more weight, she would be too thin, and if she exercised any more, she would have no time for anything else.

In fact, Vasiliev's dedication to making herself better made Gāo feel guilty at least once a day. Sometimes it was for eating an extra pastry at breakfast; sometimes it was for the caffeine she ingested like a lifeline; sometimes it was for skipping an extra walk around the ship.

Gāo loved Vasiliev. She was the second-best assistant Gāo had ever had, after Cali Baker. But Baker had gotten promoted, and then got promoted again. That was the problem with the good ones. They moved on in their careers—or rather, Gāo let them move on. She'd seen what happened to superior officers who blocked transfers and promotions of their excellent staff members.

Those staff members eventually withered and became ineffective. Everything that made them the best slowly faded away. And slowly, the senior officers lost their effectiveness because their staff had become useless.

Gāo wouldn't have Vasiliev long either, but Gāo would value Vasiliev as long as she worked in this position.

"What do you have, Lieutenant?" Gāo asked. She never berated her staff for interrupting her. She believed that training them *when* to interrupt her was as important as dealing with the interruptions themselves.

"We got a coded communication, for you." Vasiliev's chocolate brown eyes, as curved as the rest of her, narrowed. Her arching eyebrows—the same brown as her eyes and hair—moved downward, making them look like someone had drawn wings on her smooth forehead.

She extended the tablet, almost as if it hurt her.

"Did you open it?" Gāo asked.

"No, sir," Vasiliev said, "because it says *eyes only*."

Vasiliev was Gāo's eyes. She was supposed to open the *eyes only* communications, and help Gāo deal with whatever was inside. Vasiliev had the clearance for that duty, and the chops as well.

Gāo had come to rely on her assistants for their great advice, a trend that had started with Baker, and continued on to Vasiliev.

"Any reason you didn't follow office protocol?" Gāo asked. She had learned the hard way not to reprimand someone for a choice when she didn't have enough information to understand the choice.

"Um." Vasiliev bit her upper lip. The frown deepened. She clearly wasn't sure she had taken the right path in doing this, but she had done it. So she bobbed her head and then said, "It's, um, it's from the *Renegat*."

Gāo felt her breath catch. If she had a chair nearby, she would have collapsed into it. She almost reached out to brace herself on the columns of data beside her, but they didn't exist, not as anything real anyway.

So she wobbled a little, then took the tablet. She finally understood why Vasiliev had made that choice.

Had Baker still been on the job, Baker would have opened the communication. But Baker had left three years ago, and by that point, Gāo had reluctantly given up on the *Renegat*.

Last she had heard, the *Renegat* was entering foldspace for the sixth time. Nadim Crowe had asked for her assistance in convincing Captain Preemas to turn the ship around and bring it back to the Fleet. Gāo had ordered Preemas to do just that.

And then she had heard nothing.

She had pinged the *Renegat* hundreds of times, and received no response. Baker said that at one point, it seemed like something had gotten through, but there was no real way to tell.

Later, as Gão had examined the logs of all of those sent communications, she had seen a familiar pattern. When a ship got lost in foldspace, the system often thought it did not exist.

The first few communications Gão had sent seemed to go to the ship, and then get blocked. After that, the communications went nowhere. As if the *Renegat* had ceased to exist.

More than that, though, it seemed like the *Renegat* had *never* existed.

That sort of reading often happened with ships that had gotten lost in foldspace. The Fleet couldn't communicate with them. No one could. They simply vanished, and the system seemed to lose faith in their reality, even if someone had been in touch with them just hours before.

It had taken her years to get past the loss of the *Renegat*. Gão had believed—hell, she *knew*—it was her fault. She had known that ship wouldn't make it through the long journey. There were too many problems.

The mission had stalled any promotion Gão would have gotten in the past five years, but it had utterly destroyed Admiral Hallock's career.

Everyone had known that the *Renegat's* mission had been her baby, even though she had tried to pass the responsibility on to Gão. Hallock had played a lot of political games when it became clear that the *Renegat* was lost, trying to destroy Gão. Hallock had claimed she was badly served by her subordinates, but too many other vice admirals had been in those meetings.

Too many other people had known about Gão's doubts—about the doubts of anyone with sense. And most of the people involved hadn't wanted to find out what was going on *behind* the Fleet. Everyone in the Fleet looked forward.

Hallock's argument that she was trying to close down past mistakes wasn't a compelling one, not for people who didn't care about fixing lingering mistakes from the past. Hallock sounded more and more out of touch, particularly as *her* superiors realized she had deliberately sent a ship into danger without the proper backup.

Her secondary argument, that everyone on board the *Renegat* had no real business being in the Fleet, fell apart when the survivors, the ones who had left the *Renegat* on Sector Base Z, had told various committees that Preemas was doing his best with a crew picked for him, a crew that didn't have the ability or the experience to handle this kind of mission—and wouldn't have been able to deal with it, even if they had had the experience.

Because the *Renegat* wasn't a DV-Class vessel. It had not been built for this kind of extended travel.

Hallock had finally retired last year, broken but unrepentant. She still believed that the Scrapheaps were dangerous as well as a waste of resources.

Gão hadn't quite taken up the rallying cry. But she had paid attention. She was concerned about the Ready Vessels. Try as she might to locate the history of them, she couldn't find much, and what she did find led her to believe that the Fleet should stop seeding the Scrapheap with working ships. The Fleet had never used them. To her knowledge, no one else had either, but Hallock had been right about that; those ships were a danger to the Fleet itself.

It was one thing to leave a Scrapheap of mostly destroyed vessels, protected by a force field. Other cultures, particularly those not as developed as the Fleet, wouldn't always be able to reverse engineer the ships. But to leave intact and functioning vessels in a secondary force field, one that the Fleet wasn't policing, was inviting disaster.

Especially in Scrapheaps that were only a sector or two away from where the Fleet currently was.

"The *Renegat*," she repeated. "Are you sure?"

Vasiliev nodded. "I've checked everything against our files. I consulted with Cali Baker too. This message definitely came from the *Renegat*."

Gão took the tablet from Vasiliev. "Is it recent?"

Vasiliev shook her head. "It took a long time to reach us. We're not quite sure how long, but long. Would you like me to stay while you see what the message actually is?"

Gão thought about it. It would be easier to have someone else here, but it would be harder as well. She had no idea what was on the message, so she had no idea what her own reaction would be.

It would be better if Baker had been handing her the tablet. But Vasiliev only knew of the *Renegat*. She hadn't spent weeks (months) listening to Gão describe her own hesitations about it all.

"If you can remain nearby, that would be good," Gão said. "But I'd like to watch in private."

"All right," Vasiliev said, as if she had expected that response. She reached across the tablet, pulled it down, and pointed at a small area on the front. "Tap here. In theory, you should see a hologram. If it doesn't work, let me know."

"I will," Gão said.

Vasiliev nodded, then stepped out of the doorway. The door slid closed, leaving Gão alone with data streaming around her.

Instead of freezing the program, she shut it down. The towers of data winked out as if they had never been.

The room looked empty. The walls were blank. Her favorite chair looked abandoned; she had shoved it into a corner, and there it remained. If it weren't for the coffee cup on a nearby table, the room would have looked forgotten.

She moved the cup, set the tablet on the tabletop, and touched the spot on the tablet that Vasiliev had showed her.

Immediately, Nadim Crowe appeared. The holographic image was full-size. It seemed like he was standing in the study with her—or it would, if part of one of his legs wasn't being bisected by the table itself.

Vice Admiral, he said stiffly, as if he wasn't used to talking alone in a room, to someone who wasn't really there. *The situation on the* Renegat *has become dire. I waited to hear from you after our last contact, and heard nothing. I consulted with Captain Preemas, who told me that you had convinced him to forge on to the Scrapheap....*

A helpless fury rose in her so fast that she had to take a small step backwards, as if Crowe was actually standing in front of her. She paused the hologram, freezing him in place.

He looked exhausted. The shadows under his eyes were deep, and worry lines hollowed his cheekbones. He probably hadn't been eating.

Not that it mattered. Since this was an old image, from years ago.

Her hands clenched, nails digging into her palms. She had known Preemas was going to ignore her. She actually had a plan for dealing with that.

She had set that plan aside years ago, when she deemed the *Renegat* lost.

She had to remind herself that she could do nothing about this. Preemas had taken his action long ago—he had *disobeyed* her long ago—and unless he survived, which she now doubted, she could take no action at all.

Even if he had survived, she could take no action. Because he might not ever return to the Fleet. He might have found himself somewhere else entirely, doing whatever he could to keep his ship and his people alive.

But she doubted that. She doubted he would do anything for anyone else except Ivan Preemas.

She squared her shoulders, and opened her fists one finger at a time. Then she started the hologram up again.

Nadim Crowe grew more comfortable as he talked. He shifted from foot to foot a bit, but his body loosened up. His face got sadder, the lines in his skin deeper, his eyes bottomless pools of sorrow.

He hated telling her about the condition of the ship—about the things Preemas had ignored, the risks he had been taking.

And then Crowe got to the fact that Preemas had deliberately sabotaged the communications between the Fleet and the *Renegat.* Sabotaged any way for Gão to get in touch with him.

All that worry, all those efforts, and he had *deliberately blocked her?* The fury was back, doubled. And with it, frustration. Even if he was alive, she wouldn't be able to touch him. He was too far away. He had won their little contest of wills, and the hell of it was, she hadn't known it.

She had feared for them, worried about them, took the blame for their loss.

When that blame could have been put squarely on Preemas's shoulders, for disobeying orders. And taking the *Renegat* into foldspace without notifying his chief engineer? While the ship was having problems?

Preemas hadn't been thinking clearly.

No wonder Crowe had contacted her.

She paused the playback again, looking at the image of the exhausted man before her. Exhausted but not defeated. Worried, but not broken. Not yet.

Or rather, not then.

She had no idea what had become of him, and she wasn't sure how she could find out.

Whatever had happened had already happened. She had no idea how to fix that, not even in her own mind.

She took a deep breath, calming down. She believed Nadim Crowe. She had had enough encounters with Preemas to know the man was a wild card. And her experiences trying to contact the ship more or less proved Crowe's point. Something had happened to their ability to communicate, even after Crowe had reestablished the system.

After all, it had taken years for this message to reach her.

When the message ended, she would trace the route it had taken to get to her. She would see how long the message actually took. Because sometimes, ships went into foldspace and stayed there for a short time by their measure, and by the Fleet's measure, it had been years.

That was backwards from what usually happened—usually ships were in foldspace for years in their experience and only days in the Fleet's—but this way happened as well.

She knew she was being unreasonably optimistic, but that was the only way she could listen to the rest of this message, especially given how defeated Nadim Crowe already seemed.

He had a long list of things to tell her. She listened as attentively as she could, given how distraught she felt. She would have Vasiliev listen as well. Together they would see what they could do, maybe even try to find the *Renegat.*

Although Gāo knew that was a long shot at the very best.

Crowe finally moved, as he showed her the injuries he had received as the *Renegat* bumped its way through foldspace. His seemed minor, but he told her there were others, because Preemas had been so reckless.

By now, she was calmer. She had a plan, although it wasn't much of one.

Then Crowe put his arm down, and said, *Vice Admiral Gāo, I humbly request that you relieve Captain Preemas of duty. I ask that you do so by patching into our entire communications system shipwide…*

Her breath caught. Crowe looked deeply uncomfortable as he spoke, as if he knew he was walking some kind of line.

He said all the right things—that he didn't need to lead the ship, just that someone other than Preemas did. Crowe said he was following regulations, and he was more or less. He was notifying Preemas's superior officer in the only way that he could, begging for help.

He ended with this, *I don't think the* Renegat *will be able to handle the foldspace journey. I am not certain we can make the journey back to you, either…*

And she stopped him. She couldn't listen to any more.

His thoughts were probably correct. She hadn't responded, so Preemas sent them into foldspace, and Crowe, good man that he was, followed orders.

Or Preemas sidelined him somehow.

Or Crowe took over the ship after all, inspected it, tried to fix it, and tried to return.

And the journey through foldspace hadn't worked, any more than receiving this communication in a timely manner had worked.

Gão ran a hand over her face, wishing she could apologize to Crowe. Wishing she could apologize to the entire crew of the *Renegat*. Regretting the day she had failed to trust her instincts about Ivan Preemas.

She could have prevented this. She hadn't.

And she would have to live with that for the rest of her days.

PART TWENTY-THREE
THE RESCUE
NOW

THE *RENEGAT*

Floating series of impressions: the darkness of the bay, illuminated only by the lights on all the environmental suits. The man, the rescuer in charge, grabbing Serpell's arm and not letting go. Serpell's panic that he was going to rip her suit worse. The roughness of his voice in her comm system, asking if she knew how to open the doors.

Of course she didn't know how to open the doors. Why didn't *he* know how to open the doors?

Then Kabac helping with the doors, and that moment of fear as she realized that Kabac was touching the controls. She really didn't trust him. She would have said so, but the doors opened, revealing this wide-open, well-lit maw filled with cushions and no controls as if she was stepping into a gigantic playpen for babies in zero-G, and then before she could say anything about Kabac, warning about him, the man, the rescuer in charge, shoved her into the life raft as if she was just a bit of luggage.

Other people were also shoved into the life raft. Lights were on—and she hadn't realized just how much she had missed lights. Good lights, lights that illuminated everything.

And everything here was just soft walls on all sides. Designed, probably, for people who had no environmental suits or who had been injured. There were straps on each wall and there appeared to be built-in sleeping compartments, like bags attached to the walls.

It took her a moment to realize those bags were for people who were unconscious or injured or unable to hold on to straps themselves.

Things could be a lot worse. Everyone could have been so damaged they wouldn't have been able to move on their own.

She swallowed, still too lightheaded for her own good.

The cargo bay door closed. She couldn't see the interior of the bay. She couldn't see Kabac. She assumed he was still there, but she wasn't sure she cared. Or maybe she did care, but not in a good way.

A film covered the opening between the closed bay doors and this life rafty thing. Now she was really inside some kind of cube, even though it wasn't dark.

Yay! It wasn't dark. She wasn't sure she would ever be able to handle the dark again.

Welcome, said an androgynous voice in her helmet. *You are on a small rescue vessel on its way to* Aizsargs Rescue One, *a large rescue ship that will take you to the* Aizsargs, *a vessel in service to the Fleet. In less than a minute, the atmosphere will reestablish itself inside this vessel. You will be able to remove your environmental suit's helmet, should you be wearing one. You do not have to remove the helmet if you are more comfortable with it on.*

Serpell let out a small sigh of thanks. She would be all right after all.

She felt heavier than she had in hours, maybe days, and she realized that the gravity had reestablished itself too. Her feet actually touched the part of this vessel that was currently serving as the floor.

Everyone around her had hit that part of the floor too. A few people hadn't held straps and had fallen onto the floor. No wonder it was made of soft material. She wondered how long it had taken the Fleet to realize it needed soft interiors on its rescue rafts for just this moment, when gravity reasserted itself, and some people fell so hard that in any other environment they would have been injured.

There, the voice said, as if it had heard her thought. *Atmosphere has been reestablished. You may now remove your helmets if you are so inclined.*

Serpell clawed at hers, her gloved hands unable to find purchase for a moment, before she remembered she had to unhook from the inside, with a very simple command.

Her brain wasn't functioning well—probably due to diminished oxygen.

She pulled off her helmet, and felt cool air on her face. She took a deep deep *deep* breath, and realized just how long it had been since her lungs had truly been filled with air.

A couple of other people removed their helmets as well, and shook their heads like they were getting rid of dust. Maybe they were. All of them had hair matted to their scalps, which told her that their environmental suits hadn't worked well either.

Apparently no one had tested the damn suits in some time, if ever, and that was wrong all by itself.

She took another deep breath, enjoying it, not realizing until now how much she had feared never being able to breathe like this again.

Your journey to Aizsargs Rescue One *will not take long.*

The voice clearly wasn't just playing in helmets. It was also being broadcast into this little ship. Into the *atmosphere* of this little ship, where sound waves actually had something to vibrate through.

She wanted to clasp her hands together in another spontaneous applause moment, but she didn't. No one else would understand it if she did.

Once we have docked, you will be able to step off this vessel onto Aizsargs Rescue One. *From there, you will receive instructions on where you will go next. Please exit quickly upon arrival. This vessel is designed to return to the site of the rescue to remove more survivors. The quicker you exit, the more likely we will be able to help your friends, family, and colleagues.*

Serpell leaned against the wall, but she still couldn't let go of the strap that had been holding her up. Nor did she completely set aside the helmet, just in case something else went wrong.

Again, welcome aboard.

She didn't care that the words came from a recording. They comforted her, and they seemed to calm the others—at least the others who had their helmets on.

Everyone still seemed tense though, and no one let go of the straps. The people who had never grabbed them in the first place just sat where they had landed on the floor, as if they were afraid to move.

It didn't quite seem real, this rescue. And maybe it wasn't. Maybe she had died.

But she didn't think so. Because she was breathing.

And that, all by itself, was the greatest thing she had experienced in weeks.

One breath in, one breath out, gave her a feeling of safety that she would have scoffed at months ago.

One breath in. One breath out. Safe.

Finally.

Safe.

PART TWENTY-FOUR
ARRIVAL
100 YEARS AGO

THE *RENEGAT*

He didn't hear from her. The week Crowe had bought from Preemas was now up, and he hadn't heard a single word. Gão had not responded at all.

Crowe had thought she would. He still checked the logs, but not as obsessively. If he hadn't heard by now, he suspected he was never going to.

And that meant he had to make some choices. But he wasn't quite sure how to make them. He had hoped—oh, truly, he had *expected*—Gão to come through for him, so that he would accept leadership, not take it.

Now, his choices were stark. He could do nothing and try to shepherd the *Renegat* through the long foldspace trip. Or he could try to wrest control of the ship from Preemas before the journey began.

The problem with wresting control without doing any of the groundwork was that Crowe had no idea who supported him enough to rebel against their captain. Crowe might succeed, or he might spend that entire foldspace trip in the *Renegat*'s brig.

Or he might end up dead.

He wasn't afraid of dying. He was afraid of losing lives because he had made the wrong choice. Right now, when the *Renegat* went into foldspace, that choice would be Preemas's, not Crowe's.

But Crowe had made the choice, maybe as much as the week before, when he decided to wait for Gão. Maybe he had been deluding himself. Maybe he didn't want to take over the ship at all. Maybe he wasn't as strong as he thought he was.

Because he stood in Engineering now, finishing up the last of the tune-ups to all the various systems, while he awaited Preemas's shipwide order to send the *Renegat* into foldspace for the longest journey on record.

The entire Engineering crew was stationed throughout the ship. Stephanos was on the bridge, near the *anacapa* drive. Willoughby was near the officer's mess (not the captain's mess) where a secondary unit existed that allowed access to a few of the systems.

Those two women, his best engineers, could handle repairs and generally keep the ship together should something happen to Engineering itself.

Crowe was going to try to prevent that, but he had no idea what kind of strain there would be on the systems. They had all suffered some kind of wear and tear, and they had all needed some kind of tweaking. A few systems had actually needed major repair and improvements.

Crowe had done the best he could, given the supplies they had. What the *Renegat* needed was a stop at another sector base just to have experts other than him and his team look at some of these specialized systems.

But of course, there were no other sector bases nearby. There was nothing Crowe could do for some of those systems, not here, not on this trip. He had brought as many supplies and replacement parts as he could, and that hadn't been enough.

Every engineer was awake and on duty. Many of them were in Engineering, but others were scattered throughout the ship, so that they could handle localized outages. He had technicians and former engineers standing by as well.

Crowe was handling the *anacapa* systems here in Engineering. The redundant systems that might or might not cause issues. He had placed Willoughby's most trusted assistant, Luc Tosidis, near the communications *anacapa*.

Tosidis had great instincts and great credentials. He also thought fast on his feet, which Crowe appreciated. And Tosidis wasn't afraid to ask for help, either. Crowe wasn't that far away from the communications array, so he could go there, if need be.

Sometime during this excessively long (yet somehow short) week, Crowe had given up keeping the Fleet's secrets. He had told the entire engineering team about the communications *anacapa*. However, he did swear them to secrecy. He didn't want everyone on the ship to know about it.

He just wanted the people who could actually work with *anacapa* drives to understand that there was a tiny one in the communications array. He had shown them the sliver of a drive, explained how it worked, explained the problem he had found, and told them that they would do more work on it after this journey.

That way, if something happened to him or to Stephanos, someone else knew that the little drive existed.

He and Stephanos had opened the drive so that Tosidis could observe it, and maybe work on it, if need be. Crowe and Stephanos had debated that action. They worried whether or not to leave the drive completely contained like it usually was on journeys, or make it observable as it had been on that earlier journey. They had finally decided on observable.

Tosidis had one small screen open to his left, reviewing the data that Crowe had gathered from the previous foldspace journeys where he was able to look at the communications *anacapa*. Tosidis was small, his hair a yellow-blond with black highlights that made his dark skin look sallow. He had a wisp of a beard underneath his chin, and that beard was a reddish brown. He didn't seem to mind that his own personal colors clashed with each other.

In fact he didn't seem to give much attention to his appearance at all. His shirt was on inside out, and his pants were a little too loose. When Crowe had first met Tosidis, Crowe had worried about Tosidis's lack of attention to his own appearance. Now Crowe knew that Tosidis mostly lived in his head. His attention to detail—on his work—was almost as good as Stephanos's.

Tosidis seemed to feel Crowe's gaze. Tosidis looked up, and Crowe nodded back.

They were as ready as they were going to be. Now it was all up to Preemas.

Preemas had said they were going into foldspace within the hour, and the hour had already passed. Crowe was about to contact Stephanos, quietly, to see if there was some kind of problem on the bridge, when Preemas's voice boomed into engineering.

"As you know, we are heading into foldspace this afternoon. This will be a long journey in distance. We're not sure how long we'll be in foldspace, but given the bumpy ride we had the last time, we thought we should warn you that this trip will commence in five minutes or so. Put any liquid or loose items near you away, and if you're so inclined, find somewhere to strap in. This will be your only warning."

The announcement wasn't as elegant or as informative as Crowe would have liked. Nor had it come early enough for the crew to prepare the way he would have wanted.

But at least they had warning this time.

Crowe peered around the equipment. He could only see three of his engineering crew besides Tosidis. They had braced themselves as if the journey had already begun.

Then Tosidis frowned and peered at the communications *anacapa*, a faint light illuminating the side of his face.

That light was the only real warning that Crowe had. The *Renegat* bumped and vibrated as if it were a much smaller ship heading into some planet's atmosphere. The bumping changed to a kind of thudding, and then an irregular rolling that almost made Crowe lose his footing.

The hair on the back of his neck and his arms rose. He glanced down at his skin. It was pebbled with goosebumps. The air had a charge to it, as if some kind of energy had been released.

The light on Tosidis's face had faded. Then one of the other crew members lunged at the panel in front of them—just as the ship's automated voice warned that environmental controls were being compromised.

Two other engineers hurried toward the environmental controls tower, tripping over their own feet as they went. They reached it as Crowe could feel the gravity getting lighter. He could still stand, but he felt floaty, one of those senses that usually happened before gravity disappeared altogether.

The rolling had become bumping, but it was less noticeable as the gravity faded. Then Crowe felt heavier. The gravity had returned. Someone let out a weak

"Yay!" from the engineering corner, that got covered up as the ship's automated voice said,

Danger averted. Environmental controls stabilized.

Crowe had no idea if that voice had spoken to the entire crew or just in engineering. He didn't have time to think about either implication. The bumping made his teeth chatter.

All of the readings in his little area were just fine. Then that pebbly feeling increased. He could feel energy on his skin. It felt like he had walked into some kind of charge. It washed over him, prickly and filled with some kind of static.

If that was what had happened the last time, then the attitude controls might have been taken out by some kind of static charge, not by anything inside the *anacapa* drive itself.

"Hey!" he said to the crew through his communications link. "Don't touch anything right now."

He saw Tosidis nod. Crowe couldn't quite see anyone else. He hoped no one on the bridge touched anything either. Or maybe they weren't even feeling this.

The sense of being inside some kind of prickly energy field increased. The prickling grew into tiny painful stabs, as if he were being jabbed with a thousand needles on all of his exposed skin. He closed his eyes, protecting himself from the sensation there at least. Then the prickling/stabbing started on the edge of his ears, on his lips, on his cheeks. He wanted to brush it off, but he couldn't.

He wasn't sure he dared to move.

The tiny stabbing sensation grew worse. It felt like something was puncturing his skin. He could now feel those stabs through the thin parts of his clothing—his sleeves, his pants around his upper thighs, and the tops of his feet where his socks slid into his shoes. His skin was swelling in response to that continual stabbing pressure.

The ship continued to bump and roll, the foldspace journey going on forever and ever and ever. He wasn't sure how much longer he could take the pain. He wanted to check with his crew, but he didn't want to open his mouth, afraid that the prickling/stabbing sensation would go to his vulnerable gums and tongue and the inside of his cheeks. Maybe even go right down his throat.

The bumping grew in teeth-chattering regularity. He felt his feet slide across the floor, but the gravity remained on. He resisted the urge to put out a hand to steady himself, hoping his static/energy-covered body didn't slide into nearby equipment.

Then the bumping stopped. It took a moment for him to realize it had stopped. The hair went down on his arms and the back of his neck, and the prickling/stabbing sensation eased. But his skin hurt, as if he had a thousand tiny cuts on each inch of exposed flesh.

He waited one more minute before opening his eyes. When he did, he looked down at the backs of his hands first. They were red, and still pebbled, like as if he had been bitten by teeny tiny bugs.

But that staticky feeling was completely gone. The air no longer felt charged. He no longer felt like he was under attack.

But his entire body ached. His jaw hurt because his teeth had chattered into each other so hard it felt like he might have cracked one of his molars.

He made himself blink, felt tears—not from pain (he hoped) but from some kind of relief.

Then he took a tentative step forward, saw Tosidis looking at his hands, so Crowe knew that strange experience had been universal.

Something crackled, then Preemas's voice boomed into engineering. *In case you haven't noticed, we have left foldspace. You can continue your duties.*

Preemas didn't say that they had arrived wherever they had planned on arriving. He wouldn't even have had time to check or not. Preemas and Breaux were probably examining the records—what few they had of the area around that Scrapheap.

Crowe couldn't think about any of that anyway. He needed to concentrate on the equipment.

"Damage reports?" he said to his team.

"Nothing so far," said Torrey Spade. She was one of the people who had run toward the environmental system.

"I don't want to touch anything," said Benjamin Bakhr. He was young, but he had proven himself reliable over the past week. "But it all looks good."

Others checked in as well, and found no problems.

But their voices shook as they spoke, and their eyes looked haunted. Crowe didn't ask, but he had a hunch the rest of them felt like he did; they didn't want to go back through foldspace for a long, long time.

And if Preemas made them take that same kind of journey on the return trip...

Crowe didn't want to contemplate it.

Tosidis was the only one who hadn't answered him. He was still standing near the open communications array. Crowe stepped closer to him.

Tosidis's skin looked raw, as if someone had slapped him repeatedly all over his face. Crowe wondered if he looked the same way, but didn't ask. He would deal with the physical fallout later—if there was any.

"I'm sorry," Tosidis said quietly. "I didn't watch the drive. I closed my eyes. The pain—"

"I know," Crowe said. "I have no idea what that was, but I've never experienced it before."

"Me either," Tosidis said. Bakhr nodded from his station. Apparently their voices carried just enough.

Tosidis waved a hand at the small drive. "We started into foldspace, and another foldspace window formed. I was about to send in the probe when that sticky feeling started."

Crowe hadn't thought of it as sticky, although that wasn't a bad description either. Whatever it had been, it didn't feel natural.

"And I just closed my eyes." Tosidis was whispering now. "I completely lost track of what I was doing, and then you said not to touch anything, and the next thing I know, we're here."

Wherever here was. Crowe nodded. He wasn't going to yell at Tosidis. He wasn't going to yell at any of them. Whatever had just happened to them had been extreme. He saw no point in reprimanding them for acting like human beings instead of some kind of unfeeling creature.

Crowe moved as close to Tosidis as he could, so that he could see the tiny *anacapa*. It rested in its little bed, looking completely normal. There was no evidence of a foldspace window or of that light that Crowe had seen reflected on Tosidis's face.

The area around the little *anacapa* drive seemed normal as well. The fact that the *Renegat* had just gone through the longest foldspace journey ever didn't seem to have made a difference in the little *anacapa* drive.

Crowe glanced at Tosidis. Tosidis wasn't looking at the drive. He was looking at Crowe. Crowe shrugged, then reached into the small space around the drive.

Crowe hadn't touched anything since he had told the crew to keep their hands off the equipment, but he had walked to this spot. If the static had remained, he would have noticed it as his feet touched the floor.

His gaze held Tosidis's for just a moment. Tosidis looked scared. His skin was pale and his eyes seemed even more sunken than they had earlier.

Crowe, he just realized, wasn't scared at all. He was ready to determine what kind of mess Preemas had gotten them into, and to figure out a way out of that mess.

Crowe was ready to take real action for the first time since this mission began.

And the first step in this real action was pretty simple: he had to touch the small *anacapa* drive.

He had held *anacapa* drives off and on throughout his career. No one became an engineer, let alone a chief engineer, without the ability to touch an *anacapa* drive. The energy in those drives sometimes made people anxious or angry or terrified, which meant those people couldn't work on the drives at all.

He had none of those problems. He had always approached the drives with respect, but never trepidation.

Until now.

He swallowed hard, then turned his gaze onto the little sliver of a drive. Then he extended his right hand, and brushed the drive with his index finger.

The drive felt smooth and just a little warm, like active *anacapa* drives usually did after going through foldspace. He felt a faint echoing energy filtering through his bones. His teeth hummed slightly, not like they had while the ship was in foldspace, but like there was some residual energy that had made its way to his mouth.

He brought his hand back, then let it fall to his side.

"I have no idea what I expected," he said, "but it appears that nothing is different."

"That's good, right?" Tosidis asked.

Crowe didn't answer directly. "Anyone seeing anomalies?" he asked through his comm.

He got some denials, and that was it. No one said they were encountering problems.

"Um, Nadim?" the voice was soft. It belonged to Stephanos. It sounded like she was trying to keep her communication with him hidden.

"Yes, Natalia?" he asked.

"Have you looked outside the ship?" she asked, in that same subdued tone.

He hadn't. He had been so focused on the changes inside the ship that outside seemed very far away to him.

"Problem?" he asked.

"Almost," she said, her voice nearly a whisper.

That caught his attention. He brought up a holographic screen and looked at the external view of the ship.

The *Renegat* hovered at the edge of a Scrapheap—at the very edge, as close to the Scrapheap as a ship could get without being inside the Scrapheap.

Crowe's heart started pounding, hard. They had nearly opened a foldspace window inside a Scrapheap, something he hadn't done ever, something the experts believed caused the disaster that had destroyed that Scrapheap in his youth.

He made himself breathe. He was the first officer and chief engineer of a ship of the Fleet, not the boy who had gotten his friends killed. The *Renegat* hadn't appeared inside that Scrapheap. The disaster had been averted—if, indeed, it would have been a disaster.

Although, judging by Stephanos's tone, she had thought it would have been.

"I guess we're here, then," Crowe said as calmly as he could. "I guess we're finally here."

THE *RENEGAT*

Crowe called up a holographic image of the area around the *Renegat*. He wanted as clear a view of that Scrapheap as he could get.

He could just see the edges of it. It was large—larger than he expected. The protected area was much bigger than the area from the Scrapheap he had helped destroy.

He didn't have exact figures, but he knew that this Scrapheap was huge and unwieldy, just from the glimpses he got now.

The edges of the Scrapheap sparked and glowed. The force field around it didn't look like anything he had seen before. It was visible to the naked eye, for one thing, which wasn't at all like the usual Fleet force field. Behind it, he caught glimpses of ships and ship parts. Some of the ships had the curved design of a DV-Class ship, but others were round. Most of them had damage—at least the ones he could see easily.

He frowned at the Scrapheap, thinking it represented yet another problem that he would have to deal with.

But at least they were here. Which was going to make Preemas ecstatic, thinking that his method—the method that Crowe did not recommend—had worked.

Crowe had no idea what was happening on the bridge. He almost didn't care. He figured that Preemas was celebrating his own wisdom in getting them to the Scrapheap, without seeing the fact that he had nearly gotten them killed.

Clearly, Stephanos had seen how close they had come to disaster. And if she had seen it, others had as well.

But Crowe couldn't concern himself with the others right now. He couldn't concern himself with the personality details inside the ship. He needed to deal with the Scrapheap first.

He walked to the center of engineering, to an area that he had been using when the engineering crew had been working on its deep systems check of the ship. He called up several different views of the Scrapheap—some large, some very small.

Willoughby had left the officer's mess once they came out of foldspace. She had hurried to engineering, joining him, her face taut.

"We need to look at the energy readings," she said.

She was right. The way that force field was sparking was a visual warning for them.

"Do so," he said. "And move a team to diagnostics here on the *Renegat*. Let's see how well we survived foldspace."

He was giving the orders almost reflexively. He needed to see this Scrapheap almost more than he needed to check on the ship.

He wasn't quite sure where the need was coming from. Maybe from a fear he wasn't sure he wanted to acknowledge.

It only took a few minutes for him to get holographic images of the Scrapheap set up the way he wanted them to. He placed a three-dimensional image of the Scrapheap in the very center of all of his floating screens. The three-D image floated a few inches off the floor.

At first, he thought that the image's resolution was poor. Then he realized that the Scrapheap was filled with holes. The center of the Scrapheap only had a handful of ships, stationary, as if something was holding them in place. Parts floated around them like waves around rocks.

He had never seen anything like that before.

He moved away from the two-D floating screens to study the three-D image more closely. He walked around it, hands clasped behind his back. His skin was no longer pebbled, and although it ached, it didn't feel as bad as it had.

Small blessing, while he was focused on all of this.

He peered at the three-D image, thinking that something was wrong with it. Then he turned and saw the two-D images were sparse as well.

There appeared to be holes in the force field. There were also gaps throughout the Scrapheap.

And a darkness in the middle that made his stomach twist, although he didn't know why.

"I don't like the energy readings," Willoughby said from behind him. "That Scrapheap is giving off waves of energy like nothing I have ever seen before."

"*Anacapa* energy?" Crowe asked.

"I don't know," she said.

He wheeled around, and headed to the screens she had been using. The energy readings included familiar energies, the kind given off by standard Fleet drives, mixed with some *anacapa* energy, the kind dying drives gave off as well as the kind that drives in rest mode gave off. But there were several other kinds of energy as well, things his system couldn't readily identify.

They mixed and floated together, creating some kind of bubble. He couldn't tell if that was deliberate, either, or if it was some kind of defensive measure, designed to attack anything that got too close to the Scrapheap itself.

He cursed. "This ship has to move, now."

Only he knew that Preemas wouldn't order the move. Preemas would see that as some kind of rebuke against what he had just done. Preemas would probably want to remain as close to the Scrapheap as possible.

"Are you going to go to the bridge?" Willoughby's voice wobbled as she said that, and he realized that she was scared to have him leave engineering.

He didn't want to leave either. There were too many unknowns here.

"No," he said. "We'll move the *Renegat*. Right now."

"Sir?" Willoughby asked.

He didn't say any more. He just went to the backup controls and programmed a course away from the Scrapheap. As he did so, he locked out the bridge command.

He worked fast, so that no one on the bridge could respond to any notifications or warnings.

The *Renegat* responded quickly, moving as fast as she could away from the Scrapheap.

"How far does that energy bubble go?" he asked Willoughby. He could see what he thought was the end of it, but he needed someone to double-check his numbers. He had no idea what would happen if he miscalculated, but he didn't want to find out.

She told him, and her numbers were the same as his.

He reset the coordinates, sending the *Renegat* twice the distance needed, just to be safe.

"What the hell are you doing, Crowe?" Preemas's voice boomed through the entire engineering department. "I order you to restore the command to the bridge immediately."

The way Preemas's voice echoed, it might not have gone to just the engineering department. Preemas might have been broadcasting to the entire ship.

Crowe's mouth went dry. He had taken a step to save their lives, and it ended up being the step that he had tried to get Gão to take for him. He had taken over the ship, without really thinking about it.

"Are you going to answer him?" Willoughby asked, that wobble still in her voice.

"I've got more important things to do right now," Crowe said. He had to make sure that the bubble wasn't designed to pursue them. He doubted it was, but he had no evidence. He had seen nothing like it.

He veered the *Renegat* away from the Scrapheap, running parallel with it before heading perpendicular again.

The energy bubble grew, but didn't seem to follow them.

"Crowe!" Preemas's voice was louder and filled with what Crowe had once privately called Preemas's command bark. "Cease what you're doing and return control of the ship to me this instant!"

The *Renegat* mapped nearby areas of the system. There were several good-sized planets, some of which could easily sustain human life (and probably did). He wasn't looking to see if any of them had space travel capability. He was actually looking for a safe place to hide the *Renegat* from that bubble, and he finally found it in a secondary moon off a cold and dead planet.

He placed the *Renegat* on the opposite side of that moon from the Scrapheap, then let out a small breath.

"Crowe!" Preemas shouted. "Crowe, I demand that you cease this instant."

Crowe finally decided to answer him, publicly, through the comm.

"Or what?" Crowe asked. "Or you'll send us back to the Scrapheap? Because if we had stayed there much longer, the ship would have exploded."

"You're making that up," Preemas snapped.

"Which is precisely why I didn't consult with you before taking the ship away from the Scrapheap," Crowe said calmly. "We needed action, not argument."

"You have no right to take such actions without my okay," Preemas said.

"I'm your First Officer and Chief Engineer," Crowe said. "I have every right."

Then he shut off the comm. He was wrong, and he knew it, but he didn't care. The crew needed to hear the argument, and needed to hear it from both of them.

Crowe ran a hand over his hair, smoothing it against his scalp.

Willoughby was standing near him, twisting her hands together. Her eyes seemed bigger than he had ever seen them.

"I don't want to bring you into the middle of all of this," Crowe said.

"I'm already in the middle," Willoughby said. Her voice was calmer than her hands or her eyes for that matter. She looked terrified.

"All right," he said. "If you're willing to help me..."

"Of course," she said just a bit too fervently. "Why wouldn't I be?"

He could think of a dozen reasons, all of them good, but most of them traditional. They were in new territory. He was aware of that, but Preemas clearly wasn't.

And Crowe had no idea how many other people on the ship were aware of it either.

Clearly, Willoughby was.

"I need you to monitor the controls here in engineering," Crowe said. "I need you to make certain that no one manages to route control back to the bridge."

She nodded, her lips thin.

"You do realize that I'm asking you to help me disobey the captain," he said, just to be clear.

She opened her mouth, as if she was going to say something sarcastic. Then she seemed to think the better of it.

"Yes," she said. "I do."

And before he could ask her if she was willing, she moved in beside him and called up a few more screens so that she could handle whatever came her way.

"What else do you need?" A voice behind Crowe made him jump. Tosidis was standing there, looking nervous.

"Helping me right now is probably not a good idea," Crowe said.

"I don't see the logic in that," Tosidis said. "You're the one keeping us alive."

Crowe let out a small breath. "All right," he said. "Let's seal off engineering until we know exactly what we're dealing with."

Rather than opening the comm to everyone in engineering, he stepped back into the center where his hologram was, and raised his voice.

"Hey, everyone! I need your attention."

The engineers who were assigned the Engineering bay came out of their alcoves.

He met their gazes one by one. Everyone looked nervous. The only person in the entire area who wasn't watching him was Willoughby. She continued to monitor the command controls.

"You all heard my interaction with the captain," Crowe said. "He's going to be angry at my behavior."

Hell, he already was angry. But Crowe didn't correct himself.

"I'm going to seal off engineering. But before I do, I wanted to offer those of you who feel I'm in the wrong the chance to leave. I don't want the captain to blame you for what I'm going to do."

"What are you going to do?" Hadley Ellum asked. Her voice was soft, as if she wasn't sure if she really wanted to know his answer.

"What we're trained to do," Crowe said. "We're going to study that Scrapheap before we get close to it again. We're going to figure out what that energy bubble was and whether or not it was a direct threat."

"That seems sensible," Bakhr said.

"Yes, it does," Tosidis said, almost angrily, as if he couldn't believe that following procedure might cause problems with the captain.

"I'm going to seal off engineering while I do it," Crowe said, "and keep control of the ship here. That's what the captain will object to."

"Maybe you should give him a chance to actually object....?" James Rodriguez said.

Crowe looked at him. He looked gray, his eyes sunken into his face. Rodriguez was clearly scared and overwhelmed. Crowe didn't blame him. This trip—this command—these events were hard on everyone.

"The captain and I have been going round and round about the best way to handle this entire trip," Crowe said. "I have followed his procedures until today. You all know why I moved the ship. You can double-check my data if you like."

No one moved. They knew how meticulous he was. Several of the engineering crew had told him they liked that about him.

"All right," Crowe said after a long minute. "Whoever wants to leave should do so now."

A couple of the engineers shifted slightly. Hadley Ellum peered around the edge of her alcove, as if to see if anyone else was contemplating leaving. No one else moved. Then she looked in the other direction.

Rodriguez tilted his head just a little. She nodded.

Together they stepped forward, and started to the door.

She stopped in front of Crowe, a slight frown on her face.

He braced himself for recriminations. Instead, she said, "You know this isn't personal, right? I really respect you, sir. I just—it's the rules. I mean, you're doing something kinda like mutiny. And I can't be part of it."

There was that word, the one he had been avoiding in his head. *Mutiny*. If he ended up taking over the ship, over Preemas's objections, that wasn't *kinda like mutiny.* That definitely *was* mutiny.

A couple of the other engineers shifted in place as well. Apparently, they hadn't thought of his behavior in those terms.

"I understand," Crowe said. "That's why I offered all of you the opportunity to leave now. I don't want any of you to get blamed for my actions."

Two more engineers stepped out of their alcoves. One shot Crowe a worried glance, but said nothing. The other kept his head down as he walked to the door, maybe ashamed of what he was doing.

Or maybe he just didn't want to face Crowe at all.

Crowe remained motionless, waiting for them to leave. As they stepped out, he said, "Anyone else?"

No one responded.

"You're about to miss your chance," he said.

Everyone stood very still. Their faces were serious; their expressions taut. A few were threading their fingers together the way that Willoughby had earlier.

"All right." Crowe reached to the small screen floating in front of him, and pressed the controls. "The doors are closing."

The doors rattled as they sealed, which he thought was somehow appropriate. It was almost as if the entire engineering department was nervous, including the equipment.

He made himself take a deep breath. Mutiny.

That was a problem he would have to deal with when—if—when he returned to the Fleet. This ship had to survive the next few days first.

The doors shut, and then beeped as they sealed.

He closed the small screen, and looked up at the hologram of the Scrapheap.

"Okay," he said. "Let's figure out what we're facing."

He nearly added, *Outside of the ship*, but he didn't. They all had a hunch about what they were facing inside.

But outside—that was the key. And that was the great unknown.

He nodded at all of them, and then got to work.

THE *RENEGAT*

Captain Preemas slammed his hand on the arm of his captain's chair.

"I want control back on this bridge and I want it now!" he shouted.

Half the bridge crew ducked. Natalia Stephanos hadn't moved away from the *anacapa* drive, her head down. Milton Atwater shot Justine Breaux a panicked look.

Atwater was standing only a few yards away from her, watching as he always did during a foldspace journey. He had looked tense on this one. He had thought the prolonged trip one of the worst ideas he had heard of. He had actually advised the captain against it.

Breaux hadn't given any advice at all, but she had gently told Captain Preemas that she had no real maps of the area. The historical record wasn't just spotty. It was non-existent.

She had found some information about the Scrapheap by modifying the notices that the Scrapheap had sent, the notices that had pushed the *Renegat* onto this path in the first place.

But the information hadn't been visual. It had been a signature, one from the Scrapheap itself.

She had to modify the equipment she had been using so that it could track the signature of any Scrapheap they had come into contact with.

When they had arrived, so close to the Scrapheap that it took her breath away, she had double-checked the signature. It was the same. But, as she tried to tell the captain, that didn't mean it *was* the same. She wasn't sure her equipment could handle the reading or if the ancient Scrapheap before them was the actual Scrapheap they were looking for.

Of course it is, Captain Preemas had snapped. *It's at the right coordinates, and it has the right signature. Just because we don't have maps doesn't mean we're wrong.*

He had seemed charged even then, and that was before First Officer Crowe had somehow shut down the bridge. He had moved the ship without the captain's permission, which infuriated Preemas, making him scream at everyone.

"He's completely sealed us off," said Yulia Colvin. She was talking about Crowe. "We can't do anything from here."

"That's impossible," Preemas said. "We should be able to reroute the equipment so that we have control of the ship."

"It's not impossible." Stephanos spoke up. She was standing straight, her expression flat.

Breaux got the sense that Stephanos didn't want Preemas to know how she really felt.

"Oh?" Preemas asked. "You should be able to fix this."

"Technically, you're right, sir," Stephanos said, in a very flat voice. It almost felt as if she was talking to a wayward child. "But it seems that First Officer Crowe initiated invasion protocols."

Breaux frowned. She had never heard of this, but it sounded straightforward.

"Impossible," Preemas said. "Only a captain can do that."

Stephanos tilted her head slightly, either acknowledging him or disagreeing with him. "First Officer Crowe is one of the best engineers in the Fleet," she said.

The implication was clear. If anyone could initiate that programming, it was Crowe.

Breaux held her breath. Her heart was pounding. She had a vague feeling of being out of control right from the start of this journey, but she had welcomed that feeling. She had done her best to set that feeling aside. She was good at ignoring things.

Only now, she couldn't ignore the feeling. The captain didn't have control of the ship. First Officer Crowe did, for reasons she didn't entirely understand.

And they were far away from backup, from help, from any assistance at all.

She stood rigidly and watched as the conversation played out.

Captain Preemas glared at the floating screens in front of him as if he could change them. Then he ran his fingers on the arm of his captain's chair.

Other controls were there, specific ones. Breaux had seen them, but she had no real idea what, exactly, they did. Preemas seemed frustrated by them. His fist curled above them, as if he wanted to pound the arm of that chair as hard as he could.

Then he straightened, and looked at Stephanos.

"You will go down to engineering and fix this," he said to her.

She still had that odd, impassive look on her face. It was as if her face had frozen into one expression, and one expression only.

"Chief Engineer Crowe has sealed off engineering," she said.

Captain Preemas cursed, long and loud. Inventive language that Breaux had never heard before.

She almost glanced at Atwater, to see how he was reacting to all of this, but she didn't. Because she had a strong feeling that if she did look at him, and if his gaze at all mirrored hers, she would burst into tears.

Oh, get ahold of yourself, Justine, she thought.

She had been the one to put her life in their hands. She had been the one who volunteered to come here, even after dozens of others had left the ship. She had thought it would be an adventure.

Well, it *was* an adventure, and she was now paying for that.

It was what she had wished for.

She clenched her own fists, and continued to watch, trying to mirror Stephanos's expression. Show no emotion. Just get through this. One moment at a time, if need be.

These people were experts. They knew what they were doing.

Her heart thudded against her chest. She didn't believe that last. She was beginning to understand that none of them understood what they were doing. This was as new to them as it was to her.

And that terrified her even more.

"Are you refusing to go to engineering?" Preemas asked Stephanos.

"It won't do any good," she said. "Do you know a way to unlock an invasion override? Because I sure don't."

Preemas turned his back on her and walked to the ready room. He reached for the door, as if the answers lived inside that room. Then he stopped.

"Yeah," he said. "I do know how. And so do you. We're going to my quarters."

Stephanos's hard expression finally cracked. She seemed uncertain. "If he has invasion protocols on, you won't be able to use the controls in your quarters."

"There's an override that I always activate whenever I command a ship," Captain Preemas said. "I can get control of the ship back, but I would like your help."

Breaux's gaze was on Stephanos only. And Stephanos finally looked scared. Was that because she supported Crowe? Or because she felt like this plan wouldn't work?

Breaux had no idea.

The pause after Captain Preemas's comment went on too long. Everyone on the bridge stopped whatever they were doing and looked at Stephanos.

"I will go with you," she said.

Captain Preemas was studying her. Something in his expression told Breaux that he didn't trust her. Not entirely.

And then Breaux realized that Captain Preemas had asked Stephanos to come, not ordered her to. Had he suspected her loyalty all along?

"The rest of you," Captain Preemas said as Stephanos stepped around her console. "You need to see if you can override whatever it is that Crowe's doing. And also be prepared for the control to come back to the bridge. Because, at that moment, we are going to shut him down."

Whatever that meant. Breaux almost asked Captain Preemas what he wanted her to do, but she didn't. She didn't want to get into the middle of this at all.

She would find out more about the area, double-check her own work, make sure they were at the right Scrapheap.

She glanced at the image of the Scrapheap on the tablet still clutched in her left hand. The Scrapheap, which everyone seemed to have forgotten. The Scrapheap, the point of all of this, the reason they had come here.

The Scrapheap, looming over all of them, as if it was waiting for them to decide what to do next.

PART TWENTY-FIVE
THE RESCUE
NOW

THE *RENEGAT*

It took Zarges more time than he wanted to disengage his helper from the cargo bay doors. The man—and it was a man—wanted to continue helping until the last person had left the *Renegat.*

Zarges had no idea who this guy was, but he seemed scarily determined. He wanted to control those doors, as if they were the most important thing in the cargo bay.

Zarges let the guy do the job for a while, as Zarges bodily pushed half of the survivors onto the life raft. It wasn't that they didn't want to leave—they clearly did—it was that they were also afraid to get onto the life raft itself.

He wasn't sure what had happened to these people but they were the most timid group he had ever rescued—at least the most timid group of Fleet members. If they were Fleet members.

He was starting to have his doubts.

He had just heard from Iqbar. As she prepared to close her life raft in Cargo Bay Two, three more stragglers had found their way to her. She contacted Zarges, asked him if the remaining six people had arrived in his Cargo Bay.

"Not yet," he said. But Palmer had. And so had Khusru and her team.

He was loading the last of his evacuees onto the life raft. He didn't see any lights coming down the corridor or reflecting off the cargo in the bay.

But he couldn't leave six people behind.

"This ship is pretty unstable," Palmer said. "We can't wait."

"I know," Zarges said to him. "Here's what I want to do. I want you and the rest of the team to get into the life rafts and go back to *Rescue One.*"

Palmer brought his head up as the others, listening in on the comm, made noises of protest.

"What will you do?" Palmer asked.

"I'm going to find the missing six," Zarges said. "Get the life raft back to *Rescue One*, then send one last life raft here."

What he didn't add was that if the ship blew, they might lose a life raft. But he didn't really care. He was willing to risk losing one life raft to save six lives.

Besides, if it didn't work, he would not be around to face the consequences. If the Fleet got pissy about the loss of equipment, everyone could blame him.

Rightfully.

"I'll stay too," Palmer said.

"No," Zarges said. "They're probably not that far from here. I just have to wait and get them on board. I know how to work the doors now, and I can do this without help."

"Are they nearby?" Palmer asked *Rescue One*.

Rescue One was tracking life signs. Zarges was finally convinced the life signs *Rescue One* had seen were all of the life signs on board the *Renegat*.

"The six people are not nearby," Ranaldi said from *Rescue One*. "But they will arrive within ten minutes."

Palmer flicked his light on inside his helmet so that Zarges could see his face. Palmer shook his head, his mouth a thin line.

His message was clear. He didn't believe they had ten minutes.

But he wasn't going to say that because, like Zarges, he didn't want someone to overrule them and keep the life raft away from the *Renegat*.

Those six people needed a chance.

"I'll wait for them," Zarges said. "You need to go. I want *Rescue One* as far from this ship as possible. Once the life raft disengages from this ship, then *Rescue One* can come get us. Not a moment sooner."

Palmer closed his eyes for just a moment, the blink long and slow and deliberate. They both knew the timing would be dicey at best. Life rafts were slow things, without a lot of power. Even though Zarges could control it from the inside, he wouldn't be able to get it out of the blast radius quickly if the ship followed the projected schedule.

Rescue One might decide it was too dangerous to pull the final life raft to safety.

And that was a decision he would be fine with. They all would in different circumstances.

Even waiting for these six people was probably a bad idea. But he wouldn't be able to live with himself if he didn't. He couldn't. He would always imagine them arriving just as the bay doors closed a final time, waiting in the dark and cold for a rescue that was never, ever going to come.

He couldn't be responsible for that.

Not after the last time. He had lost dozens of people on that rescue.

He wasn't about to lose six more.

THE *AIZSARGS*

"He's going to do *what?*" Dauber asked. She looked at the kaleidoscope of images rising about her tablet, all in three dimensions. *Rescue One* hung back, two life rafts heading toward it, with a third making a repeat visit to the disabled vessel.

Everyone on the bridge looked at her. She had never used that tone before, not with this team. Maybe she hadn't used the tone ever. It had a tinge of panic. Because she knew what was coming.

Damn Zarges. He was gambling. She hated it when her crew members gambled.

To the credit of the bridge crew, none of them gamed his chances of success. They were as alarmed as she was, maybe more so.

The trail of atmosphere from the *Renegat* had finally ceased, and she didn't like that. She also didn't like the look of the telemetry she had scrolling on one side.

There was an increase in energy. Unstable energy, the kind she'd seen coming out of foldspace in the past.

She had ordered the fighters away from the ship almost an hour ago, and she'd been sweating *Rescue One*. The readings from the *Renegat's anacapa* drive showed that it was terribly unstable, and the resulting explosion would be catastrophic.

Rescue One already had one hundred survivors on board. She could order *Rescue One* to return to the *Aizsargs* now, but that bordered on cruel. She had—she hoped—the extra few minutes for the remaining two life rafts to dock with *Rescue One*.

But the third one? That was a wish. Not even a prayer. It wasn't going to survive.

"He thinks the missing six passengers will arrive in time," Ornitz said.

"I knew I shouldn't have sent him," Dauber said. "He's gotten soft."

"It's not soft to try to rescue six people," said Lauritz.

"It is when it will cost more lives and equipment," Dauber snapped. "Zarges knows that. He knows what the regulations are. Throughout his entire career, he's made the right call. This is the first time he hasn't."

"The first time he's been out in almost a year," Almadi said softly. "Perhaps he wasn't ready."

"Or perhaps," Ullman said just as softly, "he decided he didn't want to lose anyone again."

"He doesn't get to make that decision," Dauber said.

But Zarges had. Because she couldn't recall the life raft. It was nearly to the *Renegat.* And he had already stayed behind.

One of her best officers, and he was on a suicide mission to save six people he didn't even know, people who might have nothing to do with the Fleet, people who could be thieves or murderers, people who didn't deserve his sacrifice.

She folded her hands together, then squeezed them tight. Damn him.

Damn him for taking the choice away from her.

Damn him for making her watch this, even when she knew it was going to go all wrong.

PART TWENTY-SIX
CONTROL
100 YEARS AGO

THE *RENEGAT*

The Scrapheap was huge. It covered an area that could have encompassed two large planets—and all of the distance between them. To Crowe's surprise, however, the Scrapheap wasn't full. It wasn't even close to full.

He stood in the middle of all of the data he had pulled from that Scrapheap, trying to ignore all the crises around him. Occasionally Preemas would bleat something through the comms, something about getting control of the ship back.

Crowe could ignore that. He liked being able to concentrate on something else. And right now, the Scrapheap—and the energy it was giving off—was more important than Preemas.

Crowe had Preemas under control, at least for the moment. Occasionally, Crowe would glance at a screen that showed the bridge. Everyone on the bridge looked flustered and confused. Some of that was because they weren't the most experienced bridge crew, but most of it was because of the crisis Crowe had caused, and Preemas's reaction to it.

The remaining engineers seemed less nervous than Crowe expected. Maybe it was the work that faced them. They needed to figure out what was happening with the Scrapheap, and they were all good at focusing at the expense of everything going on around them.

Thank goodness.

Even he felt less tired, less panicked, than he had felt before. He had a task now—several tasks—and he had somehow found the concentration to deal with them.

Maybe because he liked a good puzzle.

And the Scrapheap was proving to be a puzzle.

Parts of the Scrapheap—at least that his system registered—glistened in the way that very old security fields glistened. Old fields like that were dangerous and hadn't been used in centuries. Crowe had come across those old fields when he trained on the first SC-Class vessel he'd ever served on.

Those old fields were unstable, and didn't always protect areas that they seemed to be covering. And sometimes they worked too well—shooting down nearby ships that should have received only warnings.

He couldn't believe that this Scrapheap would attack the *Renegat*, but he did not know for certain. He was glad that he had moved the ship away.

"When we first got information on that Scrapheap," Tosidis said, "it looked full."

Tosidis had moved closer to Crowe, probably so that he could see the Scrapheap better. And Tosidis was right: the Scrapheap seemed to have a lot more ships in that information that had made it to the Fleet.

But some of that information got rebuilt from the data stream. So the guesses that whoever rebuilt the data made could have been wrong.

"We have no idea how old that information was," Crowe said, "or how long it had been traveling to get to us."

"Judging by how empty this thing is, it must have been decades."

"Or not." Crowe had examined those logs early in this voyage. "Ships were returning every five days. Whoever had taken ships out of this Scrapheap had done so in a systematic way."

He wasn't as concerned with the loss of DV-Class vessels that the Scrapheap had suffered. Most of those vessels were at least a thousand years old. He was concerned about the loss of their *anacapa* drives, which he knew had happened because those drives had gotten the ships out of the Scrapheap in the first place.

The major concern, though, and the one he and Preemas had discussed when they were still discussing things, was that it appeared that the Ready Vessels area had been compromised. Crowe knew, given the scattered information that the Fleet had received, that the area he considered the Ready Vessel area might not have been filled with Ready Vessels.

It might not have been anything other than another storage area. He wasn't even sure the Fleet stored Ready Vessels in Scrapheaps this old.

But Crowe had to act on the assumption that the Fleet had, and if it had, then the situation around this Scrapheap was much more dire than Crowe had initially imaged.

Because Ready Vessels had been designed to maintain their systems, and keep them activated. Those ships were to move themselves into the main part of the Scrapheap if they no longer worked properly—ostensibly to await repair, but mostly to suffer a slow decline.

Those ships weren't just state-of-the-art at the time they had been hidden in the Scrapheap. They were also completely functional vessels with no flaws at all. If someone stole one of those ships, that someone could have used the vessel for decades with no serious problems at all.

Crowe wouldn't be able to check on the Ready Vessels until he figured out the Scrapheap's codes. He had also worked on that early in the voyage, but hadn't gotten far.

Although that wasn't his most pressing problem.

Preemas had just left the bridge. He was probably going to his quarters to regain control of the ship.

He wouldn't be able to.

And that was the moment that would seal Crowe's fate as a mutineer, should he ever get tried inside the Fleet. Because removing the command closet in the captain's quarters showed that Crowe had planned to take over the ship for some time—even if the message he sent to Gão had never gotten through.

Crowe's stomach did a slow flip.

He glanced around engineering. Everyone was working on the Scrapheap now, except Willoughby who was staying ahead of the bridge crew. Everything they tried to regain control of the ship, she rebuffed.

Of course, it helped that he had set up invasion protocols. That he *had* planned ahead for. He had removed all trace of Captain Preemas from those protocols, and had done so weeks ago. If someone had tried to take over the ship, Crowe didn't trust Preemas enough to handle the situation well.

Preemas couldn't regain control of the ship even if he were as smart about engineering as Crowe was. Not from the bridge. Not from the minimal systems in the officer's mess. Not anywhere.

The mistake Crowe had made, however, was forgetting that Preemas could enlist help. Crowe hadn't blocked others from taking over in case of invasion. The invasion protocols were set up that way—so that someone lower on the chain of command could act if the captain was dead or disabled.

Crowe had established himself in the captain position, but he hadn't blocked anyone else.

And it was beginning to look like Preemas had Stephanos on his side.

Crowe hadn't expected that. Natalia Stephanos was a smart woman who made it clear that she loathed Preemas. Crowe couldn't believe that she would support him over Crowe, particularly at a time like this.

And yet, she had left the bridge with him. And other than the initial contact to make sure everything was all right, she hadn't spoken to Crowe since this entire incident began.

Crowe made himself focus. They had to examine the Scrapheap, figure out what, if anything, had gone wrong here.

That was the mission, and he was going to fulfill it, just like Preemas would have. Only, unlike Preemas, Crowe was going to make sure a minimum of harm came to this crew.

Crowe was going to get them out alive—even if it was the last thing he'd ever do.

THE *RENEGAT*

Natalia Stephanos's heart pounded as she walked half a step behind Captain Preemas on the way to his quarters. She deliberately stayed behind him, half-hoping he would turn around and return to the bridge.

She didn't want to help him. She thought Crowe was doing the right thing. But she also didn't want to lose her position on the bridge. She was afraid that Preemas would replace her with someone who had no idea how an *anacapa* drive worked, and then they would all be screwed even worse than they were.

The captain's quarters were down a corridor all their own. They were not even in the crew wing, but closer to engineering and the center of the ship. The captain was to be protected at all times, at least that was what the design said, and for the most part, that was how it happened.

Preemas walked quickly. Stephanos had to struggle to keep up. She had been in this part of the ship, but only to perform maintenance and check systems in the corridor itself.

It felt isolated here, which bothered her more than she wanted to say. She didn't entirely trust Preemas. She would have said, a few weeks ago, that he would never hurt anyone. But he had gotten so volatile as the trip went on that she was beginning to think he could lash out in anger.

And she was heading to his quarters, alone.

She wasn't quite sure what she was going to do. She wanted to warn Crowe that he was about to lose control of the entire ship, but she didn't dare. And she really didn't want to see what Preemas was going to do to Crowe once this all got resolved.

She was torn between her loyalty to the others on the ship, and her desire to help Crowe who was, in her opinion, one of the only other competent people on board the *Renegat*. She would be much happier if Crowe were in charge.

But she didn't dare say that, not right now. And she wasn't sure how she felt about disobeying a captain, even one like Preemas. She was just too Fleet to make those kinds of decisions on her own. She believed in rank and hierarchy.

She believed in making the right choices the structured way because that made the ship run smoother.

But Preemas hadn't followed structure either, and she had to remember that. It wasn't as if she was feeling torn between a by-the-book captain and a rogue first officer. If anything, Crowe was much more by-the-book than Preemas had ever been.

Preemas stopped at the door to his quarters. The door was unmarked, unlike the doors in the crew quarters. Individual cabins, like the officers' cabins, had the rank etched into the door itself. Shared cabins had numbers so that the crew members could find the rooms quickly and efficiently.

But the captain's quarters were deliberately hard to find, partly because of the command closet hidden inside of it. She had never worked on this command closet. That was something the chief engineer assigned if the command closet needed some kind of repair. Often the chief engineer did the work himself.

The door didn't open automatically, the way it was designed to open when the captain was alone. Instead, Preemas had to give it a small hand signal to show that he was all right, and not opening the door under duress.

That system was even more complicated when invasion protocols were in place.

Then she heard the slight hiss as the door slid open.

"Stephanos!" Preemas snapped, as if he had thought she would linger in the hallway.

She spun away from the wall, and entered the captain's quarters.

They were smaller than she had expected. She had never been in a captain's quarters before, but she had thought they would have significantly more room than the private cabins in the crew quarters.

The cabin did have some more room, but not a lot. It had two bedrooms, with doors on the opposite side of the small living room. The kitchen wasn't much bigger than the kitchen in her cabin.

Her eye immediately went to the design. There was too much wall space near the kitchen, which meant the command closet had to be there.

She had just found the outline of the door, as Preemas pushed it open.

"Get your butt in here, Stephanos," he said. "I'm going to need your assistance here—"

And then he just stopped speaking. He was staring into the closet, his mouth open, as if he had forgotten to finish his sentence, as if he hadn't even had a chance to finish his thought.

Stephanos moved just a little closer, but she didn't want to crowd him. She glanced over her shoulder at the door to the corridor. The door had closed, and she hadn't even noticed.

She wasn't sure why that made her even more nervous than she already was, but it had.

Preemas still hadn't moved. He looked stunned. Then he started to shake his head, minimally at first, and then with a broader and broader movement.

"You knew about this, didn't you?" he said very softly. She had to strain to hear him.

"Knew about what?" she asked.

He slammed his fist against the wall beside the door. "*This!*"

He clearly wanted her to get closer, to peer inside the room, but she wasn't going to get near him.

"Knew about what, captain?" she asked again,

"Someone disassembled the command closet," Preemas snapped. He pushed away from the wall, as if he could jettison himself out of this part of the ship with that very simple movement. "You knew about this, didn't you? Your friend Crowe did this and you helped."

Preemas was probably right: Crowe had probably done this. Stephanos didn't want to contemplate it. Because that meant that Crowe's insubordination today had been planned longer than a few hours.

She finally walked toward Preemas. She had to see this for herself. She didn't get close to him, though. She got as close as she could be without being within range of his arms, and peered into the narrow closet.

Even though she had never seen an active command closet—only those in decommissioned ships or ships that needed some kind of repair—she could tell at a glance that this one had been tampered with.

The top had been removed from an entire console. There were bits and pieces of another console on the floor beside the closet's only chair.

Preemas took a step toward her, his eyes flaring, and she took a step back.

"I don't know what happened here," she said. "I've never been to your quarters before. You can check the logs."

"Oh, I'll be checking the logs." He took another step toward her. It took all of her strength to hold her position. "You can bet I'll be checking the logs."

She wanted to check them as well. She could barely believe that Crowe would do something like this. Tampering with the command closet meant that he had actually planned to take over the ship at some point.

She didn't like that. She had been willing to support Crowe when she had thought he was doing this as a reaction to the long foldspace trip and the arrival (too close!) to the Scrapheap, but to think he had been planning this for some time…

Preemas tilted his head, watching her. "You didn't know, did you?"

His voice was remarkably calm. The way that he could go from furious to calm in a heartbeat startled her. She liked to tell herself that he could do that because of his captain training, but it didn't seem like training had taken over. It seemed more like his moods were mercurial, like he could turn them off and on at will.

"I told you," she said in the calmest voice she could manage, "I did not help him."

Preemas's eyes narrowed. "Then fix this."

She let out a small laugh before she could stop herself. "You're kidding, right?"

He stared at her. She could feel his fury grow.

"I have never seen the captain's command closet or whatever you call this. I have no idea what's missing and what should be here and where it can all go. I can figure it out, but it'll take time." She still used the calm voice, hoping none of this sounded like excuses, because it wasn't excuses.

It was the truth. She had no idea how to do anything he asked.

"Your friend, Nadim Crowe, has taken over my ship," Preemas said, his hands in fists again. "We need to get the ship back, in any way possible. If you can't fix this, then what the hell can you do?"

She hoped he meant *what the hell can you do toward that aim?* because she didn't want him to use a blanket *what the hell can you do* to talk to her. Her cheeks had warmed. She wasn't embarrassed, so much as frightened and frustrated.

Nothing was as she expected it to be. Crowe had actually planned a mutiny. Preemas was becoming unhinged—and she wasn't sure she blamed him. It was his ship, after all, no matter how she felt about him or his command. She was here, and she was supposed to listen to him.

She slowly shook her head, saw his fists clench even tighter, and felt her heart rate increase.

She lifted a single finger, hoping that would stop whatever reaction he was leaning into.

"I am going to think out loud here," she said. "You know these ships as well as I do, so I would appreciate it if you have ideas."

She was actually buttering him up, because she had no clue if he knew the ship well. She doubted it, given the way he had behaved.

He moved his head ever so slightly. She had his attention, but she wasn't sure how long she would be able to hold it.

She continued, "This console will take work. We can put a team on it, but I'm not sure what good that will do. Crowe will still have the ship while we do that."

"If we have the parts." Preemas started to kick the console near him, then slowed his foot down and pushed at the equipment instead. It rattled as he did so.

"If we have the parts," she agreed. "I can try to break into engineering, but that might be a fool's errand. Because invasion procedures are in place, and that means the ship itself will fight me."

"Can I override those procedures?" Preemas asked.

She paused. She wasn't sure if he could. But he might be able to.

"It depends," she said slowly. "If Crowe used your information to take over the ship, then you can shut down those procedures...with a working console."

"The ones in the bridge—"

"Are disabled." She stepped away from that depressing little closet and looked at the rest of the captain's quarters. They weren't much better. Neat as a pin, except for the open door to the bedroom, which looked a bit like it had been through zero-G and no one had bothered to clean up afterwards.

"There's access on every level," Preemas said.

"Yes, there is," she said, "and Crowe would have thought of that." In fact, she believed, that invasion procedures shut down those consoles as well.

On DV-Class vessels, there was a single override in a special area known only to the command staff. But there was nothing like that here, except…

"The weapons room," she said more to herself than Preemas.

"What?" he asked.

"The weapons room," she said louder, as if that made a difference. "It has its own entry codes and a self-contained system."

She wasn't sure if Crowe would have thought of that. She certainly hadn't until now.

"You think Crowe would leave weapons unattended, when he's trying to overthrow my ship?" Preemas's tone was filled with venom.

She didn't know how to explain what she thought. Crowe wasn't trying to take over the ship as much as he was trying to make Preemas do what he wanted.

Or so she had thought before she had seen this messed-up room.

She took a deep breath.

"I have no idea what Crowe would do," she said. "I didn't expect any of this. But I do know he's not focused on weaponry, so he might not have thought of that entry point into the systems."

"And if he has?" Preemas asked.

She took a deep breath, and took yet another half step away from Preemas.

"Well, then," she said using that calm voice as protection. "If Crowe has thought of that entry too, then we just wait."

"Wait?"

"Yes," she said. "Because, if that's the case, the ship belongs to him."

THE *RENEGAT*

Crowe glanced at the small screen above the images of the Scrapheap. He had been monitoring the corridor outside of Preemas's quarters, wondering what was taking Preemas and Stephanos so long. They'd been inside for a while.

Engineering was quiet. Everyone was working hard. Which was good. They had more work ahead of them than Crowe had expected.

Crowe wasn't the only one monitoring the bridge, and the Scrapheap itself, but he was the only one monitoring the corridor outside the captain's quarters. He probably should be monitoring other parts of the ship as well, but he just didn't have the ability right now.

He was taxed almost to his limits.

Preemas had clearly discovered what Crowe had done to the command closet. Crowe was less worried about what Preemas thought of it than he was about Stephanos. What had she thought?

She couldn't activate it again, not without a lot of work. Crowe had removed a lot of the equipment. But that might not stop her from trying.

Which worried Crowe. He wanted her to monitor the *anacapa* drive, especially considering how close they were to this ancient Scrapheap.

The Scrapheap was a mess. A tangle of different energy signatures, a failing force field, a security system that seemed to work intermittently, some tractor beams of a type that Crowe had never seen before, and bits and pieces of ships, untethered from the moorings inside the Scrapheap, floating around like possible weapons, should they collide with the wrong part of an already damaged ship.

Crowe had finally found the control tower in what had once been the middle of the Scrapheap but was nowhere near the middle now. It was about as far from the *Renegat* as possible and still be inside the Scrapheap, which disturbed him, because he wanted to pull information from that tower without sending a ship into the Scrapheap.

He didn't think that was possible now.

Although the tower did seem to be working. He couldn't ping it—his technology was so very different from the tech running this ancient Scrapheap as to be almost designed by a different species. But the tower's energy signature appeared correct—as correct as he could guess it would be.

He would need to verify whatever it was, and maybe get Atwater or Breaux or one of the other researchers to figure out what kind of language, what kind of codes, the tower would find acceptable. From what Crowe understood, the Fleet's language and procedures hadn't changed in the five millennia that it had spent crossing space, but he was no expert.

He truly wished he could still contact the Fleet. This wasn't a question for a resident expert on board a half-assed SC-Class vessel. This was a question for someone who worked in research, preferably on one of the school ships, someone who made their life's work something particularly esoteric, someone who could answer Crowe's question without even looking up the answer.

He let out a sigh. He was faced with more work than he knew how to do, and he was doing it without the resources of the Fleet, and without most of the resources of this ship.

Plus, he wasn't as focused on the Scrapheap and the mission as he should have been. A good third of his brain was thinking about Preemas, wondering what the man was doing now, how he was reacting, what he was planning.

Crowe needed to focus and he needed to prioritize. He had half of the remaining engineering staff examining the various energy signatures coming out of the Scrapheap. Crowe wasn't sure what caused all of them, and the last thing he wanted to do was what had happened in his youth—he didn't want anyone to accidentally ignite something inside the Scrapheap, and cause a chain reaction that would destroy everything.

That bubble of energy that had nearly engulfed the *Renegat* had scared the hell out of him. He had no idea what other tricks the Scrapheap had up its metaphorical sleeve, but he suspected there were quite a few.

He also figured it had some features that the Fleet had later discarded or improved upon, things he wouldn't know about because history of the Fleet's Scrapheaps wasn't one of his specialties.

Willoughby was still monitoring what the bridge crew was doing to get into engineering, something that was beginning to irritate Crowe. He needed one of his best people on that task, but he wanted Willoughby beside him—especially since Stephanos was either working with Preemas or keeping an eye on him or both. No matter what she was doing, Crowe figured she was lost to him.

He didn't dare trust her, not anymore.

And that was the other downside to this entire plan.

He was going to have to use some of his brain power figuring out who he could and couldn't trust. He never used to worry about interpersonal relationships. He didn't have many of them, and those he did have were pretty superficial.

He had learned the hard way that the best way to avoid being hurt by someone else was to stay uninvolved.

And now he was going to have to care about others, not because of any particular emotional involvement with them, but because he was going to have to figure out if he could trust them, maybe in less than a minute. He was going to have to make snap judgments, and he was going to have to do it with the fate of the entire ship on his back.

"Um, Mr. Crowe, sir?" Tosidis spoke softly from across engineering. He had left the images of the Scrapheap a while ago to return to the communications array.

"Yeah?" Crowe's response was curt, and it wasn't exactly professional. But he had more than enough on his plate at the moment. He didn't need anything else.

"The, um, communications *anacapa* drive, the tiny one?" Tosidis said, making that last bit a question as if Crowe had no idea what the drive was. "It's vibrating."

Crowe's heart leapt for just a moment. Gāo was contacting him! He could finally communicate with the Fleet.

And then he remembered where he was and how far away from the Fleet he was and how close he was to some of the strangest energy signatures he had ever seen on anything.

"Vibrating," he repeated, making it not quite a question.

"Yes, sir. You know how *anacapa* drives sometimes do when they're activating."

Usually *anacapa* drives only vibrated to the touch, not visibly, and Tosidis wasn't standing close enough to touch anything.

That meant the drive was actively moving—more than vibrating. It was bouncing.

"Has it opened a foldspace window?" Crowe asked.

"Not yet," Tosidis said, "but if it keeps behaving like this, it's only a matter of time until it does."

Crowe fervently wished that Stephanos was still at her post on the bridge, that she hadn't decided to work with Preemas, that she was available for Crowe to contact.

He wanted to know if the drive on the bridge was acting the same way.

"With us using invasion protocols," he said to Willoughby, "can we still see what's going on with the *anacapa* drive on the bridge?"

"We should be able to." Her voice was tight. She had heard everything that Tosidis had said, and she knew what it meant. "And—ah—maybe we should move a little farther away from the Scrapheap?"

If the drives were activating because of some kind of cue from the Scrapheap, it was too late to move farther away. But Crowe didn't say that. Instead, he just nodded, and said to Bakhr, "Has the energy from the Scrapheap reached us here?"

"Not any more than expected," Bakhr said.

"Expected?" Crowe said. He hadn't expected anything. He wasn't sure what Bakhr was talking about.

"Scrapheaps under duress give off excess energy," Bakhr said. "Entire systems would feel a little impact."

"How do you know that?" Crowe asked. He didn't know it. He could tell from the startled faces in the room not many of the others knew it either—if any of them did.

"I grew up in one of the sectors with a Scrapheap," Bakhr said. "We had to deal with excess energy all the time."

It would have been good to know that before they started on this trip.

"How did you deal with it?" Willoughby asked, and then looked down at one of the holoscreens floating near her. Something had caught her attention.

Crowe looked over her shoulder at the screen but couldn't see what it was.

Bakhr didn't seem to notice that Willoughby's attention had gone elsewhere, or maybe he felt it wasn't important. He said, "We adjusted for a basic level of energy coming out of the Scrapheap. We monitored it continually, and when that energy changed, the entire community took action."

"What kind of action?" Tosidis asked.

Bakhr shook his head just a little. "I was a kid. I wasn't part of the discussions, even though I knew it was important. It was one of the things that got me interested in engineering, though, to figure out what was going on around me."

Crowe's brain was still stuck on what Bakhr had said earlier. That Scrapheaps under duress gave off excess energy. That excess energy, even if it was expected, might interact with *anacapa* drives.

"Can you get a reading from the drive on the bridge?" he asked Willoughby.

"Not and keep monitoring what they're doing to get into engineering," she said just as tightly. "Someone else will have to check."

Crowe realized he didn't trust anyone else to check. He was feeling paranoid, and deeply uncomfortable.

He moved to one of the consoles, and opened a window. He would have to access bridge information without allowing the bridge to gain access to engineering.

It would be tricky, but if he didn't do it, and that *anacapa* drive was also being activated, then they had other problems besides the rebellion against Preemas and being in this ancient quadrant.

Crowe built a window into the bridge, making himself work slowly. He guarded that window with protections and codes and firewalls that only he could change. He knew that was risky. He knew some of it was flamboyant enough to call attention to what he was doing, if someone was paying attention and cared.

But he also knew that their best engineer was currently with Preemas in the captain's cabin, so there was a chance that no one would notice.

There was even a better chance that if someone had noticed, they wouldn't know what to do about it.

He found the *anacapa* controls and examined them, making sure his window didn't activate anything either.

The bridge's *anacapa* drive was humming. Not quite vibrating, but not quite active either.

He wasn't sure what to do to stop it. He knew what *not* to do. He knew that activating the *anacapa* drive and sending the *Renegat* into foldspace would probably cause all of the excess energy from the Scrapheap to mix with the energy from the *Renegat*, and cause some kind of chain reaction.

The memory of that old Scrapheap igniting ship by ship dominated his mind, just for an instant, until he shook it all away. He had to concentrate.

He had to make the right choice here, and he wasn't sure what that was.

He let out a small breath, realized that not making a choice was the same as choosing, and made himself activate the helm.

Willoughby was right: they had to move farther away. But he wasn't sure how far.

"I need to know," he said to Bakhr, "how far that energy extends. We have to get beyond it."

"It's going to pretty much blanket this entire solar system," Bakhr said.

They couldn't move quickly out of this solar system. They couldn't get anywhere quickly without their *anacapa* drive.

So moving wasn't really an option after all.

Crowe let out a small breath. "All right then," he said. "We stay. We'll have to monitor the *anacapa* drives."

And do what? he would have asked, if someone else had given that order. He didn't know. If they activated, he would at least be informed. Maybe informed just before he died.

Monitor the bridge, monitor the *anacapa* drives. And do nothing, except keep Preemas out.

Crowe needed to stop reacting and start acting.

He needed a plan. And he couldn't consult the engineers for it.

He had taken over the ship, whether he wanted to admit it or not. So he needed to guide the ship.

He had to choose: complete the mission as the Fleet designed it or do something else entirely.

And he had to choose fast.

THE *RENEGAT*

Weapons storage was in its own wing, three decks away from the captain's quarters. It took Stephanos longer to get there than she wanted.

But she made Preemas take a stealthier route rather than the direct route. If she had taken over the ship the way that Crowe had, then she would have monitored Preemas's movements from the start. She would have considered him a major threat, and would have acted on that threat.

Hell, she might eventually slap some lightlocks on him and take him to the brig.

Crowe might still do that. She had no idea what he was planning. She wasn't sure how the crew would react, though, when they saw their captain imprisoned.

They were Fleet, after all, even if they were Fleet screw-ups. They still believed in the Fleet way of doing things, or they wouldn't be on this ship. They would have taken whatever opportunities they had to leave and moved on, away from all the rules and regulations.

Stephanos's stomach felt like an iron ball, and her shoulders ached from tension. She was grinding her teeth together, even though she kept trying to stop herself from doing so.

The weapons room might have been a bad idea. Because arming Preemas could mean some kind of shoot-out on the *Renegat* herself. The crew, fighting each other for control, trying to settle whatever this was while they were as far away from the Fleet as anyone had ever been.

The entry to the weapons room curved, with doors leading into various areas. Everyone on the ship had their personal weapons, generally some kind of laser pistol. Most people on the ship never carried those weapons, unless they worked security or unless they felt the ship was under threat.

Her own personal weapon was locked in her quarters. It was keyed to her handprint and useless to anyone, including her at the moment.

She wiped her sweaty palms on her pants, then peered at the various doors. Behind each was a different type of weapon. In one area were the laser rifles and weapons with a lot of firepower that could be carried into some uncertain situation. Behind another was handheld nonlethal weapons, things that flashed or exploded, but did no harm.

A third area contained backups for the ship's weaponry, as well as tools for repairing the smaller weapons. SC-Class ships like the *Renegat* actually had as much or more firepower than DV-Class vessels, just because SC-Class vessels found themselves in difficult situations, as they tried to rescue damaged ships or counter some kind of threat to a sector.

DV-Class vessels used their firepower in more aggressive situations, if they encountered a hostile space-faring power, or if they found themselves blundering into some kind of war.

Stephanos hadn't been in any of those situations, which was probably why she hadn't given the weaponry any thought until now. She hoped that it had been the same for Crowe, so that he wouldn't have given this place any thought.

Preemas had already taken a few steps ahead of her. He contemplated the various doors as if he were looking at his own options. She felt a chill run down her back.

By bringing him here, she might have started the path into one of those in-ship civil wars she had only heard about. She couldn't imagine any of her colleagues dead, nor could she imagine them fighting each other, but she knew it was a possibility, one Preemas might have been thinking about now.

Preemas continued staring at the doors, his jaw working as if he was grinding his teeth as well.

He had choices here. He could get the weapons and blast his way into engineering, or he could see if the controls worked. Or he could do a variety of other things.

Somewhere along the way, she had started clutching her hands into fists. She didn't say anything though. Preemas was the captain, and he could make his own decisions.

Then he pivoted, and placed his palm on the panel on the smooth wall, the one that hid a small group of backup controls. If he could get that open, she might be able to use the tools here to get her into other control panels.

The panel flared red.

Security code outdated. Access denied.

Preemas sucked in air, then glanced at her. "What the hell does that mean?"

It meant that Crowe was even smarter than Stephanos had thought. He hadn't installed himself as captain or even changed any of the structure inside the various panels.

It meant that Crowe had disabled Preemas's security access after activating invasion protocols, probably reporting to the ship that Preemas was incapacitated in some way or injured or compromised by the "invaders."

"Well," she said, "the good news is that the ship still recognizes you."

Preemas's eyes narrowed. "That's not good news. That's ridiculous news. It needs to respond to me."

She nodded. "It is responding to you," she said. "That's the problem. It recognizes you as captain but won't give you access."

"Why the hell not?" Preemas snapped.

"It thinks..." she sighed. "Invasion protocols, remember? It thinks—"

"I'm being used by someone who has taken over the ship? Anyone who knows me—"

"It doesn't matter," she said. "The ship doesn't know you. The ship is a machine, and somehow Crowe has convinced it that you're not trustworthy."

But she might not be on that same list.

"Let me try something," she said, and stepped beside Preemas. She had to wait until he moved away from the panel so that she could try it.

Preemas took a reluctant step back.

She put her palm on the same panel. It didn't immediately flare red, but it didn't open either.

She knew what it was doing, and she felt her heart sink. It was reporting the attempted access to Crowe.

She didn't tell Preemas that either.

Secondary security clearance needed to open this panel. Contact the first officer for emergency code.

Preemas cursed and slammed his fist against the wall next to the panel. The panel shook. So much for any other attempt they could make. His use of force just precluded anything they could try to trick the system.

He had just confirmed what the system thought it knew. The system believed it was under attack from the outside. The system believed that Preemas was compromised.

And, as far as the system was concerned, he had just proven it.

Preemas pushed past her and shoved his fingers inside one of the door handles, trying to get to the weaponry. She opened her mouth to warn him, but couldn't get the warning out quickly enough.

He yelped, and brought his hand back. The system had shocked him—a minor shock, as a warning, but if he tried again, it would get worse.

Preemas clutched his hand to his chest and whirled on her. "What the hell does Crowe think he's doing? He's not in charge of this ship. *I* am."

Well, not anymore, she thought but didn't say.

"Get to engineering," Preemas said. "Break in any damn way you can. We're going to get this ship back from him, no matter what it takes."

Stephanos started to protest, then thought the better of it. She had no idea how to break into engineering. Had Preemas blocked himself in Engineering, she would have gotten in easily, but this was Crowe. And he knew more about ship systems than she did.

All she could hope for was that he had overlooked something.

"What are you going to do?" She almost didn't pose the question; part of her didn't want to know. But another part wanted to be prepared, just in case something awful happened.

"I'm going to figure out what weapons we do have," Preemas snarled, "and I'm going to get my crew, and we're going to take the ship back, no matter what it takes."

"Sir," she said, before she could stop herself, "we're alone out here. If something happens to the *Renegat*—"

"What, do you think I'm *stupid*?" He was still clutching his hand. He looked like a vicious little boy who had been burned and was now vowing revenge. "I know that we have no backup. Although, have you looked at that Scrapheap? There're hundreds of ships inside."

Centuries old. They probably didn't function. But she wasn't sure she should say that. She wasn't sure she should say anything else.

Everything she said seemed to enflame him even more.

"You going to tell me to be careful?" he said, pushing his face close to hers. "You think I don't know how desperate this situation is? Your friend Crowe, he knows too. He thinks I'm too much of a coward to even try to take my ship back. But I'm not. And he's going to pay for this when it's all over, Fleet or no Fleet."

Then Preemas stomped down the corridor, still clutching his arm.

Stephanos watched him go. She looked helplessly at the weapons room, at the lost opportunity.

Her heart was pounding. She had to do something to stop the collision between these two men, but she wasn't sure what she could do.

She wasn't sure how to save any of them. She was afraid they were all going to die here, and she could do nothing to stop it.

THE *RENEGAT*

Crowe quickly rearranged the workload inside of engineering. He made Bakhr monitor the bridge *anacapa*. Crowe also made Bakhr monitor the energy waves coming out of the Scrapheap, looking for changes or increases in energy. Crowe had one other engineer examine the energy waves as well, just in case.

Crowe needed more help figuring things out quickly, but he didn't have the personnel. Time was pressing in on him. He couldn't just research and gather information.

He had to make some decisions.

That's what captains did, sometimes without enough information. And even though he wasn't the captain, he controlled the ship.

The decisions were his to make now.

He walked to the gigantic holographic image of the Scrapheap. More parts of it had filled in. There was a blank spot in the middle, just like he had expected. An area that was impossible to scan. That was usually something that only ships or crew that had gone inside the Scrapheap could notice, and they probably wouldn't have thought anything of it.

It was where the Ready Vessels were stored—at least in modern Scrapheaps, the kind he was familiar with.

Only, as he walked around the hologram of the Scrapheap, he realized that a small corner of that blank sensor area looked ripped away. Something had destroyed the force field that protected the Ready Vessels (or whatever was stored) inside that Scrapheap.

Crowe opened another screen, and created a hologram of just that area, zooming in as best he could. The *Renegat*'s sensors couldn't gather all of the data needed. Getting some of what he wanted would require him to tweak the sensors, and again, he didn't have time.

For a brief moment, he considered sending in a probe. But that would force him to send or use someone outside of engineering. It would definitely alert the rest of the ship to all the things he was doing.

Crowe used the equipment, moving the smaller hologram of the Scrapheap to show him inside that corner.

And his breath caught.

The guarded interior storage appeared empty. At least at this angle. He would have thought it was going to be full.

But he wasn't sure why. Someone had clearly broken into the Scrapheap, and might have done it centuries ago. If that someone had managed to crack the codes in the Fleet ships they stole, then they might be able to figure out that better, more functional ships were hidden here.

Crowe kept zooming in on the hologram, kept refining the image as best he could from this distance, and with all the energy interference. Was that interior empty? Or was there another force field, something that made it hard to see what was actually inside?

He thought he saw a shadow of something, something large. So he filtered the images, and changed the algorithms slightly.

He had been wrong: there were ships inside, and they were cloaked somehow, or protected in ways that he couldn't quite filter through given the equipment he had, and the distance he was at.

The muscles in his shoulders loosened ever so slightly. More ships. And maybe functional ships.

He let out a breath as the beginning of a plan started to form in his head.

If he could get everyone on the ship working together again, then maybe they could fulfill the Fleet's mission and curtail Preemas's ego. Or rather, harness it.

Maybe the *Renegat* could become a tiny fleet of ships—an armada of some sort—with the crew members who had trouble with Preemas on a different ship, all of them heading back to the Fleet—to use Preemas's phrase—"as victors."

And maybe waving one arm would make all of this conflict go away.

Crowe smiled grimly to himself. He was being too optimistic.

But at least this plan was a chance to hold the entire crew together, maybe even a way to have backup *anacapa* drives to allow the ships to get through that long foldspace journey back with a minimum of trouble.

Provided the *Renegat* survived the energy waves coming out of that Scrapheap.

Provided Crowe could convince Preemas to work with him again.

Provided the *anacapa* drives didn't accidentally open a door into foldspace.

So many contingencies. So many things that could still go wrong.

But for the first time since Crowe had sealed off engineering—maybe for the first time since he found out that Preemas had been lying to him—Crowe felt a measure of hope.

THE *RENEGAT*

Break into engineering, he said. As if that were possible. As if she wanted to do it.

Stephanos's hands were shaking.

Preemas expected her to break into engineering. He had asked her to get into it before, and she had investigated, then told him it was impossible.

But now, he had used the words "break into" engineering, which meant he expected her to use force. *He* was going to use force.

He was going to gather a team and somehow, *somehow*, get into engineering, and maybe kill Crowe.

Maybe kill them all. The rest of the crew would be collateral damage in this fight. The *Renegat* would be collateral damage.

They could all die, and die horribly.

Stephanos stopped in the middle of a corridor, realizing that she had been walking blindly in the opposite direction from weapons storage. She hadn't been heading to engineering at all.

She hadn't been going anywhere, just walking in her great distress.

She put a hand on the wall panel, feeling its cool surface beneath her palm. At least the walls felt normal, even if nothing else was.

She had no good choices here. Either she followed what Preemas wanted her to do and broke into engineering—if she could—and sided with a man who might be crazy, a man who was certainly angry, a man who wasn't going to listen to reason at all—or she tried to work with Crowe somehow, and then where would that get her? Where it would it get any of them?

Stephanos bowed her head. She couldn't think of a third option, something that she could do, something that no one else would think of.

Unless *she* took over the ship somehow. A third faction, one that stressed—what? Unity? It was too late for that.

And she had no idea what was going on with the Scrapheap. She was the one who had warned Crowe. It had been obvious to her that *Renegat* had arrived too close to the Scrapheap. There was a danger from the outside and one from inside as well.

If they survived this, it would be a damned miracle.

Unless she brokered a truce.

That was the third option.

Or it would have been, if she were some kind of damned diplomat, which she most decidedly was not. She didn't know how to talk to people, how to get them to do what she wanted.

And what did she want?

She let out a small breath and pushed off the wall.

She wanted them all to get along. She wanted the *Renegat* to be a real Fleet ship, not this makeshift thing.

She wanted to go back to the Fleet, and be an officer, and she would never ever ever misbehave again, not ever. She was so sorry for all the demerits that had relegated her to Sector Base Z, for that "inspired" moment when she jumped to the *Renegat*, thinking she could work on a ship again. She was so sorry for everything that she had ever done wrong, for the way that her entire life had led her to this moment.

If she had it to do over again—oh, God. She didn't want to live it all over again. Not ever.

And now she was here, stuck here, *trapped* here.

Where she was supposed to break into engineering, for god's sake.

She wiped a hand over her face. She couldn't do it. She *wouldn't* do it.

Crowe was her friend and he was a good man—or so she had thought—and he was an excellent engineer, and they needed him on their side no matter what Preemas said, particularly now.

And she needed to tell Crowe that.

She needed to let him know that he and Preemas could work together, and she would make that happen somehow. She had to.

She squared her shoulders, took a deep breath, and let all the fear out. Or tried to. Because she had to do this. No one else could. And she had to be calm while she did so.

She pivoted, and headed down to engineering. It wasn't a long walk, and if anything, her resolve grew.

She found it fascinating that no one else seemed to be around—no one was in the corridors, and no one was peering out of their quarters or hanging out in the mess. This hadn't been a particularly chummy ship—Preemas's captain's style prevented that—but it had been a talky ship, again because of Preemas's style and the way he had changed all of the jobs. People tried to work together to figure out how to do their new assignments and how to handle this "ignore rank" thing.

And now, they weren't in the corridors, they weren't talking, they weren't doing anything.

She felt more alone than she ever had.

She finally reached engineering. The doors were closed, just like they often were when the team was taking on some major task.

It looked normal here—workday normal—and that felt odd to her. But it might work in her favor.

She stood for a moment before those closed doors, then she reached to the panel on the side, and pressed her palm against it. There was a chance—even in invasion protocols—that she could get inside, especially if Crowe hadn't thought to block her in any way.

A red light flared around her fingers, and heat shot through her palm. Not extreme heat. Just enough to make her pull her hand back. Warning heat.

Apparently, Crowe had blocked her. Or he had blocked everyone who wasn't already in engineering.

Maybe he knew she had gone with Preemas to his quarters. Maybe Crowe now believed that Stephanos was on Preemas's side.

She hated even the thought of sides, but that was the reality now.

She paced in front of the doors for a moment. Break in. The thing was, she even had an idea how to do it. With the proper tools, she could break the seal on the doors, and then she would be inside.

She put a finger on the panel, felt the extreme heat. Not a subtle warning now. A threat.

"Nadim," she said.

She wasn't sure what to call Crowe—First Officer Crowe, Chief Engineer Crowe, Usurper Crowe, Captain Crowe—so she opted for his first name.

"Nadim, please. Talk to me."

Her stomach was jumping. The heat had worked its way into her finger, deep, into the bone. She was going to have to pull her finger off that panel any second now, because she could feel the skin starting to blister.

"Nadim," she said. "Please."

"I don't have time." His voice sounded echoy and annoyed. She pulled her finger off the panel, and glanced at the fingertip. Yep, it was red, but there was no blister, not yet. Still, she wished she had something cold to put it against.

"None of us have time for this, but please, let me in. We have to talk. Preemas knows." Her voice didn't sound good either. Wobbly and scared, no matter how hard she tried to sound strong.

"Natalia, we'll talk later," Crowe said.

"No," she said. "No. No! We have to talk now. Nadim, he's getting weapons."

There was a long silence, long enough that she thought Crowe had cut her off and hadn't heard that part at all. She took a step forward and was looking at the panel, wondering if she would have to sacrifice another fingertip when Crowe's voice filled the area near the doors.

"Knows what?" he asked, sounding leery.

"That you've been planning this," she said, trying not to sound judgmental, trying not to add, *God, Nadim, what were you thinking? You never struck me as the type to take over a ship.* "He found the captain's quarters."

"You have no idea what's been going on," Crowe said. "Preemas cut off our communications with the Fleet. He made talking to them impossible and lied about it."

Her breath caught. Then she let it out, slowly. The details didn't matter. None of it mattered, because Crowe had been right the first time: they didn't have time for this.

"We can talk details later, Nadim," she said, letting herself sound as panicked as she felt. "We can figure it all out then, air grievances, do whatever you want. But right now, you have to hear me. Preemas is gathering *weapons*."

"Stop bluffing me," Crowe said. "I know you've been to the weapons room. I know you couldn't get in."

She let out a small breath. She had expected him to monitor them—*she* would have monitored them—but to realize he had actually done it unsettled her just a bit.

No wonder he didn't trust her.

"I'm not bluffing," she said gently. "I'm not. We were all issued personal weapons when we joined the Fleet, remember? Most of us just don't carry them day-to-day. Not even security does. So the fact that he didn't get into the weapons room just means that he doesn't have *all* of the weapons. That's what I mean by *gathering*, Nadim. He's going to break in, and he's going to literally take prisoners. I assume you don't have any weapons in there with you."

There was another long silence. She wasn't even sure Crowe had heard her.

Then he said, "What kind of talking do you think will work, Natalia?"

"We can agree to work together," she said, realizing how stupid that sounded right now. "Maybe you can convince him why you took this action, maybe we can figure out how to work together until the crisis has passed."

"I need you on the *anacapa* drive," Crowe said. "It's vibrating on the bridge. We think something in the energy from the Scrapheap has started a slow activation, but we don't know, and we can't go investigate."

She was nodding as he spoke, trying not to smile. They were going to work together. He had skipped over the agreement part, and moved right into the help part.

"I can do that," she said.

"Then do it," Crowe said.

"Will you let me into engineering so you can brief me on everything that's going on?" she asked.

"No," Crowe said. "Let's work on the *anacapa* first. Briefing will happen later. And I'll open the doors to engineering when I think it's safe to do so."

A little chirrup echoed in the small space near the doors. Crowe had activated the sign-off sound, so that she knew he had cut off communications—at least right now.

She felt buoyed by the fact that he was willing to work with her. Scared that there was an *anacapa* problem. Worried that Preemas would misunderstand why she had moved to the bridge. And she was slowly beginning to understand why Crowe had taken such drastic action.

She half-walked, half-ran toward the bridge.

She would work with Crowe on the *anacapa*. If Crowe's information proved correct—and she had no doubt that it would—then it would go a long way into convincing Preemas that the threat outside the *Renegat* was real, that they all needed to band together to solve that threat before dealing with the issues *inside* the ship.

Maybe this would get solved and they would be all right.

Maybe.

For the first time in hours, she actually had some hope.

PART TWENTY-SEVEN
SURVIVAL
NOW

THE *AIZSARGS* RESCUE ONE

The life raft vibrated, and then the other end opened, like a curtain pulling back. Some of the people in the very back tumbled out.

Serpell's heart rate increased. For a half second, she thought everyone had fallen into the vast darkness of space. But then she saw lights and walls and signage, all of it in Standard, which made her heart rise.

Please exit the life raft in a quick and orderly fashion. The faster you leave, the faster we can rescue your friends and family.

She let out a breath she hadn't even realized she had been holding. She scooted forward, eager to get off the life raft, away from the *Renegat*. A few others vaulted across the life raft's squishy floor, bouncing toward the exit and then jumping out of it, almost as if they were pushed.

She didn't even try to stand up. The way the floor was bouncing, she wouldn't be able to get purchase anyway. She continued to scoot forward, like a few others were doing, and she reached the edge of the raft faster than she expected.

It had docked on some kind of platform. Her legs dangled over the edge. A few of the people who had run and jumped were moving forward, away from the raft.

She wanted to linger, but she didn't dare. Everyone on the *Renegat* needed the life raft.

Everyone left on the *Renegat*.

She was so happy she would never see that ship again. She had lost everything on board that ship. Everything except her life.

She pushed herself off the lip and onto the floor. As she did, several versions of the same sign in Standard floated around her.

Please follow the yellow lights. They will take you to Decontamination.

She shuddered. What did these people think she had brought back from the *Renegat*? How in the universe could anyone be contaminated from riding on a ship, anyway?

She glanced over her shoulder, looking for familiar faces, but most people were still wearing their full environmental suits. She didn't blame anyone for doing that. It had been terrifying on the *Renegat*, and even though everything looked fine here—wherever they were—that was no guarantee it was fine.

The yellow lighting rose around her like her own personal hallway. Only it was just a bit out of reach, guiding her forward. She finally reached the far wall in the area where the life raft had docked. The yellow lighting illuminated an actual door, and she stepped through it, into a smaller area, dim and a little cold.

Remove your clothing. Covering will be provided for you once you are through decontamination.

They were going to take her clothing? Serpell had been through decontamination before, but mostly as a formality. She had never had to remove her clothing before.

There wasn't even a place to be private. She gripped the shoulder of her environmental suit, and tugged. It ripped in her hand, something she hadn't thought possible.

She stared at the edges in stunned surprise. They were ragged, filled with stressed fabric and microtears. No wonder the suit kept telling her it was compromised.

It wasn't just compromised; it had been disintegrating.

She let out a small involuntary bleat. Until that moment, she hadn't realized just how close she had come to dying.

She peeled the rest of the suit off herself. Some of it adhered to her shirt and her pants. She knew that an environmental suit shouldn't have done that. It should have remained separate, creating its own little world. Instead, it had glommed onto her and her clothing.

She had been wearing a short-sleeve shirt. She looked at her arms, saw some of the suit was still stuck to her. She dug at it, felt it loosen, and then come off.

Maybe she did need decontamination, just for the suit. She kicked the remains of the suit away. It skittered until it hit the hairy leg of Anthony Varasteh. He looked up in surprise, saw Serpell looking at him, and covered his private parts with both hands, turning away from her. His naked buttocks looked vulnerable, his back curved.

She had never seen him naked. She hadn't seen many on the ship naked, including the women.

Serpell didn't say anything to put him at ease. She wasn't at ease; she had no idea why she felt the need to put others at ease.

And there were others here, people she could finally recognize now that they were out of the suits.

They were staggered along the floor at what looked like irregular intervals, so that it didn't seem like they were lining up as much as standing in their own little booth, waiting for the next turn.

Until she had kicked the suit, she hadn't realized how public this space was. Part of her brain marveled at the design feature, making this entire area seem private when it wasn't.

She had never seen anything like it.

Please step forward. Decontamination will take approximately two and a half minutes.

She glanced around, trying to see if anyone else had heard that voice. No one else seemed to. So she stepped forward, through that yellow lighted door, and into a small area. The area was dark. The outlines of the yellow light still reflected along her eyeballs.

The area was also cold, and a little damp, which made her feel like the place was contaminating her rather than decontaminating her. First something that smelled of antiseptic blew on her skin, followed by a tingling that she didn't like, particularly when it invaded all parts of her.

She groped herself, like Varasteh had, trying to keep that feeling out. Then the tingling stopped and the air got so dry that her lips chapped almost immediately. She felt a growing sense of claustrophobia. She needed to get out of this area. She wanted her clothes. She wanted normality. She wanted—

Then a door she hadn't seen opened in front of her. White light filtered toward her, making her blink.

Proceed.

She did. She was in a small room now, barely the size of an airlock. A robe hung from the wall.

Put on the clothing, then exit. You will receive further instructions once you leave.

She nodded, as if the damn voice could see her response. She put on the robe. Its softness felt good against her hands, but scraped the skin of her arms. That scraping feeling was either from the suit or the decontamination procedure.

The door didn't open when she put on the robe, like she had expected. She wasn't sure if she should pound on the door, or call out. God, somehow, she had become terrified of small spaces, of being trapped, of never escaping. She was not on the *Renegat* anymore, but she still felt hopeless and frightened and—

The door slid open. She didn't even have to wait for the voice to say, *Proceed.*

She did, almost leaping out of the room, like some of the others had bounced out of the life raft.

The room she stepped into was large, filled with soft chairs and tables in groupings so that a small cluster of people could sit together. Thick carpet, soft as the robe, covered the floor, and felt good against her bare feet. There were several doors on the far side of the room, but they were closed and marked *Crew members only* in Standard.

Food sat on a side table, but what kind, she couldn't see. There was also a sign not too far from her that said *Beverages*, but she couldn't see what kind either.

Ten others stood in the room, all wearing robes, all barefoot, all with wet hair. She touched her scalp and realized that her hair was wet too. The dampness must have caused it. Or maybe she just hadn't noticed when that tingling started.

Varasteh stood a few yards from her. She almost walked over to him, to apologize for kicking the suit, but he turned away, clearly too embarrassed to talk with her.

She was thirsty and exhausted and scared. She walked toward the beverage area, and as she did, that voice returned.

Welcome to Aizsargs Rescue One. *Once your friends and family have joined us, we will take you to the* Aizsargs. *Until that moment, take whatever refreshments you need and rest. We will let you know when we will leave for the* Aizsargs.

The *Aizsargs*. That was the ship the people on the bridge had said they were from. Serpell let out a small sigh of relief. Her knees nearly buckled under her.

This was a transitional vessel. It would take her to a larger ship, where, maybe, she could actually relax.

She stopped in front of the beverage table, saw a screen with some simple choices like water and tea, and other choices she had never heard of.

She was only a linguist, but she had served on a number of ships. She had never seen anything quite like this. It almost felt like she was on a vessel for a culture she had never seen before, one that recognized the Fleet way of doing things, but wasn't Fleet.

The thought made her shiver.

Then she took a deep breath. She was having catastrophic thoughts because she had narrowly averted a catastrophe. She was going to be unsettled for a long time.

She had to accept that.

At least she was alive. She had survived.

And that was all that mattered.

THE *RENEGAT*

Finally, Cargo Bay One.

Breaux let out a small breath, feeling the relief. She was here. *They* were here.

And the doors leading into the cargo bay were open.

She pushed off the corridor's wall with a little more force than she had planned. She was so *thrilled* to be here. The wall vibrated, making her uneasy.

If her memory was right, there had been a lot of damage down here when the ship got attacked outside of that weird planet. But she didn't see any damage now.

Except that wobble. That wobble took some of the thrill away.

Still, the force of her push made her zoom into the bay, and then she ducked, because something floated by her. The duck caused her to spin, and she was losing control, so she activated the gravity on her boots, hoping they would find the floor, not a wall.

They found a wall. She was jutting out just like a badly designed light fixture. And she felt stupid, because the rest of the crew would see her like this.

She walked down the wall, put a tentative foot on the floor, and saw the rest of her little troop float in. Their lights illuminated the floating cargo, and just a small section of the bay.

And that was when she realized there were no other lights. She couldn't see other people in environmental suits. She didn't see anyone else.

Her heart sank. They were too late. They had missed the rescue because she had gotten lost, because she hadn't known how to get to the cargo bays in the dark.

Maybe this was the wrong bay. Maybe this was something else.

But the map had led her here, and this *looked* like a cargo bay. It had to be a cargo bay, right? It couldn't be anything else.

She turned, slowly, picking up her sticky gravity boots and moving. No. No one. No other lights.

And she had no idea how to get around the ship, let alone find the escape pods.

If there were any left.

Then she saw a lighted figure directly ahead of her. For a moment, she thought she had imagined it.

It looked like an angel. A glowing, beautiful, human-shaped angel.

"Hello?" she said tentatively.

"Hurry up," the angel said. "Get to the cargo bay doors. We have one last life raft coming to get us. How many are with you?"

"There are five," she said, then looked around her. The others were pushing forward, trying to get to the angel. "Six, counting me. I'm not sure if their comms work properly. They haven't said anything to me since we started."

"Can you hear me?" the angel asked them.

A couple of people nodded. Of course. She should have asked that.

"Can you respond?" he asked, and no one did.

Breaux felt her cheeks heat. At least there was a reason they had glommed on to her. She could communicate with them.

She walked in her activated boots, and when that worked as poorly as it had back in the rec room, she shut off the gravity. As she pushed off the floor with her feet, she aimed her body at the angel.

He had moved to the side of the bay doors, and was doing something over there. Then the doors rose, and a lighted room appeared.

Light, with a lot of empty space. A rescue vehicle, just like he had said.

She entered it, with the other five. They bounced in, and he followed.

"Where's everyone else?" she asked.

"You're the last," he said, then did something with his hand. The door they had come in sealed up.

"Who are you?" she asked, feeling stupid that she hadn't done that before. She had been panicked and not thinking, and even though the panic was fading, she still felt a little on edge, as if she couldn't quite believe she was rescued.

"My name is Raul Zarges," he said. "I'm with the rescue team. I'm taking you to our ship. It'll take a little longer than usual. But you're safe now."

Safe. She wanted to hug him. She wanted to scream with relief. Instead, she felt herself get heavier as gravity came on.

Then an androgynous voice said, *Welcome. You are on a small rescue vessel on its way to* Aizsargs Rescue One, *a large rescue ship….*

And she felt herself relax.

She was safe. *They* were safe.

They had been rescued.

And it was over.

PART TWENTY-EIGHT
THE FIRST DEATH
100 YEARS AGO

THE *RENEGAT*

The air on the bridge felt odd. Breaux stood near Atwater, brushing the hair on the back of her neck. The hair kept rising, not because she was unsettled—which she was—but because something kept drawing it up, like static electricity. It wasn't static electricity, though, because when she touched something, she didn't get one of those little shocks.

But something was off, and it wasn't just everyone's mood.

She and Atwater were leaning over the console, comparing the data that she had been organizing since she joined the *Renegat* with the feed from the Scrapheap. They were working hard at this because no one had given them orders on what to actually do.

Captain Preemas was angry at First Officer Crowe, and had left the bridge with Natalia Stephanos to investigate some other way of regaining control of the ship. And Breaux didn't want to think about any of that, particularly given the charged way the air felt around all of them, as if the ship herself knew that something was horribly, horribly, horribly wrong.

She was trying to focus on the work, trying not to think of it as make-work. Everyone else on the bridge was talking in low tones, using words like "invasion protocol" and "override" and "impossible." A couple of people had moved away from their consoles, as if the consoles themselves were at fault.

Most of the others, though, were clustering, working, trying to get control back to the bridge.

Atwater would occasionally look at them longingly, as if he wanted to help them, rather than work with her.

She elbowed him a few times, worried that in the middle of all of this consternation, the real important thing would be lost: they were near that Scrapheap, and there was evidence someone had tampered with it.

Why was no one concerned that the thieves would come back and harm the *Renegat*?

Or maybe that had been First Officer Crowe's concern all along. Maybe he was focused on that and worried that the captain was too excitable.

She had no idea. If she had had experience on ships, she might know more about what was going on, but she didn't. And she wasn't sure she wanted to.

Then the doors to the bridge slid open and Captain Preemas strode through them, alone. No Natalia Stephanos.

In his hands, he held laser pistols—three per hand, which seemed to be all he could hold. More were strapped to his waist, and over both shoulders, he carried laser rifles.

The conversation on the bridge halted. Everyone looked at him.

The charged air seemed even more electric. Breaux almost forgot to breathe.

"We can't get into engineering," Captain Preemas said in a very calm tone. A surprisingly calm tone, considering how he looked—wild-eyed and covered with weaponry. "Crowe has been planning this mutiny for weeks, maybe for the entire trip. He dismantled the captain's command system in my quarters, and he disabled the secondary command system near the weapons room."

Tindo Ibori's eyes were wide. Breaux clasped her hands together to keep them from shaking. Atwater still leaned on the console as if he needed it to hold him up.

"So, we're going to break into Engineering," Captain Preemas said. "India Romano, I need you to contact Fernando Oshie. We need to gather all the personal weaponry we can. We're going in, and we're taking back control of this ship."

Security Officer Romano, a tall dramatically dressed woman who usually lurked near the back of the bridge looked startled that Captain Preemas even knew her name.

She nodded and frowned at the same time. "But...um...why Oshie? I'm sorry, I'm not clear—"

"Because he's head of security now," Preemas snapped. "Didn't you study the chart on personnel changes?"

"I didn't memorize it, sir," Romano said. Her tone implied that there might be more changes. Or maybe Breaux was just reading into it from her own assumptions.

"Well, you should have memorized it, shouldn't you," Preemas said. "I need the rest of you to pair up and leave the bridge, heading to your quarters to recover your personal weapons—if you're not already carrying them. And be warned, I'll be keeping track of who doesn't come back. I need you *all* on this."

Breaux winced, and timidly raised her hand. She wanted to stay invisible, but she couldn't, not after this.

"This is not a classroom," Preemas snapped. "Ask your damn question."

Breaux's cheeks heated. She took a deep breath, hoping she wouldn't sound as terrified as she felt. Although she wasn't sure why not. Maybe because she believed that Preemas wouldn't respect her anymore if he knew how scared she was.

Not that she was sure he respected her now.

"Well?" he snapped.

"Um," she said, and winced again. "Some of us weren't issued personal weapons, sir."

"What?" Preemas asked. "First Officer Crowe was thinking ahead again, I see."

"No, sir." Atwater raised his head. But his hands were still braced on that console. "I think it was an oversight, sir. Those of us from Sector Base Z didn't go through the usual arrival protocols."

Preemas studied him as if trying to figure out whether or not Atwater was being critical or just being honest. Then he must have come to some kind of answer in his mind, because he half-smiled, and adjusted the laser pistols in his hands.

He set two of the three in his right hand on the nearest console, and tossed the third at Atwater.

Atwater stood, caught the pistol and held it.

Breaux tried to sink back into the wall. She didn't want a weapon. She also didn't want Preemas to yell at her for not having one. She was still dithering when Preemas whirled, grabbed another pistol, and tossed it at her.

She barely caught it. The pistol was heavier than she expected, and it yanked the muscles in her arm. She brought it up, looking at how Atwater was holding his. He gripped it on the non-business end, and his fingers were nowhere near anything that looked like something that might activate the pistol.

Preemas was watching her, half amused, half annoyed.

He was scaring her even worse than he had a moment ago.

"I-I-I don't know how to use this, sir," she said.

"Then learn," he said and turned away from her. "Anyone else not issued a weapon?"

No one else on the bridge responded. Breaux couldn't tell if they were being willfully silent or if they had all received weapons. Since the rest of them had been on the *Renegat* from the beginning, she would assume they all had weaponry—and knew how to use it.

"We'll figure out who doesn't have a weapon, and we'll hand out the extras," Preemas said. "I'm putting you in charge of that, Atwater, since you know so much about the Sector Base Z people."

"I—um—" Atwater started. It was clear that he was going to deny he knew anything.

Then Preemas glared at him.

"Right, sir. I'll get right on that, sir. Justine, I'll need your help." Atwater looked at her meaningfully, but she didn't understand the look. Except that he wanted her help and she was supposed to understand what that meant.

She nodded, her head bobbing ridiculously.

Preemas had already moved beyond them, talking to the rest of the bridge crew, asking about their progress.

He no longer looked like a perfect captain, but more like a renegade who had taken over the ship.

Odd that it was him that looked like the renegade when First Officer Crowe was the one who had disobeyed orders.

Atwater took Breaux's arm. His grip was a little too tight.

"Come with me," he said. Then he made her hold up her laser pistol. He adjusted something on its side, and moved her fingers so that she held it differently.

She looked up at him, feeling stupid and scared and like her body was covered in little prickles of energy.

"You were holding it wrong. It won't go off now, unless you want it to," he said.

She didn't want it to. She didn't want any of the weapons to go off. Why had she joined this ship?

Oh, yeah. Adventure.

How stupid had that been?

Atwater glanced over his shoulder at Preemas, who was still talking to Ibori. Something about breaking into engineering, moving the ship, the Scrapheap, not having success.

Breaux couldn't catch all the words, but she wasn't sure she wanted to.

Atwater tugged at her arm, and said so softly she could barely hear him, "Come on. Let's get out of this mess."

If only it were that simple.

Still, she smiled at him, and let him lead her off the bridge. Somewhere safe, she hoped. Or at least, somewhere out of the line of fire, wherever that might be.

THE *RENEGAT*

Stephanos reached bridge level just as two of the newer recruits were heading out the doors. She hung back in the corridor so that they wouldn't see her. The woman, whose name was something something Breaux, was the one who handled the mapping of the past sectors for Preemas. The man who was with her had been supposed to work with Stephanos on the *anacapa* and foldspace, but she had blown him off weeks ago. His knowledge was all theoretical and maybe that would be useful one day, it certainly wasn't right now.

What she wouldn't give for someone who actually knew as much about *anacapa* drives as she did. Crowe was good with them, but they weren't his specialty. And his comment that the drives were vibrating made her even more uncomfortable.

Although that could possibly explain why she felt so off balance—besides all the events going on. This deck felt charged, as if something had activated and was adding some kind of ionization to the air. The hair on her arms and the back of her neck had risen. She knew that feeling. Sometimes it came from a malfunctioning *anacapa* drive.

If whatsisname—Atwater?—knew as much about *anacapas* and foldspace as he thought he did, he would have known that this ship had yet another problem that needed a real solution, and needed it fast.

Part of her felt oddly relieved, though, that Crowe hadn't sent her on a fake mission. Something really was wrong, and he wanted her to solve it. So he still trusted her abilities, if nothing else.

She slipped through the still open bridge doors, only to stop right inside of them.

No one stood at their stations. No one was paying any attention to what was going on with the ship. They had all crowded around Preemas, who was standing near his captain's chair, loaded down with laser rifles and laser pistols.

Tindo Ibori and Yulia Colvin were hanging back, as if they wanted nothing to do with any of this, but everyone else was watching with great interest.

Stephanos stomach twisted, and for a half second, she thought about fleeing.

Then Preemas turned around. His green eyes met hers and narrowed.

"I trust this means you got into engineering," he said. "But then, that begs the question. If you did, why are you here?"

She gave him a nervous smile, which just made her want to kick herself.

"It's complicated," she said.

"Actually, it's simple," Preemas said. "Either we control the ship or Crowe does. And right now, Crowe does. You've done nothing to help that."

She slipped around the outside of the consoles, closer to the walls than to Preemas. She glanced at her usual post near the *anacapa* drive. At least the drive's protective cover wasn't glowing. There was that, anyway.

"There's a problem with the *anacapa* drive," she said.

"Uh-huh, sure," Preemas said. "Something he caused, I suppose."

"No," she said, her voice sounding shakier than she wanted. "No. It's something else. The Scrapheap maybe. Can't you feel it?"

"What I feel," Preemas said, "is anger at your failure. Now we'll just have to blast our way in."

She had reached the *anacapa* drive and, to her relief, Ibori had joined her. He at least understood how the drives worked.

"I think we can get in if I confirm what's going on with the drive," she said.

"You mean, Crowe sent you on a mission and you *took it*?" Preemas sounded even angrier than he had a moment ago. "You're listening to him?"

"I'm double-checking him," she snapped. "If he's right, then all of this—who runs the damn ship—doesn't matter all. We'll all die here. Right here. As close to succeeding in our mission as we'll ever get. And no one, *no one*, will know what happened to us."

India Romano looked up from a console near the captain's chair. Her eyes were comically wide. They were lavender, matching her hair, which only served to make her look ridiculous.

"I'm sure that's what Crowe told you," Preemas said. "It's a distraction, Stephanos. Now, get your weapon. We're heading to engineering."

"I am going to check on this," she said, realizing that she too was now defying orders from the captain. "Because if Crowe is right—"

"Oh, he'll be right," Preemas said. "He set this up as something that will convince you he's right and I'm wrong. And you'll move to his side, and so will everyone else because we have 'an emergency.' And it's just manufactured, Stephanos. So get over here."

She shook her head. "I need to check."

Preemas grabbed one of the laser pistols that had been sitting on the seat of the captain's chair. He pointed the pistol at her.

"No," he said. "Either you follow my orders or you get off my bridge."

She looked at the pistol, her heart pounding. He was actually doing this. He didn't care about any of them.

She froze for just a moment, then she realized she couldn't follow his orders even if she wanted to. Not and live with herself. If they survived, which she wasn't sure they were going to.

"Look," she said, and to her surprise, her voice wasn't shaking. "You might actually have a point. Crowe might be making this up. But if he isn't, then we're screwed, Captain. It won't matter who is on your side or who is on his. So I'm going to check to see if Crowe is telling the truth. And if he's not, I'll walk right over there and join you. But if he is, then I'm going to solve this, because whatever happens here is irrelevant if the *anacapa* drive is malfunctioning."

No one else said a word. No one else moved.

Preemas didn't move either. His hand was steady, his gaze narrowed. She could actually see his brain working. He was trying to see if there was a percentage in shooting her. Or having someone restrain her. Or removing her from the bridge. Or doing something to shut her up.

She could stand here and let the bastard think, or she could ignore him and do her work.

She gave him a hard look, an *I dare you* look, then walked the remaining distance to the *anacapa* container. The air felt alive here. She got goosebumps on her skin in addition to the raised hair.

Something was happening, but she wasn't sure what it was.

Out of the corner of her eye, she could see Preemas. He continued to hold the pistol on her. Her heart rate increased to a level she had never experienced before.

He was going to shoot her when she wasn't looking at him, when she was trying to save the ship.

Then he lowered the pistol, still watching her, as if he couldn't decide what to do with her.

She moved to the console closest to the *anacapa* drive, where she usually ran the drive. She didn't want to go to the *anacapa* container, in case Preemas actually shot her. If he missed and hit the container after she had opened it, well, then there was no telling what would happen.

He whirled away, pistol still clutched in his hand, as if he didn't care about her at all anymore. He went back to the group he had been talking to before she arrived, as if she hadn't interrupted him at all.

She let out a small breath. Ibori moved closer to her.

"I can monitor the controls," he said softly, "if you want to look at the drive."

She swallowed, then said in a near-whisper, "I'd rather you watch the captain."

Ibori nodded. "I can do both," he said.

Her heart rate spiked. It was almost painful. She was either going to have to trust Ibori, or she was going to have to do it all herself, which would take even more time.

"Let me look at the readings first," she said a little louder, so that it didn't seem like the two of them were whispering against Preemas.

Ibori stepped away from the console, and gazed at the group around Preemas. They had shifted positions slightly, blocking his view of Stephanos, and hers of him. She hoped Ibori could see more clearly from his vantage.

Then Stephanos bent over the console. The *anacapa* controls hadn't been activated, so the *Renegat* should not go into foldspace. But if what Crowe said was true, then *shoulds* didn't matter. Whatever would happen was going to happen.

She couldn't see any evidence of Crowe tampering with the *anacapa* drive either, but she only gave it a cursory look. She didn't believe that Crowe would tamper with the drive just to get her attention, no matter what Preemas said.

Of course, she hadn't expected Crowe to take over the ship either, but given the way that Preemas was acting right now, she was beginning to have some sympathy for Crowe.

Stephanos let out a shallow breath. Preemas had every right to try to get his ship back, but he was not calculating the danger the ship was in.

Maybe she should just talk to him, get him out of that paranoid space.

After she dealt with the drive.

Her heart rate had slowed as she focused on the drive controls. They looked just fine.

But she wasn't letting the controls and their readings dictate her behavior. Or maybe she was unwilling to believe that Crowe had lied to her to get her away from engineering.

"Okay," she said to Ibori, her voice sounding steadier than she expected. "You monitor the controls. I'm going to open the container and peek inside."

And that was all she was going to do. Peek. She wasn't going to open the container all the way, she wasn't going to activate anything. She was just going to look.

Her heartrate spiked again. She hadn't been this nervous ever, in her memory. Not ever.

She took the five steps over to the container. On this ship, the container was a small black box, that looked like someone had committed a weird flaw in the design of the floor of the bridge. The box grew out of that floor—seemingly—although with a closer look, it became clear that the box was attached to the floor, but not part of the floor.

She decided to follow the training for a malfunctioning *anacapa* drive. If the drive looked fine on the controls, there were ways that an engineer could determine if the connection between the controls and the drive was flawed.

She put her hands on the sides of the box. It felt just a little hot, and that sense of something ionized—something electric—something charged—grew just enough to make her shiver. Something was happening here, but what she didn't know.

Did Crowe have the ability to tamper with the *anacapa* drive and not have it show up on the controls?

She tried to banish that thought before it finished crossing her brain, but she wasn't able to do so. She had no idea what Crowe could or couldn't do. And she didn't want to think about whether or not she had the capability of doing something like that.

She only knew she never would.

She quieted her thoughts. If she went at the *anacapa* drive in a panic, she might miss something.

The bones in her hands ached. She put her teeth together as an old instructor had taught her to do, and she felt a hum inside her mouth.

Active *anacapa* drives sometimes caused that hum. It was a vibration that became some kind of sound, something that communicated as soft music rather than as something that registered on a more sensible level.

That instructor had had her hold an *anacapa* in the lab. That old drive hadn't been attached to anything, no ship, no controls, and yet it had felt alive.

She hadn't felt anything like it in all the years since.

Her stomach flipped, and she had to swallow hard to keep down fear-caused bile. Something was going on here. She'd touched this container dozens of times, and it had never felt like this.

She didn't look up at Ibori, or over at Preemas. She couldn't focus on them right now. She needed to focus on this.

"I need everyone to back away from this part of the bridge," she said as clearly as she could.

No one moved. They all seemed to be waiting for Preemas to tell them what to do.

"Now," she said. "If something is wrong, then I want to be the only one hurt."

Or killed, she thought.

Ibori didn't move. A couple people shifted, but no one stepped away. No one looked at Preemas either, although she could tell they were all waiting for him to tell them what to do.

"For God's sake," she said, raising her voice. "*Move! Now!*"

A couple people stepped back—those who weren't in Preemas's immediate line of sight. Two others looked at Preemas, who gave her a small smile.

"They don't believe there's any danger," he said. "They think you're a tool of the traitors."

She shook her head, which aggravated the hum in her mouth, and made her feel as if she were falling apart. Tears of frustration pricked at her eyes, which made her realize just how unsettled and on edge she was—partly because of the situation, but partly because of the *anacapa* drive. When it got into the bones, like it was right now with her, it upset a person's entire system.

"All right, fine," she said. "I can't protect you, and the captain's clearly more interested in being right than your well-being. Do what you want. I don't have the time to mess with any of you."

She bent over the container, knowing that she had sounded a little unhinged. But they were all unhinged. That was the problem, wasn't it? The entire ship had gone completely mad.

She took a deep breath, trying to expel the hum, even though she knew that wouldn't work. Then she worked the edge of the container with both thumbs, like she had a dozen times before.

The lid on the container stuck—not because it was sealed shut, but because some additional force held it in place. If her hands were trembling, she couldn't feel it now. Because her entire body was vibrating on a tiny level, as if some kind of gigantic machine had activated on a lower level and was rattling the entire ship.

Out of the corner of her eye, she could see Ibori's feet. They hadn't moved. She hoped that meant he was still monitoring the controls.

And then she mentally shook herself, forcing herself to focus only on the container.

It would take more than the pressure from her thumbs to open the lid. She was going to have to move her hands, something she hated to do, because that meant the container could move a little too.

So, she crouched, then braced the container with her knees and thighs. The vibration moved to the lower half of her body, making her warm, and interfering with her concentration.

She slipped the tips of her fingers around the lid, using her nails to slide into the tiny gap between the lid and the rest of the container. Some kind of force kept pulling the lid down.

She braced herself even more and did something that was against regulations. She tugged upwards, hoping she wouldn't dislodge the container.

It moved ever so slightly against her knees, and she felt a little frightened, a little floaty. And then the lid popped up.

"Oh, thank god," she breathed, knowing she had spoken aloud and not really caring. No one else seemed to care, either. They hadn't even looked at her.

The *anacapa* glowed golden, just like it was supposed to. A thread of pink ran across it, as if something had bled on it and the blood had found a slight crack in the drive.

She had never seen that thread of pink before.

She needed to touch the drive, but she had to do so properly.

She moved her knees away from the container, grabbed the gloves she kept in the container's side drawer, and slipped them on. They felt warm against her skin, which was new.

Then she put her left hand on the side of the container. Before she reached inside with her right, she examined the entire area.

No foldspace window had opened, at least that she could see with the naked eye.

"How are the readings?" she asked Ibori.

"It says everything is normal," he replied. "But the light coming out of that thing looks a little weird."

So apparently the pink was showing up in other ways.

"No indications of foldspace activation?" she asked.

"Not here," he said.

"Okay." She took a deep breath, then reached inside the container.

Her hand vibrated in the air itself. The air actually felt thick, almost like water. And it shook as she forced her hand through it.

The hum in her teeth grew. It seemed to come from the bones in her hand, going up her arm, into her skull, and down the other side.

Now the tears pricking her eyes were from pain and the incredible headache she was getting just from reaching into the container.

She had to do this fast, before something else went wrong.

She put her hand on the *anacapa* drive itself. It felt smooth through her gloves, like it was supposed to, but it also moved. More than a vibration, less than an actual shaking. It was as if the drive was trying to escape on its own from the container, but didn't yet have the power to do so.

Something hot crossed her upper lip. She licked it, expecting sweat, but tasted blood instead.

That wasn't good. None of this was good.

She tried to pull her hand off the *anacapa* drive, but the glove stuck to it. She had never seen anything like that, but she had heard about it, and it wasn't good.

None of this was good.

She could either pull her gloved hand off the drive or slip her hand out of the glove and leave the glove on the drive. But she had no idea what that would do, if it would change anything, or if it would make matters worse.

A drop of her blood dripped into the container, hitting the edge of the drive. The blood didn't look like that pink line at all. Instead, the drop of blood spread over the surface like little balls of mercury that had escaped onto a floor.

She felt warmth against her back. Ibori stood beside her. "Should I pull you free?" he asked.

She shook her head, making herself dizzy. The blood was spattering on the edges of the container. Tears were running down her cheeks. She had to do this herself, because he could get trapped in here with her.

But her thoughts were coming slowly, and she knew her thinking had become impaired. If she stayed much longer, she would pass out or—

She wouldn't let herself think about that.

She put her free hand on the side of the container, gripped the inside of the glove so that it moved with her other hand, and yanked.

For a moment, she thought it wasn't going to come free.

And then it did, with such force that she fell backwards, slamming her back and shoulders against one of the consoles.

"You've told me not to mess with *anacapa* drives ever since we got on board this ship." Preemas was sneering. He couldn't even bother to ask if she was okay. "Maybe you should have taken your own advice."

Her brain felt loose inside her skull, her head was swelling—or it seemed to be—and blood ran from her nose. Ibori was gesturing at someone, whom she couldn't see, and a few people were shouting.

She wanted to close her eyes, just close them and rest for a minute.

But she couldn't. She had to say something. She had something to tell them. Only her thoughts were so sluggish, she couldn't remember what that something was.

A woman knelt near her, and put a cold compress on her nose. People were shouting about the med bay, about getting Stephanos there. She didn't want to think about the med bay, and the shouting hurt her ears.

"Close the container," she managed to say, trying to focus on Ibori's face. His skin was gray, and he looked terrified. "Don't touch it with your bare hands. Just close it."

The voice didn't even sound like hers, all gravely and wrong. Her mouth tasted of iron and salt—blood and tears. Her face felt like it was caving in on itself, even though she knew that was impossible.

She had been chosen to work on *anacapa* drives because she did not have a physical reaction to them; some people did, but not her. Never her. This was different.

This was scary.

That's what she had to tell them.

She grabbed Ibori's arm. "The problem isn't the *anacapa* drive," she said as clearly—as strongly—as she could. "The problem is the energy that's surrounding it. It's causing—"

Words were failing her. She couldn't remember the term. That angered her, deep down. She needed to remember the term.

And then the term hit her brain. If only she could have patience, she would do fine. But they didn't have time for patience. None of them did.

Ibori was leaning close to her. Wasn't she speaking loudly enough? Or was it the others, still shouting, gesturing, seemingly upset. And Preemas, who was blaming her for this injury, using words like *stupid* and *difficult* and *why was she tampering with it after being told not to?*

She blinked, then pulled Ibori even closer.

"Chain reaction," she said, using the words she had nearly lost first. Those were the most important thing. "That energy is causing a chain reaction, creating something new, something dangerous…."

She was having trouble finding the air to push out the words. Her eyelids felt heavy, and her teeth ached. She had had no idea that teeth could ache like that.

"Tell Crowe," she said to Ibori. "Tell him it's not the *anacapa*. It's the other energy. Get us out of here. Tell him."

Ibori was nodding.

"Crowe?" Preemas asked. He had moved toward her. She could see him at the edge of her vision, just barely, looking disgusted. At her? At her words? At her face? "*I* run this ship."

She waved a hand—or tried to. "I don't care. *Someone* has to get us out of here. Someone…"

She couldn't talk anymore. It took too much effort.

She closed her eyes. They would have to solve this without her. She needed rest. She needed quiet. And she was getting it. The voices were fading. The pain was easing.

She sighed.

And she was done.

THE *RENEGAT*

She was dead.

Tindo Ibori crouched beside Natalia Stephanos, still clutching her hand in his. She hadn't acknowledge the clutch. She had grabbed him and pulled him closer, and hadn't done anything more when he took her hand, squeezing it tight.

Her face was black and blue. Blood vessels had burst under her skin. Her eyes, still open, were red-rimmed. The tears that leaked out of them were pink. Blood caked along her nose and mouth. Her forehead looked shrunken, as if it was collapsing on itself.

Yulia Colvin rocked back on her heels. She had put a compress on Stephanos's nose, but Ibori had taken it off, because it was interfering with Stephanos's ability to talk. He had needed to hear what she was saying. She had died telling him about the *anacapa*.

Telling him not to touch the damn thing, and close the container.

He looked at it like it was the enemy. The lid was back, and the *anacapa* drive glowed golden, just like it was supposed to.

Or at least, like he thought it was supposed to.

Ibori had had minimal *anacapa* training. It had all been theory. He hadn't touched one or interacted with one or done much more than look at one throughout his entire career.

He knew how to use the controls to turn them on. He knew how to handle a ship entering foldspace.

But he didn't know how to deal with a broken *anacapa* that had just killed someone.

"If she hadn't listened to Crowe, she would be fine," Preemas was saying to the sycophants around him.

"You don't know that," Ibori said, almost to himself.

"Crowe rigged the *anacapa* drive so that it would hurt anyone who touched it," Preemas said. Ibori couldn't tell if Preemas was responding to him or if Preemas was still just mouthing off.

"I don't think you can rig an *anacapa* drive," Ibori said, a little louder.

"He's trying to take over the ship permanently by getting rid of everyone who helped me," Preemas said. "I tried to tell Stephanos that, but of course, she didn't listen."

Ibori put a hand on Stephanos's shoulder. Her skin, through her soft uniform, was still warm.

"Stop blaming her for doing her job," Ibori said even louder this time.

Preemas looked down at him, and clearly saw Stephanos's body. Preemas's mouth formed a moue of disgust, and then he looked away.

Ibori shot to his feet. "Don't you look away," he said. "You did this to her. And you'll do it to all of us."

Preemas's eyes narrowed. "I told her not to—"

"You haven't listened to anyone since you received command of this ship, and now one of us is dead," Ibori said. "Horribly, awfully dead, killed by the thing *she* was the expert in. She—"

"Yeah," Preemas said. "She was the expert so Crowe took her out."

Ibori took a step toward Preemas. Ibori wanted to punch the man in the face, and end it all right, there.

"Even I know how impossible it is to tamper with an *anacapa* drive," Ibori said. "And I'm not captain. I haven't had the years of training on *anacapa* drives. I haven't commanded ships that had *anacapa* drives, forcing me to understand them, in theory. I am frankly scared that you know so little about the drives. I'm worried—"

"If you're scared of the work on the bridge," Preemas said, picking up the exact wrong word. The wrong message, the wrong word, "then you can step down."

"We could all die like this," Ibori said, sweeping his hand toward Stephanos's body. "Because she couldn't fix it in the time she had, and everyone else who can has bolted themselves into engineering trying to save the ship."

Preemas's eyes narrowed even more. His silence was palpable. No one else on the bridge moved.

"Is that what you believe?" he asked, finally. "You believe that they're trying to save the ship? From me?"

Ibori's career was already over. He'd already made his choices. And Stephanos's body, still oozing blood near his feet, made him realize the stakes were more than doing the right thing. The stakes had moved to survival.

"I believe," he said slowly, "that once we arrived in this sector, we were in some kind of trouble, and everyone in engineering realized that you wouldn't listen to them or take the right action. I mean, the first thing they did was move the ship away from the Scrapheap."

"The Scrapheap's the reason we're here," Preemas said. "They're showing cowardice."

Everyone was watching them both, but no one was speaking up. The rest of the bridge crew held their positions next to Preemas. They were watching, but they weren't participating. They weren't *helping*.

Didn't they realize their lives were at stake as well? Or had they already given up? Or did they just find it easier to follow orders, even if the guy giving the orders was a clueless idiot who was going to kill them all?

"They're showing initiative," Ibori said. "Natalia said that there's some kind of energy interacting with the drive. And she thought the energy was coming from the Scrapheap."

At least, that's what he had understood her to say. But he wasn't an engineer. His specialty was navigation.

He looked at that container, his heart pounding so hard in his chest he was amazed that his chest didn't burst open.

"She told me to put the lid back on the container," Ibori said.

"Probably the only sensible remark that she had made all afternoon," Preemas said.

That was it. That was all Ibori could take.

"Then you fucking do it," he snapped. "Because I'm not touching any of this. And I'm not helping your little raid or whatever it is. I want Chief Engineer Crowe to handle this emergency. He's smart, and he actually knows how ships work."

"You're being insubordinate," Preemas said.

"I'm being sensible," Ibori said.

"You close that container, then get a weapon and join me as I go down to engineering," Preemas said.

"No." Ibori didn't add the other thing that almost blurted out of his mouth. He didn't say, *If I had a weapon, I'd turn it on you.*

The fierceness of that thought startled him. He wasn't a violent man.

"Then I suppose we should start the arrests." Preemas looked at Fernando Oshie, the new head of security. Ibori hated Oshie. The man had muscles on muscles, and often used them to shove some of the crew around. "Let's take him to the brig and get him out of our way."

A ripple of movement went through the bridge crew. A few people looked stunned. Were they finally realizing just how serious this could be? Was it the fact that someone—anyone, one of their colleagues—could go to the brig that caught their attention? More than Stephanos's death did?

Ibori held up a hand.

"Tell you what," he said. "I'll take care of Natalia here, since none of you seem to even acknowledge she's dead, and then I'll report to the brig like a good soldier."

He sounded convincing, but even as he spoke, he knew he was lying. After he got Stephanos to the med bay, so that she could be preserved until they could deal with her body, he wasn't going to report anywhere.

Except maybe engineering.

Preemas tilted his head just a little as he looked at Ibori. Ibori got the sense that Preemas was also watching the rest of the crew out of the corner of his eye, trying to figure out how far he could push them before they bolted from him.

Ibori wasn't sure the crew supported the arrest. Preemas had to have seen the movement and discomfort as well, because his face softened just a little.

"All right," Preemas said. "You've served this ship with honor, and now you want to honor one of our dead. I will allow that."

Ibori let out a small breath. Preemas was coming to his senses after all.

"But," Preemas said, "if you do not report to the brig after you have taken her to the med bay for disposal—"

Ibori winced at that word.

"—we will hunt you down and deal with you in whatever way we deem appropriate. Do you understand?"

Whatever way they feel appropriate. In other words, if they were in the middle of some kind of battle, they would kill him.

The captain just threatened to kill his navigator. A man who had never done anything wrong.

Ibori opened his mouth to tell the bridge crew that, and then stopped. They were smart. They could figure this out on their own. Or choose to ignore it, on their own.

Ibori didn't answer Preemas. Instead, Ibori crouched beside Stephanos. The blood had stopped oozing. It was drying black against her skin. She looked sunken and broken. She really didn't look human anymore.

He glanced at the open container. He really should close it, but he didn't dare. Look at what happened to her when she tried.

He wasn't that courageous. Or maybe, he wasn't that kind of courageous. Because he was standing up to the captain of a ship he had agreed to serve on.

Standing up in a mutinous way.

Ibori looked at Colvin. "Will you help me get her on a gurney?"

Colvin shook her head slightly. She either didn't want to be involved or she didn't want to touch Stephanos's body any more than Ibori wanted to touch the container.

He was going to have to bring one of the floating gurneys here, which made him queasy. More tech moving in the vicinity of the *anacapa* drive simply meant more things could go wrong.

"I will help," said a voice he didn't recognize.

He looked up. It took a moment for him to recognize India Romano. Her hair was lavender today. She always looked well put together. He noticed her, but she had never noticed him, which was probably good, considering she was married to one of the linguists below deck.

He had thought Romano was a linguist too. Then he saw the small badge attached to her sleeve, and realized she had been moved to a new position. She was security now.

Was this another ploy by Preemas? A way to make sure that Ibori actually went to the brig?

He hadn't seen them consult, so he wasn't sure how the ploy worked. Maybe Romano just took it upon herself to ensure Ibori's compliance. Or maybe the offer of help had nothing to do with Preemas at all.

"Thank you," he said. "I was worried about bringing the single gurney, because I didn't want it interacting with the *anacapa*."

Romano nodded, as if she had thought of that herself. "Yulia, get the regular gurney out of the storage closet. We'll carry her to it."

Ibori grimaced. He really didn't want to touch Stephanos, but he was going to have no choice. He grabbed the gloves from his navigation console, and slipped them on.

As he did so, he saw Romano walk over to the *anacapa* container. She looked down on it. Her hair was standing up around her head, not a lot, but as if she had walked into a slight field filled with static.

"I don't think you should touch it," he said.

But even as he spoke, she bent over, grabbed the container lid with her bare hand, and slammed the container shut.

The bang echoed across the bridge. Ibori's heart rate spiked so badly that he couldn't catch his breath. A couple of people ducked. A few more took a step back.

Preemas's hand had tightened around the laser pistol he had turned on Ibori.

"Wasn't hard," Romano said, turning away from the container. She wiped her hands on her pants. "You are all big babies."

"Touching that killed Natalia," Colvin said.

"Touching the stupid drive killed her," Romano said. "My first lover was in *anacapa* training until they made her touch a drive. She went mad. Literally. Those things are dangerous, which is why we have them in containers."

She took a few steps back to Stephanos's body. Then Romano's gaze met Ibori's.

"No offense," she said to him, "but you're no expert on the drive. For all you know, just touching the drive after it had been used so many times is what killed her."

"That's not what she said." Ibori spoke softly. He would never get her damaged face out of his mind, her hand clasping his, the urgency in her voice. "She told me as she was dying that it was the energy from the Scrapheap interacting with the drive."

"Yeah, sure," Romano said. "We're all so reliable when we're injured or dying. I'm sure her perceptions were spot on."

Her tone, her lack of respect, her complete idiotic confidence made Ibori want to tell her to stay away from Stephanos's body. But he didn't.

He needed the help.

The gurney was out of the storage closet and floated a few steps up, near one of the large screens. That screen had been showing the Scrapheap, but was now dark.

Ibori had no idea when anyone (Preemas, probably) shut the screens down.

More denial, or whatever Preemas was doing. Ibori couldn't quite figure it out.

But he didn't have to. He needed to do this first, before he could do anything else.

He crouched beside Stephanos's body.

"You ready?" he asked Romano.

"Yeah," she said. "I'll grab the feet."

The feet. As if Stephanos was a thing, and not a person. Which, Ibori realized, she was now. Because Stephanos wasn't in that body anymore. He felt a tightening in his throat, and made himself breathe, just to calm himself. It wasn't working.

He just had to get through this.

He slipped his hands under her shoulders. The blood had oozed there and was already tacky against his fingers. Stephanos's shoulders felt thinner than he would have expected. She had loomed large in his life—the person who knew how the *anacapa* drive worked, the woman who barked orders at him, the other person on the bridge he could share a smile with—so he never thought of her as small. And she had been.

And fragile.

Romano's gaze met his. She didn't seem disturbed by any of this at all. Her eyebrows went up, as if she was asking whether he was ready to do this.

He nodded.

"On three," she said. "One…two…three."

He lifted with his knees, not that the effort was all that necessary. Romano didn't have Stephanos by the feet. Romano had gripped Stephanos's thighs. Together Ibori and Romano carried Stephanos up the incline past several consoles to the floating gurney.

The gurney adjusted to the proper height, sliding under the body. Ibori let Stephanos go. His hands were covered with her blood, and it had dripped on the floor. He didn't look at the spot she had fallen. He suspected it was one large blood stain right now.

"I'll go with her," he said to Romano, and then realized that Romano had already left him, going back to Preemas and the upcoming fight.

Ibori put his filthy hand on the gurney, gave it the verbal instruction to go to the morgue wing of the med bay, and it moved faster than he would have liked.

He had to walk quickly to keep up with it.

A few people, still near the stations, watched it go. But no one said anything. He had no idea what they were thinking.

He didn't look back. He couldn't.

But he had trouble looking at Stephanos too. The body no longer resembled the woman he had known.

She was dead, and as deeply as that disturbed him, another thought had entered his brain, one that disturbed him even more.

He had a hunch that she was only the first.

THE *RENEGAT*

India Romano wiped her hands on a sanitizing cloth that Colvin handed her. There really hadn't been goo from Stephanos's body on Romano's palms, but she cleaned her hands just in case. She'd made Ibori take the top part of the corpse because that's where all the ick was. Who knew that death could happen so fast and so horribly? One mistake and—that.

Romano shuddered, wiped her hands a second time for good measure, and then she tossed the cloth aside. The bridge was already a mess; one more piece of garbage didn't matter. She surveyed that mess for a minute—the horrid black pool of body fluids from Stephanos, sending out a waft of stink like the worst backed-up toilet. Suddenly, Romano wanted off the bridge. It was creepy. The abandoned consoles made the bridge look almost empty, even though a crowd of people had formed near the captain.

Also near the captain, more weapons than Romano had seen outside of weapons training classes in school. She knew how to use all of these, because they were personal weapons—standard-issue laser pistols, and a few rifles that everyone received training on before joining a ship in any kind of official capacity.

She didn't recognize the tiny things—the hand-sized balls—but she figured they were explosives of some kind. She half-smiled to herself. As one of the security officers now, she should know how these things worked, and she didn't.

Just more to learn.

She let out a small breath, forcing herself to focus on the crisis at hand, not the one she had just grumpily solved because no one else on this stupid bridge had been willing to step up and deal with Ibori and Stephanos.

Now that the gurney with the body accompanied by yet another living traitor had left the bridge, everyone could settle down to business. Including her.

She rejoined Captain Preemas, pushing her way through the other bridge crew members who had gathered around him. He had stacked a pile of weapons on top of a floating table. He was leaning on the arm of his captain's chair, and looking at a tablet he had placed on its seat. She had no idea why he wasn't using screens. She suspected that he was worried Crowe would hack into what the bridge crew was doing.

She wiped her hands on the back of her pants. Her hands felt like they were coated with something, although that was probably her imagination. She had never handled a dead body before.

Stephanos's thighs had been thin, bony, and squishy. Her skin, through her pants, had still been warm, which Romano hadn't expected. But Stephanos had been heavy, like a sack of rocks, and it hadn't felt like Romano had been carrying a human being at all.

That thought had kept her calm while she was handling the corpse, but clearly she was bugged by it, or she wouldn't keep wiping her hands.

But that wasn't the only thing that bothered her about her hands. They were tingling. Her whole body was tingling on some low level. The air felt alive.

She had no idea if the tingling had gotten worse when she grabbed the container lid and slammed it shut or if everyone was experiencing this kind of tingling.

She wanted to ask, but she didn't want to draw attention to herself.

Although she was irked that she hadn't gotten any kudos for touching that container lid. She was still pissed at Ibori for being a baby about handling the *anacapa* drive container; she was pissed at Crowe for putting them all in this situation; and she was pissed at her wife for continually pinging her in their shared link.

Romano had told her that there was a situation on the bridge, and Romano would talk to her later. Romano repeated that message twice after that, and then, finally, she had cut the link to Serpell.

Serpell had been difficult since Romano switched from linguist to security officer. Apparently Serpell hadn't cared that Romano was happier in this position.

Their relationship was doomed; Serpell just didn't know it yet. And Romano didn't have the guts to tell her. Not yet. Besides, Romano didn't want to be stuck on a ship with an ex. Better to avoid the actual wife, than exacerbate things by confronting Serpell about the failure of the relationship and then having to see her every single day.

"At least a dozen others have weapons that we'll be able to use," Preemas was saying. He seemed a little more animated than usual. The man was one of those fidgeters, always moving. But today, he was moving even more, clearly unable to stay still.

Romano didn't blame him. He had just been betrayed by the person he trusted the most. Crowe had been planning to overthrow Preemas for weeks, maybe since before he got on the ship.

It had been a brilliant plan, too, as far as Romano could see. Crowe had waited until they were as far from the Fleet as they could get, and then he seized the ship. What could the Fleet do, after all? Send *another* ship? They'd already filled this one with the dregs of the Fleet. It would take them weeks, maybe months, to fill another ship like this.

Not that anyone could send a message back to the Fleet anyway.

Preemas had explained all of this to the team—how Crowe had tampered with everything, then made it seem like he was a good guy so Preemas promoted him. (*He fooled me*, Preemas said. *I'm man enough to admit that. He fooled me just like he fooled you all.*)

Crowe had used all of his access to cut off communications with the Fleet, make sure that Preemas's secondary command center had been shut down, and had isolated the bridge.

Preemas was doing everything he could to find a way to get information that Crowe couldn't access. Romano didn't know a lot about systems, but she knew that Preemas did, and she had to trust him on this.

"The problem is that we don't have engineers," Preemas was saying. "Crowe has polluted them all. Even the ones who left engineering aren't really getting involved. I've confined them to quarters. I've already sent someone to confiscate their weapons, but we don't have time to wait for extras."

No one else spoke. Romano wiped her hands again, hating how they felt. It was almost as if they were going numb.

She glanced at her right hand, her dominant hand. It looked paler than usual. The blood vessels were visible through the skin, something she'd seen on people with lighter skin, but never on her hands before.

"Are we boring you, India?" Preemas snapped.

She raised her head and dropped her hand at the same time. "No, sir. It's just—." She interrupted herself, deciding not to tell him what was happening after all. He probably wouldn't care, for that matter. "Um, it's just that I'm ready to go after the bastards now, sir."

Preemas's frown changed to a grin. He laughed. "Good point, India," he said. "The more we talk, the more time they have to figure out how to keep hold of the ship."

He waved a hand at Fernando Oshie, who had started acting as his second in command. "Hand out the pistols. Who here has been trained on laser rifles?"

Titus M'Ghan and Jorja Lakinas raised their hands.

Preemas nodded and handed them each a rifle. "We'll use the rest of them," he said, "only if we need them. People who know how to use them, but haven't been trained, take the others. If I give the command, we'll just fire randomly."

Romano shuddered. She wasn't sure what caused that. She'd like to blame the tingling. But the idea that people like her who only knew how to use the rifles in theory actually using the rifles made her nervous.

But…this was the situation that Crowe had put them all in. She would do what she had to do.

Preemas picked up one of the small round things. "These are charges that we usually use planetside. They have a small explosive power, enough to open doors and blast through walls. It's risky to use them on a ship, but I see no other way to get into engineering."

Romano stood very still. Now she knew that the shot of nerves that ran through her had nothing to do with the growing tingling feeling throughout her body. The idea of blowing anything up on a ship in space terrified her.

Yulia Colvin shot Romano a glance. Colvin looked terrified. Lakinas's lips thinned, and she clutched her rifle tighter.

"The great thing about these charges," Preemas was saying, apparently not noticing the growing unease in the people around him (or not caring), "is that they can be controlled. We change the force and the power of them. Fernando and I have both used them before. We will set them outside of engineering, and blow open the doors before we storm the place."

He raised his head, then met everyone's eyes. When his gaze locked on to Romano's, she felt her breath catch. It was as though he could see all her doubts and fears, and he felt the same level of contempt for them that she had felt for Ibori.

She made herself give him what she hoped was a confident half smile and a nod. She was ready, even though it would be hard.

"This is a straightforward assault on the sealed room. We blow the door, we enter, and we shoot," Preemas said. "Because it's engineering, though, we have to be careful where we aim. If you're not an accurate shot, then reserve your firepower until I give the order. We want to hit the mutineers, not the equipment around them. Is that clear?"

A shootout in engineering. Clear. Yeah, it was clear. It was clearly terrifying.

But they were at a stalemate and someone had to do something, or Crowe would hurt them all worse.

She wasn't quite sure what the worse was, but that wasn't her concern. Preemas knew Crowe. He knew what Crowe wanted, and why Crowe took over the ship. And Preemas felt it was enough of a threat to everyone that he had to take drastic action.

That was good enough for Romano.

When Preemas's gaze met hers this time, she had a half smile plastered on her face. His gaze moved from hers quickly this time because he couldn't see her fear.

Which was good because her fear was irrelevant.

"Sir?" Colvin asked. "Won't First Officer Crowe be expecting us to do something like this?"

Irritation crossed Preemas's face, then disappeared so quickly that Romano questioned whether she had interpreted the micro expression correctly.

"He has sealed off the weapons' room," Preemas said. "He thinks we don't have access to weaponry. He thinks he controls the entire ship. We'll show him that he doesn't."

Romano swallowed compulsively. The hair on her arms stood up, as well as the hair on the back of her neck. She blamed that on the tingling, whatever that had been. It continued. Her hands ached as the tingle grew worse.

She flexed them, and they moved the way they were supposed to. That was all that mattered. She would worry about the growing ache in her bones later.

"All right," Preemas said with a determined grin. "Get your gear. We're going in."

PART TWENTY-NINE

THE END OF THE *RENEGAT*

NOW

THE *AIZSARGS*

If Dauber had less training, she would have been watching events unfold in real time with her hands covering her mouth. As it was, she had to thread her hands together so that she wouldn't show the tension that had woven its way through her body.

The entire bridge crew had stopped any pretense of working. They were all watching screens or holoimages, staring at data flow, whatever was the easiest for them to either process what they were seeing or to remain distant from it.

She didn't reprimand any of them. They knew, as well as she did, that this was a crucial moment. She almost saw it as a gesture of respect for Raul Zarges. He was taking a hell of a risk, and she hoped it would pan out.

She watched, but she also made herself concentrate on the next steps.

Rescue One had 193 of the people from the *Renegat* safe and sound in the hold designed especially for that purpose. No member of *Rescue One*'s crew was allowed to mingle with the evacuees, because they had arrived from foldspace, with some kind of time differential.

Fleet rules: anyone who had gone through some kind of time change like that needed to be informed of that change slowly. In the past, the Fleet had simply told the ship's crew of the change and expected them to deal with it. But most hadn't dealt with it at all.

The Fleet had lost valuable crew that way. Some had quit, others had spiraled downward, losing their ability to function in any capacity that required them to travel in and out of foldspace.

Dauber was following regulations, even if Zarges wasn't.

She watched the life raft leave the dying *Renegat*, moving much too slowly. At least all the other vessels were nowhere near the *Renegat*. The energy spikes were getting more and more frequent and erratic. Dauber didn't like what she was seeing.

She had a hunch her team didn't either, although they weren't saying anything.

Everyone was waiting for that damn raft to get as far from the *Renegat* as possible.

When this was over, she would recommend to the brass that any future rafts built by the Fleet would have some kind of faster engine built in. She knew the rafts didn't have them because they were designed to be operated from a distance or by injured survivors.

The Fleet had learned the hard way not to give the inexperienced a lot of choices.

But they had needed this choice right now.

"How far is safe for that life raft?" Ornitz asked, breaking the unofficial silence.

"Dunno," Ribisi said, and if the Chief Engineer didn't know, then no one did.

The life raft moved at an excruciating pace no matter what image Dauber looked at.

In two dimensions, the life raft seemed like a flat rectangle that wasn't moving at all. In three dimensions it was a cube that barely inched forward—which she could only tell by the stars and planets behind it, appearing or disappearing as the cube blocked them.

Only in telemetry could she really see how well the life raft was gaining on *Rescue One*.

"At this pace, it'll take them about twenty minutes," Ullman said, but for whose benefit Dauber didn't know. She had seen the timing, and she was sure the rest of this bridge crew could see it to.

Twenty excruciating minutes, as the energy spiked and whipped like something she had never seen before. Twenty excruciating minutes—

Ribisi cursed.

Dauber raised her head, searched the images for an anomaly, saw it on the sensors first. Something was actually registering as hot on the far end of the *Renegat*.

"Where is that coming from?" she asked Ribisi.

"The *Renegat's* bridge," he said.

And she knew. She *knew* it was all over.

She knew it before that heat image engulfed that entire part of the *Renegat*, before the anomaly became light on the two- and three-dimensional images she was monitoring, before the light spread outward like hands clawing at the edges of space.

Before the light engulfed the life raft, and it disappeared completely.

She should have ordered *Rescue One* to move even farther away from the anomaly, but she didn't. Because she knew they would ignore that order, and it would be on the record, and she didn't want their disobedience on the record.

Because they were waiting—hoping—Zarges would get out.

The light spread outward, the edges of it reaching—reaching—reaching—toward *Rescue One*, and then falling off, as if the edges couldn't maintain.

The light faded and disappeared almost as a unit.

She glanced at the area where the *Renegat* had been, half-expecting to see debris, but she saw nothing. She also expected to see the edges of a foldspace opening, but she didn't see that either.

It was as if the *Renegat* had not existed.

And there was no life raft.

She would have sunk into her chair, if she had allowed herself a captain's chair. But these sorts of moments were exactly why she didn't.

She had to be strong for her crew.

"Any sign of the life raft?" she asked, sounding much calmer than she expected. It sounded like she had had no emotional reaction at all.

"No." Ullman's voice shook. "They're gone."

"Did that explosion send them into foldspace?" Lauritz asked. She clearly wasn't used to seeing other ships go into foldspace.

Dauber was. She knew the answer before Ullman spoke up.

A ship gave off a certain signature when it headed into foldspace. There was no signature here.

"No," Ullman said. "The ship—the derelict ship, and the life raft. They're gone." Then he cleared his throat. "Destroyed."

That last word reverberated into a growing silence.

That word would demoralize the crew if Dauber wasn't careful. She had to handle it correctly, right now.

"One hundred and ninety-three survivors will arrive on this ship within the hour," she said. "We need to prepare for them. We lost Raul Zarges, but these survivors have lost their home and their friends. Follow protocol. Let me handle the difficult information. And remember one thing."

Everyone was looking at her, their expressions bland, but their eyes filled with anguish.

"We *rescued* one hundred ninety-three people we hadn't even known about when we got out of bed this morning. One hundred ninety-three lives. Saved. Keep that close to your heart as you mourn Raul."

She didn't add the one thing that might also have given them comfort. He had *chosen* to go back, chosen to violate her orders, chosen to take a risk that she knew—they all probably knew—wouldn't pay off.

If she had mentioned that, it would seem like she approved of his actions in retrospect, and she did not. His heroics cost her a good crewman and one life raft.

And would interrupt her sleep for years.

The bridge crew was still looking at her. For a moment, she wondered if those thoughts had floated across her face. But she hadn't felt like she moved at all.

She took a deep breath and said softly, "After we get the newcomers settled, we will plan a memorial for Raul. But we have work to do first."

That settled it. Heads bent, fingers moved, Lauritz left the bridge to coordinate the arrival of the survivors of the *Renegat*.

And Dauber wished for a big, welcoming captain's chair, to enfold her and support her, just for a few minutes.

But she didn't have one. So she stood, and moved through the rest of her day.

Just like she was supposed to.

PART THIRTY

PREPARING FOR BATTLE

100 YEARS AGO

THE *RENEGAT*

Crowe stood in the center of a variety of floating screens of all sizes, monitoring half a dozen things, and he had to force himself to concentrate. He had finally decided that keeping track of the people outside of engineering was as important as all of the other tasks he was working on.

The crew in engineering itself were working hard, keeping their heads down. He would occasionally lift his out of the circle of screens to make sure that no one was upset or collapsing under the stress.

Because the stress was massive. Too many crises all at once. Since he was monitoring the environmental system, he noted that the oxygen usage in engineering had gone up slightly, even though the number of crew members in engineering had gone down.

Everyone was breathing a little too much, trying to calm down.

There was also a slight smell, a funk of human body odor and stale sweat that the environmental system couldn't overcome. It was a sign, he knew, that everyone was as terrified as he was, and they were doing their best to overcome it all.

He was monitoring the environmental systems for a variety of things, not just oxygen usage. He could see life forms on the rudimentary environmental controls. The environmental controls automatically showed life signs for anyone with engineering access, so that an engineer (or an upper level crew member) could figure out exactly how much stress on the system the people in a given room were causing.

He could dig into other systems, access the crew identifications, since the ship monitored where everyone was at all times. But that would mean he would have to access systems that would flag his activity to the bridge. He could shut off the flag, but even that would call attention to itself.

He didn't want to do that. He didn't want Preemas—or someone who still allowed Preemas to tell them what to do—to know what Crowe was working on.

According to the environmental logs, the systems were working well in most parts of the ship. The only exception was the bridge, where that extra energy he had noted from the Scrapheap seemed to have dried the air more than it should have.

He couldn't dig in and see what caused that, and from what he could tell by crew placement, no one was working on that, either. Some of the bridge crew had left the bridge. A couple of people were heading for the mess.

They weren't the only ones moving. The entire crew seemed to be shifting positions all over the ship. He hadn't heard any announcements from Preemas, so either word was getting out in a different way, or everyone was on edge because they were here, at the Scrapheap.

Some crew members were going back to their cabins in the middle of a workday. Still others had gone to the bridge.

And then there was the trip one person was taking with a gurney toward the med bay.

Crowe couldn't get an exact reading on who that was without revealing himself. If he asked for too much information from the systems, someone who was good with watching what others did—just like he was—would be able to figure out what he was thinking. More or less, anyway. If they were organized enough to watch everything.

Otherwise, nothing had changed. He had his relatively small crew monitor the Scrapheap to make sure that its energy levels weren't changing. He also had Tosidis keep an eye on the communications *anacapa*, and Willoughby was watching the bridge *anacapa*, as well as the bridge itself. The vibrations were continuing, and that made Crowe nervous.

Bakhr had said they couldn't move far enough away in this solar system to avoid that energy. Crowe was trying to see if Bakhr's experience from that past Scrapheap applied to this one.

He was having trouble concentrating, though.

He hadn't heard from Stephanos. And he had no idea why. He was beginning to become convinced that he had been played for a fool. They wanted him to think that Stephanos had come back to his side, but why?

The answer came just a few minutes later. The crew members he was monitoring on the bridge had left the bridge en masse. Only two people remained on the bridge, which startled and alarmed him. A ship this size needed a full crew compliment on the bridge, no matter what was going on.

But apparently the idiot captain didn't think so.

Everyone else was heading out of the bridge, taking the elevators down, and Crowe knew where they were going: they were going to engineering.

"Can we see what's going on with the main *anacapa* drive?" he asked Willoughby.

She was shaking her head. He had no idea if she saw the bridge crew heading this way, but he suspected she did.

"No one seems to have made any change," she said. "It's like they've forgotten they're on a ship at all."

He felt cold. He had that sense as well, and he wasn't sure why.

But since the bridge crew was mostly *off* the bridge, Crowe was going to risk figuring out who was where.

He went into the main system and monitored each crew member individually.

The two people on the bridge were Titus M'Ghan and Yulia Colvin, neither of whom had engineering training. M'Ghan was a terrible pilot, whom Crowe avoided at all times and had hoped would leave the ship at Sector Base Z. Of course, that hadn't happened.

Colvin meant well, but had never risen to the level of competence that should have allowed her to command a runabout let alone run the bridge on an SC-Class vessel.

That alarmed the hell out of Crowe. They wouldn't know what to do if there was some kind of energy flare from the Scrapheap or if the *anacapa* started to thrust the ship back into foldspace.

Preemas was leading most of the bridge crew, several security officers, and a few crew members Crowe had had no interaction with toward the elevators.

Crowe's mouth went dry. He felt lightheaded, then realized he wasn't breathing.

It had finally come to this. And he had received no other warning from Stephanos.

But, considering who the two crew members left on the bridge were, Crowe didn't have to worry about subtleties anymore. He entered the main system, moved all its information onto yet another screen, made it float in front of him at eye level, and then turned on the visual.

Preemas stood in front of the bridge-level elevator, with almost twenty people around him, and more on the way. Preemas wore two laser rifles, and some kind of bandolier with small charges packed in it. He had a laser pistol on each hip, and he held another laser pistol in his right hand. He was gesturing with it, the idiot.

The lightheadedness returned, along with an adrenaline spike that made it feel as if Crowe's innards were trying to slam through his ribs. It was one thing to know that he and the captain were at odds; it was another to see the captain and the small army he had assembled prepare to march on engineering.

"You seeing this?" Crowe asked Willoughby, deciding not to be specific.

"Something with the *anacapa*?" she asked, which meant she hadn't noted what Preemas was doing.

"The captain," Crowe said.

"I see it," said Tosidis.

"Me, too," said Bakhr.

The remaining engineering crew chimed in one by one, all of them monitoring what was going on. So Crowe enlarged his various screens, and placed them around the main part of engineering, so that everyone could see in great detail what they faced.

He counted a dozen laser rifles, with two others besides Preemas carrying two. A few of the people with laser rifles looked uncomfortable with them. Everyone who was with Preemas had at least one laser pistol. And one other person carried a bandolier just like Preemas was doing.

Crowe scanned the faces, and he also looked at the computerized identifications. No Stephanos. She wasn't one of the two people left on the bridge either.

He didn't like what he was thinking. He called up another small screen just as Tosidis said, "Sir, you see those shape charges?"

"I do," Crowe said, trying to find the gurney on his smaller screen.

"If they use them all—"

"We have no ship left," Crowe said. The gurney had entered the med bay.

"They wouldn't do that, would they?" asked Bakhr.

"I wouldn't have thought that so many armed crew members would be willing to storm engineering," Crowe said, and immediately regretted it. These people didn't need his anger; they needed him to guide them.

But he was distracted, because the med bay had only one other life form in it. When he turned on the identification, the computer told him the person there was Ibori, not Stephanos.

Crowe didn't go to a visual now. He couldn't quite bear it. And he didn't have time to think about it, not with Preemas and his people—*his people*, who would have thought that?—getting on the elevator to engineering.

Crowe could trap them in the elevator. But they would probably try shooting their way out. And that would do even more damage than attacking the doors of engineering—provided they only used one or two of those shape charges, not the entire lot.

He couldn't think about Stephanos right now. Or what might happen with the *anacapa*. He had to deal with the nearly two dozen armed people heading here.

Preemas was going to try to break in, and do it physically. Crowe had expected that, but had hoped Preemas wasn't going to do it.

At least, Crowe had prepared.

He shut down the feed from the med bay, but kept the rest of the ship information live. He just made it smaller.

The screens showing Preemas and his crew remained large and a focal point. Seeing his colleagues look determined as they headed toward engineering was more disheartening than guessing that such an attack might come.

If Crowe was disheartened, the other engineers had to be as well.

He took a deep breath.

"All right, everyone," he said. "We knew that this attack might occur. We can deal with it."

With little or no loss of life, he wanted to say, but he knew that was unrealistic. He wasn't going to make promises he couldn't fulfill.

"Daria, I need you to continue to monitor the bridge and the *anacapa* there. Benjamin, I need you to make sure the energy readings outside this ship remain unchanged."

Willoughby nodded. Bakhr looked both serious and frightened.

"The rest of you need to listen carefully," Crowe said, "because here's what we're going to do."

THE *RENEGAT*

Somehow, Captain Preemas managed to gather over thirty people to make this attack on the engineering bay. No one seemed nervous or hesitant. They followed Preemas's lead, and Preemas was determined.

Romano's hands still ached, but she ignored that as best she could. The fingers worked, and her arms followed her commands. That was all she cared about.

That, and the fact that the tingle through the rest of her body eased the moment the doors to the bridge closed. That tingle was half a memory by the time she squeezed into the elevator with the rest of the troops.

That was what Preemas was calling them: *troops*. As if they were an army marching against a shared enemy, which, apparently, they were. Hard to think of former friends and colleagues as enemies, but they were. Fortunately, she hadn't known anyone in engineering well. She could hate with impunity.

She half-smiled as she left the elevator. Serpell said that Romano was good at hating. It was a skill she would put to use now. She would show none of those betrayers any mercy. They had endangered the *Renegat*. She would make them pay.

That thought of Serpell made Romano double-check her comm. She didn't want to be interrupted by her panicked wife in the middle of the attack. Romano couldn't take the entire thing off-line, but she could set it only to respond to contact from Preemas and the bridge crew, which she did as she stepped into the wide corridor.

It was filled with people—Preemas's troops. Romano hadn't been able to stay exactly at his side, but close enough to be in the front of the action. She gripped her laser pistol. Preemas had made them all go through a quick refresher on the bridge—this was how the pistol worked, how to aim it to avoid the troops, how to concentrate the beam.

She went over each detail with him, even though she remembered clearly how to use the weapon. And she was ready to use it.

Her heart pounded, but with something akin to joy, not fear. She was ready for this. She had needed this. It banished that trapped feeling which had been growing during the journey to the Scrapheap. She finally felt useful, really useful.

She hurried past a few members of the bridge crew, walking slowly, as if they weren't sure they wanted to be beside Preemas. She practically shoved them aside so that she could trail him.

He was talking to Oshie about the shape charges.

"...don't want to blow a hole in the ship," Preemas was saying. "I want to use just enough to open that damn door. You think four, strategically placed?"

Oshie tugged on his own bandolier. He was wearing shape charges too. Romano wished Preemas had trusted her enough to give her some extra weapons.

She would prove herself to him this afternoon, though.

"We have to be careful," Oshie said. "The fewer charges the better."

Romano managed to reach Preemas's left flank.

"What about just one?" she asked a little too loudly. Her adrenaline was really pumping. She couldn't even properly modulate her voice. "Right at the door's latch?"

Preemas didn't even look over his shoulder so that he could see her. "That's fortified, and then the fortification triples in invasion mode. That's the one area we probably can't blow."

He let out a small laugh, as if it all amused him.

"In fact, that'll probably stay latched while the door blows inward."

She didn't find that funny, even though she could see it in her mind's eye. She felt her cheeks heat. Sometimes it was really clear just how much training she missed when she went to school for linguistics.

And if she had stayed a linguist, she wouldn't be standing here, at her captain's side, about ready to retake the ship. She'd be hiding somewhere with her useless soon-to-be-ex-wife, crying and terrified and wondering when it would all end.

"Door's four corners is what I'm thinking," Oshie said. "Charges set on the lowest level."

"And I'm thinking the control panel," Preemas said. "The door gets fortified in invasion mode and the panel is impossible to access, but no one ever thinks of the way the panel's attached to the wall. It's a separate unit. If we can remove that unit with a charge, we cripple Crowe's ability to control the door, and we have access to the room."

Romano wanted to say, *what about both,* but she was beginning to realize just how out of her depth she was.

"Eight charges, set at the lowest setting," Preemas said. "The door, because it's expected, and because we might be able to weaken it, and the panel."

Oshie nodded "If we set them far enough apart, they won't become one gigantic explosion. That should keep the hull of the ship intact."

"Always a good thing," Preemas said with a feral grin. He stopped walking, and Romano almost stepped into him. She leaned back just in time, then stepped to his side.

They were almost to the engineering alcove. They had stopped just shy of it, the troops filling the corridor, shifting uneasily, as if they didn't want to stop moving.

"All right, everyone," Preemas said. "Remember your orders. No weapons until I say so."

Heads nodded around Romano. She didn't nod. She just held her laser pistol as tightly as she could.

"You will hang back here, while Oshie and I set the charges. We'll come back and join you. Lakinas, are you able to access the corridor control panel?" Preemas asked.

Romano looked in the same direction Preemas was looking. She hadn't even noticed Jorja Lakinas, one of the few people who had said she knew how to use laser rifles. Lakinas apparently knew some engineering tricks too.

Dammit.

Lakinas had crouched near the corridor control panel, apparently without being told to. Initiative, that all-important initiative.

But it seemed like she wasn't having much luck. She had the panel door open, but she was shaking her head. Her face should have been illuminated by various blinking lights, but it wasn't.

Her features were shrouded in shadow.

"I can access it," Lakinas said, "but I can't use it. Even that has been compromised by First Officer Crowe."

Every time someone called Crowe *First Officer*, Preemas's expression narrowed. It was as if he took Crowe's former rank personally, as if Preemas hated to be reminded of the mistake he had made.

"I expected that," he said. To Romano's surprise, Preemas's voice remained level—or maybe tinged with just a hint of disappointment.

He took a deep breath, and his entire posture squared up, as if he were bracing himself.

Captain Preemas was nervous? Romano hadn't expected that. Perhaps he had wanted Crowe to give in. Crowe had to be seeing this. Perhaps Preemas thought the presence of so many armed crew would make Crowe give up.

Romano had half-thought about it as well. She had kinda hoped for it. Part of her didn't want to attack at all. That same part of her wanted to hide.

But she wasn't going to. The other part of her was ready to go. She was shifting back and forth on her feet, not enough for everyone to notice, but enough so that she felt the movement, knew it was out of her control. It was her way of managing the adrenaline and the stress. She wanted to move. She hadn't had a lot of training (she hadn't had *any* training), but she knew that if she let that energy out wrong, she would get trigger happy. And she didn't dare. Not in such close quarters, with people she valued near her.

"All right." Preemas reached into his bandolier and grabbed one of the shape charges. It fit into the palm of his hand. He hefted the charge as if he were weighing his decision.

Then he looked up.

Romano followed his gaze, saw the faint green light of an active camera—the kind that existed on top of all of the department doors. She had no idea if anyone was monitoring that camera, but she would be surprised if it were unattended.

She would be watching Preemas closely if she had rebelled against him.

Preemas lifted the shape charge, then hefted it again. The threat was obvious. *Come out, or we will blow our way in and…*

Kill you all? Capture you all?

Romano didn't know the rest of that threat, but that wasn't her concern. She had her orders.

She focused on her hand, the one holding the laser pistol. She was going to have to concentrate to make sure she didn't move too fast, didn't let the adrenaline take over. And she had to watch her grip as well, given how her hand ached.

She couldn't quite tell how much tension was in her fingers, so she kept her finger away from the trigger.

At least for now.

No one responded to Preemas's threat. Maybe no one had been watching.

Preemas looked at Oshie.

"Let's do it," Preemas said. "I'll take the control panel. You handle the door."

"Got it," Oshie replied.

Romano held her breath, and watched as the men stepped forward.

And so it began.

PART THIRTY-ONE
SURVIVAL
NOW

THE *AIZSARGS RESCUE ONE*

Close to two hundred people crowded the room on *Rescue One*. When Serpell had initially arrived, she had thought the room large. Now it seemed small, with bodies pushing against each other.

Part of the problem was that no one wanted to sit down. Every time a new group entered, the automated voice made that announcement again, about welcoming them to *Rescue One*, and waiting while the ship finished the rescue. Everyone knew they weren't going to be here long and, it seemed, no one wanted to get too comfortable.

Serpell had sucked down two large bottles of water, placing them into the recycling when she was done. Each time she did, another bottle popped up on the beverage table. There was no glassware, just like there were no plates or dishes on the food table. Everything was in small containers, and floating instructions told anyone taking the food to recycle it.

The fact that all the instructions were in Standard was something she was clinging to. She was truly a linguist deep in her soul. The language she had grown up with gave her comfort.

She could have handled one of a dozen different languages easily, and another twenty not so easily, and a whole bunch of variations on Standard, but regular Standard? That eased her mind more than almost anything else.

Except that the oxygen, the gravity, the fact that this ship—or at least this room—was clean.

She had gone to the restroom once, and found a crew member she knew by sight leaning against the sink, sobbing. The crew member didn't even seem to know Serpell was there. Serpell opened her mouth to say something, then changed her mind.

She wasn't sure she could give comfort—not sincere comfort—so she hadn't tried.

Her lack of compassion had bothered her after she left the restroom. She finally got enough nerve to go back in, but the sobbing person was gone, and Serpell didn't know how to look for her.

It was hard to tell who was who in this large room. Everyone was wearing robes, and the robes were all the same whitish beige. Some people she recognized because of their unusual height. A few others had their hoods down, so that she could see their hair or their faces.

But most people left the hoods up and had hidden their hands in their sleeves, as if the robes were a different version of an environmental suit.

Serpell kept her hood down, only because she wanted to be able to see everything around her. But she felt so very unsettled that she wished for the comfort of her own clothes. She wanted her possessions, what few she had left.

Mostly, she wanted the jewelry that India had given her for their wedding. The relationship had been horrible at the end, but it had been good in the beginning. Serpell had held on to the jewelry like a talisman, placing it inside a cubby in her quarters so that the jewelry would make it through tough times with no gravity.

Maybe, when the rescue was over and this *Aizsargs* ship's crew figured out what was wrong with the *Renegat*, everyone could go back on board and retrieve their stuff.

Serpell wanted to ask questions like that, but there was no one to ask. Since she arrived on board, she had only seen crew members from the *Renegat*. No one else had talked to them. Everything had been automated.

That fact unnerved her. She wanted to ask questions from real people. She wanted to find out what was going on.

She finally saw Kabac. He was hovering near the food table as if he couldn't decide if he was hungry. His black hair was matted against the back of his head, and his beard looked crushed against his face.

She pushed her way past dozens of robed figures to reach him. No one looked at her. Most didn't even acknowledge her when she touched them. They were just standing, waiting, maybe not even completely conscious, as if they had shut themselves down the way that computer systems did when those systems weren't being used.

Maybe they had. Everyone knew how close they had come to dying.

That was bound to sober up anyone.

She reached Kabac's side as he set down a container of food without opening it. His hands lingered over another container, before he let his hand drop to his side. He turned, and saw Serpell.

His hands instantly came up, as if he thought she was going to hurt him somehow.

"You volunteered to run the door," she said quickly, so that he would know she wasn't going to yell at him. "And now you're here. Does that mean everyone got out?"

His eyes were sunken in his face. He didn't just look exhausted. He looked defeated.

"I don't know," he said. "The guy—that one from the ship? He stayed behind. He made me get in a life raft. He said there were six people who hadn't arrived yet, even though we were well past the countdown."

Kabac's voice was shaking. His eyes were lined with tears.

"I didn't think we'd make it." He looked down.

Serpell's throat closed. That was the emotion. It wasn't relief. It was disbelief. They had survived, and yet it didn't feel like survival. Not at the moment. It felt like they were still waiting.

"I haven't seen him," Kabac said. "I haven't seen them."

"Do you know who the six were?" she asked.

A few other people were watching, as if they were awaiting news of friends. Maybe they were. But Serpell had not seen anyone from the *Renegat's* crew ask where their companions were. Maybe they had found those companions on the life raft.

But she had been just as guilty. Although she had no one close on the *Renegat*. Not after India died.

"I don't know," Kabac said. "I don't know who made it and who didn't."

He didn't sound curious. He sounded tired.

"And I have been watching for six stragglers to come in here, but I haven't seen that either." He glanced at the food again, but didn't get any.

"I think it would be hard to tell," Serpell said. She wasn't trying to comfort him. She meant that. It would be hard to tell, what with the robes and the silence and the subdued nature of everyone here.

"Maybe," Kabac said. "But something's off. Doesn't it seem like something is off?"

She nodded. Everything seemed off. She had never felt this dislocated in her life.

"I wish they'd tell us what's going on," she said.

"Me, too," Kabac said. "But they're probably waiting for everyone to get through decontamination."

He sounded like he didn't believe that. It was as if someone had told him to speak the words.

But that was the logical assumption. Or maybe they were traveling to the bigger ship, the *Aizsargs*, and no one was going to talk to them until they arrived.

Was *Rescue One* completely automated, like the life rafts? That very idea made Serpell's stomach twist, and she nearly lost the water she'd drunk. She didn't want to be at the mercy of any ship, not ever again.

She had never craved land before.

She did now.

She patted Kabac on the arm. "You should eat something," she said. "It's okay to eat."

"Yeah," he said in a way that made her think he wouldn't eat at all. "I know."

Then he gave her a tentative smile.

"I'm glad you got out," he said.

"You too," she said, and meant it.

She was glad they had all gotten out.

PART THIRTY-TWO
BATTLE
100 YEARS AGO

THE *RENEGAT*

Shape charges. Even after he saw all of them laced through the bandoliers, Crowe hadn't believed that Preemas would use them. Crowe had believed, somehow, that Preemas was smarter than that.

Crowe stood near all of his screens in engineering, mouth slightly open. He felt dumbfounded. Preemas had to know what those charges would do, not just to the door, but to the people around him.

Preemas had stood in front of the main camera into engineering and made his plans clear. The bastard. He clearly hadn't thought it through. Placing the shape charges all around the entrance to engineering would have an impact throughout the ship.

Preemas was going to use eight—on the lowest setting as he had said—but eight, in a small alcove, where the explosions would send debris and shrapnel into the alcove and the corridor, probably injuring the idiots who were standing side by side with Preemas.

Crowe tried not to look at the faces of his colleagues. His former colleagues. People he had helped, people he had worked with. He had to think of them as something other now, which he hadn't had a lot of experience with. He had spent his life in engineering so he wouldn't have to make these kinds of decisions.

There was so much equipment built into the walls, so many connections between the control panel Preemas was going to blow and the control panels throughout the ship, that the greatest threat to the ship had just become her captain.

Everyone in engineering knew it. Tosidis had said something under his breath about fools. Willoughby had contacted a friend or a lover, telling them to brace themselves. Bakhr actually muttered *what the hell?* when the shape charge appeared on the screen, as if he too couldn't believe what the ship's captain was planning to do.

Crowe moved closer to the controls he had modified. He was going to execute his own plan. No one else. And if they ever made it back to the Fleet or if someone challenged what they had done, he had already instructed his engineers to say that he had coerced them. He had to, because his plan was extreme.

The situation was extreme.

He tried to remind himself of that, but it still disturbed him on a level he wasn't sure he wanted to analyze.

Preemas walked to the control panel and pulled it open—the damn idiot. That would make things even worse.

Then he grinned at the camera above the door again, even though his face was five times larger in the cameras around the control panel.

That grin said, *Try and stop me.*

"Okay," Crowe said. He clenched his fists, knowing he couldn't turn back from this.

None of them could turn back from this.

Then he punched the controls, and braced himself.

Captain Preemas had opened the control panel. Then he grinned at the engineering camera, his right hand still clutching that shape charge. He held the control panel door with the other hand, then stepped in closer, bracing the panel door open with his shoulder.

The threat was clear. He was going to place the charges if no one opened the doors.

Romano held her breath. Her heart pounded. Part of her prayed that the engineering crew would open the doors now, but of course, they weren't going to.

Then Preemas raised that single shape charge and pressed it into the top right corner of the control panel. He was actually whistling, some kind of jaunty tune she didn't recognize.

He was enjoying this. She couldn't believe that. She just wanted it to end.

Oshie was crouching near the edge of the door, pulling a shape charge off his bandolier.

Everyone else was shifting, moving ever so slightly, all that nervous energy, just like Romano had.

Preemas turned slightly, grinned at them, and said, "First charge is in place."

And then he reached for the next, when burning orange light came out of the panel and drilled into his forehead. The light went right through him, like some kind of projectile, slicing a neat round hole through his head.

People scattered, moving out of the way as the light continued across the corridor, narrowly missing Romano. She felt its heat sear past her left arm, adding to its ache.

Preemas remained standing for a good long moment, his hands dropping to his sides. And then he fell over backwards, landing with a loud thud.

The light had vanished. Romano looked behind her, because she couldn't help herself. The light had not drilled a hole in the corridor wall. The only damage that light had done was to Captain Preemas himself.

A targeted shot, from inside engineering.

Oshie was also on the ground. The hole in his head was at the top. Apparently, another light beam had struck him, but on the crown of his head, not the forehead.

He huddled in a fetal position, and for a brief half second, she thought he was still alive.

But he didn't move.

Neither did Preemas. But he wasn't ever going to move again. His eyes were open. The burn hole in his forehead was black around the edges and dark as it went through.

There was no blood.

The stench of cauterized flesh filled the alcove.

No one moved. No one said anything. The silence was as damning as the action had been.

Romano looked at that panel, and for a brief moment, she wondered if Preemas had touched something that had sent out that beam of light.

But he couldn't have. Because a similar light hit Oshie in a completely different position and killed him too.

A woman to Romano's right made huff-huff-huffing sound as if she were about to start sobbing. A man behind Romano said softly, "Oh, my God."

And his words seemed to galvanize everyone else. A few ran, but the rest looked around as if they expected someone to tell them what to do.

There was no one to tell them what to do. No one to lead. The First Officer was Nadim Crowe and he was behind that door, perhaps even the one who had sent out that charge.

Perhaps? He *was* the one.

And that thought caught Romano. Her fury returned. She looked at Preemas, on his back, his eyes open, a hole in his forehead, and then she looked at the door, trying to see the cowardly first officer hiding behind that door, and she raised her laser pistol as high as she could.

"Get them!" she screamed.

Then she fired into the ceiling before leveling her pistol at the doors. Debris and bits of ceiling panel rained down on everyone.

It didn't matter that they no longer had someone who knew how to use shape charges. They would shoot their way into that engineering bay, and they would make sure the traitors died.

She shot into the panel, at that thing whatever it was that had killed Preemas. The red light from her shot expanded across the panel and then dissipated.

At that moment, everyone else started shooting too, except for Lakinas, who grabbed her rifle and used its butt to pound on the doors.

Shots hit the walls around her, doing some damage.

They were going to get in. They were going to get in.

And then everyone inside would die.

So far, no one else had died. But they sure were trying hard.

The idiots were firing laser weapons in a small space, their bodies jumbled together, the weaponry aiming at nothing as far as Crowe could tell.

The shots had surprised him. He had thought everyone in the Fleet had enough training to know that firing in that contained area was a terrible idea—for the shooters—but apparently not.

He was about to order his crew to activate the shields, but before he could even voice the order, the standard shields in front of the engineering doors activated.

The shield in front of the control panel had activated the moment Crowe had fired those shots, killing Preemas and Oshie. That shot India Romano had fired had dispersed throughout the shield, adding power to that shield.

Now, the shots were ricocheting back on the small army that Preemas had assembled. Someone screamed in pain, and Crowe didn't even bother to look to see who had been hit.

There would be more screams and more deaths from those idiots, if he didn't stop them.

"Now," he said to Tosidis.

Tosidis nodded, then surrounded the entire corridor in shields. Now the entire space where the small army was gathered had become a shooting gallery. More people screamed, and a few fell, screaming and clutching their arms, their torsos, their faces.

If Crowe didn't act fast, the entire army would kill themselves.

Using the environmental system, he isolated the area inside that killing chamber, and then he carefully removed the oxygen content. A few more people dropped immediately, but others kept shooting, their eyes wild.

Romano whipped around, as if she had just realized what she had unleashed. She started shooting at the edges of the shields, as if she could break them.

Crowe kept lowering the oxygen content but only a few people were dropping. He didn't know what he could send into that shielded area to make everyone else pass out.

It was as if the adrenaline released in the fighting was giving them extra strength, was making their bodies' use of oxygen even more efficient.

And then he realized: It was.

The longer it took him to lower the oxygen, the greater the chance that those who had already passed out would die.

So he just removed the oxygen altogether. He was watching Romano's face throughout. It turned purple, then she gasped like someone dying in space, and then, finally, she fell.

The others fell as well. Crumpling onto each other, laser pistols skittering on the floor, and bumping against the shield.

He brought up the oxygen just enough to keep everyone inside that shield alive, but not enough to wake them.

Then he staggered backwards, leaning against the pointed corner of his own alcove, trying not to fall as well.

He had no idea how many of them were dead. But there were more injuries than he had seen in years. Blood was oozing everywhere, and somewhere in the middle of that pile of humans, blood spurted.

"We have to get to them," Willoughby said.

She saw the spurting too.

He nodded. He couldn't think about what he had just done.

He had to save lives now.

"Use oxygen masks. You won't need full environmental suits," Crowe said. "I'm going to keep the levels in the corridor low."

He sent for automated gurneys from the med bay. He had no idea who was working the med bay right now, or whether any of those people were now lying on the floor, dying.

Dying.

His team was already gathering their masks. He had to give instructions.

"Remove the weapons first," he said, surprised at how authoritative he sounded. "Get those inside engineering. We'll continue to use this as a base, just in case this was only the first wave."

"Someone's dying out there. We have to get out there," Willoughby said. "I don't give a damn about weapons."

She already had her mask on. Her voice was muffled by it.

She used the side of her fist to activate something on one of her screens, but it didn't work, because Crowe controlled the shields.

"Go," he said. "Get that bleeding stopped. The rest of you, take care of the weapons first. Then restrain those who aren't visibly injured. We're going to have to move them to the brig."

He would probably need more gurneys for that, but he'd worry about that after everyone was restrained.

He unlocked the doors, and shut down the shield protecting engineering. He hadn't even finished giving the command when Willoughby left her post at a full run. The doors had only hissed partially open, as she squeezed through them.

Others followed. Tosidis held a mask to his face and followed. As he passed Crowe, Crowe grabbed Tosidis's arm.

"No," Crowe said. "I need you on the bridge. You and Bakhr."

Tosidis shot a worried glance at the door, as if he would rather go through and work to save his former colleagues.

Then he blinked and turned to face Crowe, arm still trapped in Crowe's hand.

"I'm not an *anacapa* expert," Tosidis said, then looked at the pile of humans outside the door again.

Through the corner of his eye, Crowe could see his team moving through them. Willoughby was crouched in the middle of the bodies, hands down. He could hear her voice faintly, as she shouted orders at the others who were working around her.

Tosidis leaned toward them all, and Crowe wondered if someone special to Tosidis was in that pile.

"I know," Crowe said, "but Stephanos—"

Crowe stopped himself, reconsidered telling Tosidis that Stephanos might be badly injured (or dead), and instead said, "Stephanos—I can't find her. She's not in that group, but she's not on the bridge."

"I'm not half as good as her," Tosidis said. "Surely, you have someone else."

Me, Crowe thought, but he couldn't stretch himself that thin. "You know what the problem looks like. I want you to take Bakhr and go to the bridge. You're authorized to do whatever it takes to keep the *anacapa* from malfunctioning."

Tosidis was shaking his head. "It's not my specialty. I don't know what I can do."

In that moment, Crowe realized that the shooting had caused Tosidis to panic. Or maybe, the death of Preemas had done that.

Odd. After the initial discomfort, it had calmed Crowe down.

Crowe grabbed Tosidis by the shoulders and shook him. Tosidis raised his head to Crowe, eyes cloudy.

"You have to hold it together," Crowe said. "I *need* you. You're the only one who knows what the communications *anacapa* has been doing. We don't have a lot of resources right now, and we're all a little out of our depth."

Including Crowe, but he didn't say that.

"I need you calm. I need you thinking clearly. And I need you on the bridge." Crowe shook Tosidis again, although not as hard. "Is that clear?"

Tosidis blinked, then a frown covered his face.

"We're not up for this, are we?" he whispered.

Crowe felt a flash of anger. "If we're not, we die."

Tosidis swallowed, then glanced at the pile of passed-out people. Since the shield had gone down, more oxygen was probably getting into that area. That meant some of them would be waking up.

But a few of his crew were already carrying weapons into engineering. Colin Vezner held up a laser pistol and, with his other hand, pointed down an alcove, clearly asking if Crowe wanted the weapons stored in that direction.

Crowe nodded, then turned his attention back to Tosidis. Tosidis had been watching everything Crowe did, eyes wide.

"I need you to do this," Crowe said as firmly as he could. "I need you to do whatever you can to keep the ship safe, while I'm dealing with the crew crisis."

"And find Natalia?" Tosidis asked.

Crowe realized in that moment that Tosidis didn't trust himself. He didn't believe he was up for the job, and he needed to believe he would have backup.

"As soon as I find her, I'll send her to you," Crowe said, mentally adding, *if she's even capable of coming to you.* But he didn't say that. He didn't say any of it, because he needed Tosidis working. He needed everyone at their best.

Tosidis's shoulders relaxed. He almost smiled, and then seemed to stop himself, probably because he believed the expression was inappropriate.

"Please send her," Tosidis said. "I don't have the training, and I doubt Bakhr does either."

"You are going to have to do your best," Crowe said, trying to keep the irritation from his voice. He needed to stop this damn pep talk and get back to work.

He let go of Tosidis's shoulders, and resisted the urge to give Tosidis a little shove.

"Now," Crowe said. "Go. Get that done."

Tosidis stepped back, then looked at the pile in front of the door. Getting around everyone would be difficult, and it might send Tosidis over the edge again.

If Tosidis couldn't do the job, Crowe didn't know who else to send.

He scanned around the room, looking for Bakhr, then realized that he was helping with the people pile.

Crowe almost told Tosidis to get Bakhr, but that would mean that Tosidis would have to wade into that pile of people, and their presence already disturbed him enough.

Crowe walked over there himself.

"Benjamin Bakhr," he said, making sure his voice had a bit of command in it. "Tosidis needs your assistance."

Bakhr lifted his head. Some blood was smeared along his cheek where he had clearly been wiping at his own face. Crowe almost said something, and then decided against it.

"I prefer to help here," Bakhr said quietly.

Was everyone going to question Crowe's command now?

"I don't care what you prefer," Crowe said. "We need your expertise. Go. Now."

Bakhr bit his lower lip, then glanced down at the people pile all around him. Crowe couldn't tell who Bakhr was looking at, but clearly that person meant something to him.

Then Bakhr nodded. He stepped around some bodies, and worked his way to the edge.

Crowe watched him for a moment, then turned his attention to the mess in front of him.

The weapons were already gone, except for the bandoliers around Preemas and Oshie. A laser pistol was on Preemas's hip, and his body was partially resting on a laser rifle.

Clearly no one had wanted to touch their dead captain.

So Crowe did.

He bent over and slipped his hands under the bandolier. Preemas's body was still warm, his eyes open. That cauterized hole in his head, though, made him look smaller somehow.

And the smell of burned flesh near the body made Crowe gag. It wouldn't do to have the man who had murdered his captain vomit all over him.

Crowe willed his stomach to behave, then grabbed the bandolier and worked it over what remained of Preemas's head. Crowe tried not to think about what he was doing, because that was the only way to keep himself calm.

He slipped the bandolier over his left arm, then bent down again, and lifted Preemas's right shoulder. The body was ridiculously heavy—not a person any longer, but a thing, with no tension in its muscles at all.

Using his foot, Crowe pushed the laser rifle away from Preemas, and onto the main part of the floor. He let Preemas's shoulder fall. It landed with a faint meaty thunk.

Crowe grabbed the laser rifle, then took the laser pistol off Preemas's hip. Crowe carried everything inside engineering and placed the bandolier, rifle, and pistol in the alcove he had been using, rather than having the shape charges anywhere near the rest of the crew.

Bakhr was talking to Tosidis. Tosidis was gesturing at the door.

Crowe frowned at both of them.

"The bridge," he said. "*Now.*"

"Yes, sir," Bakhr said, and put a hand behind Tosidis. Tosidis opened his mouth as if he was going to object again, but Crowe glared at him.

Tosidis closed his mouth. Then he let Bakhr push him toward the exit, going to the door farthest from the pile of bodies. The two men were still going to have to walk around injured and dying colleagues, because there was no other way to the bridge.

Crowe didn't want to watch them pick their way across.

Even though he had to go back to that pile to get the weapons off Oshie.

Two of Crowe's engineers were going through the pile, pulling up people's arms and locking them in laser restraints. Crowe felt a jolt of surprise at that. Of course, they were using laser restraints. The physical restraints were in the weapons room.

He hadn't prepared for that.

A few members of Preemas's army were stirring in the growing oxygen, but no one had spoken and no one had tried to push their way through the pile of people. The entire scene was eerily quiet. Only the sound of restraints pinging shut and the rustle of his people, moving through the pile, reached him.

Crowe went over to Oshie. He looked worse that Preemas—his head smashed downward by the laser that Crowe had programmed. Oshie had no features left, except his jaw, chin, and neck. But there was no blood here either, although Crowe could smell blood.

It was probably coming from the pile. That spurting—

"Where are the gurneys?" Willoughby was beside him. Crowe hadn't even heard her approach.

"I sent for them," he said. "As many as we have. They're on their way."

He had double-checked before coming out here. She could have done so too.

Then he looked up, over his shoulder at her. Her torso was matted with blood, her face speckled with spray.

She looked furious.

"We're going to have to get half of those people to the med bay," she said.

"I know," he said. He didn't want her to tell him about any of this. He wanted to get the weapons out of the corridor, and then he wanted to get back to work. He felt the pressure of that *anacapa* drive, bearing down on him.

"We lost one," she said. "He bled to death. I couldn't stop it in time."

She *was* furious. Her words were tight and clipped.

"We're going to lose more if we don't get them to the med bay," she said.

What the hell do you want from me? he nearly said. *I can't change this, and more people will die if we don't secure the ship.*

Instead, he said, "We're doing what we can. You can continue to help the injured if you want, but I need the most qualified engineers on the Scrapheap problems. I'd prefer it if you work with me on saving the ship. That'll save lives."

He said that last with a bite, then realized he wasn't as in control as he thought he was.

She stepped back as if he had struck her. Then she glanced at the pile. More people were moving now, and the entire engineering crew was out there, restraining the others, and doing what they could with the wounds.

Only Crowe, Tosidis, and Bakhr weren't helping, although Crowe was out here too, gathering the last of the weapons.

"I don't want to leave them to die," she said so softly he almost didn't hear it. Her voice shook.

"One thing at a time, Daria," he said as gently as he could. It felt odd to speak gently, while he was holding the bandolier of a dead man—a man he had killed.

"We have to secure the ship. Then we worry about the wounded."

"I don't even know if there's any staff in the med bay," she said, that quiver growing. Apparently, she was closer to an edge than he realized.

"I don't either," he said, and he should have known. He was the first officer, after all. He should have known who was staffed where.

He did know that Preemas let most of the medical crew move to other positions if they wanted to. Preemas, who apparently (mistakenly) believed he was immortal, hadn't seen much reason for a medical staff, not on a trip like this one.

Crowe felt the edge of panic. He willed it away, and that mostly worked.

"We'll just send them there, and let the bay itself sort it out," he said. "Our expertise is what we need for the ship, and we're going to have let others deal with the medical emergency."

Willoughby swiped at her face, smearing the blood spray rather than wiping it off.

"Clean up," Crowe said, "and then get back to work."

She stared at him as if he had said something in a language she didn't understand.

"Daria," he said in that gentle tone. "It's all we can do right now."

Her eyes changed, became clearer. Apparently, that got through.

She nodded, and walked back into engineering, before he could ask her to help him remove the bandolier from Oshie.

Oh, well. Crowe would finish here and then go back into engineering to figure out what to do next.

He knew it wasn't very straightforward, but he would do his very best.

And try to keep the panic at bay by reassuring himself that his very best was all he could possibly do.

THE *RENEGAT*

Tindo Ibori stood in the empty med bay, next to the body of Natalia Stephanos. The automated signage had stopped him, the opposite of what it had been supposed to do.

But he stared at the two choices the signage gave him—going to the actual medical part of the med bay or taking a body into the morgue—and it had stopped him. Even though the sign hadn't said *morgue.*

It had said *storage and disposal.* It was the automated voice that had tried for reassurance that had made him vaguely ill.

The gurney you have brought here carries someone who is beyond medical care. If you want to accompany that body, please go to the left. Otherwise, remove your hand from the gurney's side, and the gurney will proceed on its own.

He looked down. He was holding on to the gurney. He hadn't even realized he had been doing so. He really should let go, but as that thought crossed his mind, he tightened his grip instead.

He was not really ready to leave Stephanos.

He hadn't realized how much he relied on her, how much she had seemed like the center of the ship to him, not Captain Preemas or Chief Engineer Crowe. After receiving an order, Ibori had always looked to Stephanos for her reaction.

Sometimes she rolled her eyes. Sometimes she smiled as if she found the order amusing. And sometimes she nodded seriously, as if to say that Ibori should take the order seriously as well.

But she wasn't going to do that anymore, not that there was anyone left who was going to give sensible orders. Those weapons on the bridge, the anger in Preemas's eyes, the way everyone clustered around him, Ibori had never seen any of that, not on any ship he had ever served on.

Or the shuffling of the crew, or the uncertainty, or the distance from the Fleet.

Without Stephanos, he was truly alone here, and he didn't know what to do.

His hand tightened on the gurney so hard that the bones in his fingers ached. He didn't want to let her go, because that would mean he would have to make choices. He would have to go back to the chaos that this ship had become.

But he didn't want to look at her either. She didn't look like herself anymore. She wasn't *there* anymore, and he knew it, but he didn't know it, not deep down.

He swallowed hard, then looked up at those impersonal floating signs. He had never noticed how creepy they were before, words floating in the air with no background, allowing the walls, the equipment, and everything in the room to frame them.

The automated announcement repeated.

The gurney you have brought here carries someone who is beyond medical care....

"I know, I know," he muttered back at the voice. He almost pleaded with it to help him, but he knew it would do no good.

And that was when he realized he was alone in the med bay.

He hadn't seen another person at all. Wasn't there supposed to be someone in the med bay at all times? Or had Captain Preemas changed that rule as well?

...Remove your hand from the gurney's side, and the gurney will proceed on its own.

Choices. The system wanted him to make choices. Him, of all people. Choosing whether or not Stephanos would have a service, or if she would go into a funeral pod for jettisoning almost immediately.

He wasn't qualified to make these decisions. And he didn't want to think about her in that pod—where she would end up either way. The pod igniting from the inside out, burning the body and then itself, ashes spreading through space.

If there had been another person here—another *living* person here—he would have abandoned the body, saying that he wasn't close enough to Stephanos to make these choices, which was, sadly, true. He had no idea what kind of service she would have preferred, what her family customs and traditions were. He had no idea if she had left family behind in the Fleet, if she had been married or had children or had been as alone as he was. Probably alone, or they wouldn't have brought her on this journey.

Or maybe estranged, because a few folks on the *Renegat* had been permanently estranged from everyone they knew. He had talked to them. They hadn't even seemed bothered by it.

Something rustled in the actual medical part of the bay, the one where everyone living got treatment. Then he heard another rustle in the *storage and disposal* wing.

"Hello?" he yelled, feeling a little relief. Someone else *was* here. Someone could help him with this decision. "Hi, I need some assistance here."

Not like medical emergency assistance, but assistance all the same. Someone to make a decision, someone to maybe talk to. Someone who might not even know about what Preemas was doing or how far the ship had fallen apart.

The rustling grew stronger and then doors banged. A metallic smell grew in the air, and he felt a slight breeze. Then the door to the other wing opened, and gurneys—empty gurneys—floated out.

Flat and long and automated, just like the one Stephanos was on. His heart was pounding. Who had ordered those up? And why so many?

They floated three to a row, four rows high. As they reached him and Stephanos, three levels of gurneys in the middle row paused, as if waiting for him to move. The gurneys on the top floated over him and Stephanos, leaving a faint scent of cleaning fluid in their wake.

Then the next row rose up and floated over them, and each row thereafter.

The doors to the med bay opened, and the gurneys in the two side rows were leaving, with the gurneys from the center row following one row at a time.

He had never seen anything like it. His heart pounded. He was terrified.

Someone had ordered up a dozen or more gurneys. He hadn't counted exactly, but a lot of gurneys. Those weapons—Preemas had used those weapons.

And a lot of people had been injured. Maybe even dead.

Ibori's heart sank. He didn't want the engineering crew to die. They were the people he spent most of his time with, the people he worked with. They mattered to him as much as Stephanos, even though he had been trained to be loyal to his captain.

Ibori had been loyal. He had been as loyal as he could be. Which was why he left with Stephanos, so he wouldn't have to choose to bear arms against his friends.

Who were, apparently, dying now.

His fingernails dug into Stephanos's gurney. That gurney hadn't even tried to move.

He could hide in here, wait until it was all over, or he could see what was going on.

If someone had ordered gurneys, it was mostly over.

Or so he would assume.

He looked up at the floating *storage and disposal* sign. He would have to send Stephanos's body in there, and he would store it. Yes, he would store it, because maybe there would be a service for everyone who died.

More banging from inside the storage and disposal part of the med bay. Maybe that was where the other person was.

"Hello?" Ibori called again. "Is anyone else here?"

Maybe they had received orders to send the gurneys. Maybe—

Then more gurneys floated out of the *storage and disposal* side of the med bay. Those gurneys were also in formation. This time he counted. Three across, four rows up, three gurneys per row.

Why would they need so many gurneys?

Plus the ones from before.

His stomach churned. What had happened out there?

It had to be over because they ordered the gurneys, right? No one ordered gurneys if the fighting was still ongoing, right?

Then, as if they heard his thought, all the gurneys stopped moving. They floated, as if awaiting instruction.

He looked at them as if they were their own rebel army, waiting to attack someone. Waiting to attack him.

Then, one stacked group of gurneys moved forward. Twelve. Only the middle rows, the ones that would have plowed into him and Stephanos, moved sideways, the gurney on the lower row moving to the left, and the gurney on the upper row moving to the right.

They went first. The others followed.

He was shaking. He could hide here, and no one would know where he was. Unless the gurneys weren't ordered for bodies but for the wounded. They would all crowd in here, and he would be stuck helping with bleeding and crying people and watching even more of his colleagues die, just like Stephanos.

Ibori leaned over her, as if she were alive. But any illusion of her still being alive vanished when he saw her sunken face. It looked even worse than it had on the bridge.

"I'm sorry," he said to her. Or what was left of her. Or how he imagined her. "I'm so sorry. I'm going to have them store you for a while. I'll worry about what to do with you later. I'm sure others will want a remembrance."

He wasn't sure, and he felt a little odd, trying to placate a dead woman.

He let go of Stephanos's gurney, glanced at the various signs for the verbal command he needed to store her body, and then uttered the words.

Her gurney floated by itself into the *storage and disposal* part of the bay. He had an odd sense that this was the last time he would ever see her.

Which might be true, if the ship didn't make it.

Or he didn't make it.

He let out a small breath, then clenched his fists. If he hurried, he would be able to catch up with those gurneys.

He had to see where they were going.

He had to know what, exactly, was going on.

THE *RENEGAT*

Crowe stood in the middle of his floating screens, but he had lowered them so that he could monitor his engineering crew. He didn't know their psychological profiles and personal histories well enough. He fully expected the events of this afternoon to break some of them, and for some, it did seem close.

A few of them were a little too focused. They would probably break down once the crisis was over—if they survived the crisis.

Willoughby was working near the communications *anacapa*. She had taken over from Tosidis, monitoring the *anacapa* and handling the strange energy that was still filling the ship.

She hadn't wiped the blood spray off her face. The spray had dried black, so it looked like she had weird freckles on her skin. Or the spray would have looked like weird freckles if it weren't for the blood still coating her shirt and pants.

She was working hard, just like Crowe wanted her to do, somehow changing her focus from the dead and injured in the corridor to saving the ship.

He was having trouble changing his focus, despite his ability to compartmentalize. He kept wondering how badly he had destroyed his own cause. How many more deaths did he have to add to his own personal tally? And how many of those deaths should he count? Because Preemas would have destroyed the ship, which would have taken out hundreds of lives.

How did Crowe balance the lives lost with the lives he might have saved?

And why was he thinking about that now, when they could still all die from Preemas's stupidity?

He forced himself to concentrate. He didn't look at anyone else in engineering.

Instead, he focused on the screens, particularly those showing the energy readings flooding the ship. He thought he could feel the energy change. The air had a tingle to it, as if the molecules themselves had a vibration he didn't recognize.

But he wasn't sure if that tingly feeling was just something he imagined because of the readings or if it came from his own distress at the events in the corridor.

What he did know was that he couldn't shake the feeling, no matter how hard he tried, and he wasn't sure he should ask anyone else about it. He didn't want to plant the idea in their minds, but he also wasn't sure if he could trust their perceptions anyway.

They were even more upset than he was.

Engineers didn't kill people, even in major battles. Sure, engineers provided support and sometimes released a ship's weapons. But watching people die in front of them? Watching their *colleagues* die? Engineers didn't normally do that.

He made himself take a deep breath, then he bit the inside of his right cheek hard, tasting blood. He turned his entire attention to that pain, vowing to do it again if his attention wandered off the first task at hand.

Because he had to figure out how to stop that energy from making the *anacapa* drives vibrate. He had to figure out what, exactly, the energy was doing to the drives. And he had to somehow isolate those drives, just in case the energy activated them. The last thing he wanted was for the *Renegat* to return to foldspace, particularly if the *Renegat* did so without any help from her crew.

Crowe slowly slid his teeth off the inside of his right cheek, although his tongue played with the new injury.

The energy was coming from the Scrapheap, just like Bakhr had said. And the energy wasn't just one kind of wave. Crowe had been mapping the signatures, finding hundreds of them. He had color-coded all of them, then switched to a view that showed how the colors mixed.

He ended up with a muddy reddish orange that tended toward black in some parts. There were too many colors, too many different kinds of energy, some he didn't even recognize.

He had no idea how he was going to isolate them. This was the kind of work that would take months—separating the energy strands, figuring out which one was doing what and finally determining which one was interfering with the *anacapa* drives.

The work would also take an expert, like Stephanos. No one else knew the drives like she did, not deep down. Except maybe that Atwater kid, even though he had no hands-on experience. He did understand the theory, maybe better than Crowe himself.

If theory was all Crowe could get, he would take theory.

But before he tried to track down Atwater, he would see if his team of two was making any headway on the bridge.

He contacted Tosidis, and actually put him on a screen. Not because Crowe needed to see Tosidis, but because that gave Crowe an excuse to see the bridge.

Tosidis was standing near the captain's chair. Behind him, the ready room door stood open, but Crowe couldn't see inside, not from the screen's angle.

Tosidis looked gray. He hadn't looked good after the attack, but he looked worse now. He looked like he was a few days from death himself.

"It's bad up here, sir," he said, his voice shaking. "You have no idea."

Whatever Crowe expected, it hadn't been that. He had hoped to find Tosidis and Bakhr working on the *anacapa* drive.

Crowe didn't ask to see the rest of the bridge. He called it up on a different screen and scanned. The bridge was mostly empty except for two, Yulia Colvin and Titus M'Ghan, who looked as sickly as Tosidis did.

Bakhr was standing near the empty navigator's console. He was wearing gloves, and gingerly working a screen in front of him, one that Crowe couldn't see.

Two laser pistols sat on top of another console, and a laser rifle littered the floor near the ready room door.

The screens on the bridge were off, and the rest of the consoles were unmanned.

"She died up here," Tosidis said. "After she touched the *anacapa*."

Crowe had been about to ask who she was, then realized the rest of what Tosidis had said had answered his question. She. Stephanos.

Colvin, standing off to the side as if she didn't really want to be part of this conversation or *any* conversation really, gripped her hands tightly in front of her.

"She bled everywhere," Colvin said, voice shaking. It was as if Stephanos were still on the bridge. "There's a stain near the *anacapa*."

"It's too big to call a stain," M'Ghan muttered. His face was squinched up into a scowl of disgust.

Colvin continued as if he hadn't spoken at all. "Her face just collapsed in on itself. She didn't even look like herself anymore."

"After she touched the *anacapa*?" Crowe asked. He wasn't sure who he was asking. Tosidis looked like he was about to be ill. The other two seemed to have gone past looking ill into being in some kind of shock.

Crowe was missing a small section of the bridge from his screen, and he hoped that was where Bakhr was.

"I wasn't watching her closely," M'Ghan said. "But she was working over there, and then there was this big kerfuffle, and Ibori was helping her and the captain, he didn't think anything was wrong…"

M'Ghan's voice trailed off, and he shook his head, as if he was trying to get the images out of it.

"What did the captain do?" Crowe asked.

"He was more concerned with what you were doing," M'Ghan said. "He thought you rigged the *anacapa* to hurt her."

Crowe let out a small breath of surprise. *He* had? He didn't know anyone who could manipulate an *anacapa* like that. Not even Stephanos.

"A lot of the crew believed him," Colvin said.

"But you didn't?" Crowe asked.

She shrugged one shoulder, and looked down. He took that to mean yes, she had believed it.

"Ask India Romano about it," M'Ghan said. "She's the one who closed the *anacapa* container lid."

Crowe blinked. Romano? She had moved from…something intellectual to security over his objections. She had never seemed like the brightest person he had encountered.

And unless he was mistaken, she was the one who had shot first after Preemas had died.

He didn't tell the two remaining crew members on the bridge that he couldn't ask Romano. She was unconscious.

"Sir?" Bakhr's voice seemed to come from everywhere and nowhere. Crowe didn't want to move his view of the bridge, so he opened a smaller second screen near the first. The two screens side by side made it look like Bakhr was standing in a room by himself.

In reality, he was working one of the consoles that Crowe usually preferred. It had a lot of easy-access scientific information, all set-up to appear as screens with a touch.

"It feels really odd up here," Bakhr said. "Like the air is actually alive."

Colvin and M'Ghan were nodding.

"It feels to me like I'm being pricked by a hundred needles," Tosidis said.

That was when Crowe realized that Tosidis was nowhere near the *anacapa* drive, even though monitoring the drive was the reason he had been sent up to the bridge.

"Have you looked at the *anacapa*?" Crowe asked Tosidis.

Tosidis shook his head, very slowly. "After what happened to Stephanos, I wasn't sure I should touch the container."

"Yet Romano did," Crowe said, trying not to let too much of his irritation out.

"Yeah." Tosidis said, as if that didn't really matter to him, as if he wanted to be anywhere else.

"I need to know what's happening with the drive," Crowe said. No one had time to be delicate. Not right now. Because delicate could get them all killed.

"Yes, sir," Tosidis said, but didn't move.

Bakhr's mouth had formed a thin line, as if he were keeping words back, words he really wanted to say.

"I'd check it for you, sir," Bakhr said, "but I'm trying to sort out these energy signatures. I've never seen so many. They're intertwined, as if they were different kinds of vines that had grown together over time."

"Don't bother," Crowe said. "I'll handle those."

"Sir," Bakhr said quietly, as if they shared a private conversation rather than one overheard by the three others on the bridge. "This isn't like anything I've ever seen."

"I thought you said it was similar to what happened when you were growing up," Crowe said.

"Similar, yes," Bakhr said. "But a thousand times more intense. This Scrapheap is so old, and so many ships inside have probably decayed, not to mention all the different energies have some kind of impact on each other. This is…I don't think it's something the *Renegat* can just deal with, sir. I think we're going to have to do something."

Crowe didn't answer that, because he didn't have an answer for that. He knew they had to do something. He just didn't know what it was.

"Figure out if using the *anacapa* to get the hell out of here would be worse than not using it," Crowe asked, but even as the words left his mouth, he wondered if he was asking the impossible. They had no idea what these energy signatures were or what was causing them.

He had no idea if anyone had even seen anything like this before. He did know that he needed time to solve this, and he wasn't sure he had time.

"None of us want to get near the *anacapa*, sir," Bakhr said. "That's why I'm working here. I'm trying to see what I can through the instruments."

Crowe felt a surge of exhausted anger run through him. Did he have to do everything? Was this entire ship incompetent?

Then he blinked, remembered the answer. Yes. Yes, it was. Incompetent, expendable, useless.

"It's worse near the *anacapa*," Tosidis said. "That alive feeling in the air? If I had to say what it was, sir, I'd say that it's just like the communications *anacapa*. The air is vibrating, sir."

Crowe raised his head, the words finally getting through to him. The *air* was vibrating, which meant the *environmental system* was vibrating, which meant that the entire ship was probably vibrating.

"As if we're under attack," he muttered.

"Sir?" Bakhr asked, followed only a fraction of a second later by Tosidis. The other two crew members were frowning.

Crowe started, "Give me the status of the…" and then he realized he could figure things out faster himself. He switched one of the screens from the inside of the ship to the outside, looking at the shields.

The shields were down.

Everyone had been so focused on the internal conflict on the *Renegat* that they had forgotten to deal with the external threat. Even Stephanos hadn't thought to check what was going on with the ship's exterior—although Crowe didn't know that for a fact. She might have died before she could implement anything.

He let his mind skitter past her name, not wanting to think about the details he had just learned about her death. Instead, he double-checked the shields, making certain they were in working order.

Then he raised them, and reinforced them, as if the *Renegat* was taking on heavy enemy fire.

"Something changed," Willoughby said from across engineering. "The communications *anacapa* is no longer vibrating."

Crowe's arms, legs, and face ached. Anywhere he had exposed skin actually hurt, but the hurt was different than the tingle had been. The hurt was apparently what he had been feeling underneath that tingle, blocking out the hurt because it had been too much to deal with.

He rubbed a hand over his arms, feeling goosebumps beneath his palm. As he glanced around engineering, he saw several of the others doing the same thing.

"Sir?" Bakhr was speaking from the bridge. "The energy signatures have changed. I'm only reading a few, and they are very weak."

"I put up the shields," Crowe said.

Tosidis let out a shaky laugh. "Who would have expected it to be so easy?" he asked.

"It's not easy," Crowe snapped. "Now we have to figure out if all of that energy damaged our *anacapa* drives, including the backup. And we have to do it without our best person."

His voice wobbled a bit. He didn't want it to. He wished the wobble away.

"Are we going to proceed to the mission, then, sir?" Tosidis asked.

Crowe frowned. The Scrapheap. Discovering who, if anyone, had raided it. What the Fleet should do, if anything. If the warships were taken. If they even existed.

The mission. It seemed so unimportant and so far away.

"*Anacapas* first," he said. The mission wouldn't matter if they couldn't get back to or communicate with the Fleet.

Crowe didn't want to think that the *Renegat* might be stranded here, but he was already thinking it. And the thought made him nervous because it felt true.

Stranded here, with potentially damaged *anacapa* drives, and a rebellious crew. A dead captain, injured fighters, and a good three-quarters of the crew who had no idea at all about what had just happened.

He was exhausted, but he couldn't quit. Not now. He was still going to have to compartmentalize, still going to have to figure out how to deal with the crew, while inspecting the *anacapa* drives, while figuring out what, exactly, killed Stephanos, while dealing with the energy signatures from the Scrapheap itself.

He let out a long breath. He was going to have to take it all one crisis at a time.

Because he couldn't do it any other way. He was already overwhelmed. If he thought too much about the odds of his success—of their success—he would give up.

They all would.

And he couldn't let that happen.

PART THIRTY-THREE
SOMEWHERE NEW
NOW

THE *AIZSARGS*

It took two more hours before *Rescue One* docked inside the *Aizsargs*. The fact that the rescue ship could easily dock inside the *Aizsargs* told Serpell just how large the *Aizsargs* was. It was one of the largest DV vessels, which meant it had to be brand-new.

Although the *Aizsargs* didn't seem new. As she, and the rest of the survivors, were led off *Rescue One* into a section of the docking bay, she noted areas that seemed worn, items stored along walls not built for storage. The *Aizsargs* looked like a well-used vessel that had run more than its share of missions.

Maybe that was how they knew how to funnel the survivors along one side of the docking bay, away from most of the equipment. An opaque screen had been set up on one side, blocking any view of the other ships in the bay.

Which made sense to her, considering that the crew of the *Aizsargs* often had no idea who they were rescuing. They seemed to know about the *Renegat*, so they should have trusted the crew here.

So maybe she had been observing standard procedure.

She didn't know that, considering she never served in the administrative capacity of a ship. She usually hid in her research area—or she had until this horrid horrid trip back to the Fleet.

She had been among the first people to leave *Rescue One*. She had lost track of Kabac, which didn't break her heart. She was happy he had survived, but she didn't want him to be her survival buddy, somehow becoming close to him because they were the only two left who understood how bad it had been on that bridge.

The entire remaining crew of the *Renegat* trudged through the protected area, toward some double doors. This time, there was no overall announcement, and there still weren't any people. She was beginning to get terrified all over again.

What if they really weren't on a Fleet ship? What if they were on something that looked like a Fleet ship?

And did the kind of ship matter, really, considering she was breathing real air and walking in real gravity and wearing a robe that was soft against her skin? She had none of that on the *Renegat*. Given the condition of her environmental suit, she probably would have been dead by now.

She shuddered at the very thought, but still felt the terror lurking underneath. She had no idea where she was or what she was supposed to do. She had no vision of her future at all.

She barely understood her present.

She was the thirteenth person through the double doors. They opened into a gray corridor that looked like it might have been made out of nanobits, but she wasn't certain. The gray material glistened in a muted yellow-white light that she had never seen in a Fleet vessel before.

There were no control panels on the walls, and no decoration either. Either the ship was very minimal or this section had been stripped down.

Up ahead, the first person off *Rescue One*, a person who was still wearing the robe's hood, stopped. Serpell leaned to the left and saw that person was talking to someone in a gray uniform with silver accents. Serpell had never seen that particular uniform before, although it was similar to other uniforms she'd seen throughout the Fleet.

Her mouth was dry, even though she had drunk four bottles of water on *Rescue One*. And that thought alerted her to the fact that she needed facilities again.

The person in the uniform—whose gender Serpell couldn't yet determine—smiled and swept an arm toward a different corridor. The first person off *Rescue One* trudged in that direction, and the next person stopped there.

The others hung back. Serpell couldn't tell if they were encouraged to stand back or if they wanted to.

The survivors of the *Renegat* seemed lost in their own minds right now, maybe too overwhelmed to do much more than continue forward.

She wanted to run forward, shoving the others out of the way, as she got wherever it was the crew of the *Aizsargs* was going to take them. She wanted to know what was next, not stand in yet another line, letting people decide for her.

It was probably that impulse, which she recognized from the first few days after they had left the Scrapheap, that had probably put her in charge of the *Renegat* in the first place.

She had learned after dealing with India to ask questions, to push forward, to get the news *now* rather than wait for someone to deign to tell her.

When Serpell reached the front of the line, she realized that the person before her was male, someone who had grown up on ships and was thin and wispy from living in artificial gravity and, perhaps, preferring zero-G.

He had a smooth face, dark eyes, and short hair. His uniform was clean—as it should have been. So was his face, and so were his fingernails. She envied all of that, and wished—hoped—she would get a chance to clean up as well.

He had a nice smile.

"Welcome," he said. "I'm Emile Parizo. I'm going to give you a room assignment and directions. You'll be able to clean up and rest. There will be food in your room as well."

"And then what?" she asked. As the words came out, she realized she was being rude. She hadn't even introduced herself. "I'm sorry. I'm sorry. I'm Raina Serpell."

"Nice to meet you, Raina," he said, and he didn't ask her rank, which was good, because she really didn't have one, at least as far as anyone here understood. Or so she assumed, since he hadn't given her his rank either.

If he had one.

"To answer your question," he said without a change of inflection in his voice, as if her rudeness hadn't bothered him at all, "we will have an overall meeting once everyone is settled and refreshed. We're thinking that won't be for at least twelve hours, giving you time to sleep."

She didn't want to sleep. She needed answers first. But she was at the mercy of the people here.

"At least tell me where we ended up. How you found us. What—"

"Everyone wants to know those things," he said. "We'll tell the entire group when we have the meeting. Until then, take care of yourself and tend to your own needs."

She swallowed, knowing she wouldn't be able to pull more information out of him.

She clenched her hands into fists, then released them, willing herself to remain calm somehow.

"Now," he said in that annoyingly reassuring tone, "would you like to share a room or have a private room? We have both available."

He sounded like the concierge at a hotel, not a crew member on a Fleet vessel. And how could a functioning vessel have rooms available? What was that about? Especially a *choice* of rooms?

She opened her mouth to ask again, and then realized that wouldn't work. He would tell her to wait in that annoyingly reassuring voice, designed to sooth her fractured nerves and the damn calmness was just making her feel worse.

Or maybe she would feel worse anyway, no matter what he said and how he said it. She had suppressed her emotions so much, just trying to get through, and now they threatened to engulf her.

He was watching her with a patience she could barely understand. Out of the corner of her eye, she saw the others in line behind her shifting. They were probably as distraught and restless as she had been, and she was holding them up by being indecisive.

If she shared a room, then she would have someone to talk to. The downside of that, though, was that someone, whoever it might be, might want her to act like the leader everyone had thought she was.

She couldn't take more pressure. Not right now. Particularly after she had failed so very badly, nearly destroying the ship on the journey home.

"Private." The word croaked out of her.

If she had a private room, she could shower and sleep and eat whenever she wanted to. She could cry, maybe. Finally. She could sit there and shake. She could have a reaction that might let out the tension.

"Wonderful," he said. "You'll head to room 1145, down this corridor. A word of warning: the door has a standard lock, not something coded. We'll give you a code after we see how the arrangements work."

"How the arrangements work?" she repeated, unable to keep the panic out of her voice.

He gave her a soothing smile—or maybe something he intended to be a soothing smile. "You might think you want privacy, but after a few hours, you might change your mind."

"Oh," she said, and felt the fury rise. She really wanted answers.

"Room 1145," he said again, and this time she heard something slightly different in his voice. He was pushing her, trying to make her move.

She bit back anger and nodded. Then she started down the corridor.

Room 1145. Her next destination on this never-ending trip.

PART THIRTY-FOUR

AFTERMATH

100 YEARS AGO

THE *RENEGAT*

Breaux, Atwater, and six other people who had moved from Sector Base Z to the *Renegat* sat in the secondary mess, with the lights off and the doors closed. Atwater had brought them here, in the silence. No one used the secondary mess. The primary mess was the domain of Danika Newark, the former first officer turned chef, and everyone preferred to eat there.

Only Atwater and Breaux had weapons—the laser pistols that Preemas had given them. Those weapons were sitting on a long table in the middle of the room, and the eight people in that room were staring at them, as if the weapons were at fault for the situation they found themselves in.

Atwater had contacted all of them on the way here, asking them to join him. He wasn't doing anything else, wasn't building a coalition, wasn't gathering supporters of Captain Preemas or First Officer Crowe.

The eight had hidden inside the mess for hours now. No one had come for them. No one had asked about them. No one even seemed to know they were here.

Breaux wanted to contact the bridge, just so that she knew what was going on. She hated not knowing anything.

It was quiet here, and somehow she thought that was a bad sign.

She ran her finger along the laser pistol that Preemas had given her. The thing terrified her. Using it against her colleagues terrified her more.

Atwater walked over to the doors. They were sealed shut. Breaux had done that after they all arrived. She had done it without asking. She wanted to be safe, whatever that meant.

She had never really been in a situation like this before, where her fate was so intimately tied to what other people were doing. It felt odd to her. It felt wrong.

"You going to use that?" Gary Trubetor asked, nodding toward the pistol. He was short, with hair that he seemed to shave to stubble every day, and a tiny little beard that formed a triangle under his lower lip.

She hadn't known him on Sector Base Z. She had seen him around the *Renegat*, but she hadn't really talked to him here, either.

He made her uncomfortable for reasons she didn't want to analyze.

Breaux moved her hand away from the pistol. She looked at it as if it were the enemy, not the situation itself.

"I don't know how," she said. Then she looked up at him.

Everyone was watching them, including Atwater.

"Do you know how?" she asked Trubetor.

"I've had a little training," he said. "You want to give me that? I'll guard the door."

"Against whom?" she asked. "Who are we fighting?"

Trubetor shifted, then glanced at the woman standing beside him. Breaux hadn't caught her name. Sally or Susan or something plain. Breaux hadn't seen the woman before either, but Atwater seemed to know all of them, everyone who had left Sector Base Z.

The woman—Susan or Sally or whatever—looked down, as if she didn't want to be responsible for answering that question. A few of the others were watching Breaux, only to look away when she met their gaze.

"I suppose we'll have to choose a side," Trubetor said quietly.

"And how do we do that?" Breaux asked. "The captain wants us to shoot people. The first officer wants to take over the ship."

She reached toward the pistol again, then pulled her hand back as if the very air around the weapon was hot.

"I don't want to do either of those things," she said. "I don't want to shoot anyone. I don't want to fight. I didn't sign up for this."

There. Finally. She had voiced the thought that had been rattling around her head for hours, maybe days.

One of the men turned away, wiping at his face as if her words had physically hurt him. The Susan-Sally woman bit her lower lip, keeping her head down.

Atwater rocked back to his heels, as if Breaux's words surprised him.

They shouldn't have. He had let her know he felt the same way.

As they hurried to the mess, he had said ever so quietly, *I don't think they'll find us here.*

Didn't that imply that he too did not want to get involved?

"Well, we can't stay here forever," Trubetor said. "We're going to have to leave at some point."

"Why?" The Susan-Sally woman spoke in a near whisper.

When no one answered her, she looked up. Her lower lashes were spiky, as if they had been coated with tears.

"I mean," she said, "we have enough food to survive for weeks, and there's a bathroom on the other side of the kitchen. The cushions in the booths are soft enough to sleep on."

"We hide for *weeks*?" Trubetor asked. "Are you nuts? This is a crisis, here. We should do something."

Breaux nodded. She agreed. They should do something. But there was nothing to do. Not now. The crisis was here, and it was forcing them to pick sides.

If they were going to do something, they should have done it weeks ago, when they joined the ship. When they—she, really—realized just what a disaster this ship was.

Only she had been flattered by the captain's attention. She had felt honored that he asked her to find the old maps so that the *Renegat* could complete the mission.

Breaux had completely overlooked the turmoil, figuring it would sort itself out, telling herself that because she had never served on a ship before, she had no idea how the inner politics worked, how all ships probably seemed dysfunctional from the inside out.

"Maybe they'll all just kill each other, and we won't have to worry about it." That from Leena Capacete. She was a thin, dark-haired woman who always seemed to have a perpetual frown on her face.

Atwater whirled on her. "And then what would we do?" His voice had more anger in it than Breaux expected. "Do *you* know how to operate this ship? Because I sure as hell don't. I don't know how to do much of anything here. This thing is huge, and powerful, and everyone who knows what they're doing seems bent on fighting each other."

That anger had dissipated by the time he reached the end of his speech. He raised his eyes toward Breaux, as if he expected her to have answers.

She didn't have answers. How could she have answers? He was the one who brought them here. He was the one who had gotten them away from the fighting, and for that she was really grateful. But she wasn't sure what to do next, if anything.

"If only we could go home," said Susan-Sally, still not looking up. "We could just take one of the small ships, and go back."

"A ship with an *anacapa* drive?" Trubetor asked. "Because that's what we would need."

"Smaller ships don't have *anacapa* drives," Atwater said. "The Fleet discovered that was too dangerous. People were using the ships without training on the drive, not to mention the kind of pull one of those drives has on the ship itself. Some of the ships never made it out of foldspace."

His words echoed in the large room. *Never made it out of foldspace.* Everyone in this situation—all eight of them—had known getting stuck in foldspace was a risk. Apparently, they had all accepted that risk, just like Breaux had.

But they had thought that getting stuck was the big risk, not this civil war that they found themselves in the middle of.

"Does anyone here even know how to do anything like pilot a ship?" Susan-Sally-Whatever asked. She finally raised her gaze upwards, looking around at the seven serious faces surrounding her.

Breaux's cheeks grew warm. Except for short hops into orbit around Sector Base Z, she hadn't even been on board a ship before volunteering to serve on the *Renegat*. The idea of piloting one, even on autopilot, made her really nervous.

A couple of people shook their heads slightly, as if shaking them hard would attract attention. Trubetor focused on Breaux, as if he expected her to say that she had flown a ship before.

She shrugged at him.

Then he looked at Atwater, who hadn't moved at all.

"Have you flown a ship before?" Trubetor asked.

"It doesn't matter if I have or not," Atwater said. "Where would I pilot to? I'm not expert enough to take us in and out of foldspace repeatedly, particularly in a small ship."

"If the small ships on the *Renegat* even have *anacapa* drives," Susan-Sally Whatever said. "I don't think they do. I really don't."

"You're forgetting something." Capacete spoke very softly, yet her words stopped the conversation. She took the time to turn her head, meeting everyone's gaze, and saving Atwater for last.

"I'm sure we're forgetting a lot of things," he said, sounding irritated. Breaux didn't want him to be irritated. She didn't want any more turmoil, from anyone, anywhere. "What, in particular, are you thinking of?"

"The Scrapheap," Capacete said. "It's filled with old ships."

"Thousands of years old," Breaux blurted. "I wouldn't get on one of those, ever. Even if we thought it was in perfect shape, and how would we know? I mean, do we have any engineers in this room? Do we?"

No one responded. Susan-Sally looked down. Capacete raised her chin slightly, a half smile on her face, as if she felt good about provoking Breaux.

"This talk about us piloting a ship," Breaux said, "it's just talk. We need all those fighting people. We can't do this without them. We're out of our element here."

She was breathing harder than she wanted to be. She was more upset than she wanted to be. In her imagination, she was a strong woman who could do anything.

That imagination had brought her to the *Renegat.* That imagination had led her to believe she could handle anything.

But she couldn't handle a small ship on her own, let alone a large one.

"You're saying we should wait for the outcome of the fight," Susan-Sally said.

Breaux nodded.

"How are we going to know that it's over?" Trubetor asked. "We going to send out a message saying we've been hiding while you people settle your problems, now welcome us back into the fold?"

"That's not such a bad idea," Atwater said. "It's not our fight, after all."

"We could make it our fight," said that woman whose name Breaux never learned.

"That's what the captain wanted us to do," Breaux said quietly.

"And what's he going to do to us when he realizes that we didn't help with either side?" Trubetor asked. "He strikes me as a very vindictive man."

Breaux had to keep herself from nodding at that. If she was being honest with herself, and apparently, that was what she was doing now, then Preemas hadn't seemed very stable to her either.

But Crowe had, and he was the one who started this crisis.

Or so Preemas had said.

"I wish we could contact the bridge," she said.

"I'm sure there's a way," Atwater said. "Probably from the kitchen area."

He looked at her as if he expected her to do it.

"The captain was going to leave the bridge, right?" she asked Atwater. "I mean, that was why he had all the weapons."

"I say we wait," Susan-Sally said.

"I say we leave this place now and pick our side," Trubetor said.

"And I say we find a ship and a pilot and get the hell out of here," Capacete said. "We don't owe these crazy people anything."

Two of the others, the ones Breaux didn't know at all, nodded at that.

"There have to be habitable planets in this area," one of the others, yet another woman, said. "I mean, the Fleet wouldn't have set up a Scrapheap here otherwise."

"Some planet around here might have been habitable thousands of years ago, Žofka," Atwater said, "but who knows what has happened in the meantime."

Žofka rubbed her hands together as if she was trying to twist the fingers off. She clearly didn't like the uncertainty any more than Breaux did.

"We can search, though, right?" Žofka asked. "And if we find one, we can go there in a small ship on autopilot. That wouldn't take any *anacapa* work at all."

"And who knows what we'll find," Susan-Sally said. "Civilizations hostile to outsiders, or people so advanced they might not even recognize us."

"Or some culture that has never even thought of space travel before," said Vladislav Shelstein. His lower lip was cracked and bleeding. As she watched, he chewed on it, showing just how nervous he was too.

"Still," Capacete said. "It's an option. It'll get us off this ship."

"I think we should consider it," Trubetor said.

Breaux looked at Atwater. For some reason, she expected him to be sensible. Rational. He would come up with the right answer.

He gave her a sheepish half smile, one that held no amusement at all. Then he shrugged.

"It's an option," he said quietly. "At least we're finding a few. I thought we had none when we came to the mess."

Breaux's heart sank. She thought he had more of a plan than that when he brought them here. Instead, he had been fleeing Preemas and his decision to use weapons just like she had.

Then she realized everyone was looking at her. They had done that a lot in this conversation. Did they think she was the one in charge? Not Atwater?

Even he was looking at her, expecting her to make some sort of decision.

How could she without knowing what was happening outside those doors? She needed to know if there was a big battle, if anyone survived, or if those "options" Atwater had mentioned were simply wishful thinking.

Maybe she was the one in charge of this little band. No one else seemed to be making the hard decisions.

And she wasn't sure she was up to them either.

"Let's give it a few hours," she said. "Let's see if this crazy situation resolves itself."

"And if it doesn't?" Trubetor asked her.

She was right. Everyone was thinking she was in charge. They were all still staring at her.

"We'll pick an option," she said. "Based on what we know at that point."

If they knew anything at all.

THE *RENEGAT*

Ibori actually had to jog to keep up with the gurneys. They were moving at a rapid pace. He had no idea they had such speed built into them.

His heart was pounding. He wasn't used to moving this fast. He had never used the treadmills that were recommended to the crew so that they could stay in shape. He always figured walking the corridors was enough.

He had been wrong.

The gurneys wound their way through a path he almost didn't recognize. They weren't heading to the bridge, which was what he expected. It took him several minutes to realize they were going toward engineering.

His heart sank. He did not want to see his engineering colleagues dead.

But there were more gurneys than colleagues, so he assumed that some of the people Preemas had brought with him were also dead or dying.

Ibori's lower lip trembled. He tried not to think about all of the implications of that.

He also didn't like the fact that he was the only person in these corridors. Was that because everyone else had been in the battle? Or because everyone was in hiding? Had he missed a verbal order from Preemas to the entire crew, to stay in their quarters or to shelter in place?

Ibori could have, he supposed, considering the fact that he had been in the med bay. Sometimes shipwide announcements were muted there so that patients could rest. He hadn't seen any patients, but that didn't mean that there weren't any.

He hadn't gone into the section for living people, after all.

The thought made those tears he had suppressed rise to the surface. He was overwhelmed. This was the problem that had moved him from ship to ship.

Too sensitive for his assignments, one of his captains had said, with great disapproval. Ibori had tended to one of his colleague's feelings after the captain had yelled at him, and the captain hadn't been appreciative.

There had always been reasons that Ibori could cite for the reprimands he got, blame he could give his superior officers.

But he was beginning to think they were right. Stephanos's death had left him so deeply shaken that he wasn't sure if he was going to be useful to anyone for anything.

He could veer off and go to his cabin. It was small and out of the way and no one would find him there for some time, maybe a day or two.

By then, this crisis might be over.

But he couldn't imagine himself there, hiding and wondering what the hell was actually going on.

Despite his "sensitivity," he was a doer. He had to be in the middle of things. He had to participate. He was built that way too.

A small equipment chute opened at the end of one of the corridors. The gurneys tilted sideways and entered it one by one.

He couldn't go that way even if he wanted to. The chute wasn't much wider than the gurneys themselves. Besides, he didn't want to be jammed in there with the equipment.

He headed to the nearby elevators, knowing this was his chance to go to his quarters, to avoid whatever was going on.

But he also knew where that small equipment chute opened, and it confirmed his hunch: everything was heading to engineering.

And now he couldn't stop.

The elevators—all of them—opened for him, which freaked him out more than he wanted to admit. He wasn't sure he had ever seen that. The elevators usually had someone else waiting for them somewhere. That was why he often used the tunnels and chutes, going down the ladders rather than waiting for an elevator to reach him.

He almost pivoted and went to the nearby crew ladder, but he didn't. He got on the nearest elevator and rode it down to engineering, half-hoping his hunch had been wrong.

Of course, it wasn't. The elevator doors opened to reveal a parade of gurneys floating past.

His stomach lurched. He stood in the elevator long enough for the doors to start to close. He had to use an arm to keep them open as he slipped out, and then he had to be careful to avoid getting hit by a gurney.

He plastered himself against the wall, before he remembered he could change the gurneys' pattern just like he had done with the elevator. He stuck out one arm, and the next gurney in the center of the row closest to him moved up. All but the lower gurney shifted to adjust.

He had to stick out a foot as well to make it work, and for a moment, he thought the lowest side gurney would slam into his leg.

It didn't. It moved into the middle row of gurneys. The lower level gurneys all floated into that row.

He stepped into the empty space he had made and walked with the gurneys, all of the ones in his row avoiding him, but still making him nervous.

Not because they nearly hit him, but because they weren't empty like he thought.

They all had neat packages of bandages in the very center of the cot part, ready to be opened and used by whoever had ordered the gurneys.

He'd ordered an automated gurney or two in his career (before Stephanos. He winced), and they all had the packaged bandages and small medical scanners, designed for use by someone with no medical experience whatsoever.

If the gurney itself determined that no one would use the package, it would open a small compartment and the package would drop inside, protected against fluids and any other ick from the body on top of the gurney.

There had probably been one of those packages underneath Stephanos.

He winced again, then focused on the gurneys around him. It almost felt like he had ordered them up, and he was leading them to whatever carnage they were heading toward.

He smelled the carnage before he saw it, which made him shudder. The smell was faint at first—blood mixed with offal mixed with the faint odor of burned metal.

At first, he thought that smell had lingered in his nostrils from Stephanos (dammit, again), but the smell grew stronger as he got closer to engineering.

It took a powerful array of odors to overcome the environmental system's automated scrubber. His heartrate, which had slowed down, sped up, and he swallowed hard against a dry throat.

The gurneys weren't some kind of system glitch, then. They were actually needed.

He glanced over his shoulder, finally willing to flee. But he couldn't get out of the gurney mess without bumping into one, and weirdly, superstitiously, he didn't want to do that.

He let them move him along, around another corner.

The wall nearest him was scored with burn marks. Some were from laser pistols, but some seemed to be from something even more powerful.

He rounded the final half corner, and saw it, the carnage so much worse than he expected.

A pile of people lay on the floor, some on top of the others. Somehow they were all in a relatively small space, even though there was room on the sides.

The air smelled of burned flesh here, as well as that overpowering stench of blood. Hot metal and the tang of laser fire also filled the air.

The doors to engineering were open, though, but he could see no people inside.

He didn't recognize anyone in the tangle of limbs and bodies. They all seemed like parts to him, even though they were attached.

The gurneys divided here as well, with the bulk of them going to the left and the rest off to the right.

That was when he realized that people stood on either side, directing the gurneys. Only three people, two on the left and one on the right.

Engineers. Colleagues. The people he had been worried about.

Strangely, he hadn't worried about the captain at all. But now he did. Was Preemas inside engineering? Had he taken over that part of the ship—or rather retaken it?

Ibori was stunned to realize he didn't want Preemas inside engineering. He wanted First Officer Crowe to be handling everything.

Ibori had picked a side and hadn't even realized he had done it.

The two people on the left guided the first gurney down to the pile of bodies. Ibori stepped out of the gurney line and looked down. He couldn't tell where one person began and another ended. They lay in a sea of blood, and he couldn't tell who that came from either. But it had already gotten on his shoes.

He didn't see weapons, either.

"What happened?" he asked, louder than he expected to.

The woman on the left raised her head in surprise. It was Mi Bajaj. Her face was speckled, probably with blood, her eyes wide. She pointed a laser pistol at him. Her hands, blood-covered, were shaking.

He doubted she had ever fired a laser pistol outside of training.

Except maybe today.

"I'm sorry, Tindo," she said, her voice shaking as well. "I need to know why you're here."

He put his hands up, without moving his arms at all. Almost in a *stop. Don't hurt me* motion.

"I followed the gurneys," he said. "I was in the med bay with Natalia."

"Oh good," Bajaj said. "She's all right, then."

He shook his head, half-expecting the tears he'd been fighting to start again. But they seemed to have dried up once he saw all the bodies around him.

"No," he said. "She's dead."

All three of the people cleaning up turned toward him. He recognized the other two, DeShawn Hagen and Tasneem Zhang, although he had never worked with them. They were both coated with blood as well. Zhang had a smear across her forehead, as if she had tried to wipe some off.

"Natalia's dead?" Hagen asked, as if he couldn't believe it. "Did the captain kill her?"

"Um." Ibori didn't know how to answer that. Preemas certainly hadn't cared that she was injured and he had treated her terribly. But kill her? No. Unless the situation itself had caused her death. "No. Not directly. No. She…"

His voice trailed off. He wasn't ready to talk about that.

Zhang grabbed a gurney and held it just the way he had held Stephanos's gurney. She was guiding it down.

"What happened here?" Ibori asked again.

"They tried to storm engineering," Hagen said. "They failed."

Ibori let out a small, scared breath. "And the captain?"

Hagen waved a hand toward the open doors. Ibori had to stand on his toes to see over the pile of people. Then he saw a huddled form near the control panel on the side. He recognized the pant legs, of all things. They were the bottom part to the captain's uniform, something that Preemas usually wore with a nontraditional shirt.

Ibori's mouth went dry. Not possible. The captain had to be alive.

But that body was Preemas's. He had a hole in his forehead. He was clearly dead.

Ibori felt a trembling beginning in his torso. He wasn't sure if it was fear or disbelief or sheer terror that caused it.

He swept his hand toward the pile of bodies.

"Are they all dead?" he asked.

"Oh, no," Zhang said. "That's why we have to hurry this. We have to get them to the brig. Do you have a weapon?"

"Me?" Ibori said. "No."

He knew that Preemas had been handing them out, but he hadn't taken one.

Preemas. The captain. Dead somehow. And everyone else unconscious.

"Are you willing to help us right now?" Bajaj asked. Something in her tone told him that if he didn't, she might truss him up as well.

"Um," he said. "I guess."

His shoes were already coated.

"There's a lot of blood here," he said.

"Some people are injured," Hagen said, then he nodded toward Zhang on the other side. She was guiding the gurneys to the most wounded, and using the bandage kits on automatic, letting the gurneys determine what exactly needed to be done.

Already a handful of gurneys were heading down the corridor, moving even faster than they had before.

"Where are these going?" Ibori asked.

"Brig," Bajaj answered.

Brig. That meant the battle was over. The fighting was done. There were good guys and bad guys, and the bad guys were being locked up. But Ibori looked at the faces—those he could see—of the people sprawled along the floor, and he didn't see any bad guys.

He saw colleagues. He saw people he didn't like who had ganged up with Preemas. He saw folks he had shared a drink with.

"What are we going to do with them all?" he asked.

"Not my concern," Hagen said as Bajaj said, "Get them to the brig."

They looked at each other, then shook their heads.

"One thing at a time," Bajaj said to Ibori by way of explanation. "That's all we can do."

"You could go with them," Hagen said. "We need someone to supervise this transfer."

He had a hopeful expression as he looked at Ibori. Ibori's mouth gaped open. He would manage prisoners in the brig? He wasn't sure he had ever been to the brig. There had been no tour of the ship when he had come on board, and he had purposely avoided some areas.

"You can't do that," Bajaj hissed. "You don't know what side he's on."

Hagen gave Ibori a speculative look. "Preemas is dead," Hagen said coldly. "You upset about that?"

"Of course I am," Ibori blurted. "He was a human being."

Hagen's eyebrows went up. Bajaj shook her head, as if she couldn't believe what an idiot Ibori was. Zhang ignored them all, continuing to work as if the rest of them weren't even here.

Ibori was shaking. He had lost a friend today, and it looked like he had lost a lot of colleagues as well. Everything was different, and it had changed in the space of a few hours.

"I don't know what you people thought you were doing," Ibori said. "I don't know what *anyone* thought they were doing, but this—this was a colossal mistake. What the hell?"

Bajaj glared at him, then bent over a woman on the floor and attached wrist locks before guiding a gurney over. He was startled to realize it was Jorja Lakinas.

Slowly, Bajaj eased Lakinas onto the gurney.

Ibori watched it all, feeling the horror all the way to his soul. He had had lunch with Lakinas not two days before. They had laughed over the tensions in the ship, saying that it was probably some residual terror about taking such a scary mission.

And now she was going to the brig? For defending the *captain*? For following Fleet protocol?

Although Ibori didn't know if they had been following protocol. It certainly wasn't protocol to march on an engineering department, even if the Chief Engineer had gone rogue.

"I didn't take a side," Ibori said. "I was in the med bay with Natalia."

They didn't seem to care, those three people. Bajaj still looked at him with suspicion. Hagen shook his head, then looked away. The gurney he had been guiding floated near him, bumping him occasionally as if urging him to continue the work.

Zhang eased wrist locks onto another person. Ibori couldn't even tell if she was arresting a man or a woman. She grabbed a gurney and eased it down, as if she were working on some sort of automated line.

Bajaj watched him, even as she sent the gurney with Lakinas on it into the queue in the corridor.

The gurneys were floating, waiting.

But the pile of unconscious people on the floor was looking more like people huddled together and less like a collection of limbs, torsos, and heads.

"What are we going to do with all these people?" Ibori asked.

Bajaj glared at him. "Just stop asking questions, okay? We don't know. *I* don't know. We're taking this from moment to moment. These people *attacked* us and tried to kill us. We defended ourselves. We won. And now we have to make sure they don't attack us again. You got that? We have to protect ourselves and this ship."

She pushed another unconscious person onto a gurney. This person, a man, was someone Ibori did not recognize.

"I don't have answers," Bajaj said. "I doubt First Officer Crowe has answers. He told us to do this job, and we're going to do it. That's all. Then we move to the next thing. We really need someone in the brig to organize these prisoners."

Ibori wasn't going to do that. He wasn't going to be a jailer, no matter how hard Bajaj pushed.

But he understood what she was saying. He remembered the craziness on the bridge, the way that the crew had huddled around Preemas, the way that their eyes sparkled with a hatred Ibori had never seen before.

The way they refused to see Stephanos as a casualty and instead, saw her as a problem to be solved.

"What about the med bay?" he asked.

Hagen was easing a badly injured man onto a gurney. "What about it?"

"Who is working the med bay?" Ibori asked. "When I was there, I didn't see anyone working it."

"That doesn't mean no one is there," Bajaj said.

It didn't, but Ibori had a hunch that was the case.

He didn't want to be in the middle of any of this, and he only saw one way out.

"I'll take everyone to the med bay," he said. "You find someone else for the brig."

"You have medical training?" Bajaj asked.

"Field training." Ibori said. A long, long, long time ago. And it had only been a theory class. The first truly bloody person he had ever seen had been Stephanos.

"Well, that's more than I've had," Hagen said. "Good. You go with them."

Ibori sucked in a breath. He didn't take orders from Hagen. Technically, Ibori outranked Hagen. But Preemas had said that rank didn't matter. Not as the ship got reorganized. (And looked how well that turned out for him.)

Besides, if Ibori went to the med bay, he would just have to work. He wouldn't have to fight anyone or weigh in. Or think about what was actually going on.

He made his way around the pile of people still on the floor. Someone was moaning.

He wasn't sure what he signed up for, but he realized it was a sign of just how little he wanted to be here that he was willing to deal with the injured and the dying rather than pick a side.

"Okay," he said as he helped Zhang load a young woman he didn't recognize onto a gurney. The gurney immediately lit up, as it started the program to assess the woman's injuries.

All Ibori could see was burns. A lot of them. Laser burns.

She was going to be in horrible pain, real soon now.
And he would have to deal with it.
His stomach twisted.
He had no good options.
But he was going to have to choose one.

THE *RENEGAT*

Serpell couldn't concentrate on her work.

She sat at her work area, because if she stood, she would pace. She couldn't reach India. She had tried and tried and tried. The last time they spoke, India was curt with her.

Everyone else in the research area was working, heads down, hands moving, looking serious. A little earlier, one of the men had said that a friend had told him the crisis between the captain and the first officer was coming to a head, and that they should all brace themselves.

But no one knew what that meant, so they just continued to work. Work had been their refuge since the long trips through foldspace. Everyone had braced their work stations, so that if the gravity disappeared again or the attitude controls failed, they wouldn't lose much. Nor would they injure each other.

In fact, all of them were using the built-in stools now. The stools raised and lowered into a hole in the floor. Serpell was the only one sitting on hers. Everyone else had theirs tucked away.

She had never seen that before, and half-suspected they all wanted a quick getaway.

Not that she knew what a quick getaway meant. There was nowhere to go.

Although they had arrived at the Scrapheap. And that was something, at least. It was what everyone was working on. They were all comparing the Scrapheap to the images that came through the first communications. They also searching for something that the captain called Ready Vessels, to see if they remained in the Scrapheap.

And they were supposed to figure out if there was a direct way in or if they would have to use what looked like breaches in the force field protecting the Scrapheap.

All of the researchers were working on this, all five of them, plus people with different specialties like Serpell. She had hoped that her linguistic skills would be put into play by now, but maybe they would be useful once the *Renegat* investigated the Scrapheap itself.

A couple of the researchers had left about an hour ago. They had joined the ship on Sector Base Z, and they had never really coalesced with everyone else working in this area.

Still, the fact that they left, along with the rumors that the captain and the first officer were coming to blows, made Serpell even more nervous than normal, especially since India wasn't contacting her.

Serpell didn't know how to deal with that at all, and she didn't want to be here, and she felt like she was here because of India (well, she was) and now India was unavailable. It felt like a betrayal on top of all the danger and the uncertainty of this trip.

The betrayal was making Serpell alternately clingy and angry. So she mostly tried to work. Work had been her salvation so far, but it wasn't helping right now.

"Anyone know what's going on?" she asked.

Clyde Hammersmith, who worked on the console closest to her, said, "I haven't been able to get any information at all. No one is answering on the bridge and engineering is cut off."

"Cut off?" someone asked in a strangled voice. Serpell couldn't see who that voice belonged to. Fear had changed the tone enough that the voice sounded only vaguely familiar.

"My messages keep bouncing back," Hammersmith said.

Serpell's mouth was dry. Maybe India hadn't deliberately cut off communications. Maybe it was an order from the captain.

"What could be going on?" she asked, and her voice sounded a bit strangled with fear too.

"I don't know, exactly," Hammersmith said quietly. "But I've been trying to find out. I don't have high enough clearance to get into some of the systems."

"Me either," said Ariel Dover. "And I've been trying since a friend contacted me, asking if I still had the laser pistol I'd been issued when I joined up."

Serpell raised her head in surprise. She still had hers, but India hadn't asked. India knew where it was though, and India knew the password to get the pistol out of the storage panel Serpell kept it in.

India wouldn't do that, though, would she?

Serpell wasn't sure anymore.

"Why would they want our personal weapons?" Hammersmith asked.

"No one can reach engineering," Dover said.

"That's not a reason to use weapons," Serpell said.

No one responded. They all looked down at their consoles.

Serpell stood up. India was out there, and she was doing something, and it might involve laser pistols. Weapons.

"I'm going to go see what's happening," Serpell said.

Hammersmith grabbed her arm. "You don't want to do that," he said. "What if they are using weapons? You're going to get into the middle of something—"

"My wife is out there," Serpell said. She had no idea what she could do to help India. Serpell wasn't even sure India wanted help. But Serpell wasn't going to let India go into danger alone.

Serpell looked down at Hammersmith's hand. He let her go.

"You don't want to be out there," he said. He knew more than he was saying. She could tell from the set of his head, the way his eyes glinted.

"I'm sure India doesn't want to be there either," Serpell said.

"If something's going wrong, you're not going to be able to save anyone," Hammersmith said.

Serpell nodded, just once. He was probably right.

But at least she was going to try.

PART THIRTY-FIVE

SOMEWHERE NEW

NOW

THE *AIZSARGS*

"They're hiding something from us," Kabac said, his arms crossed.

He had scuttled over to Serpell's side just as the meeting started, and she had not moved or rolled her eyes, although she had wanted to do both.

The meeting was in a large room that clearly could have several different functions. There were circles in the floor for furniture to rise up and populate the room. But for the purposes of this meeting, the only furniture were sideboards lining three of the four walls. One of the sideboards was broken up by the only visible door, which the survivors of the *Renegat* had entered through.

The fourth wall seemed blank. A few of the survivors had walked up to it to investigate, but stopped doing that when crew members entered, pushing a few of the survivors in wheelchairs.

The wheelchairs were smooth and sleek and clearly could have brought the non-mobile survivors on their own. But for some reason, someone in charge of the *Renegat* felt that these survivors needed help getting here.

Serpell recognized several of the people in the chairs. Most hadn't been injured the last time she saw them, but a few were survivors of Preemas's battle for the ship. They had sustained terrible injuries and no one on the *Renegat* had the skills to do much more than keep-them-alive repair. Not even the automated programs in the med bay could handle some of those injuries.

Serpell found herself staring at Jorja Lakinas, who tilted sideways in the chair, arms twisted and legs useless. Lakinas had been taken to the med bay that horrid day, not to the brig, and she had gotten enough help to continue breathing. Although whenever Serpell had tried to talk with her—and Serpell had tried several times—Lakinas's bitterness made Serpell cut the conversations short.

Serpell had finally given up spending any time near the remaining wounded from that battle, primarily because of Lakinas. Intellectually, Serpell was glad that Lakinas had survived, but emotionally, Serpell still couldn't deal with her.

Just like she wanted nothing to do with Kabac. He had hovered near her during the entire talk, watching the woman who was in charge of the entire group speak to them calmly and slowly, as if everyone were injured as badly as Lakinas.

Serpell had had a feeling that something was off too. She just didn't like discussing it with Kabac.

She stood near the back of the room for the entire speech—and it had been a speech, filled with cautions and rules, although it was couched in welcoming language.

The woman who talked with them, Anna Vail, hadn't given her rank but she was clearly not the captain. She said her specialty was coordinating things, and apparently the survivors of the *Renegat* were things to be coordinated.

She had answered some of Serpell's questions, though. The *Aizsargs* was in this sector on a mission when they saw the *Renegat* emerge from foldspace. And she broke the news that the *Renegat* had exploded after all but six had escaped.

Who the six were that died was something she and the team of the *Aizsargs* would help the rest of the survivors figure out. If anyone was missing relatives or friends, though, they were to talk with Vail.

And a few people were already lined up to talk with Vail. Serpell had had to move slightly to the left to see Vail, because she was a small woman. But she was visible amongst the survivors. Every survivor wore white, beige, or light gray shirts. Every survivor wore black pants and sandals. Vail had told them that they would be able to customize their clothing later in the day, as the system readied itself for the demand. The ship was recycling most of the clothes that the survivors had arrived in, since the clothes were unworthy of salvage—whatever that meant.

Not that Serpell wanted to keep the outfit she had been wearing underneath her horrid environmental suit. But the loss of the clothing felt like an odd blow. The clothing had been the only thing she had managed to salvage from her entire life, the only thing she had brought with her off that ship, and now that clothing was gone.

"I mean it," Kabac said. "They're hiding something. Something big."

Serpell looked over at him. He had deep shadows under his eyes. He had trimmed his beard, and his hair was no longer matted. He looked like a real person now, albeit one who was under severe stress.

"Why didn't you ask Vail about your suspicions after she was done talking?" Serpell asked.

Kabac's mouth thinned. "What kind of question is *what are you hiding*? Besides rude. I mean, they did save our lives."

"Yes," Serpell said. "They did."

And they were doling out information in organized chunks. Serpell leaned against the lip of the sideboard. She had been standing far away from most of the food. Her appetite had not returned, although she did make herself some eggs for breakfast in the tiny private kitchen of her room.

The room was nicer than anything she had ever seen on a ship. The room had a couch/bed combination that she could change as needed. Built into the wall, it had three cushions in its couch form, and one very soft mattress in its bed form. There was the small cooking area, and a counter with a chair so she could eat.

And a wall full of entertainment options, none of which contained news or the ability to contact anyone off ship.

She supposed that was all right. After all, no one on the *Aizsargs* knew this crew. They hadn't known who they had picked up.

That was one of the first things Vail had told them: the rescue was following strict protocol and the survivors wouldn't be allowed shipwide access unless or until the captain of the *Aizsargs* determined it was necessary.

They were being taken to the nearest base, although Vail did not say whether it was a sector base or a starbase, which Serpell also found to be unusual.

"I'm sure they'll tell us what they feel we need to know," she said, sounding more passive than she felt. But Kabac's paranoia fed her own.

"Exactly," he said. "'What they feel we need to know.' Why are they keeping us in the dark?"

She frowned. There were always Fleet policies that kept crew members in the dark. Officers knew more than regular crew. And then there were missions that no one knew about—or very few. Like theirs.

"Maybe they're on a top secret mission," she said.

Kabac leaned his head back, his frown deepening. "Or maybe they can't find us in the records."

"What do you mean?" she asked.

"Our mission was probably top secret too." He scanned the room as if he were looking for someone.

She did too, and saw that Vail had left. Most of the other survivors stayed, though, and were taking food off the sideboards and talking quietly. She wondered if they felt as uncomfortable as she did.

"There's no one to ask right now," he said, "but I'll bet that's it. Maybe they think we stole the ship."

"The ship will be in the records," she said. She knew that for a fact. She'd been researching so much at the behest of Captain Preemas that she knew what was in Fleet records and what wasn't. "And so would we. But there wouldn't be any record of this particular mission or it would be blocked from view. If someone on board has the proper clearance, they could see it."

He nodded, but looked distracted. It was almost as if he hadn't heard her.

"If no one does," she said, making sure she sounded reasonable, "then they're probably contacting someone with the proper clearance."

"I'm sure you're right," he said and walked away.

Serpell felt a surge of irritation. She greatly disliked that man, and the dislike had not changed since they arrived.

She scanned the room again, and looked to see if there was someone else she wanted to talk with. She saw many familiar faces, but those faces belonged to people who had pressured her at one point or another, demanding that she do something for them as acting captain (which she hadn't been, not technically) or screaming at her for all of the things that had gone wrong on the ship.

She didn't want to talk with any of those people.

Exhaustion hit her. She hadn't been able to sleep much in that new room, and she had been so tired before. She was really tired now.

She wiped a hand over her face, and started out of the room. As she passed the others, she overheard wisps of conversation.

"...never seen a bed quite like the one in my room..."

"...the coffee tastes weird. Doesn't it taste weird to you? I used my regular settings..."

"...even in the corridor, the design is different. I mean, it curves where it should be straight..."

She had reached the door by the time the words penetrated. Everyone felt dislocated, and not just because they were new to this ship.

The ship was unfamiliar in a non-Fleet kinda way. The details were off. Her heart started to pound, and the exhaustion took a step back.

Once again, she had that sense that she wasn't on a Fleet vessel, but on a vessel that mimicked the Fleet.

She glanced at the door as she walked through it. Whoever had been speaking had been right: the door didn't have edges. It seemed vaguely rectangular until she really looked at it. And then she saw the curve in the design.

She hadn't been on the Fleet's newest ships. She didn't know much about their designs. And she had been gone on this journey for nearly a year. A lot could have changed.

But this ship hadn't been built in the past year. She'd served on new ships, and it took five years for all the flashy-shiny new to wear off. The new had worn off here. This ship looked used. The sideboards had a few scratches—gaps where the nanobits didn't repair themselves as well as other parts of the surface. Because the sideboards weren't essential systems, either no one noticed or no one cared enough to fix them.

She didn't know what this meant. She also didn't know what she could do about any of it, except worry. And she'd done enough worrying.

She was here, and safe for the moment at least.

Maybe she was wrong.

Maybe Kabac's paranoia had rubbed off.

Or maybe nothing was as it seemed.

PART THIRTY-SIX

AFTERMATH

100 YEARS AGO

THE *RENEGAT*

Crowe was going to have to inspect the *anacapa* drive himself. He didn't want to. He really wanted someone else to do it, someone with more expertise. But there was no one.

He had to leave engineering, which he really did not want to do. He wanted to stay there and work, but of course, he could not.

He also didn't want to cross the bloody part of the corridor. It still smelled like burned flesh, and that particular sharp stink caused by fear-sweat. The smell alone made the hackles rise on the back of his neck, not counting the smears of blood and other fluids all over the usually clean floor, and the holes in, and near, the equipment.

The weapons were gone at least, and so were the bodies, finally. The injured were heading to the med bay, and a few of his people—people he couldn't afford to lose on the engineering side—were taking everyone else to the brig. They'd be ensconced there, until Crowe could figure out what to do with them

He'd already made certain that only he and Willoughby could authorize anyone being released from the brig. He was still afraid someone would turn on them—heck, he was afraid most of the ship would turn on him.

He carried a laser pistol now, which he had never done on any ship he had worked on throughout his long career. The pistol felt heavy against his hip. He wasn't even sure he could fire the damn thing.

But he might have to.

He took the elevator to bridge level against his better judgment—considering what was going on, he should probably never trap himself in any small environment—but he was in a hurry. The sooner he solved one problem, the faster he could move on to the next.

The elevator opened onto a better-smelling corridor. The air was fresh, which surprised him. He half-expected it to still feel "alive" as Bakhr had deemed it, but the residual effects of that energy seemed to have dissipated.

He was having Vezner in engineering monitor the shields, making sure that the energy didn't compromise their integrity.

He would put someone else on monitoring those shields as well, as soon as he had someone else.

Crowe rubbed a hand over his face, willing the exhaustion away. He had a lot to do before he could execute any commands—any *real* commands.

Because he wanted—he *needed*—to get the *Renegat* out of here. Given what Bakhr had told him about the sector in which Bakhr had grown up in, and given what Crowe was seeing from the readings, he couldn't just move the *Renegat* to another part of this sector. That energy probably permeated the entire region.

What he needed to do was start the long journey back to the Fleet.

The very idea made him wince.

The moment he got back, he would be court-martialed. It was inevitable. From the day the Fleet had decided to forgive him for destroying an entire Scrapheap, the court-martial was only delayed. Some would probably have said that killing the captain was inevitable as well.

Crowe staggered a little as he approached the bridge doors. He felt like a very old man, because his body ached from the stress and the aftereffects of that energy slamming into him for hours.

He also felt like a kid, about to be tested on a subject he had never studied. He had never in his entire life been so completely out of his depth.

The doors to the bridge stood open, which was not standard procedure. He didn't even remark on that, as he walked through them, because who really gave a damn about standard procedure on this day? Even if standard procedure protected them all.

The two crew members that Preemas had left behind, Colvin and M'Ghan, were huddling near the wall, beside one of the more useless consoles. Neither crew member was near those consoles, as if they had abandoned all idea of working on the bridge at all.

Bakhr hunched over the science console, his fingers moving across its smooth surface. Apparently he didn't like working on floating screens.

Tosidis had moved to the edge of the captain's chair, that little bunker that Preemas had designed to keep himself informed. Tosidis, Crowe was happy to see, had started working again, even if his fingers shook as he moved.

A stench in the bridge made the smell in the corridor of engineering seem miniscule. The odor here started more as a sensation, but as he walked past all of the empty consoles to the navigation panel, the smell grew more and more foul.

Organic rot, like decayed flesh, tinged the air, combined with the scent of old blood. His stomach flopped, and he couldn't keep quiet.

"How come this place hasn't been cleaned up?" he asked M'Ghan.

"A lot of it has," he said. "The environmental system is on scrub."

"But we left the area near the *anacapa*," said Colvin, "because we were afraid to run any equipment near it."

"Probably wise," Crowe said, wincing as he spoke. He didn't want to see where Stephanos had died, but he would have to. He needed to understand it.

He made his way past Bakhr, past the screens that Tosidis was working, unable to see exactly what Tosidis was doing. Not that the details mattered. Tosidis was trying to figure out the *anacapa* without going near it, which might be useful, if he could figure it out.

Crowe doubted that was possible, but he had doubted a lot of things that had become true.

Like the condition of this bridge. Even though he had seen it on a three-D rendering in engineering, it wasn't the same as being here. The place represented the turmoil of the entire ship.

This bridge was all about that kind of abandonment. Some of the consoles were on. Others had shut down. The door to the ready room stood open, and inside were even more weapons, as if Preemas hadn't found enough people to use them. Or maybe Preemas had been stocking them for later.

Some of the chairs were turned away from their consoles. Most of the stools near somc of thc consolcs were only half up, as if someone had tried to store them in the floor, but hadn't had the time to finish.

And then there was the area around the *anacapa* drive.

He braced himself. He knew that Stephanos had died there, but he wasn't sure exactly what had killed her.

He walked down to the front of the bridge, around the navigation console, and made himself look.

The area was worse than the area outside of engineering, mostly because he knew that big blackish-red blood pool had come from only one person. There were no smears on the wall, like there were near engineering, no holes in the console, not even any spatter on any of the nearby furniture.

Just that blood pool, and a few footprints beside it.

The smell was stronger here, of course. He had expected that, but it still overwhelmed him.

Then he looked at the container. The lid was closed. There was no blood on it.

He turned, about to ask exactly what had happened to Stephanos, then realized he was better off replaying the events.

He crouched, opened a small screen, and shut off the sound. No reason the others had to hear this, not right now.

He went back to the moment Stephanos arrived on the bridge. At that moment, the bridge was packed with people, but most of them surrounded Preemas.

He was handing out weapons like they were candy.

Then Preemas looked at Stephanos. They were clearly having words. Finally, he raised one of the laser pistols and held it on her.

Crowe's breath caught. Had she been injured because Preemas shot her?

Stephanos raised her chin, said something to Preemas, and he got that look—the look Crowe had hated the most—the one that implied that he hadn't meant what he had said just a few minutes ago, and that he would blame someone else for the "misunderstanding" if he possibly could.

Then he turned away. Stephanos moved to the console closest to the *anacapa*, said something to Ibori, who nodded.

She worked on the console. Crowe couldn't see what she had done from this angle, but he could replay images from a different angle if need be. Then she walked over to the *anacapa* container.

Crowe could see the container clearly. It looked fine, but then, he hadn't been near it. And to his eye, Stephanos seemed leery. He couldn't quite put his finger on what made him think that, but something did.

She tried and failed to open the lid. He'd never seen that on a container before. He expected her to go to the console and change some settings, but instead, she used brute force, finally managing to open the container.

The golden glow of the *anacapa* looked just fine to him. It illuminated her face. She was biting her lower lip, and it wasn't just because she was concentrating. Something was bothering her.

He wished he could peer over her shoulder into the *anacapa* drive itself. But the way the bridge cameras were set up, he wouldn't be able to do that.

She licked her bottom lip, closed her eyes for a brief second, then reached over and grabbed gloves.

Now, it was Crowe's turn to panic—even though he knew she was dead.

He also knew that something around that drive had killed her.

Something in there made her want to touch the drive. He hadn't had a lot of *anacapa* training but he'd had enough to know that touching the drive was an unusual move.

She placed one hand outside the container, then held the other above it. Through it all, she was talking to Ibori. Crowe might have to listen to that conversation later.

Stephanos squared her shoulders and slowly brought her left hand down toward the *anacapa* drive.

The movement was odd, as if she were slicing through water instead of air. He made the image larger, saw that her entire body was vibrating.

Her eyes leaked tears. Then her nose started to bleed. Blood dripped onto the drive itself, but that didn't change the color of the light.

Although Stephanos's face looked different in the light. It was as if the light were illuminating her from within, as if the light was a part of her like it was part of the *anacapa* drive.

Blood dripped out of her ears, as well, and the tears falling down the sides of her face looked more pink than clear.

Still, she didn't let go of the drive.

He had no idea what she was trying to do. He had thought he would be able to figure it out just from watching her, but he couldn't.

The energy that had been flowing into the ship from the Scrapheap had somehow altered the *anacapa* drive, and caused this reaction.

Ibori noticed that she was in danger. He stepped toward her, but she said something to him, and he stopped. Preemas was sneering at both of them, and in that moment, Crowe was glad he couldn't hear what was being said.

Stephanos leaned forward, blood pouring out of her nose now, and pushed so hard with her left arm that Crowe could see her muscles working.

She appeared to be stuck to the *anacapa* drive. Then she flew backwards, falling onto the spot where the blood pool was now.

Ibori leaned over her, and Crowe couldn't tell what was happening now.

Except that the *anacapa* drive glowed golden, the light even stronger than it had been a moment before, as if the blood had refreshed it.

He didn't like that thought. He didn't like any of his thoughts.

Anacapa drives weren't supposed to work like that. *Anacapa* drives usually showed different colors if they were failing, not the normal healthy golden color.

He fast-forwarded through the images, saw people fighting, saw Preemas turn his back on Stephanos, saw others trying to save her, saw Ibori look more and more stricken.

And all the while, the *anacapa* glowed golden, the light getting brighter and brighter.

Finally, India Romano looked at everyone with contempt, then walked across the blood and slammed the lid closed.

She came back to Preemas's group, but she rubbed her hands against her legs as if her hands bothered her.

And light filtered out of the container's sides, as if the container could no longer house the drive.

Crowe's heart was pounding as if he had done something wrong.

He looked at that container.

No light leaked out of it now. It looked perfectly normal.

He stood, realized that he probably should not have crouched like that, moved his shoulders, and straightened his back just a little.

Then he went to the console closest to the *anacapa* drive, trying to see if the drive's readings had changed.

They hadn't. The drive read as normal from the moment the *Renegat* came out of foldspace until this very moment. It was as if whatever had happened to the drive did not register on the equipment.

Then he looked up to see if that light had had some kind of impact on the ceiling. The light shouldn't have, but it shouldn't have grown in intensity like that either.

But the ceiling looked just like it always did. Disgustingly normal.

It was as if the light had had no impact at all.

Although it had—or something from the *anacapa* drive had had an impact. The air had felt charged, and then when Stephanos had touched the drive, even with her gloves, she had bled.

He opened a small screen on the console, and made himself look at Stephanos, not from the angle he had used before, but from the one above her, as she lay dying.

Colvin had been right: Stephanos no longer looked human. Her face had collapsed in on itself. Some of the crew members who had been watching at her had turned away, as if they couldn't bear to look.

Crowe could hardly bare to look either. But he did.

Because he had never seen anything like it before. Not ever in his entire career.

It was as if the container holding Stephanos together—her bones and her skin—had collapsed in on themselves, lost structure, lost integrity.

He shut off the image of her face. He couldn't look at it any longer.

But he stared at the blood pool.

Lost integrity. Lost structure.

"We need to check the ship," he said to the four others on the bridge.

"What?" M'Ghan. "What do you mean?"

"Full automated inspection," Crowe said. "Hull integrity, systems integrity, everything."

And they should probably check the crew too, but he didn't say that. Not yet. He wanted to see if his theory was correct.

Whatever had mixed with the *anacapa* energy might have started disassembling the ship at a microlevel.

And if it had the same effect on humans, then maybe some of the behavior he had seen—he had been part of these last few hours—had not been because of simmering tensions but because everyone had literally been falling apart.

He leaned on the console.

What had happened this day was probably not that simple. It had been building for a long, long time. But the emotions, the boiling anger, the screaming he had seen in the corridor as the crew Preemas had brought down from the bridge charged, those might have been exaggerated because the *anacapa* had been affecting everyone.

Stephanos had just gotten a larger, quicker dose because she had touched the drive.

Then Crowe half-smiled at himself. He wanted that to be true. He wanted this entire mess to have happened because the crew had become irrational, not because they had made the choice to attack each other.

He took a deep breath, realizing that he had stopped compartmentalizing.

He had work to do. He had to figure out how to examine that *anacapa* drive, and how to do so without harming anyone.

He wasn't sure that was possible.

But he would try.

THE *RENEGAT*

Something bit into her wrists. And her hands ached.

India Romano kept her eyes closed, cataloging pains. She couldn't even feel her left shoulder. It was numb. She remembered something—shrapnel?—hitting it. Her right thigh burned.

And her chest hurt as if someone had slammed a piece of metal against it—hard. So hard that it hurt the inside of her chest, and yet somehow hadn't broken her ribs.

No. That hurt wasn't from the outside. It was on the inside. Air.

She hadn't been getting enough air. She remembered gasping, and seeing lights in front of her eyes, then thinking she couldn't breathe, the bastards had removed the oxygen, she was going to die…

Her eyes flew open, and she saw the rigid rows of lights along both edges of a corridor ceiling. Her entire body was still tingling—that sensation she had felt earlier.

She lifted her head slightly, which made her dizzy, but she held the position and looked.

She was on a gurney. *Strapped* on a gurney, and not the kind of straps designed to keep an unconscious person in position. No. The thick straps used for prisoners.

Her feet were apart, and each calf had a strap, which wasn't regulation. She should have had one over her thighs as well, and along her ankles, but nothing was on her ankles or her thighs—except a white bandage over her entire right thigh, a white bandage that was slowly turning color along the side of her thigh—turning from white to a brownish yellow. She was bleeding or oozing puss or something.

She couldn't catch her nonexistent breath in this position, and the back of her neck ached, but she didn't lower her head yet. Instead, she slowly moved her head to the right, saw Odafe Yarleque on a gurney beside her, unconscious, small bandages dotting his arms and covering his face.

She hadn't even realized he had been fighting with them. She had thought he worked in the med bay.

She turned her head left—even slower, because moving her neck hurt so badly she almost teared up—and saw Bruno Moratis, also unconscious—or maybe just giving up—tears leaking out of his eyes like a slowly moving river. He was strapped properly for a prisoner, a large strap across his chest, another over his hips, thighs, ankles, hands restrained inside the gurney, far enough apart that they couldn't touch anything important.

Moratis had been fighting beside her just a moment ago—or what had seemed like a moment ago. But Crowe had done something, firing back at them—murdering the captain. *Murdering* the captain.

Romano let out what breath she had and her head fell back onto the gurney, rocking it a little. It managed to right itself easily. And that was when she realized it was moving forward, slowly, and so gently she could almost not feel the movement. Only the changing lights on the corridor ceiling told her that she was in motion. They were splitting as the corridor split into three different directions.

"Hey," she said, her voice thin and reedy. She barely had enough air to speak. "What's going on?"

"Shut up, India," Yarleque said, his voice stronger than hers. "You're the one who got us into this."

She was? She had come down to engineering to defend her captain like everyone else. She had just been following captain's orders.

"What did you say?" Yarleque continued. "*Get them*? Well, they got us now."

The gurney on her left veered left. The gurney on her right stayed beside her.

She raised her head just a little more. The gurneys on the left were heading down another corridor. She squinted, trying to make out where she was, ignoring the dizziness.

They were heading to the med bay. They had to be, considering everyone was unconscious and looked—oh, God, ragged, broken. Not like the impatient group of crew members turned fighters who had crowded into that elevator not too long ago.

She blinked and leaned her head back down, not willing to ask any more questions. The dizziness remained.

If the unconscious were going to the med bay, where was she going?

She turned her head and over the edge of the gurney, she stared at Moratis. He was unconscious too, and he was traveling her direction.

She closed her eyes for a half second, realized that made her dizzier than keeping them open. She made herself take a deep breath, which hurt. Her lungs ached from emptiness.

She remembered that feeling from childhood. They always locked the teenagers up in some room, and slowly removed the oxygen—enough that it hurt, but not enough to injure them, just so that they all knew what it felt like to go without an environmental suit. It was teen-training, trying to make sure they wouldn't be reckless.

It had taken nearly a day to get her air back. She had resented the feeling then, and it angered her now. Crowe had subdued them all so easily.

And murdered the captain.

She opened her eyes, and saw that the lights above her had changed color again, a brownish amber that made the entire corridor unpleasant. And that's when she realized where she was, and where she was going.

The brig.

Of course.

She had seen the brig after joining the security team. All of the new security officers had gotten a tour of the security features on the *Renegat*. The *Renegat* was an SC-Class vessel, and SC-Class vessels sometimes had to handle major security breaches, so the brigs on these things were huge.

And cold. And dark. Designed to make prisoners uncomfortable. Designed to keep them quiet—or as quiet as could be.

She had hated the brig when she saw it that day. She had thought that she would never, not ever, willingly put someone in there—unless that person had done something really bad…

Like murdering the captain.

She did not want to go to the brig. Couldn't they see she was injured? She shouldn't be in the brig, she should be in the medical bay.

Even though there were medical facilities in the brig. Just not as good as the med bay. But places for prisoners who were too mobile to risk at the bay.

Her heart rate increased, and that breath she'd been struggling with grew even more ragged.

She was not going to go to the brig. They couldn't make her. She wouldn't.

She thrashed on the gurney. She was going to overturn the damn thing, knock the others aside, get out of here, do…what? She had no idea, but she'd develop a plan once she was free.

She rocked the gurney hard, but it kept reestablishing its own balance. It was fighting her, but she would overcome it.

She would win.

Then the straps tightened, and another snaked across her hips, forcing her deep into the gurney's folds. The new strap scraped against her injured thigh, sending pain through her so intense that she gasped.

She couldn't move to fight. She couldn't move at all.

And the pain made it almost impossible to want to.

What were they going to do to her? To all of them? They were so far from the Fleet, away from any kind of organization. To shut up everyone who sided with Preemas in the brig would require some kind of maintenance, and lots of care, care there wasn't the personnel for.

She'd assume that Crowe didn't have the stomach to kill them all, but he had killed Preemas, so Crowe was clearly willing to kill for what he wanted.

She leaned her head back, cursing the tingling, the ache, and that pain that kept coursing through her right side. Adding to it, the pinch of the straps and the no-longer-smooth glide of the gurney, and she was done. Defeated. At least for the moment.

She closed her eyes against that dark amber light. Maybe she would try something when they all arrived at the brig. Maybe she would unite them.

If she could. If anyone would listen.

THE *RENEGAT*

Crowe returned to engineering, but he didn't go to his safe circle of screens in the alcove. Instead, he walked directly to the communications *anacapa*. He had a lot of figuring to do.

All the way back to engineering, he'd been thinking about what he'd seen. The images of Stephanos's death, besides breaking his heart, also baffled him. No *anacapa* drive should have worked like that. Nothing that he knew of in the workings of the *anacapa* drives had killed someone with a single touch.

Although he mentally had to correct that. Had killed someone who had worked with *anacapa* drives for years.

He knew that anyone training with *anacapa* drives who couldn't handle the feel of one was removed from their presence immediately.

But even that wouldn't have helped Stephanos. Her death had occurred fast. If something like that had happened on a school ship, the *anacapa* drives would have been considered a lot more dangerous than they already were.

He did not know if she had touched the driver previously on this journey, nor did he know what had caused her to touch it.

Those thoughts so preoccupied him that he had been startled as he reached the corridors outside of engineering. The stench of blood and death remained, even worse than it had been.

He glanced at the mess, saw the stains turning black, the imprints of hands against the floor, the pooled blood and bits of clothing, parts of weapons, and one single shoe. His stomach turned. He stepped around everything, and went into engineering itself.

He probably should have programmed the environmental and cleaning systems to at least clean up the blood, but he had hesitated twice now on that.

He wasn't sure why; maybe he expected someone to officially investigate what had gone wrong. Perhaps that was his training kicking in. Or his horrid experience as a young man.

He didn't have time to contemplate his own psychology, so he was ignoring it. He was ignoring all of it.

He had moved Willoughby away from the communications *anacapa*, telling her that he needed her to supervise the orders he had given from the bridge. He wanted to know how the *Renegat* herself was holding up after the onslaught of strange energy from the Scrapheap.

Willoughby had given him an odd look, and it made him wonder if she could see inside his head, if she saw that he wanted the energy to be to blamed for everything that had gone wrong.

But she didn't say anything. She had moved to the command post he had been using before he went to the bridge. The other engineers were following her bidding. Most of them hadn't moved out of their alcoves in hours.

Crowe wasn't sure if that was because they were dedicated to their work or if it was because they felt trapped by the mess outside the door. Maybe they didn't want to accept what had happened either, and were using the same method—ignoring it—as a way of pretending it never happened.

Willoughby had been monitoring the communications *anacapa*, with its little container closed. She had opened it to check to see if it was still vibrating, and then closed the container completely.

Crowe did not tell anyone what he was about to do. He needed to examine that tiny drive, and he needed to do so following protocol. His stomach was in tight knots. He placed a shield around the entire alcove he was working in. If something went wrong, he didn't want anyone to try to grab him and pull him away.

The shield shimmered into place. The shimmer only lasted a second or two, but it caught Willoughby's eye. She frowned at Crowe. The frown was filled with disapproval.

He half-smiled at her. He couldn't pull off a full smile for anyone today, but he wanted to reassure her.

He also liked the fact that she had noticed what he had done. If something happened to him, the ship herself would be in good hands with Willoughby.

Then he banished those thoughts, and focused on the work. He braced the door to the panel housing the communications *anacapa*. That way, if there was a small surge of energy, it would not accidentally slam the little panel door shut.

Then he pressed the controls that made the container and its housing slide out of the compartment. It was easy to remove the container's lid; there was actually a tiny hinge that pulled the lid up.

He used the automated hinge. The less he touched the *anacapa* housing, the better.

Then he slipped on the gloves that he had brought with him. He almost slipped on two pair, but realized if there was still an energy problem, the number of gloves he wore wouldn't matter at all.

Willoughby's frown deepened as she saw him put on the gloves. He had no idea if she had seen the images of Stephanos dying. He suspected Willoughby had: the woman was thorough, and understanding what had happened to Stephanos was important to all of them.

Willoughby's gaze rose to his, and she shook her head just a little. She didn't want him to touch the drive. But he had to in order to examine it the way he wanted to.

He wasn't going to justify his actions to her. That was precisely why he hadn't told her what he was going to do. He didn't want her to cause a stink about it.

The light from the tiny *anacapa* drive—something he thought of as a slice of an *anacapa* drive—glowed golden against the raised lid of the container. If he only looked at the light, he would have thought everything was just fine—the same as the main *anacapa* drive on the bridge.

But as he looked down at that slice, he saw bits of pink flowing through it. He had never seen pink in an *anacapa* drive before, especially not pink that looked like it had found veins in the drive itself.

He never thought of the drives as having veins, like rocks with metals inside of them. He always thought of the drives as one unit, even though he knew they weren't.

In his *anacapa* classes, decades ago, he had seen how different the drives could look from generation to generation, and also how different they looked as time and wear had had an impact on them. But they had never had veins. That was new.

He swallowed hard. All of the controls around the drive said that it was working just fine, exactly like the controls around the larger drive on the bridge.

In circumstances where the controls and the appearance of the drive differed, the common procedure was to use different equipment to scan over the drive. But he understood why Stephanos hadn't done so. She had been worried that introducing yet another energy signature into the mess would cause even more trouble.

There was less energy around the drive now that he had put up shields around the *Renegat*. But he still was loathe to try another piece of equipment.

Which meant he had to examine the drive physically.

And that was exactly what had killed Stephanos.

Crowe flexed his fingers. He would be looking for pitting, fractures, or more vibration in one area or another. Such things would be easy with the regular-sized *anacapa*, but this tiny one would be a challenge.

Even if his large fingers could hold the communications *anacapa* properly, he wasn't sure if his fingertips were sensitive enough to find pitting on something as small as his thumb. The gloves wouldn't help. Their membrane was thin, but that would still put an extra layer between his skin and the drive itself.

And, if he were being really honest with himself, he was scared to put the drive close to his eyes, so that he could examine the surface up close.

He touched the top of the *anacapa* drive, expecting to find a rough surface. Instead, it was as smooth as it was designed to be. It didn't even hum, like the drives sometimes did when they were glowing golden like this one.

He tried to trace those pink lines. If they were fractures, he should feel the fracture, but he didn't. He didn't feel anything.

Which was a problem.

He set that problem aside for the moment. One thing at a time. He was looking for damage in the drive itself first, and then he would deal with the way it operated after he finished with its structure.

Sometimes the two—structure and operation—were deeply intertwined, and before he delved into the operation part, he wanted to make certain all was fine with the structure.

He needed to slip his fingers around the slim little drive itself, but as he started to do so, Stephanos's face rose in his mind, the blood coming out of her nostrils, her tear ducts, and her ears.

He didn't feel ill. He didn't feel anything at all. But he almost wiped at his face with his free hand, and it took an act of will to stop himself from doing so.

He was going to fine. He had to be fine. There was no choice in the matter. This ship couldn't keep losing its most experienced *anacapa* engineers.

As if wishful thinking worked. He felt a surge of amusement at his own ability to delude himself and then made himself focus on the work.

He finished slipping his fingers around the tiny drive, and paused, half-expecting it to jab him or send shooting pains through his hand, or make his entire body vibrate.

None of those things happened. He was fine.

At least as far as he could tell.

Then he picked up the communications *anacapa*.

It only weighed a few ounces. The average *anacapa* drive weighed at least fifteen pounds, if not more. But this thing weighed next to nothing. That surprised him, and he knew it shouldn't have, because the thing was barely a fraction of the size of an average *anacapa* drive.

Still, he thought it would have more mass, the way a piece of solid metal had more mass than a hollow piece of glass.

This felt like a glass tube, even though it wasn't.

The drive also felt fragile, as if he could crush it with his fingers.

And that thought caught him. He made a note of it, then gingerly shifted the drive from his palm to holding it on its edges, using his thumb and forefinger.

He had to force himself to bring the drive up to eye level, and he tried not to think about what could happen.

He stared at it, saw no pits or external groves. The golden glow seemed even more harmless than a sharp beam of light being directed at his retina. When he blinked, he did not see a reflection of the light at all.

He had no idea if that was normal. He hadn't ever given the light coming out of an *anacapa* drive any thought.

The pink, though. The pink was something else entirely. He had thought it illuminated fractures in the drive. But viewed up close like this, he realized that the pink spiderwebbed into a series of lines, rather like a bottle made of string. It was as if something had been built inside of the *anacapa* drive, like a parasite taking over the drive, hollowing it out and creating its own little nest in the interior of the drive itself.

He let out a small breath, realizing just how much tension he was holding in his body. More than he wanted to consider.

He slowly and ever so carefully lowered the drive into its container, then let out another breath as he moved his hand away from the drive.

He felt no different—unless a profound sense of relief could be considered a difference. But physically, he felt the same. He hadn't been harmed by the drive—at least that he could tell.

He closed the lid on the container, and sent the container back into its holder. Then he removed the shield he had placed around the alcove.

Willoughby was watching him. He looked at her, raising his eyebrows in an unspoken question. Did he look the same? Was he injured and just not feeling it?

She shrugged. And he wasn't sure if that shrug meant he seemed fine to her or if it meant that she had no idea what he was asking.

But if something had been visibly wrong with his face or his posture, she would have let him know. He had to trust that.

He nodded at her, then removed the gloves and inspected his hands. They looked no different than they had before and they felt fine.

He turned his palm over, and rubbed his thumb against the fingertip on his forefinger. The skin felt like it always did, smooth and warm.

Then he turned his hand back over, shook it out because of the nerves, and made himself focus again.

He had one question, and only one other person could answer it.

He opened a screen so that he could see Tosidis on the bridge.

Tosidis answered, his face drawn and tired. His lips were chapped and bloodied, because, Crowe knew, Tosidis had been biting them. Tosidis was still standing inside the cocoon of screens that Preemas had built.

"If you want an update on the ship," Tosidis said before Crowe could speak, "we're still analyzing."

"I know," Crowe said. He'd been monitoring what they were doing on yet another screen. He hadn't seen any flagged information yet, but he hadn't been watching closely.

He probably shouldn't have been that dismissive, but he was focused on the *anacapa* drives first. One problem at a time, as he often told his staff.

"I need something else," Crowe said. "I can't find where you catalogued the weight of the communications *anacapa*. Do you have a recollection of how heavy it was?"

"Oh, my," Tosidis said. "I'm not sure I catalogued the weight."

Crowe didn't nod. He knew that Tosidis hadn't cataloged the weight or Crowe would have been able to find it. Crowe had just learned to approach someone from the perspective of *I'm looking for the correct data, so tell me where you stored it* instead of *why the hell didn't you do this right?* People usually admitted their mistakes this way, just like Tosidis had.

"But I did remember thinking it was much heavier than I expected," Tosidis said. "You know, when you work with full-size *anacapa* drives, you're not surprised—or, I guess, *I* wasn't surprised—that the drive is heavy. You kinda—*I* kinda—expected it, you know?"

Crowe nodded, his heart sinking as he listened.

"But I had never handled one of the small ones before," Tosidis said. "That one was much heavier than I thought possible."

"Anything else you noticed when you touched it?" Crowe asked. He knew better than to ask a leading question, because he might influence Tosidis's recollection.

"Yeah," Tosidis said. "It had that same alive feeling that a regular drive had, and by that I mean, it had the same intensity. I would have expected it to be just a fraction of the same intensity, you know what I mean?"

Crowe did. He felt even worse than he had a few minutes before, and he hoped it didn't show on his face.

"And no pink threading through the drive, right?" he asked, this time asking a leading question.

"Pink?" Tosidis asked. "You saw pink?"

Crowe didn't answer. He just waited.

"I never saw any pink," Tosidis said. "Is that part of a normal drive? Because I don't remember it."

"Don't worry about any of that at the moment," Crowe said. "I'll keep an eye on the *anacapa* drives." For now, he added mentally. "I need you to focus on the ship itself."

Because if the *Renegat* had been gutted the way he was now believing that the *anacapa* drives had been gutted, they were in even worse trouble than he had thought.

He leaned his head forward, wishing he understood more about *anacapa* drives. Wishing he knew how they worked exactly.

Because he couldn't just rely on Tosidis's memory here. What Tosidis might consider "heavier than expected," Crowe might consider "lighter than expected."

Although on some deep level, he doubted that. The pink construction inside, that parasite analogy that had risen unbidden in his mind, the loss of Stephanos so quickly, all led him to believe something else was going on.

He rubbed a hand over his face, then stopped himself. That nervous habit was getting old.

"Daria," he said to Willoughby. "Do you know who the acting physician is supposed to be?"

He should have known that, because he was the First Officer on top of everything else, but he couldn't remember. He might not even have registered that position or, possibly, hadn't noticed if it went completely unassigned.

"Orlena Seymont," Willoughby said. "I think. Last I checked."

"Do you think we can get her to autopsy Stephanos fast?" Crowe asked.

"In the middle of all this?" Willoughby asked. "We sent nearly a dozen people to the med bay. And I'm not even sure Orlena was even there."

He had known the injured were there, and he silently cursed himself for failing to see if the acting physician was actually in the med bay. For all he knew, she had been standing alongside Preemas when they attacked.

"Can you find out?" he asked.

"Why is an autopsy more important than saving lives?" Willoughby asked.

"Because we need to know what killed Stephanos." He wiped his fingers on the side of his pants. His fingers felt no different—his hands felt no different—but clearly touching the tiny communications *anacapa* still bothered him. "This has to take priority."

Willoughby frowned. "You think this could harm the rest of us?"

"I don't know," he said.

"But that's what you're worried about." Willoughby was pushing.

He nodded. He didn't want to give voice to it, all those fears swirling around inside of him.

"And how are we supposed to tell her to prioritize an autopsy?" Willoughby asked. "With real patients there?"

Willoughby seemed to assume that she was part of the command staff. And Crowe was going to let her assume that. It would make his job easier.

"Tell her that the work she's doing on the real patients is all for naught if Stephanos died the way I think she died," Crowe said.

"And how is that?" Willoughby asked.

Crowe shook his head. He wasn't going to lead her either.

"Let's just get it done, okay?" he said. "I'm heading back to the bridge."

"Why?" Willoughby asked.

"To examine the regular *anacapa* drive," Crowe said. Because if it was as hollow as the one down here, then there would be no way back through foldspace, and he would have to make other choices.

But he was getting ahead of himself.

He needed more evidence of what had happened to the *anacapa* drives before he had put up the shields.

And he needed it fast.

PART THIRTY-SEVEN
MYSTERIES OF THE *RENEGAT*
NOW

THE *AIZSARGS*

Dauber sat in her ready room, hands threaded through her hair. She had opaqued the door so that no one on the bridge could see inside, which was probably a good thing.

Her frustration wasn't with her crew.

They had done their job. They had done better than she could have hoped, really. They had saved 193 people from the *Renegat*, and those 193 people were now housed on two lower decks. The *Renegat* survivors had the run of those decks, but they couldn't access any of the upper decks.

The decontamination procedure that the survivors had gone through hadn't just cleared them of unknown organisms and strange viruses. It had also proven that they were who they said they were.

The records that had been the easiest to find were the identification records for the individual crew members. These survivors were who they said they were; they had been on the *Renegat* when the ship embarked from Starbase Rho a hundred years before.

These people had been a part of the Fleet then, and should be considered part of the Fleet now.

So Dauber followed protocol for foldspace survivors who had gone through a time jump. She made certain that there were no news sources that the survivors could access, no Fleet histories, in fact, no histories of any kind. The entertainment was lower level standard, so that it didn't look too advanced.

There was also no way for the survivors to contact anyone outside of the ship. Right now, Dauber—and no one else—controlled who approached the *Renegat* survivors, and she was keeping those approaches to a minimum.

Not only had she sent crew members who had done this before, but she had also sent her least chatty crew members. The ones who wouldn't linger and have a conversation with the survivors, the ones who wouldn't accidentally let something important slip.

All of that was standard procedure, but none of it led to her current frustration. She rested her elbows on the small desk she kept in her ready room mostly for form's sake, and closed her eyes for a long moment.

The records concerning the *Renegat* were a complete and utter mess. Dauber had spent the last three days going through them, and she only knew two things for certain: The *Renegat* had been given a classified assignment and sent by itself on a long foldspace journey that caused people consternation at the time, and the *Renegat* herself had been written off as lost about fifty years ago.

But that particular action was simply a formal acknowledgment of what the Fleet had accepted as reality three years after the *Renegat*'s communications ceased.

The Fleet knew that the *Renegat* had taken a long foldspace journey, and that it hadn't responded after one of the foldspace legs of that journey. So, as the Fleet often did, it assumed the *Renegat* was trapped in foldspace.

Only the Fleet had not followed standard procedure at that point. Standard procedure would have required the Fleet to send foldspace search vessels after the *Renegat*. At least three ships should have gone to the place that the *Renegat* had last entered foldspace, and then proceeded to do a grid search.

They hadn't.

And the Fleet—or rather the admirals and vice admirals who had planned the *Renegat's* mission—had decided against rescue before they even sent the ship on its mission.

Dauber had no idea if the captain, Ivan Preemas, had known that he was on his own from the very start, but she had a hunch he had. His actions—the ones she had found—had been unusual. A captain who knew that the Fleet wasn't going to come after him to enforce protocol might make the decisions he made to give his ship a fighting chance.

And deep down, Dauber didn't blame him. He had been sent on a dangerous and unusual mission with a crew that looked like it wasn't up to the task. He had been sent in an old SC-Class vessel without the usual backup. And he had no way of getting help if he needed it.

They were headed to an ancient Scrapheap, for reasons she still hadn't found. And she couldn't understand what was behind the mission.

She had found a number of Fleet records marked classified, but they were above her level of classification. Not much was. She needed to be a vice admiral to access some of the information about the *Renegat*.

And she needed to be on a sector base or a starbase, since that information wasn't even in the *Aizsargs's* files.

What was in the *Aizsargs's* files were the records pulled from the *Renegat* before it exploded. But most of those records had to do with the *anacapa* drive and other engineering problems with the ship.

Dauber had told her team to pull what they could, starting with the *anacapa*, before she had realized she had a major mystery on her hands.

And the survivors of the *Renegat* weren't really helping. They had no rank structure that she could find. Some of that was due to the fact that they needed rescue. Something terrible had happened to them, and she wasn't sure where or when.

What she did know was that the upper levels of the crew, from captain and first officer through the engineering department, had not been on the ship when it had come through foldspace this last time.

That explained some of the problems—the lack of environment, the damage—but not all of it.

Dauber felt like every time she found an answer, it raised more questions.

Her staff was still digging, still trying to figure out what was going on, but they were finding nothing.

And most of her staff—no matter how good and reliable they were—had never experienced a time-gap foldspace rescue. They knew the theory, but they hadn't participated in one.

Dauber had. Like all captains of her generation, she had been required to serve on a foldspace search vehicle for six months. That service had been the gloomiest of her career. Unless the crew rescued out of foldspace had been gone—by their own lights—less than a week, they were screwed up.

In a foldspace rescue, it wasn't uncommon to be missing a lot of crew. Usually, after years had gone by, most of the crew would leave the ship—sometimes to get more supplies, sometimes to find a new place to live.

What was unusual about the *Renegat* was that the missing crew members were senior officers, not the rank and file. She'd participated in three rescues in which most of the crew had left the ship that had been trapped in foldspace, but in all three cases the crew that remained were the senior officers.

She couldn't rule out that the *Renegat* had somehow operated differently, because its mission had been so unusual and its staffing had been nontraditional.

Still, it didn't feel right—any of it.

She didn't quite know what to do with these survivors. Her obligations toward them differed depending on what had happened. If they had spent all of their time in foldspace, trapped and lost, then they could go back to the Fleet in some capacity.

She would need guidance for that from her own superior officers. They would probably want to take the *Renegat* survivors back as a unit, rehabilitate them, and send them to the same place, be it a sector base or a starbase or some ship that went on routine missions without going into foldspace.

She'd even heard of foldspace survivors who would teach units to engineers who handled *anacapa* drives, to impress on those engineers just how important it was to keep the use of the drives as error-free as possible.

That kind of decision was not hers to make.

But she needed more information before she even contacted her superiors. Because her gut told her that something else was going on here.

The *Renegat* had suffered a lot of damage and not all of it lined up. The exterior damage didn't match all of the interior damage.

What disturbed her most was the information that had come from Stanley Palmer, who had been inside the *Renegat*'s engineering department, trying to salvage the ship at that last minute. He said that the control panel outside of engineering had been damaged. He also said that there was evidence of tampering with some of the equipment inside engineering, tampering in ways that didn't make any sense to him.

He had told Dauber that the tampering could have come from the inexperienced crew members trying to fix the ship, but something about it had struck him wrong. In engineering, at least, the tampering looked like it had been done by someone with engineering skill, someone who had known what they were doing, someone who had a real purpose behind their actions.

Then Palmer had grinned at her. *But I was only there a few hours, and I was a little busy trying to save the ship. I could easily be wrong.*

He could have been wrong, yes. But she trusted her crew. And she also knew that impressions made while doing something else were often reliable, because the eye saw things that it didn't have time to analyze. Those observations went into the subconscious and slowly came to the surface; they were usually purer than observations made with the intent of "understanding" something.

A few of her team—Vail, Parizo, and others who had interacted with the *Renegat* survivors—believed that the senior staff had died.

Which raised even more questions. Because senior staff as a unit rarely died on any Fleet mission. Some of the senior staff died, along with rank and file crew members, particularly if the mission was dangerous, like this one had been.

Dauber didn't like what she was thinking; losing the entire senior staff bothered her on a deep level. It also was exacerbated by the handful of survivors who had serious injuries, the kind of injuries that they had barely survived.

She'd seen images of three of them. They had the kind of injuries soldiers usually got from laser battles, not from flying debris in a space battle.

If her darkest suspicions were correct—if these survivors had somehow done away with the senior staff—then they had to be taken to the nearest starbase, and given to the judicial branch of the Fleet. The prosecutors could figure out what to do with them, if anything.

Before Dauber took such drastic measures, though—before she even *suggested* them, she needed to satisfy herself that her suspicions were justified.

She needed to talk to the crew herself.

And to start, she needed to talk to the one person everyone seemed to refer to as the person who had headed the mission home.

A linguist, of all things. A woman with no leadership experience, named Raina Serpell.

PART THIRTY-EIGHT

AFTERMATH

100 YEARS AGO

THE *RENEGAT*

Once upon a time, Orlena Seymont drank. A lot.

And that was why she was standing in the middle of the biggest disaster of her entire career, surrounded by moaning sobbing collcagucs, who had—apparently—inflicted a bunch of wounds on themselves.

She was in the actual medical part of the med bay, not the part where bodies were taken for disposal, in the area where at least two other physicians should be working, but of course there were no other physicians. All of them left on Sector Base Z, and the person who had joined the medical unit—some worthless creature named Bosley something (or something Bosley)—had only been here once that she knew of.

She hadn't been able to hail him all day, which told her nothing, because she hadn't been able to hail him any other day either. And when she complained to Captain Preemas, Preemas had laughed and said, *More opportunities for you to rebuild your reputation, then.*

She'd curse out Preemas, but she didn't have the heart. Preemas was in the other part of the med bay, very clearly dead. She had to preserve the body, because god knows what was going to happen to the entire crew when the Fleet figured out that the crew had murdered their captain, but that was a problem for another day.

There were enough problems for today—all of them crowded into this space. The gurneys kept coming, and what she saw were wounds, bleeding staunched, faces pale or gray or slack, burns everywhere.

And then there were the smells: scorched flesh, evacuated bowels, vomit, and urine. Things she normally tuned out, but which overwhelmed here. The same with the cries of pain, the hands grasping for her, begging her to help, the yells and the screams and the moans—things she'd been trained to hear and evaluate, just so that she could make a diagnosis when the patient couldn't communicate clearly.

She needed a drink.

More than anything else, she needed a drink, and she would never ever ever have one again. She'd stopped drinking when she was assigned to this ship, and she'd maintained that throughout everything and she had to maintain it now.

But holy shit, she needed something to hold her up right now, and there was nothing. Nothing and no one.

Just her, and the injured, crowding over one another, three levels deep.

She had finally grabbed a tablet and used it to process everyone, using (in part) the recommendations of the gurneys themselves. The patients came in pre-triaged, decided by computer, of course. This person should get treatment first, that person should get treatment second—and not all of the triaging made human sense.

The medical program was designed by rank, like everything in the Fleet, and Preemas had screwed with the ranks. Seymont had no idea who was running what, even though the system told her that nearly unsavable person needed all of her attention.

Hell, that stupid ranking system was why she had been required to check in Preemas's body in the first place, even though he was long past her help.

Half the people here were past her help. She didn't have the skills for this. And the ship had half-assed medical facilities. They were designed to work with the *Santé Two*. Some doctor or surgeon somewhere who specialized in some esoteric technique would virtually assist the system to handle whatever it faced.

There was no connection to the Fleet, no connection to the *Santé Two,* no way for Seymont to even approximate good medicine for the truly truly damaged people in front of her.

And now, she was being pinged by the geniuses in engineering.

She put a hand to her ear, and nearly shut off the link to engineering—to the entire ship, really—but she didn't dare. She needed to stay in touch in case they were going to send more gurneys or fucking shoot themselves up again.

So she answered the ping with, "I don't have time to talk to you people. What I do need is anyone you have with even a modicum of medical training. Right now."

"We have another problem." The person who responded wasn't First Officer Crowe or whatever he called himself now. It was Daria Willoughby.

"I don't need another problem," Seymont said. "I have dozens of them, most of them unsolvable. So sorry, I'm cutting off—"

"Orlena." Willoughby's voice was sharp. "We think there's some kind of rapidly moving pathogen. It might be what killed Natalia Stephanos."

"Yeah, probably. It's probably stupidity. That's a virus—"

"No," Willoughby said. "I'm serious and you have to pay attention. You need to autopsy her—"

"No." Seymont tapped her tablet, moving the gurneys by severity of injury, not by rank. Damn the system. "I do that, more people die."

"You don't, and we all could die." Willoughby said.

Seymont stood very still for just a moment. She should just walk away. Drink until she couldn't think any more. Let them all die. Fuck them all, anyway.

"You don't know medicine," she said. "You have no idea—"

"At least cut her open," Willoughby said. "We need to know what's inside."

"You do know that autopsies are not done with scalpels, right?" Seymont asked.

"We need to see inside her," Willoughby said. "Computers might not find this. She was holding the *anacapa* drive when she died, and—

"For god's sake," Seymont said. "If there is something transmitted by touch, the worst thing you can do is send your only physician in to look at it."

"We don't have anyone else," Willoughby said.

"Neither do the dozens of wounded people you just sent to me," Seymont said, and cut off the contact.

She continued to sort, trying to figure out resources. No one here had minor wounds. Those must have gone elsewhere, which was what the system was set up for whenever there was a mass casualty event.

She didn't even care about the minorly wounded. The gurneys, with their own medical supply cabinets built in, could take care of them. The problem was the people who could have been saved in a normal situation. She wouldn't get to all of them in time.

They were going to die, and she couldn't do much to save them.

Old-fashioned triage. That was what she was going to have to do, and she was going to have to do it through her skills alone. And she didn't have a lot of them.

Then something pinged, and an image of some kind of device floated out of her tablet. Damn the engineers. They were doing something to communicate with her.

The device had pink veins.

We're looking for that inside Stephanos. Willoughby's voice floated with the image. *If it's inside her, we have to figure out how it got there and what we can do to stop it.*

Seymont sent a quick message back. *Then do it yourself.*

And she cut off all communications with everyone. Screw them.

She had lives to save.

And she was going to do it, no matter what anyone else wanted her to do.

THE *RENEGAT*

Serpell had slipped out of the research room before she opened one of the control panels and used it to find India. To Serpell's surprise, India was in the brig.

Serpell had to use the ship's map to find the brig. She had never seen it before. She had figured if she was going to see it, it would have been to interpret for some prisoner they had captured at the Scrapheap. At night, when India was out doing whatever India had been doing lately, Serpell had been boning up on all the various forms of Standard that she could find, figuring that someone they found in the ancient Scrapheap might be speaking a form of Standard so old that it wouldn't sound familiar.

But there were no outside prisoners. No one had been captured. No one had even gone to the Scrapheap yet.

And those rumors that something had happened.

Serpell was seeing no evidence of it in the corridor outside the research room, but then they were so far away from everything, that she probably wouldn't see evidence of anything.

The trip to the brig took her to an elevator bank that she had never seen before. The elevators were wider than the others, as if they were built to accommodate a lot of people. Or maybe people in custody.

Of course, the elevator bank would be somewhere other than the regular elevators. No one wanted the prisoners to be anywhere near the crew.

Her mouth had gone dry, and she continually wiped her sweaty palms on her pants. The brig was on its own deck, which made sense. She remembered learning somewhere that the brigs in SC-Class vessels were huge, in comparison to brigs on other vessels, because SC-Class vessels specialized in security.

When the elevator opened onto the bridge floor, she was assaulted by a stench she hadn't ever encountered before. It wasn't quite rotted and decayed, but close, as if something had died nearby. Or gotten really really sick. Or a lot of people had gotten really really sick.

She could separate out a few smells—vomit was one—but mostly the stench was a miasma that seemed like a live thing. It made her eyes water. She put an arm over her nose, and peered around the edge of the elevator to see a corridor filled with gurneys.

Gurneys? She checked her map. The med bay was nowhere near this part of the ship. So why were gurneys here?

Her heart started pounding really hard. The system said India was here. Since she was security, she was probably shepherding the gurneys.

They were stacked one above the other, three high, and there was a gap of a yard between each one. People moaned on them, and stirred. An arm hung off of one just in front of the door—a thin arm with a bracelet that Serpell sort of recognized. She couldn't remember whose it was right now—her brain wasn't working that way—but it was familiar.

The stench was making her queasy. She brought up the collar of her shirt and put it over her nose and mouth, not caring that it exposed her stomach. The air down here was hot and humid. Clearly, the environmental systems weren't working as well as they could have been.

Something had happened. Something bad.

"India?" she shouted.

"Raina?" India's voice came from a few yards away, and sounded weak. India never sounded weak.

Serpell pushed her way past the rows of gurneys. Hands reached for her. One coated her forearm with gooey wetness. She looked down and saw what seemed to be blood.

She wiped that off on the back of her shirt.

She couldn't see India anywhere. Then she heard her name, spoken impatiently, as only India could do.

Serpell turned, saw one of the gurneys rocking, and caught a glimpse of India as the gurney turned toward her for a half second.

Serpell backtracked, caught the bottom of the gurney, and said, "What the hell?"

India looked over at her from the center of the gurney. Straps covered her, holding down her torso, legs, and arms.

"They killed the captain," India said, but she didn't sound sad. She sounded angry.

"Captain Preemas?" Serpell asked.

"You know any other captain?" India snapped.

"For godssake, Romano," said Odafe Yarleque from nearby. He was strapped to his gurney too. "You want someone to help you, you be nice to them."

Serpell's face heated. India's face looked bruised. She had scorch marks on her shirt, and a gaping hole in the cloth near her hip. Her skin had turned an ash gray, and her eyes had sunken into their sockets.

"What happened to you?" Serpell asked.

"She was stupid enough to tell people to open fire in a crowded alcove," Yarleque said.

"Shut up," India said. "I didn't hear you taking point. And someone had to defend the captain."

"Who was already dead," Yarleque said.

Serpell was trying to process everything. Captain Preemas was dead? Someone had lashed not just India but all the others to their gurneys and sent them to the brig? Because they had *shot* at each other?

"Get me off of this," India said. "We have to get to the bridge."

Then the gurneys started to move forward, all in a unit, the middle row swerving just a little to avoid hitting Serpell in the face.

"You set anyone free, and I'll arrest you." The voice came from the open doors to the brig.

Serpell looked toward it. DeShawn Hagen stood there, holding a laser rifle against his shoulder. His face was streaked with blood.

She usually thought of him as an elegant man. Now, he looked like a soldier of a type she usually avoided. His gaze was flat, measuring.

"What did they do?" she asked.

"They tried to kill us all," he said, then waved his free hand. The gurneys moved again.

She realized now that the top row of gurneys were heading the other direction, going back toward the med bay. Those gurneys were empty.

"India's injured," Serpell said. "Let me take her to the med bay."

"Your wife isn't that badly injured," Hagen said. "She's staying here."

India mouthed *asshole* but didn't say anything, which startled Serpell. It meant that India was afraid of Hagen, afraid of what he could do.

"Please, DeShawn," Serpell said. "I'm standing right next to her and the bandage on her hip has worked free. Let me—"

"The people in the med bay need surgery, not bandages. We'll get the minor injuries tended to here, in the brig, after we've saved as many as we can in the med bay." Hagen was curt and sharp. His gaze cut into her. "What were you doing a few hours ago?"

"Research." Serpell's voice came out small. "I had no idea that this was going on."

He raised his chin slightly. Then he shook his head. "Your lovely wife got a bunch of people killed. I'm not sure how many, but enough that we're keeping her in the brig until we get back to the Fleet."

"We're going back to the Fleet?" Serpell asked. "Now?"

He let out a sigh of dismay. "This ship isn't even working right now."

"Then she might be in the brig indefinitely. You can't keep injured people locked up. It's not fair—"

"One more word about this, Raina, and I'm putting you in there with them." Hagen's free hand had moved to the top of the laser rifle, almost as if he were going to yank it down and use it on her.

Her mouth opened slightly. "What are you doing?"

"Saving the ship," he said. "What are you doing?"

"Trying to save my wife," Serpell said.

"Then bring her supplies once she's locked up. She killed people, Raina."

She had never seen Hagen looking like this, strong and impossible to move beyond.

She glanced at India, whose eyes were cast down. She wasn't defending herself for once. India, who usually fought any slight, wasn't fighting right now.

For a moment, Serpell thought maybe India had passed out. But she hadn't. Her eyelids fluttered just a little, showing just a bit of her eyeball. She was actually watching Serpell, watching for Serpell's reaction.

Serpell's breath caught. Was Hagen right? Had India caused a bunch of deaths?

The gurneys moved forward again, and this time, India's moved into the brig. The area was huge and darker than the corridor. There were individual cells, most of which were empty, and then there were cells with bunks stacked against the walls. Those cells had five people each in them, some lying on the bunks.

Hagen grabbed India's gurney and held it. He peered over her at Serpell.

"What are you going to do with her?" Serpell asked.

"She's going in a cell by herself," he said.

Serpell frowned. He made it sound like punishment, when she at least would have wanted to be alone.

"He doesn't want me talking to anyone," India said. "He's afraid of me."

Hagen smirked. "Yeah, I am," he said. "But not of your mouth or your ability to convince people to do things. I'm afraid of the depth of your stupidity."

India thrashed on the gurney, clearly infuriated. Serpell took a half step back, shocked at what she was seeing.

This was not the ship she was used to. Not the way the Fleet operated. She wasn't sure exactly what had happened, but it was devastating, and she didn't even understand the implications yet.

"Take me to the med bay, Raina," India said, still trying to buck the gurney out of Hagen's hands.

"I'll bring supplies to you," Serpell said, because she didn't want to get locked up too, and she was convinced Hagen would do it.

"You are completely useless," India said. "You should be getting us out of here. Raina. We were defending the captain. Hagen and the others, they mutinied."

That was a word Serpell never though she would hear on a Fleet ship. Her gaze rose from India's to Hagen's. His jaw was set. His eyes glittered.

He wasn't denying the charge.

The gurneys were stopping in front of cells. The doors would open, gurneys would go inside, and then they would tip their passengers into the bunks. No one got up and ran for the doors, leading Serpell to think that either everyone was trussed really well or they were drugged somehow, or both.

Her gaze met Hagen's again. He hadn't moved. He seemed to be waiting for her to do something.

She backed away from India's gurney. "I'll bring you things," Serpell said, and then hurried down the corridor.

She was shaking. She would pay for leaving India behind. Whenever she didn't do what India wanted, Serpell got in trouble. But it would be hard to get in trouble at the moment, because India was locked up.

Which, oddly, relieved Serpell, and terrified her at the same time. She needed to find out what was really going on. And she needed to figure out where she fit.

If she fit anywhere at all.

THE *RENEGAT*

Ibori followed the last of the gurneys into the med bay, and was astonished to see them peel off in two directions. The entry, where he had had to decide what to do with Stephanos, didn't seem to be asking questions anymore.

Doors opened to the Storage and Disposal area without prompting. Lots of gurneys went in that direction. Even more went into the med bay proper.

And Ibori thought he heard a voice coming from in there. Then he tilted his head, and the voice stopped.

He was probably imagining it. Wish fulfillment, because he wanted—he needed—someone else to be here.

He started to follow the gurneys into the med bay, when a barrier fell from the ceiling, preventing his entry.

You must suit up and decontaminate before entry.

He blinked, having never seen that before. He'd visited folks with cuts and scrapes in the med bay more than once, and no barrier had fallen, nothing had told him to clean up.

But it made sense. Given the wounds inside, the fact that something (at least) was trying to save lives, the extreme medical protocols had probably started up.

He cast about for a suit, saw that a closet door had slid open, and the protective gear designed for severe medical situations hung inside. He looked for the decontamination unit, found it just next to the suits, and stepped inside. The unit demanded that he remove his clothing, and as he looked down, he saw why.

He was covered in blood and goo and other stains he couldn't even identify. He'd had no idea that his clothing had essentially turned into stiff boards of drying liquid. He wasn't as aware as he thought he was.

First, the decontamination unit rinsed him off, then it covered him with that reflective light he had experienced after coming back from missions on strange planets. He had never experienced this kind of intense cleansing in the med bay before—really, anywhere inside a ship, particularly when traveling from one part of the ship to another.

The decontamination brought the anxiety he thought he had buried to the surface. His hands were clammy. He threaded them together, only to have the system demand that he separate them again.

The cleansing seemed to take forever, even though he knew it hadn't. The door opened on a different side, showing him a small alcove, with a variety of white shorts, t-shirts, and socks on shelves. He grabbed one of each, slipped them on, and then opened the back door to the protective gear.

The gear was easier to put on than an environmental suit, partly because the gear was looser. He wanted to keep the hood off, but the suit wouldn't finish assembling without it. At least the hood was clear on all sides. He hated the way that some environmental suits restricted his vision.

He slipped out of the small area, back into the med bay entrance proper. The gurneys were gone, and he couldn't hear that voice anymore. But the door to the medical part of the med bay was still open.

He finally saw why as he got close. So many gurneys were stacked inside that it was impossible for the door to close. And that room inside the bay was large.

He didn't hear someone speaking anymore, which disappointed him. But he did hear moaning, and the occasional cry. People were alive in there and suffering. He needed to get inside.

That anxiety rose—almost a panic—but he made himself take a deep breath. He needed to be as calm as he could, whatever that meant. Especially since he would be the only functioning person in the room.

He wasn't sure exactly what was going on in there yet. He couldn't quite see. But the gurneys were shifting position, based on the colored lights underneath. He didn't understand the coding, but yellow lights were joining yellow lights, brown lights were joining brown lights, and blue lights were joining blue.

He let out a small breath. He was going to have to wade into this mess and see if human hands could make a difference, even inexperienced human hands.

He hated being the only one down here, the only one mobile. But it was better than trying to cope with this already devastated ship, and following orders he wasn't sure he believed in.

At least, he would be doing something constructive.

As he ducked between two rows of gurneys, someone said, "*Stop* bothering me."

He peered over one of the gurneys, expecting to see two injured people clashing with each other.

Instead, a woman he recognized but didn't know stood in the middle of the gurneys, clutching a tablet and looking fierce. She was stocky and strong-looking, but her face was filled with broken capillaries, which suggested she was (or had been) a hell of a drinker.

Of course. If she was a doctor stuck on this ship, there had to be a reason. Substance abuse was a good one.

She had one hand on her ear, and she was clearly speaking to someone who wasn't here. "I've told you. Handle it yourself."

And then she added, “I’m cutting off all contact now.”

The stench in the room was overpowering, just like it had been outside of engineering. Only here, the smell wasn’t as much about blood as it was suppurating flesh and discharged bowels. The moans seemed fainter than they had before, or maybe he was just getting used to them.

The woman didn’t seem to notice him.

“Hey,” he said as he pushed past the first row of gurneys. “Can I help?”

She started and nearly dropped the tablet. Then she looked at him as if she didn’t believe he was there.

“Who are you?” she asked.

“Tindo Ibori,” he said.

“I don’t suppose you’re a medical professional,” she said.

“Sorry,” he said. “I worked on the bridge until earlier today.”

“And you’re here because, what, you have a hangnail?” Her tone was vicious, something he hadn’t expected at all.

“No, no,” he said. “I came with the gurneys.”

Something in her expression changed. It was still fierce, but now it was measuring.

“What, did they send you here to make sure I healed the right people first?” she asked.

“No,” he said. “I chose to come here. I didn’t know you’d be here, and I thought someone should be with these people.”

All the fierceness left her face, and for a moment, it looked like she might cry. Then her expression hardened and she nodded.

“Do you have any medical experience?” she asked.

“I had field medicine training a long time ago,” he said.

“So, no,” she said. “You have no experience. And I don’t have time to train you.”

Then she raised her chin, just a little.

“But the people who think they’re in charge have a mission they believe is more important than saving lives. You can do it.”

“I’d rather save lives,” he said.

“Oh, the people who think they’re in charge believe that this mission of theirs will save lives.”

He frowned, not understanding at all. “Who—who are these people?” he asked.

“First Officer Crowe, ostensibly, and Daria Willoughby, who used to be one of the most sensible people on the ship.” The woman shook her head slightly and then swiped at her tablet. More gurneys moved, some into another room.

The survivors, then. He let out a small breath. “What do they need?”

“They think something infectious is on board this ship, and they want me to stop everything I’m doing to perform an autopsy. I just told them to go to hell.” Her dark eyes measured him. “But you—”

“I don’t know how to perform an autopsy,” he said.

"You don't have to. They want to look inside one of the corpses I have in the other part of the bay and see if it has some infection. You're already suited up, so no known pathogen will get on you. And they all assure me that this will save lives."

"I don't know how you would perform an autopsy without performing an autopsy," he said.

"The system in the other room will do it." She grabbed a tablet off a small ledge behind her. She pressed her fingers on the tablet, then handed it to him over the barely conscious body of a woman on the nearest gurney. "Just do that, and get in touch with Willoughby. She'll tell you what she's looking for."

"Is it necessary?" Ibori asked. He would rather be here, providing an extra pair of hands.

"How the hell do I know?" the woman asked. "I don't have time to debate anything. I want them off my back, you'll get them off my back, and the faster you do it, the easier it will be for you to come back and help me here. Okay?"

An autopsy. He let out a small breath. As if this day wasn't bad enough already.

He took the tablet, saw some blinking commands, as well as an order in which he was to perform them.

"All right," he said. "Does it matter whose body I use?"

He hated the question. It sounded strange and cold and disrespectful.

"Apparently so," she said. "You're to examine the first body of the day. Natalia Stephanos. I guess she died holding the *anacapa* drive."

"Yeah." He was surprised he could get the word out. "I was there. She died fast."

And horribly. And he didn't want to see her body again.

"I was the one who brought her here," he added.

Compassion touched the woman's face, but only for a moment. "I'm sorry," she said, and if he hadn't seen the momentary compassion, he wouldn't have believed her words. "You don't have to do this."

She had opened a door. He could stay here. But he couldn't get one word out of his brain.

"They think a *pathogen* killed her?" he asked.

"I'm guessing," she said, moving yet another gurney.

"And they think it's contagious?"

"You can't get anything in that suit," she said. "Trust me on that."

He nodded, not sure if he did trust her. But it probably didn't matter. If there was a pathogen, he had already been exposed.

Although it hadn't showed up in his decontamination.

As if reading his thoughts, she added, "They tell me the computers won't see what they're looking for."

Great. If he didn't die from all the incompetence on this ship, he would die like Stephanos had, melting and dissolving, his face collapsing in on itself.

"I'll do it," he said, before he could stop himself.

The woman grinned at him. The grin was grim, if grins could be considered grim.

"Good man," she said. "Contact Willoughby, follow the instructions on that tablet, and get back here as fast as you can."

He nodded. "Okay," he said, and was about to duck under one of the gurneys again, when he stopped. "I'm…um…you didn't introduce yourself."

She raised her eyebrows, as if she couldn't quite believe he was insisting on niceties at this moment.

"I'm the idiot in charge," she said, "but you can call me Orlena."

"Okay, Orlena," he said. "I'll be back as soon as I can."

"Make it sooner," she said. "People are dying here."

Yeah, they were. And he wasn't sure if what he was about to do was going to make things worse.

THE *RENEGAT*

Crowe hurried to the bridge. He was already wearing his favorite environmental suit, the hood down. He didn't know if the suit would prevent any contamination from the *anacapa* drive, especially when he touched it, but he was going to use every single tool he had.

He also carried with him a small box of *anacapa* specific tools, tools he hadn't used since school. He had stayed as far away from *anacapa* drives as he could, preferring to let people who loved them and their mysterious workings, like Stephanos, handle the drives.

He had done everything he could from afar, while doing the exact minimum for the training he needed as an engineer.

His lack of continual experience with an *anacapa* drive was going to bite him now. He knew that, and it bothered him, but it couldn't be helped.

Even if he had a person who was an *anacapa* expert—and not some theory expert like Atwater—on board this ship, he wouldn't make them touch that drive.

This was something Crowe had to do by himself.

The door to the bridge was open. He walked in. The four crew members glanced up at him, but didn't say anything.

Then they all returned to work—which both pleased and surprised him. He hadn't expected them to be so diligent.

It was hard to be diligent today.

Tosidis was still sitting in the captain's chair. He had opened some of the captain's screens, which were designed so that only the captain could see them and only when the captain was seated. As Crowe walked down toward the center of the bridge, it looked like Tosidis was conducting a symphony or playing with the air.

Bakhr was still at the science console, frowning as he worked. He wasn't using holoscreens at all, his fingers dancing along the top of the console. Colvin stood beside him, watching his every movement, and occasionally, saying something softly to him.

Apparently, Bakhr was trying to teach Colvin something or get her to be a proper assistant. Crowe silently wished Bakhr luck with that.

M'Ghan had moved to a different console, and as Crowe passed, he saw that M'Ghan was staring at the bridge's environmental system. It looked like he was trying to boost the scrubbing capability.

Crowe wanted to tell him that boosting wouldn't make any difference; the key here was cleaning up the mess that was all around the *anacapa* drive.

On a normal vessel, the captain would have ordered the area preserved while the ship itself took images and created a holographic memory of what happened, including samples from the fluids that had soaked into the carpet, as well as readings taken from the *anacapa* container and the drive itself.

But there would be no investigative team, no one on the ship to analyze anything—except Crowe, of course.

He made his way to the edge of the goo-covered floor, and pulled up his hood. As he did, Tosidis said, "What do you need from us?"

"I need you to get the hell out of here if something goes wrong," Crowe said.

Colvin looked alarmed, but Bakhr put his hand on her arm, apparently trying to soothe her. M'Ghan nodded, head down.

Tosidis straightened his shoulders, as if he expected to launch himself out of that chair at any moment.

Crowe couldn't think about any of them right now. He needed to examine that drive.

He paused at the mess in front of him. He was acutely aware that it had once been part of a woman he respected. It felt like he was harming her in some way just by walking across that. He knew he was being fanciful, but the feeling was hard to shake.

He recognized it, though. He had had that same feeling off and on over the years, as he learned engineering, and advanced in his career without Tessa.

His heart twisted. He banished the thought of her, like he often did throughout his career, unable to think about her and the path that her death had lead him on.

The path that had led him here.

He crossed the mess. It squished underneath his boots, black liquid rising around him. He knew that the fluids would have to be tested at some point. He recalibrated his boots to gather some of the liquid, so that it would be preserved.

Then he reached the *anacapa* container.

He pulled out a small handheld scanner, no bigger than his thumb. The scanner was recalibrated to examine all types of permutations of *anacapa* energy. The scanner knew if an *anacapa* drive was dying, if it had used up most of its energy, if it was solid and would last for a long time, and if it was giving off odd signals.

It also could identify where the *anacapa* drive had come from. Many of them were smaller parts of a larger piece. He wasn't sure if that would be relevant, but he didn't want to discount anything.

His mouth was dry, as he approached the container. He knew that Romano had slammed it shut and she had clearly not suffered any ill effects—or at least any visible ill effects (he couldn't vouch for mental ones).

But it still unnerved him to touch the container itself. And he had to lift up the *anacapa* drive to weigh it.

Although, he reminded himself, he hadn't felt anything when he touched the communications *anacapa*. And, as far as he could tell, he was all right.

He crouched beside the container. It looked like most *anacapa* containers, dark and closed, the nanobits intact and solid. It didn't gleam or call attention to itself in any way. If some non-Fleet person came onto the bridge, they would simply think it part of the design, not a container for the most important part of an SC-Class ship.

He ran the scanner around it, and got no abnormal readings at all. He had set the scanner on its highest level of sensitivity so even if something was just infinitesimally off, the scanner would find it.

And it found nothing.

He rested the scanner on his right knee, and studied the container as if it could reveal all of its secrets right now. It didn't, of course. Maybe it had no secrets to give.

He clenched his gloved hands, then stretched them, then clenched them again. Then he activated all of the gloves' sensors. He couldn't delay this any longer, no matter how much he wanted to.

He put his hands on each side of the container, half-expecting to feel a vibration or something going awry. Nothing was. And nothing unusual showed up in his glove sensors either.

Considering what had happened to Stephanos, he would have thought something would show up, even if it was something very small.

He caught his mood, suddenly, and half-smiled at himself. He wanted something to show up. It was what one of his counselors had called his desire to be punished to expiate the guilt he felt from someone else's death.

He shook off the emotion, then used his thumbs to hit the latches on the lid. It rose up slowly, just like it was supposed to, revealing the *anacapa* drive inside, glowing with a perfect golden light.

This drive was shaped like a kidney with some knots on the top side. He leaned a little farther forward, dislodging the scanner from his thigh. He managed to catch the scanner before it fell onto the mess below.

He shoved the scanner into one of the side pockets on his suit. He would deal with the readings later.

Then he eyeballed the drive. He was seeing some pink etched alongside the gold veins in the drive. The drive also had some dried blood on its surface. He stared at those stains, wondering why they hadn't been dissolved, then he realized that something had been shut off inside the container.

Before he touched the drive, he rocked back on his heels and peered at the container controls.

They were closed. He pushed the little door with the knuckle of his right hand, and the door popped open.

All of the internal scrubbers for the environment around the drive had been shut off.

"You can help me," he said to Tosidis. "I need you to find out if anyone on the bridge shut off the *anacapa* container controls."

"We haven't seen it in the security feeds." Bakhr answered, not Tosidis.

"Yeah, I understand," Crowe said. "But I'm not interested in who walked over here. I want to know when those controls were shut off. It might have been months ago, or maybe even at Sector Base Z, when the drive was inspected. I just need to know, and Luc has access to that through the captain's command center."

"I'll look," Tosidis said.

Crowe did not wait for Tosidis to find anything. Instead, Crowe inspected all of the controls. Most of them were on—the ones that would actually contain an unplanned surge of energy from the drive and those that would notify the bridge should something start going awry with the drive itself.

Just the environmental controls were off.

"And, Titus," he said to M'Ghan, "stop messing with the environmental controls on the bridge itself."

"What do you want me to do?" M'Ghan asked.

"Nothing," Crowe said. He didn't trust M'Ghan. Crowe looked over his shoulder at Bakhr. Fortunately, Bakhr had been watching him. Bakhr gave a small nod.

Crowe hoped that meant Bakhr had understood Crowe's unspoken command. He wanted Bakhr to examine the bridge's environmental system, to see if any parts had been shut off, and when.

And he didn't want to give that command aloud, worrying that M'Ghan might have caused the problem himself.

If Bakhr didn't understand, Crowe would look all of that up later.

He did not change any of the controls inside the *anacapa* container. He would leave them alone for the moment.

He wanted to get to that drive.

He flexed his fingers one last time. He was done stalling now. He had to do this.

Slowly, he reached inside the container and put his hands on the drive. It flared a little, as drives sometimes did when touched.

As the light inside the drive changed, he saw even more pink stuff, meshing with the golden light, as if it were following the same pattern that the golden light was. It was almost as if the lights were operating simultaneously.

But the pink had expanded beyond the veins of light as well. It seemed to coat the very middle of the drive. The pink did not look like veins there. Inside the center of the drive, the pink had a pattern, like snowflakes before they hit the ground. Only snowflakes reformed into bits of snow, but this pattern remained intact. Each tiny bit of pink attached itself to other bits of pink, creating something that was more like a web than a vein.

It was pretty, and it attracted his eye. He made himself blink, and raise his head, wondering if the attraction was part of the problem.

He let out a small breath, then carefully hefted the *anacapa* drive, and nearly tossed it over the back of his head.

He had been using too much force. The drive was so light that it felt like it could float away on its own. He could easily crush it between his palms.

And crush wouldn't be the right word, because *crush* implied effort. If he didn't move with complete ease and precision, the drive would shatter.

Every *anacapa* drive he had ever held felt like he was holding a living, vibrating, rock. This felt like a gigantic egg shell—although most egg shells he had held in his life had been thicker and sturdier.

Plus, this drive wasn't vibrating. It didn't feel alive at all. Usually, holding a drive this long would make his teeth ache—although he had never held a drive with a full environmental suit on.

He almost pulled off his gloves to see if he could feel the vibration, then decided against it.

He had enough information for now. The drive was compromised.

Hell, compromised was too small a word. The drive had been hollowed out and destroyed.

He was holding a husk of a drive. But, curiously, it still looked like it functioned.

"Benjamin," he said to Bakhr, "what readings are you getting from this drive?"

"It's normal," Bakhr said without hesitation. Maybe he hadn't been looking at the environmental system at all. Maybe he had thought Crowe's silent command was all about the *anacapa* drive.

That was all right too.

Normal. The drive was anything but normal.

The drive had been destroyed from the inside out. Maybe Stephanos had been holding it while the destruction occurred, and that was what had happened to her.

But Crowe didn't know, and he wasn't going to guess.

Gingerly, he replaced the drive in the container, and closed the container's lid manually.

Then he commanded the gloves to retain every bit of dust or dirt or bits of the drive they had come into regular contact with just because he had touched it.

He peeled off the gloves and put them in another pocket, resisting the urge to wipe his hands on his environmental suit.

He stood, slowly, his knees creaking because he had been crouching so long.

"Is it lighter?" Tosidis asked.

"Yeah," Crowe said. He didn't want to explain any more. He had to check the backup drives before he spoke the words he knew he couldn't take back.

If the other drive was as damaged as this one, the *Renegat* was screwed. It would never be able to travel back to the Fleet. The *Renegat* would never be able to leave this sector.

It would be stranded here, forever.

THE *RENEGAT*

Ibori didn't get sick. He considered that his major accomplishment of the day. He didn't get sick as he watched a beam of light slice into what was left of Stephanos's body, and claws from the table her body was lying on stretch her skin back as if peeling an environmental suit off her.

He had gone into the storage and disposal section after talking to Daria Willoughby for a few minutes. She had sounded stressed and frightened and apologetic, none of which he expected from her.

He finally asked her to send images of what she was looking for, and she did, so rapidly he was almost afraid the tablet he was using had malfunctioned.

The storage and disposal area was empty, compared to the area he had just left. The gurneys had taken bodies of his colleagues and placed them into storage pods, where someone would deal with them later (or so he supposed).

All of the gurneys had moved into a decontamination area. Once they were through it, they would return to their docks, to await being summoned again.

God, he hoped no one would need to summon them.

After talking with Willoughby, he understood why the engineers were so panicked. He also felt convinced that their diagnosis was plausible.

He had never seen anyone die like Stephanos had, and even though he had guessed at the time that the *anacapa* had caused the problem, he was willing to entertain other thoughts. And while he was entertaining them, he was tamping down his worries about his own health.

The tablet that Orlena had given him worked beautifully. He tapped the first command, and the pod holding Stephanos's body opened. Everything followed after that, one thing on top of the next.

First, the area around Stephanos's pod was isolated. A small chamber that reminded him of a clear interior shield formed around the pod. He actually had to give the system a verbal command to allow himself into that chamber, and before he entered, the system verified that his protection gear was functioning properly.

Then a table rose out of the floor. The pod floated onto the table. The table conducted the regular autopsy, which involved a computerized examination of her internal organs without opening her up.

Ibori had been congratulating himself on his ability to watch all of this, when the surgical laser appeared, and, without ceremony, sliced open Stephanos's torso, shirt and all. That hadn't been as bad as he expected. But when those claw-like things rose out of the sides of the table, and peeled her skin back, and her skin made a crinkling sound like chicken skin did when it was deep fried and he peeled it off the bone himself, he gagged.

He managed to hold back the vomit—which was good, because vomiting in any kind of suit was always a frightening proposition—but he did have to shut down the sound in the suit for several minutes.

He also looked away while the peeling was going on, sneaking an occasional glance at her body to see if the work was actually finished.

When it was (and that seemed to take forever), he leaned forward to look inside her. In his field medicine training, he had had to examine the interior of the human body. It was a simulation, but a realistic one, with smells and touch and temperature thoroughly controlled. While he was trying not to look at Stephanos's body being torn apart, he forced himself to remember that old experience, so he could make comparisons.

He didn't have to recall anything to see the difference.

The engineers had been right.

Her body was threaded with pink goo. It looked like lace. If he hadn't been so startled, he would have thought the pink stuff beautiful.

Instead, he peered at the gloves of his suit, terrified that somehow the pink had made its way over to him.

It took him a lot of concentration to realize he needed to take images of Stephanos's body and send it to engineering. Then he contacted Orlena.

"The engineers were right," he said. "Her body is full of something icky."

She didn't respond. He figured she couldn't, so he sent her the images too. And then he asked her what she wanted him to do next.

Get out of there, she sent. *Decontaminate again. Put your suit in the burn pile. Suit up again, and wait for further instructions.*

She didn't tell him what to do with Stephanos's body, so he left it on the table. But before he did, he double-checked the system, making sure it was isolated. Then he had one of those horrid claw things take a sample of the pink stuff. It needed to be tested to see exactly what it was.

As the claw thing dipped into Stephanos's body, Ibori frowned. He had been so surprised by the pink that he hadn't seen what else was going on—and he should have. After all, he had just recalled what a normal human's insides looked like.

Normally, they were packed together—colon here, kidneys there, heart and lungs and ribs, spine, hips, and all kinds of blood vessels and muscle tissue.

Most of that was gone from Stephanos's body. Anything that had liquid seemed to have leaked and deflated. The bones looked gray and pockmarked. The spine had almost completely vanished.

He sent notification of that to everyone too, and then he bent at the waist, wishing he had a chair so that he could collapse for a moment.

This could be happening inside of him, albeit slower than what happened to Stephanos.

It could be happening to all of them.

They were screwed. They were all going to die horribly.

And he had no idea what to do to stop it.

PART THIRTY-NINE
MYSTERIES OF THE *RENEGAT*
NOW

THE *AIZSARGS*

The captain ordered her presence. Serpell sat in the tiny meeting room, which was barely bigger than her quarters here on the *Aizsargs*, and threaded her hands together.

One of the junior officers had placed her here, brought her a specially made green tea that she was slowly falling in love with, and offered her a raspberry pastry. The last thing Serpell wanted was food, even though the pastries here were unexpectedly delicious.

The pastries—the food—it all was better than anything she had had on the *Renegat*, even the stuff cooked by Danika Newark.

Once the tea arrived and steamed in its thick mug on the table before her, Serpell didn't want anything to drink. If she was going to sit here for a long time waiting for the captain, she would need the facilities, and, depending on the kind of discussion this was going to be, the facilities might not be in the offing.

She clasped her hands tightly, fingers pressing against the spaces between her knuckles so hard that her bones ached. She didn't want to be nervous, but she was. She didn't want to be frightened, but she was.

There was no reason for the captain to talk to her—not when the captain hadn't spoken to anyone else. The captain was singling her out because—

Serpell shook her head. Even after her stint as leader of the *Renegat*, she still didn't understand captaining a ship. She had never thought of herself as captain. But she wasn't sure if that made a difference now.

The walls in this room were black and shiny. They absorbed the bright lights from overhead. The shine wasn't from light reflection. It seemed to be from something else—something more like a glistening of the material itself.

The walls almost seemed alive. Or maybe that was her imagination. She was getting tired of being inside rooms with nothing to do but wait. She had always worked, usually on the research or linguistic problems, but then, after she had to run the *Renegat*, she was busy every moment she was awake.

And now, here, she felt as if she had been dropped into emptiness and forced to sit very very still.

The door opened, and the captain of the *Aizsargs* walked in. She was taller than Serpell expected. The captain's shoulders were narrow, her face careworn, as if she had lived hard and long. Her eyes were an odd brownish-gray, and her hair looked like it had been recently and reluctantly combed.

"I'm Captain Dauber," she said, extending a hand as she leaned across the table.

Serpell had to stand to take Captain Dauber's hand. Serpell's cheeks warmed just a little as she realized she should have been standing from the moment Dauber entered the room.

"Let's sit," Dauber said, as if she could read Serpell's mind. "This isn't the most comfortable room, is it? Unfortunately it's what we have on this level, unless we want to use one of the excessively large meeting rooms."

Serpell nodded, her voice already caught in her throat.

"I know you have a lot of questions," Dauber said, "and we will answer them strategically. Some things have changed since you were away, and it's best to discuss those changes with all of the survivors."

Serpell swallowed hard. She nodded again, then felt just a little stupid for doing so. She probably should talk. She probably should have introduced herself, even though that was one of those societally stupid things—making introductions when both parties knew who the other was.

"First though," Dauber said, seemingly unconcerned that Serpell hadn't spoken yet, "I need to know a few things. We've gleaned from the others that you were the one who brought the ship back to the Fleet…?"

Serpell let out a small sound of surprise before she could even block it. "No," she said. "I don't know anything about operating a ship the size of the *Renegat*."

Dauber frowned. "That's not what we heard. We heard that you were in charge."

Serpell resisted the urge to close her eyes. She didn't want to be singled out. She didn't want anyone to pay attention to her again.

"Not exactly," she said. "I, um, no one was, um…."

Dauber watched her, not saying a word. Serpell would have spoken up if someone else were having this much trouble talking to her. She would have said something soothing like, *It's okay. Take your time.*

Dauber did nothing to put Serpell at ease. It was almost as if Dauber wanted her to be uncomfortable.

"I…um…I'm a linguist," Serpell said.

"That's in your file," Dauber said.

"And a control freak," Serpell said.

That got a half smile from Dauber.

"When everyone was refusing to take on the captain's role, and it became clear that someone had to make the decisions, I made them." Serpell was now speaking too fast, but she couldn't stop herself. "I mean, um, no one else would, and we had to move forward, so I did my best. I had thought that the ship would just get us home, but it wasn't that easy."

"It never is," Dauber said.

Was that sympathy? Serpell couldn't tell.

"Only a handful of people listened to me anyway and only when we got into trouble. I…um…am not cut out to lead anyone. That was clear. I just did some things because no one else would."

Then Serpell bit her lower lip, and shook her head. Kabac would probably contradict her on that, so she had to address it.

"I mean," she added, "the one or two people who really really really wanted the job were the ones who shouldn't have it."

Dauber's face changed ever so slightly, as if she felt like Serpell had revealed something important.

And maybe she had. Because if she went too far down this road, she'd have to discuss India, and India was the last topic she ever wanted to broach with anyone.

"You know what I'm talking about," Serpell said, trying to sound as friendly as possible and not sound desperate. "You've met Yusef Kabac."

"You're the first person I've talked with," Dauber said. Her voice was flat, almost like an automated voice.

Serpell's heart rate increased. Of course she was. Because that was just her luck. And Dauber, apparently, saw her as someone in charge.

"Well, then, you'll see what I mean," Serpell said. "Yusef was the only person left on the ship who had been on the bridge crew, but he was fired long before we even got to the Scrapheap. I let him handle the *anacapa* drive because he was the only one who knew where the controls were, and you saw how that ended up."

Dauber's eyes narrowed slightly. Serpell replayed what she had said, heard *I let him* and winced. Here she was, denying that she had had anything to do with running the ship in one breath and then in another, saying she had let him do something.

"Well," Dauber said after a moment. "You're the only one who even approximates leadership on the *Renegat*, and so I need to talk with you first. I need to know what happened on your mission. I'm not even sure what it was."

Serpell swallowed. She had thought about this meeting every day since she had arrived on the *Aizsargs*. And it scared her.

It wasn't that she was unprepared. She had discussed this with the bridge crew ever since they started the trip back from the Scrapheap. Eventually, they had a meeting with the entire crew—after the debacle near that weird planet Amnthra. Everyone knew what to say.

But, faced with it all now, it felt inadequate, as if it was clear that every word she spoke was a lie.

"You need a high security clearance to know what the mission is," Serpell said.

"I have a high clearance," Dauber said.

"I'd rather you talk with Vice Admiral Gāo," Serpell said. She had never spoken with Vice Admiral Gāo. In fact, she had only heard Vice Admiral

Gāo's name raised a few times before Serpell left on this mission, as in *Vice Admiral Gāo chose all of the crew personally,* and *Vice Admiral Gāo believes in this mission.*

Serpell saw more about Vice Admiral Gāo in Preemas's records, enough to know that Vice Admiral Gāo had chosen a group of failures on purpose and that Vice Admiral Gāo hadn't believed in the mission at all.

"I'm afraid that's not possible," Dauber said. "You'll need to tell me what the mission was, exactly."

Serpell shook her head. The entire group had decided not to talk about the mission, not that they understood all of it. She did now, after seeing Preemas's records, but still, she wanted to hold fast, just like everyone else would.

"It's not for me to say." Serpell swallowed hard. "I'm sure that the Fleet knows. You can contact someone there. But it's my understanding that this is too high up to talk about."

Dauber's expression didn't change, yet Serpell could feel a change in the room. Frustration, maybe? Anger?

"What happened to the captain?" Dauber asked.

There it was. The question that Serpell had been waiting for.

She tugged on her lower lip with her teeth, even though she had promised herself she wouldn't fidget or have nervous gestures at all.

"Captain Preemas was…unorthodox," she said. "And a whole lot of the senior crew didn't like him. They fought against him, and then they literally fought against him, shutting down engineering and taking over the ship. There was a big battle just outside of engineering. Captain Preemas died. So did a lot of others."

Dauber's face remained impassive. Serpell realized, in that moment, that Dauber already had an idea about how Preemas had died. Or else Dauber had an incredible ability to control her expressions.

"Where were you during all of this?" Dauber asked.

"Below decks where a bunch of us were researching at the beginning of it," Serpell said. "And then I went to look for my wife."

Those last two words came out soft, because as she spoke them, she remembered she hadn't wanted to say anything about India.

"Where was your wife?" Dauber asked.

"Fighting with Captain Preemas," Serpell said. "At his side."

Her heart was pounding so hard that she was convinced its drumbeat was visible through her shirt.

"But you weren't there," Dauber said.

"She was on his security team," Serpell said a little too quickly. "I was still just a linguist, although all I was doing at that point was researching."

"So you weren't in the fighting," Dauber said. It didn't sound like a question.

"No," Serpell said.

"What happened to the rebels?" Dauber asked.

Serpell had half a dozen answers to that question. That was the one everyone had discussed, worrying it. Trying to figure out how to answer it properly.

She finally defaulted to the answer that the group had decided on. They figured it would work because it was the truth.

"I'm not sure," she said.

Dauber nodded, then sighed. She looked away, and seemed about to say something, but then appeared to think the better of it.

She turned her head back toward Serpell, but it took another minute for Dauber to meet her gaze.

"How did the *Renegat* get so badly damaged?" Dauber asked.

"We tried to get more supplies on our way back, but the planet we approached attacked us from the moment we got into its space. We barely got out of there."

That was all true. She was shaking.

"The records cut off just before that battle," Dauber said, her voice even. "Why?"

The question sent a bolt of adrenalin through her. Dauber had checked the *Renegat's* records? How? How had she gotten those? The *Renegat* was gone, along with all of its information.

Or so Serpell had thought.

If the Fleet had all the records, then everything changed.

She thought the survivors of the *Renegat* were completely in the clear.

She was wrong.

THE *AIZSARGS*

Dauber made herself sit rigidly in her seat, working as hard as she knew how to make certain she revealed nothing as she spoke to Serpell. The small room helped. It had very few distractions. Just the table, four chairs (two of which were against the wall), and a door that she had changed from clear to solid from the bridge before the meeting.

Dauber could concentrate on Serpell, and, quite frankly, she didn't like what she saw.

Serpell looked terrified. She was an unremarkable looking woman, with big brown eyes on light brown skin that might've been lovely once, but was now a wan grayish color.

Dauber had remarkably little sympathy for her, and Dauber should have had a lot. Because, even though Serpell said she hadn't led the ship, the logs said otherwise. Serpell had taken command when no one else wanted it, and somehow she had gotten the ship across a long distance and 100 years, almost by herself.

But Serpell was lying now, and doing so badly. Dauber didn't entirely know why. She knew that something awful had happened at that Scrapheap they had traveled to, something that had left Serpell in charge.

The records Dauber had been able to go through hadn't been clear on that, partly because most of them were kept by people who had not made it back to the Fleet. Combine that with the fact that Captain Preemas had changed rank and duty assignments, and Dauber wasn't sure what records to look through when.

She had decided to hold the meeting sooner rather than later, because she needed to know where to take the *Renegat* survivors. And in the middle of this interview, she knew.

She would have to take them to Starbase Sigma, and leave them in the hands of the legal system there.

The attack on the captain alone suggested that, even though Captain Preemas had been a divisive figure. Had Preemas been the only death, however, Dauber might have taken the survivors to the nearest sector base, and let the authorities there decide what to do.

After all, it had been 100 years or more, and the mission clearly had been unorthodox. Dauber would have argued that the survivors never serve on a ship again, and the problem would be solved.

Not that they probably could serve anyway, given the 100 year time jump. Fleet technology changed slowly, but it changed enough—and norms changed enough—that foldspace rescues who had returned after 10 years missing had trouble enough assimilating. This group would find it almost impossible.

But the lying. It made Dauber even more uncomfortable than she expected.

Something had happened to half the crew, and Serpell had been involved in that.

Still, Dauber didn't approach it directly. Not again. Serpell had to settle down.

Besides, Serpell's answers on that seemed rehearsed. Dauber had a hunch she would hear the same answers from the others she spoke to.

But Serpell's reaction to the question about how the *Renegat*'s exterior got damaged seemed authentic. The question itself terrified her.

Perhaps it was the memory of the battle itself, but Dauber had seen a lot of crew members who had bad reactions to difficult and stressful situations, and they had never reacted like Serpell had.

Serpell hadn't answered Dauber's question about the records. In fact, Serpell seemed stunned that there were records at all.

Dauber decided to throw her a fake lifeline. "We got as much of the *Renegat's* records as we could," Dauber said. "At first, we were looking for *anacapa* anomalies, but we're finding a lot of other questions."

Serpell swallowed visibly. Her eyes had widened, and Dauber hadn't thought that was possible at all.

"We got a lot of material, but the bridge records disappear in the most crucial time," Dauber said. "They stopped just as the *Renegat* was heading to that planet that your system identified as Amnthra. What happened?"

She had backed into asking the question again. And this time, she would wait for the answer.

Serpell shifted slightly in her chair. "Um, they were probably destroyed during the battle. We took a lot of hits."

"Fleet ships are designed with a lot of redundant systems, particularly when it comes to keeping track of what happens to the ship herself. I'm sure we'll find other information—

Serpell's breath caught. It seemed involuntary.

"—but what we have at the moment suggests that someone went back and erased all of the information from that battle forward. Why would anyone do that?"

Serpell's cheeks turned pink underneath that grayish pallor. Her eyes glittered, almost as if she was trying to hold back tears.

If Dauber had to guess, she would guess that Serpell herself had deleted the records. But she couldn't figure out why.

Half of the crew was already gone. It was pretty clear that the survivors had no idea what they were doing, and that going to Amnthra was a poor decision, but one that the crew insisted on.

There seemed to be nothing to hide here, especially considering that the records from the part of the journey that saw the loss of half of the crew were still intact.

"What happened?" Dauber asked, making her voice gentle. Maybe that would work with this woman.

The glittery look left Serpell's eyes, and the color faded from her cheeks. But her voice shook as she said, "It was just really hard. I…listened to the crew. They wanted more supplies, and we shouldn't have done that. Once the weapons on that planet started firing on us, I hit every single control panel I could think of to defend us. None of us knew how the weapons' system worked or what to do with the shields. So I poked around and got lucky. I probably deleted the records or did something wrong right then."

Dauber was believing her until she added that last part about probably deleting the records. Battles could be confusing, and if the *Renegat* was fired upon for violating the space of a region that guarded the area around a planet vigorously, the battle might have been sudden.

But the weaponry controls and the defensive controls were completely separate from the recording systems. There was no way to hit one while working with the other.

So what Dauber was getting was a half-truth.

Dauber decided to stop pressing. She needed a lot of information from Serpell, but she wasn't going to get it in this setting.

Besides, Dauber had made her decision when she realized that Serpell was lying. They were going to Starbase Sigma.

All of this would become someone else's problem.

Even though Dauber still had one problem left.

She had to tell the *Renegat* survivors that they had returned 100 years in the future. And that discussion would not be pretty.

Dauber braced her hands on the tabletop and used the surface to help herself stand. Then she nodded at Serpell.

"Thank you for your time," Dauber said.

"I thought we were going to—." Serpell cut herself off. "I mean, I have questions."

"I know," Dauber said. "And we need to answer them all. Call your people together. We'll tell you everything tomorrow at noon."

"Tomorrow?" Serpell breathed. "Why not now?"

Because, Dauber wanted to say, *I have to inform my staff that none of you are trustworthy. I have to contact Starbase Sigma. I have to get the plans ready to get rid of you people, so that you won't be my problem anymore.*

"Because," Dauber said, "this is information that can't slip out."

"I won't tell anyone," Serpell said, and Dauber believed her. Serpell might be a bad liar, but she was clearly tight-lipped.

"I see that," Dauber said, trying very hard not to sound sarcastic. "But I don't dare take any risk."

"Is this ship in trouble?" Serpell asked.

"The *Aizsargs*?" Dauber asked, surprised.

Serpell nodded.

Dauber smiled before she could stop herself. "No," she said. "But we have protocols to follow so that we stay out of trouble. I have to implement them now."

She walked to the door, then stopped. Serpell was watching her every move, looking even more panicked—if that was possible.

"Thank you for your time," Dauber said. "You're free to go."

Serpell nodded, but didn't stand up. And Dauber wasn't going to wait for her.

Dauber let herself out of the small room and into the corridor.

She hadn't realized how tense she was until she got out of that room. She made herself walk slowly from the area, and then, when she thought Serpell couldn't see her, Dauber rolled her shoulders to get out some of the tightness.

She hated being lied to, particularly by someone she had been trying to help.

There were still a lot of mysteries to the *Renegat*, and Dauber was beginning to believe she might never find out what all of the answers were.

PART FORTY

SAVING THE *RENEGAT*

100 YEARS AGO

THE *RENEGAT*

Crowe ordered all of his engineers to the bridge. He understood how that looked. It looked like he was captain of the ship now. But he was acutely aware that he was no more captain now than he had been when he pretended to be captain of the *Br2 Scout3*. His position hadn't been sanctioned by the Fleet, nor had the crew chosen him.

He was leading this ship by default.

The bridge was still a filthy smelly mess. He was loathe to clean up the floor near the *anacapa* drive, until he knew exactly what was going on. He was probably being overly cautious, or not cautious enough. But he did know that all of this evidence of bloodshed—both here and in front of engineering—would distract his people. And since they were going to be distracted, better to be distracted here than in engineering itself.

Unlike Preemas, Crowe had turned the screens on. He had a small holographic image of the Scrapheap floating to his left, away from the *anacapa* container and the mess on the floor. He would make the image larger when the rest of the engineering staff showed up.

He still had his environmental suit on, but the hood was down. He had found another pair of gloves, but he hadn't put them on. The scanner remained in one of the pockets of the suit, although he would use the scanner again, if need be.

He had taken over the captain's chair from Tosidis—aware yet again of the symbolism—and had used its easy command controls to find the engineers who had abandoned him when it became clear he was going to fight Preemas.

Now that Preemas was dead, Crowe had to decide what to do with those engineers. He had said he would be understanding—and he would—but if they so much as blinked wrong, he would send them to the brig as well.

He didn't need more distractions. He needed experts—or what passed for experts on this ship.

Because he was scared and exhausted and worried that with all of his own distractions, he wasn't making the right decisions.

He wouldn't present that to any of the crew members who were starting to file onto the bridge. He was going to talk confidently to them, and then have them play around with his ideas. But he was going to present the ideas as something he was willing to change, given the right circumstance.

Tindo Ibori had reported to him from the med bay. Apparently, Orlena Seymont had commanded him to perform the autopsy on Stephanos—or, rather, observe the automated systems perform the autopsy. Ibori had looked green when he contacted Crowe. Ibori had sent images of Stephanos's insides, coated with that same pink that Crowe had seen in the *anacapa* drive.

Ibori had clearly been shaken, but he had taken some initiative—he had checked with Seymont to see if any of the crew members she was treating had that pink stuff floating through their systems.

So far, none of them had.

But Crowe wasn't satisfied. He remembered seeing the imagery of India Romano slamming the *anacapa* container closed, and then, surreptitiously, rubbing her hands together. Crowe wanted to know if she was infected as well.

It had taken a bit of discussion, but Crowe had convinced Ibori to bring Romano to the med bay. She needed treatment for minor injuries, according to the system, and that would allow Seymont to examine her for the pink stuff as well.

If Romano was afflicted, they would have to see if she had contaminated anyone else—if she even could contaminate anyone else.

He had asked Willoughby to barricade herself in engineering after everyone left, and he made her promise that she would run the ship if something happened to him and to the others.

She had wanted to join this meeting—and she would, virtually—but he needed someone he trusted in the only other part of the ship that could control the ship.

He threaded his hands together, mostly to stop himself from rubbing them against the knees of his environmental suit. He knew he hadn't been compromised—yet, anyway—but he wasn't sure if it was a matter of time or not.

Besides, he had more pressing problems to worry about.

He had Bakhr continue his analysis of that energy wave that had flooded the *Renegat* before Crowe had put up the shields. Tosidis was now helping with that, and they were using Colvin as their go-to person for any research questions they had.

M'Ghan had stopped working on the environmental system. Instead, Crowe was having him map where the entire crew was. Not everyone had participated in the fighting, and Crowe wanted to know where they had spent the last twenty-four hours.

When Crowe looked, he had found most of them in their cabins. But he wasn't sure everyone had been there during the worst of the conflict.

Hadley Ellum had already arrived on the bridge. She walked to the captain's chair with her back straight and her head held high. Crowe watched her approach through a small screen that opened directly in front of him. He didn't have to turn around at all.

She was trying to show that she had no regrets about fleeing engineering when Crowe offered his people the chance to stay out of the fighting. Her posture, which was usually sloppy, made her nervousness obvious. She was pretending to be confident just so that he would think she was.

Instead, Crowe could see how scared she was.

James Rodriguez came in shortly after Ellum did. Rodriguez had his shoulders hunched forward, and his gaze was darting from person to person, as if he expected to be yelled at.

Crowe didn't have the energy to yell at anyone. He needed as many people as possible here, and they all had a mutual interest: Survival.

Atwater came in last, all of his confidence gone as well. His pale skin turned even paler as the stench hit him, a sure sign that he hadn't served on ships before. Occasionally smells overwhelmed the environmental system, and while the crew didn't always like that, they got used to it.

Atwater had probably never experienced it before.

"We don't have a lot of time," Crowe said. "I need you all over here, near the captain's chair."

Rodriguez glanced at Ellum who shrugged. Atwater came down an aisle separate from them. Tosidis had stepped to the left of the captain's chair, M'Ghan beside him. Colvin remained next to Bakhr, standing by the science console. Crowe called up Willoughby, setting a holographic image of her next to him.

She glanced around, seemingly surprised that Rodriguez and Ellum were on the bridge.

"You really want me too?" Bakhr asked.

"Yes," Crowe said. "Just for this short meeting."

And it had better be short, because the more time they spent discussing was time away from trying to survive.

"You remember that wave of energy that hit us when we got here?" Crowe asked.

Everyone nodded.

"I'm pretty sure that something in it destroyed our *anacapa* drives. All of them, including the communications *anacapa*, are hollowed out and useless." He had checked the backup drive before calling this meeting. It had been destroyed as well.

Ellum closed her eyes and raised her face to the ceiling, as if she were calling on a higher power. Or maybe she had just hit maximum overwhelm. Rodriguez looked at his shoes.

None of the four who had been on the bridge moved at all. Neither did Willoughby. Crowe couldn't see Atwater clearly, but he seemed motionless.

"To make matters worse," Crowe said, "Natalia Stephanos tried to fix the *anacapa* drive here, and died while doing so. The same material that destroyed the *anacapa* drives is all over her system. I'm no doctor, and neither is the person who observed the autopsy in the med bay, but we both believe that the same material tried to hollow her out as well."

"What does the system say she died of?" Atwater asked. The rules guy. The guy who hadn't served on a ship.

"That's the problem," Crowe said. "Everything we have, from the smallest scanner to the largest piece of equipment, tells us that there's nothing wrong with the *anacapa* drives. According to our equipment, the drives are in perfect working order."

"I was asking about the autopsy," Atwater said. Clearly he didn't see Crowe as a captain, because Atwater was comfortable interrupting him.

"That system did not register the stuff either, although we were able to get images of it." He enlarged the holograms that Ibori had sent him. Crowe used the one that included Stephanos's damaged face, so no one could accuse him of substituting some other person or image.

Even though he had seen this before, it was still shocking. Stephanos barely looked like herself.

Tosidis made a gagging sound and turned away. Willoughby visibly bowed her head.

But Atwater actually took a step forward. "It's pink. Like lace. I've never seen anything like it. What did the med bay autopsy say she died of?"

"Natural causes," Crowe said flatly. "We ran the data again, and then we got old age as the cause."

Rodriguez swore softly. Ellum placed her hand over her mouth.

"Is this happening to all of us?" Tosidis asked.

And that was the important question.

"I don't know," Crowe said. "Have you found any of this in our systems?"

He had been supposed to check.

"I've been doing an automated check," Tosidis said. "Of course, nothing is showing up."

Crowe hadn't specified a physical check. He cursed himself for that.

"I opened the environmental system," M'Ghan said. "It's fine. There's none of that stuff in it."

"And I've been checking systems here in engineering ever since we saw the communications *anacapa*," Willoughby said. "I'm not finding anything bad here either."

Crowe let that information in, but he wasn't going to let himself relax because of it.

"Natalia touched the *anacapa* drive while that energy was flowing through it," Crowe said. "India Romano touched the container with her bare hands. She's on her way to the med bay right now, and we'll look at her as well."

"I thought she was in the brig," Willoughby said.

"Yes," Crowe said. "But we need to know what this stuff is and how it spreads. I've collected quite a bit of it, and the team in the med bay are examining it right now as well."

If he could call Ibori and Seymont a team. Seymont was still trying to save lives. Ibori was just asking her questions on occasion.

"Right now," Crowe said, "Benjamin is trying to isolate the various strands of energy that bombarded our vessel, maybe isolate whatever that was."

Bakhr nodded.

"We're pretty convinced that we blocked whatever caused this pink stuff," Crowe said. "Once we activated the shields."

Once he thought to do that. He had been mentally very harsh on Romano and the others for the choices they had made in the alcove, but he had made bad choices too.

"Do you think that whatever this energy was caused the uprising?" Atwater asked.

Crowe shrugged. "The thought has crossed my mind. But I'm also aware that the crisis we just went through was building for a long time. If I hadn't taken over control of the ship—"

"We would be dead, I get that," Atwater said, as if it were a minor thing.

"And the captain reacted badly," Willoughby said primly.

"I'll say." Ellum crossed her arms.

"Logically," Rodriguez said, "if that energy wave had corrupted our thinking process and put that stuff inside all of us, wouldn't we still be corrupted? Wouldn't we still be responding like we had before?"

"I don't know," Crowe said. "And we don't have the time to figure that out. We're going to have to do a series of things at the same time. We're going to need to figure out what that pink stuff is, especially if we're infected with it. After I leave here, I'm heading to the med bay, and we will examine me to see if I'm infected."

He didn't want to go, but he would. It was necessary.

"What I need from all of you is help. We're going to need to do some hands-on science work, yes, but we're also stranded here. We need options." Crowe glanced at all of them.

They had deep care lines in their faces that hadn't been there the day before. They were as tired as he was. And they knew they were nowhere near the end.

"I need a team to find us a habitable planet or a starbase or a moon, some place that we can go if we have to, preferably someplace that won't mind an extra few hundred people," Crowe said. "The Fleet used to build Scrapheaps far away from inhabited areas, but this Scrapheap has been here forever. I'm going to assume the sector is very different than it was thousands of years ago."

"We're going to be stranded here, aren't we?" Ellum asked.

Crowe was shaking his head before he even realized it. "We have no good options, Hadley. Even if we find a way back to the Fleet, our captain is dead. There will be a court-martial. I'll take the blame for all of it—"

The blame was long overdue for him. He should have been punished years ago.

"—but I can't guarantee that they'll listen just to me." Crowe placed his hands on the arms of the captain's chair. "That's a risk if we go back."

"It's also not a worry, since we're not going to be able to go anywhere without an *anacapa* drive," said Colvin. She sounded a lot more sensible than Crowe had expected.

He glanced at her. She seemed calmer than everyone else, also something he hadn't expected.

"Yeah," Crowe said. "Which brings me to my next point. We might be able to get *anacapa* drives."

Rodriguez and Ellum glanced at each other in surprise. Atwater brought his head back as if Crowe had shocked him. But Bakhr and Willoughby didn't move at all.

"If you're thinking of getting them from the Scrapheap," Tosidis said, "the ones in there are probably contaminated like ours is."

"We don't know that," Crowe said.

"If it's coming from that energy wave," Tosidis said, "then any *anacapa* drives remaining in the Scrapheap have been subject to that wave."

"Maybe, maybe not." Crowe slid forward on the chair so that he could look directly at Bakhr. "Did that wave come at us directly?"

"Like a weapon, you mean?" Bakhr asked.

"Yeah," Crowe said.

"A lot of the energy we were dealing with is just bleeding off the Scrapheap itself," Bakhr said.

"But not all of it," Crowe said.

Bakhr inclined his head. "But not all of it, no."

"I seem to recall in our original briefing," Crowe said, "we were told that someone broke into the Scrapheap, stole DV-Class vessels, and left their own vessels behind."

Bakhr shrugged. Not everyone had been part of those briefings.

"Yeah, that's true," Willoughby said. "I remember that. I remember thinking that piece of information was irrelevant because whoever had done that would have had to have been long dead by now. We'd never catch them."

"But that wasn't the point, was it?" M'Ghan said quietly. "We weren't sent to catch them. We were sent to see what they had taken."

Crowe shook his head. "We were sent to see if they had taken the Ready Vessels."

Everyone looked at him, and he realized not everyone on the bridge had the kind of clearance that let them know about Ready Vessels.

So he explained them, as quickly as he could.

"We've been salting the universe with *warships*?" Atwater asked when Crowe was done.

"In theory, to protect ourselves," Crowe said. "But I don't know how that theory would have worked, since the Fleet never went backwards."

"I always heard it was for the people we left behind on sector bases," Willoughby said. "If they needed fighting ships, then they had the ships."

Bakhr was shaking his head. "Sector bases are never near Scrapheaps."

"It doesn't matter," Crowe said. "We could speculate for hours about Ready Vessels, and we will never know the exact answer. I had always been taught that they were warships, reserved for the Fleet when it was in the area, and, if need be, able to be retrieved with a short foldspace journey."

"Then logically, we should have cleaned the ships out of the Scrapheaps when the Fleet moved on." Atwater sounded almost angry.

Crowe gave him a small sideways smile. "Don't expect logic from the Fleet on everything," he said. "It stops a lot of disappointment."

Atwater was shaking his head.

"You're saying there are Ready Vessels here," Bakhr said.

"And they look untouched," Crowe said.

The bridge was silent for a moment.

Then Bakhr said, "So much would have to go our way. We would have to see if that energy wave did, in fact, cause the problems you found. We would need to get into the Scrapheap without problems. We would have to be able to get into the Ready Vessel area without problems. And then we would have to find intact and functioning *anacapa* drives."

"If we don't find the drives," Colvin said, "we're stuck here."

"Nadim already said why returning to the Fleet isn't in our best interest," Bakhr said.

"But staying in this sector might not be in our best interest either," Colvin said.

She was standing just a bit too close to Bakhr. Was Crowe misreading the tension between them? Was there something more than workplace camaraderie?

He shook his head slightly. He didn't need to know unless it affected their work.

"Yulia is right," Crowe said. "We might not want to stay in this sector. For all we know, this energy wave has flooded most of the region, and has had some kind of impact we don't know about."

"Or we might not be able to find somewhere friendly to stay," M'Ghan said.

"That too," Crowe said. "I would feel better if we had a working *anacapa* drive, even if we choose never to return to foldspace again."

"At least we'd be choosing," Willoughby said.

"Exactly," Crowe said. "I want it to be our choice, rather than us feeling trapped by circumstance."

"So let me be clear," Atwater said. "One: We need to see if we're all infected with this stuff. Two: We need to see what we can find out about the region of space that we're in. Three: We need to see if we can find working *anacapa* drives. Am I missing anything?"

"Four," Bakhr said, "and really, it should be number one: We need to find out what caused that invasive pink stuff in the first place."

"We don't have enough staff for this," Willoughby said quietly, almost as if she was standing next to Crowe rather than being projected from the bridge.

"We don't have enough staff for anything," Crowe said. "But we're going to have to make do. That's the other thing I want. I want a work schedule. Or, rather, a sleep-and-eat schedule. We're going to have to run this like the tightest of tight ships for a while. Because we also have injured."

"And prisoners," Willoughby said, just a bit louder.

Crowe nodded, hating the word prisoner, even though it was true.

"We're going to have to keep guards on them, relieve our medical staff at times, and maintain the ship's systems as well," Crowe said. "It's a lot of work, and those four things that we just named are over and above the regular running of the ship."

He didn't add that there was one other thing they had to do. They had to ensure regular order on this vessel. They had to quell all those emotions that had boiled over on this horrible day.

He wasn't sure how to do that. He had never been the emotion guy. And he was standing on the bridge with mostly engineers, none of whom were known for their emotional sensitivity either.

He had no idea how to resolve that one. He wasn't sure it was solvable.

So he met everyone's gazes and said, as forcefully as he could, "Let's get to work."

THE *RENEGAT*

Romano didn't fight anyone when they pulled her out of the brig, because they told her she was going to the med bay. Given the way her hands ached, she welcomed any respite. Her hip looked bad, and was probably getting infected, but her hands. They had never hurt like that before in her entire life.

DeShawn Hagen had called down a gurney and strapped her into it. And he had strapped her the way that she had been strapped before, with every single limb separately held in place.

She knew she couldn't fight, but she didn't even try.

It would be easier to escape from the med bay after all.

After they dealt with her hands, of course.

She was also relieved to get out of the brig. The thirty people being held were in terrible shape. She couldn't tell if they were all injured, but a number of them sat on their bunks and sobbed.

If she could have come up with a plan, she would have, but her mind was hazy. Some of that was because that bastard Crowe had cut the oxygen and it was taking her body a while to recover. Some of that was from her injuries.

She suspected that the original gurney had shot her up with painkillers, and that led to fuzzy thinking as well.

If she knew how to make this gurney shut off the pain meds, she would have—or maybe not. Because the closer she got to the med bay, the better she felt.

Hagen walked alongside her, the laser rifle on the other side of her, so she couldn't somehow escape from her straps, reach over and grab the damn weapon.

Hagen wouldn't look at her and wouldn't talk to her. It was as if the gurney was empty. Only the placement of the laser rifle let her know that he was aware of her.

He had complained when Tasneem Zhang had told him to take Romano to the med bay. He hadn't seemed happy about being in the brig either, but apparently he found that preferable to seeing all the severely injured and the dying.

If Romano had been feeling better, she would have berated him, told him how he and Nadim Crowe and their cohorts had caused all of this. Then Hagen would have said that she had fired the weapons, and she would have said she wouldn't have had to if he had followed Fleet protocol, and…God, just thinking of the arguments made her tired.

Everything did, including the fact that Serpell had left her behind. Romano had begged Serpell to get her out of the brig, and Serpell had refused, apparently still thinking she had some kind of career to protect. Or maybe she just believed that she had to get along so that she wouldn't go to the brig.

Serpell was such a spineless creature. Usually she was easy to boss around, but right now, even Serpell could see how powerless Romano was to do anything.

The corridor opened wide around the med bay, and the gurney slid right in. The lighting here was bright white and cold, not soothing at all. The med bay was divided into two sections—one for actual medicine and one for the dead.

Romano had been here once before, and when she had arrived, the med bay itself had offered her a choice between care and death stuff. But there was no choice in the offing right now.

In fact, there were at least three doors on her left that glowed red, meaning that she and Hagen couldn't go in them if she wanted to.

"Hey," Hagen said, sounding confused like people did when something didn't go as they expected. "I brought the prisoner."

The prisoner. He could at least have said her name. She turned her head slightly and glared at him, but he still didn't look at her.

A door on her right slid open, and Tindo Ibori stepped out.

She had been expecting one of the docs, whose names she could never remember. Sycophant or sillyphant or something. Both of the medical professionals Romano had run into had been women. So Ibori's presence surprised her.

He was wearing an environmental suit, which also bothered her. He had the hood down, but he was wearing gloves.

"In here," he said and swept one of his gloved hands toward the open door.

She thought that the right side was for dead people.

"Hey," she said. "That's not the operating theater. And you're not a doctor. What's going on here?"

"Do you need me to stay?" Hagen asked, still talking to Ibori. It was as if Romano didn't exist at all.

Ibori sighed. He looked exhausted and more than a little sick himself. "I don't have a weapon, so I suppose I do need you to stay. You'll have to suit up."

Hagen nodded.

"Suit up?" Romano asked. "What is this? I thought I was going to get medical care. You don't need an environmental suit for that."

Ibori glanced at her. She felt ridiculously grateful at being seen. "Just give me a few minutes, India, okay?"

"You're not a doctor," she said.

"Yeah, I know," he said.

Hagen had his back to her. He still clutched the laser rifle, but he wasn't paying attention to her. He was looking at a rack of suits. They weren't really environmental suits. More like the kinds of suits she saw around decontamination containers.

He apparently was taking Ibori's suggestion to wear a suit very seriously.

Hagen would be preoccupied with that for a few minutes. If she was going to escape, now was the time. Not that she could even move. She thought about struggling against the restraints, then remembered how painful that had been before. And how fruitless.

Then the gurney jerked forward. No one was touching it. But clearly Ibori had done something. The gurney ended up in the center of a narrow room, with all kinds of equipment on the walls. Lights flared around her and she recognized what was happening.

They were isolating her, with some kind of security chamber.

"Hey!" she yelled. "I'm already strapped down. You don't need the chamber."

But her voice echoed back in on her.

Ibori and Hagen were in the door. Hagen held a suit in one hand and the laser rifle in the other. Ibori was pointing at Romano, and Hagen shrugged, more than once. Then he handed Ibori the laser rifle, and slid the suit on, slowly.

Ibori looked at the rifle as if it was going to shoot him. Romano remembered him on the bridge, the way he had crouched over Stephanos, trying to help her, and then looking at Preemas as if the man had been crazy when he started talking about weapons.

Ibori had tried to pretend like he wasn't going to take a side, but he had. He was on Crowe's side, even if Ibori had never taken a weapon and shot at Preemas.

Romano looked at the security chamber. It wasn't quite clear. She could see the occasional rainbow of light streaming down one side as something on the equipment around her beeped.

She couldn't see a way out even if she wanted one. What the hell were they going to do to her? And why Ibori? What about Doctor Sycophant? Had she died along with everyone else?

Romano shivered. She'd rather take her chances with the medical programs than with Ibori. The man was a navigator, for god's sake, and clearly wasn't good at anything, or he wouldn't be on this ship.

Hagen pulled at the suit, adjusting it over his shoulders. He kept the hood down for a moment. He looked somehow larger in his suit than he had out of it. He took the rifle from Ibori, then nodded at him.

Both men put up their hoods. They didn't look quite human anymore. She had trouble seeing their faces through the security chamber's so-called clear walls and then through their so-called clear hoods.

There was a click and she could hear whooshing and the hum of the environmental system.

"India," Ibori said. "How do your hands feel?"

The question startled her. She hadn't expected that at all. She had expected Ibori to grab a medical scanner and run it over her hip or maybe have the entire gurney send him a reading about her internal injuries. (If she had any. She wasn't sure what kind of injuries she had. The very idea made her heart flutter.)

"My hands?" she asked. "Why are you asking about my hands?"

"Because you seem to be favoring them." That was Hagen, and it was a lie. He couldn't have seen the way she rubbed her hands.

She couldn't call him out on the lie, though, because she really did need help with her hands. The ache had moved from a tingle in the beginning to full blown screeching pain, almost like someone was holding her hand on top of a hot surface.

"I thought you guys were going to work on my real injuries," she said, letting her tone sound as sarcastic as she felt.

"As you said, I'm not a real doctor." Ibori sounded calm. "I'll be bringing Orlena in here soon, but I need to know the extent of all of your injuries. Some of them are obvious, but your hands aren't. So what's going on with them?"

Orlena. Doctor Sycophant was alive after all. So there was a medical professional, and she would come into this weird little room on the death side of the med bay to…what? End it for Romano?

That wasn't possible, was it?

"My hands hurt," Romano said.

"Did they always hurt?" Ibori had glanced to the side. She realized now that he was working off a holographic screen she couldn't see.

"You mean all my life or just today?" she asked.

"Is it normal for your hands to hurt?" he asked.

How stupid was that? "Is it normal for *your* hands to hurt?" she asked.

He raised his chin slightly and frowned at her. At least she thought that expression was a frown. It might have simply been a bit of shadow crossing his face.

"India," he said. Amazing how one word could be so condescending. "We're trying to help you."

She snorted. "By locking me up and then bringing me here and putting me in a security chamber, being examined by a *navigator?* Really, Tindo, you're trying to help me?"

"Yeah." His voice remained even.

Hagen adjusted the laser rifle slightly. The movement was some kind of threat. It had to be.

"No, my hands did not hurt before today," Romano said.

Ibori glanced at that place to his side again. "When did the pain start?"

"It didn't start as a pain," she said. "It started as tingling. Like your body does if you sleep on your arm funny or something."

He raised his head again, and this time, she saw his eyes. They met hers. She felt his confusion.

"Tingling?" he asked.

"Tingling is tiny pains," Hagen said. "Just not severe ones."

"Thank you, Doctor Hagen," Romano said.

He shifted the rifle again, and ostentatiously turned his head away from her, as if she was not worth his time.

"When did the tingling start?" Ibori asked.

She felt her face heat. This was his fault, all of it. He hadn't wanted to close that *anacapa* container. So she had shown him that she wasn't scared of it.

She had stupidly grabbed the thing without gloves. Or maybe she should have kicked it shut with a booted foot.

She hadn't thought that through. She just wanted to show him that the container was harmless.

And now, she was going to tell him she had been wrong.

"India?"

She mentally cursed him. Then took a deep breath. No one could help her if she stayed silent about this stuff. Dammit.

"The tingling started right after I slammed the *anacapa* container closed." Her fury, at herself and at him, made each word vibrate.

Ibori bowed his head. Hagen tilted his backwards. They had expected that answer, and they hadn't wanted to hear it. She found that odd.

"I'm sorry." Ibori's voice was slightly muffled.

She knew what he was apologizing for. Hagen didn't, and looked at him with surprise.

"Something got me, didn't it?" she asked.

Ibori lifted his head.

"That same thing that killed Natalia," Romano said. "That's what got me, right? Am I going to die?"

"I don't know," Ibori said. "I'm not a doctor."

"You keep saying that." Romano raised her voice. "Where is the damn doctor then?"

"Saving lives," Hagen said flatly.

Romano raised her head as high as she could. The strain made her neck and shoulders ache.

"You think mine isn't worth saving?" she asked. "You really want me to die like Natalia did?"

"You won't die like she did," Ibori said.

"You don't know that," Romano said.

"I do," Ibori said. "Because you'd be dead already. Whatever happened to her happened fast."

That was true. Romano had seen it.

"You think I got, what, a minor dose of whatever it was?" she asked.

"Just let me finish with the questions, okay, India?" Ibori asked. "Then we'll figure out what to do."

"You and me and your pet security guard?" Romano asked. "Because none of us are doctors."

"I told you," Ibori said. "Orlena will be here shortly."

"I want to see her now," Romano said.

Ibori didn't seem intimidated by her anger. Instead, he smiled sadly. "Yeah, I would too," he said. "But we don't always get what we want."

Romano clenched the fist on the far side of Ibori, so that neither he nor Hagen could see her movement. Clenching was hard. It was getting harder and harder to do anything with her hands because the level of pain was growing more and more intense with each passing moment.

Maybe that was because she was focusing on the pain. She needed to think about something else.

But she had touched the *anacapa* container, and Stephanos had died by touching that *anacapa* drive, and what if the two things were related? Romano had never seen anyone die like that, not that quickly and not that horribly.

And she might be next.

Ibori took a small step toward her. He peered through the security barrier. She could see his face fully now. He seemed to be looking at her with compassion.

She had to wrench her gaze from his before she teared up.

She wanted compassion less than she wanted to fight. Fighting, at least, she understood.

"Tell me about the pain," he said softly.

And she did.

THE *RENEGAT*

Seymont slid out of the operating theater and leaned on the wall. She closed her eyes for a moment, then felt sleep edge close to her consciousness. When she'd been studying medicine on the *Santé Two*, she had often fallen asleep standing up.

She didn't want to do that here. Not now. And she couldn't use any stimulants.

She needed her mind clear.

She opened her eyes, and made herself take several deep breaths, then shuddered.

Three people had died so far. She didn't have the skill to save them. She wasn't sure anyone did. Maybe in concert with one of the experts on the *Santé Two*. Maybe not.

She had never been in a war zone or even a major battle, although she had heard that it could be like this.

Hearing about it and living it were two different things.

And she really didn't have the time to rest. Right now, she had the virtual medical assistant scanning the second-stage triage patients, trying to see if they had worse injuries than the gurneys reported or if the injuries were causing a cascade inside the patient's system.

She was most worried about Jorja Lakinas. Even if she survived, she might not walk again. Something the lasers had done had fused her spine in a way that Seymont hadn't seen before.

If she had time, she might be able to reverse the damage, but right now, she didn't have time. She really shouldn't even be standing here, in the quiet between the two sections of the med bay, but she was.

Because she was supposed to go into the death wing and see what, if anything, was growing inside India Romano.

Seymont had taken a short, short, short break an hour—two hours? Three hours?—ago, and looked at the weird pink webbing that had threaded its way through Natalia Stephanos's body. That webbing had wound itself around all of her internal organs, squeezing them as if it had been wringing out a washcloth. The webbing had paralleled Stephanos's veins, and had essentially followed their path into Stephanos's heart.

The entire thing looked like some kind of late-night medical quiz, something one of her professors would have foisted on the medical students somewhere in the middle of their final year. But it wasn't a quiz.

It was real life, life here on the *Renegat*, and, according to Crowe, that stuff was all over the *anacapa* drives as well.

If that stuff was inside of India Romano, then it was game over.

Of course, Romano hadn't died rapidly like Stephanos. But Romano hadn't touched the *anacapa* drive. Just its container.

And that, according to the information Tindo Ibori had sent to Seymont, had been enough to make Romano's hands hurt.

Nothing showed up on any scan. But, then, nothing showed up on the scans after Stephanos's death either. For some reason, that pink crap was invisible to all of the Fleet sensors.

Seymont had initially ordered Ibori to use some of the equipment in that morgue to slice into Romano's hand to see if there was pink stuff alongside her veins.

But Ibori had balked.

It's one thing, he had said, *to let the machines help me examine a dead body. It's another to slice into someone's hand and pray there won't be any consequences at all.*

He was right; of course he was right. And so was Crowe. If this stuff was everywhere, and if it killed its hosts like it seemed to, then the entire crew was at risk.

It was just that Seymont wasn't really a creative physician. She was a get-by physician, whose entire career had piggybacked on the shoulders of her betters. When she had a great coworker, she did a great job. When she had a mediocre coworker, she did a mediocre job. And when she had no coworker…

Ah, hell. She just wanted to go to sleep.

Or have a drink.

She licked her lips, then pushed off the wall. The moment she thought about alcohol, she had to move. She had promised herself that. She had to stay busy, so the drinks wouldn't become the very next thing she did.

Besides, she didn't want to die in the same way that Stephanos had.

She stopped at the storage closet, and grabbed another bio suit. She took off the suit she'd been wearing and put it in the cleansing unit. She hadn't been following cleanliness procedures exactly. She'd been cleaning up properly, but she hadn't really been decontaminating, figuring everyone had bled together in that alcove, so they had already contaminated each other—if there were any airborne pathogens.

But this was a completely different matter. She was going to wear the highest level of suit, and she was going to follow extreme conditions procedures, just to make sure she didn't get contaminated (if she wasn't already).

The suit went on quickly. She put up the hood before she stepped into the morgue, concerned that Ibori and Hagen hadn't followed procedure in there.

But she needn't have worried. The isolation chamber glimmered around the gurney. India Romano was strapped to that gurney. She looked gray and ill, eyes sunken into her face, lips chapped and bleeding. Her hair, which she had colored a bright lavender, looked like some kind of fake string cast about her head instead of the fashion statement that Romano was known for.

Romano didn't see her, but Ibori did. His shoulders visibly relaxed, as if Seymont held all of the answers. Or maybe Ibori didn't want the responsibility anymore.

Hagen saw her too. He nodded almost imperceptivity. He was still clutching his weapon, as if Romano—who was strapped onto her gurney and held inside that isolation chamber—could suddenly leap out and try to kill them all.

Seymont pushed past both men. She opened a holoscreen and scanned the answers to the questions she had made Ibori ask Romano. Seymont had examined those answers before, and on some low level, they had terrified her. But she had to set her own feelings aside.

She also had to keep her mind open. Just because Crowe thought that Romano had been infected didn't mean she was. And that ache in her hands might have been caused by some malfunctioning weapon in that alcove. The tingling could have been *anacapa* vibration and completely unrelated to the pain now.

Seymont had seen stranger things just that afternoon. Hell, this entire journey had been strange.

She then examined the information that the gurney had provided. The wound on Romano's hip was a straightforward laser burn. It would heal just fine with standard treatment, provided there wasn't any pink parasitical thing slowly cannibalizing Romano's insides.

Better to see if that pink stuff was threaded through her before handling the hip wound.

Romano was watching her warily. They had never liked each other. Romano had come into the med bay a few times, complaining of minor ailments, and trolling for medication.

Seymont had never given her any, which continually made Romano angry. Slowly, Seymont figured out that one of the three medical professionals who had left the *Renegat* on Sector Base Z had been giving Romano something to keep her calm.

Which, given what had happened in that alcove, had probably been a better decision than Seymont had originally thought it was.

"You gonna do something to help me or are you just going to take readings?" Romano asked.

Her voice didn't sound normal. It was a little wobbly. She apparently was going for defiance, but it wasn't working.

India Romano was scared.

Seymont felt a second of surprise, but tamped the emotion back. Sure Romano was scared. They were all scared. Seymont was scared. And she wasn't going to try to calm anyone down. That wasn't her job.

Not right now anyway.

She set the tablet aside, and closed the screens around her.

"I need to see what's going on inside those hands," Seymont said.

"Okay," Romano said. "I can't help you trussed up like this."

"Actually, that won't matter." Seymont was going to have to explain this and she really didn't want to. "Natalia Stephanos was killed by something that infected the *anacapa* drive. There's a chance that same something infected you."

"I'm not dead," Romano said, as if Seymont lacked the ability to notice that.

"Obviously," Seymont said, keeping her tone even. "But you didn't touch the drive directly. The problem is that this material doesn't show up on any of our equipment."

"Grrr-eat," Romano said, lengthening out the word.

"I'm going to have to open part of your hand and examine the interior myself," Seymont said. "You're right-handed, right?"

"What do you mean 'open'?" Romano asked.

"I'm going to make a small incision, then look inside the area," Seymont said. "Right-handed, right?"

"Is it going to hurt?" Romano asked.

"I don't know, given the pain you're already feeling. You're already medicated. I don't dare give you any more."

"Medicated?" Romano frowned. "I don't feel medicated."

Probably because she had a tolerance. But Seymont wasn't going to say that, nor was she going to assume it. The pain that Romano was experiencing might have been so severe that the medication didn't block it.

"I'm going to put yet another protective barrier around your left hand," Seymont said, since Romano still hadn't told her which hand was her dominant one. "Then I'm going to make a small incision. I'm going to peel back the skin just a bit to take a look, and then I'll close everything up."

If it looked normal, that is. If it didn't, Seymont was going to have to make some decisions on the fly.

"If you want," Seymont said, "we can knock you out. It might be easier on you if we do."

Romano's eyes narrowed, as if she didn't trust Seymont. And then Romano shook her head slightly. Apparently, she wanted to stay awake.

"I don't want to see this," Romano said. "Shut me down."

That surprised Seymont. Maybe Romano had been weighing the pros and cons of staying awake. Most people would have. Apparently, Seymont hadn't expected Romano to act like most people.

"All right," Seymont said. She adjusted the controls on the gurney, and within seconds, Romano was unconscious.

Seymont felt herself relax. She really hadn't wanted to do this tiny procedure under Romano's watchful eyes.

Ibori had moved beside Seymont. She almost told him she was feeling crowded, because that was what she normally would have done, if she were doing a little bit of hands-on surgery. But, she realized, she wanted him there.

She needed his vision to augment hers.

She activated the internal hands on the isolation chamber, and used one of those hands to lift up Romano's left hand. Then Seymont created an isolation bubble around Romano's hand and the surgical device. She had the surgical hand turn the index finger into a laser scalpel. The third finger became a collection unit, so that she could rub the finger along whatever she saw, if she needed to.

The second finger had a tiny camera on the tip. She pointed that down.

Then she moved so that she could eyeball the incision as well. Ibori got out of her way. She appreciated that. Most medical students didn't have that kind of sensitivity.

Through the surgical hand, she could feel everything as if she were doing the surgery with her own hands. The palm of Romano's hand rested heavily on the other surgical hand. Dead weight.

Although, as Seymont thought about it, the hand shouldn't have been dead weight if it were being cleansed of fluids the way that Stephanos's system had been. Or, as Crowe had described the *anacapa* drives, if the hand had been hollowed out.

That all was a good sign, then.

Seymont bent as far forward as she could. She had opened yet another screen, so that she could glance at the interior of Romano's hand—if the camera showed anything at all.

It probably would, since it had with Stephanos's corpse.

Then Seymont banished all speculation, and, with a steady finger, sliced between the delicate bones on the back of Romano's hand.

Seymont had chosen that area because there were a lot of muscles, veins, and nerves in that tiny area, but nothing that could cause Romano to bleed out quickly.

The cut wasn't deep. All Seymont wanted to see was the dorsal venous network, since the pink stuff had traveled alongside Stephanos's veins.

Seymont expected to see the red veins, the rich meaty look of the muscles, the yellow of the fatty tissue, and the whiteness of bone. But the first thing she saw was a purplish-blackness coating everything, like mold.

Ibori swore next to her. That made Hagen crowd over.

"Back away," she said. "Let me work."

She sent the camera finger as close to the moldy stuff as possible, trying to see if the stuff was actually attached or if it had layered itself across the surface.

As far as she could tell with just a look, the stuff had attached to the nerves, and was choking them off. Or had been choking them off.

Unless she missed her guess, that purplish-blackish stuff had once been pink.

She took the gathering finger and slid it over the material. It wiped free, like dirt on glass.

"Tindo," she said, "see if the scanners can read this stuff now."

Now that the hand was open, she meant. But it didn't matter if he entirely understood. She just wanted him to scan and see.

"They're showing damage to the nerves, but not any of the stuff around it," he said.

That was what she was afraid of. She was going to have to figure this out on her own. She ran a diagnostic of the material the container finger had gathered.

It read an unidentifiable foreign substance.

She queried the operating system with her free hand. Could the surgical finger clear that material from inside Romano's skin?

That system said it could. So she set it to remove the purplish-blackish stuff in the area that had been cut open.

The finger did as it was told, collecting the material and dropping it into a container it created out of the surgical hand's palm.

This operation was going to take time—maybe a lot of time, depending on the extent of the contamination.

Seymont raised her head and peered around the double isolation chambers. In the actual operating theater, a dozen injured people waited. Jorja Lakinas needed attention now.

Seymont didn't have the time she needed to clean this stuff out of Romano. Nor did she have the time to teach Ibori how to do it.

Seymont took a deep breath. Then she removed her hands from that set of tools.

"What are you doing?" Ibori asked.

She didn't answer him. Instead, she dropped another small isolation bubble around Romano's left biceps. Seymont set up another surgical hand, and carefully sliced open a bit of skin near the veins on the top of the arm.

No blackness, no purplish debris, no mold looking stuff, no pink stuff. Just normal healthy tissue.

Seymont let out the breath she had taken. Then she moved to Romano's right side, and examined the biceps there.

Nothing out of the ordinary. Nor was there anything out of the ordinary on Romano's forearm or on her thighs.

Whatever had infected her had only infected her hands.

Which made Seymont's choice a bit easier.

She could clean out the hands, save the strange material, and analyze it later. If Crowe wanted it analyzed sooner, he could find someone to do that.

Seymont set the isolation systems on the biceps, forearms, and thighs on automatic, letting them seal the skin. She hoped nothing had gotten through the isolation chambers, because if it had, Romano would feel the tingling (as she had described it) when she woke up.

Otherwise, she wouldn't feel a thing.

Then Seymont set to work. She took images of the damage inside Romano's hands. Then Seymont cleaned it all, wiping and scraping, being careful to avoid any damaged area.

She wasn't going to worry about repairing Romano's hands. That would have to wait until Seymont dealt with the more seriously wounded people in the next room.

But Seymont would clean out the contaminant, and then, later, she would check to see if it had regrown.

She was hoping for a one-time contamination.

But she was learning on this godforsaken voyage that whatever she hoped for invariably did not come true.

THE *RENEGAT*

Crowe slipped inside the med bay, expecting chaos. Instead, he found an empty entry, with a discarded bio suit on one bench, and some clothes on another. The usual automated voice did not come on, directing him to either the med bay proper or the ship's morgue, which the *Renegat* had some fancy term for.

He stood there for a moment, tired and woozy, expecting to see someone at least, or a crowd, clamoring for the attention of Orlena Seymont. As far as he could tell, she was the only remaining doctor on the ship, and she had to be pretty overwhelmed by now.

He stopped at the main med bay door and peered inside. It was slightly shaded, so that he couldn't see anything clearly, but he could identify a stack of gurneys, which meant even more people were waiting to be helped.

He wondered if Romano was in there. He really didn't want to see her, but he would if he had to, particularly if he had to move her forward, and force Seymont to care for her.

A door slid open behind him. As he turned, he saw Seymont standing just inside it. She was wearing a bio suit, with the hood down. She looked as exhausted as he felt.

"Mr. Crowe," she said, with a slight wry emphasis on *Mr.* Apparently, she had no idea what title to give him. Neither did he, not at the moment. "To what do I owe this pleasure?"

He wanted to stick his hands out at her, and tell her to examine them. He wanted to get all of this over with.

Instead, he made himself turn until he faced her.

"Have you looked at India Romano yet?" he asked.

"Yes," Seymont said. "And it was quite fascinating."

He felt a chill. "So she was infected."

"She was," Seymont said. "Emphasis on *was*. The material had died inside her hands. I cleaned up the residue, stored it so someone someday could figure out what it was, and then came out here to find you."

"It...died?" It took him a moment to process that. "It was organic?"

"I think it was," Seymont said. "I didn't study it closely. I was thinking of it as a parasite, but Tindo says he thought of it as a virus. Whatever it was, it was starting through her system, albeit much more slowly than it had gone through Natalia's. But then, India hadn't touched the drive directly."

Crowe clenched his hands. The gloves covering them creaked. "I touched the communications *anacapa*," he said. "I want you to examine my fingers."

She was shaking her head before he even finished. "I don't have time," she said. "People in that operating theater will never recover properly if I don't get in there."

"And if this stuff contaminates anyone who touches it with their bare hands, we might have something going on that threatens the entire ship." He kept his voice level. He didn't want to panic her, but he did want her to understand the urgency.

"You realize I'll have to cut your hand open," she said.

"Start with the fingertips," he said. "That's where I held it."

Her mouth formed a thin line. Then she sighed.

"I'm going to do this fast, and we're going to do it in here." She swept her arm toward the morgue.

He nodded, then followed her inside. He didn't have to go far. Romano's gurney took up most of the space. Ibori was looking at something on a floating screen, and DeShawn Hagen was standing to one side, holding a laser rifle. Both men were wearing bio suits.

They glanced at him. Ibori nodded, and then went back to whatever he was doing. Hagen watched Crowe as if he expected Crowe to do something to Romano.

Romano was out cold—thank god, because Crowe did not want to listen to anything she had to say.

She was covered in an isolating bubble, and her hands had extra bubbles on them. Both hands had long red marks along the back, apparently where Seymont had cut her open.

"Over here," Seymont said, leading him toward a small table near a row of equipment that he could barely identify. Something medical and important, something he was too tired to think about.

He stopped beside the table.

"I'm going to put both of your hands inside an isolation bubble," she said. "You're going to remove your gloves. Then I'm going to isolate each hand separately. I don't have any gurneys to offer you, to numb you or put you out. I can give you some medication to ease the pain."

"Will the medication interfere with my thought processes?" he asked.

"You'll be fuzzy for several hours," she said.

"Then no," he said. "Just do what you're going to do."

"In that case," she said, "I'm adding an extra pair of surgical hands to hold you in place. The last thing I want is for you to jerk around while I'm digging into your skin."

It all sounded unpleasant, but he could deal with unpleasant. He almost told her that but then realized that he wasn't sure if he could control his reactions to that kind of isolated pain.

"Do what you need to," he said.

She put on extra gloves over her gloves, then took him gingerly by both wrists. "Keep your hands there," she said.

An isolation bubble formed over them. It covered half of his forearms as well.

"Remove your gloves," she said.

He did. His fingertips on his right hand were tingling, but he wasn't sure if that was simply the power of suggestion.

He let the gloves fall onto the table—or, at least, that was where he thought they would end up. Instead, they landed on the bottom of the isolation bubble. It had more solidity than he expected.

"All right," she said. "Now move your hands slightly apart, palms up."

He did. Two more bubbles formed over each hand. Then a surgical hand formed underneath each one, cupping the back of his hand. The surgical hand was warm, which surprised him.

"Which hand held the communications *anacapa*," Seymont said.

"I touched it with both," he said, "but I held it with my left hand."

"All right," she said, then did something he couldn't quite see without moving his entire body.

More hands appeared inside the isolation bubbles. None of the new hands touched his.

"Forefinger and thumb?" she asked.

"On the left hand?" he asked.

"Yeah." Her voice was curt as if he was getting in her way, by clarifying questions.

"I cupped it with all of my fingers. It was very fragile."

She leaned forward just enough that her expression became visible. She was frowning.

"Show me," she said.

He moved his hand into position, as if he were still holding the communications *anacapa*. He could feel just a bit of tingling in all of the places that touched the *anacapa*, and he wasn't sure if that tingling was simply memory or if the tingle actually existed.

She moved something on her screen, then shoved her hand forward. One of the hands inside the isolation chamber gently grabbed his pinkie.

"I suggest you look away," she said.

He didn't. He would rather watch this.

The hand that she was clearly operating inside the chamber had, instead of a forefinger, a scalpel. It sliced into his pinkie, making him gasp from the sharp pain.

"Told you," she said. "Painful."

His fingertip was bleeding profusely. One of automated fingers became a suction tube, gently pulling out the blood. Then Seymont grabbed the edges of the skin and started peeling it back.

That was when Crowe looked away. Looking away didn't help the pain, but it settled his stomach.

Next to him, Seymont sighed.

"Look here," she said.

He looked at his finger, which didn't look so much like a finger as a tiny peeled (and bloody) banana.

"No," she said. "*Here.*"

He glanced sideways, saw the three-D image she had turned toward him. The interior of his fingertip, filled with things he couldn't easily identify.

But he did recognize the pink stuff. Just a bit of it, alongside the blood vessel she had sliced.

His heart sank.

"I touched that drive maybe two hours ago," he said.

"We could inspect your whole hand," Seymont said, "and see how the stuff has spread."

He wasn't sure what to do. He looked at the pink stuff, looking like healthy lace, then said, "Can I see what was in Romano's hands?"

Seymont opened another three-D image, showing what was recognizably a hand, but with the skin pulled back, showing him things he didn't recognize, but which looked like those models of the human body he had seen decades ago in school.

Overlaying all of it was blackened crud. If he squinted hard enough, he could see some of the same patterns he saw in the delicate lacy pink stuff that he saw.

He raised his gaze to hers. "You think that's dead."

"It's dead," she said. "I calibrated the instruments to make sure, but it's dead."

Two pieces of news in that, which she clearly hadn't realized would benefit him. That something had killed the stuff inside Romano's hands, and that Seymont had recalibrated the instruments to recognize the stuff.

"If you've calibrated the instruments to recognize this stuff," he said. "Can we scan for it?"

"Not yet," she said. "But I can compare it. And it's clear: what exists in your hand is alive, and what was in hers is dead."

"But mine isn't growing," he said.

"We don't know that," Seymont said. "It's just not growing as rapidly as Natalia's did or as India's initially did."

Then Seymont straightened her shoulders, and glanced at the door.

"Now," she said, "unless you want me to examine the rest of your hand, I need to close you up and go back to my other patients."

"You don't need to examine me anymore," Crowe said, "but I want you to look at Tindo."

"What?" Ibori spoke from behind them, almost like a man coming out of a dream. "Why me?"

"Because you touched Natalia," Crowe said. "Because you've been around all three of us who've been infected."

"I'm not sure I want to know," Ibori said.

"You don't have a choice," Crowe said. "If you've been around us and haven't become infected, we have a piece of data we didn't have before."

"That this spreads only by touch," Seymont said, as if Ibori didn't understand that.

"By touching the *anacapa* drive or anything nearby that…" Crowe stopped. Thought. Realized there was something at the edge of his consciousness.

"What?" Ibori asked.

"…absorbed the *anacapa* energy," Crowe said, slowly. "Whatever this is, it might have to mix with *anacapa* energy to infect us."

"Which means I'm still vulnerable," Ibori said, "because that container lid was off for quite a while, and *anacapa* energy was thick on that bridge."

Crowe suddenly wanted Seymont to conduct more autopsies, to see what was going on with Preemas and the others. But he knew she would refuse.

"Are you seeing any of this in your other patients?" he asked.

"I'm not cutting them open," Seymont said. "I'm healing them."

He nodded. He might end up telling her to look for this. But first, Ibori.

"Please, Tindo," Crowe said. "Do this."

Ibori bit his lower lip. If he refused, Crowe wasn't sure what to do. Crowe hadn't really taken over yet as captain. Would this force him to make the final leap into leading this ship all the way?

"All right," he said. "But where would you look?"

He addressed that last at Seymont.

"You touched Natalia with your bare hands, right?" Seymont asked. "We start there."

Then she turned to Crowe. "I'm going to let the machine close you up."

She didn't ask his permission. She just decided to do that.

And he was all right with it.

He didn't have to look at what the automated hands were doing. And besides, he needed time to think.

He was on the edge of a breakthrough.

He just wasn't sure what, exactly, it was.

THE *RENEGAT*

The bridge smelled different. Justine Breaux felt her stomach turn as she stepped through the main doors and scanned the emptiness. Normally, this place was abuzz with activity, and Captain Preemas had been at the center of it.

Now, there were only a handful of others on the bridge besides herself, and they all seemed really busy. Except Atwater.

He gave her a tentative smile and then made a microshrug with his shoulders, as if he didn't want anyone else to see it.

She should have listened to him. He had contacted her, asking her to help with the research, but encouraging her to go back to her usual research station.

She didn't want to be alone, anywhere, though, and so she decided to come here. Some of that was because she found his presence…not soothing, exactly, but something akin to soothing. Comforting? No. Familiar?

Maybe.

He was one of the few people who actually understood how she felt. When they had all been hiding in the mess, it had been clear that the fighting occurring on the *Renegat* had nothing to do with them.

Now she felt like she was being sucked back into a conflict, one she didn't entirely understand.

She stepped onto the bridge proper, almost ready to bolt. If she went to her quarters, no one would see her for a long time. She could order food, sleep, stay quiet. And get really restless.

And even more scared.

She took a deep breath, then regretted it. That foul smell was underneath everything. Atwater had warned her—he had said that the environmental system on the bridge wasn't keeping up with the mess, and no one had cleaned it up—but she hadn't entirely understood what "the mess" meant.

She could see edges of it, black on the carpet near the *anacapa* container.

No one stood over there. That entire part of the bridge looked neglected.

Atwater was standing near a console that he had never used before. She joined him. Patches of sweat covered his shirt. Since the bridge wasn't overly warm, she had to conclude that the sweat came from nerves. She couldn't smell him, though, because of the underlying stench that seemed to coat everything.

We might have to stay here, he told her when he contacted her. And by *here*, he meant this sector. Far, far away from everything she had known and loved.

She hadn't thought about it much as she came up to the bridge. All she had known was that she didn't want to work alone in the research room. But now that she was here, her stomach twisted.

"Finding anything?" she asked him.

"I'm not working on the local issues," he said.

She found his choice of words odd. *Local issues.* As if they were just dealing with some kind of minor crisis.

"I'm investigating the Scrapheap, at least from here. Doing some other work," he said, apparently being deliberately vague. "You can work over here."

He moved her to a console near his. It looked like one of the tables she used in the research room.

"I'm looking for somewhere we can live," she said, surprised the words didn't twist in her throat.

"Not a habitable planet or moon or even a starbase," he said. "We can find those."

Of course they could. They didn't need her for that.

"Look for something that had been the Fleet's once," he said. "Somewhere that might be familiar. Or something that would accept us."

"How am I supposed to know that?" she asked. "The Fleet hasn't been here for—"

"We know," Atwater said. "Just see what you can find."

Then he went back to his console, his shoulders hunched forward. He seemed defeated, somehow, and she wasn't quite sure how, or what he had learned in the short time they had been apart.

She didn't like the mood up here at all. No one else spoke to her. They all seemed deeply involved in their own work.

A history with the Fleet didn't really matter. The Fleet wouldn't be real to these people, not in this sector. Or would it? Would it be something mythical? Or part of their history? Or would these people here be like the Fleet themselves, people who threw away their history?

Breaux ran a hand through her hair, and tried to figure out how she would even start her search. She needed to access information about the sector, as the sector itself reported it.

She hoped that systems in this sector spoke to systems on the *Renegat*. She hoped that the language was the same. She hoped that somewhere, some culture would be amenable to the crew of the *Renegat*.

Or did she?

Because if she didn't find anything, maybe that would convince everyone on board the ship to try harder to get home.

Home.

She half-smiled at the word. Home was lost to her now. She meant back to the Fleet itself.

The Fleet was home.

And she regretted running away.

Ibori did not seem to be infected with the pink stuff. Short of recalibrating all of the instruments and then trusting that recalibration, Seymont couldn't be sure, of course. But she thought Ibori was clear, and so did Crowe.

He couldn't quite explain the relief he felt when he realized that Ibori was clean. If anyone else should have been infected, it should have been Ibori. And he wasn't.

Which meant that the infection started whenever someone made direct contact with the *anacapa* drives or the containers.

Crowe remained at his table, his hands still isolated, his pinkie throbbing. He didn't mind the throb. It made him realize he had to solve this pink stuff problem before he moved on to anything else.

And he couldn't solve it until he knew what had happened with Ibori. Now that Crowe knew, however, he felt that tickle in his brain grow more insistent.

Only three people had touched anything related to the *anacapa* drive—that he knew of—after the energy blast from the Scrapheap. Him, Romano, and Stephanos. Crowe had put up the shields after Stephanos had died, but before Romano had been tested.

Logically, if the shields had killed whatever was in Romano's hands, the shields should have killed what was in his hands as well. And it hadn't.

So something else was different. Something else had caused the change.

Seymont set Ibori free from the isolation chambers, then turned to Crowe.

"I don't know what to do with you," she said. "Or India for that matter. I don't think you're contagious, but I'll be honest, I don't have the brain power for any of this. I need to get back to the others."

He started to nod, then stopped himself. "Orlena," he said, "do you think that something in Romano's system could have repelled this stuff?"

She gave him a sympathetic look. "I'm sorry, no," she said.

"Convince me," he said.

"It would have done so from the start," she said. "And I saw clear evidence that the pink stuff grew and compromised her blood vessels and nerves, maybe even her muscles. I'm not sure if she will ever heal properly, and I don't have the time to try to fix her."

With that, Seymont started for the door. It was clear that she was thinking about the other patients.

"Wait, Orlena," Crowe said.

"I can't wait," she said. "I've waited long enough."

"Something was different between her and me and Natalia," Crowe said.

"Then figure it out yourself," Seymont said. "She did something different that the two of you didn't do."

"Natalia didn't have time to do anything." That was Ibori, speaking quietly. His voice was shaking. "Her nose started bleeding immediately, and then…."

He shook his head.

Crowe frowned. Nothing like that had happened to him, but by the time he was investigating the bigger *anacapa* drives, he was suited up. The energy field had also been mostly blocked.

Seymont shook herself, as if she had been caught by Ibori's emotion. "Look," she said, "I'll work on this when I have a chance. But right now, it's just the three of you. No offense, Nadim, but I have more pressing problems next door."

And then she pushed her way out of the morgue. He wanted to stop her, but he knew that she was right: she needed to get to the others.

Leaving him to figure out the mystery of what was different.

It had to be something physical, something that had happened to Romano or that she had done that he hadn't.

For the first time, he looked over at her, and wished that she was conscious. He would take the arguing and the viciousness, just to figure out what had changed. Because—

His brain finally stopped tickling.

She was unconscious.

She had been unconscious earlier. He had made her lose consciousness by depriving her of oxygen. Her system had been starving when she lost consciousness.

"Grab Seymont," he said to Hagen.

"She'll be furious," he said.

"I don't care. Get her *now*."

With one quick movement, Hagen set the laser rifle down, and bolted from the room. It only took a few seconds for him to return with a furious Seymont.

"You're wasting my time," she snapped.

"I might be saving your life," he said in return. "I need to know something."

She crossed her arms and leaned back.

"The major physical difference I can think of," he said, "is that I starved Romano of oxygen until she passed out."

"Her and half the people in the med bay," Seymont said, "all of whom need me."

"Would that have starved this...parasite...as you're calling it?"

"I have no idea without conducting experiments I don't have time for," she said.

"What about testing it on me?" he asked. "Can you set that up?"

"You know how dangerous that is," she said. "If I calculate wrong..."

"Then I get what I deserve, at least according to everyone here," he said. "Let's try it."

She glanced at Ibori, and then at Hagen, who had come in behind her.

"We need to replicate the conditions exactly," she said. "Tindo, figure out how long these people were without oxygen, and how slowly the oxygen returned to their systems. When you know that—"

"I'll do it," Hagen said. "I was there. I know mostly what it was."

"Fine," Seymont said. "Once you have it set up, we'll need an isolation chamber for Nadim here—"

"A security chamber," Crowe said. "Let's replicate as much as possible."

"*Fine*," Seymont said, her irritation clear. "Set up the chamber whatever you want it to be, set up the timeline, and come get me. I'll run the damn thing and then I'll check your hands, Nadim."

She had dropped the *Mr. Crowe* somewhere along the way. Crowe was glad of that.

"Sounds good," he said.

"Fine," she said a third time. He was amazed how one word could convey so many moods. This time, the *fine* was dismissive.

She left the room as quickly as she entered it.

"All right, gentlemen," Crowe said. "You heard her. Let's get to work."

THE *RENEGAT*

It took about fifteen minutes to get all of the information that Seymont wanted, and set up the security chamber around Crowe. He had made her take the isolation bubbles off his hands, resting them on the table, wincing slightly at the pain in his little finger.

The tingle in his other fingers remained. He wondered how quickly the pink stuff spread into his system. Another thing to study—if he had time for study.

He had theories too, that he hadn't told any of the other three. Because he was afraid of damaging the experiment they were trying. He didn't want any expectations at all.

But he had already thought of this pink stuff as some kind of weapon that latched on to something in the *anacapa* drive. If the pink stuff remained dormant until it was touched by oxygen, then it became even more lethal.

Because *anacapa* drives only ran in oxygen on occupied ships. The drives could operate without a full environment, and sometimes did, but they thrived in a regular environment as well—an environment with oxygen.

If this pink stuff spread by touch, then it would destroy the engineers who understood *anacapa* drives, and prevent those engineers from solving the problem in any kind of timely manner. It would, effectively, destroy any ability for a vessel with an *anacapa* drive to travel through foldspace, maybe for good.

Crowe didn't understand the rate of the spread—at least in the human body. Maybe it had something to do with the degree of exposure or perhaps it was more complicated than that. But the pink stuff did spread quickly through the *anacapa* drives, which, he suspected, it was built to target.

And who would have done such a thing?

"You ready, Nadim?" Hagen asked.

Crowe looked up. Seymont had returned. She was shifting from foot to foot as if she couldn't wait for this to get underway.

She probably couldn't. She still had a lot of patients to deal with on the other side.

Just like he had an entire ship to deal with, once this was solved.

Crowe's chest hurt. His heart was beating faster than it had a moment ago. They had cut the oxygen before they had told him they were going to do it.

He thought about holding his breath, then changed his mind. None of the people he had knocked unconscious outside of engineering had held their breath. They hadn't realized what he was doing until too late.

And Hagen was doing the same thing here.

Crowe met his gaze, then gave Hagen a half nod of respect. The nod hurt.

All of Crowe's muscles started to ache. Or maybe they had already been aching. He wasn't sure. But he did know that he was starting to feel pain everywhere, and the places where there had been pain hurt even worse than they had before.

Even though he knew what was happening, he tried to take a deep breath, and got nothing. A panic built inside him. He needed to get out of this security barrier. They weren't going to let him out either. This had been his idea, and he was going to die here.

Part of his brain watched the panic with expected amusement. He had panicked at the loss of oxygen on all of his environmental suit tests back in school—or rather, he had felt panic, but hadn't acted on it.

You would've been captain-track if you didn't have so many blemishes on your record.

One of his teachers had told him that. But who, he couldn't remember. He couldn't remember anything. He couldn't remember the insights he had had a few moments ago about that pink stuff.

The insights were important.

Saving the *Renegat* was important.

Sitting here was important.

He just didn't know why.

THE *RENEGAT*

When Crowe passed out, he fell sideways, hitting his shoulder on the barrier, and then bouncing in the other direction, and slamming his head on the table. The sound reverberated in the small space, making Ibori jump.

"Will that make a difference?" he asked Seymont.

She was looking at the readings on the screen floating in front of her. So was Hagen, the laser rifle near the door. Romano was still asleep on her gurney. Ibori had realized, sometime in the last hour, that Romano's unconsciousness had nothing to do with her injury any longer and everything to do with convenience.

"Will what make a difference?" Seymont asked. She sounded annoyed. She'd been sounding annoyed for some time now, and Ibori didn't blame her. Apparently, she hadn't even been able to finish working on the case she had started before Crowe arrived in the med bay.

"Him hitting his head!" Ibori's voice rose even though he didn't want it to. He sounded almost panicked, or maybe he was panicked. He didn't want to watch anyone else die today.

"Oh." Seymont looked up. Apparently she hadn't even noticed. She stared at Crowe for a moment. "No. The oxygen is what we care about."

One of Crowe's hands had fallen off the table, and the other was sliding down slowly. Ibori couldn't see from his position, but he thought maybe there was some blood on the table too.

Head wounds bled. He remembered that from his field medicine training. Head wounds bled more than expected. He couldn't panic.

But he was.

He was so tired that everything was a crisis. Then he let out a small laugh. Maybe everything seemed like a crisis because everything *was* a crisis.

"You're waking him up, right? What if he doesn't—"

"Stop, Tindo." Seymont sounded exhausted. "We're following the plan."

"But he hit his head. If he doesn't—"

"That's why I'm here," she said. "I'll deal with whatever comes up."

Crowe's other hand slipped off the table, and swung just a bit. He wasn't waking up. Ibori shot a glance at Hagen, who was looking at numbers as well.

"How long did it take the others to wake up?" Ibori asked.

"We brought them back slowly." That wasn't a real answer, and Hagen knew it. "The question is, how long should we wait to check to see if that stuff died in Crowe's hand?"

He addressed that to Seymont. It was as if Ibori wasn't in the room.

He kinda wasn't. He had no function here, which was probably also why he was fluttering around like a worried child. He made himself take a deep breath—saw the irony in that—and then shook his head slightly.

He needed to calm down. There was a lull in all of the activity and it was making him react—or rather, letting his reactions come to the surface.

He still didn't have time for reactions. He needed to focus, and to figure out what to do next.

"I think we can check as soon as he's conscious," Seymont was saying to Hagen. "If the lack of oxygen caused the die-off in Romano, then it would have happened fast."

Crowe moaned and brought his right hand to his forehead. He didn't lift his head, though.

Ibori was glad to see the movement, glad to hear the moan.

Hagen and Seymont didn't seem to have an emotional reaction at all, though. They continued, as if Crowe hadn't done anything.

Crowe sat up. Blood had run down the right side of his face from a cut on his forehead. His right hand was on the cut, even though he probably shouldn't have touched it.

"Nadim," Seymont said. "I'm going to need to slice another finger."

That had been so painful. Ibori thought he had been able to handle pain well, but having Seymont slice into his finger, not an hour ago, had been one of the most painful things he had ever experienced.

He had mentioned it to her, and she had laughed. *It's the nerve endings in the fingertip*, she had said. *Fingers are designed to be extremely sensitive.*

And they were. His index finger on his right hand still ached from the slice.

Crowe winced, nodded, and then winced again. "Same hand?" he asked.

"Yes," she said. "Hold that hand above the table. We're going to have to clean the table off anyway."

"My head hurts." Crowe was speaking slowly.

"I bet it does," Seymont said. She had no bedside manner at all. It was clear that she wanted to be somewhere else. "We'll worry about that in a minute. Hand up, please."

Crowe half-closed his eyes, started to raise his right hand, then stopped. He raised his left hand, and held it, palm up.

One of the isolation bubbles formed around the hand. Ibori moved slightly to the right, so that he could see. He had already opened a small screen that was tied to the equipment Seymont had used before.

Ibori wanted to see if this experiment worked—in real time.

A surgical hand formed underneath Crowe's left hand, holding it in place. When that surgical hand had held Ibori's, the grip had been firm and impossible to shake off.

The second surgical hand formed inside the bubble, a scalpel instead of the index finger. This time, Ibori looked away. He didn't need to see that again—and be reminded of how it felt.

Even though his own finger throbbed in sympathy.

Crowe's entire body jerked.

Ibori looked at the screen floating near him. He remembered what he had seen before—the pink against the veins, the abnormal material nestled under the skin.

He had been relieved when that hadn't shown up in his reading. He was still relieved.

It took a moment for the small camera to focus on the interior of Crowe's finger. There seemed to be dirt on the lens. Ibori was about to tell Seymont to wipe the dirt off, when he realized what he was seeing.

The pink stuff had died.

Crowe had been right.

The lack of oxygen had killed it.

"It worked?" Ibori breathed.

"Looks like it." Seymont sounded so matter of fact. And yet, this discovery, this thing that had just happened, might well save all of their lives. For good. She should have been more excited.

"It worked?" Crowe echoed. He tilted his head back, his skin a weird shade of greenish gray, probably from the lack of oxygen.

"Let me finish before I declare victory." As Seymont said that, the scooping finger ran over the wound in Crowe's finger.

Hagen was tapping the screens in front of him as she did so.

"Yeah." Hagen's voice lilted upwards with the beginnings of a disbelieving joy. "Yeah. It's the same stuff you pulled out of Romano. The lack of oxygen killed that shit dead."

Ibori let out a half laugh. He had hoped for it, but hadn't expected it.

Seymont leaned her head back and closed her eyes.

Crowe laughed. Ibori wasn't ever sure he had heard Crowe laugh before.

"What does this mean?" Ibori asked. "We're going to pull the oxygen from the *Renegat*?"

"No need," Hagen said. "We can deal with the *anacapa* drives on their own, and anyone who might be contaminated, we do this to."

Ibori nodded, weak-kneed with relief.

"What does this mean?" Crowe repeated, as if Hagen hadn't spoken.

"It means we had a victory," Seymont said. "I hadn't realized how much I needed one."

"It means," Crowe said, his voice stronger than it had been a moment before, "that we have a future. We just need to figure out how to implement it."

PART FORTY-ONE
A CENTURY AND CHANGE
NOW

THE *AIZSARGS*

Dauber was beginning to recognize the survivors by their faces alone. Not that she had met everyone—she hadn't—but she had looked at quite a bit of footage from the *Renegat* as she was trying to figure out exactly what had happened to it.

She watched the *Renegat* survivors slowly enter the same large room where Anna Vail had first talked with them. That time, the room had been set up for a short meeting. None of the furniture had arisen from the floor. There were sideboards with food, but not a lot.

This time, the sideboards remained but they had abundant food of all types. There was water as well, but no stimulants and no alcohol. Rows of chairs had risen out of their places in the floor, as tight as Dauber could make them and still have room for the nearly 200 survivors from that ship.

Counselors and security were strategically placed between the sideboards, and a few were already standing in the back, doing their best to blend in to the dark wall.

Dauber fully expected half of the survivors to melt down somehow. She'd seen it before, when she had done her short stint on foldspace search vehicles. Then, she had only had to observe as the captain of the search ship informed a dozen crew members of a rescued ship that they had lost twenty years.

Twenty years had been traumatic, but at least most friends and family had still been alive when those dozen crew members had returned. She doubted anyone that the *Renegat* survivors had known were still living. Long life was rare, particularly among the traveling Fleet. She had heard of people living longer than 150 years, some as high as 200 years, on some of the former sector bases, but most humans barely made it past their 130s.

Anyone the survivors had known would have had to have been very young when the survivors disappeared. And, Dauber knew from the research, most of the survivors had left no friends or family behind. Maybe that would make this news easier.

Last night and this morning, she had reviewed the protocol for telling survivors of foldspace that they had lost time. Few people reacted well. And, the materials said, the ones she had to watch out for the most were the ones who responded stoically, because they might get ambushed by their emotions at a much later date.

That was for standard crews, lost in foldspace on a routine mission. Nothing had been routine for the *Renegat*.

Dauber stood on the small raised platform at the front of the room, and watched as the survivors made their way inside. A handful had wheelchairs and other apparatus that still startled her. Fleet medicine was good, more than good enough to repair serious damage that people suffered.

But only when they had access to the proper care and the right kind of medical professionals. She hadn't really realized, until she saw the *Renegat* survivors, how important connection among all the Fleet ships truly was.

It took a lot of restraint for her to keep from nodding at the various faces she recognized. So far, she had only personally met with six survivors, and the longest meeting she had had was with Serpell. It had also been the most frustrating.

But the others hadn't really been helpful either. They all seemed to tell the same story, and sometimes it was spoken slowly and cautiously as if the person speaking was trying to remember the proper words they had been told to say.

The last of the survivors straggled in. The most severely injured gathered near Dauber's left, far from the door.

Everyone else stood in front of the chairs but didn't sit down. Either they were waiting for permission to take a chair or they weren't sure exactly what they were supposed to do.

"Please sit," Dauber said. Three of the people in the front row glanced at the chairs as if the chair might hurt them. But they sat.

Only a handful of people in the back continued to stand, and Dauber realized that there were no empty chairs near them. She waved a hand at Vilma Lauritz, who was in the back with the counselors. Lauritz and several members of her security team were nearby in case some of the survivors reacted violently.

Having them seated would minimize the impact. If they fainted or their knees gave way, they would already be sitting. If they wanted to hit something, they would have to stand, which would automatically draw attention to them.

Lauritz touched controls on the wall, and brought up two more rows of chairs in the back.

The rest of the survivors then sat down.

"Thank you all for coming," Dauber said. "I'm Captain Kim Dauber. I am pleased to have you all on board the *Aizsargs*."

Raina Serpell sat in the very center of the room, her hands folded in her lap, her head down. Yusef Kabac sat at her left, and kept glancing at her. Dauber worked hard to avoid Kabac's gaze. The man had been annoying in their short session. He had been trying to impress Dauber, and his know-it-all attitude had pushed her away instead.

If she hadn't seen the report from some of the survivors identifying him as the one who got the doors to one of the *Renegat*'s cargo bays open at the potential risk of his own life, she would have thought him a worthless idiot. Instead, she figured he was clueless and directionless, the kind of person who didn't learn easily and didn't take advice well.

"I'm sure many of you have noticed some of the unusual restrictions we placed on you when you boarded the *Aizsargs*," Dauber said. "These are part of a protocol that we are required to follow in cases like yours."

"There are cases like ours?" one of the injured women—Lakinas?—muttered just loud enough for Dauber to hear.

Dauber did not acknowledge the comment. She wasn't going to let anything pull her off script.

"There is no easy way to tell you all this," she said. "So I am going to do so bluntly and with no dancing around. The *Renegat* left on its mission more than one hundred years ago."

There was a collective gasp around the room.

"By the time we found you," Dauber said, "you had been officially considered lost for over ninety years. Unofficially, the Fleet considered you lost two months after your last contact with the vice admiral who had approved your mission."

"Vice Admiral Gāo?" someone asked.

That comment Dauber did acknowledge. "Yes," she said into the direction of the voice.

All of the survivors were looking at her directly now, even Serpell, whose face was a mask of anguish. Dauber's heart twisted, but she didn't let her emotion show on her face.

"They wrote us off?" someone else asked. "We were doing something dangerous *and they wrote us off?*"

Dauber couldn't tell where the voice had come from, but the security team toward the back left moved just enough to let her know they had seen the person who had spoken. One of the counselors put a hand out, blocking the team from doing anything.

Apparently, the counselor wanted them all to wait, to see how this played out.

"Unfortunately," Dauber said, loudly enough to keep the survivors' attention, "the Fleet has had to develop systems to deal with a loss of time in foldspace. The systems—"

"We didn't lose the time in foldspace," a woman yelled. "I know we didn't. We kept track of everything. We weren't becalmed or anything. We weren't trapped—"

"Please," Dauber said, holding up her hand. "I know this is hard."

"You have no idea," Lakinas said. "You have no damn idea. You're—"

"Please," Dauber said, more forcefully this time. "Let me continue and you'll—"

"Continue?" Lakinas said, even louder this time. "So that you can cover your ass with the Fleet. Yes, Admiral. I followed procedure. They were still upset—"

Dauber clapped her hands together. The sound reverberated off the walls.

"Now that I have your attention again," she said, "we will be following a procedure developed after you folks disappeared. It has been shown to ease the transition."

"*Ease*?" a man yelled from the back. "You can't *ease* one hundred years."

"The Fleet knows, from experience," Dauber continued, "that it will take a long time and a lot of counseling to deal with what's happened to you—"

"You have no idea what happened to us," a woman named Jane Zerpa said, her voice wobbling. Zerpa had been one of the few Dauber had talked with. "The deaths, the fights, the attack. You have no idea. And now we're here. It was getting back to the Fleet that drove us. Don't you understand?"

Dauber did understand. She would have been the same way.

She gave Zerpa, a large woman who seemed to be forever on edge, her most compassionate gaze.

"I do understand," Dauber said. "I would have wanted to come home too."

Voices rumbled beneath hers as the survivors turned toward each other, or tried to ask questions, or moaned into their hands, which were now covering some of their mouths.

"The Fleet is eternal," she said. "It's not that different than it was a hundred years ago."

Although she didn't know that for certain. She wasn't sure if she was lying or not. She assumed not, but she couldn't know. She was certain small things were different.

"The Fleet has a system for finding relatives," she said.

"They chose us because we didn't have relatives," Declan Connolly said. He had spent a lot of time on the *Renegat*'s bridge, which was why Dauber had talked with him. During their short interview, he had had trouble meeting her gaze.

"I know," she said. "But you had friends. You had a life."

A number of people were shaking their heads.

"We will help you through this," Dauber said, deciding to go back on to the script. "There are counselors in the back who will meet with you. All of you need to have at least one mandatory meeting with a counselor. You can choose to have more if you want."

And the counselors might choose for you, was the next sentence she was supposed to say, but she didn't. These people seemed stressed enough.

They were shifting in their chairs. Some had their heads down, hands stuck in their hair, maybe even covering their ears.

A few were watching her with tears streaming down their faces.

"I'm not going to say that everything will be all right," she said. "You did go through hell to get here. We realize that, and we know that will have an impact on everything that happens to you going forward."

A few more people looked up.

Dauber's gaze met Serpell's. Serpell was one of the stoic ones the Fleet protocol warned about. But her nose had turned red, and her teeth were visibly holding down her lower lip.

"We are going to take you to Starbase Sigma," Dauber said, "and there—"

"*Sigma*?" Kabac said, his voice nearly a wail. "The Fleet just finished Starbase Rho."

Serpell closed her eyes, and a tear caught the light as it meandered its way down her face.

Dauber nodded. "You will have a lot of disconcerting moments like that one," she said. "I'm not trying to normalize it. I am trying to warn you. A number of things are different. We will get you to Starbase Sigma. They have facilities that will help you—"

"You're going to incarcerate us there," Lakinas said. "The Fleet sends survivors to sector bases, not starbases. Starbases handle legal."

"They did," Dauber said, not quite lying. Starbases still handled legal. "Please do remember, as you try to filter information we're telling you, that some things are different in this time period."

"God," someone moaned, and that led to a cacophony of sound—yells, cries, sobs. People were hunched over, their shoulders shaking. Others had their arms around each other.

Still, a handful continued to gaze at Dauber as if she could give them some kind of answer that would make them feel better.

Not that she could.

She clapped her hands again. The sound carried, and several people jumped as if they had been shot.

But the noise stopped.

"You will remain on this deck," Dauber said, "unless you're being escorted to a counseling appointment. We're going to open up the computer network a bit, so that you can read the history of the past hundred years, and catch up on Fleet business."

"But we can't try to contact anyone we used to know, right?" Connolly asked, his voice bitter.

"Not yet," Dauber said. "Some of the things you will want to do are beyond our capability here on the *Aizsargs*. You'll be able to do most everything when you get to Starbase Sigma."

She hoped. She didn't exactly know, but at that point, these people wouldn't be her problem anymore.

She didn't tell them that they would be debriefed. Nor did she tell them that she had already sent all of the *Renegat* records to the justice unit on Starbase Sigma. That unit would decide how to handle these people.

Her decision-making for them was done. She had decided that she couldn't deal with everything that had gone wrong on their ship, and that the Fleet itself needed to figure out what to do with these survivors, not her.

Maybe that was the coward's way out. It seemed that way as she looked at nearly two hundred distraught people. She felt an incredible compassion for them and their situation—they had survived hell, probably by thinking about home.

Only their home was gone. Everything they knew had been destroyed.

And she, in following procedure, was going to make things worse.

Because she suspected they had done some things in their quest for survival that went against all of the Fleet's protocols.

"I don't suppose we have a choice." Serpell spoke with great force. Dauber finally understood why the others had followed her.

They all looked at Serpell now. The crying had stopped, although sniffling continued from various points in the room. The counselors had moved a bit closer, but still hadn't joined the group.

Dauber wasn't sure she understood the question. "A choice?"

"We can't ask you to drop us somewhere else," Serpell said. "We have to go to Starbase Sigma, don't we?"

Fascinating idea, that they could chose to end up somewhere else. Dauber wasn't sure where that came from. Maybe Lakinas's comment about the legal ramifications of their journey.

"I don't have a choice," Dauber said. "Fleet procedure for rescues like this requires me to bring the survivors to a place of the Fleet's choosing."

She left off the part that she had recommended which of the two options the *Renegat* survivors would have to take.

"Where you go from there," she said, "is not up to me. I don't know that procedure. I've never been a part of it."

"We have to go to Starbase Sigma, whether we want to or not," Serpell said.

"Yes," Dauber said. "We will arrive in just a few days. Please use the time you have here to talk with our counselors and figure out how to move forward again."

"Yeah," said that male voice she couldn't identify. "Because moving backwards worked so damn well for us."

Half the survivors laughed, a strange bitter sound.

Dauber frowned. They had gone backwards, at the Fleet's direction. She hadn't really thought of that in depth before, how unnatural that trip must have seemed.

"I wish I had better news," she said to the group. "But we will do everything in our power to help you."

Then she beckoned the counselors and security to move forward, and essentially surround the survivors.

Conversations rose, mixed with cries of anguish and some ugly sobbing.

Serpell continued to stare at Dauber as if Serpell were trying to figure out Dauber's motivation.

Dauber wanted to say, *If you had been honest with me, maybe you would have been able to go to a sector base. Maybe you wouldn't have to go through that extra step.*

But she didn't, of course. She couldn't.

Besides, she wasn't sure that comment was true. The Fleet did have procedures, particularly for ships that returned without their captains.

The *Renegat* had no senior officers at all, and that was suspicious.

It seemed even more suspicious to Dauber now. Serpell seemed almost angry at this turn of events—not at the lost time, but at the destination.

Then Dauber turned away from her, away from all of them, and reminded herself that the anger might have been misplaced. The anger might have been about the lost time, but Serpell (and some of the others) might choose to blame Dauber instead.

Dauber glanced over her shoulder. A number of the survivors were standing now. A few were holding each other. The counselors were talking to people on the fringes of the crowd, and some of Dauber's junior officers were standing near the door, taking names of the people who were trying to flee the room for somewhere more private.

She slipped out the side, entered a small corridor that allowed her to walk back to the elevators undetected.

She leaned against the wall and closed her eyes.

She had known today would be hard. She had even anticipated the anger. But she hadn't quite understood what was behind Serpell's stare. Fury yes, but something else.

Betrayal? Terror?

Dauber closed her eyes. In sending the survivors to Starbase Sigma, she had vacated any right to solve the mysteries of the *Renegat* herself.

And, she realized, she was all right with that.

She wanted these people off her ship. They felt dangerous to her—and she wanted them gone.

PART FORTY-TWO

SAVING THE *RENEGAT*

100 YEARS AGO

THE *RENEGAT ORBITER ONE*

Crowe felt like a nervous boy again, about to embark on something he knew was wrong. Only he wasn't waiting for his team in the children's mess. He stood in the cockpit of the *Renegat Orbiter One*, something one of his former captains called a ship-to-shore vessel, after long ago sailing vessels.

Crowe had chosen *Orbiter One* because it did not have an *anacapa* drive, but it did have speed. It had the most powerful force fields of all the small ships on the *Renegat.* And *Orbiter One* also had some laser canons and a few directional weapons should anything go wrong.

His palms were wet, and his fingertips still ached. The fingers that Seymont had sliced open hurt when he brushed them against anything, but that was a small price to pay for the knowledge he had gathered.

The knowledge made him confident, and the confidence had helped him officially take over the *Renegat.* As he told the entire remaining crew, someone had to lead them. He made a shipwide announcement after he'd had some sleep and things settled down in the brig.

He had told everyone about the threats from the Scrapheap, and the weapon he had discovered. He called the pink stuff the anti-*anacapa* weapon, since it chewed up *anacapa* drives from the inside. He told the ship that they were lucky that the small medical and engineering team had figured out how that weapon killed humans as well, and how to stop it.

He wiped his hands on the outside of his environmental suit. He had brought six others with him on *Orbiter One*. Bakhr sat near the console, monitoring the energy coming off the Scrapheap.

Ibori was piloting. It turned out that he had a lot more experience in that realm, particularly with small ships, than Titus M'Ghan did. M'Ghan remained on the bridge of the *Renegat,* along with Atwater, Ellum, and Rodriguez.

Willoughby ran engineering, which Crowe still kept guarded as if it held all of the secrets.

Tosidis sat nervously beside Ibori, threading his fingers together. Tosidis hadn't done much outside-the-ship work, past his training, but he was a smart engineer and he knew a lot about systems.

Crowe missed Stephanos tremendously. He needed an *anacapa* expert now, and he didn't have one. He was going to have to rely on the team he had here.

Most of them sat in the cockpit, pretending to be relaxed. Tasneem Zhang even had her head back and eyes closed. Everyone else was studying the Scrapheap as it loomed ahead of them.

Besides Crowe, only two others stood. Yulia Colvin was actually pacing, and next to her, Danika Newark continually adjusted her environmental suit, as if it didn't quite meet her standards.

Newark was the surprise. Crowe had brought her along because of Colvin.

Crowe had learned, by examining the records, that Colvin had a lot of exterior repair experience. She had often gone outside of ships, investigating problems on ships' hulls and patching equipment in zero-G environments.

Her various promotions had taken her away from that. When Crowe had asked her about her experiences, she had smiled. *I loved working in space*, she had said. *I'd love to explore those ships in the Scrapheap.*

But she had had one condition: she wanted to bring an experienced partner.

Apparently, on some ship in their history, they had actually been repair buddies. According to Colvin, Newark was one of the few people who knew how to stay calm when working outside of a ship.

Crowe had started to protest, and then he remembered the one thing that Preemas had taught him about the *Renegat*: almost everyone had been in the wrong job for the wrong reason. Crowe had thought that Preemas found Newark's expertise when he moved her to the chef position, but Preemas had ignored her extensive experience working in zero-G.

Maybe Preemas hadn't thought he would need it.

When Crowe looked up those experiences in Newark's record, he found commendation after commendation. Then she had been promoted above her skill level and, apparently, over her own protests. She hadn't wanted to move up. She had wanted to keep the job she had trained for.

She seemed a lot calmer now than the woman he had known as first officer. She had actually given him a small smile when she had boarded *Orbiter One*.

He hadn't smiled in return.

This mission was a serious one, made more serious by his history with Scrapheaps.

In the few hours of sleep he'd managed over the past few days, he'd had two memory-nightmares about the Scrapheap exploding.

This Scrapheap was completely different. It had a malfunctioning and half-ruined protective force field, a lot of empty places where ships had been, pieces of older ships so damaged as to be almost unidentifiable, and a central tower that looked like someone had dug holes into it.

The Ready Vessels still seemed protected, but he could see the ghostly shapes of them through their force field. And that told him either the force field was malfunctioning or it was slowly losing power.

He also knew it was possible that it had been designed differently than the force fields he was used to.

He'd been thinking a lot about force fields and shields lately because, he realized as he worked on understanding the anti-*anacapa* weapon, that the Fleet had encountered it before. The shields on the *Renegat* had been designed to block the weapon's infiltration of the vessel.

Preemas's failure to arrive in this sector shielded had caused the weapon's invasion. Although Crowe couldn't put the failure entirely on Preemas. If the Fleet kept track of its history, the entire *Renegat* would have known that there were weapons that had targeted the Fleet's most essential drive, and the *Renegat* would have been prepared.

Crowe did not like to think about the implications of the weapon—that some culture somewhere had targeted the Fleet so specifically, and so effectively, causing severe problems. The weapon also showed a sophisticated understanding of the *anacapa* drive, which meant that whoever had developed this weapon might have had a better understanding of the drive than the Fleet did.

Atwater had wanted to discuss all of that, but Crowe had brushed him off. What Crowe had needed, he told Atwater, was a way to guarantee that any drive brought back to the *Renegat* was free of the weapon. Atwater was now searching through the databases, trying to see if the Fleet had—in its distant past—developed a test for finding the weapon.

Crowe also had Willoughby put a team together to reverse engineer the block against the weapon in the shield. If the shield could stop the weapon's energy, then the shield could identify the threat in that energy.

Crowe needed the *Renegat's* computer system to be able to identify the weapon as well.

He ran his right hand over his face. His skin was damp, mostly from nerves. The environmental system in the cockpit of *Orbiter One* was working just fine.

But he was on edge, and that edge got sharper and sharper as he got closer and closer to the Scrapheap.

The plan was that *Orbiter One* would enter the Scrapheap in the biggest opening in the Scrapheap's force field. Crowe had already set up *Orbiter One*'s shipwide identification band, so that it reflected not just modern Standard, but a version of Standard that they had found in the information that had gotten sent to the Fleet all that time ago.

One of the linguists, Raina Serpell, had helped him design that, even though a few people in engineering had told him not to use her assistance. She was married to India Romano, and although she hadn't rebelled with Romano, most of the crew saw Serpell as compromised by Romano.

Crowe didn't care who was compromised by whom. As he had said in his shipwide announcement, the crew had to work together now to survive. They needed each other.

He wished he had the full crew complement, but he had to leave the worst of the rebels in the brig. And then there were the injured and the dying in the med bay. Some of them, Seymont told him, would never recover fully, even if they survived.

Crowe moved to the pilot's chair, standing slightly behind Ibori, trying not to let his own tension infect anyone. Like he had done all of those years ago, Crowe had actually modeled this trip into the Scrapheap. He had run simulation after simulation, looking for the best way in. He had had Bakhr run similar simulations.

They both found the same entry into the Scrapheap, and the same possible cautions near the force field surrounding the Ready Vessels.

From what Crowe could tell, there were still working *anacapa* drives in the Ready Vessels. He couldn't get readings, but the Ready Vessels looked mostly untouched.

He hoped they were.

The *Renegat* needed two working *anacapa* drives and a communications *anacapa*, if they could find one. If they couldn't, he wasn't going to worry about it. Communications *anacapa* drives were luxuries. He didn't need to contact the Fleet right now anyway, especially given what had happened a few days ago.

He resisted the urge to ask Ibori if he was clear on the plan. They had gone over the coordinates half a dozen times already. At one point, Ibori had given Crowe a sideways look.

"What are you worried about?" Ibori had asked.

That this ship will cause the entire Scrapheap to explode. The thought had crossed Crowe's brain before he could stop it. But he didn't say that. He also didn't say, *Nothing*, which was his default response.

Instead, he had answered honestly. "I'm worried about this entire journey," he had said. "We need this."

Strangely, he wasn't worried about his part in it. He hadn't worked in zero-G outside of a ship in a decade or more. And he hadn't been particularly good at the work when he had done it. He preferred to work and think in the comfort of an engineering bay or a bridge. He didn't like working with gloves covering his fingers, and an environmental suit his only protection between him and the coldness of space.

But he was going to do it now. He needed to look at the *anacapa* drives himself. Right now, he didn't really trust anyone else.

"Okay," Ibori said. "We're approaching now."

Technically, they had been approaching all along. But what Ibori meant was *Orbiter One* was finally nearing the space around the Scrapheap where—in modern Scrapheaps at least—the Scrapheap's defenses would activate.

Crowe probably should have sat down and strapped in. But he didn't. He placed his hands on the back of Ibori's chair, making Ibori turn slightly and glare at him.

But Crowe didn't want to move. He wanted to see this as the pilot did. Ibori had a circle of screens around him. Colvin had called up some floating screens and was monitoring *Orbiter One's* passage as well.

Crowe appreciated that. She clearly had a system for working outside of the ship, and he wasn't going to interfere with it.

Bakhr had a group of screens floating around him as well. Crowe had given Bakhr permission to alter the shields on *Orbiter One* as needed to compensate for any energy coming off the Scrapheap. That Bakhr also thought the Scrapheap might target them made Crowe feel a little better.

His mouth was dry, though, and he kept quiet. He knew he was too distracted to command this little ship at the best of his ability. He had to trust the others here, and he was.

Tosidis leaned forward and called up a holographic representation of the Scrapheap and *Orbiter One. Orbiter One,* glowing yellow on the hologram, looked like a speck of dust about to enter a planet.

Crowe did not look at the representation anymore. Instead, he watched what Ibori was watching, *Orbiter One* moving ever closer to the edge of the Scrapheap.

The Scrapheap's force fields crackled and flared, as if they were malfunctioning in some of the smaller areas. Crowe was beginning to think that most of the Scrapheap's defenses were down, when a red light spread across the remaining ships.

The red light sent a jolt of adrenaline through Crowe. For a brief, ugly, half second, he thought maybe *Orbiter One* had somehow ignited the interior of the Scrapheap, even though he knew that was impossible.

Orbiter One hadn't even entered the Scrapheap yet.

"What's that?" Tosidis asked as the red light circled around the entire Scrapheap.

"Central tower." Ibori sounded preoccupied.

"Doing what?" Newark asked.

"If I knew, I'd tell you," Ibori said.

"They got our identification?" Bakhr asked, with just a tinge of panic in his voice.

"I sure hope so," Ibori said. "I've been sending it since we left the *Renegat.*"

Crowe willed himself to remain calm. It was hard. That red light had ignited all those old memories, which weren't buried as deep as he had hoped.

He could almost hear Tessa's voice: *You better pay up, buddy.*

Pay up. He'd been doing that his whole life. And now he was trying to do it again. He needed to save the remaining crew of the *Renegat.*

That thought made him focus.

"Use that old channel we set up," he said to Ibori. "Put the identification message in old Standard on repeat from that channel."

"I'll do it," Tosidis said. Clearly Preemas's structure remained with this crew. Orders were something to be ignored, or not followed to the letter.

Crowe only half-cared. He wanted the crew to get this done, no matter how they did it.

The red light caught *Orbiter One*. He could see it on the representation first, and then on one of Ibori's screens.

"Has that light changed the energy readings around the Scrapheap?" he asked Bakhr.

"Nope." Bakhr sounded calmer than Crowe expected. "The energy readings are still a complete mess of various signatures, but nothing is ramping up."

"Good," Crowe said. He glanced at that central tower in the representation. The tower wasn't that far from the gigantic hole in the Scrapheap's force field.

He had measured that hole as he ran the simulations. It was the size of a small moon. They had a pretty clear path from that entry point to the Ready Vessels. Most of the large ships had been removed from that area. Even the ones on the imagery sent back to the Fleet—the ones that had been replaced with non-Fleet vessels were gone.

Orbiter One's trajectory took it through the center of that hole, into the very middle of the emptiness. Although emptiness wasn't really what they faced. More like an area filled with small traps, mostly composed of parts of ships and unidentified pieces of technology.

Crowe hadn't even tried to figure out what tech was causing the various energy signatures. When Bakhr ran his simulations, he tried to figure out the energy signatures first, and had no real luck. He had come to Crowe and said that to figure out the signatures first would take at least a week, maybe more.

They both had agreed that the *Renegat* didn't have that kind of time.

Not because the *Renegat* was low on stores or because of any kind of pressure from the outside. But because the remaining crew was restless. Many of them were terrified of being trapped in this sector. They all wanted the freedom that the *anacapa* drive gave them—even if the entire ship decided never to use the drive again.

Crowe's fingers dug into the back of Ibori's chair, prompting Ibori to give Crowe another filthy look.

Crowe almost lifted his hands off the back of the chair, but didn't. He couldn't, really. He needed the support—especially as *Orbiter One* slid firmly into the Scrapheap itself.

The young Crowe—the Crowe with imagination and dreams—had thought the interior of a Scrapheap would be a magical place, filled with great ships that had had stirring histories and equipment that he had only seen in ancient tech blueprints.

The actual inside, of this Scrapheap, anyway, was a lot more prosaic. The name suited it. The junk *Orbiter One* threaded its way through was—as far as he could tell—just that. Bits of ships and parts of equipment that seemed to have no use at all.

The only difference from what his younger self had expected was that these pieces were stationary. There was something in the Scrapheap that held all the various ships and parts of ships in place.

But that something didn't have an impact on *Orbiter One*. The ship managed to follow its plotted trajectory as if it were being pulled forward by one of those beams of light.

Crowe glanced at the representation of the tower again. The light had shut itself off. The tower looked dormant.

He wondered if that meant that the tower had accepted *Orbiter One* as a Fleet vessel, or if that function had been completely shut off.

"Wow." Newark was watching a smaller hologram, one that showed the area around *Orbiter One* in three dimensions. "Is that a Dignity Vessel?"

She actually used a phrase the Fleet refused to use. Dignity Vessel was the original name of DV-Class ships, but somewhere along the way, the Fleet had not only dropped that name but actively started discouraging its use.

So when she said Dignity Vessel, she meant a Dignity Vessel.

Crowe looked at the ship Newark was pointing to. It looked ancient. Its design was smaller than the DV-Class ships he was used to, and it looked like it had been soldered together with some kind of ancient tool. The ship didn't appear to be made of nanobits, but of some kind of metal instead.

But it had the familiar frame of a DV-Class vessel, minus the curves over the small winged area, and it was definitely a Fleet design.

Newark looked over her shoulder and gave him a grin. He hadn't seen her this animated since her first day as the ship's chef. He had no idea she loved old ships.

He didn't. He liked newer, more modern equipment, and he was going to say so, but by then, *Orbiter One* had gone past the Dignity Vessel, and was wending its way through a bunch of square objects, that looked like parts of the Dignity Vessel itself.

"We'll be at that secondary force field in less than five minutes," Ibori said. His voice held no trace of nerves whatsoever. Which was good, because Crowe had become a basket of them.

The secondary force field was the third major hurdle that *Orbiter One* had to get past. First the external defenses. Then entering the Scrapheap. And finally crossing into the Ready Vessel area without a hitch.

This time, Crowe went to the chair he had assigned himself toward the back of the cockpit.

"Let's strap in this time," he said to Newark and Colvin. "I have a hunch this is going to be harder than it looks."

THE *RENEGAT ORBITER ONE*

Ibori felt more alert and alive than he had in nearly a week. He had forgotten how much he liked to pilot small vessels. *Orbiter One* was a great, responsive little ship. He could move it with the touch of a finger.

He had practiced on it before they had left, and had been pleased to discover that it also had an excellent autopilot function. If he couldn't operate the ship at full capacity, the autopilot should accurately follow any trajectory he programmed into it.

He had programmed their trip into the autopilot before they left, and had instructed it to avoid any pieces of debris in its path. He had only set up the autopilot as a backup.

He was piloting the ship by hand, simply because it gave him such pleasure—and pleasure had been in short supply recently.

He had thought he would need all of his skills to pilot *Orbiter One*, though, because he had expected a lot more random debris and pieces of ships along the trajectory he had chosen.

So far, there had been no debris or pieces of equipment or detached parts of ships, which led him to believe that he was following an actual path, something carved out of the Scrapheap by the thieves who had been here long before the *Renegat* ever arrived in this sector—maybe thousands of years before Ibori had even been born.

The Scrapheap itself was a marvel. The ships and debris were held in place by strong waves of energy that actually made the space around them seem solid. The energy waves buffeted *Orbiter One*, rocking it along the path.

He had had to concentrate when he first entered the Scrapheap because he hadn't expected the energy waves to have an impact on *Orbiter One*. When he realized that they did, he had moved slightly to one side, and that was where he had discovered the path. It was almost like a pocket trail built into the Scrapheap itself.

He suspected that, if he had time to analyze everything, he would find some kind of small force field around the area he was traveling through, preventing those waves from hitting *Orbiter One* too hard.

He could see the end of the path, looming ahead. Several ships of a type he didn't recognize closed in around the edges of the secondary force field, the one around the Ready Vessels.

Ibori was pretty sure those ships weren't Fleet vessels. He had already scanned them. They didn't have any life signs, nor did they have active energy signatures.

And unlike several of the ships that *Orbiter One* had already passed, those ships in front of the force field didn't have an *anacapa* drive either.

Ibori had spent the day before this trip with Crowe and Bakhr, going over the simulations that both men had run. Ibori had run his own simulation, and he had also done his own research.

He had found several ships closer to the opening in the Scrapheap's force field that had active *anacapa* drives, ships that weren't Ready Vessels and weren't protected by that secondary force field. He had presented that information to Crowe, and Crowe had nodded.

I don't want to trust drives that old, Crowe had said, as if he knew somehow that the *anacapa* drives inside the Ready Vessels would be newer.

Ibori reminded Crowe that no one knew how old some of the *anacapa* drives the Fleet was still using were. And Crowe had called that information irrelevant.

Ibori had felt stung. But not because Crowe had treated him badly—he hadn't. But because Crowe wouldn't even listen to the argument.

Ibori had had *anacapa* training just like the other engineers, and he had been fascinated by the *anacapa* drives grown from ancient roots. Most drives were manufactured, but some were developed off old pieces, using a technology he had ultimately chosen not to explore.

Not that it mattered right now.

At the moment, it had become very clear to Ibori that Crowe had been right: the ships outside of the Ready Vessel area were ancient. It wasn't that their drives were too old. The containers were either nonexistent or had broken down.

Crowe's *irrelevant* phrase had also turned out to be right, because the equipment around the *anacapa* drive was untrustworthy, and the drives themselves could be contaminated with all kinds of junk from inside the Scrapheap.

Of course, the Ready Vessels could be contaminated too. But the *Renegat*'s sensors hadn't been able to penetrate all of the noise inside that Ready Vessel area. Those ships might be new and pristine, like they were advertised to be, or they might be as decrepit as the remaining ships outside the area.

There was no way to know without getting inside.

"Um," he said, still not sure how to address Crowe—or really, how to address anyone. "Are you all looking at this? It seems to me that the ships in front of that secondary force field have moved."

He hadn't charted it. He was too busy piloting *Orbiter One*.

"I think," he said when no one responded immediately, "that they might be trying to block us."

"They have no life signs," Newark said, which surprised him. Her level of engagement surprised him completely. He had written her off once she quit working on the bridge.

"So they're programmed to block ships?" Tosidis said.

"Maybe," Crowe said. He had strapped in, to Ibori's relief, because for most of the trip, Crowe had been tugging on the back of his chair, which was extremely annoying.

"Or Fleet ships," Bakhr said.

Ibori felt a chill.

"Maybe it's just to prevent something that had broken free from getting in," Colvin said.

"I don't care about theory," Ibori said. "I need to either go around them or get through them. Ideas?"

"I'm sending you a new path," Crowe said. "Try that."

The coordinates appeared in front of Ibori, and he moved *Orbiter One* accordingly. As he did, the other ships shifted too.

"Let's just shoot them," Zhang said.

"No." Crowe's voice was harsh. "We don't fire weapons in here. I thought I explained that."

He had, but he hadn't explained his reluctance to do so, at least in full. It seemed like he was spooked. Although, Ibori knew, Crowe didn't spook easily.

"The Scrapheap has already recognized us," Bakhr said. "Why don't we just ask it to open the secondary force field."

"Ask it how?" Ibori said. "We didn't plan to communicate with the Scrapheap itself."

"Except with our identification," Bakhr said.

"It's a good idea," Crowe said. "Let's just send a normal entry signal. See if that does anything."

The same signal the Fleet used with all of its small ships, asking for entry into a larger ship or to dock on a starbase or to land on a sector base. Ibori sent the signal, but he didn't have a lot of hope. Surely, the signal would have changed over the centuries.

"Something's opening," Tosidis said.

"The force field is clearing below us," Bakhr said at the same time.

Ibori saw it at that moment too. The problem was the ships on this path were starting to shift as well.

He sped up *Orbiter One*, going five times faster than he had a moment ago, hoping that opening in the force field wasn't an illusion.

Orbiter One ducked under the ships, then sped into the opening in the force field. Ibori winced as *Orbiter One* went through—half of him was convinced it would bounce off the force field and back into the main part of the Scrapheap.

But it didn't.

It arrived at the edge of the Ready Vessel area, surrounded by ships that made the *Renegat* look small.

The force field closed behind *Orbiter One*. Ibori hoped that the same signal would open the force field a second time.

"God," Tosidis said, "these ships are huge."

"And in great shape," Bakhr said.

"And old," Zhang said.

Ibori nodded. They were old, just like the bits of the ships outside the secondary force field. Apparently, the Fleet had been preparing Ready Vessels for a very, very long time.

"Any particular ship you want to target?" he asked.

"If only we could choose a newer one," Zhang muttered. Her words were probably deliberately loud enough for everyone to hear.

"We don't have time to search," Crowe said. "Follow the original plan."

The original plan had been silly, in Ibori's opinion. They hadn't been able to see the Ready Vessels clearly through the force field, so Crowe had simply chosen the nearest ones to their entry point.

"Do those vessels have *anacapa* drives?" Crowe was asking Bakhr. Apparently, Crowe was referring to the vessels he had targeted initially.

"Yeah," Bakhr said. "And it looks like they're functioning, given the energy readings I'm getting."

"All right," Crowe said. "Get us as close as you can, Tindo."

"Are we going to hook up to the ships?" he asked.

"Maybe we should see if they let us into one of their docking bays," Newark said.

"No." Crowe used that same firm voice he had used before. "I don't want these ships to activate. We're going to hook up like we're doing a rescue."

"Grappler or space bridge?" Tosidis asked.

"Both," Crowe said.

Ibori had already known that was the plan. Both the grappler and the space bridge were ready. He just had to find a good entry into the nearest ship.

His heart was beating hard. This would be the tricky part for him. He hadn't done this kind of hookup with another ship in more than a decade.

He scanned the edges of the ship that Crowe had chosen. That ship was twice the size of the *Renegat*. The ship was black, unlike many of the others, and looked like it was composed of nanobits. So, in that, at least, it was newer.

Ibori hoped the grappler would work. He had no idea if it would have worked on the older, metal ships, so he was glad that this ship appeared to have the right kind of material.

"All right," he said. "I've picked an entry point. It's as close as I can get to that *anacapa* reading that Benjamin found."

That entry looked very far away from anything, though. Which made sense. The Fleet's bridges were always well hidden.

"We're going to have to go in and out very fast," Crowe said to Colvin and Newark. Apparently those three were the ones heading onto the designated ship.

Ibori had no idea how they were chosen. He was just grateful he wasn't one of the people traveling to that dark and empty ship. He had done his required exterior work on shuttles and DV vessels, using gravity boots to hold him onto the sides of the ships, and those had been the most terrifying weeks of his training. He hated being outside a ship, and the worst thing, in his opinion, would be to go from inside a warm and comfortable fully functional vessel into one of the dark and cold ones, a vessel that might or might not operate properly.

"All right," Colvin said, as she put up her hood. Newark did the same. Then they both checked their gloves.

Crowe slid his on, wincing a little, probably because of the surgeries on his hand. Ibori's finger still ached as well, but he hadn't been infected with that stuff. He had no idea what other kind of pain Crowe might be feeling.

Then Crowe started to put his hood over his face. He stopped and made eye contact with Ibori, Bakhr, Tosidis, and Zhang.

"We're going to stay in close and active communication," he said to them. "If we run into trouble, we'll tell you if we can."

Ibori nodded. None of the others did. They just waited.

"However—and I want you all to pay attention to this—if one of us tells you to leave the vicinity, you leave immediately." Crowe looked pointedly at them all again. "Got that?"

"What are you worried about?" Tosidis asked.

Crowe looked down, then back up again. He took a deep breath as if it took extra strength to talk.

"I once saw something go wrong with an *anacapa* drive inside a Scrapheap. That caused a catastrophic reaction inside the Scrapheap. I don't think that will happen this time, but if anything goes awry, I want you all to get out of here as fast as you can. Do you understand?"

"Not entirely," Zhang said. "Are you saying that something that happens inside that ship could hurt us?"

"I'm hoping that won't happen," Crowe said, "but the possibility exists. There's too much weird energy inside a Scrapheap for us to expect everything to work as we think it will."

"Whatever that means," Zhang said.

"If I knew," Crowe said, "I would plan for it better. Just leave if I tell you to."

"Or if either of us do," Newark said. She shot a questioning look at Crowe, as if she worried that he would be upset at her clarification.

"Exactly," he said.

Ibori's entire body had stiffened. He had known this was a dangerous mission. He had also known that without it, the *Renegat* would never function properly again.

But he hadn't been prepared to flee the Ready Vessel area quickly.

While the team was gone, he was going to have to reprogram the autopilot. And that would take time. He would have to be very careful not to trigger anything else.

And somehow, he was going to have to account for that automated signal—the request to the Scrapheap itself to open the secondary force field.

He had a lot to do while they were gone.

He glanced at Tosidis, Bakhr, and Zhang. He would ask them for help as well. But he was going to wait until Crowe, Newark, and Colvin were gone.

"The energy waves buffeting these vessels might interfere with communications," Bakhr said.

"Let's hope they don't," Crowe said. "I'm going to need all of you on this."

Then he looked at Zhang. "Make sure no oxygen leaks into that storage container on the outside of this vessel. Luc, make sure that the environmental systems in all of the exterior storage areas are off."

"I will," Tosidis said.

"Remember," Crowe said, hands on the edges of his hood, "any oxygen near these *anacapa* drives and we're screwed."

Ibori nodded. The others did as well, even though none of them had actually seen the difference between the healthy pink whatever it was and the dead stuff that had turned up after the oxygen source ended.

None of them had watched anyone die from that stuff in real time.

"We'll be careful," he said.

He would make certain of it.

UNKNOWN VESSEL

Crowe entered the airlock on the unknown vessel. Immediately a light appeared in front of him, welcoming him to the ship and asking him to wait as the environmental system powered up.

Panic flared through him. The last thing he wanted was for one of these old vessels to power up in any way. He cast around for some shutoff mechanism, and then saw it in the middle of the well-lit announcement.

He pressed the shutoff mechanism, and for a moment, he thought it wouldn't take. Then the system blinked green, acknowledging his countermand.

He activated the gravity on his boots and gloves so that he could lean, just for a moment, and let the panic flow through him. Panic would not serve him at all on this mission.

Panic might kill him.

The airlock timer started—a blue light above the inner door.

He had seen something like that years ago, as a young student on the *Brazza Two*, when they had been allowed to explore the systems of a very old ship. He hadn't seen it since.

The door to the interior of the ship opened slowly, almost sticking as it moved.

Since he hadn't allowed the environmental system to activate, the ship wouldn't need to use the airlock.

He hoped that this ship would work the way all the other Fleet ships did, and not close the interior airlock door quickly.

But he had to plan for the worst. So he leaned into the space bridge, and beckoned Colvin and Newark to join him. They moved quickly toward him, Newark slowed a little because she was carrying an *anacapa* travel container.

They probably should have brought two containers, but he didn't want two of the three explorers to carry something extra. He was making a lot of decisions like that for this trip, based on a judgment he wasn't exactly sure was sound.

Technically, he should have let Colvin lead this mission. She had a lot more experience exploring old vessels. But Crowe couldn't put her in charge, partly because he didn't trust anyone, not after what had happened with Preemas, but partly because she didn't know exactly what they were looking for—and Crowe did.

He was glad he had made that decision now, because he wouldn't have wanted Colvin to accidentally start the environmental systems in this ancient ship.

The three of them squeezed into the airlock and then pushed into the ship itself.

There were no maps of this vessel, at least not in his suit's storage, and none on *Orbiter One* either. This vessel—whatever it was—was so old that blueprints of its interior didn't seem to exist anywhere—or at least anywhere that he could find.

The fact that he could talk to it, and read its notifications, seemed like a small miracle to him. He wondered if the Fleet had stored these vessels here centuries after the Scrapheap shut down, and knew that, at the moment, he had no way to find out.

He pulled the scanner he had brought with him, and turned it on. He was holding his breath. He had to force himself to stop doing that. But each time he used one of his own pieces of tech, he worried that he would ignite something.

The scanner monitored *anacapa* energy. He could have monitored that through his suit, but he didn't want to. He wanted to be able to easily shut off the tech and toss it away from the team, if he needed to.

When he had described that, before the mission started, everyone looked at him as if he were being paranoid. And maybe he was. But he liked to think he was being cautious instead.

The *anacapa* energy on this ship was low level and came from one area only. That area was to their right and one deck above them.

He told Colvin and Newark that in two quick sentences. They nodded their response.

"Yulia," he said, "you lead. But should anything unusual happen, you stop and wait for me."

She knew how to find good handholds, how to work in this kind of zero-G, and what to avoid. It only made sense that she would be the one to lead while inside.

"You sure?" she asked.

"Go," he said.

She pushed past him, setting a pace faster than one he would usually have set. She turned on all of the external lights in her suit except for the lights at the bottom of her boots. That way she wasn't blinding the other two, but she was illuminating their journey.

Crowe hadn't thought to do that.

He was now positive he had made the right decision.

He turned on the lights in his gloves and along the sleeves of his suit. He also turned on the hood lamp on his forehead, but left the rest of the face lights off. He hated using those, because they sometimes blinded him.

Newark brought up the rear, and like Colvin, she had all of her suit lights on. Together, the three of them brightened the corridor considerably.

The corridor had sharp angles and corners on its doors. The floor seemed to be carpeted, although Crowe couldn't tell just from looking at it. None of the doors were open. Panels jutted out of the walls, right about the height Crowe was traveling, so he had to be careful not to hit them.

The corners and angles and sharp edges made him nervous. Any one of those edges could compromise his environmental suit.

Colvin kept a killing pace. She would push off the control panels or the walls themselves, then use an outstretched hand to right herself, half-floating, half-propelling herself down that corridor.

Crowe struggled to keep up. He had never traveled like this, not fast, anyway, so his technique was nowhere near as good as hers.

Newark stayed with him, although she would occasionally pull ahead, and then seem to remind herself that she needed to bring up the rear. He would have told her to go forward, but he was worried that he would get hopelessly behind, and then get confused in the dark corridors.

No one said anything. The comms were open, though. He could hear the occasional grunt or a harsh intake of breath. But no conversation at all, which he appreciated.

Once they started moving, he stopped worrying. They had to get through this, see what condition the *anacapa* drive was in, and figure out if their sensors were leading them astray with the drives. If the drive was as it seemed, then it wouldn't take a lot of work to get the needed drives.

If the drive wasn't as it seemed, then they had a lot of work ahead of them, and he wasn't sure if the crew of the *Renegat* was up to that task.

Colvin finally veered to the right. He followed, a little slower than he wanted to. She had stopped near an elevator and was using one of the scanners she had brought to probe for some other way to the next level up.

As Crowe started to reach for his scanner, she set hers back in its pocket, and grabbed at something he couldn't quite see clearly. He moved a little closer, so that his hood light illuminated what she was reaching for.

It was a handle.

"Scan the underside first," he said. "Sometimes, in the old, old, vessels, these handles were fake."

They were traps for the unwary, designed to slice into environmental suits.

He was pretty sure this ship predated that trick—apparently, it had been developed when Fleet ships were routinely getting boarded by strangers—but he couldn't be sure of anything.

"Thanks." Colvin moved to one side and angled the scanner toward the back of the handle, turning on one of the scanner's exterior lights.

Newark reached them, and turned on the gravity in her boots, sinking to the floor. She approached that handle as well.

"It's clear," she said.

Colvin pocketed her scanner, then grabbed the handle. She braced her feet on the wall below, then turned on the gravity in her boots, and tugged.

Debris rose from the area around the handle. The debris floated past Crowe, startling him. The debris was not black or gray like sloughed off nanobits, but shiny and silver, like shaved metal.

"Need help?" he asked.

"Give me a second," Colvin said, her voice straining. The muscles in her back became visible through her environmental suit.

Newark stood to the left, her hood illuminating a different side of the handle. Crowe was about to turn the gravity on in his boots when the gigantic door around the handle popped open, just slightly, as if it didn't want to open all the way.

Colvin swore, but the sound seemed more like relief than anger.

"Okay," she said. "Now let's all try this thing."

Crowe moved closer. The handle wasn't really on a door so much as a hatch. And the hatch was anchored at what he considered to be the top, which made him realize that had the gravity come on in the ship, Newark would have been standing on the ceiling.

That also explained the awkward placement of the control panels. They had probably been placed deliberately low, and if the ship's environment were on, they would probably have light tabs on their sides, so that they'd be visible from a long distance off.

Newark moved closer and put her hands on the handle. Colvin moved slightly to the right. Crowe remained to the left. Once the hatch opened farther, he would reach inside and shove it the rest of the way.

The debris floated around them, catching the light. He wasn't sure where the debris came from. The edges of the hatch seemed smooth and round, just like they were supposed to.

Maybe there was dirt inside the tunnel connecting the decks.

If there was, he didn't like that. A ship shouldn't be quite that filthy, even after it had been left for a long time.

Although that depended on whether the environmental system remained on.

He couldn't make assumptions. As he had learned on that horrible night on the *Br2 Scout3*, assumptions could kill.

Colvin got the hatch to open just a bit farther. Newark scanned the hatch's edges and stuck her scanner inside as well. Apparently she had been listening too.

"It's clear," she said to Crowe. Then she tugged on the handle along with Colvin.

Crowe reached inside and gingerly put his hand on the back of the hatch. He attached his boots to the wall, just like Colvin had done, and shoved that hatch door.

The hatch flew open and, had they not been anchored, the women would have flown backwards as well.

Instead, they banged against the hatch.

"You okay?" he asked.

"Fine," Colvin said and Newark said at the same time, "Yeah."

Crowe leaned into the opening from the hatch, using the lights on his gloves and his hood light see what was next.

This was not a maintenance tunnel as he had expected. It was wide enough to accommodate a number of people. It was also square, with edges, just like everything else. Rung ladders covered all four walls. There was no floor that he could see, which made sense, since this team had entered on a middle deck.

This tunnel, housed next to the elevator, was the main way to travel between decks. How horribly inconvenient. But it was an efficient design.

"All right," he said. "We're going to climb up. I'm going first."

That wasn't the procedure they'd been following, but he wanted to see what was on that deck. Some Fleet ships had the entire deck for their bridge. Others had a separate bridge entrance.

If this one was all bridge, he wanted to see that. He also wanted to prevent another query from the ship, offering to turn the environment on in the bridge only—provided this ship had that feature.

It felt strange, not knowing the ship's layout. He never went into a Fleet ship without knowing its basic plan.

He climbed up the rungs, using the lack of gravity to pull himself up several rungs at a time.

He could tell the women were following him, because their lights bobbed, illuminating this wide space.

He almost missed the next level, but his scanner vibrated against his leg, telling him he was close to the *anacapa* energy.

That was when he saw the hatch. It didn't have a handle. It had a wheel that he had to turn and push.

"We have another door," he said as he stopped next to it. He used the knuckle lights on his gloves to make sure there was nothing sharp about that wheel.

There wasn't anything visible. So he leaned over from the rungs, then locked his left foot first, then his right onto the wall, using the full gravity in his boots. He put his hands on that wheel, testing it. It moved more easily to the right, which relieved him, for some reason.

The wheel was as he expected, then.

He turned it carefully, and unlike the hatch below, this larger door popped open as if it had been waiting years to do so.

He leaned forward, using the door as a shield, and peered into what seemed—at first—to be a corridor. Then he saw chairs and consoles dangling from what he thought of as the ceiling, and long columns of equipment alongside them. Between the columns of equipment were screens, located almost directly across from him.

Apparently whoever had designed this vessel liked their screens up high, rather than at eye level.

The scanner was buzzing vehemently against his leg. He was very close to the *anacapa* drive.

He shut off the gravity in his boots, then pushed himself up and onto what had to be the bridge. He pushed himself a bit too hard, floating upward. For a half second, he wasn't sure what to do, then realized he could turn on the gravity in his boots.

He floated down, landing softly, shaking his head at all the skills he had left behind.

"Yulia, Danika, come on up," he said, glad they hadn't been able to see his error. Working in zero-G had never been his strong suit, and it certainly wasn't his strength now.

He pulled the scanner from his pocket. His sore hands wrapped around the scanner, holding it tight. It was still vibrating hard. He turned 360 degrees, ever so slowly, trying to find where the bulk of the *anacapa* energy was coming from.

He found it, finally, in the place he expected it the least.

That tall cabinet behind him seemed to be the place where the *anacapa* energy was coming from. He squinted at it, unable to see any protections or containers for the drive.

Maybe there was one inside the cabinet.

He walked over to it and crouched, looking for a way to open the cabinet.

He found a latch on the side—an old-fashioned flip latch that he could manipulate with his fingers. He did, wincing as his sore finger brushed against what his gloves identified as metal.

Metal and *anacapa* drives. He had been taught not to put those things in close proximity.

He opened the door, and blinked as a faint golden light reached him. What looked like a rock rested on a cushioned cubby in the middle of a shelf. That rock glowed slightly amber.

The scanner nearly jumped out of his hand. He turned the scanner off, and slipped it back into his pocket, locking the scanner in place. Then he peered at the rock.

It was a very old, unrefined *anacapa* drive. No one had lopped pieces off of it. It hadn't been augmented or protected in any way.

"Found it," he said, so that the other two team members knew what he was doing. "Stay back please."

He reached into the other pocket of his environmental suit and pulled out the protective gloves, designed for use with an *anacapa* drive. This was the main reason he had come on this mission: he knew he could touch an *anacapa* drive.

In theory, Newark should have been able to as well, but it wasn't a theory he wanted to test, since not everyone could handle a drive safely.

He leaned just a bit closer to the drive, trying to see if any pink threaded its way through the drive.

He didn't see anything, but that didn't mean that the drive was all right. The others hadn't been.

"Danika," he said, "open the container and hold it near me."

She moved up beside him. Out of the corner of his eye, he saw her set the container near his right thigh. She held the container tightly in both hands.

He slipped his double-gloved hands under the drive, getting ready to lift. If the drive felt too light, he would leave it in place. It should feel very heavy, and thrum with power, even through both gloves and the environmental suit.

The moment his gloved hands touched the drive, his teeth chattered against each other. He had only felt something this powerful once before, holding a large *anacapa* drive when he was still training as an engineer.

He slowly lifted this drive, and felt the solidity of it. It was lighter than it should have been because of the lack of gravity, but he could still feel the drive's mass.

Nothing had hollowed out this drive. And it was filled with power, more than he had held in a long time.

He still examined it, turning it over in his hands, even though it felt like his bones were going to vibrate out of his skin. He was getting a headache, but that was normal for him when he held *anacapa* drives. He wasn't sniffling, he couldn't taste blood, and nothing else felt awry.

This drive was fine. Maybe even better than fine. It still had peak energy, something most of the drives the Fleet used did not have after a few decades in service.

He hefted the drive to the container, then set the drive inside. He kept one hand on top of the drive as he brought the container lid down with the other hand. He removed his hand from inside the container at the very last minute.

The second he stopped touching the drive, the thrumming in his teeth and bones stopped. The headache receded.

Newark sealed the container closed, then looked up at him. The lights on her hood nearly blinded him, but he gave her a reassuring smile anyway.

"Can we use this drive?" she asked.

He grinned at her. He felt a little giddy, and he knew that was relief.

"Oh, yes, we can," he said. "It's probably better than the drive we came out here with."

She let out a small hoot of joy. Colvin laughed at the sound, and Crowe's grin widened.

They had a lot left to do. They needed to get this drive to an environmentally free area near the *Renegat.* Then they needed to make sure the drive wasn't infected.

But Willoughby said she was close to a system on that. Crowe knew it wouldn't take much.

They would be able to use the *anacapa* drive again.

The *Renegat* was free to travel in foldspace again. It could go wherever it needed to go.

That thought made the panic that had been underpinning Crowe's every move ease.

They weren't trapped in this sector. *He* wasn't trapped in this sector.

They had choices again.

And until this moment, he hadn't realized just how much he needed them.

PART FORTY-THREE

LONG-LOST COMMUNICATIONS

85 YEARS AGO

THE *SPRÁVA*

Three months before her official retirement, Admiral Gão had finally found the information she had been searching for.

She sat in the gigantic suite that had been her home on the *Správa* for decades. She had dedicated an entire room to the study of Scrapheaps, and one Scrapheap in particular.

She still collected information on that old Scrapheap that the *Renegat* had been heading toward when the ship got lost. She had actually brought in an assistant to design a program that would tell her if there was any change to the daily information the Scrapheap sent through those old back channels.

Over the years, the program had found several changes, mostly of ship thefts that were similar to the thefts she had seen before, and erosion of the systems around the Scrapheap. Apparently, the force field into the Scrapheap continued to decay.

A parade of lieutenants who became her assistants for a few years before promotion seemed to believe that the old Scrapheap was an obsession. Gão had even heard them discussing that Scrapheap as a seminal moment in her career, something she couldn't get past.

That was probably true, but, in her eyes, irrelevant. The Scrapheap/*Renegat* incident had taught her to speak up, even when the risk was greater than she wanted it to be. She learned to fight harder than she ever had before, and she had made a lot of difference in the past fifteen years.

One thing she had done: she had gotten the Fleet to change its practice with Ready Vessels. She had found enough proof to show that the program was useless and a waste of time as well as resources. Future Scrapheaps would not hold Ready Vessels, only old and useless ships.

She couldn't quite convince the Fleet or herself to destroy old ships, although she had laid the groundwork for some other enterprising leader to make that change in the future.

She hated being at the end of her career, but she knew it was time. She had narrowed her focus too much, and she felt irritated at some of the younger Vice-Admirals who made suggestions for things she had suggested decades ago. She wanted those young Vice-Admirals to understand that their ideas weren't new or even timely, and no one was going to implement them without a lot of work that the Fleet did not want to do.

The moment she realized she was thinking like that, she realized she was done with this part of her life. She always wanted to be a forward thinker, not someone who quashed souls and ideas. She failed as much as she succeeded at that, but at least she tried.

And then she would come back to this suite, check that program for the Old Scrapheap, which ran continuously, and note the lack of change (most of the time). The handful of changes she had seen turned out to be exciting blips in a week or a month, but nothing major.

She had no idea what she'd been hoping for, but she would know it when she saw it.

For the past month, she had made arrangements to have the entire system moved to her new quarters on Starbase Sigma. She had signed up for the retraining program designed for captains, commanders, and admirals at the end of their active career. There, she would find another, less demanding career—not quite something to do with her time, but something to keep her mind engaged.

And as part of that quest, she had thought, maybe, she should let this program go.

If she could.

So when she walked into the room to check the stats, what she found startled her so much that she sat heavily on the creaky old chair she'd been using for more than a decade.

A ship had entered the Scrapheap. Not just any ship, but a ship the system recognized.

It was one of the *Renegat*'s orbiters. And it had opened the force field leading into the Ready Vessels.

She let out a small breath of air, and felt tears prickle her eyes. The *Renegat* had actually made it to the Scrapheap. The ship had done the impossible, even with all of the crew issues, and gone into the Scrapheap to investigate the problems that had originally sent the *Renegat* there.

She blinked, hard. One of those tears traced its way down her face. She rubbed the tear away with her thumb, and made herself smile.

They tried. They had actually done better than she thought. They had somehow continued forward, even though they had more problems than they could deal with.

That meant, somehow, the Preemas situation had been resolved. And the *Renegat* had done what it was supposed to do, under someone's command.

She swallowed hard, then shook her head, wishing she had someone to share this with. Cali Baker had moved to a completely different sector and was overseeing the building of some new sector base. None of Gāo's other former assistants really understood the depth of the issues with the *Renegat*.

All of the former vice admirals who had been part of the decision to send the *Renegat* out were either retired or in other parts of the sector. And none of them understood her obsession with the *Renegat*. They all looked at its loss as one of those incidents in their careers, one of those things they were part of that hadn't worked out.

None of them felt the *Renegat's* loss like she had.

"Well," she muttered to herself. She had her answer. She was going to keep the system. She would move it to Starbase Sigma.

She might never hear anything about the *Renegat* again. Something might have happened with the Ready Vessels or with the ship herself. But the idea that they had made it—that they had done something she had believed impossible—filled her with relief.

She had known that the chances of the *Renegat* succeeding were slim. But she had wanted them to have a chance at redemption. When Nadim Crowe had contacted her, and she had seen his plea all those years ago, she had figured the *Renegat's* politics had prevented it from doing its job.

But the fact that the orbiter had gone into the force field, the fact that the crew of the *Renegat* had somehow continued in the face of those long odds, made her feel so much better.

Made her feel less responsible.

If the ship failed—and it did, because it hadn't returned—it wasn't because of the crew she had put together. It had been because of the dangers of the foldspace journey or working so very far away from the Fleet.

She took a deep breath, stood, and then scanned the room, with the screens running everywhere, processing information from a Scrapheap she had never seen, a Scrapheap that she felt she knew intimately anyway.

She hadn't realized she had been carrying such a burden from the *Renegat*. Her obsession, after all.

Now, finally, she felt like she could step away from this career. She could move on.

She had an answer.

She still didn't know what happened to the *Renegat*, but she did know that the ship had continued to function, long after she had thought it impossible to do so.

She leaned against the chair and realized that the *Renegat* had held her back in a way she hadn't expected. Part of her mind had been back there, blaming herself for its fate.

And she didn't need to do that anymore.

She would continue to monitor, because she was curious. But she could feel the obsession leaching from her.

This was the answer she had been seeking.

And she was content.

PART FORTY-FOUR
REPAIRING THE *RENEGAT*
100 YEARS AGO

THE *RENEGAT*

Crowe sat cross-legged on the bridge of the *Renegat*, right next to the *anacapa* container. He had never sat cross-legged in an environmental suit before, but it was surprisingly comfortable. He wore double layers of gloves, and had his hood up, although privately, he felt like he didn't need to have his hood up at all.

He had become quite comfortable working in an environmental suit, something he had never thought would happen. He had also become quite comfortable with the *anacapa* drive, enough that it worried him. He didn't want to be too confident in his own abilities, especially since he was sitting where Stephanos had died.

In the weeks since the *Renegat* had been near the Scrapheap, the crew had done a lot of work on the vessel. Crowe had directed it all.

The very first thing they had done was pull up the carpet where Stephanos had died. He didn't want the environmental system to try to clean that area, nor did he want various bots and the crew to clean it either.

Instead, he had bots remove the carpet and replace the flooring with a strong nanobit seal, as it should have been from the beginning. He had no idea why the bridge on the *Renegat* had been carpeted. It had always seemed like a strange choice to him, but it was one he had decided he could live with, until Stephanos had died here.

If he could have replaced the *anacapa* container, he would have. The container had been cleaned and sterilized of that anti-*anacapa* weapon, but he didn't entirely trust the container's integrity, no matter how it came out on various scans.

He couldn't replace it, though. He didn't have the materials to build a better *anacapa* container, and so far, none of the fifteen Ready Vessels his teams had explored had an actual functioning *anacapa* container, at least not one he would have trusted.

Some of those vessels had rudimentary containers, but they looked more dangerous than no container at all.

The entire engineering staff was on the bridge at the moment, except Colin Vezner, whom Crowe had in engineering proper.

Ever since the incident with Preemas (and that was how Crowe was allowing himself to think about it), Crowe kept one person he trusted in engineering at all times. He wanted to maintain control of the ship, and the best way to do that was to control both the bridge and engineering.

The engineers were at different consoles, and Tosidis sat in the captain's chair. Most systems could be activated from that chair, with the proper clearance and with screens that opaqued to private.

Crowe had thought about altering those screens to be functional throughout the bridge, but as he solidified control, he changed his mind. He wanted several areas where only one person could access the important controls. He had one in his quarters (he had rebuilt the captain's command center), another in engineering, and a third in the command chair here on the bridge.

The *Renegat* was now his ship. No one seemed to question that he was the leader now, although he did not have them call him captain. That seemed to be the wrong way to go—made the mutiny and the death of Preemas seem too calculating, which it was not.

The crew did listen to him, except for the six people in the med bay and the dozen people still in the brig. He had gone down to talk to the prisoners in the brig on three separate occasions, offering to free them if they worked with him.

All of them refused. All of them blamed him—rightly—for Preemas's death. None of them saw that there had been any need to get rid of Preemas, and a few had told Crowe that they would not have let him imprison Preemas in the brig had Preemas lived.

Crowe had never even thought of imprisoning Preemas, although, Crowe supposed, that would have been the right step. If Crowe had convinced Preemas to step aside, Crowe would have isolated Preemas to quarters, which was one of the many reasons that Crowe had gotten rid of the captain's control closet there.

Crowe did not regret killing Preemas. As time went by, Crowe was beginning to think it had been the only thing he could have done.

Preemas had not been the kind of man who would have allowed himself to be confined for long.

The crew certainly wouldn't be repairing the *Renegat* if Preemas were still alive. These last few weeks, the crew had worked on the *Renegat* as if it were about to leave on its maiden voyage rather than having gone through the longest journey of its existence.

Even so, Crowe worried about the ship. Without the support of a sector base, he couldn't improve the ship in the ways he wanted to. It wasn't just the *anacapa* container. There were a dozen—maybe a thousand—little details that made this ship less than suitable for...what?

That was what he had to figure out. Because if the *Renegat* went back to the Fleet, half the crew would be up on charges, if not all of the crew. And staying here, without any Fleet support, didn't seem like an option either.

But he was noodling all of his choices, and what he had come to was this: He would make the *Renegat* the best ship possible. He had already made sure that the ship could run easily on automatic pilot—at least in a sector. Handling foldspace would still require someone who had worked with *anacapa* drives, but he didn't want the average untrained person touching an *anacapa*.

But he did want the contingency in place that someone could run this ship with a minimum of work. To do otherwise, after they had lost so many knowledgeable crew members, would be foolish.

He wanted to be prepared for everything.

With that in mind, he had taken a lot of equipment from the Ready Vessels, and used that equipment to augment the *Renegat*'s systems.

He was also toying with the idea of improving one of the Ready Vessels, should any be suitable, and maybe making it into the primary ship for this crew. He wasn't sure exactly why he would do that.

He just wanted options.

In all cases, though, he had to make sure that there was no trace of that anti-*anacapa* weapon anywhere. He and the engineering staff had worked out a system to make sure that the weapon wasn't a threat to the *Renegat* and maybe not to any of the other ships.

And, as Willoughby had said to him, threats were another factor to consider. The Fleet had apparently built a lot of response to threats they had faced in the past into the technology of later ships. The *Renegat* would not have survived if the shield hadn't blocked that anti-*anacapa* weapon.

Who knew what other threats lurked in these forgotten sectors of space, threats that the Fleet had faced and had incorporated into their various systems.

So much to think about.

Crowe looked at all of the tools scattered around him. He was at the last stage of the ship repair. He was going to handle the *anacapa* drive himself, mostly because of Stephanos. If someone had to die on this day, it would be him.

Although he didn't expect it would come to that.

So far, the crew had cleared out that anti-*anacapa* weapon from all of the systems. It had taken some stellar work by Willoughby and her crew, reverse engineering the block in the shields and applying it to the various systems so that they could scan for the weapon in all of its various forms.

The engineering staff had used those scans to clear the *Renegat* of all traces of the weapon. They also used it to isolate the energy that had infected the *Renegat* with the weapon.

The weapon hadn't come from the Scrapheap's central tower, as Crowe had initially thought, but from the vessels that had been left in the Scrapheap when those vessels' owners had left the ships behind and taken Fleet vessels out in their stead.

Initially, Crowe was going to send a team into one of those vessels to see if they could find a timeline for the thefts, but Atwater had talked him out of it. Atwater had said that it didn't matter when the thefts occurred. It had been long enough ago for the messages to travel all the way to the Fleet, which meant that the *Renegat* was in no immediate danger from those attackers.

In fact, Atwater said, it looked like the Fleet had met up with those attackers later and dealt with them in some kind of final way, which was why the protections had been built into the shields and nowhere else.

That had a certain logic. Crowe was going to accept it, and not worry about outsiders trying to get at his *Renegat* crew.

He had enough to worry about.

He sensed unease among the crew, although no one spoke to him directly.

They were all uneasy about the future. Once the *anacapa* drive was hooked up and functioning, the entire crew had choices to make.

Normally he would have made the choices for them—that's what captains did—but he wasn't an official captain. And he wasn't sure this crew—one that had overthrown a previous captain—would follow his lead on anything.

They didn't even agree on everything. Half of the crew wanted to return to the Fleet, and the others were afraid of doing so. Maybe *afraid* wasn't the right word. The others recognized the personal dangers of returning.

Their lives were going to be different no matter what choice they made. Not everyone seemed to understand that.

Some of the crew were delusional enough to believe the Fleet would welcome them with open arms.

He had already tried to disabuse several crew members—including Kabac—of that idea. In fact, it had been Crowe's conversation with Kabac that made Crowe worry about the future of this crew.

Nothing held them all together, and he wasn't popular enough to bring the crew together just based on his personality alone.

The team he had with him on the bridge trusted him though. All of his engineers—even Ellum and Rodriguez—would do whatever he said, no questions asked. They had become his core supporters, partly because they knew how hard he worked, and partly because they—more than anyone else on the *Renegat*—understood how close the entire crew had come to dying.

He glanced at the travel case that housed one of the *anacapa* drives he had pulled off a Ready Vessel. It had taken weeks to pick the right drive. He had brought six working *anacapa* drives onto the *Renegat*, clearing each one of traces of the weapon. Some of the drives, which had looked good on their Ready Vessels, didn't seem as solid on the *Renegat* itself.

The first drive he had chosen on that very first day was actually too large to fit into the *anacapa* container on the *Renegat*—and Crowe didn't have the skill to modify the drive to fit.

He hadn't replaced it, though. He had been storing the excess drives in different corners of the *Renegat*. At some point, though, he would have too many *anacapa* drives in a single vessel. He might have to leave the excess drives behind, although he was contemplating another solution.

The *Renegat* had a lot of small ships in its docking bay, too many small ships for the crew to ever use. Crowe was considering placing one of the small ships a safe distance from the *Renegat*, and storing some more drives and excess equipment there.

He hadn't told the crew yet—or rather, his engineering crew, whom he was thinking of as *the* crew. Everyone else, with the exception of Colvin, Seymont, and Newark, really weren't worth his time.

And that wasn't a captain's attitude either.

Whenever he came across the non-captainlike attitudes inside of him, he thought of picking someone else to lead the *Renegat*, but there was no one else he trusted.

At some point, that person would disagree with Crowe, and because Crowe had installed them as leader of the ship, that person would have the final decision-making power.

Crowe wasn't ready to give that up.

Just like he wasn't ready to give up control of the *anacapa* drives.

He slid the travel case toward him. He was wearing double gloves. He had the regular *anacapa* container open. He just had to move the drive and make sure all of the parts worked.

The very idea of doing it twisted his stomach. Once that drive was installed in the container, there was no going back.

He put his hood up, sealing it in place.

"Make sure you're suited up," he said to the team.

The precautions probably weren't necessary, but he was going to do them anyway. He wasn't going to lose another team member to an errant *anacapa* drive.

Tosidis put his hood up fast, and so did Bakhr. But Ellum shook his head slightly, because he believed Crowe was overreacting, and had said so. That had led to an argument among his engineers about the dangers of the drives, and Tosidis saying that everyone should watch the images of Stephanos's death before they stopped taking precautions.

Crowe wasn't going to make anyone watch what had happened to Stephanos. He would never be able to get that out of his mind, and he didn't want others to be stuck with the same imagery.

His gaze met Willoughby's as she slowly brought up her hood. She agreed with Ellum, thinking that the precautions were no longer necessary. But she didn't take it personally when Crowe overrode her argument.

She gave Crowe a small half smile, as if reminding him that she was indulging his caution, and then sealed her hood.

He looked around the bridge, making sure everyone's environmental suit was sealed. As he did, he realized that this bridge looked nothing like Preemas's bridge.

This bridge was pristine, so clean that the cleaning bots would have had trouble finding a speck of dirt. Some of the surfaces sparkled. All around them, the large wall screens showed different parts of the sector—some focused on the solar system, others focused on individual planets, and still others showing the Scrapheap itself.

The screens had become a backdrop to the work here, like screens usually were on a bridge.

Crowe felt a lot less isolated with the screens on.

He nodded at the bridge crew, then double-checked the interior of the *anacapa* container. All of the systems were on and blinking bright green, just like they were supposed to.

He'd worked with containers like this in the past, so he knew how they should feel—what their weight should be, and how the interior should look. Even though this one had been cleaned deeper than any other container he'd ever seen, he still thought he could see the faint ghosts of Stephanos's bloodstains.

He also knew that was probably his imagination.

He squared his shoulders, then braced his legs, and pivoted toward the travel case with the *anacapa* drive inside.

This drive was smoother than the one they had found in that very first Ready Vessel. This drive had been cut from another, larger drive, which made Crowe believe this drive was newer—although he had no real way of measuring that.

After each engineer had examined this drive, and had made certain it had no sign of being infected by the weapon, he and Willoughby had gone over it and over it, making certain that it functioned properly. Both of them were relying on training decades old, but they were the only two with training that extensive. They had done their best.

And now, this was the test of everyone's skill.

He leaned forward, and wrapped his hands around the drive. It hummed under his fingers, and that humming went deep into his bones—like it was supposed to.

He welcomed the feeling even as it made his stomach flutter just a bit. He hefted this drive upward and into his arms. Then he pivoted his torso again, and gently set the drive in place.

The container was supposed to handle the hookup itself, something he had seen a few dozen times. He knew what the hookup should look like. He watched as each light went from green to white, and then shut off, just like it was supposed to.

The drive was—theoretically—in place. But he wasn't going to take any chances. He switched the knuckle lights on his gloves on, and examined each connection, making sure it looked proper to him.

Out of the corner of his eye, he saw movement. Willoughby crouched beside him, holding a thin little light in her right hand. She shone that light on every connection, and as far underneath the drive as she could.

The drive glowed golden, and had no trace of pink. The drive made an ever-so-slight humming noise as it settled in.

And then, just like that, it looked like it had been part of the *Renegat* forever.

Willoughby tilted her head just a little, as if to say, *Well, that's all we can do.*

"The computers say that the drive is functioning," Tosidis said.

"Actually," Bakhr said, "our original drive did not have this kind of power. This drive is stronger than any drive I've seen before."

"Is that good?" Ellum asked.

"I have no idea," Bakhr said.

And neither did Crowe. None of them did. The mysteries of the *anacapa* drive.

The problem was that there would be no way to accurately test the drive before the *Renegat* went into foldspace. And Crowe had already vetoed the idea of traveling into foldspace as a test of the drive.

If they decided to go into foldspace, they would be taking their chances—maybe even more than they had on any other trip.

Or maybe they would be safer. He had no idea.

He rocked back on his heels, and realized he was feeling better than he had for weeks.

The *Renegat* could travel in foldspace again.

He smiled at the crew. A few of them blinked in surprise—he certainly didn't smile all that much.

But Willoughby smiled back.

"We did it," she said.

"We certainly did," he said. "We certainly did."

THE *RENEGAT*

"You know they're going to make us stay in this godforsaken sector forever," India said.

She was lying on her back on the top bunk of her cell. She shared the cell with two other mutineers, who spent most of their time trying to avoid any contact with her.

Serpell had noticed that the very first week, after India had had the surgery that had repaired her hands—or rather, had mostly repaired them. India said she had lost a lot of function, and when Serpell got the chance, she had checked with the medic, Orlena Seymont. Seymont said that India had lost a lot of muscle and tissue in that attack, but with the right kind of treatment, it could all be replaced.

India figured the right kind of treatment did not exist on the *Renegat*. Serpell thought maybe it did, but Seymont had her hands full, dealing with several people who had nearly died.

India hadn't, although she wouldn't acknowledge that. She was convinced that she would have ended up like Natalia Stephanos, given enough time.

The brig was mostly quiet. Serpell was the only person who visited the prisoners—at least that she knew of. And she was beginning to think she was only doing so because India had guilted her into it.

Serpell sat on one of the benches outside of India's cell. Serpell could see three other cells, with their prisoners sleeping or trying to amuse themselves with some kind of gambling, done with clothing.

No one was allowed any tech at all. The guards—a rotating group of volunteers—could program some entertainment to play on a holographic screen in the middle of each section of the brig, but most of the guards didn't.

It seemed that no one wanted to coddle the prisoners at all.

Serpell couldn't tell if that was because Nadim Crowe didn't coddle them, or if the rest of the crew blamed them for placing the ship in this position.

"How would you know what 'they' are going to do?" Serpell no longer moderated her tone with India. In the past, Serpell had tried to avoid sarcasm.

Now, she didn't. She was a half step away from stopping the daily visits. She already had an excuse, saying she would have too much work to make seeing India regularly possible.

India already hated Crowe and company. Making up that lie would only increase India's animosity—not that it mattered. She couldn't do anything from the brig anyway.

"I hear the guards talking," India said. "Everyone's afraid that we'll get court-martialed if we go back to the Fleet."

Serpell bit her lower lip. "Not all of us were involved in that fight," she said, and then wished she hadn't. It meant that India had won—India had engaged her attention somehow.

"Some of us were on the right side of that fight," India said. "If we do go back to the Fleet, you can bet I'll make sure they know who fought with the captain and who murdered him."

Her voice rang out, louder than it needed to be. The guard, Vladislav Shelstein, gave her a sideways look, filled with contempt.

Serpell let out a small *huh* of exasperation. None of this conversation had been for her benefit. It had all been about India, trying to make everyone uneasy. Maybe even trying to let her out of the brig.

Serpell stood.

"You can't leave yet," India said. "You haven't told me about your day."

As if India cared about her day.

Serpell made herself smile. "We've just been cleaning the ship."

India laughed. "Why? Is someone expecting an inspection?"

No, Serpell nearly said. *But it is amazing just how disreputable the ship had gotten under Captain Preemas.*

If Serpell had said that to India, though, India would have chastised her for criticizing Preemas.

India's laughter faded as if it never was. She swung her legs off the bunk and jumped down, coming over to the clear nanobit enclosure that separated her from Serpell.

"You don't want to stay here, do you?" India asked.

"I'm not even sure where 'here' is," Serpell said.

"We're Fleet," India said. "We don't live in places where we've been before."

"We haven't been here before," Serpell said, but she felt uneasy. What was India trying to do?

"You know what I mean," India said. "The future is forward. We were told we could go home."

Not that India had had a home.

But Serpell had. She had had friends too. And she missed them. She missed the Fleet more than she wanted to say.

"What're you going to do when Crowe tells you that you need to stay in this sector for your own good?" India asked.

"He's not going to say that," Serpell said.

But Shelstein gave her the same sideways look he had just given to India. Did Shelstein know something Serpell didn't? Were they going to stay here?

Why would they?

Except the court-martial thing.

She could understand why Crowe would want to stay. Crowe and all the people who helped him. But everyone else, they had no reason to stay here. They had been promised a return to the Fleet too, and now that the ship was back in order, they could do it.

"You are so naïve." India shook her head. "Sometimes I wonder what I ever saw in you."

Someone to do your homework, Serpell nearly said. *Someone to help you with the job you couldn't do. Someone to boss around.*

But she didn't say any of it, and probably never would.

"I have to get back," she lied.

Then she kissed her fingers and pressed them to the wall near India's mouth. India raised her eyebrows as if she couldn't believe she had just seen that, and then walked back to the bunks, hefting herself onto the top bunk as if she barely had enough strength in her arms to do so.

Serpell frowned at her, wondering at India's health, including her mental health.

Serpell turned around, though, before India could see her. Because India's words were ringing in her head.

You know they're going to make us stay in this godforsaken sector forever.

Serpell didn't want to stay here forever. She really didn't want to stay here for another month.

She wanted to go back.

She wanted to go home.

And she wasn't sure she ever would.

PART FORTY-FIVE

ARRIVAL

NOW

THE *AIZSARGS*

The *Aizsargs* was only a day away from Starbase Sigma when Dauber made a discovery that took her breath away.

She had been in her quarters, going through the *Renegat* records. Brett Ullman had developed some kind of program to organize those records and reconstruct them. He hadn't really examined them, not after Dauber had told him that she was going to bring the *Renegat*'s crew to Starbase Sigma.

Ullman's gaze had met hers.

I think that's probably for the best, he had said.

She had a feeling then—and it was compounded now—that he knew a lot more than he was saying. He probably would have told her if she had asked, but she hadn't.

She wanted to dig for herself. After speaking to most of the survivors of the *Renegat* over the course of the journey back to the Fleet, she knew that her decision to bring the *Renegat* survivors to the legal arm of the Fleet was the right one.

She just hadn't realized how right until now.

She stood up, then walked to the kitchen in her quarters, and made herself a cup of green tea. She held the cup in her hands, letting it warm her. Although she wasn't sure anything really could warm her.

Because she had finally found what the *Renegat* crew had been hiding—what they had been lying to her about.

They had abandoned part of their crew. Just left them behind. The crew had been on a mission somewhere, and Raina Serpell, Yusef Kabac, and the others had activated the *anacapa* drive, and left the sector entirely.

Dauber leaned against the counter, clutching the tea. She hadn't taken a sip, wasn't sure she could take a sip. Wasn't sure her stomach could handle anything right now.

She put the cup down and closed her eyes.

No wonder the crew of the *Renegat* had lied to her.

No wonder they had a matching story.

They had left more than sixty people behind, with only small ships and no *anacapa* drive at all—and no way to hook one up. Sixty people who might or might not have found those supplies, who might or might not have made it through the next few weeks, let alone the rest of their lives.

She rubbed a hand over her face, thinking about what she needed to do.

She had planned to dump them on the starbase's justice system, then give all of the records the *Aizsargs* had recovered to the proper authorities. She had wanted them to make a decision about what to do with these survivors.

And if she were honest with herself, she had felt a lot of compassion for them. One hundred years in their future, their ship lost, their friends gone. Sent on a mission with no hope of surviving.

But that compassion was gone.

What they had done was horrifying.

And because she found it so horrifying, she knew exactly what she needed to do.

She let her hand drop, felt her resolve grow. Her stomach settled.

She had a lot to do, and very little time in which to do it.

STARBASE SIGMA

Captain Dauber told Serpell she needed to leave the *Aizsargs* first. As the de facto leader of the *Renegat*, Serpell was the one everyone looked up to—or so Dauber had told her.

Serpell stood in the *Aizsargs's* docking bay, which, ironically, was where she had arrived on this ship. Behind her stood the 192 other survivors of the *Renegat*. They all shifted slightly, but there were no real conversations. Several people held mesh bags provided by the *Aizsargs*, filled with clothes that the ship had provided.

The instructions the survivors had received before they were to depart had said that they could take the clothes or toiletries.

Serpell chose not to bring anything other than the clothes on her back—a loose, long-sleeved tan shirt and matching brown pants. Nothing else here belonged to her. She would get new clothing on Starbase Sigma.

The instructions also said that they would be provided with housing, clothing, food, and some income until their situation got sorted out.

Clearly, the instructions were standard for all rescues of Fleet ships that the *Aizsargs* had participated in. Nothing in those instructions was specific to the *Renegat*, which made Serpell deeply uncomfortable. That meant enough other people had been in this situation that the ship had impersonal lists for everyone to follow.

She swallowed hard, glanced at those bags in the hands of her colleagues—soon to be her former colleagues. This adventure, if she could call it that, was nearly over.

As the *Aizsargs* got closer to Starbase Sigma, she had decided she would start her life anew here. She wouldn't even tell people she was a widow. She might not mention the *Renegat* or the lost 100 years, unless things were so different on the starbase that she would seem clueless otherwise.

She would get new clothing, and a new home, and maybe even train in a new profession. She didn't want to travel any longer. She would probably stay on the starbase, just so she could see different groups come through. Sector bases were too isolated for her, unless she worked in the sector base itself.

And she was thinking that if she trained in a new profession, it would be something unrelated to the Fleet. Maybe some kind of service offered on the starbase. There had been retail stores on starbases she'd visited in the past, and restaurants, and bars, and all kinds of entertainment. There were literary societies and debating groups and organizations she didn't entirely understand.

She would investigate all of it.

She would start moving forward again, only this time, the forward would be with her own life.

She rubbed her hands on her pants. Her heart thumped hard against her chest, not with panic so much as with anticipation.

She was anxious, yes, but it was a good kind of anxious. The kind that she got when she was looking forward to something special.

And this would be special.

She didn't even mind going first, although it was not something she normally would have chosen.

Her conversation with Dauber had been short. Dauber had appeared holographically in Serpell's little cabin. Dauber had seemed even more imposing than usual. She had her arms crossed, and she had glared at Serpell.

I need you to leave the Aizsargs *first,* Dauber had said. *You are the leader of the* Renegat. *You get to lead one last time.*

Serpell heard something in Dauber's voice that made no sense, some thrum of importance, or some emotion Serpell couldn't quite identify. If Serpell had known Dauber better, Serpell would have said that Dauber was angry.

But Dauber didn't look angry. She had seemed very calm.

I don't know why it's necessary, Serpell had said. *We're all ready to take the next step.*

That was a lie. She had no idea how the others were feeling. She hadn't asked them. *She* was ready to take the next step. She wanted off this ship—off all ships, really—and to move forward.

As people in the Fleet always did.

Consider it your last official duty, Dauber had said and had signed off, leaving Serpell alone in her quarters, staring at an empty space in the center of the room.

Last official duty. One more. Not that she had ever had official duties as a leader. Not that she had wanted them.

But she had executed them just fine. She had gotten her people home. Except India. India had died at Amnthra, and Serpell really didn't miss her.

She rubbed her hands together, hating how sweaty they were. She probably should have brought a bag, just so she had something to do with her hands—maybe shift it from hand to hand or something.

She threaded her hands together and took a tiny step forward. She was afraid to look at the other survivors. She didn't want to catch Kabac's eyes.

She had had enough of him. If she never saw him again, she would be a happy woman.

If she never saw any of them again, she would be content.

She made herself take a deep breath. Then a side door opened near the bay door.

For some reason, she had expected the bay door to open all the way, but of course, it hadn't. They weren't moving ships in and out. They were moving people, and people could go single file through the doors.

Two of the *Aizsargs* crew, a man and a woman that Serpell did not know, stood on either side of the door.

She reached them, and they nodded at her. They didn't even say goodbye or anything. Or wish her good luck with her future.

For some reason, she had expected that. Had hoped for it, really. A kind word. A half gesture. Something to acknowledge what they had all been through.

Instead, the man spoke to the person following her.

"Wait here," he said. "It will take a few minutes to process each person."

Serpell frowned. She nearly turned back to ask what that meant. No one had told her about processing. She had already gone through decontamination and all kinds of other checks when she boarded the *Aizsargs*. There was no need for more processing.

She'd never been processed when she'd gone to a starbase before.

But that had been more than 100 years ago. Maybe things were different now.

The thought turned her anticipation into something closer to anxiety. New things were fine, she reminded herself. Everything was going to be new for a while.

If she could figure out how an SC-Class vessel worked (more or less), she could figure out anything.

She stepped off the *Aizsargs* into a narrow corridor. The lighting was dim, and the walls were gray. She had entered through a dozen different corridors like that throughout her years on ships. The corridor felt reassuringly normal.

Even if she was the only one in it. No one followed her—at least not yet.

Her mouth had gone dry. This didn't feel right. When she had disembarked from other ships, she had always walked with a group. No one had left individually, unless they were being dumped at a location.

The thought made her turn back. Dumped. They were leaving her here? By herself?

But that made no sense. And it didn't matter anyway. She was on Starbase Sigma, which was someplace she had never seen before. The *Aizsargs* was someplace she had never seen before either. She had survived it.

She had nowhere else to go.

That thought made her face forward again. The corridor wound around one corner and then another. And then a door opened, letting in light.

She let out a small breath. Finally, she had arrived.

She walked through the doors, only to step into a booth, not a room.

More damn decontamination units. The *Aizsargs* crew should have warned her. Dauber should have warned her.

She stepped inside the booth, and the door snapped shut behind her.

Raina Serpell. The androgynous voice startled her. She hadn't expected to hear her name. But the *Aizsargs* had given her a new identification chip, so she shouldn't have been too surprised. *Place your hands on the counter in front of you.*

She didn't see a counter. And then she realized that the counter was clear. She lifted her hands and placed them on the smooth surface.

This was the oddest decontamination unit she had ever encountered, but each system was different.

Then something wrapped itself around her wrists and shoved her hands together so hard that her thumbs slammed into each other.

She gasped, startled.

The counter disappeared, and her arms fell forward, elbows jamming into her stomach, hands slapping into her thighs.

Raina Serpell, you are under arrest for mutiny and 60 counts of murder. These major charges as well as several minor charges shall be enumerated as you are processed into the Fleet Judicial System. You will not speak until you are asked to. You will be assigned an advocate for processing. You may change advocates when processing ends.

"Sixty counts?" she asked. "What do you mean, sixty counts?"

Your questions will be answered once your advocate is in place. Step forward.

The doors opened in front of her. The area was labeled holding. There were signs and arrows popping up in front of her, telling her what direction to move in and how she would be processed.

"This is some kind of mistake," she said to the air. There were no people here. Of course, there were no people here.

And this was what Dauber had meant by processing. They were taking Serpell first because she had been the leader of the *Renegat.*

Sixty counts.

Her breath caught. They were blaming her for the deaths of Crowe and the others.

Crowe had been the leader of the mutiny against Preemas. It had all been Crowe's fault, not hers. She had done the right thing, the only thing.

She had brought everyone back.

She had saved the entire crew.

Except the engineers and some of the senior staff and India.

But they had been in the way. They had wanted to stay away from the Fleet.

Something beside her shoved her forward, taking her to a station off to her right to continue processing. The room was set up for a dozen people to go through at one time, but she was alone.

Then she heard a snap, as the doors to the processing booth shut. Another *Renegat* survivor was getting arrested.

Processed.

No wonder Dauber had seemed curt and angry.

She had found something. Or learned something.

Sixty was a really specific number.

Someone had talked to the crew of the *Aizsargs* and told them what had happened to Crowe and his team.

Crowe.

He had said that if the *Renegat* returned, the entire crew would be charged as mutineers. Serpell had thought he was wrong.

He hadn't been.

That was the irony, wasn't it? He hadn't been wrong at all.

She squared her shoulders. The hope she had been feeling only moments ago was dashed.

Her future wasn't a new life in a starbase, with freedom and a new career.

Her future was defending herself against charges of mutiny and murder.

She hadn't come back here for this. And yet, here she was.

She had made the wrong choices from beginning to end. From hooking up with India to returning to the Fleet.

She couldn't blame India for this one. Serpell had ultimately made this decision. And stupidly, she had hoped that she would finally settle into the kind of life she actually wanted.

She had hoped for a real future on a starbase, and she was going to get one.

Just not the one she imagined.

And not one she ever would have wanted.

PART FORTY-SIX

FINAL DECISIONS

100 YEARS AGO

UNNAMED VESSEL

Crowe knew the risks.

He had been planning this day for nearly a month. Once he had found the newest vessel in the Ready Vessel section of the Scrapheap, he knew that he had to test it, see if it was the kind of ship he wanted.

But he also knew that the test would take dozens of personnel. He had no idea how to conduct the test otherwise.

He stood on the bridge of the vessel. It probably had a name and a designation, but he didn't know what either of those things were. He also didn't know exactly how old the vessel was.

It had features he had never seen before. It had an actual working backup *anacapa* drive in engineering, more weaponry than he had ever seen in a Fleet vessel, and shields that looked state-of-the-art for his time, rather than the time here.

He and the engineering staff had spent nearly a week on this ship, testing systems, seeing how old it was, and whether or not it was a ship from their era.

It wasn't, but Atwater believed it had been a prototype for the kind of DV-Class vessels that the entire crew was used to.

Crowe stood on the bridge of this vessel, legs slightly apart, hands clasped behind his back. He had gotten the screens working ten days before, and they showed all the other ships in the Scrapheap. The holographic imagery worked well.

The command controls seemed to function.

His entire engineering team was here, in various parts of the ship. That was the risk he was taking. He had brought every competent person off of the *Renegat* to run this final test.

And, he was going to talk to them, to see if they would help him convince the rest of the *Renegat*'s crew to stay in this sector. To build and improve ships, in space itself, and maybe discover some kind of mission on their own.

He wasn't sure that suggestion would work, and he was open to several others. But he didn't want to talk to the dead weight in the *Renegat's* crew. He wanted to talk with these people.

After this test.

He swallowed hard, then leaned forward and tapped the console in front of him. He would have to modify it to make smaller, working, holographic screens for this ship—should it become the main ship.

He wasn't sure why he wanted it to be the main ship, except for a feeling he had about the *Renegat*. He wasn't usually a superstitious man, but that ship felt cursed to him. Maybe because so many crew members had died stupidly on board the ship.

Maybe because he'd had to repair it so many times—most recently with parts that didn't quite fit into the ship itself.

Or maybe he just wanted to lay the ghost of Preemas to rest, and Crowe couldn't do that onboard the *Renegat*.

The entire console was lit up before him. Each working section of the ship was lit green. Inside the green were blue dots, indicating where each crew member was. He hadn't logged them into the computer—that was a system that could be set up later—so he couldn't tell who was who except by section.

He had Danika Newark in the mess. She had come over with him earlier and set up the food system. They had even brought a few supplies—the minimum amount to test with. On this day, they had brought more (but not much) because he wanted a feast of celebration to end this test—if it worked, of course.

If not, the food would wait until the next test or the next.

Willoughby was in engineering. The rest of the engineers were scattered around the ship's most important systems. He had even given Atwater a job. The man was going to monitor the controls in the captain's quarter. Apparently, the captain's control closet had been part of the Fleet even as far back as this ship.

Atwater couldn't touch those systems, but he would let Crowe know if those systems worked or not.

Crowe clenched his fists and then unclenched them. The test was both simple and complex.

The crew would turn on every single system simultaneously. If it was possible to make that particular system run at full capacity without causing issues inside of the Scrapheap, then the person in charge of that system would run it to capacity.

Crowe had run simulations of this, and he had done so on the ship. The ship's systems had told him it would all work together.

But, after the experience with the anti-*anacapa* weapon, he had learned that he couldn't trust what ship systems told him.

"All right," he said on the shipwide comm. "We will hit *go* in three...two...one..."

The ship shuddered, which he did not like. And then the consoles around him lit up. The bridge gained a hum that both surprised and pleased him. He hadn't realized the hum was missing. It was here now.

It was the sound of a ship that functioned.

He smiled slowly. Even if some of the systems broke down or didn't work quite the way he wanted them to, they could run together. This ship was functional.

He hadn't expected that.

He had hoped for it. But there had been so many failures on this trip, that any kind of hope seemed foolish.

This didn't.

Not any longer.

And now, he had some choices to make.

THE *RENEGAT*

The *Renegat* shuddered, then bumped and rolled.

Serpell recognized the feeling, and gripped the wall of the corridor in panic.

The *Renegat* had gone into foldspace. Why had it gone into foldspace? Was it the new *anacapa* drive? Did it do something strange?

She ran to the elevators, and headed up to the bridge before she could even think about it. She didn't see anyone else in the corridor or the elevator, not that they would have been dumb enough to travel through the ship during the foldspace window.

But the bumping stopped, and the ship had righted itself, at least as far as Serpell could tell.

She burst out of the elevator, and ran to the bridge.

The door was open, and the bridge was empty. Her breath caught. She had been right. The *anacapa* drive had sent them into foldspace on its own.

She moaned, and that's when she saw movement near the drive.

Yusef Kabac stood next to the drive, working the console closest to it.

"What the hell did you do?" she asked.

He looked up, as if he hadn't realized she was there.

"They were going to make us stay in the sector," he said. "You know that, right? That backwater primitive place, without the Fleet? They were going to make us stay."

"You don't know that," she said, even though deep down, she knew he was right. Everyone had been talking about it, arguing it, worrying over it.

Most people she spoke to had wanted to go back, no matter what the dangers were.

"Of course, I know that," he said. "They're scared of traveling back. But they isolated themselves, all of the rebels. They were going to get court-martialed. We won't."

She stared at Kabac. He stared back.

"Where are we?" she asked.

"I'm not sure," he said, "but the system tells me that we're at the exact coordinates we want to be for our return trip. I was just about to contact Justine Breaux to have her confirm with her little research materials."

Where they needed to be. Heading back.

Serpell swallowed. "We should probably go back and get the others," she said.

"Travel back to that Scrapheap?" Kabac said.

She nodded.

"Why?" he asked. "So we can have the inevitable fight? You saw how they treat people who disagree with them. It was only a matter of time before they either killed or imprisoned the rest of us."

She leaned on a nearby console.

"Who'll run the ship?" she asked, and with that question, she knew that deep down, she agreed with Kabac. She had been afraid of speaking out against Crowe and his team. She had been afraid of what they would do to her.

"We don't need anyone to run it," Kabac said. "We just head back. We follow the coordinates, and retrace our steps, and we're home."

"You make it sound easy," she said.

He shrugged. "We're not trying to do anything else. If we were trying to go on a mission or something, it would be harder. But we have one goal, and we can do it."

She nodded. As she did, some other crew members ran onto the bridge. She knew some of them by name. Garja Blaquer. Declan Connolly. Anthony Varasteh.

They all started talking at once.

Kabac smiled at them and gave them the answers he had given her.

They didn't seem upset.

Serpell walked around them, and headed out of the bridge. Weirdly, she wasn't upset either.

She was relieved.

They were going home.

Finally.

Where they would be safe.

UNNAMED VESSEL

"Nadim."

Crowe frowned, not willing to move away from the various control consoles. The ship was working beautifully, better than he expected. He felt a certain joy in that.

"Nadim."

He looked up, saw Tosidis standing right in front of him, arms crossed. Tosidis never called him "Nadim."

Something was wrong.

"What's happened?" Crowe asked. He was braced for something wrong. This ship hadn't been used in a very long time, if much at all. The strain on the systems from them running together might have shown a weakness that wasn't appearing on his consoles.

"The *Renegat* is gone," Tosidis said.

"What?" It took Crowe a moment to understand Tosidis's statement. Crowe had been lost in the details of this ship, not the *Renegat*. "What do you mean, gone?"

"Gone," Tosidis said. "It's not in the sector."

"What?" Crowe asked again.

He manipulated the screens on this ship, and then had them search for the *Renegat*. Nothing showed up.

"Look." Tosidis tapped a different console, bringing up a holographic image that showed the past few hours. The hologram ran forward quickly, showing the *Renegat* in the area where Crowe had left it.

And then the *Renegat* glowed golden for a half second before the silvery shadow of foldspace opened around them.

The *Renegat* hadn't disappeared.

It had left them.

All of them.

His mouth opened, and he had to work to close it. Had the *anacapa* drive caused this on its own? He'd never heard of that, but that golden color wasn't quite normal—not for modern *anacapa* drives.

"We're going to have to get them back," Crowe said. "If we can figure out where they went. We're going to have to—"

Tosidis put a hand on Crowe's arm, and shook his head. "No."

Tosidis didn't understand. There were 199 people on that ship, people Crowe was responsible for. He wasn't going to add 199 deaths on his shoulders. Not on top of the fifty.

Not on top of Preemas, and the others.

"We have to figure this out," Crowe said. "They're not equipped to handle this kind of emergency. They—"

"It's not an emergency," Tosidis said. "At least for them."

Crowe frowned.

Tosidis looked up and nodded at someone behind Crowe. Crowe half-turned and saw Colvin standing near a communications console, rubbing her hands over her biceps as if she were trying to stay warm.

"Play it," Tosidis said.

She nodded, then reached forward.

Yusef Kabac appeared, larger than life-size, a grin making his stupid beard look like it had grown outward several inches.

"We're heading back," Kabac said. "We don't want to stay here, and you're going to make us. No one on this ship now will be court-martialed. We'll be fine."

And then Kabac vanished.

Crowe shook his head slightly. Kabac, the only person Crowe had left on that ship who knew how to work the *anacapa* controls.

Kabac, delusional as always.

Kabac, who had no idea what he had just gotten them all into.

If Crowe had known that Kabac wanted to try something like this, Crowe would have...

He had no idea. He couldn't have brought Kabac here. Crowe hadn't wanted Kabac to screw up this test.

And yet, Kabac had done that.

"That's it?" Crowe asked. "That's the entire message?"

"Yeah," Colvin said, her voice shaking. "Now what do we do?"

Crowe frowned. Then he looked at the emptiness where the *Renegat* had been.

They could do a search and rescue on the *Renegat*, try to recreate the trip that the *Renegat* had chosen to take—if Kabac followed predictable coordinates.

If the *Renegat* didn't get lost in foldspace.

If, if, if.

Crowe ran a hand over his face.

They had more pressing problems than finding the *Renegat*. There was enough food on board to last maybe a month, not counting whatever the normal supplies were in *Orbiter One*. If they rationed the supplies.

But this ship worked. It was, in many ways, better than the *Renegat* could ever be.

And the dead weight of the badly chosen crew had just disappeared, leaving Crowe with all of the competent people remaining on the *Renegat*.

That joy he had felt a moment earlier had returned.

He was free. Free of the Fleet. Free of the strictures that had prevented him from being the kind of man he had wanted to be. The kind of leader he wanted to be.

"What are we going to do?" Crowe repeated.

Colvin nodded. Tosidis shifted slightly, nerves evident.

"We're going to make this an opportunity," Crowe said.

"What?" Colvin asked.

"We've got ships," Crowe said. "We have tech. We need to figure out how to find food, but we can do that."

"And then what?" This time, it was Tosidis.

"And then we build." Crowe was thinking on the fly, but as he did, he realized he'd been contemplating this ever since he found the Ready Vessels.

"Build what?" Colvin asked.

Crowe grinned. He couldn't help it. Kabac and company had just given him the gift of a lifetime, and they hadn't even realized it.

"Our own Fleet," Crowe said. "We build our own Fleet."

Just the way they wanted it. Without the baggage and the rules. With a mission all sixty of them could agree on.

He felt giddy, and ready to work, all at the same time.

He was finally going to captain his own ship.

And he would do it right.

Colvin and Tosidis were looking at him like he was crazy. And maybe he was.

They needed more than a future vision. They needed what to do next.

"First things first," Crowe said. "We let the others know. Then we assess our supplies. And then, we look at those maps that we have, and find a culture that'll provide us with some food."

"You already have this figured out," Tosidis said in surprise.

"No," Crowe said. "It's just logic."

But it was more than that. Captains didn't panic. Captains dealt with the situations they found themselves in.

Captains saved their crews.

Captains built.

And that was exactly what Crowe was going to do.

I value honest feedback, and would love to hear your opinion in a review, if you're so inclined, on your favorite book retailer's site.

Be the first to know!

Just sign up for the Kristine Kathryn Rusch newsletter, and keep up with the latest news, releases and so much more—even the occasional giveaway.

So, what are you waiting for? To sign up go to kristinekathrynrusch.com.

But wait! There's more. Sign up for the WMG Publishing newsletter, too, and get the latest news and releases from all of the WMG authors and lines, including Kristine Grayson, Kris Nelscott, Dean Wesley Smith, *Fiction River: An Original Anthology Magazine, Pulphouse Fiction Magazine, Smith's Monthly,* and so much more.

To sign up go to wmgpublishing.com.

ABOUT THE AUTHOR

New York Times bestselling author Kristine Kathryn Rusch writes in almost every genre. Generally, she uses her real name (Rusch) for most of her writing. Under that name, she publishes bestselling science fiction and fantasy, award-winning mysteries, acclaimed mainstream fiction, controversial nonfiction, and the occasional romance. Her novels have made bestseller lists around the world and her short fiction has appeared in eighteen best of the year collections. She has won more than twenty-five awards for her fiction, including the Hugo, *Le Prix Imaginales*, the *Asimov's* Readers Choice award, and the *Ellery Queen Mystery Magazine* Readers Choice Award.

Publications from *The Chicago Tribune* to *Booklist* have included her Kris Nelscott mystery novels in their top-ten-best mystery novels of the year. The Nelscott books have received nominations for almost every award in the mystery field, including the best novel Edgar Award, and the Shamus Award.

She writes goofy romance novels as award-winner Kristine Grayson.

She also edits. Beginning with work at the innovative publishing company, Pulphouse, followed by her award-winning tenure at *The Magazine of Fantasy & Science Fiction*, she took fifteen years off before returning to editing with the original anthology series *Fiction River*, published by WMG Publishing. She acts as series editor with her husband, writer Dean Wesley Smith.

To keep up with everything she does, go to kriswrites.com and sign up for her newsletter. To track her many pen names and series, see their individual websites (krisnelscott.com, kristinegrayson.com, retrievalartist.com, divingintothewreck.com, fictionriver.com, pulphousemagazine.com).

Printed in Great Britain
by Amazon

36701222R00461